THEN

Julie Myerson was born in Nottingham in 1960. She is the author of seven previous novels: *Sleepwalking* (1993), *The Touch* (1996), *Me and the Fat Man* (1998), *Laura Blundy* (2000), *Something Might Happen* (2003), *The Story of You* (2006), and *Out of Breath* (2008). Her non-fiction books are *Home: The Story of Everyone Who Ever Lived in Our House* (2004), *Not a Games Person* (2005) and *The Lost Child* (2009). She lives in London.

JULIE MYERSON

Then

VINTAGE BOOKS
London

Published by Vintage 2012

2 4 6 8 10 9 7 5 3 1

Copyright © Julie Myerson 2011

Julie Myerson has asserted her right under the Copyright, Designs
and Patents Act 1988 to be identified as the author of this work

First published in Great Britain in 2011 by
Jonathan Cape

Vintage
Random House, 20 Vauxhall Bridge Road,
London SW1V 2SA

www.vintage-books.co.uk

Addresses for companies within The Random House Group Limited
can be found at: www.randomhouse.co.uk/offices.htm

The Random House Group Limited Reg. No. 954009

A CIP catalogue record for this book
is available from the British Library

ISBN 9780099554721

The Random House Group Limited supports The Forest Stewardship
Council (FSC®), the leading international forest certification
organisation. Our books carrying the FSC label are printed on FSC®
certified paper. FSC is the only forest certification scheme endorsed
by the leading environmental organisations, including Greenpeace.
Our paper procurement policy can be found at:
www.randomhouse.co.uk/environment

Printed and bound by CPI Group (UK) Ltd, Croydon, CR0 4YY

For Helen 1924–2010

I

Sometime in the middle of summer, the temperature drops so low that animals bite off their own tails and small birds come falling down out of the sky.

People are eating the birds. We see some lads crowded round a brazier on Houndsditch, fighting over a handful of scorched sparrows. Laughing and shouting as they pull flesh from bone and cram it in their mouths. The rest is chucked in the snow. Dogs are waiting.

It isn't the first time we've seen the birds die. Back in March, or was it April, the streets were full of them. Only now there are bigger things too. Rats and squirrels. Foxes. Cats curled up and frozen to rooftops. Even a stupid pony, leaning up against the old wheelie bins, its eyeballs white, its breath turned to ice in its throat.

And then, one dark afternoon, making my way back along Camomile Street, I step over a puddle and see a pale face staring up at me. A tiny child, no more than one or two years old – I can see the stubby bottom teeth – frozen under the ice. She must have fallen in and knocked the back of her head. The eyes are bright blue and astonished, the lips parted as if on the edge of crying out.

I take a breath and walk away fast.

All I want is to get back to the building, but on the corner of Houndsditch and Bishopsgate a man steps out from the blackest part of the shadows and grabs me.

I hear myself cry out, but just as I am about to struggle, I look down and see what's there: two gloved hands holding on to mine. The leather shabby and cracked, a sharp rip in the thumb, as if someone has used a knife on it.

Graham, I say.

Every time I see him I have to recognise him all over again. All that black hair. The staring eyes. He is hardly any taller than I am. I know that I am not afraid of him. I think that he used to be a lawyer. He would hike up mountains in his spare time, or so he says.

Graham. He stares at me now and he shakes his head. I ask him what he wants.

What do you mean, what do I want?

Why are you following me?

I'm not following you. I came to look for you. And you're lucky someone else didn't find you first.

What? I say. Who would have found me?

He takes a breath. His fingers tight on my wrists.

Look. It's almost dark. What the hell are you doing out here on your own?

On my own? I try to think what the answer to the question might be. Nothing comes. I am glad when he lets go of me. Now his eyes are softer.

Seriously, he says. Why did you run away like that? We looked everywhere for you. We didn't know where you'd gone.

Neither did I, I tell him, and for a moment or two the words do feel true. But then the face of the child comes back at me, and with it confusion.

Graham is frowning.

I was worried about you, he says. We all were.

Ted and Sophy wouldn't worry, I say, and he doesn't contradict me.

You can't just disappear like that, he says.

Disappear? I stare at him. For a second or two, splinters of light seem to flash around the corners of his eyes. When I blink, they are gone.

He sighs

You don't remember a thing, do you? You've no idea what happened.

I hug myself.

Maybe, I say.

Really? You remember what you did?

Did?

I feel my stomach twist.

The little incident. With the kid. This morning.

The kid. The sound of that word makes my two hands clench into fists.

Leave me alone, I tell him. I don't want to talk about it.

Don't want to talk about what?

Graham, I say, I never touched him.

Snow is falling now, a pillow of cold feathers shaken down. I look at his face again, the face of this man whose name I have forgotten again – where are the clues? In his eyes? Recognition, it comes and goes. I'm still staring when he mistakes my look for something else and pulls me to him. Working his hands, the gloves off now, inside my coat.

No, I say, because I know what's coming.

Come on –

I tell him not to do it, but he doesn't listen. He does it anyway. His fingers on me, making me shiver.

I want to go now, I say.

What? he says.

I want to go back to the building.

Shh. I feel the wetness of his lips on the side of my ear. What's the hurry? Just let me hold you a moment.

Why?

Because I want to.

But I don't want to.

I keep myself stiff and unhelpful in his arms. But then, as he hugs me closer to him, the hot smell of his skin loosens a memory.

Am I your wife? I ask him.

A pause. His laughter in my hair.

My wife? Ha. That's a good one. Not exactly, no.

But have we . . . I mean, do we . . .?

He laughs again, not quite the same laugh.

I'm glad I'm so memorable, he says.

He is still for a long moment. Dusk wrapping itself around us. He's right, it's dark. I tilt my head back and there's the big cold face of the moon, the only light you'll find right now in the whole city. I think about the building. Its wide, dark spaces.

So what happened? I ask him at last. Did something happen to him?

Happen to who?

To the kid, of course.

He takes a little breath.

His name's Matthew.

Matthew. The name drops into my head. The fact that there's already a Matthew-shaped space for it tells me I knew it. Some quick, dark pictures go through my mind: the kid's chopped brown hair and surly face. His brown tracksuit bottoms. His fat and grubby hands. The sudden change when he enters a room.

4

And yes, he continues. Something did happen to him.

Something? I breathe, try to keep myself steady.

Oh, I say. What was it?

He bites his lip, hesitates.

I'm sure you didn't mean to do it, he says.

We live on what was once Bishopsgate, between Wormwood Street and the old Liverpool Street train station. Thirty-five storeys that once contained lawyers and bankers. There are more buildings still standing in this part of the city, Graham says, than anywhere else. It's the way they're built. Structures of glass and steel. Windows that go from ceiling to floor. Men used to go up in cages to clean them, but they aren't clean now, even though the sun still shines in most days. Dust and silence. A hundred or a thousand empty desks. No one will ever work here again.

I walked in one bright loud morning, the air ringing with stillness. I don't know how long ago it was. I remember the bang of the door shutting behind me. I know that I stood for a moment, waiting. I didn't know what I was waiting for, but the waiting felt right. And I couldn't remember why I'd come, but I knew I had a good reason. The good reason settled around me, warm and solid and certain.

I'm here, I told the silence. I'm here.

I let myself walk around. Acting as if she owns the place, someone might have said – and maybe they did say it and maybe I did own it, for I recognised everything. Everything. Nothing was strange to me, nothing was new. The lifts, dead and defunct since the power left the city. I knew those lifts. And just along from them, a door – heavy, with a big steel handle. I'd touched it before, that handle. I pushed it and found

5

myself in a dark and grainy stairwell. As I knew I would. The door sighed shut behind me. I smiled. I began to climb the stairs.

On the second or maybe it was the third floor I found them, the two of them. Sitting in a slumped and gloomy silence right against a wall – a boy and a girl, teenagers, with bony starving frames and anxious faces. They were very shocked to see me – in fact the girl looked terrified. She gasped and even the boy shrank back as I opened the door.

What's wrong with you? the girl said. Your hands and face – what happened?

I looked down at my hands. I couldn't remember where the blood had come from. I touched my face and wasn't surprised to find it sticky. Every part of me was shaky and bruised. As I stood there, something liquid slid down my leg.

I don't know, I said. It's nothing.

Did someone attack you?

I'll be OK, I said.

The boy asked me how I got in.

Got in?

How did you find the entrance? We thought that no one could see it. From the street.

Oh well, I said. I'm sure they can't. I think someone might have brought me here.

This seemed to frighten them even more.

Someone? said the girl who was called Sophy.

In my head I tried to wade backwards.

I think there was a man, I said.

And where is he now? said the girl.

I hope he's not coming back, said the boy, who told me his name was Ted.

Where is he now? I thought about this. The thought hurt.
I pushed it away.

It's OK, I said. He's not.

Not what?

I don't think he is. Coming back.

We walked around the building. We went up the stairs. We had
little juice left in our hearts and bones but we got as far as the
sixteenth floor. Panting and dizzy. Sophy wanted to keep on
going – the higher we go, the safer we are, she said – but Ted
said no, sixteen was far enough. He told us he'd been here
before, in this building.

How come? Sophy said, frowning at him.

He thought for a second.

I worked here.

She laughed.

But you're only about fifteen. You're nothing like old enough
to have worked here.

Ted seemed to think about this. I saw that his face was
unhappy.

I think it was work experience.

I realised I felt sorry for him. Confusion could tip you up
just like that.

It doesn't matter, I told him. You're here now.

We crossed a landing and found ourselves in an office. Dust
over everything. Pigeons had been in and there were streaks
on the backs of chairs, on desks. A high-pitched noise in a filing
cabinet turned out to be a nest of mice, grey-skinned and hair-
less. In the corner of the office was a bundle of clothes and
inside them was a man.

The man's head was on his knees. His hair was long and

matted and his beard was black. At first we thought he was dead, but after a moment he lifted his head and started rolling a cigarette.

Ted stared at the cigarette. The man saw him staring and, after taking a suck himself, he held it out. Ted looked amazed. But he went over and took it. He had a puff, then handed it back, but the man held up his hand as if to say keep it.

Ted looked even more amazed.

Cheers, mate, he said.

With the cigarette in one hand, he put himself down at one of the dead screens. Touched the mouse. In his eyes was the look boys get when they are near computers.

Hey, maybe we can go on Facebook? he said.

For the first time, the man in the corner made a noise. It was laughter. The man was Graham.

Later that day we found the kid. Down in the old basement kitchen, a solid and sullen-looking boy, maybe thirteen years old. He was sitting up on the shiny metal counter and using a blunt knife to hack into a can of beans, the orange kind that you used to have on toast.

Sophy ignored the boy and rushed over to the cans and started picking them up as if they were little babies. There was sweetcorn, the one with the giant on it. Tuna. Peas. Chopped tomatoes. She nursed six or seven of them in her arms at once, before putting them down again.

On the table by the counter was a stack of white sliced bread that someone had ripped open and left. The slices were blue, green and grey. There was a freezer too. Sophy went over and pulled up the lid, but the smell was rank and she banged it shut very fast. The smell of rotting flesh lingered. She looked at the kid, who was still stabbing the can.

Isn't there an opener? she said.

He said nothing.

She went over and looked in a cupboard. Several packets of something, maybe crackers or biscuits, had spilled over a shelf. She snatched one up and tried to cram it in her mouth but as soon as it touched her fingers, it was dust. The kid was watching her.

There's some that are OK, he said. Over there in the other cupboard.

How long have you been here? Ted asked the kid. How did you get in?

The kid stayed where he was. He didn't answer and he didn't look at Ted. He swung his legs against the counter so his boots scuffed and banged. He put down the blunt knife and felt around in a drawer for a sharper one. Then he began attacking the can of beans again. The blade kept on slipping. Soon there was blood on both his hands.

Stop it! Sophy cried. What are you doing? Can't you see you're hurting yourself?

I asked you a question, Ted said. How did you come here?

The kid wiped his hands on his tracksuit bottoms. He looked at me.

With her, he said.

What?

I came with her.

At his words, I froze. I shook my head.

He did not, I said.

Keeping his eyes on me, the kid stabbed the knife into the can again.

9

But I brought you here, he said. After I found you. After the men had hurt you. You don't remember?

Ted was looking at me.

I thought you said it was a man who brought you?

A bright hot flush went through me.

It was, I told him in a steady voice, though my heart was beating crazily. I don't know this boy. He's just a kid. I've no idea who he is.

The kid gave up on the can and dropped it on the floor. It hit the concrete with a dull sound.

She's lying, he said, but he said it as if that was the end of the subject, and he did not look at me.

I've never seen him in my life before, I told Ted and Sophy. And I don't like the look of him either.

You could see Ted trying to decide what to think. In the end, he sighed.

If you want to stay here with us, he told the kid, you've got to join the team.

The kid stared at him.

What team?

I mean you've got to do what we say.

The kid looked at him then and he nodded. He looked younger suddenly, and solemn. There was something else, too, on his face – was it sadness, or was he sulking? I felt excited.

And now I have hurt him. Is it so surprising? That I've hurt the bloody kid? I have no memory of whatever it is I am supposed to have done, but that doesn't stop everyone else shaking their heads and knowing it. And now here they all are, waiting for me to say I am sorry.

Am I sorry? Am I? I try to think about what sorry might

feel like and whether or not it's in my mind right now. Sorry. No, I do not think that sorry will come.

I do not like the kid and I never have, but still I can't think what he might have done to make me want to hurt him. I am not a violent person, and I don't think I would ever lash out at a child for no reason.

Look at him, now, lying there. Ted and Sophy have made a pile out of some of the coats and blankets and laid him on it. He doesn't look good. He looks like someone has picked him up and dropped him from a great height.

What's he called? I ask them, more out of politeness than anything else.

Graham looks at me.

You know what he's called. I told you just an hour ago.

I shrug.

I always just call him the kid, I say.

He's Matthew, Sophy tells me in a voice that sounds like she wants to catch me out. Matt. We call him Matt.

Matt. I say the word to myself and then I say it again. An angry word. I pull my big brown cardigan up to my chin.

I think I'll just call him the kid, I say.

They all watch me. Ted — pale and skinny and heartbreaking the way some teenage boys are — watches me. He can make you feel guilty in three seconds flat, Ted can. And Sophy, the blonde and mouthy one, kneeling right next to the kid now and holding on to his hand the way girls like to do with people who are lying down. She keeps on glancing up at me, to check I've seen her.

And there's a nasty ripening bruise on the kid's head. And maybe a cut as well, because someone has got a cloth off one of the old tea trolleys and ripped it to make a bandage. The edges are black and blood has also leaked into his hair, one of his ears. His eyes are closed, his face full of shadows. I peer at him more closely.

Are you sure he's not dead?

Sophy gasps.

Would you even care if he was?

I look at him again. That sullen face. That lumpen, accusing presence. Would I care? It's a difficult question.

Graham is watching me.

Do you remember now, what you did?

Several different and violent possibilities are going round in my mind. I put the brakes on, reach out for one of them.

Did I hit him?

Sophy looks at Graham and claps her hand to her mouth as if to stop a laugh. I look again at the kid lying there on the coats. His bloody hair. The bruises on him. Then a new idea wells up.

He went for me first, I say.

This time Ted speaks up.

No, he says — and I notice that he blushes and keeps his eyes fixed on the floor, as if it somehow costs him to be saying it. No way. It's not true. I was there.

Graham looks at me. I hold up my hands, feeling sorry suddenly for Ted.

OK, I say. OK. Whatever. He didn't.

Graham looks at me and shakes his head.

You'll say anything, won't you? Whatever comes into your head, whatever you feel like saying, you'll just go right ahead and say it.

And I turn to him, about to deny it — but then, for a few quick, strange seconds, I see that he has on a suit, a clean shirt, his hair is sharply cut and his beard shaved. I smell coffee, hear a staticky hum that I think is electricity.

What is it now? he says when he sees me staring at him.

I don't answer. I notice his clean fingernails, the glint of a watch on his wrist, the newspaper in his hand. I shiver and take my eyes to somewhere else – as far away as possible, out of the window. Someone has lit a bonfire on a rooftop somewhere far off towards Bank. You can see the bright flames jumping into the black night sky, puncturing the darkness of the city.

I keep my eyes on the flames for a moment and then, when I look back at Graham, he's as he should be – dressed in his old dark and greasy clothes, skin parched and dirty, face all covered with hair.

The main entrance of the building – the big, grand entrance, with its turnstiles and leather sofas and dead and curling trees – is on Bishopsgate, but that stays shut and we come and go through the side entrance on Wormwood. Ted and Sophy and Graham are very afraid that someone else will find it. It's all they talk about. I can't bear listening to their worries any longer.

It won't happen, I tell them. I mean it. No one's going to come in.

Graham looks at me.

How on earth can you know a thing like that?

I hesitate, trying to collect up the words that will seem right to him. I know that the kid is watching me.

Because I feel it.

I know as soon as I say it that it's the wrong choice. Sophy rolls her eyes.

You feel it?

Yes.

But what do you feel?

I just know what's possible and what's not.

No you don't, Graham says. How can you?

Look, I tell him. It's not what's going to happen.

Now Sophy starts to laugh.

So, what? You're saying you know what's going to happen? You know the future?

You don't know who you are or where you came from, Ted points out. You've got no memory at all, even less than us. But you know what's coming?

Yes, Sophy says, and she shoves her pale hand in my face. Do you tell fortunes too? What can you see? Tell me everything. What's going to happen to me?

I don't look at Sophy's hand. I don't need to.

You'll be OK, I tell her.

I can't look at the kid, but I know that he has looked away.

This place. In the day, sun crashes through the windows. The air warms up. It can almost feel like the old world in the day. But at night, the temperature drops. At night, you hear things. Screaming and crying. Sounds that could be animals but aren't animals.

Sometimes in the morning there are bodies in the street. Terrible injuries that no one could survive. A day later the bodies are gone. We don't know who takes them. There are other bodies too, piles of them stacked in the old bus shelters, in the post office, under the canopy where the market used to be, or left out on the street to freeze.

It has been some time now, no one knows how long, but still the dead are everywhere. Some days the cold can stop a human heart in less than thirty minutes. You see people on the ground exactly where they sat down to rest, faces black and surrendered, clothes torn off in their hurry to cool down. You walk down Bishopsgate and see drifts of snow with human hands and feet sticking out of them, the fingers and toes black with frost, the nails falling off. Or part of a face – the eyes gone and the skin dark and swollen, the expression of terror otherwise perfectly preserved.

Mostly the freeze keeps the smell of death at bay. In that way, the city has become a perfect morgue. But then you find yourself turning a corner into some sheltered place where the walls and roof are still intact, the air ripe and warm, and you back straight out again, heaving.

All right, Graham says. I'd better tell you. If you really can't remember.

It's the middle of the night, a full bright moon. We are lying down quite close together on the blankets and coats by the window. At night, this is often how we are. Sometimes he puts his hands on me, sometimes not. Sometimes I want him to. Other times I don't care whether he does or not. His hands are his own – my body never feels like mine.

The blankets are the cleanest thing we have, the softest. I don't know where we got the blankets – maybe Ted and the kid found them somewhere in the city. You can still find things in shops sometimes. The coats smell of cigarettes and soap and scent, of the places and things that people used to smell of. I know the coats were already in the building. On the day it happened, the air began to burn before it froze and nobody took their coats.

I look at Graham. His face green in the moonlight.

Tell me what? I say.

What you did. To the kid.

Oh.

You pushed him down the stairs.

A quick fizz of surprise runs through me.

I did? I pushed him — what's his name again?

Matthew.

Matthew. I pushed him down these stairs?

Yup. You gave him a shove and he went flying. Ted saw it. He says he went down a whole flight of steps.

I think about this. I try to picture it — the moment. The feeling of my hand on him. The sudden lightness as he goes. But it's not anywhere in my memory. It's hopeless. I shake my head.

I just don't have it, I tell Graham.

Don't have what?

The memory. I don't have it in my head.

He thinks for a moment.

Well, I'm telling you, it's what happened. It's what you did.

I'm silent.

And is that all? I ask him then.

What do you mean, is that all?

Is that all I did?

Christ. Isn't that enough?

I didn't mean to hurt him.

Well, he says, did you see his head? He's lucky to be alive.

Alive. Dead. Graham is the only one who makes such big distinctions.

In what way lucky? I ask him.

I mean he could easily have died.

For a moment, I wonder what it would be like if the kid did

do that – if he did die. I suppose it would be simple, that we would put the body out in the snow with the rest.

I feel Graham looking at me.

I don't understand you, he says.

I shrug. I step away from the idea and also from the conversation. In my head I take a sharp fruit knife and begin to make a strip of peel. It falls in a long, loose circle. I smell its lovely acid perfume. Such a relief, to be able to stop thinking and watch it fall.

What are you thinking? Graham says, still looking at me.

I was thinking about an apple, I tell him.

He is silent a moment and then, in a slightly angry way, he laughs.

I saw a little girl, I tell him a few minutes later.

He waits.

A girl?

Yes. A baby really. On Camomile Street.

He carries on waiting, as if he expects me to tell him more. I wait too. I shut my eyes for a quick second, struggling to remember. Is there more?

Go on, he says.

What do you mean, go on?

And? What happened?

Nothing happened. She was dead, I think. Just lying in a puddle and dead. She was right under the ice.

He says nothing. He rolls away from me and he sits up. I wait, yawning, as he smoothes the foil and strikes a match. Soon there's a smell of burned sugar in the air.

There are dead people everywhere, he says at last.

Well – but this one was just a baby.

17

He doesn't say anything. His face is expressionless. For a few moments, it's him and the foil and the flame. When he turns back to me, his eyes are glittery, the skin on his face raw and tight.

There are babies everywhere, he says.

I watch as he chases the flame along the foil. And I let myself think of him, then – the lawyer on Bishopsgate. In his dark suit, hurrying along. I see sunshine, the last waves of heat over the city. I feel sick. I hold my breath. He sees my face.

What? he says. What is it?

You worked here, I tell him. In this building.

He flicks a look at me.

You know I did. I've told you that.

When did you tell me?

I don't know. Lots of times. You've just forgotten. I'd been here coming up to three years. My office wasn't on this side. It faced out towards St Paul's.

St Paul's?

The man's name throws me for a moment. Then I remember: it's a church. And then the rest of it comes back.

That he was at work. It was a Tuesday. That he still remembers every last detail of his journey in that morning – the man who sold him a newspaper, trying to eat a bacon sandwich at the same time and not wanting to have to put it down to give him change. The long queue to renew his pass for the train. The fact that for once he shelled out for a six-month instead of a three-month.

And the fact that it was an especially glorious and sunny morning. Hot, in fact. Much hotter than it should have been. That high blue sky, cloudless and soaring. The fact that he loosened his tie and took his jacket off in the street because it was so unseasonably warm. Sweat on his face. You should not have sweat on your face in February.

He went in the building, through the turnstiles, past security. People were already talking about what could have caused the rise in temperature. Some people were laughing and joking about it, saying to enjoy while it lasted, others were worried. He didn't worry. The building was air-conditioned and anyway he was Graham and he had work to do.

He went up in the lift. He smelled coffee as he stepped into the corridor.

And then – and then.

He says that when he woke up, when he arrived back at something he could call consciousness, the air was scorched, an odour of burning fat, and the city was dark. The blue air and the sunshine had gone. There was ash and there was ice – and something else, something metallic, something that in some unholy way seemed final.

Final?

I can't explain it. It was like nothing I've ever felt. The worst sensation. Oppressive. As if something had happened that was beyond simple weather. As if the air or perhaps the whole of the sky had changed.

And yet even then, even after all that, he still failed to grasp what had happened.

Would you believe, I actually set off for London Bridge, he told me, his voice cracking with disbelief, to get a train home?

Home?

I mean, seriously, what in fuck's name was I expecting?

I wake in the night. His leg nudging mine. His hand on me. His breath in my ear.

Come on, he is muttering.

I don't bother saying anything. Instead, I lick my lips and I try to taste what is around me. The salty darkness. The silence above us and below. And then she comes flashing into my head — those blue astonished eyes, the little stubby teeth — and my heart sinks.

Come on, he is saying. I like you. I've always liked you. You're so fucking lovely. Even if we'd met in real life, I'd probably have hit on you —

In real life?

In the old life.

He leans up on one elbow and looks at me. I can tell by the way that his eyes touch my face then carry on going straight past it that he is still high.

I look away from him, listening. In the dark sometimes I can hear things. The distant sound of an office photocopier, sliding backwards and forwards, heavy and slow, dropping its pale rectangles into the tray. If I open my eyes, I know I will see shadows moving along the wall, sliding across the furniture. I don't know whose shadows they are.

I could tell you I loved you if you wanted, he is saying. Is that what you want? Would that make it better?

I look at him. I am hardly listening. I am thinking: why did I walk away from her? Why did I leave her lying there?

I lift my head then. A different sound.

Do you hear that?

Hear what?

That dog.

What dog?

There's a dog barking.

He yawns, scratches himself.

It'll be outside.

No. Listen. It's right here.

I can't hear anything, he says, and he tries again to pull me on to him and this time I don't bother struggling too hard. I can smell the burned sweetness of his breath. I rest my lips on his face. At last the barking stops.

I can tell from the loose shape of him that any moment now he'll be asleep and sure enough I am right and he is.

Most of the moon has slid away under thick dark cloud by the time I creep out of the building. It is the deadest time. Vicious cold. Enough to make even something as simple as breathing feel like a rough and complicated act.

The streets are empty. I see almost no one. Just one or two souls hurrying back towards the old synagogue. I don't know if they are women or men. They have dark hoods pulled down over their faces. As we pass each other, I see their teeth flash white and I hear the squeak of their boots, but they leave me alone and I am grateful for it.

I am on a mission, my heart is high with it. But as soon as I get to Camomile Street, my hopes crash. I realise it is hours or maybe days since I was here and nothing's the same. New snow has fallen, blurring everything.

I look around for anything I might remember, but the picture has changed completely. It might as well be a whole different street. I don't recognise a thing.

The building to my left is entirely burned out, its roof gone, walls charred, windows smashed. Near to it is a set of recent footprints. And a bright yellow stain in the snow where someone, maybe a man or maybe a dog, has pissed.

I look up and see a wall with red and blue paint on it and a faded and peeling sign that says Fresh Italy – Beautiful Food Fast, but even that means nothing. One frozen puddle in a big white landscape like this. What was I thinking? How could I ever have hoped to find her again?

The air above my head is black and silent, the odd flake of snow drifting down. I take a deep breath and walk about twenty paces to my left, then the same to the right. Then back to the left again. Then I turn and, as I wait, something changes. Lines and shapes settling, everything less distant and confused – the street around me beginning to make sense.

I go back a few paces in the original direction.

No, I think. Wrong. I slide a little the other way and test the ground with my foot. Nothing. I move along and do it again, harder. Still nothing. But the third time, there it is. The faint creak of ice. I stamp on it hard with my boot and feel it give.

It could be any puddle, I tell myself. There's no reason why it should be the right puddle.

Getting down on my knees, heart banging so hard that a taste comes up into my throat, I use my gloves to wipe all the soft fresh snow off the puddle's icy surface.

I look down. And there she is.

She is looking straight at me. I pull off my glove and rap my bare knuckles on the ice. Her eyes are blue as the bluest flower. Wide open and still. Nothing in her face moves.

I'm going to get you out, I tell her.

Pulling my glove back on, I go to look for a stone – a sharp one. And on the far side of the street, I find it – stacked in a pile along with all the other sharp stones. Left there for me.

I bring it back, heavy in my hands. Making sure to keep it away from her face, I begin to tap and chip at the ice, which is surprisingly tough. In the end I have to lift the stone right up in the air and smash it down hard.

Forgive me, I whisper. I don't want to hurt you.

The ice breaks with a pop and a hiss and I lift whole shards off, chucking them in the snow, where they fall against each other with a musical sound. Then I tear off both my gloves and plunge my two bare hands into that freezing water.

The cold is agony. At first there is nothing – my hands crash around and don't find a thing. But then my fingers close on something solid and I know that I have her. The chill of her flesh, the tangle of her hair, the rigid weight of her small body. As I brace to scoop her out, I think I even hear her sigh or gasp. Is it possible?

In my arms, she is a piece of ice. It hurts to hold her. Still, I sit back there in the snow with her slumped hard against me. Strands of her hair dripping over my wrists, her cold face against me, her blue skin that smells of old pond water, her clothes wetting mine.

I look down and see blood on my hands. And that's when I lift my head and notice her standing a few feet away – the dog. Head on one side, intent, an ear cocked up, the other flopping over.

I hold out my hand to her, but she pulls back, lifting her lip and snarling. Breath. Deep in her throat, the beginning of a growl.

Come on – I pat my leg to try to get her to come to me. Come on, come here.

Straightaway she takes a step back, her ears flat, tail tucked and curled between her legs. I snap my fingers at her and she backs still further away. I make my voice into a whisper.

Come on, I say. It's only me.

She shows her teeth.

I try to laugh.

OK, I tell her. Have it your way. Go on – off you go.

As she turns to go, I look down and see that my lap is full of water.

2

It grows colder. Every day the city alters a little more. There are icicles a metre long on Lombard Street. A young lad puts his tongue on some icy railings at Aldgate and gets stuck there for an hour or a day depending on who you want to believe. Trees that have stood on the Embankment for three hundred years split apart with a crack so loud that you see people fall to their knees, thinking they've been shot.

Familiar landmarks fall away, gone in an instant. A multi-storey car park near our building, which has withstood the weight of years, gives in and sinks to the ground in the space of an afternoon. One day the Monument is still up there, defiant and intact; the next it has crashed down across King William Street, the piece of sky it used to occupy left blue and ravished behind it.

London Bridge is still there, and so is Southwark, but Tower Bridge is long gone, plunging down through the ice to rest on the bed of the Thames. Ted says that if you're on the river on a bright day, you can look down and see it lying there, a massive shadow, darkening the water.

If you stand on the ice, you can see all the fish that have swum up towards the light and been blinded or suffocated. Some boys bring picks and shovels and hack away, determined to get at them, but the ice is so thick they soon give up and use the picks to threaten passers-by instead.

The police and the army are long gone and vandalism and

menace are commonplace. Heartlessness has become the law and no one cares any more who they hurt. An old woman is tied to some icy railings and her boots and jacket pulled off, and, even when she is half-naked, no one has the decency to release her so she can crawl to safety. Ted says she must have died hallucinating, because she tells everyone she sees a unicorn, a white beast with a single horn, heading straight for Fenchurch Street.

You'd think that Sophy has seen enough dead people by now, but when she hears about the old woman, she cries.

Meanwhile, the kid is getting better. He is much better. His cut has all but healed and his bruises have turned violet, then blue, and now a sinister mottled yellow.

He still complains of a pain in his shoulder but Graham tells him that will go away too. Graham isn't a doctor, but he has the knack of making people believe what he says. The kid certainly falls for it. He laps it up. He refuses to have anything to do with me, but that suits me fine.

You're not my friend, he says when I happen to pass him in that strange grey portion of corridor by the lifts.

Good, I say. You're not mine either.

I hope he will carry on walking past, but he doesn't. Instead, he stands still for a moment, the black holes of his eyes still on me. I try to meet his gaze. I'm not going to let myself be daunted by a stupid kid.

Why do you tell lies? he asks me then.

I try to smile.

I don't tell lies.

You do. You know you do. You told the others that we didn't even know each other. Why did you do that?

I don't know you, I tell him as firmly as I can. I don't know you and I don't want to know you either.

He shakes his head. I'm not even close to him but I know already how he'll smell. Mean and musty, of old skin and hair. The dirt that is boy.

You're evil, he says. I mean it.

I could say the same about you, I tell him without missing a beat.

There's something really wrong with you.

Ditto, I say.

He looks at me with a brief flicker of interest, as if someone has turned a switch and upped the voltage in his head. I make sure to return the gaze without wavering. I feel very alive, excited even.

Just try me, I think. I'm ready for you.

He has on a long red jersey full of ratty frayed holes, and over it a dirty brown hoodie with some kind of a logo on it – I don't know what, something to do with America or sport, I guess. He is a solid boy – wide-chested and fat-necked and big-thighed.

Where are you going? he asks me as I turn to walk away down the corridor.

I say nothing. I walk, looking straight ahead.

I don't want to turn back, but after a moment or two I can't help it. I do. He has turned around and is looking out of the window. I notice with a quick snag of pleasure that his track-suit bottoms are wearing out at the back and soon you will be able to see his dirty grey pants showing through.

Another time, though, he comes and finds me on purpose. This time the look on his face is forced and jaunty. As if someone has put him up to it. As if he is carrying out a dare.

So how come you don't like kids? he says.

I give him what I hope is a cool look.

I do like kids. I like them very much. It's you I don't like.

He looks at me with interest.

Haven't you got any of your own, then?

I feel myself flush.

Got any what?

Kids.

I don't know, I say. I don't think so. It's none of your business, is it?

He looks at me and I look at him. There are sullen purple shadows under his eyes and I can see that his nose is running. He sniffs and wipes his nose on the sleeve of his hoodie. I watch as he inspects the sleeve.

It must be weird not to remember anything, he says.

I don't know, I say. Is it?

He gives me a hot little look.

I remember lots of stuff. I know my own name. I know that I know you, that I brought you here.

I shake my head.

What? he says. You don't think I did?

I know you didn't.

How did you get here, then?

I try to think. I can't answer the question.

He sniffs again.

And I know that we used to play together.

Play?

I try not to laugh.

Maybe your kids are dead, he says then, as he agitates one part of his clothing against another to absorb the slick of snot. Maybe that's why you had to play with me.

I wait a moment. I can feel the blood jumping into my throat.

Get lost, I tell him. I mean it. Just fuck off and leave me alone.

He looks impressed.

You shouldn't talk to a child like that.

You're not a child.

A new look of respect goes over his face. He licks his lips.

How do you know?

How do I know what?

That I'm not a child. How do you know it? And why do you always go around the building?

I stare at him.

What do you mean, go around it?

I hear you, all the time. Walking around. Up and down the stairs. Going into all the rooms. Even at night you do it.

I say nothing.

Well? he says. What is it? What are you looking for?

I feel my heart contract. I manage to take a step away from him.

Is it a person? Is there someone else here?

I shiver.

I don't know what you're talking about, I say. Any more questions?

He doesn't get it, the sarcasm.

Yes. What happened to your hands?

I can't help it. I glance down at my hands. They look like someone has scratched or bitten them. I pull my sleeves down to cover them.

He gazes at me.

Sometimes I feel so sorry for you, he says.

I move myself away before the temptation to reach out and strike him becomes too much.

Later that day, or maybe it's the day after, I walk into one of the offices on the floor above and I know that someone else has only just walked out.

I glance around me. The light is wavy. Shadows darting here and there.

Who's there? I whisper. Who is it?

Silence.

The room is a large one, a corner room. I haven't been in it before. I go over and sit in the big swivel chair, touch the cold metal of the arms, swing myself from side to side, lay a hand on the computer keys. A layer of dust comes off on my fingers. On the floor, a glass photo frame lies smashed, the photo inside long gone. I slide open a drawer – noiseless, clean, not much in it. I slide it shut again.

I wait then. I wait for a long time. I don't know what I'm waiting for.

After I've been there a while, I get up and go out into the corridor. The air feels like someone has already used it – sucked it in, breathed it out.

I stand by the lifts for a moment, shut my eyes, take a breath. I smell some things that should not be there. Apples. Ink. A blown-out candle. Blood. I think I hear voices, laughter. Far away, a siren. I know that none of this is possible.

Ted is always hungry. When we first came here, he roamed the building looking for vending machines. He smashed the glass wherever he found one and sat down and stuffed himself with M & M's, Ribena, Doritos. Now he goes out looking for food but mostly he comes back with nothing. He dreams of steaks, of sausages, of popcorn, of jacket potatoes with their insides scooped out, loaded with butter and cheddar cheese, of prawn sandwiches . . .

Sophy looks at him.

Prawn sandwiches?

You know the pink fat ones that used to be frozen, with lots of mayonnaise? I wouldn't even mind if they were in brown bread. And I think I'd eat broccoli now. Oh, and I've been thinking a lot about those crispy cheese things you used to get, do you remember, in a yellow packet with a cow on it?

He comes and stands in front of me and pulls up his T-shirt.

What? I say. What am I supposed to be looking at?

Just fucking well look!

I look. His ribs are like something you could play music on. I look away.

Well?

I don't know what teenage boys are supposed to look like, I tell him.

He glares at me.

Well – um – let me see. I think they're supposed to look more or less human.

You do look human, Ted.

I look like a freak.

It's true you haven't got much of a tummy, I say, trying not to look at the trail of small dark hairs that disappear down into his underpants.

He rolls his eyes.

I'm a fucking skeleton.

I watch as he tucks his T-shirt back into his jeans.

He makes me listen to a list of the food he used to get through in one school day.

Two fried eggs at home before I left, a mini-pizza or a BLT at break, chicken and chips at lunch and maybe a roll and butter too. Then maybe a piece of cheesecake or a doughnut when school finished and some crisps and a drink on the bus home. And then a big hot cooked dinner that my mum . . .

His voice tails off. He looks furious with himself. I notice that his ears are very dirty.

Oh Ted, I say.

He swallows back saliva.

I don't want some big emotional conversation about it, he says. I just want something proper to eat.

Another night, he comes back. His speech is thick and his breath is like old perfume.

What? he says.

You've been drinking.

He looks away. His eyes are hooded.

Not really.

I know what alcohol smells like. Where did you get hold of something to drink?

His eyes darken.

You can halt your shit right now, he says, and he tries to take a step forwards but staggers back instead.

Ted, I say. Don't speak to me like that.

Don't chat shit like you're my mum, then.

I say nothing. He sighs. Throws himself backwards into a chair. The chair has wheels. It moves under him.

Well? he says as he uses his feet to get the chair over to the desk. Don't you even want to know where I've been?

32

I look at him.

I don't know.

What do you mean, you don't know?

I'm not sure I want to talk to you when you're drunk.

Fuck's sake! I'm not drunk.

He puts his feet up on the desk. A white salt tidemark on his boots.

I went to a party, he says.

Oh, I say. Did you?

Yes.

He tilts his head back, shuts his eyes. Sophy comes in. She has a scarf wound around her neck and up to her chin. Her cheeks are pink and there are bright shadows under her eyes.

My throat, she says. It really hurts.

She looks at Ted.

What's wrong with him?

Ted pulls off his jumper. For a second or two the room is filled with the peppery smell of his sweat. I look at Sophy.

Ted went to a party.

She stares.

He didn't!

No. I don't think he did either.

It was on the river, Ted says. They had a fire on the ice. Some kids were skating.

Skating? Sophy says. Where did they get the skates?

Well, not real skates. They'd tied bones or something on to their boots so they could slide along. And they were roasting an animal. I think it was a cow. It was bare tasty –

Sophy's mouth falls open.

You had some?

And something that was a bit like vodka. And there was

33

music. And there were all these little kids paddling around in these pools around the fire where the ice had begun to melt and —

There wouldn't have been kids, I say quickly.

Why not? Ted tries to get to his feet but almost falls off the chair. Why wouldn't there be kids?

Is it still going on, do you think? I ask him.

The party? I guess it is. He hesitates, looks at me. You don't believe a single thing I say, do you?

Sophy goes over and touches Ted's shoulder.

Do you think there'll still be meat? Can we go there? Will you take us now?

It is almost the end of the night by the time we make our slow way down to London Bridge. Dawn, but you can see that it will be a dark day. The sky has a violent flush to it. The streets are silent.

We don't wake Graham, but the kid catches up with us as we leave the building, pulling on his coat. I try to tell him he can't come.

But why?

You're too young.

He looks straight at me for a second and then he laughs.

But I'm the same age as you.

Ted catches hold of my shoulder, steadying himself.

What's the problem if he comes? he says. The more of us the better.

I say nothing. I let him come. I have to. But I do my best to ignore him as he trails along behind us, a sturdy, silent, irritating presence.

Look at him, I mutter to Sophy. Nothing stops him, does it?

34

She looks at me. Her face is tired, her cheeks hollow, eyes watering.

What do you mean, nothing stops him?

I glance back at the kid.

The way he keeps on going. He's never affected by anything.

She looks at me and takes a sharp breath.

But don't you realise, exactly the same thing is true of you?

What's true of me?

You're just like him. You're the same. You don't get cold. You don't even get tired. You seem to eat nothing and yet – I'm not saying you're fat, right? – but look at you.

I hug myself. I am warm and solid under my coat. I shrug.

We're all different, I tell her. And anyway, I don't always feel so great. I just don't go on about it like everyone else.

She gives me a long look.

What?

But she doesn't say anything. She keeps on looking.

What? I say again, sick of her eyes on me, annoyed at how her silence makes me feel I have something to prove.

But still she won't speak.

No one could say that Ted is not affected by things. I've never seen a teenage boy so skinny and so vulnerable. Even walking down the street he seems to tilt off to one side, like a young tree sent off kilter by the slightest gust of wind.

And that's when he's sober. Right now he's still a little giddy and drunk. Sophy has to hold on to his arm to keep him upright. It looks all wrong, the slight, pale girl supporting the tall boy. I think that we must make an odd little group, the four of us, with the dog following on behind.

She joined us almost as soon as we left the building and now, every time I glance around, there she is, hurrying along some

35

distance away, nose down, tail lifted, paws moving over the ice and snow.

After a few minutes, I ask Sophy if she's seen her.

Seen who?

The dog.

She turns around.

What? she says, eager to see what I see. Where? What dog?

Back there. Behind us.

She looks. So does Ted.

But where?

The dog stops exactly where she is. She holds one paw in the air. Only her nose moves, sniffing the cold air.

You really don't see her? I say to Sophy. Just over there?

Ted gives me a look.

How do you know it's a her?

I ignore him.

OK, I say. But can you see her?

I can see her, someone says.

I look around. The kid. Trying to muscle his way in. I say nothing.

Sophy begins to cough. A sound like someone tearing paper. When she finishes, her eyes are wet. She looks up. Looks straight at the dog.

I think it's in your imagination, she says.

We walk on. I don't think I've been so far from the building before. Every step we take, the sky loses a little of its bloody darkness.

There are few sounds. A soft crump as snow makes up its mind to slide off a rooftop. Someone sobbing from the dark insides of a burned-out shop, or from an alley piled high with rubbish, or an upstairs window that's had all its glass punched out.

We pass a pile of rubber tyres, partly burned, and a bright plastic sheet with a hand sticking out from under it. You can't tell if it's a man or a woman. One finger is gone where someone has sliced it off to get at the ring.

A bag of rubbish has spilled open and you can see the old containers of things people used to eat. Cardboard cereal packets, bleached by wet and cold but with the curly writing and pictures of cheery brown animals still there. Plastic cartons for milk. The squeezed-out halves of a lemon, still fresh-looking. Some yellow nylon netting that once had fruit in it.

A black metal railing still has a bicycle chained to it. The chain is rusty but the bicycle's all in one piece as if someone has just ridden up that moment and got off. But the kid kicks it as we walk past and the whole thing falls apart – all it was waiting for was a touch from his boot.

One or two people are crouching in the doorways of buildings. It's hard to tell if they are alive or dead. We walk past a row of what were once shops. They're looted and burned inside but the names are still up there: Monsoon. Alliance & Leicester. Hugo Boss. Accessorize. Robert Dyas. Outside the one that says Robert Dyas, a child lies on his back on a flattened-out cardboard box. He's well wrapped up, with an anorak and gloves and a hat that someone has bothered to do up under his chin, but his eyes are dull and nothing at all is going on in his face. Next to him, a youngish man with wild eyes and red, matted hair is sobbing and crying and shouting for someone called Suzanne.

As we pass him I see that half his face is eaten right down to the bone. He has no gloves on and his hands are like two

37

bunches of black bananas. Some of the fingers still have thick dark nails, others are blunted away to stumps.

There's no one around called Suzanne, but he keeps on crying and shouting the name until another voice from somewhere else tells him to shut up.

There's a weak light by the time we reach the river. I know without looking behind me that the dog has left us. The ice is the colour of milk. Up on the bridge, three or four large fires are burning and some people are shouting obscenities at one another. There's no sign of any kind of party.

Well? Sophy says, shivering and looking at Ted.

Ted stares at the frozen water. He yawns. His eyes are red. He rubs at them and then he yawns again.

I just want to crash out and sleep, he says.

Near to us is a bench. Someone has cleared the snow off it and the wood shows up damp but clean. Ted looks at it. I look at it too and something inside me jumps.

What? Sophy says. What's the matter?

I don't know, I tell her. That. Something about it – it reminds me of something.

What? The bench?

I don't know.

You've seen it before?

No, I don't think so. I don't know.

I know I have nothing to lose by sitting on it, so I do – I go over and I sit. Immediately, before I can stop him, the kid joins me. I don't want him there, but I feel him. I feel the slats of the bench adjust themselves under his bulk. Then – even less likely – his arm in its rough coat sleeve, it comes up and rests around my shoulders.

I can't believe it. He is shorter than I am, so he has to lift his arm at an angle to get it up around me. Even then it doesn't reach. I try to push him off but he won't let me. Sophy is laughing. So is Ted.

What the hell do you think you're doing? I say.

He wants to be your boyfriend! Sophy says, still laughing, the laugh turning into a cough.

You and Matt, Ted says. Look at you. You look like an old married couple, sitting there.

I look at the kid. I look at his face, the dimples in his fat cheeks like two stitches pulled up tight. For a moment, he looks like someone else, someone I ought to know. And then, for a few quick seconds, I don't recognise him at all. He's no one. And then that all changes and I do – he's the kid again.

There isn't any party. Or if there ever was one it has left no traces on that flat icy surface that is the river. No remains of a bonfire. No meat bones, no skate tracks – if Ted is to be believed about the skates, that is – nothing at all. It is true that Ted seems to have been drinking, but he could have got hold of something to drink anywhere – a looted pub where someone forgot their stash, a locked-up storeroom that no one has had any luck breaking into.

Soon, though, we smell meat. Under the bridge, two boys are hunched over a brazier. One of them has on a padded jacket that is ripped down both sides and his face is dark with either dirt or frostbite. The other has no hair at all, not even a hat to cover the white dome of his head, which is pitted with scars. Two more boys are hunched near them on the ground, silently pulling the feathers off a pile of birds. Dogs are watching them.

Black and grey smoke curls up from the brazier. You can

smell the fat coming off the carcasses. Sophy swallows and licks her lips.

It smells like Christmas, she says.

Yes, I say. It does.

She glances at me. I see that her lips are cracked and sore. She licks blood off them.

You don't even remember what Christmas is.

I say nothing.

Well, do you?

Christmas. It's hard. I close my eyes and see a fat girl baby sitting under a Christmas tree. A spray of tiny white lights. Something velvety. Laughter. I don't know which Christmas it is and I don't know whose baby.

Well, do you? Sophy says again.

I swallow to get the feeling away. Why does she always want to make things hard for me?

I don't know, I tell her.

Leave her alone, says the kid. What does it matter if she remembers or not?

Sophy turns around and looks at him, surprised.

She's not got anything to prove to you, he says.

Sophy holds his gaze for a moment and then she shrugs.

Anyway, she says at last. Christmas isn't like that.

Isn't like what?

It isn't something you don't know about. You either remember it or you don't.

OK, I say.

She remembers it, says the kid.

I stare at him.

How do you know if I remember it or not? I say.

But before he can answer, one of the boys spots us and starts yelling and chucking lumps of ice. The dogs start barking. It is all over. We hurry away.

That night I wake. I know it's the sound that wakes me. And the air. Colder than it has ever been. Icy cold. I sit up. My breath is sharp and rough in my chest. I look around for Graham but he isn't there. I wait. It comes again.

I hear Sophy sitting up.

What? she says. What is it now?

I turn my eyes towards where I know she is but I can't see her.

Listen, I say.

Listen to what?

That.

What?

You can't hear it?

Hear what? What am I supposed to be hearing?

I tell her to be quiet. I keep my head up, listening. At last I let out a breath.

It's OK, I tell her.

What's OK?

I think it's stopped.

What's stopped?

Nothing. Forget it.

I lie back down but I can feel that Sophy's still sitting up. Even though I can't see her, I know how she'll be – hunched on the blankets, holding on to her knees like they might fall off.

What's stopped?

I hear her teeth chattering in the cold.

I told you. It's nothing. Go to sleep.

I can't. I'm awake now.

Go to sleep.

But I told you – I'm awake.

Well, that's your problem, Sophy. I never asked you to wake up.

At last she settles back down. Silence. The air gets used to itself again. Then, just as I am getting used to it too, there it is. My eyes flick open. On the other side of the room, Sophy doesn't stir.

I hold my breath. Ease myself up to sit. Straightaway I hear her sigh.

Oh, she says, her voice rising to a wail. Why are you doing this?

I'm not doing anything.

Yes you are. It's like the thing with the dog. I think you're just doing it to scare me.

I think about this.

Why would I want to scare you?

She sucks in a little breath.

I don't know, she says. I just think you would.

I listen. The sounds have all gone now. I feel my blood settle.

Go to sleep, I tell her.

I can't now.

Don't be silly. Of course you can.

When the next bang comes, I sit up so fast that Sophy yelps. I strain to see her in the darkness. The air has changed now, the light's different – wavy, grainy. I can almost see the shape of her in it.

You really didn't hear that?

Fuck's sake. Hear *what?*

It comes again. A loud bang, then a whirring sound.

That!

I look across at Sophy. The light has altered itself around her so that I can pick her out – the curve of her cheek, the pale bounce of her hair.

Sophy.

What?

I can see you. Can you see me?

I know that she can't. I watch as she shakes her head.

Just stop it, she says. I really mean it now. I don't want to know what you can see or hear. Just stop telling me things, OK?

I look around me. The room's almost light. Alive with the sound of heavy machinery. Thunking and humming.

It's the lift, I tell her.

What?

It's moving. The lift's moving.

Now Sophy laughs.

You're dreaming, she says – I watch as she runs her hands through her hair. It's a dream, she says again. She sounds relieved.

I am about to tell her that I never dream, that all of my sleep is reliably black and empty, but, just as I am about to say it, the noise stops. All of it. It drops away. Silence again.

It's over, I tell her. It's all right. It's gone.

You said that before.

This time I know it. It won't come back.

I am right. I lie back down. The silence continues. After a moment or two, I lift my head and listen again to check. But the room is dark and soft and silent and I can no longer see Sophy.

Anyway, she says after another second or two have passed, it's not possible.

What's not possible?

The lift. It couldn't move. I thought you said there was no electricity?

Of course there isn't electricity.

Then how can it be moving?

You're right, I say. It can't.

I sleep. But I wake some minutes, or maybe it is hours, later to find the kid crouching over me. He is holding a candle and by its light I can make out the dull, worn-out weave of his old tracksuit bottoms. Also his face — intent, concentrating, wobbling a little in the light from the flame. He has pulled the covers back and is looking at my sleeping body.

I sit up, snatching the blankets to me.

What? — I stare at him, trembling, hardly able to find the right words. What's going on? What the hell are you doing?

It feels like a question I've asked him only recently. He looks at me carefully.

I just want to be with you, he says.

You what?

I want to be —

What are you talking about?

He says nothing. He does not move. He doesn't even blink. His eyes are sober and sad. A thought occurs to me.

Are you asleep? I ask him. Is that what this is?

He says nothing.

Are you sleepwalking?

He does not react.

I'm asking you, which is it — are you asleep or awake?

He shuts his eyes and opens them again.

Awake.

I see then – why didn't I see it before? – that there's a long gash on one side of his face. As if he's been cut with a knife.

What happened to your face? Did someone hurt you? I ask him.

He says nothing. He nods.

Who hurt you?

He takes a breath. Says nothing.

Who did it? I ask him again. Who hurt you?

He looks at me.

You don't remember?

Remember what?

You did it.

Me?

With the piece of glass, remember?

My stomach drops.

What do you mean? What are you talking about? What glass?

The glass. The piece that I gave you to keep.

He leans a little towards me and I try to pull back from him, wrapping the blanket tight around me.

You were scared, he says. It wasn't your fault. You didn't recognise me.

I don't know what you're talking about, I tell him. It's not true. Stop saying these things.

But he isn't listening. Instead he does something that bothers me even more. He sets the candle down on the floor and reaches out and puts a hand on my shoulder. Allows it to move around to the back of my neck. Moves his fingers in my hair.

You're so warm.

I hold my breath. I want to tell him to get off but the words are stuck too far down inside me. They won't come.

He moves his hand till it's on my breast, my hip, my leg. His plump and dirty boy's hand.

Can you feel that? he asks me.

I stare at the hand.

No, I say. I don't know.

In a moment, I tell myself. In a moment I'll make him stop.

I watch as his hand goes to cup my knee. It doesn't seem like the first time he's done it. There's confidence in the movement – energy, habit.

What about that? Can you feel it?

What?

My hand – he says it a little louder and I catch a hint of childish frustration in his voice.

I can't say anything. I can't speak. Calm and happiness are flooding through me. A line of warmth running straight through from knee to thighs and up to my heart.

I'm dreaming this, aren't I? I tell him, even though I haven't dreamed anything in so long.

He keeps his eyes on me.

You're not dreaming.

I'm not?

You're not dreaming.

Silence.

If you like, I could put my arms around you?

No, I say quickly. Then, changing my mind as fast as I made it up, OK. OK. Yes.

It is light when I wake. I am still dreaming of the kid. Graham is lying on the bed next to me. I see that he hasn't undressed.

He still has everything on – his coat, his boots, the knitted hat pulled down over his ears. When he sees that I am awake, he takes hold of my hand and presses something bright and cold and round into it.

Look. See what I went out and got you.

Still confused, still feeling the kid's warm hands on me, I struggle to look at the thing in my hand.

It's an orange, he says.

I know it's an orange.

I sit up, press it to my face, to my nose. Dimpled, glossy, it looks unreal. The citrus smell is intense.

You like it?

I take a breath.

Yes, I say. It's very nice.

Nice?

I weigh it and roll it in my hand. Its oily brightness makes my fingers look even more dead. I put it to my face again, breathe in its scent.

It's lovely. Where did you get it?

There were these crates, stuck under a tarpaulin at Old Street. Crowds of people, fighting for them. I'm sorry I could only get you the one. I suppose it's been frozen all this time – will it still be OK, do you think?

I'm sure it's fine, I say, and I drop it back on the blankets.

He looks disappointed.

Aren't you going to eat it?

Later.

He picks it up, tosses it in the air.

If you don't eat it, I will.

OK.

Even though my mouth is jumping to attention at the thought

47

of that fruit, I get up and pull on my sweater and coat. My scarf, gloves, my boots.

Oh, he says. What are you doing? Don't go.

I have to.

Why? Where are you going? You only just woke up.

I say nothing. The splash of colour in his hands pulls at my eyes. He carries on moving it from hand to hand. It is starting to annoy me. At last he sighs.

At least tell me where you're going?

A thousand possible explanations roll through my head. In the end I settle for the most truthful one.

I think I need to go and find the kid.

3

I look for him everywhere. I search the whole building. I go
from floor to floor, along wide, dead and empty corridors I
didn't know existed. I go into offices and meeting rooms, rooms
left in a hurry, chairs tipped over, jackets, papers left behind.
There are used white Styrofoam cups and white plastic spoons,
some of them tipped over on the table, others knocked to the
floor. There used to be pink sachets of sugar and sweeteners,
but we ripped them open and poured them down our throats
long ago. I look in dark store-cupboards where spiders scuttle
among the polythene bags. Every place I look, he isn't in it.

I'm about to give up when I run into Sophy, who is making
her slow way up the stairs with a bucket of snow held in her
arms.

I'm giving Graham a break, she says. From fetching water
– and straightaway she blushes.

She sets the bucket down, out of breath, and I stare at her
for a moment, trying to decide what's different. She looks pale,
a sketch of her usual self – drawn a bit too quickly by someone
who doesn't care. She starts to cough. The tearing sound again.
When she's finished, I ask her if she's seen him.

Seen who?

Him. That boy.

Which boy?

I wait. I know that she's testing me. I don't mean Ted. And
certainly not Graham.

Matthew, I say, pleased with myself at getting his name.

She looks at me with interest.

But you hate Matt. Why would you want to find him?

It's private.

What do you mean, it's private?

I can't talk about it.

She looks like she's about to ask me something else but, before any words can come out, she doubles over with another fit of coughing so intense that it stops everything. When she straightens up again, I ask her if she's OK.

The look in her eyes is cold and tight.

No, she says. I'm not OK. Can't you see? I'm not at all well. In fact, I think I'm really sick.

She waits for me to say something. I can't think what to say. I don't know what I'm supposed to do about it.

She holds up her hands.

I can't stop coughing, she says. My hands hurt. I've got these bruises, look – and I feel sick all the time. I can't eat anything –

Well, I point out, we've no food anyway.

She doesn't seem to hear me.

And I haven't had a period in ages. Not in all the time we've been here. Are you still getting yours?

I consider this. The idea of bleeding without being injured. It seems unlikely.

I don't think so, I say.

You don't think so?

No, I'm not.

She hesitates, trying to decide what else she wants from me.

But – do you think they'll come back? When things are back to normal, I mean?

I stare at her. Back to normal? What exactly does she think this is? I shake my head.

You'll be fine, I tell her.

I turn to go, but this doesn't seem to satisfy her.

I don't feel fine, she says, raising her voice as I continue on down the stairs.

I say nothing. I keep my eyes on the stairwell. I think of the kid's warm hands on my neck. Surely he must be down here somewhere?

In the end he is exactly where I know he'll be — in one of the big meeting rooms on the floor above. A room I've already been into at least twice. Hunched on the dusty grey carpet, picking up beetles and arranging them in a line along the low metal window sill.

If he heard me come in, he doesn't show it. He doesn't look up. I notice with a snag of affection that there's a tide-mark of blackish dirt on his neck which his hair — always brutishly short and straight — never seems to grow to cover. I don't think I've ever seen such an unappealing hairline on a kid. Usually this thought would make my spirits sink, but this time it does exactly the opposite. It lifts me up. This time looking at him is enough. To know he's right here, in this room, close to me.

What do you want? he says at last.

Nothing.

I hear him take a little breath.

That's a lie, isn't it?

Yes.

He waits a moment, and then he twists round. The sight of his face — clever and furious — makes me catch my breath. I see that there's a smudge of something on his cheek. His eyes are red and sore.

Matt, I say – and I admit it's strange to hear myself say the name – are you OK? Have you been crying?

No.

What?

No, I haven't been crying. Can you go away now? he adds.

But I don't do it – I don't go away. Instead, I wait. I worry about what he's thinking of me, coming to him here, waiting, staying close, watching him. I worry, but not that much – certainly not enough to send myself away.

I put my hand to my face. It is burning. I watch as he carries on moving the beetles around. Deliberate, intent. The brittle slow motion of their legs, shiny blue-black shells slipping between his fingers. It's what boys do, I suppose. Play with insects.

What are you doing? he says after a few moments have passed.

What?

Why aren't you going?

I take a breath.

Please, Matt.

Please what?

Please just let me stay.

He smiles to himself. He says nothing. I ask him what he's doing.

Doing?

Yes, I say. What are you up to?

He tells me his answer as if it's a joke between the two of us.

I'm playing.

* * *

Minutes pass.

You can come and sit down here with me, if you want, he says.

So I do – I get down there on the floor with him, both of us cross-legged on the carpet like a couple of kids. I'm still wearing my coat, but I unbutton it and unwind my scarf, take off my gloves. I sneak some sideways glances at him – his dirty face, his scrub of hair. The creases in his clothes. Thick dark lashes. Flashes of something I can't name in his eyes. He points to a beetle that is struggling over the fibres of the carpet.

You want to know what this one's called?

OK, I say.

I wait, my thoughts still churning.

He's called Arthur.

Arthur? – I start to laugh.

What's funny about that?

I don't know. You have a beetle called Arthur?

I watch the beetle tackling the carpet as if it was a mountain range. Matthew looks at me.

Is it a bad name?

Not really, I say, trying not to laugh. Not at all. It's just –

What's wrong with it?

Nothing's wrong with it.

It happens to be a name I like, he says. You know, like the king with the table?

OK, I say, though I don't know what he means about the king. I like it too.

You're just saying that.

I'm not just saying it. I like it. I really do.

I smile again. He looks at me and frowns.

What's wrong with you today?

Nothing's wrong with me.

Yes there is. Why're you acting so funny?

I'm not. I'm not acting funny.

Yes you are. You're acting like you're all – I don't know – happy or something.

I gaze at him, my heart beating wildly.

I'm not happy.

He shifts his eyes back to the carpet.

OK, but I don't like it.

Don't like what?

You being like this. It's not normal. It's weird.

I wait, thinking about this. I don't know what to tell him. I take a breath.

Matt –

What?

I try to find the words to explain what I'm feeling, but before I can say anything at all, he cuts me off. The look he gives me makes my stomach flip.

What is it? I ask him. What's the matter?

He is staring at me.

Whoa, he says. I can't believe you just said that.

I didn't say anything.

Yes you did.

What? What do you think I said?

He shakes his head, rubs at his face. Then he scratches at his thighs, bulging in their dark tracksuit bottoms. I see that he can't look at me.

For heaven's sake. What is it that you think you heard me say?

But he carries on shaking his head.

I can't say it. I just can't. It's just so raw.

Raw?

It's embarrassing!

Matthew, I say, please — stop teasing me. I mean it.

I'm not teasing you.

OK.

He looks at the carpet for the longest time. Finally, he scratches his head. He doesn't look at me. His face is red.

I will if you want me to, he says at last. I can, you know. I could. I quite like you actually. What I mean is, I don't really care. I wouldn't mind doing it. If you want me to.

I stare at him.

Wouldn't mind doing what?

He waits for one more second. Then he puts his hand up to my cheek and pulls my face towards his in the clumsiest way possible.

His fingers smell of cheese.

What? I begin to say — but he leaves me no space for another word. Because a moment later he has wrapped me in a deep, tight kiss that leaves me gasping for breath and sends my body, mind and heart rocketing skywards.

We lie together on the carpet, him and me, me and Matthew, me and the kid. For a long time I cannot think, cannot move. We hold on to each other so tightly that you'd think we'd just this second discovered the use of our arms.

But after a moment or two, he rolls away from me. The sudden lack of him feels like a draught of icy air. I turn my head and I try to see him, but at first the sun blinds me — coming in through the window, lifting the dust and turning it over and over.

My cheeks are hot. I shrug off my coat.

I'm boiling, I say, and then I frown because it's not something I'd say.

He says nothing.

What are you thinking? I ask him.

He doesn't reply. He isn't even looking at me. He is staring at the ceiling where what was an old fire sprinkler has come loose. I try to look at it too – wanting to see what he sees, feel what he feels.

I ask him if he's OK.

He thinks for a second.

Not really, he says. I suppose I'm a bit scared.

Scared? What are you scared of?

Not you, he says quickly. I'm not scared of you.

I feel a longing to take his grubby hand in mine and thread my fingers into the warm damp centre of it, but I don't do it. I am, I think. I'm scared of me.

Sun moves across the dusty carpet. The palest of shadows. The lightest of touches. I'll remember this, I think, and I shiver.

I didn't mean it by the way, he says. The bit about not caring. You know, when I said I didn't mind if I did it or not? It's not true. I did mind.

OK.

Ever since I've known you, I've thought you were so . . .

I wait, my heart thumping in a mad way.

What? I say. So what?

So pretty.

Pretty? I shut my eyes to stop a laugh.

Do you believe me? he says.

Yes.

You sound like you don't.

I feel myself smile.

I believe you, Matt.

You believe me but what?

But nothing. I believe you.

Anyway, he says after a few moments have passed, it's this place, isn't it?

Which place?

Here. The building.

I sit up.

What do you mean?

You know what I mean.

I am silent for a moment. I hear him swallow. I put my hands to my face, over my eyes.

I don't know what you're talking about, I tell him.

He says nothing. Very gently he takes my hands from my eyes.

Matt?

Still he says nothing. Then I think I feel him squeeze my hand.

The next night, or maybe it's the one after that, I wake and I know that there is someone right there in front of me. It isn't Matthew.

Who is it? I say. Please? Who's there?

My heart is banging, the blood belting so fast around my body that I feel it in my jaw, my head, the backs of my eyes, my teeth. The room has turned very cold.

Tell me who you are, I say again.

The room gets slowly lighter so I can see everything. Desks, chairs, the outline of the window, the blankets and coats piled and forlorn on the floor. It stays like that for a few seconds and then it darkens again.

Nothing else happens.

Next time I wake, it is dawn. A sky like someone has chucked paint across it.

On the other side of the room, or maybe it's the next room, I can hear two people whispering to each other. One of them is Graham. I can't hear what they're saying. I don't want to. One of them laughs and then that same one laughs again. It's the girl, I think. It's Sophy.

Ted finds a couple of dozen packs of cigarettes in a cupboard on the eighth floor. He and the kid are sprawled across one of the desks, laughing together as they share them out.

Not the kid, I think. Matthew. He's Matthew.

When I come in the room, he looks up at me and there's something in his eyes I cannot name – surprise? interest? fun? – but then his gaze returns to the cigarettes.

Can you believe it? Ted is saying. Someone's secret stash. Or else they must be duty free or something.

Duty free? I try to remember what duty free is. It sounds reckless and fun.

It solves all our tobacco problems anyway, Ted says.

I stare at him.

What tobacco problems?

He makes a face.

Um – lack of. Need of. Craving for.

He holds a pack out to me.

Here, he says. And you can have more if you want.

He starts to build a tower with the rest of the packets.

I run a finger over the cellophane. It's cool and slippery. I shake the pack. The lightest sound.

I don't know if I've ever smoked, I say.

Seriously? – he snatches it back. OK, all the more for us, then.

What about Graham?

We'll keep some for Graham.

I look at the kid. Matthew. He smiles at me. I smile back. The skin at the back of my neck grows hot. Boiling hot.

I don't think you did, he says.

What?

Smoke. I don't think you ever did. I don't think you would know how to.

He does, though. Matthew does – he knows how to. He sits in the corridor with Ted and smokes one after another, quick and furious, sucking at the thing in his fingers until it reduces itself to a stub of falling ash.

At least we haven't got to worry about lung disease, Ted says when I tell him he'll feel ill if he smokes so much without any food in him.

Why not? I say. Why haven't you got to worry?

Because we'll all be dead soon anyway.

He looks at Matthew and then, as if he's only just heard his own words, he laughs.

I used to have all these panicky dreams, he says then. One was where all my teeth were loose. When I woke up I'd have to go to the bathroom and feel them to check they were there. Or I'd dream that people were chasing me, coming after me with weapons and stuff. Or the worst one was that I was in this very black room and there was this tiny point of light and I just knew it was evil. But now . . .

He stops talking and he stares into the distance for a moment.

What about now?

Ted looks back at the ribbon of smoke lifting off his fingers into the air.

Now I don't dream anything, he says.

Me too, I say. I never dream.

Matthew says nothing.

In the night, he comes to fetch me.

I know a place, he says. It's good. You'll need your coat.

I get up and pull on my coat and follow him. We go out on to the landing, past the lifts, and into the stairwell. He walks very fast. I struggle to keep up with him.

Wait, I say, but he doesn't seem to hear me.

On the stairs he stops and turns. His eyes are two holes in the darkness. He puts out a hand. I take it. His smaller hand. My large one. My hand in his. It's always been like this, I think. Always.

Three floors up, he says.

We walk up the stairs. The nineteenth floor is pretty much exactly the same as our floor, except for a lighter coloured carpet and more dead plants. Maybe a few more closed doors.

We go down a long corridor and he pushes a heavy metal fire door and suddenly we are out on a big corner terrace. A foot of snow on it, maybe more. A wall and a metal railing all around.

He lights a cigarette, smokes it, hard, not at all in the half-hearted and unsure way that Ted smokes. He smokes as if he half likes it and half doesn't, or else as if he needs it but wants it over with as quick as possible. Then he flicks the butt over the railing. When he turns back to me, his face is thoughtful.

The moon is bright. I go over to the railing and stare at the city lying there beneath and around us. The dome of the big white church I've forgotten the name of.

Towards the Barbican, or maybe it's Holborn, a bonfire is blazing. More than a bonfire. Tall flames and thick black smoke. I feel myself shiver.

Something's on fire over there, I tell him.

He nods.

What do you think it is?

It could be anything really, he says.

I look over at the fire again. The smoke is piling up, repeating itself, moving off into the paler night sky. I shut my eyes. I can't watch it for long. I shiver again.

But things aren't still bursting into flames, are they?

He stares at me for a second.

You remember that?

He gets a plastic broom from one of the rooms off the corridor and uses it to clear a space in the snow. Then he gets two or three big pieces of cardboard, flattened-out boxes that once contained computers or office equipment, and he lays them on the concrete.

Somewhere for us to sit, he says.

I ask him what we're doing out here, but he doesn't answer. He takes off his coat and spreads it on the cardboard.

No, I tell him. Not your coat. Put it back on.

But I want it to be comfortable.

It's very comfortable, I tell him. Honestly. We don't need the –

He interrupts by reaching up and putting his grubby kid's hand over my mouth. Through his fingers, I hear myself laugh.

Shut up, he says. I promise you. We need it.

I let him pull me down. We sit there for a moment, shivering. Then he hugs me tight. A bit too tight. A bit too much the way a kid would hug.

I don't want you to be cold, he says when I try to pull away a bit.

I'm not cold, I tell him truthfully as he carries on almost squeezing the breath out of me. I'm never cold.

Same with me, he says, and his teeth bang together. Or at least, I feel it and I know it's there, like right now – it's freezing – but it never bothers me.

For the second or maybe it's the third time, I ask him why we came out here. Why didn't we just go to one of the hundreds of spare offices inside the building?

He looks at me. I watch his eyes, his face, the chubby tip of his nose.

It's better out here, he says. I like it. It's our place.

Our place?

I look around me for a second. I look at the cold metal railing and the sharp angles of the low concrete wall and the burst of stars that light up the vast blackness of the sky above us.

Yes, he says. Our special place.

I listen to the words and, for a second or two, the world seems to tip, then it rights itself again.

What? he says when he sees me looking.

I don't know what happens then. Maybe I fall asleep. And, in my sleep, I see things that are not there.

A sofa. A pair of shoes – small shoes belonging to a child,

brown and scuffed with a strap and a buckle. Other things too. A baby's highchair with a row of bright-coloured wooden beads on it, the dried remains of old food stuck to them. Some stairs. At the foot of the stairs. At the foot of the stairs . . .

I wake to find the kid watching over me, worry on his face.

You really freaked me out, he says.

I struggle to sit up.

What? What is it?

You must have been having a bad dream.

I blink at him.

I don't dream. I never dream.

Well, you said the weirdest things. While you were asleep.

I gaze at his face, the dark sky beyond it. Every part of my body feels cold. My heart is racing, my mouth dry.

What things? What did I say?

He looks as if he is about to tell me, but then something happens and he seems to change his mind.

For god's sake, Matthew. Tell me.

He thinks about it for a second and then he shakes his head.

I don't want to scare you, he says.

It isn't a new thing, Ted and the kid going out on to the streets, looking for stuff to bring back. There are still shops out there that have not been entirely emptied, boxes and tins buried for so long under ice and snow and rubble, forgotten corners in places that no one has yet thought to go.

Some trips they come back empty-handed, fed up and cold, angry, hungry. Other times, though, they bring things. Cans of Coca-Cola from a vending machine, the liquid still brown and bubbling when you snap the ring. A litre of frozen milk in its waxy container. A tube of toothpaste, barely squeezed, its mintiness so bright and clean that Sophy insists on keeping it in her pocket to lick like a sweet. A rechargeable battery, useless now, but try explaining that to Ted. A lump of Blu-Tack. Shaving foam. The melted plastic casing of a mobile phone.

One time they find a hoard of chocolate money – handfuls of coins, all different sizes, light as air, shiny and gold. We rush to prise off the foil and find a dusty white bloom on the chocolate, but the taste is startling and creamy. Sophy eats her share too fast and spends the next hour being sick.

And then one day Ted brings something else. A big fat suitcase full of children's clothes. He says he found it in a burned-out car near the river. The suitcase smells of melted plastic, and many of the clothes are charred and sour. It's a piece of trash and I don't know why he bothered to bring it back. As soon as I see it, I feel light-headed, exhausted, ill.

But some of it's not been touched by the fire, he says. Some of it's fine. Look, there's some almost brand-new stuff in here. Toys, as well.

Yeah, but it's all baby stuff, Sophy complains.

I look at the clothes. Bright little folds of lilac and pink and yellow, stretchy cotton . . .

Get rid of them, I tell Ted.

He stares at me. He picks up a small pair of trainers with a scuffed picture of a pink and violet fairy on them. Thumbelina. My skin crawls.

I mean it, I say. I'm not joking. Please do it now.

But why? What's the matter?

Oh, but so cute! Sophy pulls out a light-coloured fleece with a zip and a bit of sparkle on the pocket. She holds it against her. Why can't it just be a few sizes bigger?

For a moment it looks like she's going to thrust it at me.

Oh and look! She holds up a little brown plastic animal. Sylvanians. I think I used to have some of these.

She stands the tiny creature – an eyeless, earless thing, wearing a cotton neckerchief – on her hand and holds it out to me. The room wobbles.

Get it away from me, I tell her.

She stares.

But I was only saying . . .

I take a quick step backwards. My heart is racing.

The man who is there with us and whose name has dropped out of my head now, he's trying to put a hand on my shoulder. I struggle to stop him.

Hey, he says. Come on – what's the matter? She didn't mean it. She was only fooling around.

I push him off. Graham, that's it – I push him off.

Where's Matthew? I ask them. The kid, where is he?

Graham's voice comes from a long way away.

What's Matthew got to do with it?

I don't know.

He's not here, Sophy says. I think he went to get water. Why do you want him?

I don't know.

Are you OK? Ted says.

I don't know.

For a long time afterwards, when the suitcase has been got rid of and everyone else has gone from the room, I am still there, sitting by the window trying not to think about all the things I don't know.

I go around the building.

Again I hear printers and phones, desk drawers sliding open

and shut. I hear people laughing, talking. Or the silence that falls when they are all frowning at their screens.

Sometimes I see them. Parts of them anyway. An elbow or a wrist resting on a desk. The cuff of a shirt. An earlobe with a ring or pearl in it. A whiff of perfume or sweat. The staticky shadow of a person's hair.

I smell the sourness of burned coffee when a fresh jug needs to be put on. See the sticky pink rim of a coffee cup. A cardboard sandwich packet that has missed the bin and is on the floor, its tongue of cellophane hanging out. The core of an apple, dampening the sports section of the newspaper it has been placed on. Someone's dry-cleaning, picked up in the lunch hour and hung by its metal hanger from a filing cabinet. A pair of trainers, socks stuck in them, waiting to be run home in.

And sounds too. A faraway sound of hoovering. Bursts of laughter. Doors banging. A meeting ending. A trail of disgruntled voices moving off down the corridor, discussing it.

The place is alive. It hums, it moves. Sometimes it frightens me.

Do you ever think this place is haunted? I ask the kid as we stand in silence on our secret terrace and watch the sun freeze its slow way through the sky.

Yes, he says. I told you. All the time.

I glance at his face.

You told me?

He doesn't look at me. He keeps his eyes straight ahead. The sun is red and liquid, a flame without any warmth. He keeps his elbows on the railing and stares out towards the big white dome of the church. St Paul's. Its edges turning pink.

I've done bad things, I tell him.

Still he doesn't look at me. I wonder if he even heard.

Well, he says at last, who hasn't?

You haven't.

I can promise you, I have.

I say nothing. I don't want to ask him what he's done. I am afraid that he'll say that the bad thing he's done is wanting to be with me. Being my friend. Far away, somewhere in the building, I can hear a dog barking.

Can you hear that? I ask him. That dog?

But he doesn't answer and, next time I look, I'm not even sure he's there.

And then this happens.

A dull dark morning. I am three floors up, on the nineteenth floor, standing on the landing by the lifts, when the air empties itself of any last trace of warmth. An icy wind comes out of nowhere. It lifts my hair. I gasp, I turn. And there she is.

Down at the very end of the corridor. In the grey wavy light. Standing on the dull office carpet. A fair-haired child, very small, no more than one or two years old. Sucking her thumb.

She has on a dark dress and cardigan. Her hair is mussed up at the back as if she's slept on it. I can't tell if she has shoes on her feet. I can only look at her for a second or two at a time. I look and then I cannot look. I have to look away.

I stand there in the cold wind of the corridor, looking and not looking. I let my heart bounce. I hold my breath. Whole moments go by. The room slides around. It isn't upright. Sweat bursts out on my face. I think I might faint.

Then, as suddenly as it came, the dizziness passes. I breathe. I shut my eyes. That's it, I think, it's over. When I open them again, she'll be gone.

But when I open them, she isn't gone. She is still there. If anything, she is even more there than before. The cold wind ruffles her hair. I can see her sturdy little legs, her arms in their knitted sleeves. And her head has turned, her eyes are lit up. She's seen me.

She is facing straight down the corridor towards me now. She has a light-coloured rag and she holds it up to her face with one hand while she sucks on the other thumb. Very slowly, with tottering steps, she starts to move towards me.

Mummy, she says.

I stand still. But when I see that she's coming closer, I can't help it, I take a step away. This displeases her. Keeping her eyes on me, she lets her thumb fall from her mouth.

Mummy, she says again. An accusation.

I'm not your mummy, I whisper.

She stares at me and she says it again.

Mummy?

I shake my head. My blood is jumping.

I'm not your mummy, I say again.

Everything changes then. In a matter of seconds, the wind drops and the air grows even sharper, wilder, lighter.

With one furious cry, as if someone has picked her up and thrown her, she lifts off the ground and comes flying through the air towards me.

4

Graham finds me. He finds me on the floor by the lifts. He tells me he's been looking for me everywhere. He says, What happened, what happened? He says it again and again like a dad or a mad person or something. He tells me that my head is bleeding.

I stare at him, feel a twist of confusion.

My heart?

No, he says. Your head — look.

He takes hold of my hand and lifts it to show me. My hair is warm and sticky.

I ask him how he knew to look for me here, three floors up?

He frowns.

You're always up here, he says. You wander around up here all the time.

I watch as he takes a piece of rag and makes me press it to the cut. When I keep on trying to take it away, he stops me.

You need to stop the bleeding, he says.

He puts the rag on my head again and puts his own hand over mine to show me to hold it there, but I pull it away, look at the rag. It's light-coloured, grubby, and smudged now with someone's blood. I sniff it.

Where did you get this?

What? he says. The cloth? I don't know. It was just here on the floor.

I push it back at him.

I don't want it.

But you need something to stop the bleeding.

I don't care, I tell him. I don't want this.

I fling it as far away down the corridor as I can. It makes no noise when it lands. I shudder. And that's when I realise — something is happening to my face. I put my hand up and find water there. I lick my fingers, taste salt.

Isn't that strange, I tell him.

What's strange?

She's crying.

He looks at me.

Not she, he says. You.

Me?

Yes. You're crying.

The morning runs on, dismal and flat and strange.

I lie on the blankets and coats in the weak sunshine and I stare at the sky, the city, the old life that lies frozen out there. When too many thoughts start to come, I turn myself over and stare at the wall. The wall is better. The sad little marks and stains where a shoe has scuffed or an insect has died. The row of dead-eyed plug sockets which used to bring power. The ghost of a rectangle where something once hung, a calendar perhaps, counting out the world in days and months and years. I watch the wall.

Sometimes people come and talk to me. But never the right person, never the one I wish would come.

Ted comes.

Do you want some of these? he says. I found two whole packets in the pocket of one of the coats. They're OK. I mean, they're not soggy or anything.

I look at what he's holding between his finger and thumb. A very fat worm. Fluorescent orange. Covered in a kind of dust. I don't know what I'm supposed to do with it.

Cheesy Wotsits, Ted says. Remember them? Smell it. I bet you ate them before.

He shoves it under my nose. I smell corn, salt, chemicals.

Hold out your hand and I'll give you some.

I'm OK, thanks.

Come on, you'll like it. It's nice —

Very gently he presses the worm against my lips.

Ted, I whisper, I said no.

I turn away, lick the taste off my lips. My stomach growls.

Graham comes. He puts a hand on my shoulder, or maybe it's my face. I ask him to please find the kid, but he tells me he's not around.

What do you mean, not around? Please get him.

He gives me a look I can't read, then he sighs.

He's probably gone out with Ted.

But why? Where've they gone?

I've no idea. For God's sake. They've probably gone out looking for food. Why is it so important?

I say nothing. I feel Graham looking at me. I know that the look is building up to something.

I want to show you something, he says. It's something I thought about showing you some time ago.

I shake my head. I'm sick of being shown things.

No thanks, I say.

But you don't know what it is yet.

I don't care. Whatever it is, I don't want it.

He puts a hand on my arm. I realise then that I feel all wrong — cold, shaky, sad.

I don't want it, I tell him again, thinking it will almost certainly be to do with sex. I'm not interested.

He gives me a steady look.

But it's something about you, he says. About yourself. Something you ought to know. I noticed it ages ago. I've been thinking about whether I should tell you and now I honestly think I should.

I stare at him. There's only one thing I want to know.

Can't you just find Matt? I ask him again.

He looks annoyed.

Forget Matthew. Can you please try and forget him, just for a moment? He's got nothing to do with this. I told you – it's about you. Now do you want to see it or not?

I look at him and bite my lip. I bite down hard until I taste blood.

I don't know, I tell him. It depends.

What does it depend on?

I'm worried it'll be something bad.

He hesitates.

It's good, he says. Or at least I think it is. But I have to undress you a bit, to show you.

I shake my head and pull away.

In that case, I don't want to.

I wipe my bleeding lip on my sleeve. Graham holds up his hands.

Christ, he says. Not like that, don't worry. I just have to lift your sweater a bit. Trust me, he adds. I'm a lawyer, remember?

I frown and lick my lip again.

Are lawyers supposed to be good people?

He laughs.

I don't know. Don't ask me I was joking. I'm honestly not sure I can be the judge of that kind of thing any more.

He comes and kneels by me and pushes me back on the blankets. He pulls up my sweater, my shirt too. I shiver in the sudden cold air.

And your bottoms too, a little bit.

Do I have to?

Just so I can show you.

But I pull away.

I feel dirty, I tell him, because I'm not feeling like being undressed and especially not by Graham.

We're all dirty.

Not as dirty as I am.

I'm telling you, we're all dirty.

OK.

I let him pull them down. When my belly's exposed to the air, he puts a finger on it and traces it downwards. I shiver again.

Now, he says. You see? Look at that.

I strain to look.

Look at what?

That line. You see it?

A pale brown line extends from my navel right down into my pants. It looks like someone has drawn on me with a blunt crayon.

He keeps his finger on it until I make him move it off.

You know what this means?

That I'm going to die?

Don't be silly. Of course not that.

That I'm fat?

Now you're just guessing.

Well I am fat.

He smiles.

No. Do you know what the line means?

I shake my head. He looks surprised.

You really don't?

I try to think about my body. I don't know anything about it really. Sophy's right that it isn't thin, like everyone else's. I sigh.

Is it an act of God? I ask him at last.

He laughs.

Whatever makes you say that?

Isn't it what people say? When they don't understand something?

He smiles.

I don't know what people you're talking about.

You're right, I say. I don't know either.

He's still looking at the line. I see that his face is serious now.

My wife had one exactly like this. After our first, and then an even darker one after our second.

The words thud through me like a stone.

Your second?

He doesn't look at me.

Our girl, he says. After Lara.

I stare at him.

You have a wife? You have a child?

Children, he says. I have two children. And yes, a wife. Ex-wife now. You know all of this – I've told you it all before.

You've never told me –

I have. You've just forgotten. Anyway what I'm trying to tell you is, so do you.

So do I what?

Children. Babies. That's what the line means. You get it when you're pregnant. It means that you've had children. Or a child. You have them.

A moment passes and I say nothing. Then the person who is me puts her hands over her face. Her heart stays where it is but it speeds up as a bad feeling spreads into her limbs, her blood, her bones. Dread is the word that comes to her.

He tries to take my hands off my face. Her face.

Come on, he says. You knew that already. You must have. I just don't believe it's something you could have forgotten.

I'm silent.

What I mean is, please don't be upset. I really don't think I'm telling you anything you don't already know.

He lies down beside me on the coats. I let him. We lie there and watch the sun make its slow patterns on the wall. Slipping in and out of clouds.

I'm going to forget this, I tell him.

He tilts his head to look at me.

No, he says. You won't. You mustn't.

I forget everything.

Not this.

But I want to.

Why don't you want to remember things? Don't you want to know who you are? Don't you want to go back to being the person you once were?

Once were? A sour taste comes in my mouth. I swallow it down.

I don't know, I say. I don't think so.

But why not?

I think she was a bad person. I'm glad she's gone.
When she went, it was a good thing. I don't want her to come
back.

Graham is staring out of the window with a sad face. I wonder
if he's thinking about his children. I ask him if he remembers
them.

He looks at me.

My kids? Of course I do. I think of them all the time.

Every single day?

His face stays sad.

Yes, he says. Every single day.

I think about this. I realise I can't imagine Graham with children. I ask him what their names are.

John and Lara. John's eight, or nine now I suppose. He would
have had a birthday in the summer. And Lara's five. I've told
you about them before.

I don't think you have.

I have.

OK.

I wait a moment, then I ask him about his wife. He blinks.

My ex. What about her?

What's she like? What's her name?

He's silent for a moment.

I don't know what she's like. She used to be . . . well, our
marriage kind of ground to a halt. It was my fault really. We
tried to fix it, but . . . she was a good person.

What's she called?

Caroline. Her name was Caroline.

You don't think she's alive?

He takes a breath.

I don't know. Well, I hope so, obviously. I hope they're all together and safe.

But you don't know?

No.

That must be hard.

Yes.

Another day, or maybe it's that same day, Sophy comes and finds me.

She's coughing a lot and her eyes are too blue and raw and they shine a little too hard out of her pale face. I notice that she's wearing Graham's jacket, the one with the striped lining that I've seen him in a hundred times. It's much too big on her and she's pulled the sleeves right down over her hands so that only the knuckles show.

Her thin knuckles. Just bones. She glances at my face then back down again.

Are you OK? she says.

Me?

Graham said you fainted or something.

Oh, I say. It was nothing. Look, I'm fine.

You've got a really bad cut on your head.

It's OK.

She stops. Blushes.

Graham says . . .

I watch her face.

Yes? What does Graham say?

He says you don't think you had children.

I give her a hard look.

I haven't. I know I haven't. He was completely wrong about that.

She waits a second.

But –

But what, Sophy?

I've told you before that you had kids.

I swallow, feel my face grow hot.

No, you haven't.

She says nothing. Then she takes a breath.

He also says you see things.

See things? What things?

Things that aren't there.

My heart tightens.

Aren't where?

She stares at me for a second, shakes her head.

Aren't anywhere.

Sophy, I say. How come you've been spending so much time listening to Graham?

And then I look at her pretty face, her eyes, the pretty woman she would almost certainly have grown into. And I realise that Graham hasn't tried to sleep with me in ages.

She starts to say something else then, but it is swallowed by a coughing fit. When she's finished there's something in her hand. She wipes it on her jeans. We both look at it. A brownish smear.

Is that blood? she says.

I don't know.

But what else could it be?

I don't know.

It's blood, isn't it?

Well, it might be, I say.

The sun is low in the sky – what would in the old life have been a sweet and balmy summer evening – when I go up to the nineteenth floor and stand in the corridor. Dust hangs in the air. The carpet is lit up in some places and not in others. I know that I am alone.

I try to stand exactly where I was when I saw her – was it today or was it already yesterday? I look around me. I hold myself still. I listen. Then I say it as loudly as I dare.

Are you there?

The air thumps around me. Silence. The corridor stretches on ahead, empty. I can see nothing in it and I can hear no sound. Nothing shifts and when at last I cough, the sound breaks so hard into the stillness that I jump, frightening myself.

Come to me, I say. Come. I'm not afraid of you.

When nothing happens, I glance behind me and then I take some steps. I walk all the way down the corridor towards the spot where I think I first saw her. Was it here? I try to judge the distance. I stand where I think she was. Her stout little fists and feet. Her eyes fixed on mine. The sudden cold wind that lifted her hair.

I turn back then, and look at the spot where I was standing – the place where she'd have seen me. Looking at that empty spot, a wave of something washes over me. I don't know what it is.

All down one side of the corridor are office doors, a row of them – one or two open, most of them closed. Eight altogether. I count them now. I know exactly what will be in them – desks, chairs, computers with long-dead screens, maybe some plants as well.

Each office has a glass window, an internal window that looks straight on to the corridor, each one with its blind drawn down. I walk past these windows now. Each time I come to a door, I open it and put my head into the office. Each time, as I expect, nothing. Each one empty in the same way. A row of empty offices. Evening sun shining in. An innocent sight. My mouth is dry.

I walk up and down that corridor. I do it maybe ten or twenty times, up and down, up and down, not for any reason other than that I am alone and I can. All alone. My heart unsettled. My boots dragging repeatedly backwards and forwards over that carpet.

You walk this building like a ghost, Graham once said to me and I know that I gazed at him, unsure what exactly he was accusing me of.

I'm walking past these windows for the very last time – thinking I am finally bored of this game and will go downstairs and see what the kid is up to – when I see that something has changed. About three windows along, a blind has been lifted. I creep over and look in. And draw back sharply as her face meets mine.

A child, but not the same child. A different one this time. Older, this one – long fair hair almost down to her waist, delicate limbs, small oval face. A six- or seven-year-old beauty, except for one thing. The skin around her eyes and mouth is the wrong colour – mottled yellow in some places, blue or grey in others. Her lips are almost black.

I don't know who screams first or who screams loudest. Mine bubbles up from my chest, but before I can let it out, her hands have flown to her face and she has backed away across the carpet.

It takes less than a second for the wall to absorb her. She is there and then she isn't there. No shadow, nothing, just the brightness of the space she leaves.

I look down at myself to see if I am still there. I am. My heart is hammering and my legs have lost whatever it is that keeps them up and I have sunk down on the floor, but I am — I'm there, I'm here, here I am.

Matt and I are walking up Bishopsgate towards Spitalfields. I've no idea how we got here. The sky is dark and swollen, fat wet snowflakes coming down.

We go past the old market and along Fournier Street. There are three broken-down doorways, the wood splintered and caving in. Smoke coming from inside one of them. And beyond them, a church, its door burned and broken and all its windows punched out. It must have been done recently, because glass lies all over the snow — shards in all different colours, violet and yellow and pink.

Look — he bends down and picks up a piece in each colour, arranges them on the black nylon of his glove. Do you like them?

I stare at them.

They're OK.

He takes one and holds it up. Pink. The edge jagged and sharp. He holds it up to his face. Pink light shining through. He winks at me, but it doesn't work because the other eye closes a bit as well. I watch as he plays around with the pieces of glass. I feel like a person looking at colours in a dream — you could react but what's the point?

He puts the pink one back and holds out his gloved palm to me.

Here, he says. Which one?

I shake my head.

Which one do you want?

I don't want any.

Choose one.

I don't want to.

You have to. I want you to.

When I still do nothing, he picks up the pink one and holds it out to me. I try to refuse it but he won't let me. He reaches out and stuffs it in my pocket. Then he grabs my wrist and pulls me into one of the doorways.

I let him pull me against him and I notice how clumsy he is. Really, how young.

He looks into my face.

What?

I shake my head.

What's making you unhappy? he says.

I like that he talks about happy and unhappy, that he dares to name feelings, rather than saying, as Graham or Simon would do: What's the matter with you?

Simon? Who the hell's Simon? I think.

I look at him now, this boy, waiting for an answer. Snow clinging to his awkward brown hair, to the collar of his coat. His cheeks dark with cold.

I can't explain it, I say.

He reaches up and pushes the hair from my face. It flops straight back.

Well, try, he says. I don't like it when you're unhappy.

I try not to look at him.

You're just a kid, I tell him.

He doesn't argue. Instead, he puts his arms around me and he hugs me tight. My chin sits on his hair, where the snow is already melting. He hugs like a boy, I think. Too soft, too hard, too everything.

Gently, I try to remove him. But he stays. He sticks. Finally he gives in and lets go. I smell his musty boy's breath as he pulls away from me, frowning.

I don't see what's changed, he says.

Nothing's changed.

Well then.

His fingers are moving over my breastbone, straining down to get under my coat and jumper. I don't like it. I prise them off. He laughs and pushes them back in, delving down. I take them off again.

It's not a game, Matthew.

He scowls.

You want me to go? You want me to go away from you?

I say nothing. I feel myself swallow. My hands are deep in my pockets. I find something sharp. The glass. I press my thumb on it.

Is that what you want? he says.

I don't know, I tell him as I feel the wet of the blood.

He takes a step away. Two steps. His eyes are heavy. I take my hand out of my pocket, suck the blood off my thumb.

No, I say.

No what?

No, I don't want you to go.

On the corner of Brushfield Street, two carthorses have died and fallen over. A fire has been lit and a bunch of men with knives and sticks have taken charge. Two men hack the flesh off the animals, while another three or four keep the crowd at bay. One of them shouts that if people want meat they must queue up and pay for it.

But, says Sophy. Pay with what?

I swing round when I hear her voice. I see Ted standing next to her.

How did you get here?

What do you mean, how did I get here? We came with you.

I look at Matthew, but he shows no surprise. He's watching the men.

But seriously, she says again. What are they going to find to pay with?

I look at her. Sometimes I forget that she's just a stupid teenager.

They'll find something.

Yes, but what?

Everyone has something.

She swallows.

Do we have anything?

Ted glances at me.

Don't be an idiot, Soph, he says.

Some people have already moved away, seeing the knives. A woman and a girl, both of them in brown clothes and with their hair burned close to their heads, have been put off and are hurrying away in the direction of Fournier Street.

But others are queuing up. Most do it calmly, but one or two seem frantic, trying to push their way to the front. Some young lads of twelve or thirteen get cheeky and try to grab the meat before they've given the men anything, but they are kicked down in the snow and beaten.

God, says Sophy as we watch the snow turn red around their heads.

I feel Matthew behind me. He touches the small of my back and I shiver.

A young woman, her baby in a sling at her breast, seems in a bad way, zigzagging along like a drunk. She must be desperate because she lets the men put their hands up her skirts in return for a piece of the meat. But even then they only allow her the smallest scrap and they make sure to chuck it in the snow so she has to bend over to get it.

The crowd is laughing.

God, Sophy says again. Look at that. The poor woman.

We watch as she wraps the meat in a piece of cloth and makes her slow way off down Commercial Street, past a faded sign that says National Lottery Play Here. Finally she comes to a stop and sinks down against a low wall to feed her child.

She'll be all right, won't she? says Sophy.

I say nothing. But some minutes later, we pass her and she is still sitting in the exact same place, the child at her breast, and neither of them moving at all.

We are almost back at the building when there's a shout. A man is coming through the snow towards us, shouting and stumbling and waving his arms. I can't hear the words he's saying but the sound of his voice makes my stomach clench and my breath come faster.

Quick, I tell the kids. We can't let him see us go into the building.

What? says Ted. Let who see?

I glance back at him. He is a big man, dressed in a heavy coat and a hat with flaps that hide his face. I can't see his eyes or his hair. He keeps on calling to us. Waving and shouting.

Walk, I tell the kids. Don't say a thing. Just walk away right now.

I see Sophy hesitate. Looking at Ted.

For God's sake, I tell her. Just do it.

We hurry. We do everything short of break into a run. Snow and ice creak under our feet and it's very hard to move fast without sliding around. I hope the man will give up and stop following, but instead the opposite happens and he quickens his pace as we continue along Bishopsgate and then down in the direction of Threadneedle.

Every time I glance behind me he is just in sight.

Where are we going? Sophy gasps. What's happening? Why didn't we just go inside?

I don't bother answering such a stupid question, but Ted catches up with me and touches my arm.

Can you just tell me what we're running from?

Him.

Who?

I turn around. The man is still coming. Still shouting.

Sophy gives a little sob.

I want to go back to the building.

I grab her arm and pull her along with me.

You want him to know where we live? Is that what you want?

But want who to know? Ted is asking me again.

Sophy's coughing. Her face is red in some places and purple in others. I've never seen her look so ill.

Don't be such a baby, I tell her.

But I'm scared.

Shut up. There's nothing to be scared of.

I'm scared of you, she says.

We hurry on down Threadneedle, past what was once the grand old Bank of England. Here the streets are strewn with debris.

All the once-smart shops have been looted and burned. The signs that used to advertise perfume and make-up and alcohol are all broken or defaced.

A sign still says Mint Haircutting, and another, in faded red, Dry Riser, and another Bank Tejarat. Some window-boxes hang off a building with no windows. In them you can still see the frozen ghost shapes of leaves and stalks. Everywhere, burned-out cars and lorries and buses, all of them window-deep in snow.

Now and then you see the clean, splayed bones of a hand, gripping a rolled-down window or hanging out of a car door. We make our way around an office photocopier that must have fallen out of a window. It is on its side and a pair of feet poke out from under it. One foot still has half a sock on it. The toes on both are entirely black.

Under the arch which still says Dizzy's Bar, Happy Hour, Cocktails 2 for the price of 1, two dogs are snarling and tearing at something that might once have been human. It has no limbs or features, but the long strands of hair on it are dark and matted with blood.

We're nearly at Cannon Street when I stop. The street is empty. I realise I can't see or hear him any more. But something else is wrong. Something missing.

What are we doing? says Ted. Fuck's sake. Why have you made us come all this way?

I try to catch my breath.

The man.

What man? I never saw any man.

I look around me. The silence is hard and flat. Suddenly I know what's missing. It's Matthew.

Where is he? I say.

Who?

The kid. Where's he gone?

Ted shrugs.

Maybe he went back to the building.

I stare at him.

Why would he do that?

I wish we'd gone back there too, Sophy says. She has doubled over and is clutching herself. I wish she wouldn't be so dramatic.

I look at them both.

He wouldn't do that, I say. He wouldn't just go.

Ted looks very fed up.

Well, guess what. He has.

Sophy is still looking at me.

So is it OK? she says.

Is what OK?

Has he gone?

Has who gone?

She rolls her eyes.

Whoever you thought was coming after us.

I think so, yes.

She wipes at her face with a glove. I see that there are fresh tears on her cheeks.

So can we go home now? she says.

Home. It's a funny word for it.

We head up Moorgate intending to cut through Finsbury Circus and round the back of Liverpool Street Station, to avoid going back the way we came. But we've got no further than the beginning of Lothbury when there's another shout close behind us. I glance back and feel my throat go hot. He's moving much faster now.

What is it? Ted says.

It's him. Come on, he's going faster. We need to run.

Ted is staring at me.

But I can't see anyone.

Just run!

Sophy is crying again. I try to pull her along with me but already it's too late. She trips and goes down in the snow.

Get up, I tell her.

I can't.

Sophy, get up!

She stays there in the snow. He has caught up now and is reaching out with both his hands towards her. He's solidly built. So much hair – hard to see his face.

Please, I tell him, as fear pours through me. Please. We have nothing to give you.

He looks at me then.

It's OK, he says. It's me.

It's him, I hear Ted say.

I stare at him. He speaks again, his voice is soft. He says a name which I don't hear. Then I do. I hear it.

She's not here, I hear myself say. But he ignores me, says the name again. That's when I scream.

Ted grabs my arm so tight it hurts.

What the fuck's the matter with you? What are you doing? Can't you even see who it is?

I feel the man coming close, but I am ready for him. Before he can do another thing, I raise my arm in the air and I bring it down. He staggers backwards. I watch as blood jumps out of his face and into the snow.

Sophy screams. Ted is yelling something at me. And the man, I think he is yelling too. Or howling. And I say man, but in those few terrible seconds I see the truth, that he's really much younger than I thought, quite a boy really – no more than about thirteen years old.

Matthew! Sophy cries.

I stare as Ted tries to scoop the kid up in his arms but it turns out he is heavier than we thought – almost as heavy as a full-grown man – and in the end we all three have to carry him between us.

We are inside. We sit at the bottom of the cold concrete stairwell. The kid is on the floor by a fire bucket. I want to touch him but I don't think I should.

Someone else has already done all the things that need to be done. Ted has rolled up his bloody coat and put it under his head. Sophy is doing enough crying for everyone. The kid's eyes are shut and his face is torn. I don't know who did it, and then for a quick second I do and I feel a flush of shame.

I keep my eyes on him. I watch him breathe. His chest lifting and falling. A quick excited feeling rushes through me.

He'll be OK, won't he? I say to Ted.

He looks at me coldly.

I've no idea if he will or not, he says and he looks at the floor, the way men do when something bad or important happens.

What did you use? he says at last. Was it a knife?

What?

To cut him. What was it? What did you use?

I'm silent for a moment.

Glass, I tell him.

What?

A piece of glass.

In my pocket, I put my fingers on it. Feel its sharpness and its coldness. Some of the kid's blood will be on it.

Why? says Ted.

Why?

Yes. Why would you carry a piece of glass around?

Oh, I say. That was him. He gave it to me.

Who?

Matt. He made me take it.

Ted says nothing. I know he doesn't believe me. He watches me for a moment, then he lets his head slump back against the wall, shuts his eyes.

Fucking hell, he says.

It's almost evening, the sun going down, the side of the building so fiercely bright and light it could be on fire.

I tell Graham that I will sit with the kid. He looks at me as if I've offered to chop him up with an axe.

You're not going anywhere near him, he says.

Ask him, I say. Ask him what he wants. He'll say he wants to be with me.

For a moment or two, Graham looks uncertain. But then he draws back.

Don't you understand anything? he says. You did this. It wasn't anyone else. You were the one who hurt him. All of this is your fault.

I wander the building. I walk into an office on the seventeenth floor. A corner office, at the very end of the corridor – a wide and silent and satisfying space. The air outside is turning to night, evening shadows creeping over the building. The dome of the big white church with the man's name is there against the skyline. I take a breath. I think I am alone. It takes a good few minutes before I realise that he's there.

He has on a suit, open at the neck, no tie. A shirt with some kind of pattern on it. His hair is longish, messy — almost touching his shoulders. His chin dark enough to show that he hasn't shaved for a couple of days.

He half leans, half sits on the desk in front of the window and, with one hand over his eyes, the other clenched hard against his stomach, he cries.

I hold my breath.

The room seemed very still and silent when I first came in, but now the sound is everywhere. Brutal, tearing sobs — a noise that no man would let himself make unless he thought he was alone.

I did this, I think. It is me. It is all my fault.

At last, I can't bear it any longer. I say his name. I say it a couple of times, but nothing changes. He doesn't turn or look at me. He can't see me. He doesn't know I'm here.

A few more sobs and then he's still for a moment. I hear his ragged breathing calming down.

Another long moment goes by and then he lets his hands fall and he stares out of the window. I can't see his face, but beyond his head is a sight that makes my stomach twist. The twinkling, night-time lights of the city. The occasional red dot of a plane.

I watch him. He does nothing. He does not move. He gives one final sob and takes a breath. Wipes his face with both hands. I want it badly then — the sensation of his eyes on me. So I say it again, louder this time.

Matt?

He gets up. For a moment I think he must have heard, that

he's coming over to me. Will he see me now? Will he look at me? But no. Very quickly, as if he just thought of something – a new possibility that has not been in his mind before – he turns and walks out of the room.

His step is definite, almost hopeful. As he leaves, he grabs a phone and some keys off the table. They rattle for a second, before they drop into his pocket. He walks right past me – close enough that I could easily reach out and touch him with my hand, put my finger on the rough weave of his jacket, brush the stubble on his cheek.

I could, but I don't. Because that's when I understand the truth – that we're not there together. Only one of us is there, in that room. I don't know which one of us it is.

5

Sophy isn't well. The fever has decided to stay in her body. It has made its claim. Now every part of her is sore and dark and twisted.

Her face isn't her own face any more. It has hollow parts and swollen parts and dried-up parts. The corners of her eyes are raw. She doesn't look like Sophy. She doesn't look like anyone any more.

How did this happen to her? Ted wants to know, as if it is yet another thing that I should have on my conscience.

I lift my head, look at him.

What do you mean, how did it happen? She's ill. She's been ill for a while.

His face tightens.

But I thought she was getting better. Graham told me she was getting better.

Graham doesn't know everything, I tell him.

I sit with Sophy. Her skin is the colour of dead flowers and her breath is quick and harsh. You can watch her chest moving, up and down, up and down, like a little baby's. When she isn't coughing, she sleeps. The sleeps are her main thing now, the centre of her life. She only comes out of them in order to say things, and most of those things make little or no sense.

I dreamed we found this cat, she says. Inside a cab on Moorgate. And she was dead, but in her tummy —

Hush, I tell her. Don't try to talk.

In her tummy — as she speaks, I feel her hot eyelids moving under my hand — were all these kittens.

I smooth back a sticky strand of her hair.

And I wanted to take her home, but you wouldn't let me.

Really?

No! You wouldn't let me. You told me she was dead.

I'm sure she was fine, I say.

She wasn't fine.

OK, she wasn't fine.

Her eyes are on me. She gazes straight into my eyes and out the other side. It gives me a slightly sick feeling, to be looked through like that.

Where am I going? she says another time.

What do you mean, Soph? You're not going anywhere.

I'm not?

I told you. You're staying right here.

With you?

Yes, with me.

But I just went upstairs.

Upstairs?

Didn't we just go upstairs to see the children? Didn't we go up to say goodnight?

I take a breath, try to keep myself steady.

I think you're dreaming, Sophy.

I'm not dreaming.

I touch the hot skin on her hand and I see that one of her fingers is swollen up to three times its normal size and black as a ripe plum.

I'm not dreaming, she says again.

95

I look away quickly.

OK. You're not dreaming.

Graham comes in. He stands on the edge of the room, looking in.

Any change?

Not really.

He waits, his hand still on the door.

You're doing a great job, he says.

He is about to leave, but Sophy sees him standing there. With an effort, she pushes herself up on one arm.

What day is it? she says, her eyes on his face. How long have I been here?

He looks at me, helpless.

It's not the day, I tell her. It's the night.

Her eyes widen.

The night?

Yes. The night.

Graham looks relieved. He looks at Sophy one more time and then he glances at me and he goes.

The snow has mostly stopped but sometimes a single lonely flake comes spinning past the window. Sophy gives a little moan.

In a minute, I tell her, you'll fall asleep.

I don't want to.

You must sleep.

Don't make me.

You know I can't make you.

All right, but I'm afraid to sleep.

There's nothing to be afraid of.

Please just promise you won't go away?

I won't go away.

I don't believe you.

I'm not going anywhere, Sophy.

OK.

Are you still there?

I'm here. Look, open your eyes if you want to. You'll see. Here I am.

Oh.

But later, she sits up. Her face is alert and vivid. You would almost think she was well.

How many of you are there? she asks me.

What?

Every time I look there's another one.

What do you mean, another one?

Like, you know, like there's one more of you.

I shake my head.

I don't know what you mean, I tell her. Sometimes a fever can make you see things.

She listens to me hard, her brow furrowed, concentrating. Then shakes her head.

No, she says. No, it's not that.

OK.

She blinks at me.

There it is again! There's you and then – look – there's another one.

What other one?

The one that isn't you.

Yes, but which one's that?

The one that's her.

I feel myself stiffen.

Sophy, I say, I mean it. You have to stop talking now. You have to sleep.

If I do, you won't go away?

I just told you. Where am I going to go?

You swear that none of you will go?

I draw my coat close around my shoulders.

We're all right here, I tell her.

I also sleep then. And maybe I am in her dream because there we all are, me and her and the other one that isn't me, pulling a kitten out of an upturned cab on Moorgate.

The cat is grey, its limbs unmoving.

You need to warm it up, I say. Put it in your coat.

Sophy stuffs the cat down inside her coat. I see then that her face is the colour of bone. Calcium, dust, putty. Even her hair has no colour.

After a few minutes, she pulls the cat out and looks at it. The fur is matted and rough. The ears are flat and the head sags.

It's dead, I say. It died a long time ago.

Whatever, she says. It's mine. I'm keeping it.

Ted is there. He shows us some notes he found in the cab.

Three twenties and a fifty. Can you believe it? That's more than a hundred quid.

Just pieces of paper, I tell him.

He stuffs them into his pockets.

Ted, I say. There's no such thing as money any more. It's worth nothing. It's useless.

He gazes at me with a face that is almost as colourless as Sophy's.

It's still cash, he says.

Next time Sophy wakes, her eyes are dry and bright. There's a spot of deep pink in each cheek. She sits up.

I'm ready, she says.

I put my hand on her shoulder. Like touching bone.

Sophy? – I wave my hand in front of her face. She looks straight through it. Sophy, can you hear me?

I'll be round about eight, she says.

What?

Eight. You did say eight, didn't you?

She holds up her hand. The whole thing is black now, black right down to the wrist. She twists it, then she lets it drop.

I really feel like dancing, she says.

What's it like? she asks me a little bit later.

What's what like?

Not existing any more. What will it feel like?

I look at my hands. I touch my fingers on the cool back of my neck. Put my lips to the flat inside of my wrist, breathe it in. The smell is of nothing.

I don't know, I say.

But will it be good or bad?

I don't know, I tell her. Neither.

It is the hour before dawn. A sky threaded with orange. The light turns everything strange. Sophy isn't talking. I hold a drink of water to her mouth but it's hard to get her lips to move.

Try to swallow, I say.

She tries, but begins to cough instead. After a few seconds, she pushes my hand away. After a minute or so, the blanket under her head is spattered with red.

I go out, into the corridor. The kid is there, waiting. He's been sitting there, lying there, waiting there – I don't know, even sleeping there – ever since Sophy got ill. I know he isn't doing it for her. He's doing it for me.

His face is better now. It's almost healed. The cut is a long one, a deep one, but it has knitted together well. It begins under his eye and it stops just short of his chin. Whoever did it to him managed to miss the side of his nose. I think it makes him look heroic and I told him so. When I said it, he gave me a strange look.

You don't remember anything about it, do you?

About what?

How it happened.

I hung my head.

I'm sorry, I told him. I know I was there, but . . .

He pulled me to him. Ruffled my hair.

But what?

I'm not sure I remember anything else.

He smiled. He looked like he believed me.

That's right, he said. You were there. You were definitely there.

Now I slide down the wall and sit next to him. I don't say anything. He puts an arm around my shoulders. For once, it fits exactly.

I lean my head in against him. I put my fists into my eyes. I want to punch myself. I can imagine doing it. I would do it hard. I would like it to hurt.

It has begun to get light. I go back in and shut the door and go over to where she lies. Sophy. She isn't a girl any more, but a pile of rags.

As soon as I sit down next to her, I smell it. Coffee. The air turns warm. I hear a phone ringing. I see the edge of someone sitting near us — a man, talking. His feet on the desk. Dark shoes with stitching, worn on the bottom.

The man is laughing. Laughing as he talks. It must be a person he likes. It might be a child. The laugh is kind, patient, expansive. It is right there in the laugh, how much he cares about the person.

I can't see much of him but, as he talks, I see his wetted finger move across and stab at a grain of something, pick it up off the desk. Maybe it's sugar. A grain or two spilled when he stirred his coffee. Maybe it goes in his mouth. I can't see the rest of his face. I stare. While the vision lasts, it is intense.

A moment later, I touch Sophy's dark and swollen hand.

Graham worked here, I tell her. He worked in this building. Didn't he?

Sophy doesn't react. I feel her breath come out and go in again. I decide to tell her a lie.

He loves you, I say. Graham, I mean. He really cares about you.

Her hand does not move. It is hot and hard in mine. I wish I could think of something else to tell her, something that isn't a lie. But I sit there and nothing else comes into my head.

*　*　*

Ted's tall, worried shape appears in the doorway. He beckons me into the corridor. He keeps his voice low.

She's going to die, isn't she?

I stare at him.

Ted, I say. She's young and strong. She's just got a bad chest infection.

He looks at me carefully.

It's not true, is it?

What's not true?

She's not OK. Look at her hands. Something really bad's happening to her. She's really ill.

I watch him. I see how young he looks, how his face is trembling.

What are you saying? I ask him.

He glances back into the room, then he looks at me. He bites his lip.

She needs a doctor, doesn't she?

I say nothing. I go back in the room. He stands there in the doorway, looking lost. I am very glad when he goes away.

She weighs nothing. A feather would upset the air more than she does.

When she's stopped coughing, I lift her as gently as I can and I turn the blanket over and smooth it back down so she has a clean place to lay her head. Straightaway she coughs up more. First, a spray of bright flecks that go everywhere. Then, a sudden, frightening quantity, as if someone has poured it from a cup.

The blanket beneath her head is soaked. I tug it out from under her and bunch it up and turn it around again.

She is trying to say something.

I hold her head. I can feel the frail bones of her skull, her heart pumping in her temples. Her skin is very cold. I stare at the blood.

What, Sophy? What?

She lifts her hands and grabs at the air.

I want my mum, she says.

Graham comes in again. He stands close to me, a little way from where Sophy lies with her eyes closed. His mouth is tense. He says nothing. After a moment or two, he reaches for my hand. He squeezes it.

What's happening? he says.

I don't know.

You want me to stay?

No, I say, my hand dry and loose in his.

You're sure?

Yes.

He lets go of my hand as gently as possible, replacing it by my side.

He leaves like a ghost. He leaves no imprint at all. I do not see him go.

A few minutes later, though, she wakes and stares straight at me. She licks her lips.

Why does the darkness taste of salt?

I flinch.

Sophy, I say. You're awake?

Yes, but why does it?

I glance at the window.

It's not really dark any more. Look, it's really quite light.

It's morning?

Nearly.

Which morning?

It's this morning.

Have we slept?

Not really.

But have we?

No.

I try to get her to turn her head and see how the first pale rays of sun are already scooting up the buildings, but she won't do it. She has other things on her mind.

Is this the house I used to live in?

Used to?

You know. With my mum and dad.

I shake my head.

That house was a long time ago, I tell her.

In the old life?

The old life. Yes.

But – you remember my house?

I shake my head again.

What? – her voice is high and impatient. I can't hear you.

No, I say.

But you came there?

To your house? No. No, Sophy, I didn't.

With an effort, she turns her head towards mine. I feel her trying to inspect my face. Her eyes are open but I don't know what she can see. When she speaks, her voice is a whisper.

But you did.

I try to meet her gaze.

I don't think so.

You don't remember me? From the old life, I mean?

I keep silent a moment.

I don't think so, I say again.

She shuts her eyes for a second.

But – you did. You knew my mum and dad.

I think you're mixing things up, I tell her.

She frowns.

But how many of you are there?

You asked me that before, I say, trying to smile. I told you, there's just me.

Only you?

I'm sorry to disappoint you.

Still, though, she keeps her eyes on me.

But – where are your kids?

Now my heart gathers itself.

What?

The ones I used to babysit. Where are they?

As soon as she says it, my legs turn cold. Ice dropping down them. I put my head in my hands. Feel sweat prick my scalp. I try to look her in the eye, but it's no good.

Sophy, I say, what are you doing? Why are you trying to frighten me?

The sun is up now. The sky has lightened. It is pink. It is properly day.

She lies twisted on the bed. Her hair is damp, whether from sweat or crying, I don't know. There is some fresh blood around her mouth. Her eyes have been closed again for a while now, and her breaths are struggling, painful to hear. Once or twice they seem to stop altogether, as if she's forgotten what she's doing. Then they start up again. As if she remembered just in time.

I try to look at her. The curve of her cheek. The slit in her earlobe where an earring once went. The tracing of veins on her temple. Freckles on her nose. A paler sweep of them under her eyes. The bruising on her forehead.

I don't know whether I'll remember all of it or none of it.

Outside, the sun goes behind a cloud and, for a brief moment, a shadow darkens her face. Then sunshine, spilling back over it. She lets out a long breath, but takes none to replace it.

Sophy?

I wait.

Sophy?

She relents, remembers. She gulps in air. She gives one little moan, soft and disappointed – a last protest. I keep my fingers on her arm.

It's all right, I say. It's all right. I'm right here.

She lets out another breath then and her eyes, which have been closed, open a little. She looks surprised, almost pleased, as if she's seen something or someone she knows. It isn't me she's looking at.

I wait for her to take another breath. I wait for a long time. I carry on waiting. Minutes later, nothing has changed and I am still waiting.

I wait there. I don't know how long it is. I wait until it no longer seems strange to me that although she is still lying there, I am completely alone.

Then I straighten her arms under the blankets, tucking them in so the bad, dark colour of her hand does not show. I wipe the blood from her mouth, smooth her damp hair.

I touch her face with the back of my hand. Already it has

begun to lose its heat. I try to close her eyes but they keep on springing back open and staring at the space in front of her. As if she doesn't want to miss anything.

She is still staring at nothing as I turn and leave the room.

Out in the corridor, Matthew is hunched against the wall in his boots and coat, his knees drawn up, his head resting on a frayed elbow. He looks about eight years old or a hundred and eight, depending on what thoughts are in your head when you look at him. On the floor next to him is an old brown blanket, an empty packet of cigarettes and a piece of something yellow that might be food.

I leave him sleeping and I pull open the heavy fire door and climb the stairs. Up the three flights and out through another fire door and on to the landing that is identical to ours in pretty much every way, except for one thing.

She is standing there.

She is standing there and my heart is thudding, even though this time I'm not surprised. I knew she'd be here, waiting for me exactly like before. One thumb is stuck in her mouth, the other holds the same piece of light-coloured rag to her nose. Blood on the rag. My own blood, I think, though I can no longer remember why it would be there.

She is clearer to me this time. Her hair is baby's hair, fine and light and staticky, roughed up at the back, not brushed in a while. She has on a dark pinafore dress, thick woollen tights, stout, buckled sandals. Her knitted cardigan – is it pink? – is buttoned on all the wrong holes, but done up to her chin, as if whoever dressed her that morning wanted to make sure she stayed warm.

The moment she sees me, her whole face bursts into life.

She throws her arms up in the air and moves her feet up and down, running on the spot.

Mummy, Mummy, Mummy! she cries.

Without even thinking, I take a couple of steps back, feel around for the door that leads to the stairs. But she is ready for me. Before I can touch the handle of the door, she whips her thumb out of her mouth.

Mummy not do that! Not go!

The command is wild. The wet thumb stays exactly where it is, in the air. I stand still. I don't know whether I want to stay or go. Neither feels possible. We both wait to see what will happen next.

The air is icy. I feel myself start to shiver, but I don't let it happen. I don't allow myself to feel anything at all. I don't shiver.

Mummy, she says.

This time it's not a question. When she goes back to the job of sucking, there is a little glint of pleasure in her eye. Her chin wobbles. She watches me.

I take a breath.

Sweetheart, I say. I'm not your mummy.

I know she's listening, because her eyes grow wider. So I continue.

Where is she? Where's your mummy? Shall I help you find her? Shall I? Shall we go and look for her together?

The effect is instant and extreme. I might as well have reached out and slapped her. Before I can say another word, her mouth drops open and her chin buckles and her eyes turn into two dark slits as the arms clamp down rigid against her sides.

She throws back her head and she screams.

*　*　*

In the corridor, I hear a door bang shut. Then another one. A brief scuffle and then the sound of feet running. A whoop of happiness.

It's her! It's her!

Yay!

Mummy!

Mum!

Before I can do anything, two children and a dog have found me. Wrapping themselves around my legs. Laughing. Kissing. Gripping on. Bumping against me. Saliva and fingers and hair.

I shudder and cry out, stagger backwards, try to get free of them. The dog circles my feet, barking loudly, then rushes off to do the same to the little girl, whose screams are at last subsiding into gasping sobs.

I want to do it gently but in the end it's not possible. In the end it's their fault that I have to be rough. I prise both pairs of hands off me and shove them away.

Who are you? I cry. What the hell are you doing?

They stare at me, shocked.

Mummy, says the boy at last in a small voice. You don't need to swear.

I feel my heart pounding. I put a hand to my throat.

Where did you come from? I ask him. What's going on? Who are you?

The bigger one, the girl, about nine or ten years old, claps her hand over her mouth and gasps. But the boy – round-faced, curly gingery hair, a chip on his front tooth and dirt on his cheeks – tugs on my sleeve.

Have you got anything to eat? he whines.

No. I twist my hand to get him off.

But, Mum.

Stop calling me that. I'm not your mum.

I give him a really hard look then. It works. He starts to cry.

The girl has pulled away now and is openly staring at me. I look her up and down with equal openness. She's a weedy-looking child. Her mouse-coloured hair is chopped in a bob and held back with some kind of plastic clip. Her face is thin and pale, her chin pointy. So much going on in her eyes that just looking at them makes me feel tired.

What's the matter? she says. Why won't you be nice to us?

Yes! the boy shouts. Why won't you? Can't you see you're being really horrible?

I glance over at the small girl, who is keeping herself up in a standing position by gripping on to a tuft of the dog's thick neck fur. Now and then she half hiccups, half sobs. Her eyes never leave my face.

I don't know who you are, I tell the bigger girl. I've never seen any of you before. I don't know why you keep on calling me Mummy.

She claps a hand up to her mouth again. She and the boy exchange a look of real misery.

Oh, she says. Please. Why are you doing this?

The boy has got his fingers back on me again. Worrying away at the edge of my sweater.

Yes, why are you? he says.

For the second time, I shake him off. I turn back to the girl.

Why do you think I'm your mother?

She blinks.

Because you are.

But I've never seen you before. How can I be your mother if I don't even know you?

Now she gasps and takes a step away.

Please, she says at last. I know you're just playing a funny game or something, but I really really don't like it.

I don't like it either, says the boy. But he doesn't pull away. Instead he puts his cold hand on mine. A touch like ice. I try to remove mine but he won't let me. He tilts his head back and looks up into my face.

Just please be normal, he says.

The dog is barking again. Sharp, identical, excited barks. The girl screams at it to shut up, but the animal only fixes its gaze on her and barks louder.

At last, she goes over and grabs its snout so the teeth snap shut. The dog makes a strangled sound. The boy laughs and then so does the little girl. When she releases it, the dog lets out a whine, then is quiet.

She looks at me.

We didn't mean to scare you, she says in a careful voice. We're just so very happy to see you, that's all.

We didn't think you was ever going to come, says the boy.

Were ever going to, the girl corrects him,

Were ever.

We'd almost given up, she says.

Without warning, the little girl lets go of the dog. As her legs give way, she sinks happily to the floor. The dog flops down next to her.

Why aren't you talking? the boy asks me.

Because I don't know what to say.

Why?

Because I'm shocked.

Why?

For God's sake, can you at least stop saying why?

This silences him. The girl eyes me for a quick moment. Then she marches over to the little one and scoops her up under the arms and staggers back with her hanging there.

She puts her down in front of me. The child stands there, wobbling slightly. Her face is still wet from crying. After a moment or two, she reaches both arms up into the air towards me.

Well? says the girl. What are you waiting for?

What?

Aren't you going to pick her up?

I shake my head and back slightly away. The dog yawns.

Is it because she's a bit snotty? says the boy.

No.

What, then?

I bite my lip.

Look, I just don't want to, OK? I'm not her mummy.

Immediately, the child starts to cry again – soft at first, but building to something more frantic that makes my whole body hurt. I reach down and try to pull her against my legs. It doesn't work. She cries even louder.

I wish she would shut up, I say.

The girl is staring at me.

Why don't you comfort her, then?

I shrug.

I'm not much good with babies, I say.

Get down on the floor and let her go on your lap, suggests the boy. She'll soon stop then.

I look at the girl.

Can't you do it?

She shakes her head.

It has to be you.

I don't believe her, but giving in is easier than fighting, so I do it. I put myself down there on the floor. Straightaway the little girl pushes herself against me. I put my hand on her small shoulder, her face, then I take it away again because it's wet. She nuzzles closer.

Say, There, there, Munchkin, says the boy.

Why?

Because it's what you say.

Is that her name? Munchkin?

He bursts out laughing.

Of course it isn't! Munchkin isn't a real name! Nobody would call their child Munchkin?

The girl frowns at me.

It's what you sometimes call her.

Not me, I say. I don't call her anything. I don't even know who she is.

I look down at the little girl. Her thumb has found her mouth and her breath comes in little shudders now. I feel her body relax as she settles against me. I feel mine too, relaxing.

There, there, I say. It's OK. You're OK.

I don't call her Munchkin, but at last the girl seems happy.

The boy's eyes flick from her face to mine.

I've got a wobbly tooth, look! he says, encouraged.

They all join me down there on the floor. The boy flings himself down on his stomach some little way away but I can feel him edging closer. The girl sits cross-legged, picking at her bare arms. The dog has its chin on its paws, but its eyes are open. Every now and then it sighs loudly. The little one is still snuggled against my legs.

Look, I say. I don't want to be unkind –

Then don't say it, says the girl.

What?

That's what you always tell us. If you need to start by saying that, then you shouldn't say anything at all.

Because it means you're absolutely definitely going to be unkind, mutters the boy.

I think about this. I say nothing.

But I know what you were going to say, says the boy.

Oh yes?

You were going to try and do the horrible thing of pretending you aren't our mum again.

The girl is looking at me. She pulls her knees up to her chest. Tears wobble in her eyes.

You don't like us any more, she says.

I can feel the boy watching my face.

Of course I like you.

But you don't really.

I wait, then I let it out.

I don't know you, I tell her. How can I tell if I like you if I don't even know you?

She bites her lip and hugs her knees tighter. I see that all of her fingernails are chewed right down to the quick, the ends of her fingers swollen and red and raw.

By the way, she says, if you want to know, I think you are being unkind. I think it's the very meanest thing in the world, to do this to us when we've been wanting and wanting you to come.

And I think so too, says the boy.

I look at their two pale faces, dirty hair, shadowy eyes.

But what am I supposed to do? Would you want me to lie to you?

Yes, says the boy.

The girl tells him to shut up.

Shut up yourself, he says, without conviction. His face crowds in on itself and he falls silent.

I look at the girl and see that she's crying. Her shoulders are shaking. She keeps her face turned slightly away from me and she makes a hard line with her mouth to keep out the tears. They fall anyway.

I reach out and touch her arm.

Maybe if you want I could try and help you find your real mum?

The boy gasps.

We don't want a real mum. We only want you!

Even through her tears, his sister gives him a sharp look.

Shut up, she says. Stop being a baby, Jimmy. I mean it. You're being a real pain.

Shut up yourself, he says again. He pushes his two grubby fists over his eyes. My tummy hurts, he says. Ow.

The girl pulls up her T-shirt and wipes her face. She looks at me.

He's still getting those stomach aches. Sometimes he cries all night. I think he needs to go to the doctor's.

I'm not going to the doctor's, the boy who is called Jimmy says quickly.

But there are no doctors, I tell her.

She stares at me.

The world has changed. Don't you know that? Nothing's how it used to be.

She sniffs.

I know that. Of course I know it. I just thought there might still be, like, one small hospital or something, that's still looking after people.

Well, there isn't. There's nothing like that and I don't think there will be ever again.

She looks at me and swallows.

Never? Then what will we do?

Let me have a think, I say, mainly to shut her up. I'll think of something, OK?

But what? What are you going to think of that you can't think of now?

I don't know.

You won't be able to think of anything, will you?

I'm not sure, I say.

I notice that the deep chill has left the air. It has grown softer, lighter, warmer. If you didn't know any different, you could almost think that the light flooding in through the far window was the bright sunshine of high summer.

Sunbeams move across the carpet. The dog sighs. I shift myself under the baby's soft weight. I yawn and feel my head grow heavy, but I shake myself out of it.

I can't stay here, I tell them.

Why can't you?

I just can't. I must go soon.

But why? says Jimmy, who has rolled along the carpet and is lying against my thigh now with his eyes closed. Why do you need to go?

There's a girl I was looking after, I tell him. A big girl, bigger than you.

A grown-up? he says. He opens one eye and looks at me.

Not quite a grown-up. A teenager, I suppose. And she's not well. In fact, I think she's dead.

The girl looks unmoved.

Did you kill her?

Of course I didn't kill her. But I need to go and see how she is.

But you know how she is, the girl points out.

If she's completely dead, says Jimmy, you can leave her out for the birds.

I look at him.

What do you mean? What birds?

I saw this film, right, where they put a dead person on a turret and the vultures came. It was wicked.

Don't listen to him, the girl says. It was a scary film. It was horrible. Afterwards I couldn't sleep. I wish we hadn't watched it.

But the vultures weren't bad. They were good! They were just doing what vultures are programmed to do.

The girl looks at him.

Stop talking so loudly, Jimmy.

I'm not talking loudly.

You are. You keep on shouting. You know you are. You're just showing off.

Jimmy ignores her.

What I mean is, even if you don't really think you're our mum and all that, I still really like you. I think you're lovely. I don't want you to go and see the dead girl. I want you to stay here with us.

I look down at the little one, who is now sleeping on me, the clean weight of her head against my thigh. I allow my fingers to sit in her soft hair.

So if he's Jimmy, I say to the girl, who are you?

She bites one of her fingers.

It's just a bit weird, you know, to have your own mum ask you what your name is.

I'll tell you. Do you want me to tell you? Jimmy says, but the girl puts a hand over his mouth.

I'm Iris. It's a kind of flower.

I know it's a flower, I tell her. A purple flower.

She gives me a sharp look.

They can be blue, she says. Or yellow. Quite a lot of colours really.

Well, it's a pretty name, I tell her.

She rolls her eyes.

You chose it.

The boy is leaning over even closer to me. I can feel his breath on my chin.

And I'm Jimmy.

I know that, I tell him.

He pulls back, astonished.

How? How did you know it?

Because Iris has been calling you that.

Oh.

It's James in fact, Iris says.

I look at him.

But you like to be called Jimmy?

He gives it a moment's thought.

I really like to be called Chitty.

Chitty?

Like Chitty Chitty Bang Bang.

It's a car, says Iris. A car in a children's film. And don't listen to him – he doesn't.

Yes I do!

I look at him.

OK, I say, today we'll call you Chitty. But tomorrow we'll have to see.

You shouldn't say that, Iris says. He'll want to be called a different thing every day.

I look down at the baby. She points at Iris.

Isey! she cries.

That's Katie, Iris says.

Katie points at the dog.

Dod! she says.

That's right, Iris tells her. It's a dog, isn't it? By the way, she says, turning back to me. Can you see that her cheeks are really red? Well, we need some of that stuff.

What stuff?

She looks unimpressed.

When she's teething. You used to have some stuff to put on her gums. Have you got any now?

Jimmy pulls at my sleeve again.

You know my baby tooth, the one that I chipped? Well, when it comes out and I get my grown-up tooth there, is it absolutely definite that it won't be chipped as well?

Jimmy, shush — Iris gives him an irritable look. You keep it in your handbag, she adds, turning back to me.

I'm about to tell her that no one has handbags any more, when there's another loud slam and more footsteps in the corridor and I snap my head around to see a small, fair-haired girl, maybe six or seven years old, running towards me. Before I can say anything, she throws herself at me.

Gloria, says Iris in a dull voice. At the mention of the name, the dog, who had seemed to be asleep, lets her tail beat softly on the carpet. Don't ask her anything by the way, because she doesn't speak any more.

She just gave up talking one day, says Jimmy. And that was that.

I look at Gloria's silent face and something in me tightens. I hold her away from me for a moment, at arm's length.

I've seen her before, I say.

Iris sighs.

You've seen us all before. How many times do I have to tell you?

No, I say, as Gloria looks straight back at me, cool and appraising, and I try not to shudder. This is different. It's like Katie . . .

What's like Katie?

I've seen them in the building.

We're all in the building! says Jimmy, and he jumps up as he sees that Gloria is trying to climb on my lap. I was here first! It's not fair!

You weren't, Iris says. You weren't even in her lap.

He doesn't listen. He keeps on pushing and shoving. The dog, seeing the game, stands up and starts to bark. Gloria holds on to my legs, firmly and silently keeping herself in my lap. The baby stirs, about to wake.

In the end, I push them both away.

There, I say. Well done. Neither of you can sit there. OK? Are you happy now?

Jimmy stares at me and then he laughs. So does Iris. Even Gloria's mouth twists up at one corner.

What? I say. What's so funny?

Iris and Jimmy exchange a glance.

That's what you always say. That means you're definitely our mum.

*   *   *

120

Gloria is standing there, gazing at me. Her long fair hair, which probably used to be pretty, is more like wool now, tangled and lumpy.

Has no one got a hairbrush? I say.

No, Iris says. Why would we?

I glance at her, noticing her sudden coldness.

I don't know what things you have up here, I tell her. I haven't seen where you sleep. I don't know what you have.

We don't sleep anywhere. We have nothing.

No toys or clothes?

No.

I don't even have my giraffe, says Jimmy.

It's a cuddly toy he used to like, says Iris.

But how do you manage?

She shrugs and her face makes me think of Sophy's. Almost without colour.

There's nothing to manage, is there? she says.

I don't speak. I take hold of one of the lumps in Gloria's hair and try to pull it apart with my fingers. She lets me do it for a second or two, then she shakes me off.

I could untangle it for you, I tell her.

It's no use saying anything to her, Iris says. I told you. She doesn't talk.

Why not? Why doesn't she talk?

There's something wrong with her, Jimmy says.

Iris flicks a glance at him and then at me.

She hasn't said a single thing since the . . . you know, the day.

Which day?

She gives me a tight little look.

That day.

The day the fish died! says Jimmy. The day we made the biscuits. The day you got pregnant and –

Not pregnant, Iris says. What are you talking about, Jimmy? It was the opposite of pregnant. You don't understand anything?

I do! Shut up – I do understand!

No, she says. You've got it all wrong.

Jimmy takes a breath, as if he's about to say something else, then he stops. Iris looks at me.

You don't know what we're talking about, do you? she says.

Something cold creeps through me.

No.

You're still our mum, though, Jimmy says, his voice threaded with anxiety.

Stop going on about it, Iris says to him.

Gloria is still looking at me. I keep my eyes on her. At last, she shapes her thumb and first finger into a circle and looks at me through it.

What does that mean?

Iris looks bored.

It's just something she does. It doesn't mean anything.

Gloria sits down on the floor then and thrusts her feet into my lap. Brown shoes on them, the straps undone.

She wants you to do them up, says Iris. She can't do it herself. You don't have to do it if you don't want to, though. She really ought to learn.

Gloria keeps her eyes on me. I do up the buckles on the straps, fiddling until I get the tightness right.

When I've finished, she stands up quickly and goes and sits down by the dog. Both of them looking at me.

She doesn't mean to be rude, Iris says.

Can I have a go in your lap now? Jimmy says. He stands and starts backing towards me.

In a minute, I say.

No, now!

All right.

I let him sit on me. I can smell the slight mustiness of his hair, his fingers. I had thought I would mind it, but I don't.

You shouldn't give into him like that, Iris tells me. He'll think he can make you do anything.

Jimmy says nothing. He just squashes himself harder against me.

Are you always like this? I ask Iris.

Like what?

I don't know – telling everyone what to do all the time.

For a moment she looks startled, then she sucks in her cheeks. She stops talking and chews on a fingernail.

In my lap, Jimmy twists around and looks up at my face.

You're not very nice, are you? he says in a cheerful voice.

I stare at him.

I don't know, I tell him. I don't know if I'm nice or not.

Well you're not. But I still really like you, he adds, pulling my arm tight around him.

When a few minutes have gone by, Iris chews a finger and looks at me.

Can I tell you something?

I wait.

It's about what happened.

What happened when?

On that day.

What day?

She looks impatient.

You know – the day we were talking about. The terrible day?

The day the fish – Jimmy begins.

OK, I say. What about it?

Iris glances at Jimmy, who is looking at us both with a worried face. She takes a big breath.

Well then, please don't get upset but . . . we're missing Arthur.

Arthur?

For a second, Iris shuts her eyes.

We haven't got him. We haven't seen him since – well, I'm worried we might have left him behind. At home, I mean.

Who's Arthur?

She looks amazed.

The baby, of course. Your baby!

I look down at Katie.

Not her, Iris says. Arthur's a real baby. He's the one you had just before . . . well, he's only just been born.

Like about six months ago or something, Jimmy explains.

Not six months, Iris says. Don't listen to him. It's nowhere near six. It might not even be a month. I don't know how long we've all been here. Arthur was newborn. He was tiny. He'll still be very little.

She stares at my face.

I think he must be all alone at home, she says again. I'm worried that he might not be OK.

Her mouth twists as if she's about to cry.

I look at her.

Iris, I say. I honestly don't know what you're talking about.

She shakes her head.

You don't even remember that you had a baby?

There was blood, says Jimmy, almost to himself. Lots of blood, in the kitchen. It was all over the floor.

I look at them both and feel something in me harden.

Look, I'm really sorry about the baby, I say. Whatever happened to it. But it wasn't mine. There's nothing I can do.

Iris looks shocked. She gulps down a breath, tears in her voice.

But I'm worried about him.

What am I supposed to do?

But – I don't have anyone else I can tell.

Well, too bad.

Too bad?

Can we just stop talking about this now?

That shuts her up. She says nothing after that. In my lap, I feel Jimmy's body go rigid, then soft, then rigid again as he listens to all of this.

A moment later, though, he has his hand up. His whole arm is stretched up past his ear.

Um – can I say something?

Go ahead.

He gives a little gasp.

Well, he begins, I'm not really worried about finding Arthur. I think Iris's being silly really. I don't think he's all alone in the house. Because you see we left him sleeping on that cushion on the floor and actually I think what happened is his heart just stopped and . . . and he died.

Straightaway Iris rounds on him.

Don't be such a stupid idiot! What a terrible thing to say about your own brother. Of course he didn't die. How could you possibly know anyway?

Jimmy looks at her.

Maybe the clue was that he wasn't even breathing?

Liar! howls Iris. You little liar!

Jimmy leans back against me. He shuts his eyes and puts his fingers in his ears.

I just know it, he says.

You're telling lies, Jimmy, Iris says. You're as bad as her. I hate you.

He drums his feet on the carpet.

My name's not Jimmy, it's Chitty, he says.

As if someone invisible has called to her, Gloria gets to her feet and, without looking at any of us, walks away down the corridor. The dog watches her go, ears pricked up in a hopeful and fascinated way. For a few seconds she looks like she might follow her, but then she sighs and rests her chin back down on her paws.

Where's she going? I ask Iris.

She doesn't look at me. She's still angry.

I don't know, she says. Somewhere. Away.

Is she OK?

I don't know.

She always does that, Jimmy says. She always goes away. I think she likes to go on walks around the building.

My heart flips.

Well, me too, I say. I have to go.

Iris looks at me.

Why? Why must you?

Is it because of the dead girl? Jimmy says.

He pats his leg and calls the dog to him. The dog lifts her head, thinks about it, then settles back down again.

Iris puts a hand on mine. It's colder than it should be. The chill goes through me. She licks her lips and glances at Jimmy.

Don't go, she says. I'm sorry if I was mean to you. I'm sorry I talked about Arthur. Stay here with us. I don't think we can carry on any longer without you.

We need you, Jimmy says. We've been waiting ages for you to come.

He takes hold of my other hand and plaits his fingers through mine, then squeezes a bit too hard.

Ouch, I say.

He laughs.

Why is blood warm?

I don't know, I say. Why is blood warm?

No, I was asking you!

I'm not sure. I'm going to have to think about it.

And why don't cats go on the beach? Do you think when people die they come back as animals? What kind of animal would you want to come back as?

Jimmy, I say. All these questions.

He's just trying to keep you here, Iris says.

And where do you think our dad is now? And will you still love me when I'm dead?

Seconds go by. The cold is coming back now and the light has turned bitter.

Where is your dad? I ask Iris then.

She stares at me for a second or two.

You really don't know?

How would I know?

She swallows and looks at Jimmy.

He left, she says.

127

You don't know where he is?

She shakes her head. I look at Jimmy, expecting him to have something to say about that, but he doesn't. He looks back at Iris as if she's in charge of this particular conversation.

His sister folds her arms and looks at me carefully.

I know you said you don't care, she says, picking her words, and that's OK. But I just want to know your opinion, right, because you're a grown-up? Do you think that a baby can survive all alone in a house without anyone to hold him and feed him and change his nappy and all that?

I think about this.

No, I tell her. I don't.

She turns away, puts her hands over her face.

Iris, I say. I can't lie to you. So many people have died. Don't you realise — almost everyone in the world is dead.

Jimmy's mouth falls open.

Seriously! Everyone? Are we like the dinosaurs, then?

But Iris is shaking her head.

He's not dead. He can't be. He's our little brother and he's only just been born. Don't tell me he's dead. I just can't bear to think about it.

Jimmy scrambles out of my lap and runs to the window, presses his face against the glass.

But if all the people out there were dead, there would be bodies.

He turns around, hands on hips, waiting.

Well, I say, there are.

He brightens.

If a dead body is really completely dead and nobody finds it, and they leave it for the birds, how fast does it turn into a skeleton?

Iris begins to cry.

Stop talking about it, she says. Please Jimmy, I mean it now. I'm sick of you saying all these stupid things. Just shut up.

I look at Iris, such a strange and stiff and serious little girl, and I feel bad for her. I reach out and try to touch her, but it's like touching ice. I pull my hand back.

You're so cold, I tell her.

She looks at her own arm and she says nothing.

How do you live up here? I ask her.

What do you mean, live?

Is it just the four of you? With no one looking after you?

Jimmy throws her an anxious glance.

Iris was doing it, he says. I said she could be in charge. But only until you came.

Iris nods.

It was supposed to be temporary.

But do you have food?

She blinks. Her face is whiter than ever.

Not really.

And no TV either, Jimmy adds quickly.

And how old are you?

Nine, Iris says. I'm nine.

I'm seven, says Jimmy. I'm the second oldest. Gloria and Katie are the little ones.

I'll be ten in November, Iris says, looking at me. Do you know what month it is now?

There aren't really months any more.

Her eyes widen.

Really? You mean – not at all?

Well, I suppose there are, but no one's counting them.

But why not?

Because it doesn't seem very important.

Jimmy gasps.

But that means there won't be any birthdays!

I suppose not.

So no one will get older. We'll be like aliens!

Don't be stupid, Iris says. Of course you'll still get older. You just won't know when or how much.

While Jimmy thinks about this, I begin to move Katie off my legs. She makes a noise like she's winding herself up, ready to cry. I stand up anyway. Cold in my bones.

I don't want you to go, Jimmy says again. Really I don't. I want you to stay here and make us some tea.

Iris looks at me.

It's all right. He knows that's impossible. He knows there isn't any tea.

She picks Katie up and balances her on her skinny hip. She holds her there with one hand, as if she was light as anything and not a real baby at all. Katie's shoes are off and her stubby woollen feet kick and swing against her.

I lean over and put my lips on the top of Katie's head. It almost doesn't surprise me when I feel nothing but the chilly air.

Me too! A kiss for me too! yells Jimmy.

I kiss him too, on his dirty face, but I barely feel that either. He wraps his arms around my waist to hug me and I have to look down and check to see if he's let go or is still there. Still looking at him, I reach out to touch Iris's bony shoulder. My hand goes straight through it.

Say goodbye to Gloria for me, I tell her, but even as the words leave my mouth they are dissolving. Who? Who is Gloria?

Iris is looking past me, beyond me.

Will you come back? she says. You won't just leave us, will you?

I turn my head to where the voice is coming from but find I can't look at her.

I'll try, I say.

Cross your heart?

I don't think I have a heart.

Everyone has one, Jimmy says. All mammals do. And reptiles and birds. It's what keeps you alive. He looks over at Iris. Do fish have hearts?

She says nothing. Straightaway he thinks of something else.

Do you want me to make the lift come? he asks me. I can if you want.

I glance at the lift. A button lights up for a second or two, flickers, then dies.

He's always messing around with the lifts, Iris says. I told him not to . . . But already her voice trails off.

No, I tell Jimmy. Not this time. This time I'll take the stairs.

He looks disappointed.

But definitely next time? You swear?

We'll see.

He kicks at the carpet.

That's what you always say when you're not going to do something and . . . But even as he speaks, his voice too is fading and then it slides away, it's gone.

As I walk away from them, I have a strong feeling that I'm walking away from an empty space, from nothing, from no one. No point in looking back, I think, because they won't be there. All I'll see will be an empty corridor, an expanse of carpet, the hard white sky through the square of window. All the same, just before I reach the stairwell, I can't help it. I turn.

And I was wrong. Because there they all are — a forlorn and unlikely little family, the four of them, with the dog weaving slowly between them. Iris is still holding the little girl balanced light as dust on her hip, the boy whose name I've already forgotten, and the fair-haired silent one — who must have come racing back at the very last minute to join them — standing right next to her, stiff and formal, like in a photograph taken by a stranger, their arms entwined, their faces pale and empty.

I lift my hand to them, but I don't think they see me. Maybe I'm too far away already, the shadows racing now to swallow me up. Or perhaps they're afraid of seeming too eager. I can imagine Iris murmuring under her breath to the little ones that if they all keep very still, the spell will stay unbroken and I might decide to come back.

Whatever the reason, no one, not even the little boy — Jimmy, was it? — waves back.

6

In the end, we do exactly as the little boy suggested with Sophy. We put her out for the birds.

Burying her is out of the question. The snow is thick and the ground like stone. And Graham refuses to carry her down to the street and shove her out for anyone to find.

But Matthew has told me about the perfect place, he says. There's this terrace, three floors up from here. A place where she can lie in peace and —

The perfect place? I stare at the kid. He returns my stare. His eyes are dull and hard.

I couldn't see why it mattered, he says when Graham has gone out of the room. I didn't think I'd ever see you again. I thought you'd gone.

I feel myself tense.

Gone?

I thought you'd left for ever. How was I to know you'd come back?

What do you mean, left for ever? I say. When? I haven't been anywhere.

He looks away, runs his fist across his face. When he looks back at me, his eyes are full of pain.

I knew you'd do this, he says.

What? Do what?

Try and lie about it. I just knew that's what you were going to do. I knew it as soon as you walked back in across the landing as if nothing had happened.

I look at his dark, angry face and I struggle to remember if anything did happen. In a brief flash, then, I see them again. The boy with the curly hair, standing there with his hands on his hips. The girl with the sad face and bitten-down nails. The silent blonde girl. And the baby. Her furious warmth against me. A snag of shame as I remember how I walked away from them.

I look at Matthew.

I went upstairs, I say.

He shakes his head and smiles to himself.

Oh yeah. Sure. Upstairs.

I was gone for a morning, I tell him. Not even a whole morning.

I try to remember what time of day Sophy died. I remember the long night and then the sun scooting up the sides of the buildings. Sunrise. I remember her speaking for the last time. The quantity of blood on the blankets, the dark crust of it around her mouth. I know there was a conversation which upset me. Thinking of it I flush.

Matthew is watching me.

You're a liar, he says. I thought I could believe every little thing you said. I never thought you'd lie to me.

I hold his gaze even though my cheeks are still burning.

Think what you like, I tell him. I'm not lying.

But he shakes his head.

I didn't think anything on the first day. I knew you'd been with Sophy and I thought maybe you needed to sleep. By the end of the second day, I was getting worried. On the fourth day, I thought something terrible had happened to you.

I stare at him.

But Matt, I wasn't gone for four days.

He looks away.

Sure, he says again, almost to himself. Of course you weren't.

Even though I know she is dead, it is still a shock to go in and see her lying there exactly as I left her on those bloodstained blankets.

Her eyes are still staring at nothing – but when you look more closely, you see that they've lost their blueness and got thick like old milk. When we uncover her, the stench is raw and something pale leaks out of her blackened wrists.

Christ, says Graham – he turns away and clutches his stomach, looks at me. You can't smell that?

I look around me. Maybe the kid is right, I think. Maybe it really has been four days. The room seems to have altered around her, adapting itself to her new state. As if the air itself had decided to die in order to keep her company.

Smell what? I say.

I can feel Matt watching me. I make sure to keep myself light and steady. I glance at Sophy. The rotting shell of her.

Outside, it is a sunny morning, not a cloud in the sky. A sky like the sky of the old life, hopeful and high. You can almost imagine that people are still going about their business down there in the street, walking and talking and laughing and taking money out of holes in the wall and carrying bags of things from place to place.

Matthew is looking at Sophy's feet.

I'll have the boots, he says.

Graham looks at him.

They won't fit you. They're tiny.

Matt's expression doesn't alter. His eyes are two black holes in his face. Sun on his dun-coloured hair. The ghost of a man's moustache on his fat upper lip. I look away quickly. Now is not the time to be thinking how beautiful he is.

I'm not going to leave them on her to rot.

Maybe it's the use of that word. Or maybe he really doesn't want the kid to have Sophy's boots – but Graham seems to flinch. Concern fills his face. He looks from me to the kid then back again.

But what for? he says.

What do you mean, what for?

What will you do with them?

The kid shrugs.

Swap them. Trade them.

He will, I think. That's what he'll do. I watch him with something that amounts to pleasure. I almost smile.

Graham's face is twisting with disapproval.

I think it's a bit sick. I really do. I think you should leave them.

But the kid is already unlacing a boot and pulling it off her foot. He doesn't do it very gently, and Sophy's thin body rocks as he works them off. Most of her is hard and stiff, but some parts still seem to move. When I look again, I see that a tooth is showing, making her look a little more like herself but also a whole lot more dead.

I get a sudden blue-white glimpse of a foot as one of her socks comes off with the first boot.

I said you should leave them, Graham says.

The kid doesn't even look at him. He's picking away at the laces of the second boot.

I feel Graham looking at me.

What? I say.

Come on. For God's sake.

What do you mean, come on?

You think it's OK? Him doing this?

Doing what?

Him taking her boots off her?

He looks at me with such energy and horror that I want to laugh. I look at Sophy, her boots half on, half off. Two teeth are showing now. You might even tell yourself she is smiling.

I smile back at her.

She's dead, Graham, I say. What difference does it make?

He takes a cigarette from his pocket, looks at it, as if he's about to light it.

In the old life, he says, it wasn't all that strange to be careful about the dead.

Careful?

To pay them some respect.

This isn't the old life, I tell him. And there's nothing so special about being dead any more.

I look at Matthew. I'm glad to see that he is putting the sock back on to her foot, though I notice he does it clumsily, working it up from the blackening end of her toe, and then giving up halfway through so it hangs there stupidly.

Graham sighs. He's still holding the cigarette. He looks at it for a moment as if he doesn't know what it is, then he puts it back into his pocket, unlit.

I don't think there are vultures in the City of London, though it might only be a matter of time, of course. But there are certainly gulls.

Of all the creatures of the land and the air, the gulls seem to have survived the most relentlessly. When we first came to the building, they would line their big smooth-feathered bodies up on the concrete parapet outside and train their yellow eyes on us, as if they had a job to do and we were it.

We all hated them, but Sophy hated them the most. She found an old wooden cleaning mop and used the handle to bang on the big glass windows to try to scare them off. But it never had any effect. They would lift off, make one lazy circle in the air and then settle back down, a terrible satisfaction on their faces.

Lately, though, they've become pests, swooping down on people as they walk the streets. At Fenchurch Street we saw a young child have his eye taken out. And I heard that a newborn baby was snatched from its mother's arms and ripped to pieces in the air above her so that she got showered with his blood. She fainted and the gull then went for her too, not stopping till her face was a bloody indistinct mess.

They are out there now, screaming and laughing in the heavy air as we roll Sophy out of her bloodstained blanket and on to the snowy terrace and then step back to look at her.

Because of the fever, she stripped herself down well and truly at the end. All she has on now is a dirty pink T-shirt, specked all over with her blood and gone slack at the neck to reveal the pale jag of her collarbone. And a pair of men's pyjama bottoms whose string is frayed and the edges ripped, so that you can see the top of her once-white pants and, if you look harder, the beginning of her little triangle of hair. I notice that Matt does look harder, and I'm relieved when Graham leans forward and pulls the T-shirt down to cover her.

I've brought her cardigan with me – the grey and ratty old thing that she said she had at school and which she didn't like to let out of her sight. I am about to bend down to lay it on her when I stop.

What's the matter? Graham says.

I hesitate.

You think I should put it on her face?

He presses his lips together, looks away.

I go over and lay the thing on her chest, but it doesn't look right. It makes her look like she's just having a nap. So I pull it up to cover her slightly open mouth, the barely closed eyes.

Goodbye, Sophy.

The face that we've seen for so many days and nights and hours disappears for ever under the grey wool.

Above our heads, the gulls are swooping and diving. It has started snowing again. Big fat flakes coming down.

Shoo! Graham waves his arms in the air. Get off! Go on, go away!

Matt finds a piece of brick and chucks it hard at them, but it thuds down hard in the snow and makes no difference.

He turns to Graham.

We could set fire to her? he says.

What?

Matt scratches his head. Snowflakes clinging to his hair.

To stop them eating her.

Graham looks confused.

I don't think so, he says.

I have matches, says Matt. He pats his pocket. It rattles.

I don't think so, Graham says again.

A thought comes to me then. A strong thought, but slippery and hard to pin down. Then I understand what it is. A memory of the boy upstairs. Talking about the birds.

I turn to Matt.

We want them to eat her, I tell him. That's the whole point of putting her out here.

He stares at me for a second and then he smiles. It feels like warm water splashed on my face.

I go over to the railings and stand close to where Matthew's standing. I point out the great white dome, topped with snow and wreathed in morning sunshine.

Look at that, I say to Graham. Isn't it something? That's called St Paul's.

The look he gives me is cold.

You think I don't know that? Everyone knows that. Even you would once have known that.

I can see that Matt is on the verge of laughing, but he checks himself just in time.

That night, as Sophy lies up there all alone on her terrace, the weather really does change. A storm breaks over the city. Ice and hail. It rattles through the sky, along the river, over the buildings. Everything lit up by it. Electric, intense.

I am sitting on one of the desks, my feet up against the glass, watching it all, when I realise that he's there. Standing behind me, to my right. He might be leaning against something. One of the filing cabinets maybe. I don't know how long he's been there. I hear a match. His breath as he inhales.

I don't breathe.

After a few seconds have passed, I dare to turn my head.

He looks almost the same as before. The same dark suit, but a different shirt this time, plainer, unbuttoned. The same dark, messy hair, as if he's been putting his hands through it. And this time, a tie hangs loose around his neck, as if he's just undone it and not yet got around to pulling it off.

His face is in shadow. I do not dare look at it too hard. I try to breathe. I can feel my heart going. I shut my eyes and then I open them again. He is still there. He can't see me. I don't know what to do. All I know is, I don't want him to go.

When he speaks, I jump so hard I almost fall off the desk.

Rain, he says.

What?

I said, rain.

It's his voice. Is he talking to himself, or can he see me? Blood hammers in my head. The room lights up white for a second or two, shudders, then goes back to darkness. Jags of leftover light floating past my eyes. My voice is a whisper.

What? I say again.

I hear him blow out smoke. I can tell he's smoking the cigarette in a hurried, distracted way. He can't be bothered with it. In the end, he doesn't finish it. He puts it out.

Rain. It's raining out there.

He stands up. What? I think. Is he coming over? I feel myself start to tremble.

Are you talking to me? I say.

Listen, he says as he comes closer. Can you hear it?

I do as he tells me. I listen. Tongues of light lick the sky. A faraway rumble, then such a loud crash that my whole body jumps again.

That's thunder, I say.

He doesn't reply. He is behind me. I know where he is. I can't see him but I can feel him there. He reaches out and puts a hand on my shoulder. The hand is warm. Pleasure falling through me. A feeling so intense you could mistake it for pain.

What are you doing? I ask him.

He doesn't answer.

Matt, I say. Matt – is it really you?

He lifts my hair with his hands then drops it again just as quickly. I shiver. Heat licking the backs of my knees.

Oh, I say. Do it again.

But he doesn't do it again. That's when I realise.

Can you hear me? I ask him. When I speak to you?

His eyes are on me.

Are you real? he says.

I try to look at his face, his eyes. I am sure he is looking at me.

You can't hear me, can you? I say. You can't hear a word I'm saying.

He carries on gazing at me.

I don't care if you're real or not, he says. I don't care what this is. I just don't want it to stop.

I hear it then, the sound he told me to listen for. A million rice grains trickling through fingers on to paper. I see it too. Flecks of wet on the black window. Small at first, then longer, larger ones, some of them joining up, running down. Wet flinging itself out of the sky and hitting the glass.

I try to twist around to look at him, but he won't let me.

You're not really here, though, are you? he says.

Me? I say. I am. Of course I am. Can't you see me? I'm here right now.

He smiles. Touches my cheek.

I mean, I'm sitting here thinking about you and wishing I could talk to you and suddenly you're here. I'm going mad, right?

I take a breath.

You're not mad, I say.

He doesn't hear me.

I don't care, he says. I am mad. Fuck it.

The room lights up. Another crash of thunder.

I think of Sophy lying alone on that drenched and frozen concrete, the grey wool cardigan soaked right through by now and moulded to her face.

He frowns. A tender little frown.

Fucking hell, he says. I'd give anything to see you now. I mean, really see you.

I wonder where he thinks I am. If I'm not here, then . . . My blood slows as I work it out.

He pulls his phone out of his pocket, dials.

I lift my head and look up, over his shoulder, and that's when I know. I'm right here with him but it hasn't happened yet. Rain still clings to the window, but beyond it, you can see the neon blur of all those city lights. And yes, the red dot of an aircraft. All that energy still burning away in the old life.

I watch as he props himself on the edge of the desk. Stares at the floor. He has the phone to his ear. He lifts his head and fixes his eyes on the distance, waiting.

At last his whole face changes. His chin lifts. His eyes come to life.

Hey, he says. You OK? Where are you?

Silence while he listens. Bursts into a smile.

All right, but –

He waits.

All right, but you're sure it's OK? You want me to call back later?

He waits again.

OK, he says. Oh no. Oh dear. Poor lad. Christ. How did he manage to do that?

Another wait.

Bloody hell. Oh no.

Another smile. Then a short laugh. The smile leaving his face.

I don't know about that. Well – hmmm.

A pause.

Me too, he says, and again his face loses its smile.

He reaches out and picks up a pencil from the desk. Looks at it without seeing it. Puts it down again. Sighs.

I don't know. Nothing. Sitting here in my office. Thinking about you.

Another pause.

But where's Jimmy now? Is he OK, then? He's not in pain?

Another pause.

That's good, he says. Yes, I suppose – well, until he gets his big teeth . . . Yes, tell him that – tell him I said he's a pirate.

A pause. Laughs.

OK. Yes, you'd better.

Pause.

No, of course – I just wanted –

Pause.

I just wanted to hear your voice, that's all.

Pause and smile.

Yes.

Pause.

Yes.

Pause.

You know I do.

Sigh.

OK.

He turns the phone off, but keeps it in his hand. Sits there looking at it for a moment or two as if it might spring back into life again.

Finally he puts it in his pocket and, after he's done that, he stares into the distance for a long time. He doesn't look happy and he doesn't look sad. He doesn't look anything. He is stuck there in his thoughts, whatever they are. He doesn't move.

He is there for a little while longer and then next time I look, he isn't.

Outside, the storm has stopped, but you can still hear the rain, gentler now, scattering itself on the window. The sky is dark again, dead, frozen, drained of light.

Jimmy was running along the edge of the swimming pool, racing Gloria and another kid, a friend from school, to do a dive. I had told them a million times not to run. Jimmy was a maniac. He always had been. He didn't listen.

We spent the evening in A & E. They were worried he might have concussion, but in the end he didn't. He was lucky that he only chipped a tooth and even luckier that it was still a baby one.

It would grow back. It would have grown back.

Tears are running down my face now. I lick at them and I rub my face on my jumper, but more keep coming. They keep on coming. I don't know what to do. I have no way of stopping them. They keep on coming.

I must sleep all night on that cold office floor. When I wake it is barely light. I know even before I open my eyes that something is different. It is this. There's a baby asleep in my arms.

Black downy hair, black newborn eyes, skinny baby chest, legs that have not yet quite unfolded, feet that haven't yet taken any weight or even touched earth. The soft fat animal place at the back of his neck. The dark silky hairs on the tops of his ears. Fingers you want to kiss and suck, tiny fingernails that peel and shred. The smell of his face. Just born. Sticky and warm and smelling of the insides of things. The inside of me.

It is Arthur.

I yawn and stretch and get ready to shift myself to give him my fullest most bursting breast, but even as I cup his small head so he can fix his mouth on, he takes on the quality of the air, the freezing air all around us and he runs through my fingers like a thought or a wave of the blackest of black salt water, and that's it, that's the end of the feeling, he's gone.

I go and fetch the kid. I know where he'll be. Asleep on the blankets on his stomach, fully clothed, hair flung back from his face, breathing so lightly you'd think he was dead.

I shake him awake.

What? He sits up and stares at me, frowning.

I don't take any chances. I don't even give him time to think. I fling my arms around him, put my lips against his warm and grubby face. I breathe in the asleep-boy smell of his skin. My friend, I think. He's my friend.

I need you to come with me, I say. Right now. You've got to come.

He blinks at me.

Why?

Because I need you to.

But come where?

Don't ask me, Matt. Just do it. Please. Come on.

We go upstairs. The air is cold. Everything's the same as before, the same as it's always been, except for one thing. I know why I'm here.

The first office we come to is empty. A couple of desks, grey computer screens, another dead and dried-up plant, a long glass table with chairs either side. Scattered on the table, though, are some sticks for stirring coffee. Someone has been arranging them into zigzags, making patterns before shoving the rest of them on to the floor.

My heart lifts.

Look at that, I say to Matt. Someone's been playing.

He looks at the sticks and he says something, but I don't hear what it is. I am focused on one thing now. I am excited. I reach behind me and pull him along.

The next room we come to is smaller, another office, the same as the first one – desk and screens and dead air and dust. But the last room, the one at the very end, has its door ever so slightly ajar.

I put my face to the crack. And there, exactly as I expected, fast asleep on that harsh office carpet – with no cushions or anything to lie on and nothing in the way of blankets to cover them – are my children.

My children.

There they are, I say to Matt, as I feel my face grow hot at the pleasure of seeing them, having them, knowing them.

There who are?

My kids.

He peers into the room like a blind person.

What kids? Where?

There.

He looks again. He follows where my hand is pointing. He stares at the spot and then he looks back at me.

Where? he says.

They lie there in a heap on the carpet, all of their heads

at the same end, except of course for the baby, who always manages to turn herself about ninety degrees in her sleep.

Jimmy's foot is pressed into the back of Gloria's thigh, his two hands made into fists, like someone dreaming of the perfect fight. Both of Katie's legs in their woollen tights are resting on Iris's skinny hip, her arms flung up above her head and her mouth wide open.

Iris, meanwhile, is sleeping as she always does – neat as a princess, pale hands folded under her even paler cheek. The dog is curled beside her, head down but eyes open, grave and alert.

Good dog, I think, guarding my children.

As I push the door open a little wider, she lifts her head.

It's OK, I whisper. Stay.

She looks at me – one swift beat of her tail on the carpet at the sound of my voice.

Good girl, I say.

She sighs and, eyes on my face, lets her chin drop back down on her paws. She waits. So do I. At last, somebody sighs and begins to stretch.

Look, I say to Matt. They're waking up.

That's Iris, I tell him as a thin arm unfolds into the air, twisting, fingers opening and closing. She's the eldest. She's kind of nervy, a bit of a worrier, but she's such a good girl.

And that's Katie. She's a real little rascal, but always so happy, loves her food, loves everything actually, slept through the night right from the start.

Katie rolls over on to her back and opens her eyes and, gazing happily at the ceiling, starts to chatter away to herself.

Jimmy sits straight up in one liquid movement, smiling as if woken by a joke. He rubs his eyes. Blinks.

Jimmy, I tell the kid. He'll wear you out. Seriously. I'm warning you. He never stops.

I swallow. There's something about Jimmy. I realise my eyes are full of tears.

As I watch, Gloria turns and snuggles against him and he shoves her off. She opens her eyes and shoves him back, harder. Jimmy clouts her.

Hey, I say. That's too hard. Come on, that's enough now, stop it, both of you.

Four faces turn to look at me. I wipe at my eyes. I don't want them to see the tears. The dog jumps up and comes over to me, tail wagging.

Mummy, says Katie, but she says it in a slow voice as if she's still dreaming.

Mum! shouts Jimmy.

Iris stares at me. I hold out my arms.

By the time I'm down there on the floor with them, the picture that had been hazy at first has warmed up. All the colours are brighter, the sounds louder. The whole thing has come sharp and clean.

The dusty plum of Katie's cardigan, knitted by Simon's mum when Iris was born. The washed and worn-out denim of Gloria's jeans. Jimmy's tawny, springy hair, almost red in certain lights. The warmth of their skin, the glint of a blue eye, a fat finger. Iris's dark lashes. Gloria's creamy tangled hair.

Oh, I tell Matthew. I almost forgot. And this is Gloria –

And I turn back then, ready to tell him all about her, but I'm looking at an empty doorway, sunlight falling through it, nothing there at all. And certainly no kid.

I watch the space for a moment and then I turn back to my children.

Mummy, says Jimmy. Mummy, I love you, I love you! Mummy, why are you crying?

Iris pulls on her jumper and stuffs her feet into her shoes without undoing the laces.

I knew you'd come, she says. I went to sleep just knowing it. I told myself that if I shut my eyes and banged my head on the floor and said, She won't, she won't, about eight or maybe ten times, then the opposite would happen and you'd come.

I laugh. Iris's methods have always been a mystery to me. I cup her pointy chin in my hand.

I've missed you so much, I tell her.

She throws me an anxious look.

You remember now? You know that you're our mum? You're not going to forget it again?

I put my arms around her and hold her tight.

I won't forget it, I say, and I feel her tense for a moment and then relax.

Gloria comes over, silent and smiling at me.

Still not talking? I say.

She shakes her head. I kiss my finger and plant it on her nose.

But we have to go, I tell them as I pull Katie up off the floor and on to my lap. We need to leave as soon as possible.

But leave to go where? says Jimmy.

I'll tell you in a minute.

I start buttoning Katie's cardigan. Her cheeks are red and a string of saliva dribbles down and swings there, wetting my wrist.

Poor old Munchkin, I say. You are teething, aren't you?

She makes a little noise, half a sob, half a laugh.

Never mind, I say. We'll make it better.

Better, she says.

That's right. We'll sort it out.

Mummy, she chants. Mummy-mummy-mummy.

Where are we going? Jimmy asks me again. Are we going on a trip?

Kind of, I say.

I know where we're going, says Iris.

I look at her, standing there watching me with her sad little face, and I think she probably does know.

Well come on then, I tell her. Let's get going. You're all going to have to help me. I don't want any fussing from anyone. Where are your coats? Do we still have Katie's snowsuit thing, the tartan one? It's very, very cold out there.

Colder than Christmas? shouts Jimmy.

Colder than anything you've ever known, I tell him. So get your coat.

Iris is looking at me.

We don't have anything, she says. I mean coats or anything. I told you before. We've got nothing.

She puts a finger in her mouth and tears at the nail.

Then would you mind telling me what those are? I say, indicating a pile of anoraks and duffels on the far side of the room.

Her eyes widen.

Our coats! When did you put them there?

It's probably magic, says Jimmy, and he goes over and gets his coat and puts it on. As he stuffs his arms into the sleeves, I notice how short they are. He must have grown.

And the zip, I tell him. I want it done up properly.

Hey! he shouts. My hat's here too.

He puts on the hat and then he stands, frowning, investigating his pockets.

I had some Haribo in here, he says. And some football cards. Where are they?

Jimmy, I say. It was a long time ago.

He looks at me.

How long?

I don't know how long but a very long time.

He comes and stands close to me then, his eyes full of worry.

This time you're staying, aren't you? he says.

Of course, I say.

I pull him to me and I kiss his small head.

We haven't been out of this place in ever such a long time, he says. Where are we really going?

I take his hand and I take Gloria's and I squeeze them both. I look at their sister.

Iris will tell you where we're going. Where are we going, Iris?

She gives me a careful look.

We've got to go and find Arthur, haven't we? she says. Are we going home?

That's right, I say.

Yay! says Jimmy. I don't know why, but I just knew that's where we were going!

No, you didn't, Iris says.

Yes, I did.

7

The going is hard, slippery and dangerous. Every footstep has to be negotiated.

Though the rain has begun to melt the ice, overnight the temperatures have plunged again and a light snow has fallen. The combination of freeze and thaw is precarious. Holes have opened up in the road, gaping craters which could easily swallow a truck, let alone a child. Other times, the land seems to tilt in an unexpected and frightening way because something or other has collapsed underneath it.

If she starts to slip, you let go of her, do you understand? I tell Iris, who has the dog held tight on a lead.

OK, she says.

I mean it.

I know you do.

Jimmy looks at me with interest.

But, what, even if she, like, starts sliding away and is about to be killed? You mean we're not allowed to rescue her even then?

I look at the dog and the dog looks at me.

I don't want her pulling Iris into danger, I tell him.

He's silent a moment. He has hold of Gloria's hand. We watch the dog's quick breath pumping itself out into the freezing white air.

She's only a dog, Jimmy says slowly. And the life of a human is more important, right?

Right, I tell him.

He thinks for a second then lets out a big breath.

Although I just said that, I don't think I really believe it. You see, I much prefer animals to humans. In fact, I don't really like humans all that much, apart from you, I mean –

Come on, Jims, I tell him, enough of the talking. We have to keep going.

But he stands still, remaining on the exact same spot, a frown on his face.

Because animals don't make wars, right? And they don't –

All right, I tell him. It's a good point, but can we talk about it later?

He's silent for a moment as we walk on.

Mum?

Yes, Jimmy.

But what do I do if Gloria starts to pull me into danger? Can I let go of her?

I look at the pale and silent little girl who is holding on to his hand, and for a second or two I'm not even sure she's there.

It'll be OK, I tell him. Gloria's going to be very, very careful, aren't you, Gloria?

Gloria's eyes are on me. Wordless and yet brimming with words. Exactly like her father's eyes.

It was Christmas Eve. Katie was just coming up to six months old. She sat on her bottom under the tree and pointed to something sparkly and then she laughed. Simon wanted to take a photo. He got down on the floor and looked at her through the lens.

Katie? Hey, Katie – where's my little Munchkin?

She turned and searched for his face but all she saw was the shiny black eye of the camera looking back at her. Immediately the laugh dropped away. Fists clenched, mouth turned down. The cry built to a scream.

Simon took the photo anyway. Katie screaming under the Christmas tree. She had on tartan trousers and a red cardigan that wrapped around her chest and tied at the back. The moment passed and so did the tears, but the photo stayed in our lives.

That night, the night before Christmas, I lay in bed with Simon and I took a breath and said, There's something I have to tell you.

His face didn't change.

I know what it is, he said. It's Matthew, isn't it?

I said nothing. Then I said, Yes.

Simon lay still for a moment, then he turned away.

It's not what you think, I told him after a few silent minutes had passed. Nothing's happened. We haven't done anything.

He turned back and looked at me. I'd never seen his face so empty.

I know, he said. It's worse than that, isn't it?

Matt was my oldest, dearest friend, the one I'd known since we were kids. Simon liked him too. Or at least I thought he did. He certainly didn't think of him as a threat and he was right not to. Whenever I came back from seeing Matthew, I'd make Simon laugh when I related all the stupid things he'd said, the squabbles we'd had, the various interesting ways in which he'd annoyed me.

Telling it like this made Simon feel safe about Matthew. It made me feel safe about him too.

Then, one night, we went out and we drank too much. Matthew had just finished with his latest girlfriend. I'd liked this girlfriend and I told him I thought he'd been mean to her, that I thought he was far too unkind to all his girlfriends. He admitted it was true – adding that the only person he could ever be nice to was me. We talked and we laughed and then we talked more seriously. And then we ordered another bottle.

Come on, he said when the bar staff were waiting for us to leave. I'll take you home.

We got in a taxi. Without thinking, I put my head in his lap. He put his hand on my head. He stroked my cheek, my hair, touched my lips. He kept his finger on my lips.

After less than five minutes, I sat up. But by then something had changed and we didn't know how to change it back. Or, to be more truthful, we didn't want to change it. We liked it too much.

That night, Simon and I stayed awake, crying and talking and crying again. Christmas was ruined. So was our marriage, so was our family, so were our lives.

Tell me how often you've seen him, Simon said.

We've always seen each other –

You know what I mean.

Often, I said.

Have you slept with him?

Of course not.

Have you kissed him?

Silence.

Of course you have, he said. Bloody hell. What a fool I've been. Of course you bloody have.

In the morning, though, he was different. Shaky, white-faced. He pulled me to him, put his hands on my face, touched my nose.

The thing is, he said.

I waited.

The thing is – I just don't want to lose you.

I shut my eyes, bit my lip. I laid my head on his shoulder.

Let's get through Christmas, he said, for the children's sake. We'll talk about it in January.

OK, I said.

But January came, and February too, and even March, and we didn't talk. I hardly saw Matthew. I tried so very hard not to see him. But I missed him, and when I did see him it was miserable, wonderful, terrible. Meanwhile, I hated the lies. I hated that I didn't know myself any more. I hated that when I woke in the morning, the first thing I thought about – before I fed my children or washed or dressed myself – was how not to feel this thing that I felt.

Simon never asked me any more questions. Maybe he was afraid of the answers. I know that I was afraid of the answers.

Then suddenly it was May. Katie's birthday. A blue and sunny day. She had just begun to walk. She pulled herself up on the edge of the trampoline. Gloria, bouncing, light hair flying, saw her and clapped her hands.

Look, Mummy, look! Look at Katie!

Iris came over and took her hand and led her into the middle of the lawn. We all watched as she slowly took her hands away. Katie stood, surprised, swaying slightly, then took two wobbly and important steps before sinking down on to her bottom again in the daisies and clover. We all laughed. So did Katie.

Simon had a beer in his hand. He looked at me.

You're taking all of this away from them, he said. This thing that you're doing. It's ruining our family, everything we've cared about, everything we've made. Think about it. Is he really worth all that to you?

Soon, Iris stops and stares around her. She shivers. Her nose is running. I can see that her school duffel coat is also getting too short. In fact, sometimes I'm not sure she's even wearing a coat at all. The pink of her knitted hat keeps on fading in and out, draining almost to white, and so do her gloves. Sometimes, her face looks almost to be the same colour as the snow, the sky . . .

But where are we? she says. All of this. I don't remember any of it. I don't know where we are. Do you?

I ease the wide cotton straps of Katie's sling to a different place on my shoulders.

You're getting too big for this, aren't you, Munchkin? I say. Way too big to be in a sling.

She laughs and throws her head backwards, almost throwing me off balance.

No, I tell her. You can't do that. Come on, stay still for Mummy now.

I pull her hat down over her ears, hold her small feet in the snowsuit close to my stomach and squeeze them tight. She moans and wriggles her head closer to my chest.

Well? says Iris.

The dog is tugging on the lead. She yanks it back sharply. Wipes her nose on her sleeve.

Well what?

You're not listening to me, are you? Do you even know how to get home?

I hesitate as I think about this.

I'm not sure, I tell her.

You mean you don't.

Well, probably not exactly, no.

Katie tilts her head up at me again and opens her mouth, showing her little row of bottom teeth. I kiss her nose loudly. She laughs. Iris looks annoyed.

You're not taking this very seriously, are you? she says.

I feel Jimmy watching me.

Even though you remember now that you're our mum, he says carefully, I still don't like it when you don't remember things like how to get home. It's like you're not the same person or something.

I take a breath.

Oh, darling, I tell him, I am. I'm the same person.

Well then, OK. But you don't seem worried enough.

You want me to be worried?

He doesn't mean like that, Iris says. I think he just means you're acting a bit too relaxed. For a parent, I mean.

Yeah, says Jimmy. It's like because you don't remember things, yeah, you can say anything at all, even if you don't really mean it.

You never used to be like that, Iris adds.

How did I used to be?

Well, you were always quite a careful person, thinking ahead about everything and always bringing drinks and tissues and everything.

Was I?

Yes. And you don't seem like that now. You just seem like one of us, and it's a bit scary.

The thing is, says Jimmy, you might suddenly forget us again, and then you'll turn around and without even remembering that you're leaving us behind, you'll just go!

I look at Iris.

159

Yes, she says. I'm worried about that too.

I try to think about this. I notice that Gloria is watching me with her full attention. So is the dog.

I won't do that, I tell them.

Jimmy frowns.

But I'm worried that you will.

I look at him.

Jims, I love you and I won't do it.

Yes, he says. But even though I know that, and I know you mean it and all that, still the thought keeps on coming into my head.

Well, try not to let it.

He gives a little wail.

Even when I don't let it, it keeps on coming!

Iris looks at me.

You say you won't go, but you don't know that for sure, do you?

Dad said he wouldn't go either, Jimmy says.

Shut up, says Iris. Stop it.

But it was a lie. He lied.

Jimmy, says Iris. I mean it.

But it's true.

Shut up.

I feel myself flinch. The jolt of a door slamming. A car starting up. A broken window, or was it a door? Snow falling. Rain and sun and then the whole world freezing.

Hush, I say to Jimmy. Hush, sweetheart. That's enough.

I put my hand out and touch his head, but my fingers have already drifted through his hair into another place that I can barely feel.

* * *

In late June I went to Simon. I felt ill, sad, shaky, tired.

All right, I said. You're right. I can't live like this. I agree with you about everything. I won't see him any more.

He looked very surprised. He stared at me. His face was unreadable.

You're serious? You really mean this? I can trust you?

I nodded. Trust. The word sounded lumpy and foreign as I turned it over in my head.

It has to be absolute, he said. I have to be able to be certain.

I told him I understood – well, it was true, I did understand – and that it would be absolute. I told him I loved him, and this was also true. I knew that a part of me really did love him – he was the father of my children. I loved my children. I loved him. I loved our family. I wanted our happiness to come back. I thought it all lay with me, the power to bring it back. I meant every word.

Simon watched my face for a few seconds longer, then he put his head in his hands and he cried.

I rang Matthew. I was dry-eyed, dry-mouthed. My heart was dry, bone dry. I could hear him breathing, waiting. He already knew what I was going to say. Even when we were kids, he'd known what I would say next. It had driven me crazy then. It broke my heart now.

It's the children, I told him.

Yes, he said.

I can't do this to them.

I know.

We didn't speak for a few moments then, we just listened to each other.

Don't go, he said at last. I mean right now. Please. Just stay on the line.

OK.

I waited.

I have to go now, I told him.

Not yet.

I do. In a minute I do.

He asked me to see him one more time, then – to talk it over, to say a proper goodbye.

No, I said.

No one will know about it, he said. We'll just be together for a little while, and then I'll let you go. It'll be something to hold on to. I absolutely promise that's all it will be. I won't make it hard for you.

I hesitated.

No, I told him. You know I can't.

Please.

OK, I said.

We keep on moving. We stumble over that frozen landscape as best we can, but it's hard to tell if we're heading in the right direction. So many of the old landmarks are gone.

Trees have split and fallen and are lying in the road, and so many buildings have collapsed or been burned down. The ones that are left standing make no sense without the others around them – some of them are no more than shells, half demolished so you can see right into them. Blurred and charred remnants of patterned wallpaper. The ghost outline of a fireplace. Skeletal stairs with their fresh carpet of snow.

Look at that! shouts Jimmy, and he points at a hoarding with the words T Mobile still visible on it. I definitely remember that!

He lets go of Gloria's hand for a second, but she reaches over and grabs back hold of him.

Don't be silly, Iris says. That means nothing. It's just an ad. Don't you remember, there were loads of those? Tell him, Mum. They were absolutely everywhere.

I gaze at the hoarding.

She's right, I tell Jimmy. I don't think it means anything.

Iris is pleased. She glances at her brother and then she gives me a fierce, proud look — a look that reminds me of someone, maybe of myself.

I smile back at her, even though it means looking straight through what is left of her to the fallen tree trunk behind.

Gloria is crying. If I think hard about it, I realise she's been crying for a long time. I hold the sleeping Katie against me and I bend down to her.

What is it? I ask her. Sweetheart, tell me what's the matter.

She says nothing. Her face has no colour.

I think her foot's hurting, Jimmy says.

I look at him.

What makes you say that? How do you know?

He sticks out his bottom lip.

I kind of made it up, but all the same, I do think it's true.

I turn back to Gloria.

Is that it? Is it your foot?

She stares at me. She says nothing. Then she gives a little sob. I look at her trainers, sodden with snow.

Are your feet all wet?

Iris comes closer.

I don't think it's her foot, she says. I think she wants to hold your hand.

Is that it? I ask Gloria.

Still she says nothing. But I reach down and take her hand anyway, even though it slips through mine like water.

After ten minutes, or maybe an hour, we pass a low wall with several piles of tiny bones on it. Newly done, because the snow hasn't had a chance to settle on them yet. Each pile contains maybe a hundred bones.

We all stare. Even Katie swivels her head and hangs away from my chest to get a look.

I think someone did it on purpose, says Jimmy in a dark voice.

What do you mean, on purpose? Iris asks him.

Jimmy holds out a hand. His eyes are wide.

I mean that they killed some people and then they got the flesh off the bones somehow and then they put them there, for everyone to see.

Don't be silly, Iris says. How do you know they're the bones of people? And how would they get the flesh off? And who would kill that many people anyway?

Jimmy looks at me.

Some people would. A murderer would, wouldn't he, Mummy?

I look at the bones. Some of them don't even look like whole bones. Just splinters of bones.

I don't know, I tell him.

Anyway, says Iris, they're too small to be the bones of people. Look, they're really tiny. It's probably animals or birds or something.

Or babies, says Jimmy. Maybe a murderer came along and killed a great whole lot of babies and left them there.

It's not babies, says Iris. Nobody kills babies.

Jimmy narrows his eyes.

Why not? How do you know they don't?

Because babies are helpless. They can't hurt you. You wouldn't need to defend yourself against a baby.

Jimmy thinks about this.

But what if you wanted to kill one, say, just for fun?

Now Iris looks at him and shudders.

Jimmy! What a horrible thing to say.

But some things that really happen are horrible. Some things that –

No, says Iris. They're not. And anyway, I've had enough and I don't want to talk about it any more.

But –

I said I'd had enough. Shut up!

Jimmy blinks.

Actually, he says, maybe you're right, because if they're babies, then where are the skulls?

I told you to shut up! says Iris. Mum, could you please tell Jimmy to be quiet?

At the sound of Iris's voice, the dog starts to whimper. And I'm about to speak when I realise something terrible. A weight is gone from my body. It's Katie. She's not there. She's gone.

I look down, cry out.

Mummy! says Iris. Mummy, what's the matter? What is it?

I stumble around in the wind, holding my arms out and calling her name. Katie! Katie!

But, Mummy –

I've lost her. I've lost Katie.

But she's right there! Iris shouts, almost angrily, pointing to my chest, and I look down and see that she's right, there's Katie, still in her sling, her head asleep against me.

I look down at her and now I'm confused. She seems too small. For a moment or two I don't even know if she's Katie or if she's Arthur. I'm shaking all over.

But she wasn't there, I tell Iris.

Who wasn't there?

I thought I'd lost her. I thought I'd lost Katie.

She was there, Iris says. Really, Mummy. All the time, she was there.

But . . . I thought I'd lost her.

Jimmy is staring at me.

But you didn't.

I know. I know.

You really scared me, Iris says.

I know. I'm sorry. I really scared myself.

My body knew straightaway that it was pregnant. It did not change, but the world around it did. Colours ripened, textures grew sinister crests and spikes, tastes and smells turned raw. I waited to bleed but nothing came. I felt him there – Arthur – I felt him clinging on in there.

It wasn't his fault. It wasn't the baby's fault.

I lay on the bed and I sobbed. Simon said nothing. I knew that he knew, and he knew I knew. He sat and stroked my hair. For weeks now, he'd gone out of his way to be careful with me, to be kind. The kinder he was, the more I cried. He knew what I needed. He fetched me a can of soda water.

It's a boy, he said as he snapped the ring and handed me the can, fizzing. Isn't it? You were just like this with Jims. It must be a boy, don't you think?

I said nothing. I could not look at his face. I gulped the soda. It was good; it was clean. I finished it. He opened another one for me. I tried to work out what was different about him. There was something new about the shape of him, sitting there. A different Simon. How did he manage to be so much stronger than me?

When he spoke, his voice was steady.

I want you to know that I love you. That I think we can do this. I am up for it. We'll do it together. You don't have to say anything right now. Just think about it, OK?

I looked at him. I wasn't crying any more but I could feel the sobs waiting there, deep down inside me.

Why are you doing this? I said.

Doing what?

Why are you being so nice to me?

He sat still for a moment, his head to one side.

I don't know, he said.

But why?

His face hardened just the tiniest touch. He didn't say anything else.

The following Christmas – Katie was walking properly now, she had her first pair of proper shoes – I told him the truth.

It's nothing to do with what happened, I told him. It's nothing to do with Matt. But I just can't do it. It doesn't feel right.

I saw him flinch at the mention of the name.

What exactly are you saying? What can't you do?

I looked at the ground.

It's not fair on you, Simon.

What's not fair on me? What are you talking about? Who are you to say what's fair on me?

I took a breath. Don't make me say it, I thought. But he was waiting.

I can't love you. I've tried and tried and I just can't. I just don't think I love you any more.

He kept his face steady. He did not shout or cry or even act very surprised. Back in the spring, when I'd been trying so hard not to see Matthew, we'd had a few counselling sessions and we'd both agreed that it had been a waste of time. Now, though, he asked me to go and have one more session with him.

Why? I said.

Whatever you think you've decided, I just want us to talk it through with a third party.

He told me, then, that after we'd stopped the sessions, he'd continued seeing the counsellor without me.

I stared at him.

You've been going all this time? But why?

When he replied, his voice was cold.

How else do you think I've been getting through this? How else do you think a man lives with a woman who's expecting another man's baby?

I said nothing. Then I said, OK. I'll come.

Thank you, he said, as if I was a total stranger. Thank you. I'd really appreciate that.

This time he didn't say he loved me.

It has begun to snow again. At first very light and then more heavily. Snowflakes blow into our eyes and mouths. The wind stings our cheeks. Sometimes it's so raw and strong that we have to turn the other way to get some relief.

I think we've been walking round in circles, says Iris. I mean it. I keep seeing things that I'm sure I've seen before.

I think so too, says Jimmy.

Copycat.

I'm not copying. I'm just saying what I think, that's all.

Then try and think something of your own, instead of always thinking other people's thoughts.

Hey! says Jimmy.

You two, I tell them, always fighting.

Iris sniffs.

So what do you think? she asks me. About the circles?

What circles?

Are we walking in them?

I look around me. The landscape ahead of us is both familiar and not familiar. A sign says All Bar One and another says HSBC and another says Lloyds. None of the words means anything to me.

I don't know, I tell her. I'm doing my best, OK?

Iris lets out a breath.

My arm's hurting, she says. It's really aching. Can someone else have a go with the dog?

I glance at the dog. For a second or two, she's not there at all. Then I see the outline of her nose, a whisker.

Try and keep going a bit longer, I tell Iris. Then I'll take her.

I'll take her! says Jimmy.

Iris hands him the lead, but I can no longer see an animal on the end of it. Jimmy seems unbothered. He pulls the lead along.

What would you have done, if you really had lost her? he asks me after we've walked on a bit.

You mean Katie?

Yes.

I don't know, I tell him.

What would you do if you lost us all? Not just Arthur, I mean.

I let myself think about Arthur. His dark wet weight as he came slipping out of me.

Jimmy – I begin.

Would you cry? I mean really, really cry. Would you scream?

I look at him.

Do you think that Arthur will be there? he says. When we get home?

I don't know.

What will you do if he isn't?

Jimmy . . .

What?

Oh, Jimmy. Just come here.

When he comes, I wrap my arms around him, hold him very tight. I shut my eyes.

Don't go, I say. Please don't go.

But I'm not going.

You are. You are.

I hold on, trying to feel the warmth of his body.

Hey, he groans. You're annoying the dog. And you're making all the air come out of me.

I open my eyes. As I expected, the dog's not there.

I'm sorry, I say. I just want to hold you properly.

Why?

So I can feel how warm you are.

But you know how warm I am!

No. I want to feel it.

Why?

Because I love you. Because it feels so good to hold you and know that you're there.

OK, he says, and he shoves himself hard against me, almost throttling me with his hug. Can you feel it now?

Yes, I lie. Yes, I can. Thank you. I can.

It was February when we sat them down to tell them. Iris – tense and wary, her bitten fingers resting in her lap, sharp enough to guess what was coming. Jimmy and Gloria laughing and fighting and kicking each other on the sofa, oblivious. Katie sucking her cloth on my lap. The baby's knees and elbows moving visibly under my T-shirt.

He said I should do the talking. Because this was all my doing. Because I was the one who wanted this. So I did. I began to speak the words we'd agreed on with the counsellor. The careful, difficult words. I unloaded them, in all their unkindness, in front of our little family. My voice shook, but I tried hard to keep it calm and loving. I told them how much we loved them, how we would always love them, but . . .

My voice was soft. The words were hard and terrible.

I could not look at Iris.

Their reactions were precise and entirely typical. Jimmy cried. Katie saw his face and cried. Gloria stayed silent, gazing up at her father, searching for clues. Iris stood up and ran from the room.

Sometimes the children are with me, sometimes they aren't. I have no way of knowing whether or not, when I look down, I'll see Katie's head, feel her feet hanging there. Sometimes I do manage to grip Gloria's little hand in mine, but other times my fingers hang loose and empty at my side. Mostly they hang loose.

Iris's anxious frown is still there now and then, waiting for me to say something, to do something. But more often there's nothing, an Iris-shaped space where she ought to be. Jimmy comes and goes. I never know when he'll next disappear. Halfway through one of his mad conversations. In the middle of a laugh . . .

Hold my hand, I tell him.

Oh, he says. Do I have to? I'm not a baby, you know.

I just think it's better, that's all.

But Mummy I just gave you a hug —

Yes, but this is different. I just want to know that you're still there.

But I am here! I'm right here, look!

I'd rather you held my hand. I don't know you're there if I can't feel you.

OK, he says. Can you feel that?

I look down.

I don't know, I say.

He laughs.

I just gave you a great big smack. Didn't you feel it?

No.

OK, then. Can you feel this?

What? Feel what?

I look around me.

Where are you? I say.

As we — or maybe it's just me now — make our way towards Elephant, I see people crowding round braziers, shouting things out, pushing and banging against each other. Men and boys mostly. Maybe they're fighting for something I can't see. I have no idea what they are shouting. Sometimes I catch snatches of obscenities, mostly yelling and laughter.

A small person, probably a child, in jeans and a grey hoodie, is slumped against a wall by the side of the road, legs drawn up, wrists dangling over his knees, head dipped as if in sleep. Something about the shape of him is familiar and I call out to see if he's OK, but he doesn't reply. I call again. He doesn't move. In the end, I go and ask if he's all right.

When he still doesn't respond, I lean over and touch the grey hooded head.

I won't hurt you, I tell him. I've got kids of my own. I just want to know if you're OK.

He stays so still under my gloved hand that I reach out and gently pull back the hood. Under it the bone is white and a few longish clumps of ginger hair still cling to the skull, lifting, now that I've exposed them to the wind.

The children are mostly gone, their shapes and colours, the touch of them, all dissolved, but their voices remain. Their questions.

Do you remember everything now? Iris asks me, her voice almost drowned out by the wind.

I remember some things, I tell her. I remember more than I did.

But not everything?

Not everything, no.

Maybe you don't want to remember everything?

I give her a swift look. She's always been a clever girl.

OK, but do you remember about our dad? says Jimmy.

What about him?

Everything. What he was like and all that.

I think so, I tell him.

Why did he have to go away?

It's a long story.

Do you think we'll ever see him again?

I don't know, Jims. I hope so.

And if he saw us now, say we just saw him over there walking along or something, do you think he'd remember that he was our dad?

Oh darling, I say. I'm sure he would.

A troubled look crosses his face.

And you do still remember that you're our mum, right?

Iris's voice is sharp.

What is it, Mummy? Why are you crying?

I don't know, I tell her. I don't know.

I hear her lower her voice.

Is it because of what you did to us?

I hold my breath.

What?

You know what.

She swallows. I think that her eyes are on me.

I know I ought to be afraid of you, but somehow, I don't know why, I'm just not.

What did she do? says Jimmy.

Iris says nothing. Grief sweeps over me.

I couldn't help it, she says. I was just so amazed and happy to see you again.

What did she do! Jimmy almost shouts.

Before I can think about what to do next, I feel something heavy in my arms — a fierce, dragging weight between my shoulder blades.

I look down. It's Katie. She's in my arms. She's wearing her old snowsuit, not the tartan one that she had on just now, but the other one, the red one, the one I put her in before when . . .

And there's no sling. The sling has gone. And her head is heavy and she's just about asleep, and I'm aching all over and she's a raw tired weight in my arms, this child, and I can't remember how we got here and all I know is I'm struggling to carry her just as I did when I left the house . . .

The house. We left it an hour or is it a day ago? Katie. She is mine. She is my child. I carry her in my arms. My face is on fire. I do not have a plan.

The world is still burning but the air is frozen, and once we are past Camberwell Green and on to Newington Causeway snowflakes coming down in silence – the air grows quieter. No one is screaming. No one is making a sound. There are fewer people now and those that you do see slip and stagger along in terrified silence, heads down, anxious to avoid trouble.

How many days has it been? Was it yesterday? Today?

Some carry suitcases or armfuls of blankets, but others must have left their homes as quickly as I did, and seem to have nothing. Some people sit in cars, but the cars aren't moving and they'll have to get out of them sooner or later. An oldish man with bloodied hands calls out to me for help, but I keep on walking. When his shouts grow more urgent, I move faster.

At Elephant, someone has set light to the top of the shopping centre and it's still smouldering, and all of the upper windows are thoroughly smashed. The eating places have been looted. A sign says Tai Tip Mein and then Noodle. The Eat As Much As You Like sign is hanging right off and flapping in the wind. Same for the Chinese – smashed up and burned. Bright nylon sacks of rice have been tipped in the snow. Down by the old kiosk – Chocolate-Chewing-gum-Patties-Jerk Chicken –

someone has built a snowman and forced a bright-blue plastic bag over its head.

Katie's asleep now. My arms are really hurting. I try shifting her up so she's half on my shoulder, but have to change sides so often it doesn't really work. There's some dried blood on her hands, and for a second or two I can't work out why it's there. Then, a moment later, I can, and my stomach twists. I hear a strange sound and I realise it's my own voice, gulping and wailing. I shut it off quickly. Katie doesn't budge. She stays asleep.

The freeze has already turned the trees in the middle of the roundabout black, and you can see the cars there too, stopped for ever in their rush-hour queues. You can't any longer see the people inside those cars, but there are no signs of any foot-prints across the snow.

A pretty, long-haired girl in a purple snowsuit and a fur hat is sitting cross-legged on a piece of corrugated metal on the charred back of a lorry. So still she looks like she's meditating. Her eyes are wide and the wind whips the strands of her hair around her face, and at first I think that she's mad to sit there, looking like such an easy target. But as I pass her, I see that nothing moves, not even her eyes. I'm tempted to try to get the hat, but even if I didn't have Katie, I'm not sure I'd be able to get up there without hurting myself.

By the tube is some rubble with thick snow on it and beside it a tarpaulin beneath which you can see the shapes of at least two people huddled together. The tarpaulin flaps around them. They aren't moving either. I don't stop to see if they're alive or dead.

A small red-haired person, wearing jeans and a grey hoodie is sitting against a wall by the side of the road, legs drawn up, wrists dangling on his knees, head dipped as if in sleep. I gasp and stare for a second. It looks so much like Jimmy.

Even though I know it can't be Jimmy, still I call out to him, but he doesn't move or speak and I stand there for a moment, thinking and worrying and wondering what to do. I call again. He doesn't move. In the end, I go over and ask if he's all right.

Holding Katie propped on my hip, I lean over and touch the grey hooded head.

I won't hurt you, I tell him. I've got kids of my own. I just want to know if you're OK.

He looks up at me. His eyes are empty. He isn't a child, but a man, red-haired, white-faced, a few days' growth of hair on his face. The skin on his neck is mottled with black.

Piss off, he says. Some spit comes out of his mouth as he says it.

I do as he says. I walk away, my heart thumping. When I dare to look back, he's still sitting there.

Man, says Katie.

Yes, I tell her. Man.

I stop to rest a moment, squatting and leaning against a wall with Katie propped on my knees. My face is still burning. I feel sick. The air seems to wobble. In the distance, I see another thing that confuses me. London Bridge.

I blink. It's still there. It's not possible. Surely we can't be back there already.

I look at Katie. I swallow. My throat is raw and tight.

Maybe Iris was right, I tell her. About us going round in circles.

She smiles. Dribble is running down her chin, which is getting sore.

Isey, she says and she rocks back against me. Her hair is damp and cold but it still smells like honey.

I hold my wrists up to the light and watch them moving all on their own.

I'm really shaky, aren't I? I say.

She looks at me. I can almost see the circles of her small brain going round and round. She puts a finger in her mouth and pulls it out again.

Dod, she says.

I shake my head.

The dog's not here, I tell her.

She listens. Her mouth is open. Her two new little teeth. Her fat wet bottom lip.

Isey?

Iris isn't here either.

She blinks at me.

And neither is Gloria or Jimmy and neither is Arthur, I add quickly, before she can sit there breaking my heart by running through all the names of all the other little people we'll never see again.

My mouth is dry. I scoop a handful of clean snow off the top of the wall and push it in my mouth. It tastes of cold metal and it hurts my teeth and the brief moment of pain is enough to put me back on track. I straighten up slowly and I hear his voice again. Jimmy.

Why did you do that? he asks me.

Do what?

Why did you make a face when you put that snow in your mouth?

Because it hurt when I bit on it.

Oh. Did you know it was going to hurt?

Yes.

So you're brave, then.

I'm not brave.

You are, says Iris. You are brave. You had babies.

Having babies is OK. You don't have to be that brave to have babies.

Well, I don't ever want to have a baby. I can't think it's worth it, if it hurts that much.

It doesn't hurt that much. It's hard to explain, but it's an OK kind of pain

Even though when you had Katie, you were screaming and screaming?

You remember that?

Jimmy got really scared. Dad had to send us next door to watch cartoons.

I shut my eyes and open them again, hoping to send the voices away. It doesn't work. I think about whether we should in fact head towards the bridge. If we cross it, at least I'll know where we are. I can get us back to the building. I think about the building then and I feel happier.

And what about when you had Arthur?

What about it?

That was awful.

I don't want to talk about Arthur.

Why not?

Don't, Iris. That's enough. I mean it. Don't ask me any more questions.

Why not? Why can't I ask you?

Iris.

What?

Iris. Iris.

What?

I walk on, with Katie held tight against me. The snow has stopped falling and the wind has dropped. Soon we are moving towards London Bridge.

A church has a sign outside with the words Good News! Jesus has the Answers! in big slanty letters. In front of it, a man is slumped on what is left of a wall, quite a young man, smoking a roll-up and drinking from a bottle.

He sees me and, very slowly, as if he's holding his breath, he puts the bottle down. I try not to look. The blood jumps into my throat. I walk faster, but I know he's watching me. My heart sinks when he throws the cigarette in the snow and slides down off the wall. In three seconds he is beside me.

I've got nothing, I tell him, as I feel myself start to tremble.

He looks at me and he doesn't smile. Then he looks at Katie. Katie returns his gaze.

Boy or girl? he asks me.

I say nothing. I can tell from his voice that he's drunk. He moves in closer. His breath is rank. I see that his hands are shaking.

Is it a boy, or is it a girl? he says again, louder this time.

I shake my head and he stares at me.

You what?

He keeps his eyes on me. Katie's still studying him.

Man! she says and, without any warning, her small hand flies out towards him — one of her grand toddler gestures.

Straightaway, he raises a fist and shoves it close to her nose. His eyes are hot and hard. I gasp and my heart bangs in my chest. Katie thinks it's a game. She laughs loudly.

He lets his hand fall. His eyes are on my face. Very slowly, I take a step backwards.

You got somewhere to go?

What?

I'm saying d'you want to come in?

He indicates a house whose broken windows are angrily barricaded with planks.

I shake my head but he grabs my arm, squeezes till it hurts. I see his grey wool mittens. The black hairs on his knuckles, the sliver of dirt under each long yellow nail.

What's your name? he says.

I say nothing.

Tell me your fucking name.

I bite my lip.

What? he says. You don't have a name?

I turn to face him. I'm shaking all over now.

Please, I say.

Amazingly, he releases me.

You've got lovely eyes, though, he says, as I lift Katie higher on my hip and begin very carefully to walk away.

The snow and ice are slippery here but I speed up, moving as fast as I can. I think he'll call out or come after me, but he doesn't. He doesn't do anything. I try to breathe, but it's harder than I thought. I do not breathe. I do not allow myself to look back.

The place where we are now doesn't look like London Bridge. It doesn't look like anywhere. To the left, there's a superstore, its windows smashed, already thoroughly looted. Heaps of rubbish smouldering in the car park. Beyond it, a clock tower, the hands pointing to 9.22, the moment when everything stopped.

A railway line sprawls away into the distance and I stand for a moment, confused. In front of us, a library which no one has bothered to break into. And next to that a coffee shop, also intact. I peer through the window and –

The blow comes from behind. A blow and then someone grabbing me around the waist. Almost before I can cry out, someone takes Katie from me and a big hard hand closes over my mouth. Another on my breast.

Katie begins to scream. I try to reach out for her and then I smell his whisky breath again. Right on my face.

Really sorry, he says. Second thoughts. I hope you don't mind, I brought my friend along. He's good with babies.

It's not just the friend. There are more of them. I don't know how many. Several more. At the very worst moments it feels like there might be quite a crowd.

They take us down into a basement room, blankets pinned at the windows. Flames everywhere – the yellow wobble of candlelight. The smell is of unwashed clothes, smoke, piss.

Katie is screaming.

Give her to me, I keep on begging them. I'll do anything you want. Just let my daughter stay with me.

Can you make her shut up? someone says.

I can, I cry. I can do it. I can shut her up.

No, another one says. Not her. We meant you.

Someone hits me in the mouth. My tongue swims with the bright taste of blood.

Please, I say, just give me my child.

The second blow is much harder than the first. I feel all my breath leave my body. Something cracks, but it sounds much too far away to be something of mine.

I like your hair, someone says.

More blood spills from my mouth.

The mattress is on the floor. They push me down and pull off my boots and my jeans. I don't know where Katie is. Two of them holding me while another tugs off the rest of my clothes. It feels important to try to hold on to my shirt, but they prise my fingers off easily and pull it over my head. The more I struggle, the more they laugh.

Katie, I say. Katie.

Nothing stops them. They carry on. They get the job done.

The mattress is filthy. It has a pattern of roses. Dirty satin. The word Sleepeezee. I'm reading the word over and over when I hear a match being struck and a door opening and closing. Freezing air on my bare legs.

No, I say.

A rough hand reaches out for my breast and someone else says something but I don't hear what it is.

Where is she? I whisper because I can't see or hear her any more. What have you done with my baby?

She's OK, someone says. She's having a nice time.

Yeah. She's watching TV.

A burst of laughter. I try to listen for her voice in the laughter but it's not there.

Desperate now, I list the reasons they should leave me alone.

You've got the wrong person, I tell them. I'm a mother. I've got young children. I'm bad luck. I'm already dead.

But they aren't listening. They tip something down my throat. It comes back up my nose. Whisky. I feel for my coat and try to pull it back over me. It doesn't work. Right by my face, a candle has been burning, but now someone leans to blow it out. I taste smoke and wax as the darkness unwinds itself.

That's when I begin to scream.

8

I wake. It is night. My head is in someone's lap. The person is humming. I know the tune. What is it? Is it a programme that used to be on TV?

Sophy? I say. Ted? Iris?

Oh, he says. You're awake.

I don't think so.

You are.

I can't be.

Fingers come down on my face. His fingers. I know them. I know his hands.

I do a daring thing then. I turn my head a little so my lips touch his thumb. Just the smallest touch, pulling at my lower lip slightly. I'd like to kiss the thumb, but I don't. I wouldn't dare. I hear him sigh. Lights bending and blurring, moving through the cab before they disappear again. The swish of tyres in the rain.

We shouldn't do this.

What? he says. What shouldn't we do?

I don't know. Whatever.

Say it.

I don't know.

I listen and I hear it again. The sound of those tyres.

Is it raining?

But he doesn't answer and instead it starts all over again.

You're awake, he says.

I don't think so.

I open my eyes and I look around for some sign of the building. Carpet. Desks. Windows. Corridors. Lifts. Graham handing me an orange. Sophy, hunched there, complaining on her bed of coats.

But I don't see any of this. All I see is snow. Right by my face, more snow. Above me, a black night sky sprinkled with stars.

Are we outside? I say.

Again, no one answers. Oh well, I think, and I shut my eyes.

He touches my face again.

Hey, try and answer me. Are you awake?

I yawn.

No. I'm not awake. Go away. I'm busy.

I hear him laugh.

What are you busy with?

I say nothing. I just get on with it.

Squatting down to do up the laces on Gloria's trainers, my knees pushed wide apart by the hot, hard curve that will soon be Arthur. Cutting an apple into quarters, putting one on each plate. Pulling out Jimmy's wobbly tooth for him, feeling the membrane crunch as the blood comes.

Hey, let me see it! – he takes the tooth from my fingers. But oh, it's tiny. Can I get the money now?

But just as I'm settled on the sofa with a cup of tea and Katie's backing into my lap with the same old favourite picture book, he interrupts again.

I need to wake you up. I'm sorry, but I need to see if you're OK.

I'm OK, I tell him. I'm fine.

I go back to my children.

Mum? says Jimmy.

Yes, sweetie?

I can't eat this apple. My other tooth's too wobbly.

Try eating it on the other side, then.

But that side's still sore from where you pulled it out.

OK, well then you'll just have to risk biting it on the wobbly side.

But I don't like it. I can feel the skin hanging down.

That's OK.

Yes, but I don't like the feel of it flapping and it tastes all bloody . . .

Blood. My eyes are open now. Cold air is on my hands. A dragging feeling in my stomach. I try to move my feet, but they're stuck to something. Or stuck together. I feel his fingers, picking at the knots.

I've been trying to untie you, he says. Do you know what happened? Do you remember anything? What did they do to you? Did they hurt you?

Snow is falling. It falls on every part of my face. I put out my tongue, interested to see if it will fall there too. It doesn't. Then it does. I lick my lips. I taste blood. I put up a hand and feel my teeth. They all seem to be there, a tight little row of them.

Is it mine? I ask him.

What? Is what yours?

The blood. Is it mine?

He doesn't answer. Maybe he didn't hear me. Or maybe I didn't say it.

I hear a match being struck and I smell his cigarette. I put out my tongue and let another snowflake melt there. He asks me what I'm doing, and I tell him – eating snow.

And I begin to laugh. I start and I keep on laughing. I can't stop. I feel like I've never heard myself laugh before. Or not in a long time, anyway. Isn't it funny, I'm thinking, how one laugh always leads to another . . .

I feel his hand on me again.

Oh, he says. Oh don't. It's all right. I'm here. Oh, please don't cry.

Something is crackling now – smoke coming off damp wood.

Clever, I say.

What's clever?

You built a fire.

He doesn't say anything. I have this feeling that he doesn't hear a thing I say.

Has this happened before? I ask him.

Now he answers.

What? Has what happened before?

All of it.

He hesitates.

I don't know what you mean, he says.

I put my hand up to touch my face and see that my fingers still have the brown streaks of someone's blood on them.

Whose is that? I ask him again.

What?

The blood. Whose is it?

I think it's yours, he says.

Here, he says. You're freezing. Put your gloves on.

He takes hold of my wrists as if I was a child.

I don't know why you keep taking them off, he says.

I watch with interest as my two cold hands are worked inside the gloves, each finger eased in, the thumb too, a sharp tug as they are pulled over my wrists.

Who are you? I ask him.

He doesn't hear me.

Now try and keep them on, OK?

OK, I say. But I don't know who you are.

You'll be much warmer if you keep your gloves on.

OK, I say.

After we'd sat the children down and we'd told them, Simon went to stay with his golf partner, Jock. It was what we'd agreed. Till we sorted out something more permanent. He was only a few tube stops away. He could see the children as much as he wanted.

That afternoon, the kids and I watched videos. We watched all the old ones, stuff they'd had all their lives – the more babyish the better. We watched *Thomas the Tank Engine* and we watched *Postman Pat*.

I haven't seen *Postman Pat* since I was about five years old, Jimmy said happily, as he kicked his legs in time to the theme tune.

We watched *Fireman Sam* and we watched *Teletubbies*. Even Iris watched *Teletubbies*. In fact the children were very specific about what they would and wouldn't watch.

Not Beatrix Potter, said Gloria. I don't like the fox. And not *Stingray*. I don't like the fish with the teeth.

And not *Rupert*, said Jimmy, when he saw me getting the box. *Rupert* gives me a horrible faraway lonely feeling in my tummy.

Yes, said Iris with a shudder. It's the woods. They're too dark and I don't like Algy Pug.

Why don't you like Algy Pug? Jimmy asked her.

There's something wrong with him.

What's wrong with him?

I don't know. There just is, OK?

So we skipped those and began all over again with *Thomas the Tank Engine*. We watched all curled up together on the sofa. We watched as if our lives depended on it. After a while I got up and made honey sandwiches and they all drank milk. When dusk came, I got up and drew the curtains. The outside world had never looked so dark.

Then, after a few days, Simon phoned and told me he was coming back. He'd decided he would not leave after all. It was his house just as much as it was mine. He refused to go. I would have to be the one to find somewhere else.

Why should it be me, he said, when it's you who did this?

His voice was quiet and strained. I could tell he was listening hard to this new version of himself. I listened too. My thoughts were tumbling.

But what about the children? I said.

What about them?

Where will they go?

They'll stay at home with me. The less disruption for them, the better. Remember this was all your idea, he added, when I stayed silent for too long.

But this isn't what you said before, I reminded him, when we first talked about it. You agreed it was important for me to be with the kids.

I heard him take a sip of something. He swallowed.

Well, he said, that was then. But I've talked to people now. They say I've been too reasonable. And I have to say I think they're right.

I caught my breath. Inside me the baby's feet touched my ribs.

What people? I said. I had a quick vision of the golf partner's wife, a pale, nervy redhead who had never liked me, her arms folded, a bottle of wine open on the table in front of her.

He was silent a moment.

Let's just say I've had a lot of support from a lot of people. And I've changed my mind.

That night I packed a suitcase. Several suitcases. A small one for me and huge ones for them. Everything they could possibly want. Jumpers and fleeces and jeans and socks. Gloria's favourite Thumbelina trainers. And toys. Jimmy's superhero sticker books and his dirty old cuddly giraffe. Iris's bead kit and her new guitar. Gloria's Sylvanians. Katie's raggies – the one she loved best and the other that she would only have if her best one was in the wash. All of the stuff I might need when the baby came.

I staggered out and put the cases in the boot of the car. There was only just room. I tried to get the Moses basket in but it wouldn't fit. But then I thought that the baby could probably sleep anywhere when it came. I remembered a bowl for the dog. A lead, some biscuits, a bag of food. The stained old towel she liked to lie on.

I thought for a second and then I went back to the car and pulled Jimmy's giraffe out of the case. He'd miss it if it wasn't in his bed tonight. We'd have to make sure we remembered it in the morning.

I didn't hear Gloria creep downstairs. She stood in the kitchen doorway in her socks and T-shirt, watching me. Her face was the face of an old woman.

Where are we going? she said.

Shh, I told her. You're not meant to see. It's a surprise. We're not going anywhere.

Next time I wake, I feel a man's hand touching the inside of my elbow. A dark snag of memory kicks in and I fight to sit up.

No! Leave me alone! Get away from me!

I try again to move my feet but I can't.

It's OK, he's saying. It's OK. It's only me. You're OK.

I feel my heart turning over and over, thumping and thumping. It makes my whole body shiver.

Please – don't hurt me.

Why would I hurt you? I'm not going to hurt you.

The hand is on my head again. I reach out and try to see whose hand it is, but all I can see is my own bare wrist, the one that belongs to me, with the snowflakes melting on it.

I'm here, the voice says.

You won't hurt me?

Of course I won't.

I yawn. The hand pats my head.

That's right, go back to sleep.

What are you doing?

I'm not doing anything. I just think you need to sleep for a bit longer.

Is it safe?

Of course it's safe. It's perfectly safe. I'm here.

Who are you?

You really don't know who I am?

No, I don't. Why would I?

I hear him hesitate.

I'm just a friend, OK?

OK.

I think about this.

But I don't have any friends.

Yes you do. Now you do.

OK.

I say nothing. I keep my eyes closed. After a moment or two the humming starts up again.

That tune. Now it really is beginning to get to me. Jimmy would know it. I can't think of the name of the show but I know exactly when it comes on — at 6.35, just after the news.

That night it rained and rained. It rained harder than I'd ever known it rain. Thunder and lightning, a wild storm ripping through the sky. Gloria and Katie both crying. Me getting the Calpol. Jimmy running to the loo with one of his bad tummies. The baby kicking and turning inside me. My heart in my mouth as the gutters poured.

Next morning, though, it was the brightest, bluest day. Sunshine. Uncommonly warm for the time of year. A heat-wave in February, said the radio. Already, at eight in the morning, the temperature climbing. The planet heating up. Not possible, the weatherman said. Well, let's enjoy it while it lasts, the presenter said.

I don't enjoy anything any more, I thought.

I got out of bed and water came rushing out of me. So much

water – more than I'd ever had with any of the others. Three weeks early. And it had black in it.

Gloria was standing watching me as I gazed at the wet carpet and tried to move my feet.

It's OK, I told her. It's not anything to worry about.

Straightaway she began to cry.

My head is still in his lap. It feels good. When I reach up and try to touch a part of him – his arm, his chest – a gloved hand comes and gently puts mine back down.

I think I might be a bit drunk, I tell him.

You're not drunk. You've been hurt and you probably don't feel too good, but don't worry, you'll be OK.

Who hurt me?

I don't know. Poor girl. I don't know.

It reminds me of being drunk in a taxi, I tell him. With my head in someone's lap –

I stop for a second and listen to myself.

Who's saying all of this? I ask him.

I feel his lap move as he laughs.

You're saying it, he says. And I'm surprised you remember that.

Remember what?

About the taxi.

What about the taxi?

Nothing. Don't think about it now.

Don't think about what?

It's not important. Never mind.

I can tell from the way his lap feels under my head that he's still smiling.

*   *   *

I thought I would feed them first, then call an ambulance. I wondered if I could send them all next door to Mrs Gregson, then see if I could get hold of Simon to collect them later.

I stuffed a bathroom towel between my legs and I made them all breakfast. Sugar Puffs bouncing all over the table, scattering and crunching under our feet.

It doesn't matter today, I told them, as the dog went around snaffling the spilt cereal. We're having a holiday from being tidy today.

Yay! said Jimmy, bashing the table with his fist and watching the milk slop over his plate.

Iris looked anxious.

But why? she said. Why don't we have to clear up?

Lots of complicated reasons, I told her. Just trust me, sweetheart. We don't.

But what about her teeth?

What about whose teeth?

The dog. She's not meant to have sugar. Remember what the vet said?

I was about to tell her that the dog would be all right just this once, when a pain went through me – a hard, hot cramp that stopped my breath. I bent over, held on to the kitchen table. I tried to remember how to breathe. I saw my fingers turn white as I gripped. I wondered who I should call first – Mrs Gregson, the ambulance, or Simon.

In her highchair, Katie looked at me and banged her spoon and laughed.

Again!

But Iris was staring at me.

What is it, Mum? Are you OK?

I'm fine, I told her as I took a few deep, panicky breaths. It's just a cramp.

Outside, the garden, drenched by the storm, was bone dry already. The heat of the sun had made the hellebores wilt, crisp and brown as if someone was cooking them. Petals were dropping. Leaves lay strewn and curling on the lawn, like autumn.

Far away, you could already hear sirens.

Things change. They change all the time. Now the snow has stopped and the night sky stretches high above us.

Look at the stars, I say. So many of them. You'd think they were so close.

How close are they really? Jimmy asks me. Could an astronaut touch them?

Of course no one can touch them, Iris says.

But just say they did, what would happen?

They'd burn up and die.

They're millions of miles away, I tell him. So don't worry. There's no possibility –

No possibility of what?

Of you touching one.

What are you talking about? he says.

The stars. I was telling Jimmy about the stars.

I hear him hesitate.

I think you've slept enough now. I think we're going to have to wake you up, he says.

Under my head, something shifts. My cheek sticking to something cold.

What is it? I ask him because I don't like the feel of it.

It's a bin bag, he says. Remember those?

Why've you got it?

To sit on. To keep us dry.

I don't want to be dry.

He doesn't hear me.

Do you mind if I have another go at untying your feet? he says.

What?

I blink. It's still so dark. I can barely see him. I can barely make out his shape.

Your feet. Can I untie them? I gave up on it before because I didn't want to wake you.

My feet. Something in me goes cold. I try to sit up, but I can't.

What happened to me?

I already told you. I don't know. I just found you here, lying in the snow like this with your feet tied.

But – what was I doing?

I hear him take a breath.

Well, you looked like you'd been hurt, he says finally.

And?

And – nothing. You looked like you'd been attacked. Do you remember anything? Have you any idea who did this to you?

Did what? What did they do?

I touch my face. The pain makes me shake all over. Even my hand shakes. I remember a mouthful of blood.

I think someone punched me in the face, I say.

Yes, he says softly. I think that too.

I feel some sick come up in my mouth. I swallow it back down.

Was there a baby with me? I say.

*   *   *

Jimmy went out in the garden. But seconds later, he ran straight back inside.

The fish! he was yelling. The fish! They're all floating on the top of the pond!

Iris looked at me.

That means they're dead.

I looked at her. I didn't want to upset Jimmy.

Not necessarily, I said, as I panted through another wave of pain.

She rolled her eyes.

But Mum, if they're lying on top –

Come on – I straightened up and took Jimmy's hot hand in mine. Let's go and have a look.

Out in the garden everything had changed. The light was metallic, eerie. The sun was hotter than I'd ever felt it. It burned our heads.

Ouch! said Jimmy, who always suffered in the sun.

I touched the back of his neck. It was pink, raw. I felt another wave coming.

We should go back inside, I said.

Why? said Iris.

I cupped my hand beneath my belly and felt it tighten. February. This was February. I crouched on the ground for a moment.

I don't like this weather, I said.

On the pond's steaming surface, the fish bobbed, some of them swollen, others split right open, the edges curling back as if on a hot grill. There was a strong smell.

Like fish and chips, Jimmy said. Only without the chips.

I looked at the fish and, as I looked, another pain zigzagged through me and I had to bend right over. Again, I struggled to breathe. Heat poured over me.

What's wrong with you? said Iris, and I saw that her face was wet, her T-shirt dark with sweat.

Go inside and put Katie in her cot. Then dial 999, I told her. Tell them your mum's having a baby and needs an ambulance. Tell them our address and our phone number and then open the front door and prop the hall chair against it so it stays open.

Iris ran inside, her sandals flapping on the melting path. We watched her go.

I could feel that Jimmy was about to ask me a whole lot of questions but he didn't get the chance, because, as he ran, there was a sound like a blade tearing through the sky. We watched as the house next door and the one behind it burst into flames.

Jimmy screamed. The sun disappeared. The air turned icy. Thick fat snowflakes started to fall.

He gets to work on untying me. I keep trying to see him through the darkness. Every part of me is hurting.

Did I have clothes on? I ask him.

He hesitates.

Yes, he says.

And the baby. Was she with me?

Yes – I can hear the rapid thinking in his voice. Yes. Don't worry, they were all with you.

All?

All of them. The kids.

I stop very still for a moment. I don't breathe. I don't move. This is it. The bad moment I've been waiting for.

That's a lie, isn't it?

He stops what he's doing for a moment. His hands resting on my feet.

Why do you say that?

Because it's not possible.

Isn't it?

No. You know it's not. And anyway, if they were with me when you found me, then where are they now?

He turns to look at me. I can just about see his face now, in shadow. Longish hair, down to his shoulders.

Look, he says. They're safe. I've taken them to a safe place.

Where?

It's just a place I know. A building.

I don't believe you.

I'm not lying to you.

You took them there?

Yes.

And then you just left them?

I left Iris in charge. She was fine about it. I had to come and find you. She knew I was going to find you.

I think about this. I try to imagine how the kids would be if they were left alone in a building somewhere. Would they worry and panic? I decide that Jimmy would do his best to be cheerful and that Iris would probably be pretty quick to organise them. She knows most things about dealing with Katie, I think. Sometimes she's better with her than I am. I hope that Gloria won't just mope and disappear into herself. I worry about Gloria.

Can we go there? I say. Will you take me? I want to go there right now.

We will. We'll go in a minute. I just need to get you walking first.

I can walk. I'm fine. I can walk any distance. I just want to be with my children.

He's looking at me.

Really? You think you're OK to walk now?

Yes, I say.

You're feeling OK?

Yes.

Well, good, he says. That's good.

What's the matter? Why are you looking at me like that? Don't you believe me?

No, he says.

Haven't you done it yet? I say when I see that he's still fiddling with the knots.

He says nothing. I continue to watch him – the back of his head. Hair touching the back of his coat. Something about the way he bends himself to my feet makes me feel soft.

Who are you? I ask him. Do I know you?

You keep on asking me that.

Yes, I say. I wonder why.

He laughs to himself.

Seriously? You really don't know who I am?

I remember some things very well, I tell him. But not others.

And you don't remember me?

I don't know. I haven't really seen your face, have I?

I feel the rope around my ankles give. A hand pats my leg.

There you go, he says, and he sits back on his heels and turns around. I see that he is nice-looking. Dark-eyed, a few days' growth of beard.

Someone hurt you, I tell him. On your face. That's a bad cut.

He smiles. Touches the place.

It's not too bad, he says. It's getting better.

I try to get up on my feet but I can't. He comes to help, but I don't want to let him.

It's OK, I say.

Let me help.

No.

But I want to. Why can't I?

I don't look at him.

Look, how am I going to get myself back to my kids if I can't even stand up on my own?

Don't be so hard on yourself, he says, pulling me up anyway.

I thought I was OK but, as I straighten, I feel something trickle down between my legs. All my clothes feel like they've been put on wrong. There are tightnesses in places there usually aren't. I begin to shake.

It's hopeless, I say.

What's hopeless?

I say nothing. I start to cry.

I'm so sorry, I tell him.

Sorry? What have you got to be sorry for?

For being so . . . stupid.

What? Why do you think you're stupid?

For letting myself get hurt and . . . I don't know. I feel stupid and I feel sad. I just want to get back to my kids, I say.

He looks at me.

You know something?

What?

I just want to put my arms around you.

I flush.

No, I say. Please don't.

I sway on my feet. I think I hear a dog howling somewhere. It's still dark and grey shadows are moving over the snow.

I wish it was light, I say. When will it be light?

Soon.

But will it definitely get light?

So far it always has.

I look at him.

But we can't be certain?

About what?

That it will get light.

He seems to think about this.

No, he says. I suppose we can't.

I think about this and then I hear myself laugh.

What's funny? he says.

I sound just like Jimmy, don't I?

He smiles.

You do, he says. Him and his questions.

I look at him.

You know Jimmy? You remember him?

He glances away.

I know all your kids. You think I'd know you and not know your kids?

I think about this. I look at his face and my heart lifts. I don't say anything. He smoothes out the sheet of black plastic I was lying on before. The bin bag. He doesn't look at me.

Sit down, he says.

No. Please. I want to go.

Not yet. We'll wait for it to get light. You'll feel better then.

Really? You think so.

Yes. I really do. So sit down.

I look at the black plastic.

Come on, he says. Just do it.

I look at it but I stay where I am, standing. My legs and stomach hurt. My thighs ache.

Come on, he says again, more softly now. You can at least sit down. What terrible thing is going to happen if you let yourself do that?

I look at his face again. I sit.

Upstairs in her cot, Katie had woken and was standing up rattling the bars and gasping out tears.

Maybe she'd seen the flames across the road. Maybe she'd heard the sound of next door's windows shattering, one after another. I listened to her scream for a moment and felt a prickle of panic, then I shut the sound from my mind while I got my thoughts straight. Downstairs, Iris was banging my mobile hard against the kitchen table.

Stop it! I yelled at her, as I bent forwards over the table to deal with another wave of pain. What are you doing?

The pepper mill got knocked over. It rolled very slowly to the edge of the table, then dropped to the floor. Peppercorns spilling and bouncing everywhere. We both looked but did nothing. The dog edged over and started sniffing at them. Iris banged the phone again.

For goodness' sake, I said. We need that phone and you're going to break it.

She looked at me. Her eyes were hard and scared.

But it's already broken, she said. Don't you ever listen?

That's what I've been trying to tell you. I can't even make it work to dial 999.

I grabbed the phone from her and I pressed dial and listened. Nothing. I tried punching buttons but nothing happened.

Jimmy was at my elbow.

We need to get the fire engines as well, he said.

Why? said Iris.

He was gazing at me. His face was white. He could hardly get the words out.

All the houses in the road! All the houses!

What about them? Iris said.

They're — they're catching on fire!

Iris stared at him.

They can't be, she said.

Well they are! Jimmy cried. Go and look out of the window if you think I'm fibbing.

I looked at Jimmy's small white face as another wave of pain went over me.

Go and get the cordless phone from my bedroom, I told him. Bring it here, fast.

I dropped to the floor on my hands and knees and the dog, surprised and already tiring of the peppercorns, skittered out of my way.

The air outside the kitchen window was turning thicker and greyer, like dusk but not like dusk. As if someone had stuck a lid on the world and screwed it shut. It was getting colder.

Put on some lights, I told Gloria, but I already knew what would happen when she flicked the switch — absolutely nothing.

* * *

Dawn comes. I had thought we were nowhere but it turns out we are on a road with shops and houses. Some are burned, but most aren't. There's a pound shop and a sign that says Iceland and another that says Fitness First. Also a nail shop and a betting shop and a chemist with its front smashed in, a couple of people lying dead on the ground in front of it.

Above us, the sky is an odd shade of red – almost brown in places. Everywhere, you can see smoke from all the fires that are burning. I think about the building where my children are. What if that has caught fire?

It's light now, I tell him. Can we go back?

Back?

To the place where you took the children.

He looks thoughtful.

You think you've already been there?

What?

You said back.

I tense for a second, thinking about this. Pictures turning over in my mind.

I don't know, I tell him at last. Is it in the City? Is it an office?

For a few quick seconds, I can almost see it. Empty corridors, windows that go down to the floor. A wide concrete terrace, a white dome. My heart speeds up. He looks embarrassed. As if he can see it too. He glances away from me.

Yes, he says. That's the place.

And have I been there?

He looks at me. He says nothing.

What? I say. Well, tell me. Have I or haven't I?

I look at his face. The slight chubbiness around his jaw. His dark eyes, dark lashes. The gash on his cheek.

He shrugs. His eyes are full of pain.

I don't know, he says. Maybe once.

Jimmy brought the upstairs phone, but of course it didn't work. There was pain on his face as he handed it to me. I stared at it for a moment. I couldn't think why I'd asked for it. Then I remembered.

Are you sure it's plugged in at the socket? I said, even though I already knew the answer. Iris went and checked and came back. She shivered and hugged herself as she spoke.

It's in.

What?

I said it's in.

Gloria was still flicking light switches on and off. Every light, flick, flick, on, off.

Stop it, I told her a little too harshly. Can't you see it's making no difference?

She gazed at me.

But I only want to make it be a bit light, she said in a whisper.

Me too, Jimmy started to moan. Can't you just get another light that works or something, Mum?

Can you both just shut up? Iris said as I gasped and leaned down over the kitchen table. Mummy's really hurting and she can't do anything except breathe right now.

She was right. It was all I could do. I wasn't even doing that very well. I tried to breathe, but my chest kept on wanting to empty itself and not take any air back in.

I tried to remember how it had been with the other births. I remembered the panic and the pain of Iris arriving. People shouting and running. I couldn't remember Gloria or Jimmy or Katie. I remembered the metal frame of a hospital bed,

Simon's hands, a chair with a green PVC cover, ripped so that the foam showed through — but hadn't Katie been born at home? I couldn't remember how it was, having a baby at home.

I tried to concentrate on the shape my own hands made as they gripped the edge of the wood. Sweat pricked my underarms, my back. It poured off my face.

Iris was standing and rubbing my back like I'd told her to.

Aren't you worried about our house catching on fire? she whispered.

I shook my head.

You aren't? But why not?

Trust me. I just know it won't.

I felt her take this in. I knew from the way the pressure of her hand on my back lessened for a second or two, that she didn't believe me and she didn't trust me.

I'm worried that next door is just going to burn down completely, Jimmy said.

Then what will happen to Mrs Gregson? said Gloria. Will she just scream and run out into the street, do you think?

No, said Iris. If she did we'd hear her. And anyway, she would come round here.

Well, maybe she was out shopping or something? Jimmy said.

Iris stared at him. I could feel her hand trembling on my back.

She never goes out shopping. People do her shopping for her, because of her leg. And, I think all the shops will be on fire.

He looked at her carefully. You could see he was thinking about whether or not to ask her the next question. He decided not.

Well, I hope the cats escaped, he said.

* * *

The dog was drinking water – lapping and lapping it in a frantic way as if she knew it was her last. Upstairs, Katie was finally quiet. Maybe she'd given up and gone back to sleep.

My waves of pain had lessened slightly. Was it all slowing down? I didn't know if that was a good thing or a bad thing. I tried sitting on a chair. The towel between my legs was sodden. When I sat down, I felt more water seep out.

I looked around me. The room was so dark. The children's faces were a mass of shadows. I asked Iris to fetch me another bath towel and I told her where to find candles. Gloria came and stood in front of me with a roll of kitchen paper and I almost laughed. Jimmy whispered to me that he had matches in his bedroom. Two boxes of them.

I don't want to know why you had those, I told him. And you're not in trouble this time. But never again, OK? They're not for kids.

Never again. Never again. Another, worse wave of pain came then and I got up and bent over the table again. I gasped and waited for it to finish, but another followed straight after. Three or four more coming after that.

I tried to put my hand down to feel what was happening, but I couldn't get far before another wave swept me off. Again and again, I tried to remember the breathing but the pain kept getting in the way, gripping on to me and giving my lungs no space. Upstairs, Katie started crying again.

Oh God, I said. Oh God. Oh please, oh help me.

Jimmy made a sound, halfway between a scream and a sob.

I don't want you to die, Mummy, Jimmy said. His words flew around my face and I batted them away.

Oh God, I said again.

Iris went and got Katie and brought her downstairs. Katie

held out her arms and started crying, Mummy, Mummy, Mummy!

Get her away from me, I told Iris.

Where shall I put her?

I don't know. Anywhere. Put her anywhere.

Iris stared at me for a moment, then she thrust the towel at me. I pushed it away.

There are about six houses on fire across the road, I heard Iris say. Six houses. And I don't think anyone has called a fire engine, but I suppose their phones aren't working either.

She strapped Katie in her highchair and gave her some keys to play with and also the plastic beaker of milk, which she poured straight down her front in her hurry to drink it. She cried again.

Don't die, Mummy, Jimmy was saying, and I saw that he was holding his cuddly giraffe tight against his chest and really crying now. I don't want you to die.

I won't die, I told him. But I might need to scream soon, OK?

OK, he said. His face wobbled. I could see him thinking about how to control himself. Can me and Gloria go and watch TV?

How are you going to do that? Iris said. Don't you realise, there's no electricity?

What about the computer?

That won't work either.

Gloria put her head near mine. She lifted my hair so she could whisper in my ear. The tickle of her breath was like an extra pain.

Mummy, why did you put our toys in the car? Is it OK to go and get them now?

No, I said. Of course you can't!

When I thought about the car, I wondered what on earth my plan had been. What had I been doing? Where had I imagined I was going to take them all?

No, no, no! shouted Katie from her highchair.

The room bobbed in the candlelight. Outside, the snow was falling fast. The pain had its own rhythm now and I didn't care if I died or not, I was going to follow it. Beneath me I saw a dark, wide pool on the floor. Its edges were moving, creeping outwards. I didn't give it a second thought, but Iris gasped.

Is it blood? she said, but I was in my own world now and couldn't answer her.

We make our slow way back towards London Bridge. We stick to the smaller streets, icier, more deserted. The snow squeaks beneath our feet. Sometimes I almost slip and he has to help me, but on the whole I manage it alone. I make him walk a step or two ahead of me. He thinks it's so I can grab on to him if I need to, but it isn't that. It's so I can watch the back of his big dark coat, his hair.

We walk mostly in silence, but now and then he tries to tell me things.

Do you remember where you lived? he says.

I shake my head.

Your house was pretty. Roses all around the front door and you and Simon had knocked the two downstairs rooms into one.

Simon?

Your husband.

I think about this for a very long time. I feel that he's waiting for me to say something, but I say nothing.

Roses? I say at last.

Well, I think they were. You like roses?

I don't know. Not much, I don't think.

Well, you did. You grew vegetables too. Potatoes, beans and stuff. You even had a pond, with fish in it.

To eat?

He laughs.

No, of course not. Just, you know, goldfish.

Goldfish. I feel myself tense.

I wouldn't know how to grow vegetables, I tell him quickly.

Well you did, he says. You do.

In the middle of the road, a large dog lies on its side. Its black lips are pulled up around its teeth and its eyes are wide open.

Flies dance around it and I think it's a long time since I saw any flies. And then I realise. The air's been getting warmer.

We walk around the dog.

And did you go there? I ask him a moment later.

What? Go where?

To the — to our house.

He looks at the ground.

Yes, he says. Well, of course I did, yes.

You were our friend, then?

He looks at me.

I was your friend, yes. We go back quite a long way, you and me, Izzy.

Izzy? I say. My heart drops. I'm staring at him. He looks straight back at me.

That's your name. Short for Isobel. But no one ever calls you Isobel. You really don't remember your own name?

I think about the name and I think about the person called Isobel who was never called that, and I shake my head.

I remember my children, I tell him. I remember everything about them. But I don't remember myself.

Do you want to know what my name is? he asks me a bit later.

OK, I tell him, though the truth is I don't really care about it all that much.

I'm Matthew.

Matthew? — the name twists itself in and out of shape and then settles in my head like an ache. It's a nice name, I tell him.

He smiles.

You don't really think that.

I look at him.

Well, it's OK, I say.

Suddenly he leans forward. He stares at me. He touches my shoulder.

Oh, he says. Oh, Izzy, what is it? What's the matter?

I put my fingers to the corners of my eyes, try to take away the tears. I squeeze my eyes shut, but it doesn't help. More of them come falling out. I push his hand away.

Are you OK? he says.

I shake my head.

Izzy?

I don't know, I tell him. That's enough now. Leave me alone. I don't know.

On the floor, on my hands and knees, on the towels which Iris had spread out for me, I put my hand down to feel between my legs. My fingers touched something hard and hot and wet.

It wasn't a part of me – what was it? Was it the head? I waited for a moment. I blew out more air.

In another world, very far away now, I heard the children saying things, their voices coming and going like voices on the radio. I heard Jimmy whining that he wanted to go out to play in the snow.

Me too, I heard Gloria say.

I heard Iris objecting.

But we've already got our coats and hats on, I heard them say.

All the houses are burning down, said Iris, and then she added something else which I could not catch.

We promise we'll keep away, said Jimmy.

I heard Iris say something else then, in a ruder and crosser voice.

But what are we meant to do, I heard him reply, if we can't even watch TV?

Stop moaning, Iris told him then. Stop being such a stupid little baby. Don't you see that something really terrible has happened out there? No one's to even open the back door, do you hear? Mum would go crazy. You're staying right here, both of you.

I tried to raise my head, to check they were obeying Iris. Sweat trickled down the back of my neck. I saw that their coats were off, so maybe they were. I tried to speak, but my voice was swallowed up in a bubble of pain. My breaths were coming much too fast. But too fast for what?

I cried out. Iris rushed over to me.

What's happened? Gloria was asking her. What's the terrible thing?

Maybe she thought the terrible thing was what was happening

to me, but at that moment, the world decided to answer her. Outside there was a crash like thunder, only louder and closer than any thunder should be. You would think the sky had been ripped in two.

Gloria screamed and so did Katie, and the dog ran to the furthest corner of the room and sat there panting. From where I was I could see her shaking and staring at the wall. Saliva falling from her mouth.

I saw that Iris was struggling not to cry.

I wish Dad was here, she said in a shaky voice. And then I felt her glance at me, wondering if it was OK to say that.

I said nothing. More sweat fell out of my hair and ran down the back of my neck. I tried to hold on to myself. I held myself in one place, which was all I could do. I panted hard.

When this baby comes out, I told her, you're going to have to help me catch it and wrap it in the towel, OK?

Now Jimmy looked interested.

And what happens if she doesn't catch it?

I didn't answer him. I began to push.

We walk on through those streets towards the river. It seems to take a long time. Once or twice he tries to take my arm to stop me slipping, but I don't let him and I don't slip.

I went there, you know, he tells me. A few days after it happened.

I look up.

Went where?

To your house. Well – to where your house had been.

I stare at him.

It wasn't there?

The whole street burned down, Izzy.

But – then why did you go there?

He looks at the ground.

Why do you think I went there? I went everywhere.

I'm silent a moment, trying to work this out. I try to think about everything he's told me. The roses. The goldfish. The two rooms knocked into one. The woman called Isobel who is never called that.

Matthew? I say.

What? His face softens.

Do you mind if we don't talk about it any more right now?

OK, he touches my shoulder. That's nice, by the way.

What's nice?

Hearing you say my name like that.

We reach the river. The weather has definitely changed, there's no question about it now. It's warmer. It's lighter. A fog or a mist has come rolling in. It hangs just above everything, a cloud of wetness that you can feel on your hands, your face, your hair.

We walk on to the river until we're standing right in the middle of it. In the strange afternoon light, the ice is smooth and white as a cup of milk. I lick my lips.

In front of us, some dogs are fighting – a snarling, sliding ball of teeth and fur. We both turn our heads as a man speeds past us on a bicycle, grizzle-haired and wearing black clothes, ringing the bell and spraying us with water before the fog swallows him up again.

We both stare after him.

Was that real? I say.

He laughs. He thinks I'm joking. He gives me a careful look.

Do you know what was interesting, though? Did you notice the water?

What water?

As he went past. The spray. It means the ice is melting.

I look down at my feet. It's true – there are slick, shallow puddles all over the surface of the ice.

We walk on a moment, but then he stops and feels around in his pockets and I watch as he lights a cigarette and smokes it fast, holding it down by his thigh between puffs, looking around him as if someone might at any moment come and try to take it off him. He reminds me so much of someone and I can't think who it is. And then I can. It's the kid.

He breaks off then, head on one side. Looking at me. He smiles.

What? Haven't you ever seen anyone smoke before?

No, I tell him, it's not that.

What, then?

I don't know, I say. But can I ask you something?

He looks happy. He flicks the cigarette, ash lands on the ice.

You know you can ask me anything you like.

The man who you say was my husband –

Simon.

Yes. Simon – I test the name aloud for a moment and decided it doesn't feel any more likely. Well, was he – I mean, were we happy together?

He looks at me, blows out smoke. He looks down at the cigarette, then back at my face.

Oh Izzy, he says.

What?

You're putting me in a very difficult position, asking me a question like that.

9

Arthur's bright, raw cries filled the kitchen. The dog shuffled herself under the table, terrified.

I tied the cord as tight as I could with Jimmy's shoelace and tried to get Iris to cut it with the kitchen scissors, but they weren't sharp enough and she was shaking so hard she was afraid she would hurt me or the baby, so in the end I did it myself.

Gloria screamed when the placenta slid out.

It's OK, I told her. That's just what comes out when you have a baby. There was one just like that when you were born too.

But not when I was born? Jimmy said.

You too, I said.

Oh yuck.

I told Iris to get a baking dish from the cupboard to put it in.

I don't want the dog trying to eat it, I told her. Though in fact the dog didn't look like she was capable of eating anything ever again. I'd never seen her so limp and ratty and scared.

I lifted the placenta into the dish because Iris didn't want to touch it, and she put it up on the counter. Then she pulled Katie out of the highchair, where she had got herself all slumped and grizzling, and we all went over and sat on the sofa, where I fed Arthur by candlelight.

For a while everyone was quiet. Just the sound of Arthur

sucking. Occasionally, still, the sound of glass breaking somewhere further down the road.

You have a new brother, I told them.

I hate him, Gloria said very quietly.

That's a horrible thing to say, said Iris.

You can't hate a thing that doesn't speak and is as small as a monkey, Jimmy pointed out.

I looked at Arthur. Jimmy was right. He did look like a monkey. A beautiful, perfect, adorable little monkey, with his dusky black hair and flattened nose and folded-up limbs. A flush of love made my heart speed up. I felt it in my cheeks, my scalp, just behind my ears. The sweet excitement of a new baby. I sighed with pleasure and I put my hand out and touched Gloria's cheek, but she shivered and pulled away from me.

You're just tired, I told her.

Everyone was silent again. Jimmy was holding his giraffe by its two front legs and twirling it round and round.

Can you stop doing that? Iris said to him.

Why?

Because it's really annoying me.

Jimmy carried on twirling.

He needs to do it. He needs to do his loop-the-loop, he said, and then he thought about what he'd just said and he laughed.

Iris looked at me.

Mum?

What?

He's being annoying. Do something.

Try to be still for a bit, darling, I told Jimmy.

He stopped twirling.

I thought Arthur was asleep, but when I looked down he was gazing into the distance with his big glinty monkey eyes.

He's just a few minutes old, Jimmy said. He'll never be this young again.

That's right, I said.

He thought for a moment.

If it wasn't pitch dark in daytime, and if there wasn't blood everywhere, and if next door hadn't burned down and maybe even killed Mrs Gregson, and if the TV was working, and if you hadn't just had a baby all on your own without Dad, this would be a perfectly normal kind of day, wouldn't it?

He finishes the cigarette and chucks it down on the ice. We are almost across the river now. Cannon Street is ahead of us, a creamy, blue-white line against the even whiter sky.

With every step we take, I feel a little stronger. I think of the building, with its long grey corridors, its huge wide windows, its snowy terraces.

I think I have been there, I tell him as we climb up some icy steps to what would once have been a road.

Been where?

To the building. The place where you took them. I think I know it. If you left me here right now, I think I could almost find it.

He gives me a long look.

I'm not going to leave you here, he says.

Do you know a girl called Sophy? I ask him moments later.

Sophy? Sophy who?

I don't know her other name. She has blonde hair. Very pretty. She's about fifteen.

He thinks about it.

There was a Sophy who used to babysit for you, he says.

I brighten as I realise that might be who I'm talking about.

Yes, I say. I think that's her.

Why? What about her? Have you seen her?

I try to think about Sophy. Her pale hands, coming out of Graham's jacket. A grey cardigan over her face. The rain coming down.

Yes, I say. I've seen her.

She seemed like a nice kid. Is she OK?

I hesitate.

I think so, I tell him. I'm not sure. I hope she is.

A few moments pass. He says nothing. I don't know what he's thinking. I'm thinking about all those names. Sophy and Simon and Matthew, and the woman who they never call Isobel.

Is she just the same? I ask him.

What? – he looks puzzled. Sophy?

No, I mean me. Am I the same as I was when you knew me?

He looks at me. His eyes are dark.

I recognise you, if that's what you mean.

No, that's not what I mean.

He sighs.

Well, all right, your mouth looks a bit swollen and there's a fucking awful bruise on your cheek. But if anything you look even more beautiful, especially with your hair all long and wild like that.

I feel myself flush. My hand flies to my cheek.

I wasn't talking about looks, I tell him.

He glances away.

I know you weren't, he says, and he sighs again. A long sigh. For a second he looks as if all the air has gone out of him.

You said it was OK to ask you questions, I remind him.

It is. It is OK.

Then what is it? What's the matter?

221

He says nothing. Finally he takes a breath.

What are you asking me to do, Izzy? Are you asking me to tell you what you used to be like? Or are you asking me to tell you how I used to feel about you?

The day, Arthur's birthday, rolled on. One o'clock came and so did two o'clock, three o'clock, and it did not get any lighter. We stayed in the house. We sat around. There was nothing else we could do.

Mummy? Gloria said.

Yes?

What are we waiting for?

Nothing, I told her. We're not waiting for anything.

So what's happening?

I don't know what's happening.

But — are we going to be OK?

I saw Jimmy watching my face.

That's enough questions for now, I told her.

We couldn't hear the fires burning any more, but the blackness outside remained as suffocating as ever and when Iris opened the back door to try to let the dog out, smoke and something else that wasn't smoke came in. The dog braced herself in the doorway and would not go. In the end, she peed on the mat.

Iris had a look of distress on her face.

It's awful, she said. There's nothing but snow everywhere and burned stuff. And the trees in the garden are all black.

What about Mrs Gregson's house? I said.

She gulped.

I tried to look. It just isn't really there any more.

I stared at her.

But what do you mean? What's there?

She bit her lip.

Just, I don't know, half a wall. Black stuff.

But could you see anything? Jimmy asked her. Did you see Mrs Gregson's dead body? Did you even see the cats?

Iris ignored him.

There's no sound of anyone anywhere in the road either. It's so weird and quiet. It feels like everyone has just gone away or died.

I looked down at Arthur. His face was so still that for a second or two I felt worried. Then his eyelid flickered. His mouth moved. I breathed again. I looked at Iris.

There must be someone out there, I told her. It isn't possible. Other people must be staying in their houses the way we are. We can't be the only ones.

Why didn't our house burn down as well? said Gloria, who'd been staring at Iris and listening with round, shocked eyes.

I don't know, I said.

She waited for me to say something else but I didn't have anything else to say, so I said nothing. We were all silent for a moment then. We watched Katie, who was sitting on the floor and leafing through a picture book which she was holding upside down. She realised we were all watching her and she looked up and grinned.

Butch! she said, lifting it up with such force that she almost tore a page.

Yes, I told her. Book.

Mum, Iris said to me at last, what do you think this is?

I looked at her. My mind was going round and round. Ever since Arthur had come out of me, I'd been feeling more and more unsteady.

This?

Yes. What is it? What's happening?

I held Arthur's warm damp weight against me. I put my lips on him. His head smelled of cheese.

I don't know, I said.

But do you think something bad's happened? Could it be the end of the world?

If it was really going to be the end of the world, Jimmy said, it would have been on the news.

Iris turned on him.

Shut up, Jimmy. This is serious, OK? I'm trying to ask Mum a really important question.

I reached out and took Jimmy's hand. I squeezed it. Then I looked at Iris, my anxious and speedy and clever Iris, who always worked everything out.

No, I said. Don't be silly. Of course it isn't.

But how do you know?

I don't know, I told her. I don't know anything for sure. But I just don't think it is.

You're not scared?

No, I said. I'm not scared.

She lifted her chin and she looked at me then, and I knew what the look meant. It meant she already knew the truth. That I was no use and I couldn't help her.

I'm scared, said Gloria.

I don't know if I am or not, said Jimmy.

Iris said nothing. She looked at them both for a moment and she looked like she was going to say something else, but she didn't. She went over to the window and she folded her arms and stood looking out at all that darkness.

*　*　*

We were cold. We were all so cold. Everyone shivering, everyone's teeth chattering. Katie's lips had turned quite blue. I told Iris to put another jumper on her. A jumper and a hat.

She'll never wear a hat, Iris told me, and sure enough she tore the hat off, wailing, and threw it on the floor.

I shouted at her from where I was stuck with Arthur on the sofa.

One more trick like that, I said, and you get a big hard smack.

She watched my face for a second or two and then she burst into loud upset tears.

Jimmy stared at me.

Mummy, he said. You don't smack babies.

I said nothing. I thought it was time Arthur had another feed, but he wouldn't do it. His mouth slipped off the nipple as if he didn't even know it was there. I cupped his small brittle head in my hand, touched his cheek. It felt cold. I drew him up to my breast again, tried to warm him against my own hot skin.

I was burning. My head was burning. My stomach and my legs hurt and my mouth tasted rough and sad, like old newspapers. I touched my face. My fingers slid around in the sweat.

Jimmy was sitting next to me and bouncing up and down. It was giving me a bad headache. I told him to stop it and be still. He gave one more bounce, then he looked at Arthur.

Are all new babies that funny colour? he said.

I looked at my baby.

What do you mean? What colour?

He shrugged so his shoulders touched his ears.

I don't know. He kind of looks like someone's coloured in his face with a felt-tip.

I tried to smile.

A felt-tip?

Yes, a grey one. A grey felt-tip.

I saw Iris watching me. Our eyes met for a second. She held my gaze and then she looked away.

I was hot but I knew the children needed to get warm.

You can't do anything about it, Jimmy said when I put my arms around him and tried to warm him up. There's absolutely nothing you can do.

Of course there is, I told him. Of course I can.

He gave me a sad look.

But what?

Don't worry, I told him. We'll get the room warm.

You're just saying that because you're really sick.

I stared at him.

I'm not sick, I said, but he just looked at me and said nothing.

I told Iris to look for firelighters in the cupboard behind the washing machine. She found them, but I couldn't remember if we had any wood, any coal. I didn't know where Simon would have put it. Jimmy found half a bag of kindling under the stairs, but there was nothing else.

Fetch some newspaper, I told him as I tried to keep Arthur tight and warm against me. I'm going to show you how to make a fire.

I know how to make a fire, he said, shivering all over with cold but now also with excitement.

No you don't, I told him. Not in real life you don't.

Gloria was staring at me. She was trembling. She looked empty and frightened.

What? I said. What is it, darling?

She said nothing. Her eyes were wide. I put out my hand

to her, patted the sofa. It was so cold you could think it was wet.

Come on, I said. Come and sit here with me.

She shook her head as if that was a terrible idea, and then she backed away from me as if I might grab her at any moment. She went to sit on the stairs with her chin on her knees.

I instructed Jimmy. I told him to pile up the kindling on top of the scrunched newspaper and crumble a firelighter on top of that and light it.

He looked astonished.

What? he said. With a match? You mean I'm allowed to do it all by myself?

I heard his concentrating breath as he stood back and watched the little flames dart into life. At the sound of the fire, the dog ran away to the kitchen. Jimmy sniffed at his fingers.

Smell that, he said to Iris. It's the loveliest smell, like petrol.

But what are we going to use for coal? Iris said, ignoring him.

Katie had fallen asleep on the floor by the sofa, her hat still off. I put Arthur down on the rug next to her. He startled for a second, splaying all ten of his fingers out like he'd had the most brilliant idea, then he drifted back down into sleep.

I tried to get up then. I tried to make my brain stand me up, but it didn't want to do it. The signal wasn't getting through. My legs felt like someone else's legs.

Finally, I gripped on to the arm of the sofa and I pushed. That was it. I was up. The other person's legs were hot and wet. Or maybe it was her heart, my heart. I could feel it pumping the liquid round my body and I wasn't at all sure it was going in the right direction.

The coffee table was made of some kind of lacquered pine. Simon's mother had given it to us. It was tiny, useless, ugly.

I picked it up and put it on the fire. For a second it seemed to stop the flames, but then they leaped up and embraced it, spat out some bright violet sparks.

Jimmy gasped.

We're burning the furniture!

It's all we've got, I said.

Oh my goodness, said Iris in a horrified voice. Oh, oh, Mummy, look!

She didn't mean the fire. She was staring at the sofa which was soaked dark with my blood.

Back on the other side of the river, towards Southwark, there's the sound of music. Laughter. Guitars and maybe a drum. Some singing. Flames bouncing on the ice. There's a smell of fat, of burning meat.

I remember Ted then. The night he came back drunk and we all walked to the river, looking for the party. And we never found it. But there was something else about that night — something that happened, or maybe didn't happen. Maybe it still will. It was to do with the kid. It was . . . I'm silent for a moment, trying to remember it.

He puts his head on one side.

What? he says. What are you thinking?

I was thinking about something that happened. And then I thought that maybe I got it wrong and it hasn't happened yet.

Maybe it's not the answer he wanted, because he looks disappointed. He rubs at his hair, takes a breath, looks away across the ice.

It probably did happen, he says.

You think so?

He turns back to me.

Well, what? You're saying you can look into the future?

I look at him. I don't have an answer to that.

I know what you're thinking, he says at last. You're thinking you just want to get back to the building, get back to your kids. And I'm just thinking that I would like to keep you here.

I don't say anything. Then I say, Why?

Why? – he looks at me and he doesn't smile. Why? Because I like being with you. I always did. Haven't you got it yet? Do you mind me saying that? Is it OK with you, if I tell you something that's true for once?

I listen to his words. I feel my face get hot.

I like you too, I tell him.

He shakes his head but he still looks unhappy. He swallows.

Well, thank you, he says.

I keep my eyes on him. I look at his face, the crinkles at the corners of his eyes, the dark of his lashes, the way his hair sticks up slightly on one side. I look at the hollow parts of his cheeks, the little curve at the top of his lip, the line where his beard starts.

Actually, I say, can I ask you something?

He doesn't say anything. He waits.

Did we used to . . . did we once . . . I mean, were you my . . .?

He doesn't look at me.

Was I your what?

I don't know. You say I had a husband and so –

Have. You still have a husband. As far as I know.

But what was it, then? You and me, were we somehow . . .?

He looks like he might be about to say something, then he changes his mind. His face is tight.

There's no point in talking about it, Izzy.

Why? Why is there no point?

Because it's over, isn't it? So what is there to say?

I stare at him.

Why would you want to talk about it? he says. If you don't feel it now, if I have to tell you what happened and what you're supposed to feel, well really, what's the point?

I think about this.

But, I tell him, I don't have my husband any more.

You don't know that for sure. And anyway, whether Simon's still around or not, that makes no difference. It won't come back.

It?

His face is hard.

The feeling.

But, I say, struggling to find the right question to ask, did we feel things then?

I felt things, as you put it.

And me?

There's pain on his face.

Look at you, Izzy. Look at yourself. You don't remember a thing, do you? You don't even remember what you did a moment ago.

I do, I tell him quickly. I do remember.

What did you do?

I thought about you.

And before that?

I think I thought about you then as well.

He looks back across the ice towards the party.

Everything's melting, I say.

I know.

I go over to where he's standing. I go right up close. I put my hands on him – his chest, his stomach, his thighs. I push my hands under his coat.

He doesn't move. I look up at his black eyes and I touch his face. The line of blood — I touch the edge of it. I put the inside of my wrist against his hair. When he doesn't do anything to stop me, I put my lips against his. Very gently, I put my tongue on his top lip. Then the bottom one. I lick them both. They taste of ice. I press my lips against his. He groans.

Izzy. What are you doing?

I say nothing. I pull his mouth back to mine. He doesn't speak and he lets me do it, then he draws back and says it again, less gently.

What are you doing?

I don't know, I tell him.

He shuts his eyes. I take his hand.

Do you want to go and lie down somewhere? I say.

What?

Do you want to?

He steps away from me quickly. The sound he makes is terrible. He puts his head in his hands.

I stare at him. I think he's crying.

I thought you'd like it, I tell him. I thought . . .

He doesn't look at me. He doesn't look up. His head stays in his hands. I watch him and at first I feel helpless, stupid. But after a few moments, I work out what it is I need to do. I go over to him and very gently I put my hand on his head. No kissing. Nothing. Was this how it felt, loving him?

I'm not afraid of you, Matt, I tell him. I don't care what you think. I like you best when you're like this.

Still he doesn't look up. I don't need him to.

I lied to them. I told them it was normal. I explained that mothers always bleed for a bit after they have babies.

But that much blood? said Iris, still staring at the dark slick of wetness that had begun to drip on to the floor. I mean, going everywhere like that?

Yes, I told her. That much blood.

I told them we'd get a new sofa.

But when? said Jimmy, gazing at me, hands on hips, trying to catch me out.

When the shops are open, Iris told him in a steely voice.

But when will that be? What if they never open again? What if all the shops have burned down?

No one knows whether they've burned down or not, Iris said. And anyway, even if they have, someone will build more shops and we'll go shopping again.

That's my girl, I thought.

Gloria said nothing.

I got Iris to go upstairs and fetch me every towel she could find, as well as aspirin. She brought down temazepam by mistake. I'd forgotten we had temazepam. Good, I thought, I might treat myself to one of those later.

Iris, I said, you're a great nurse. I don't know what I'd do without you.

She gave me a look that was full of doubt, but even so, she looked pleased and she insisted on carrying Arthur around for a bit, to give me a break. He looked as small as the smallest black mouse, resting there on her shoulder. Every time I looked at him, he seemed smaller and more fragile and unlikely and further away.

That night we did not move. We all slept exactly where we were.

Excellent! said Jimmy, when I told him he didn't have to put on his pyjamas or clean his teeth or go up to bed. So we're just actually going to camp in front of the fire?

If you like, I said.

To keep the fire going, I'd added the wooden bread bin and a couple of chopping boards as well as some of Simon's golfing magazines. I was tempted to put his expensive bag and the fringed leather shoes on there too, but I didn't think Jimmy who occasionally went to watch him play golf — would like that, and anyway, I worried it might make noxious fumes.

Are we just going to burn every single thing we possess? Jimmy asked me, eyeing the flames.

I smiled.

Why not? I said. But then, when I saw his devastated face — Of course not, Jims. That was just a joke. Of course not. Not really.

I looked around the room and felt suddenly brighter. With the little children and babies and firelight, and minus the blood, it could have been a scene from an old-fashioned Christmas card. My heart sailed upwards.

Well, isn't this nice? I said.

No one spoke. There was something a bit frightening about so many silent children, so I tried to encourage a bit of comment.

Is everyone warm? I asked them.

Iris glanced at Jimmy and I saw him look at her.

Kind of.

Are you having a good time?

Gloria gulped.

Not really, Jimmy said.

I touched my face. It felt damp and cold now. Even though I was burning. I'd put another bath towel between my legs and

I could tell that it was already soaking. It made a comical squelching sound when I moved. I thought how we would all probably laugh about this later. The thought made me wild and cheerful. And I looked down at Arthur, so still and sweet and peaceful in my lap and I thought how at least on that count I'd struck lucky. I didn't think I'd ever had such a well-behaved and easy newborn baby.

If it gets too hot, we'll open a window, I said.

Iris gave me a worried look.

What? I said. What's up with you now?

She shook her head and looked at the others, then she chewed on a nail.

The kids hadn't eaten for hours. Iris got some stuff from the larder and they ate hoops and beans spooned straight from the tin and they drank some milk. Then she took a torch and she and Gloria fetched pillows and duvets and blankets from upstairs.

I noticed that Gloria climbed the stairs after her and did everything she was told to do, but she did not speak. She moved in silence and in slow motion. She said nothing at all. Now I thought about it, she hadn't spoken a word for at least an hour or so.

What's the matter with Gloria? I asked Iris.

She glanced at me, trying to decide something.

She doesn't like the black outside, she said at last.

But none of us do, said Jimmy. It's horrible. And I'm not at all keen on the way everything keeps on bursting into flames.

Iris looked at him and then she looked at me. Her eyes were grave. She looked at us as if we were both fully signed-up members of the same mad team.

Yes, well Gloria really, really doesn't like it, she said.

The blood had stopped coming out of me, but I couldn't stop shaking and my teeth clattered together like the teeth of a cartoon character. I took a temazepam to deal with that. Then I showed Iris how to swaddle Arthur tightly in a towel and got her to lay him on the floor between two sofa cushions. He did not sleep, but lay awake, staring around him with his glinty monkey stare.

I picked up Katie and gave her a cuddle. She arched her back and struggled in my arms. Her fist hit my lip.

Naughty girl, I said, and I grabbed her fat wrist to pull her hand back down away from my face.

No! she said, still struggling.

Yes!

I held her all the tighter then and I shook her a little bit harder than I meant to, but I needed to show her who was in charge. She grizzled away, gazing at me with angry, worried eyes, then she stuck her fingers in her mouth and used them to comfort herself.

Just for the hell of it, I had a go at turning on my phone again. Then the lamp by the sofa. Then the television. Then the radio. Nothing. It was a fact. The world out there had fallen away.

I'm not at all well, I thought – then, quickly as it had come, I pushed the idea away. What did it matter, really? We were all here together, weren't we? That was the main thing. It was the only thing. I had all my children around me – even my brand-new little baby, my Arthur.

I felt suddenly sorry for Simon, wherever he was. Because he wasn't with his children and also because now he would never get back to the house and have the satisfaction of asserting his moral rights and reclaiming it as he'd intended. I wondered what Jock and his wife would think of that.

I realised I had no idea what time Arthur had been born. Was it lunchtime? Was it even today?

In the morning, I told the children as we fell into a strained and shivery kind of sleep, everything will be OK. In the morning, I'm sure it will be light.

On the street that looks out over the river, we come to a wall with a bench in front of it. The snow on the bench has all melted away and the wood's damp and bare. Then I notice the thing that's different from last time. On the piece of ground beneath the bench, some blades of grass are showing, coming up through the snow. The green is intense. We both stare at it as if it's a miracle.

I know what will happen next and it does. He sits down on the bench and he looks at me and, after one quick moment of thinking about it, I go and sit beside him. I am ready for this. I feel the slats move under us. And I feel it, too, as he puts his arm around me, and this time he's a man, fully grown, so his arm reaches properly around, his hand resting on my shoulder. I feel the rough of his coat sleeve, like last time. But this time, I can lean back for a moment against him.

We did this before, I tell him as my body caves into his shape.

He looks at me.

Your memory's better than mine, he says, and then he realises what he just said and he laughs.

I try to laugh too, but the sound that comes out of me is not quite like laughter.

He pushes some hair out of my face, but it falls straight back. In the end, I push it away myself. I want to say other things to him, but I don't. I don't speak at all. I sit there. I tell myself that I can even feel his heart thumping, and for a few seconds I almost think I can.

We sit there together for a long time. I don't know how long. Mist is still rolling off the river, so thick that you can no longer see over to the other side. After a while I yawn. He asks me if I'm sleepy.

No, I say.

I'm sorry, he says at last.

You've got nothing to apologise for.

Come here — he puts his hand on my face and turns it gently towards him, but I shake my head and I pull back.

I'm feeling too wound up, I tell him.

He gives me a long look.

Don't be wound up.

Or too sad. I don't know which.

He gives up and settles me back against his shoulder. He says nothing. After a moment, he puts his hand on my knee, squeezes it gently. I put my hand on his. I like the feeling of his fingers under mine.

Don't be sad, he says.

I don't know where I want to be, I tell him. Right now, I mean. I just can't stop thinking about them. Even though I know there's no point.

I know, he says. That's all right. I know you can't.

In a minute we'll go back there, won't we?

He nods.

Don't worry. We'll go and find your children.

I hope they're all OK.

They're OK.

You don't know that. You don't have to say it just to make me feel better.

None of it was your fault, you know, he says at last.

None of what?

What happened between us. I just want you to know that. What I mean is, it was all me. It was entirely me. I knew exactly what I was doing.

I twist my head to look at him. I try to think about what he might have done. I can think of nothing. When I try to remember him, my heart always lifts. To me he is blameless.

That night in the taxi, he says. Remember? I wanted it. I started it.

I say nothing. I snatch another glance at his face. Arthur's face. His dark head. The dark, dark eyes.

But it was me too, I tell him. I knew what I was doing as well. I knew what would happen and I still did it. I put my head in your lap. I shouldn't have done that.

He smiles. He touches my head again, ruffles my hair.

You don't remember do you? You were just obeying orders. I told you to put it there.

I think about this. I'm trying to remember if it's true. All I remember about the end of that evening is that I did not want to leave his side. I didn't care what happened next, just as long as it kept on happening.

I was drunk, I say.

We both were. But not too drunk. We were just about drunk enough.

Drunk enough for what?

To know what we wanted.

*   *   *

All the same, he says, when you did it, when you ended it, I honestly didn't know what to do. I didn't know how I would go on.

I say nothing. I wait. From somewhere above or behind us there's a drip-dripping sound. Ice melting.

I just wanted you to know that, Izzy, he says. How I felt about it. Not to make you even more sad, but so that you know – because I never got a chance to tell you.

I feel myself twist against him.

Even though, he continues, I'm sure you were right to do it. I'm sure you did the right thing.

You are?

I wipe my face on my coat sleeve. Then I have to wipe it again. When he answers, his arm is still around me, it's even tighter, and his voice is hoarse.

No, he says. All right. All right, I'm not.

At last, he takes his arm away. I can see that he's upset. His eyes are shaky and sad. I tell him to go ahead and have one.

What?

A cigarette. It's OK. I don't mind.

Without smiling, without thinking, he pulls them out of his pocket. He's not looking at me as he lights it. He frowns, his eyes on the flame.

I went after you, you know – that night.

What, the night of the taxi?

No, not that one – he looks at me for a second. No, I mean that last night. The last time I ever saw you. I know I shouldn't have, but I did. And I think I would probably have caught up with you, except – he breaks off to inhale – there was this bloody bomb scare. Somewhere on Bishopsgate. Police, loads of vans. They cordoned off the whole street. They wouldn't let me through.

I shut my eyes for a second, but he doesn't notice. He laughs to himself. He shakes his head.

So instead I went back up to the office. I couldn't think what else to do. I just went up there and sat alone in the dark and I cried. Maybe because you'd just been there, I could almost make myself think that you still were. All I wanted was to carry on feeling close to you. But I cried like a fucking baby, Izzy. I don't think I've ever cried so much in my whole life.

I hold my breath. I think of him sitting there on the edge of the desk in the dark. The tearing sobs.

When I speak, my voice is a whisper. Even I can hardly hear it.

And then? I say.

And then?

What happened after that?

He shakes his head.

Oh Izzy. Don't make me tell you the rest.

I shut my eyes. I see his hand, picking up his phone and keys. The brief rattle before they go in his pocket. The sensation of him passing very close to me, suddenly almost hopeful, hurrying.

What happened? I say. When you left the office? Where were you going?

He is silent for a long moment. He sucks at his cigarette. He looks at the ground. I glance at the side of his face. His hollowed-out cheeks. The terrible grey colour of his skin.

Matt? I say, suddenly afraid.

He turns and looks at me. He chucks his cigarette down. His eyes are dark.

I thought I'd go and find you anyway. Fuck the consequences. I thought I might even confront Simon, have it out with him – you know, in a calm and adult way. I wasn't going to be unreasonable. Christ, I must have been deranged that evening, because I even told myself I might be able to make him understand.

I stare at him

Understand?

That I loved his woman. That I'd always loved her. That I needed her more than he did. That I was more likely to make her happy. Yes, it was stupid and selfish of me, and it would have been a very bad idea, wouldn't it? It's not what you wanted, I know that. I'm very glad it didn't happen. I'm very glad, Izzy, that I didn't get a chance to do it.

I say nothing. He wipes his hands across his mouth, looks at the ground.

Do you hate me now? he says.

I look at his beautiful face, full of sorrow and shadow.

I could never hate you, I tell him.

He draws me to him then. He draws me close. He puts his lips against my hair, my cheek. And I know how they're going to feel before they even touch me, and I'm right, they do – icy cold.

As he speaks, his lips are in my hair. My tears are falling on his coat. A tear rolls off the rough weave of his sleeve.

Matt –

I was trying to call you, as I went across the street. But your phone was off and I didn't want to leave a message. So I started to send you a text, not saying anything really, only to tell you that nothing had changed, that I still loved you.

He looks at me and he shakes his head.

It was all my fault, I wasn't even drunk, for God's sake, but

I was in some kind of a crazy fucking dream . . . I felt nothing, no pain. I knew I was entirely to blame. And you know the worst thing? I could imagine what your face would be like, when you heard. That was the part I really couldn't bear. All I remember thinking, over and over, was that. How the hell am I going to stop Izzy finding out about this?

I stand up. The snow beneath my feet has turned to slush. I can smell soil, earth, air, ripeness. My boots are quite wet. The earth is coming back to life. When I finally speak, I can't look at him. I look instead at the smallest, greenest blade of grass. It looks so hopeful. It gives me courage.

I had a baby, Matt.

What?

I had a baby. A little boy. I had a little boy.

I was right. In the morning it was perfectly light. The darkness had dissolved, or at least it had receded, and though the
sky was still a strange, harsh colour, a sharp acid light pene-
trated the glass of the windows, illuminating the room. You
could see it all now, the things you needed to see and even the
things you'd rather not.

I saw all the chaos and mess that had crept in and taken over
the room. The sputtered-out candles. The blackened things in
the fireplace. The bloody towels all over the floor. The half-
eaten tins of spaghetti hoops. The dark sodden place that was
the sofa. The pale, untroubled faces of my children as they lay
sleeping, waiting for whatever this day would bring.

But Arthur. He didn't look at all happy. Maybe I'd never
seen him in this savage light of day before, but his skin was
yellower than it should have been and his eyes had lost their
glint and his breathing didn't seem right.

I wondered if he was hungry. I tried to remember when he'd
last let me feed him. Last night? Yesterday? I wondered if he
was cold. The room was freezing. We're going to have to find
some more things to burn, I thought, and I remembered Simon's
study upstairs full of big fat expensive art books that he never
looked at, and I smiled.

Arthur gave a little moan – it wasn't a cry. I almost wished
it had been a cry. It seemed all wrong that he wasn't crying. I
realised I hadn't heard him cry in a lot of hours.

I tried putting him on my breast but he gasped for breath and spat the nipple out. His face was naughty but I knew it wasn't naughtiness.

He's ill, I thought. He's definitely ill. And I'm not too good myself either.

I picked up my phone, stared at the buttons. I realised I was shaking. I tried to get a grip on myself. I tried to tell myself the facts: that the phone was dead, but I should not panic. What good would panicking do? It certainly would not fix anything. I tried to bring myself back – to think about normal people, normal reactions, normal things.

I thought about what Simon would do, what Simon would say, the different ways in which he would stride in and take charge. Even without the phone, I knew he would have done something – gone out to find someone, demanded someone do something, explained very calmly and clearly what he thought might be going on.

But I reminded myself that he wasn't here. That he wasn't going to be here. So I took some big breaths and tried to think calmly about my situation, ran through the kinds of things I would have said if the phone worked. I'm all alone with my four children and their new brother. And there's something wrong. The birth wasn't good. I think I might be haemorrhaging. I'm feeling very sick. I'm afraid of what will happen if I can't look after them. My eldest is only nine years old. I think I might need some help . . .

I began to cry. My crying woke Iris.

Luckily my eldest daughter was the only one who woke. The others were all still sleeping soundly, a row of little white mice under their duvets and blankets. This suited me. I told her what to do.

You're going to put on your boots and coat and go out into the street and try to find someone, I said.

She looked at Arthur, who was making a bad face and moving his tiny arms and hands in a kind of grey slow motion. Then she looked back at me. She bit on a nail.

But find who? she said. And anyway, how will I walk? The snow looks so thick. I think it'll come right up over my boots.

I tried to think. Iris was no fool. It was important to tell her something convincing.

You'll have to take a shovel with you, I told her. There's one near the back door, just behind the bins. Use it to clear a path in front of you as you go.

She stared at me. I knew what she was thinking – that I'd forgotten that she was only nine years old. Going out into the snow with a shovel was a grown man's job – the kind of thing her dad would have done. I tried to ignore the look in her eyes.

Walk along the street, I said. See which houses are still standing – there must be some that haven't burned down. And bang on the doors as hard as you can. If there's anyone in there, they must be able to hear you.

Iris blinked.

What if they're all dead? she said.

Then try going round the corner to Sophy's house. See if she or her mum are there.

Her eyes widened.

I'm really worried that they won't be there.

What makes you think that they won't?

I don't know. I just have this bad feeling.

Well then, I said — I'd had enough of her negative attitude now. Just stand in the middle of the street and shout for help as loudly as you can.

Iris scrunched up her face. She was studying me carefully, listening hard to these instructions, but I could tell she was also looking for something. She was looking for the thing that I'd left out, or not thought of, or even wilfully ignored. She was looking for the one thing in all of this that wasn't quite right.

I waited. My face was slick with sweat. I could smell my own skin, my own blood. I felt impatient but I had to admit her next question was a very sensible one.

But what exactly am I asking for? If I find someone, then what am I asking them to do? To take you and Arthur to the hospital?

I looked out of the window. The sun was still bright but the sky was the colour of tarnished metal — dead and pointless.

That's right, I said. I need a lift to the hospital. Arthur needs help. All of us, we all need some help.

She kept on staring at me. I knew that she didn't want to go. She was trying to think of a reason. She knew there was still something wrong.

But the snow — what if there aren't any cars driving?

I blinked.

Someone will think of something, I told her.

But what if I can't find anyone?

I touched her skinny shoulder. I thought that really she ought to try to humour me now.

See what you can do, I said. Just do the best you can, OK?

And I turned away, back to Arthur.

* * *

We are almost at the building now, Matt and I. The streets are light, dusty, bathed in early-evening sunshine. Even the shadows are alive with the stored-up heat of the day.

Shops are closing and bars and restaurants are filling up. Men stand on the pavements with their suit jackets off, smoking and talking and drinking beer. Women in tight dark skirts and high heels, hair swinging, briefcases under their arms, laughing loudly and talking on their phones. By the Ship Tavern someone has put a piece of chipboard on the pavement and a kid who can't be more than twelve years old is tap-dancing on it, alone and vigorously happy, without any music, hoping that coins will be thrown down into a plastic cup, which they are.

We walk along next to each other. We're not touching, not out here, but we might as well be. I'm so completely alert to the fact of his presence. His tall shape. The way the jacket of his suit swings open. The way he's pulled off his tie and stuffed it in his pocket. The hair, just long enough to touch his shoulders. The fact that I don't think he has shaved for a couple of days.

He feels me looking at him and he turns.

You OK?

I don't know.

That means no.

I bite my lip. I say nothing.

Izzy —

I suppose I'm scared.

Don't be.

Not of you. Of me. Of us.

You're scared of us?

That's about it. Yes.

He's silent a moment. A man is squeezing oranges outside

Liverpool Street Station. People rushing down the steps and escalator to get to the trains.

Izzy, he says, you've nothing to be scared of.

I say nothing.

Honestly. Do you believe me? I love you.

Don't say that.

Why can't I say it?

Another silence.

OK, I won't say it. But that doesn't stop it being true. In fact, I don't think it's ever been more true than right here, right now at this particular moment.

He stops to pick up an evening paper. By the kiosk, something awkward happens. We run into Sophy.

Oh, I say, Sophy! Where are you off to?

She looks at me quickly, breathless. Notices that I'm blushing. Also that I'm not with Simon but with Matthew, whom I think she's met maybe once before, at our house. She keeps her eyes on me, pulls a face.

Dance class, she says. Don't laugh. I haven't done it before, but you get the first three for free.

I'm not laughing, I tell her. You remember Matthew?

She nods and smiles at him and for a brief moment none of us says anything. I feel myself take a little step away from him. For all she knows, we are just friends. I ask her where the class is.

Oh, just around the corner from here. I'm just so sick of being such a blob, she adds. I want to get fit.

You're not a blob, I tell her. You're curvy in all the right places.

All the same, she says, wrinkling her nose.

Well, good for you, I tell her.

I take a breath – I really can't think of anything else to say. Matthew comes to the rescue.

I'm taking Izzy to see where I work, he says.

He laughs and so does Sophy.

OK, she says, holding her head on one side and waiting, as if there might be more to it. Which there is.

None of us says anything for about five seconds. Then she asks me if Jimmy's better.

Just about, I tell her. But he might have to have his tonsils out now.

Oh, poor thing, she says, with real feeling.

Yes, I say. It's one thing after another with him. He just seems to attract accidents and operations – which of course, deep down, he loves.

We all laugh.

I ask her then if by any chance she's free to babysit tomorrow night. I see him looking quickly and carefully away into the distance when I ask her this, as if it's not his business, not his life. She says she can't see any reason why not, but can she text me later on tonight or tomorrow morning? I say that's fine.

Well, bye then, she says, as she slings a nylon rucksack over her shoulder. Have fun.

We watch her go, bright trainers moving fast over the sunlit pavement. Matthew looks at me and feels around in his pocket for a cigarette. He frowns.

Was that difficult? he says.

I shrug.

Why should it be difficult?

I just wondered.

It was fine, I tell him. Sophy's a good girl.

OK, he says.

He threads his fingers through mine for a quick and daring second and then he lets them go again. Then he lights the cigarette and smokes it fast, but throws it down half finished, impatient to get in the building.

We go in through the main entrance and are hit by the cool of the air conditioning. A marble floor. A jazzy little fountain. Tall shiny pots with plants in them. A bank of white-leather and steel sofas for people to wait on. Newspapers and magazines spread out. I stand for a moment, looking around me.

What? he says.

I shake my head.

Nothing, I say.

The doorman is missing a front tooth. He makes a joke with Matthew that I don't understand. Maybe it's about working too hard. Most people are leaving the place, after all, not arriving. Suit after suit pouring out through the turnstile and into sunny Bishopsgate.

We have to wait for a lift because they're all so full of people coming out. One of the men who steps out is about to walk right past us, but then he turns and grabs Matthew's arm, punches it in a lively, jokey way.

He has on a suit and trainers but no tie, and his eyes are glittery and a little wired, his hair dark and springy. Under his arm, a copy of *The Times*. In his hand, an orange. I don't catch what he says. He looks at me and so does Matthew.

Izzy, this is Graham, Matthew says. Works on my floor. He's a total waster. Don't be taken in by him. Don't listen to a word he says.

The man called Graham laughs and looks at me, then his eyes change and he looks away.

Don't listen, or don't believe? he says.

Ha! Both, says Matthew. Neither.

Graham claps Matthew on the shoulder and then he looks at me again, more carefully this time, and he smiles. Then he stops smiling. His whole face alters.

What did you say your name was?

Izzy.

He hesitates, staring at me.

Have we met before?

I feel my cheeks get hot.

I don't think so, I say.

Your name doesn't ring any bells, he says. But your face — you're not a friend of Caroline's are you?

Caroline?

My wife. Well, soon-to-be ex.

I shake my head. I'd been worried he was going to say that he knew Simon. I try to smile.

I don't think I know any Carolines, I tell him.

But he seems unconvinced. He continues to stare at me.

You know where I think I've seen you? he says, chucking the orange from hand to hand as if he's about to juggle with it. I think I've seen you here.

Here?

Yes. In this building.

I laugh.

I don't think so, I tell him.

Not possible, Matthew says. Seriously, she's a very old friend of mine and she's never been here before. I'm about to give her a tour.

But Graham looks serious. He bites his lip and looks straight into my eyes.

I'm not making it up, he says. Honestly. Your face – oh God, I'll get it in a moment.

Matthew glances away across the foyer.

You're doing a pretty pathetic job of chatting her up, he says. And we're missing all the fucking lifts now.

Graham steps away. His eyes still on me.

OK, he says. OK, mate. Sorry. Go on, off you go.

He throws the orange up in the air and catches it one more time. But as we step into the lift he turns back suddenly and puts his hand on the door to stop it closing. His eyes are intent, serious.

Right here in this building, he says. I don't believe you've never been here because I've seen you. I'm not in any doubt at all. I know I have.

I take a breath. Matthew touches me somewhere.

Christ, he says, and his voice is only half warm. Come off it, Graham. What are you saying? That she's lying?

Graham keeps his eyes on me, and I feel my blood start to jump.

I don't know what I'm saying.

Matthew shakes his head.

Well, whatever it is, just leave it, OK?

I push a strand of hair behind my ears, fiddle with my earring. I look straight at Graham. I keep my eyes steady.

I've never been here, I tell him. I think I'd know if I'd been here, wouldn't I?

He says nothing. He carries on looking at me. But someone else gets in the lift then and we have to let the doors close. We go shooting up through the shaft, seventeen floors up, to the floor where Matthew works.

* * *

The room felt even colder once Iris had gone. I tried doing normal mother things. I tried walking around with Arthur drooped over my shoulder, the way you're supposed to do with small babies, but he wouldn't do it. He kept on shuddering and falling backwards, his head at an awkward angle, not behaving how newborns ought to behave. And my own head was hurting too now, a dull, throbbing ache. The more I walked, the more it throbbed.

So in the end I sat back down on the sticky sofa and laid him on his back across my knees, and I tried to take a proper, responsible look at him.

Arthur, I whispered, keeping my voice low because I didn't want to wake the others. Arthur.

His breath was coming fast and his eyes were wide open, but they weren't really looking at me. The change was subtle. Only a mother would have seen it. But it was as if he'd decided not to be there in quite the same definite way as he'd been there before.

I squeezed my eyes shut and felt a tear slide out.

Arthur, I whispered, where are you? Come back to me.

I thought I heard him whimper, but I wasn't sure. I knew that I could have imagined it. Nothing else changed.

I saw that there was a little bit of sick at the corner of his mouth. Had he been sick when I last fed him? Would I have noticed? I struggled to remember but my mind was dark.

That was the problem, I thought, as I wiped at his mouth with the cloth – he was starving. He was going to starve. The same went for all my children. I had failed them, all of them. I knew very well that the mission I'd sent Iris on was hopeless. What was I thinking? A nine-year-old girl, out on those streets. I was a bad mother, a reckless and irresponsible person. Because the world had gone, hadn't it, and it wasn't coming back in a hurry. The world was freezing, it was on fire, it was nothing, it had gone.

I sat and watched my baby. I didn't think he could see me now. Sometimes his breath seemed to be there and sometimes it didn't.

Arthur, I said again, louder. Arthur!

Katie stirred for a moment, smacking her lips together and beginning one quick little half-cry, before going back to nuzzling her raggy in her nest among the cushions on the floor.

Iris had been gone a long time. I didn't know how long, I just knew it was long. I sat there and did the only thing I could do. Kept watching my baby.

I tried to tell him things. I told him how much I loved him, how much we all did, what a special baby he was, how very much he was wanted – how sorry I was that he'd been born into such a difficult and frightening and upside-down world.

You came on the very worst day, I told him, as the tears began to fall down my face again. Honestly, it's not always like this – you should see us normally. Your brother and sisters, they're just the best, they're so funny and lively, they're such good kids. And we have a garden with a fish pond and a climbing frame – when you're older, you'll appreciate those things . . .

Arthur?

His face had relaxed, or maybe it had hardened. I was shaking all over, but I tried to keep my legs together so he would not slide off my knees. I held him there. I touched his soft cheek.

You're safe, I said. Don't worry about anything. I'll take care of you. Nothing can happen to you. I'm your mum. You're safe with me.

And maybe he'd listened to me, because he seemed to have settled. He was very still. I felt still too – still and calm. I gazed at him in silence for a while.

I thought I should really tell him about his father – about how much I'd loved him, how we'd loved each other all our lives and could never really tear ourselves away from each other, how proud and happy he would have been to see and know and hold his baby son. I wanted to tell him all of this – and for a quick second or two, I thought I could actually see it. Matt's beautiful face – his hands, his arms and fingers, the laughing way he would have scooped this child up, and then the trembly, disbelieving way he would have gazed and gazed at him.

I wanted to tell him all of this but I didn't manage it, because when I tried, when I thought about that hungry-happy look of Matt's, no words would come, only more tears.

So instead I touched the top of his small monkey head, where the black hair swirled in all directions as though it didn't know where it should go next. And I touched my lips on his tiny nose. And I put a finger in the clenched nub of his hand.

And I thought about how so much of him was new and undecided. How none of it was his fault. It never had been. So much of him was just waiting to see what would happen next.

That morning, the next morning, when Simon took a phone call from someone who knew us both, and then sat me down and told me he had some very bad news indeed about Matthew, I sat there, with my hands folded in my lap, as calm and still as anything. I know that I kept my eyes on Simon's face as he took me through it, and I know that I listened very carefully to the words, as if they were a set of instructions, which in a way I suppose they were.

Accident. Very late last night. Near his office. Instant. No one's fault. Would not have known. Nothing they could do.

Then I thanked Simon for telling me in such a kind and careful way and, even though he said he wanted to get me a brandy, a temazepam, put me to bed, hold me in his arms, I got up, and without taking anything with me – keys, bag, phone – I walked right out of the house.

I walked away in no particular direction, down the road, past the place where the builders were singing along to the radio and throwing scaffolding into a lorry, round the corner, past the newsagent's and the launderette and through the little gate that always squeaked, and across the playing field where they did the football on Saturdays.

I walked fast. The sun was on my face. It was a bright, warm morning. I went past people and dogs. The grass was dry. I saw a hedge with pink roses in it, a yellow frill at the centre of each. I saw a dead animal, on its back with some worms moving in it. I saw a little boy, crying loudly because his mum wouldn't let him go in the pushchair.

When I thought I'd walked far enough, I picked a bench, just any bench, a random bench where no one else happened to be, and I sat down on it. I felt its slats give slightly under my weight. The wood was rough and warm. It was kind. And, keeping my hands on that warm, kind wood, so that I wouldn't fly off or slip or come to some other kind of unimagined harm, I sat there and I repeated Simon's words over and over several times, until I was certain I had them properly and securely in my head.

Accident. Very late last night. Near his office. Instant. No one's fault. Would not have known. Nothing they could do.

They weren't true, of course, the words. I didn't believe them, not for one single moment. But they were all I had left of Matt now and so I clung to them. Or not quite all, because there was also that little spark of something that, even at that very moment, as I sat on the bench, was doing everything in its power to put down blood roots inside me, beyond me, around me, clinging on.

Arthur.

When Iris came back, when she stumbled in the door all pink and ragged from the freezing outside air, I think she was crying quietly to herself.

I didn't get anywhere, she said. I didn't manage to do anything. There just wasn't anything I could do. There's no one there. There are no people.

She stopped and she stared at me. She stared at Arthur. Her eyes were dark.

What's the matter? she said.

I tried not to look at her. I shook my head. She rushed to get closer.

What's happened? What's wrong with him?

I lifted my head. Felt my chin wobble.

I don't know, I said. Nothing. I'm sure he's OK. I don't know.

Iris stared at me. There was terror on her face. She said nothing. I waited for her to say something but she didn't. She just carried on standing there and staring at us both and saying nothing.

Another tear slid down my cheek. It landed on Arthur's little arm. It was uncovered. Who had uncovered it? I pulled the blanket up to keep him warm.

Iris took another step towards me. I didn't think I'd ever seen her look so afraid and unhappy.

What are you going to do? she whispered.

I shook my head.

I don't know, I told her.

I waited. And then I said something else. At first I couldn't hear what it was, the other thing I said. And then I could. I heard it. It was: Help me.

His office is huge – empty and bright, quiet apart from the faint hum of the air conditioner. The glass of the windows going right down to the floor. A corner room, so you can see everything – the cluttered city skyline, the dome of St Paul's, bathed in evening sunshine.

I sit in the big chair. I want to find out for the first and last time what it's like to sit where he sits, to see what he sees, to feel the things that he might feel.

I know that he's watching me. Even if I didn't know it, I'd still know.

I look at his dark screen, the power off, but alive and somehow alarming because it belongs to him. I place a finger on the keyboard. Lay my hands on his cool desk. Pick up a pencil, turn it around and hold it in the palm of my hand, where it sticks for a second. I put it up to my face, smell it. I slide open a drawer – noiseless, clean, not much in it really – slide it shut again.

He sees me doing all these things. He says nothing. I say nothing. He stays on the other side of the room. He folds his arms and leans against the wall. He never takes his eyes off me. He keeps on looking. I feel it everywhere in my body, his look. Shoulders, wrists, elbows, thighs.

On the desk are some papers, a magnet with paperclips stuck to it and, in a thick glass frame, a photo of some blond children.

A girl and a boy, bright T-shirts, sweet, eager faces. I pick it up.

My sister's kids, he says. Holly's the eldest, she's a nurse. The little one on the left, Ted, is coming here to do work experience in a few weeks. He's a bit bigger than that now, of course.

I put the photo back exactly where it was. He comes over then and stands very close to me. Very close but not touching any part of me. I breathe in the air between us, around us.

What are we doing? I whisper. He places two fingers on my bare neck and I shiver.

Well, he says, his voice staying low to match mine, we can either go out and find a bar, get a drink . . .

I look at his eyes.

Or?

Or, if we go two floors up from here, there's a place where we can be entirely alone and see the whole city spread out before us.

I smile.

I know, I say.

You know?

I mean that one. Let's do that one.

All the children were awake now and they all knew what had happened to Arthur. Iris had told them. She told them he'd died.

Jimmy looked amazed, impressed even.

Completely dead? You mean that's the end of him now?

Iris shuddered.

The end of him. What a horrible thing to say.

But you mean he won't ever come back to being alive, not even if he has an operation or if the doctor comes?

Iris hugged herself. I noticed that she couldn't stop shaking. Even her eyes were shaking.

He's dead, she said. Don't you know what dead means? Dead isn't a thing that suddenly changes.

Jimmy looked at me. I could see he was thinking hard. His face was white.

We're not going to die, are we?

I tried to say no, but I found I could not speak. I kept my eyes on him. I shook my head.

Don't talk to Mum, Iris told him. Just don't say anything. You've got to leave her alone for a bit. She can't talk to you right now.

Jimmy scowled.

Why?

What do you mean, why?

Why can't she talk?

Why do you think?

Jimmy ignored Iris's last question. He looked hard at Arthur's small body.

I wish he was alive, he said. Because I thought at least he would be fun when he got bigger. But I'm quite glad as well that he's dead.

Iris gasped.

What? Why are you glad?

Jimmy blinked. He looked at me. Like Iris, he was shivering.

Because at least we know what happened to him. And we don't know what's going to happen to us, do we?

At the sound of his words, something swam up in my throat and I gripped the sofa for a moment. When I recovered my balance, I laid Arthur on a cushion on the floor and tucked a blanket round him. Now that I saw him properly – his whole body too thin and his face the colour of pee – I almost laughed. How could I ever have thought he was a well baby?

From the very first moment I gave birth to him, as I'd squeezed him out, the odds had been stacked right against him, hadn't they? And Jimmy was right. We didn't know what was going to happen to us. We had no idea. But Arthur knew. It had already happened – the worst had happened and he was safe now. At least he was out of it. He wasn't waiting for the next thing.

Light blazed in through the window but the room was colder than ever. I asked Iris what the light was and she said that several cars parked in the road were blazing. She hadn't even managed to get to the end of the street. So many of the houses in the street were on fire. She said that at one point she'd glanced back down the road at our house and panicked because she thought she saw long flames coming out of the upstairs window.

But you didn't, did you? said Jimmy.

No, she said. I didn't.

Baby! Baby! – laughed Katie, and she hurled her beaker at the TV. Milk dribbled down the blank grey screen. She gazed at it and then she chuckled again. No one picked the beaker up.

Jimmy took hold of my hand and patted it.

Don't worry, he said. She's not laughing about Arthur. But she's maybe just a tiny little bit glad to be the youngest again.

Iris looked at him, a kind of disgust on her face. She was crying. She was the only one.

That's a terrible thing to say, Jimmy. And you're just making it up. You've no idea whether she feels that or not.

He gave her an uncertain look.

Stop bossing me, he said.

Iris sucked on one of her fingers. She'd bitten it so viciously it was bleeding. Every time she took it out of her mouth a bright new jewel of blood appeared.

I just can't believe it, she said through her sobs. I can't believe our brother has actually died and no one's doing anything.

I put my arm around her, tried to gather her close. I looked at Gloria, who hadn't said a word for hours now. I didn't know what I was going to do about Gloria, but I knew I would have to do something. I would have to do something about all of them in the end. They were relying on me. I was their mum.

Don't worry, I told Iris. I'm right here with you and I will do something.

As I spoke the words, they sounded like the words of a song, brave and believable in their way. Maybe Iris thought they sounded good too, because she leaned against me. She didn't look at me. She gave a last little sob.

But what, Mummy? What will you do?

I have a plan, I told her. That, too, could have been the title of a song.

I have a plan. I touched my hand to my forehead. It was icy, damp still. Outside, the sky was the colour of ash and the snow kept on falling.

We don't take the lift. Instead we walk up two flights of concrete stairs, our two pairs of feet echoing, then out into a quiet, wide, carpeted corridor, past a couple of locked office doors. I don't look at the doors. No one else is around. Just the faraway sound of someone hoovering. A snatch of music from a radio.

In the corridor, he puts a hand out behind him to take mine, and as soon as I'm joined to him like that, I feel a little less sad and shaky. Something snaps and lifts inside me. I let it.

Trust me, he says. I know what you're thinking, but it's going to be worth it.

He doesn't know what I'm thinking.

He pushes a heavy metal fire door and suddenly there we are, out on that big, empty corner terrace. That smooth grey concrete, a wall and a metal railing all around.

I stare at the city spread out beneath and around us, lazy and soft in the evening sunshine. You can see as far as St Paul's on one side and what I imagine is Whitechapel on the other. Barbican, Spitalfields, Holborn.

Above us, the gulls. Screaming and lifting and dropping on the warm evening air. The chalk line of half a dozen aeroplanes tracing their way through the sky.

He looks at me. I feel him looking at me and for a moment I can't speak. I can't do anything. I don't know what he wants me to say.

What? he says.

Nothing. Just – it's strange, I suppose.

What's strange?

This – being here.

Being here or being alone together?

Yes.

Which?

The second one. I've never been alone with you –

You have.

I think of the loud, dark bars we've been in. The taxis. The one time that we took a risk and kissed each other in the park.

I haven't. Not really. Not completely alone like this. Not without anyone else around at all. Or at least, not since we were kids.

Oh well, he says. Kids. That doesn't count.

I don't look at him. I shut my eyes. I let the building hold me.

It did count, I tell him. When we were kids, I mean. I promise you – for me it did count.

He waits. I feel him watching me. I feel the space. The silence. The possibility. I wish I didn't keep avoiding his eyes. I wish I didn't love him. I'm dizzy with all the things I wish.

I don't know what else to say, I tell him at last.

He smiles. Then he walks over to me and he touches my cheek. His hands go to my neck.

That's it, he says. That's enough. You don't have to say anything else.

It was true. I hadn't lied. I did have a plan. I told them we were going to make some biscuits.

Iris frowned at me.

But we can't cook. There's no electricity, remember? How are you going to make the oven work?

I saw Gloria watching me carefully to see what I would have to say about this. I took a breath and it came back out white. The air in the room was freezing. Now and then I thought I smelled burning, but it had to be in my own mixed-up head. My ribs and stomach hurt. My heart was clammy. I knew I was still bleeding. I didn't know how much longer I could be like this – upright, bright, alive.

Not cooked biscuits, I said, in the tight and magical voice I used when I told them stories. These are special biscuits.

Straightaway, they all adjusted their faces to match my tone. They put on their bedtime-story faces. They couldn't help it. Even Katie. Even, slightly, Iris. Wide-eyed and waiting.

Are they the sort that don't even need cooking? Jimmy said. He rubbed his nose with a grubby hand.

That's right, I told him. Well done. That's the sort.

OK, he said, rubbing his nose again.

Shouldn't we wash our hands? said Iris, glancing at Jimmy's, which were now somewhere down in his trousers. I tried to think. I knew I didn't have the strength to go through the whole thing of soap and hands and towels at the sink.

Not today, I said.

But why not?

I had a brief moment of dizziness. I stepped backwards, then forwards again.

Iris, I said, just go with me on this, OK?

She said nothing. She scowled and bit a nail, then, remembering she shouldn't be doing it, she wiped it on her jeans.

Very slowly, because I was so weak, I opened every kitchen cupboard and I got out what we had, put it on the counter. I could only lift one thing at a time, but I knew the children thought I was doing it on purpose – spinning it out, making a drama of it.

The dog saw that food was going to be involved and got up, yawned, stretched, came over. Half a pack of chocolate digestives, the one on top slightly soft and stale. An unopened box of Jaffa Cakes. Two fig rolls. Some mini-packs of Jammie Dodgers.

Aren't those supposed to be for packed lunches? Iris pointed out in a shaky voice.

I looked at her and she looked at me and I watched her face change as she worked it out. Rules didn't count any more. They were over and done with, probably for ever. I felt suddenly sorry for her then, and I did my best to make it easier.

Today is special, I told her. Today we're making works of art.

Works of art? And then we're going to eat the art? Jimmy said, getting the hang of it with his usual energy.

That's right, I told him. We're going to gobble up the works of art!

Katie laughed loudly. Not because she understood but because she knew I was doing my funny voice. I pinched her tummy and she laughed again. Her night-time nappy hadn't been changed and I noticed there was a pale pool of liquid under her highchair, but she didn't seem to mind. Good old Katie.

I found some years-old glacé cherries and also a pack of malted milk biscuits, the sort with the cows on.

Oh, not those. They're boring, Jimmy objected.

Ah, I said. But we need some boring biscuits as building blocks, you see.

Jimmy nodded as if he'd already thought of that.

On the counter was some butter. I told Iris to get icing sugar and vanilla essence if there was any.

For butter cream? she said, her voice lighting up a little, because she couldn't help it – in her heart she really loved cooking.

Yup, I told her, as I steadied myself on the counter and sweat pricked my hair. That's the glue. Butter cream is going to be the glue.

The glue for the art? said Jimmy.

You've got the right idea, my love.

Ten out of ten for knowing it? he said, an unhappy little smile on his face.

Ten out of ten, I said.

* * *

266

I lie on top of him, every part of me pressed against every part of him.

The air's still warm, but the sun is creeping away over the concrete, fast disappearing, leaving nothing but shadow behind it. His face now in sun, now in darkness. The light going. The day going.

I never thought we'd do this, he says.

I know. I didn't think we would either.

You think we shouldn't have done it?

No, I say. No.

No, we shouldn't have done it? Or no, you think it's OK?

I think it's OK – I take a breath and I lift my head to look at him. I'm very happy to have done it.

Me too, he says quietly.

I put my head back down on him.

Right now, I'm just very happy, I say.

You are?

Yes. I'm not thinking any further ahead than this moment. And at this moment, I feel happy.

I feel him stroking my cheek. My ear.

I just don't know how it happened, he says then.

What, you mean just now? This?

I feel him swallow.

No, I mean all of it. These last months. And before, actually. Everything. Our whole lives. Us.

I'm silent. I can feel my own heart beating. Or maybe it's his.

I didn't mean to fall in love with you, I tell him at last.

He laughs and I feel it, the laugh, vibrating in my chest.

I know you didn't. Ha! Never has a truer thing been said. You didn't even used to like me.

What are you saying? Of course I liked you. I've always liked you.

I feel him laugh again.

Oh come on, Izzy, not when we were kids, you didn't. In fact I think you really hated me. Remember the time you pushed me down the stairs?

For a moment I'm silent, remembering this.

I didn't mean to do that.

Yes, you did. You absolutely did. Don't you dare deny it.

I got into big trouble for it.

Rightly so, he says, kissing me.

Well, you were the strangest child. You never smiled. Or at least you never smiled at me.

I was shy of you, Izzy. I just couldn't handle it. Try and remember that in the future, will you? If a boy doesn't smile, if he ignores you, if he can't look you in the eye, it almost certainly means he likes you too much.

I think about this. I remember him then – Matthew as a kid. Lifting his eyes to mine, then looking away again.

And you had a beetle called Arthur, I tell him. Who on earth names an insect Arthur?

Arthur! I remember Arthur. Well, I like that name. It's a noble name. It suited the beetle anyway.

So, if you ever have kids, that's what you'll name them?

What? Arthur, Arthur and Arthur?

No, I say more quietly. Just Arthur.

He's silent a moment. We both are. I slide my hands under his head, feel the weight of him, his skull, the warmth of his bones. I kiss him once on the mouth, then once more. He lets me do it. Then he pulls my face back down and makes me do it again. Lifting us back out of the unhappy place.

All the same, I tell him, you were a strange kid. I never understood how you could spend so much time grubbing around with insects and animals.

He sighs.

Like I said, you hated me.

Not hate. Of course not hate. But —

But what?

Well, you were ever so slightly unappealing.

This time his laugh is bitter.

I still am, he says.

No you're not, I tell him. Not to me anyway — not even slightly. No way. Every single thing about you — I can't begin to tell you how many things — you are completely appealing to me.

He's silent for a moment.

You know that I mean it, I tell him.

I know, he says.

He touches my nose. Runs his finger from the top of it along to the tip.

You're my oldest friend, he says then. My dearest friend. And my only love. How can we just turn our backs on this? Why can't we just go on knowing each other?

I swallow. I say nothing.

Seriously, Izzy. It's a serious question. Answer me.

But I don't answer him. Instead I see my kids' tired little faces. Jimmy going on about something or other. Iris frowning and biting her fingers. I see Gloria and Katie sitting together and sticking bright foam animals on the side of the bath, content and serious-faced, without any idea that life can change shape in an instant. I say nothing.

He knows what I'm thinking.

I could make a really serious promise not to love you.

No, you couldn't.

You're right. I couldn't.

And I can't either. I can't do it. Not any more. I can't not love you, Matt.

He's silent a moment.

Maybe we could meet up just occasionally to talk about it?

Talk about what?

About how we're going to manage to stay away from each other. Though now I think of it, occasionally wouldn't be enough. Maybe we could do it weekly, or perhaps every other day would be better, or maybe even –

I start to laugh and feel my eyes fill up. I put my head down on him. I wipe my eyes on his shirt. I put my hand on his mouth.

Stop talking, I tell him.

He obeys. Silence.

You know what the deal is, I tell him and he says nothing, because he does.

We lie together and do nothing. I feel his hand moving up and down my back. After a while it stops.

Oh, I whisper. Don't stop.

He continues. I close my eyes.

You're going to break my heart, Izzy, he says at last.

I don't look at him. I turn my head to the side, still resting on his chest.

You are, you know.

I don't want to. I don't want to break your heart.

Well, you're going to.

I don't want to.

You will. You know you will.

I shut my eyes.

Don't tell me I know things. I don't know anything, I say.

A gull alights on the railing and looks at us, yellow-eyed and interested, head twisted to one side.

Fuck off, he says. Go on. Shoo. Go away.

The gull stays.

I feel my phone vibrate and reach for it. Lift it, look at it. Simon. I put it back.

You need to get it? he says.

I shake my head.

Really? You can if you need to. Talk to him, if it makes you feel –

I put my head down on him again, shut my eyes.

When each child had made their own work of art – Jaffas and Dodgers and shards of crumbling digestive held together with slabs of butter cream – I said that I was going to judge the competition.

The competition? But that's not fair! Jimmy said. You never said it was a competition.

I only just decided, didn't I?

He stuck his bottom lip out and kicked the kitchen counter hard.

It's not fair, he said again.

But, I said, as I felt another clot of blood slip out of me, would it really have changed the way you made your biscuit, Jims?

He didn't say anything. He gave the kitchen counter another hefty kick.

Any bad behaviour and you'll be disqualified, I said.

Katie was singing to herself and hanging sideways out of her highchair, oblivious, but Iris and Gloria were staring at me. Gloria had only half finished making her biscuit before giving up and trying to cram part of it into her mouth. I'd had to put my hand on her small cold one.

Not yet, I'd told her, even though she'd already had the cherry. The eating part comes later.

Why can't she eat it? Jimmy said.

Just because.

Gloria made a little circle with her fingers and looked at me through it.

Why are you doing that? I asked her.

She said nothing. She continued to look at me.

She's spying on you, Jimmy said.

Yes, said Iris. She's suspicious. She's wondering what you're up to.

I looked at her and I flushed. Then I went over to the dark, bloodstained sofa and felt around under the cushions. Where had I hidden them? I knew I'd put them somewhere.

Arthur was still lying there on his cushion on the floor and even though I knew he was in a happy place and well out of it, still the sight of his perfectly lifeless body gave me a quick snag of pain.

I love you, I whispered to him, making sure to be quiet enough that no one else would hear. I love you and it's all going to be OK. I have a plan.

The pills were part of the plan. I found them at last.

See these little white sweeties? I told the children, continuing in my special magical storytelling voice. These are the prizes – and everyone gets one. Two if your biscuit is particularly good.

Jimmy automatically reached out a hand – I knew he would take anything I gave him – but Iris was staring at me.

Those? But those are just aspirin, she said.

I held the temazepam up out of Jimmy's reach.

They're not, actually, I told her. They're something much nicer than aspirin. They're good for you and we're going to stick a couple of them in every biscuit. Really good people can have three.

Her face darkened with worry.

And then we have to eat them? But are they OK for children? I mean should Katie have them?

Katie will be fine with them, I said.

I put my two arms on the concrete and I look down at his face, trying to take it in. The precise beauty of him. The ideal spacing of his eyes, his nose. The sheer, exact brilliance of his mouth. He looks back at me.

Izzy, he says.

What?

What are you doing?

I pause. I search around for it.

I'm making a study of you. A serious, scientific study.

He keeps his eyes on me. They don't move.

Why?

So I can remember you.

He carries on looking at me. His eyes. My eyes. It feels like touching. A little flicker of something starts to move inside me.

Oh, I say, suddenly in pain. It won't stay.

What won't stay?

The picture of you. I can't keep it. I can't put you enough into my head.

273

He keeps staring at me, says nothing.

I was trying to take something from you, I tell him. I wanted to steal something of you and put it into me.

His eyes remain on mine for a second, then he turns away.

Don't say that, he says.

OK.

I mean it.

OK. I know you do.

Anyway, you already have me, he says. Look. What's here? Nothing. It's all gone. There's nothing here at all. You took it long ago, Izzy. It's all right there, inside of you.

I rest my head on him again, on his body, on the place where I think his heart might be. And maybe I sleep, because when I next open my eyes, the air is a whole different shade of velvet. Oh, I think, we're still here.

What are we going to do? he says at last.

Do?

The word jolts me out of where I was. It jolts me out of here and into there.

Yes. Oh Izzy, what am I going to do with you?

I stay where I am. I try to think.

I'm here, I tell him.

I know you are, he says. Right now you're here. But I don't think I can do this.

Do what?

I love you, Izzy. I just do – I love you. I don't think I can do what we talked about. I think I need you. After all these years. I don't see how I can let you go.

* * *

I stuck two temazepam in each biscuit. I wanted to be on the safe side. I thought about having one myself, but then it struck me that I was going to need to stay alert for quite a bit longer than the children, so I didn't.

Jimmy ate his straightaway.

Yum, he said, as he wiped the crumbs from his mouth. I think I definitely won the competition. Mine was the best.

He slipped down off his stool and went to the fridge and poured himself some milk. Drank it. Wiped his mouth again on a tea towel, just like I always told him not to. Outside, the sun was trying to come out, even though the sky was darker than ever. You could clearly see several feet of snow outside and at the far end of the garden, beyond the pond, tiny flames licked the bottom of the shed.

Gloria held on to the kitchen counter and rocked backwards and forwards on her stool, her legs hanging down like the tentacles of some silent sea creature. She picked her biscuit apart, holding it in her fingers and examining it while eating it a mouthful at a time.

I saw that one of the pills had dropped off the biscuit and on to the counter, a blob of butter cream sticking to it. I picked it up and blew on it and popped it in her mouth, and she gazed at me and I thought for a moment that she would spit it out again, but she didn't. She swallowed.

Good girl, I said, and I felt like pulling her on to my knee and hugging her so hard that she'd giggle and gasp for breath, but she didn't look like she wanted me to, so I didn't.

Katie was making a big old mess with her biscuit. She'd thrown the cherry on the floor and was bashing her fist into the rest. It was going to be hard to make sure she ate both of her pills. I stared at her for a quick and horrible moment, confused, and briefly all my strength and resolution fell away. Then I collected myself.

I'll come back to her later, I thought.

I realised I should try to get a couple of pills into the dog as well. Easy, I thought. I slipped her a piece of digestive with a pill butter-creamed on to it, but she ate the biscuit in a very slow and careful way, licking the cream off first and then holding the biscuit in her mouth as though she was chomping on something very hot.

Then, just when she'd finally swallowed the last bit down and I thought I'd got away with it, out popped the pill, clean and whole and white.

Fucking animal, I thought. I got a piece of cheese instead. It worked. She was so greedy for cheese, that dog, she forgot about all of her suspicions and swallowed it whole.

Iris licked at her biscuit and looked at me.

What? I said.

I don't like this.

You don't like the biscuit?

No. The whole thing. I don't like it. I don't like the cooking without an oven or the stupid competition or the way you keep talking in a strange voice and seem kind of happy and excited about everything even though Arthur's dead before he even had a chance to live. And I don't want to eat any of your aspirins, either, she added.

I tried to stay very calm. I knew I needed to be strong for her. I looked at my hands on the crumb-sprinkled table. Was it my imagination or were they the wrong colour? I looked at Iris.

I told you, darling. It's not aspirin.

She bit her lip.

All the same, it's medicine and I don't want to eat it.

I sighed.

Iris, sweetheart, I said. I'm only trying to make things better for everyone. It's really hard if you won't trust me. Please trust me. Please help me.

She stared at me. Her eyes were not helpful.

I love you so much, I said.

It was true. Even now I felt a raw little pain in the pit of my belly, which I knew was the dread I'd had right from the very first moment I ever held her against me – dark and keen and warm as Arthur, as all of them – that I could never keep her safe enough.

She said nothing.

I didn't want this to happen either, I told her.

She lifted her head. Her eyes were purple and splotchy from all the crying.

But Mum, she said, where's Dad?

I tried to think. None of the answers I could think of sounded right.

Does he even know you've had the baby?

Of course he doesn't. You know I have no way of getting hold of him. How could he possibly know?

She looked at me carefully.

But if he did, he'd come, right?

I thought of Simon then. The genuine kindness with which he'd tried to get me through the shock of Matthew's death. The electrically bad moment when I admitted that I was expecting Arthur. The long, hard silences in our bedroom at night.

Iris was still watching my face.

I'm sure he would, I said.

* * *

After the second time, it's like I can't stop feeling him. Rings and rings of excitement going right through me, each one smaller and tighter and brighter than the last. Maybe they'll go on for ever, I think. Maybe that's what I'll always have of him, just this delicious, rolling brightness, echoing on and on through me.

It's like a bell, I say.

What's like a bell?

Nothing. Me. I'm rocking and singing inside like a bell.

Iso-bel?

That's a really terrible joke.

But then I can't help it – I laugh. I take his wrist in my hand and he tries to grip on to me, but I don't let him. I turn it around so I can see his watch.

How much time is left?

His eyes are closed.

As much as you want, he says.

I mean what time do we have to go from here?

Any time. No time. We can stay all night if we want to.

I can't stay all night.

I know you can't. I'm just saying.

But – we won't get locked out up here or anything?

I'd like to get locked out here. It would please me very much. I could spend all night doing things to you – days and nights, I could spend months. Summer would turn to autumn and winter would come – we'd be out here in the ice and snow and the gales, just stuck here lying on top of each other . . .

I shiver. Suck in a quick, terrified breath.

To stop him talking, I kiss his face. I kiss his mouth, his nose, his eyelids, then back to his mouth again. A long kiss. He takes over the kiss. He pulls me in.

Don't go, he says.

The terrace is cool now, entirely in shadow. The sky is the colour of ink. The air smells of the river – dirt, wet, salt, bones. I shiver again.

I've been here before, I tell him.

I wait for him to say something, but he doesn't. He says nothing. I wonder if he knows. Maybe he does know, because he shivers too and he reaches out and pulls me closer.

Don't go, he says again. Please, Izzy. I feel like all we've ever done, all our lives, is say goodbye. But this time I just need a little bit longer. Don't start saying goodbye before we've even begun.

Iris ate the biscuit in the end. She didn't do it because she wanted to. She did it to please me, because she found it hard, in the end, to disobey me, her mum – because she felt that she should be a good girl and do as she was told. That was the worst part. That she did it because, deep in her heart, she was a good girl. A good and responsible girl. I knew when it came to it, that would be the worst part, the worst thing, and I was right, it was.

As she finally swallowed the last mouthfuls down, it took all my strength not to cry out and shake her and make her sick. She saw me watching her. She must have seen my face.

What? she mouthed.

Nothing, I told her as my heart turned right over. I love you.

She stared at me for a second. Her watchful little face.

Me too, she said.

What?

I love you too.

I touched her head, then turned away from her quickly.

It was impossible to get Katie to eat her biscuit. Nothing I tried seemed to work. She just wasn't having it. Her cheeks were bright red now, glazed with tears and snot, and she seemed very unhappy indeed. There was no way I was getting anything down that child.

Does it really matter if she doesn't eat it? Iris mumbled over and over again.

The pill was working now and her eyes were huge and trippy, her voice wobbling. She trudged around in tight circles, unable to decide where to put herself. It was painful to see her. It made me want to cry. Jimmy and Gloria had already lain themselves down like good children. Why on earth couldn't Iris do the same?

I looked at her and I didn't answer the question. She glanced at Katie.

I think it's her nappy, she muttered.

Iris was usually right about Katie. So I tried changing her, even though it took all my strength, getting her over to the table and laying her on it and getting the heavy, pee-soaked nappy off her, dropping it on the floor and wrapping a clean one round her.

She kicked and she cried.

As I fastened the tapes, I saw that she was red and chafed in lots of places from sitting too long in her own wet. I felt a quick flash of guilt, but there was no way I was going to get myself up those stairs to fetch her nappy cream.

By the time I'd finished changing her, everyone was properly out for the count. Jimmy in Simon's saggy old chair by the TV, sideways on, his small foot in their grey socks slung over the arm, his giraffe dropped on the floor. Gloria in a heap on the floor quite close to Arthur.

And Iris, who had finally drifted to a standstill at the foot of the stairs, one hand still on the banister, where she'd been on her way up to the bathroom to fetch her baby sister some of that cream.

We stand together on Camomile Street. The sun has gone now, but the air's still warm. The bars are noisy. I can smell beer, trees, bus fumes. Far away, the sound of sirens.

If I turned and looked back, behind me, I could still see the building, looming up at the end of the street, dark glass towering over everything. I don't turn.

He looks at me. I know that, despite the fact that his heart is ready to burst, he wants a cigarette.

Have one, I say.

What?

You can smoke. Go on. It's OK.

He looks upset, confused.

I can't, he says. But at the same time that he shakes his head, he's already feeling in his pockets. He lights it swiftly and looks at me, dragging the smoke in like it's oxygen. His face is dark.

It's very hard not to touch you, he says.

My phone buzzes. A text. I look at it.

Who is it?

Sophy, I tell him. It's only Sophy.

Can she do it?

I look up at him in surprise. I know he's not even slightly interested.

Tomorrow, you mean? Yes.

What is it? What are you going to?

Simon has a thing. A work thing.

His face falls.

Oh.

He takes two more vicious puffs of the cigarette, then he puts it out.

Come here, he says.

He pulls me into the shadows. I think he's going to kiss me then, start up the kissing all over again, and that will be the end of us, of all our resolutions, the end of everything, because I don't think I could go away from him then – but he doesn't. He doesn't kiss me. Instead he holds me very close against him. Our faces don't touch. We don't speak. We stay very still.

What are you doing? he says after a few seconds have passed.

Nothing, I tell him, as my tears fall into his shirt. I'm just trying to remember the feeling.

What feeling?

This – what it feels like – being loved.

He holds me away from him for a moment, so he can look in my face.

You're allowed to change your mind about this, he says.

I gaze at him. I can't speak. I shake my head.

Not just now. I don't mean tonight. I mean any time. Nothing will change, not for me it won't.

Don't say that, I tell him.

It's the truth.

It's not true, I tell him. You're just saying it. Things change. People change. It's right that they do. They should change. They always do change.

I might change, but my feelings about you won't.

You can't know that. How can you know it? You can't possibly know it.

I can. I can know it. Ever since I was a kid –

I don't believe you.

Try me.

Seriously, Matt . . .

I stop for a moment, confused. All our lives we have argued like this. I take a step away from him. He looks at me.

You're going? he says.

Yes.

There's a silence. It wants me to fill it by turning and walking away. I'm about to do it. I will do it. I'm about to. My legs might do it, but my eyes won't let me. I keep on looking at him standing there.

What are you going to do? I ask him.

Do?

Yes. Now. What will you do?

He shrugs. His mouth is trembling.

Fuck knows. I don't care. What does it matter? I might go back to the office for a bit.

And do what?

Nothing. Sit there. Feel sorry for myself. Cry. Think about you.

I look at him.

This is unbearable, he says.

Yes.

Finally, he is the one – he does it. He puts a hand on my cheek. I turn my head to kiss his finger, but it's already been pulled away – it's gone. He takes a single step backwards, away from me. He's trying to smile, but his eyes are doing something else. I can't look at his eyes.

OK, he says. OK. Take care, Izzy.

And I do the next bit. I do it myself. I turn and I walk away. It's easy, I think. Far easier than I imagined. It's just a question of taking some steps. One step at a time, one foot in front of another. And then another and another, until it's so many of those footsteps that the distance between us is beyond repair and I'm completely gone from him and that's it, I'm gone, I'm no longer there, I'm lost.

I don't look back. I walk away through those warm and dusty streets, still filled with people shouting and laughing and having their drinks, with the buses and the taxis and the sirens that are screaming even louder now.

On Bishopsgate, police vans are blocking the street, tape, uniforms everywhere. A suspected bomb, someone says. People are being asked to cross the street. I walk fast. I don't care where I go.

Not here, lady, a man shouts at me. You need to cross over. We're clearing the area.

Sirens. More vans arriving. A fire engine too.

I turn and go in another direction, any direction. People are shouting. I don't feel safe. and I don't want to feel safe, I don't know where I am or where I'm going – I don't think I ever will again. I don't care what happens next. My life is nothing. I don't have a plan.

Maybe I should have a plan.

Maybe I shouldn't be surprised, when, many minutes or maybe it is hours or even a whole lifetime later, I find myself back in that same blue darkness, my last surviving child in my arms, fires still burning, thick snow all around me, and even more of it coming down now, faster and harder, falling, falling, on Camomile Street.

I did the dog first. The dog was easy. She was lying on her side. You could barely see her breathing to start with. I just put the cushion on her head and I sat on it for a moment. It was quicker than I thought it would be. Easy. She didn't even whimper.

But when I got up and took the cushion off, I jumped hard – because her front leg started fidgeting, as if she was chasing rabbits in a dream. But it must have been a muscle spasm, because her breath had stopped and her tongue was out and it was clear from the emptied way she lay there that she was dead.

The dog was dead. It was a fact. I thought about how furious Jimmy would have been. With me. How the tears would have fallen down his face. The lecture he would have given me.

Dogs trust you, he'd have said. They trust you completely. Just because they don't go attacking you with guns and knives doesn't mean you should creep up and kill them.

I shut his voice out of my head and I went over to Gloria.

She was on her side on the floor and her head was back, her chin up, her small, pale face pointing across the rug to where Arthur still lay. She still had butter cream on her fingers, a trace of biscuit crumbs around her mouth. Her eyelids were a violet colour, shadowy.

Gloria. She didn't look like the rest of them. She never had. She didn't look like me and she didn't look like Simon. She was a fairy child. If you believed in changelings, then you'd say she was one. One of them. Not one of us – and certainly not mine to play this game with. She never had been.

I thought about how she'd gone silent, all the words emptied out of her, and I shivered. Had she seen what was coming?

I took her fingers and I kissed them, breathed in the warm smell. I couldn't go near her face. I couldn't put my face near hers. I had to look away at the blank TV screen as I took a breath and put the cushion over her face and held it there.

I hadn't thought I was crying, but I must have been, because, as I turned my head back, so many tears came falling on to the cushion, plopping on to the velvet and then rolling off, salt falling into my fingers, my wrists wet with them.

Gloria didn't struggle, she didn't do anything, but I thought I felt a little gasp of surprise come out from under the cushion. I also thought I saw two or three of the small fingers I had kissed clench themselves, but so very briefly and gently that I couldn't be sure.

When she'd been still for a while, I took the cushion away – only to see that her face continued to move, her mouth working away, soundless, her eyes still open and alive, gazing at me. I put the cushion back and held it there. I held it for a long time. I didn't take any chances. When I finally took it away, her face was the same colour as her eyelids, her lips were blue. There was no question.

I was shaking. Every part of me moving all on its own. I got up and walked into the kitchen and I bent over the sink, my arms on the draining board. Nothing came out. I waited. My body would not be still. My shaking arms made a cup and a bowl fall over. The bowl rolled around and around on the floor but it did not break. It still had butter cream in it. I looked away quickly.

I told myself I could stop right there, that I did not have to finish the job, but I knew it was a lie. I saw blood on the kitchen floor under me.

I'm dying, I told myself.

I didn't know if that was a lie or not.

I thought Jimmy would be the hardest, but no. Darling Jims. He always was a good sleeper, but the pills had knocked him right out. As I pressed down on his small face, I felt nothing, heard nothing, maybe the smallest sigh, but that was all.

I couldn't believe it was so quick. I waited and waited even though I sensed he was gone.

I was his mum and he trusted me. Though in some ways he was a boy who questioned absolutely everything, still you would have to admit that he accepted everything too. It was a happy balance. He would probably have grown up to be a good person, lively and content and satisfied. He liked this life, this world. It excited him. I had given it to him and I felt terrible to be the one to take it away from him.

When I'd done Jimmy, I dragged another chair over and I sat with him for a while. I did not know what I had done. I stared at him. I looked at his face, as he sagged there with his legs slopping over the arm of the chair. I laid my head back against the chair. The room went round. I lifted my head again and opened my eyes hard and steadied myself. I got up slowly, my blood was everywhere. I bent and picked up the giraffe and put it in his arms. The giraffe eyed me happily. I looked away.

I could hear some raw sharp cries coming from somewhere – the sound of a person in real distress. It took about three minutes for me to realise that the person was me.

By the time I went over to Iris I was sobbing and sobbing. I could not get my breath. I hadn't known how much strength this would take. My stomach and my arms and my legs and my face were hurting. Every part of me, inside and out, was hurting. I'll die next, I thought. It won't be very long. Give me a few more minutes and we'll all be together again.

I'd put Katie in her highchair in the kitchen, turning her to face the back door and giving her some things from the kitchen drawer – slightly irresponsible things if I was honest – to play with. A metal nutmeg grater with a not especially blunt edge. A can opener. A corkscrew with a blade on it for cutting foil. A risk, perhaps, but I was no longer a good mother in any proper sense of the word, and, more than anything, I needed to keep her entertained.

Iris's hand had slipped down off the banister and she was sleeping now with her head on her hands, the way she always did. Even in her bed she would sleep like that, with her mouth closed and her hands neatly folded, as if she'd taken sleeping lessons and passed with distinction.

I looked at her and I seemed to lose all energy. It dropped away. I put the cushion on my knees and I sat down next to her at the foot of the stairs and I put my hand on those parts of her I knew so well. The strands of dark hair that fell across her face. The small blue veins in the crook of her wrist, the inside of her little finger with its anxious, bitten-down stump of nail.

I thought about how she was my first baby, how her coming along had changed everything, made me into a different person. How there was never a moment after that when I could properly relax and not care. There wasn't a single moment when I could exist without this huge and beautiful and extraordinary thing at stake – this thing to live for, this thing to die for.

Iris.

I thought about leaving her then, letting her stay alive. But I looked outside and I saw that already the trees at the bottom of the garden were drowning in flames. And then I imagined the look on her face when she saw what had happened to Gloria and Jimmy and the dog . . .

I put the cushion on her face.

I don't know what I expected. I suppose I thought it would be like Gloria and Jimmy, but it wasn't. She gagged. She started. She struggled. She struggled hard. She fought me. The pills hadn't worked – she could not have been properly asleep. It turned into exactly what I had not wanted – a fight.

I heard her say, No! I heard her say, Mummy!

For the first time in my life, I did not answer her. I did not speak. I shut my ears, my face, my heart. I kept the cushion held right down. I could not bear it. I did not want to see her face. I did not want her to have to see mine.

Her fingers clawed at me. She had no nails, but still she managed to draw blood on my hands, my wrists. I held the cushion firm. Her cries grew weaker. Her fingers stopped moving. Her hands dropped away. She became slower, gentler. Then stiller. I heard a little moan. Then finally she was still.

Her head was at a bad angle on the stairs. She looked so uncomfortable. More than anything I wanted to make her better, prop her up, sort her out.

Iris? I whispered.

I waited.

I was so afraid to take the cushion off. I stayed there for as long as I could, holding it on her face and sobbing. I don't know how much time went by. I didn't want to leave her. I didn't want it to be the end. I wanted to tell her I was sorry. I wanted to find out that it hadn't worked after all – to have her wake

up, get up, look at me in that accusing way and take care of
me in the way she probably would have if I'd let her grow up
to be a young girl and then a woman and then . . .

Iris. My Iris.

I could hear Katie in the kitchen, happily making music with
the can opener and the nutmeg grater, banging them hard against
the table of her highchair.

I went in there and undid the harness and pulled her out of
the chair. Blood on her hands, on her face. I tried to wipe it
with a tea towel but she wouldn't let me. She drummed her feet
and yelled at me when I tried to prise the grater from her fingers.

I got it away from her, then kissed her head and shook her
hard to shut her up. She made a funny noise when I shook her.
My tears in her hair. Our faces knocking together as I tried to
pull her against me. I bundled her into her old red snowsuit –
my hands shaking so hard I could hardly do up the poppers so
in the end I didn't bother. I left it open.

There was thick black smoke in the hall and a crackling sound
coming from upstairs, as I carried her, still screaming out of
the back door. The last thing I saw as I got us away from the
house was the car, flames sneaking around the edges of the boot,
smoke pouring out – the smell of burning plastic. I thought of
all the children's things in there and, for a few stupid seconds,
I wondered if I should try to get Gloria's beloved Sylvanians.
Then the memory of why I shouldn't swung back over me and
my thoughts went dark and my legs carried me away.

I walk through the snow on Camomile Street with my child in
my arms. She is getting to be quite a big girl now, a real dead
weight. I think that her second birthday must be coming up

soon, but most of the facts have already slid away and I have no idea for sure of when she was born or even if she is definitely mine.

I don't know how we got here.

I don't know how much longer I can go on carrying her through this snow. I don't know what's been happening or how much time has gone by. I don't know what kind of person could do that to their child, their children. I don't know what kind of person I am. I don't know who I am. I thought I would be dead by now. I don't know if I am dead or not. So many things I don't know.

And across the road from us, a man is slumped on what is left of a wall, quite a young man really, smoking a roll-up and drinking from a bottle. Drunk. And he sees me staring at him. Slow motion now. He puts the bottle down.

And I wait. And even though I know exactly what is going to happen, because there are no longer any surprises – just this endless, heartbreaking loop of consequences – still my heart sinks a little when he throws the cigarette in the snow and slides down off the wall.

It won't be long now, I think, and it isn't.

In three quick seconds, he is beside me.

The one thing he got wrong, the kid: he didn't start it. It was me. It wasn't the night in the taxi – that was already right in the middle of it. We were certainly both too deep in it by then.

It was all my fault. We were children. On the carpet, playing with the beetles. And I wanted to have an effect on him. I wanted him to see me. He was not looking. He never looked. I wanted him to look. And I could not resist the shape of his mouth.

Whoa, he said. I can't believe you just said that.

What? What do you think I said?

He shook his head, rubbed at his face.

I can't say it. I just can't. It's just so raw.

He looked at the carpet for the longest time. Finally, he scratched his head. Still he did not look at me. His face was red.

I will if you want me to, he said at last. I can, you know. I could. I quite like you actually. What I mean is, I don't really care. I wouldn't mind doing it. If you want me to.

The first time we went to see the counsellor, during that first summer when I was trying so hard not to see Matthew, Simon told her it was the lies he found hardest.

Me turning my phone off, pretending I'd left it at home. Telling him I was in one place when I was in another. Telling him I had put it all behind me when, clearly, I had not. How was he supposed to trust me after that?

The counsellor looked at us both and she waited. I waited too. Was that the question? I didn't know if I was supposed to answer it. I didn't have any answers. Anyway, Simon was right. I had lied. I was not trustworthy. I didn't trust myself. That was the worst thing, if I stopped to think about it. Trust. I never had.

So I said nothing. I looked at my hands. I touched my fingers on the cool back of my neck. Put my lips to the flat inside of my wrist, breathed it in. The smell was of nothing. I looked at my knees, but they were the same ones I'd always had. They gave me no clues. I said nothing.

This, he explained to her, was why he'd told me it had to be all or nothing. It had to be over. He had to be certain there would be no contact. If I wanted our family to stand a chance. It had to be a clean break.

This had surely been reasonable, hadn't it?

Had it?

Hadn't it?

The counsellor looked at us both and waited. I waited too. I wanted to find out the answer. I didn't know the answer. I thought I would make them wait.

He throws the cigarette in the snow and slides down off the wall. In three seconds he is beside me.

I've got nothing, I tell him, but he looks at my bleeding hands and wrists and then he looks straight at the child. She returns his gaze.

Boy or girl?

Just like last time, I say nothing. I pull her against me. He moves in closer. His breath is rank. I see that his hands are moving too fast.

I said what is it, a boy or a girl?

I shake my head.

You what? he says.

There are two of them now. His friend has joined him. They stand there in the snow, the two of them. They ask me again if it's a boy or a girl. Then they ask me what it's called.

And I look down at this child who I am holding now in my arms, her eyes round with fatigue, her breath hot against my neck, and I tell them the truth — that I don't know.

The look that they exchange is quick and complicated.

You don't know your own kid's name?

I look at her again. Is she my own? I look at her hands, my hands. The blood from both of us has rubbed off on my coat.

I can't think why anyone would do that – why would anyone want to cut the hands of a child?

The first man looks at me and he doesn't smile. The child is studying him with glassy, tired eyes. Suddenly, though, she looks amused, delighted. Without any warning, her small hand flies out towards him.

Man! she says.

Taken by surprise, he doesn't wait. He raises his fist and shoves it hard in her face. As my arms open and I let her fall, he reaches out for me – for any part of me.

I smile. I knew this was coming.

The last thing I see is the water closing over her astonished face. A million crystals waiting to meld together. Ice forming.

I thought the world was frozen. I didn't know there was a puddle there. That's the very last thing I think before the world goes dark. Surprise, puddle, ice . . .

The last time we saw the counsellor – all those months later, after Matt was gone and I had decided that the only truthful thing was to leave Simon – she already knew everything, because he'd been seeing her all this time.

But still, he sat there, explaining – for my benefit, I supposed – and he asked her more or less the same question. Did she think he had acted reasonably? Had his thoughts and actions at least been understandable? Hadn't he tried his best to be loving and kind?

And I looked at him, sitting there on that sagging brown sofa with the William Morris pattern, the picture of a surprised-looking cat propped, just like last time, among the dead grasses in the fireplace. And I looked at her, with her frizzy hair and her calming ethnic jewellery and her box of Kleenex and the three untouched glasses of water lined up.

And I thought about how it was true. Simon really had been very kind, very understanding. And he was right, it was a disappointment that I had been unable to respond to his continued kindness and reasonableness with the energy and love that he felt was his due.

And then I thought about how dark and cold the world was. I thought about the way that everything that was good and kind and hopeful always had to be taken from you. I thought about how everything always ended in a cold place, bones and ashes, life sucked out, in darkness.

I shivered. And I thought about crying. But then I thought about how I'd had enough of crying, so I started to laugh.

Simon turned to the counsellor. He said nothing. He kept a very straight and level face, but his eyes said it all.

Now do you see what I'm up against?

She didn't speak. She kept her eyes on me and said nothing.

Me too – I did the same. I stopped laughing, finally, and I said nothing. I waited and waited. I pushed my fingers into the corners of my eyes, to try to keep back the tears, but it didn't work, they rolled down over my hands, my wrists, and still no suitable words came.

And I thought that I wasn't going to get away with it. I thought she would soon tell me that it was time to speak, to account for myself, but she didn't. She never did. I felt very grateful to her.

I felt Arthur hiccup inside me then. Hanging there. Keeping me in this world.

And I took a breath. I decided to speak.

* * *

I wake. It is night. Cold. Snow. My head in someone's lap. The person is humming. I know the tune.

Sophy? I say. Ted? Iris?

Oh, he says. You're awake.

I don't think so.

Fingers come down on my face. Grubby boy's fingers. I try to move my legs but my feet are stuck together.

It's all right, he says. I'll undo it in a moment.

What?

Shh.

His thumb on my lips. I know what he'll be wearing – red jersey, brown tracksuit bottoms. And I know what he'll say.

Someone hurt you. I found you here like this. I want you to come with me. I know a safe place – a place close to here.

For a few quick seconds, I see her face again. Her parted lips. The little bottom teeth. The eyes bright blue and astonished.

I shut my eyes.

The building? You're taking me to the building?

I think about its wide dark spaces, terraces, corridors. The black night sky. The world turning colder. A dog barking, children laughing – a little girl waiting to find me.

I don't open my eyes. I don't have to.

I know it, I tell him. You don't have to take me. Don't you realise? I'm already there.

Acknowledgements

Frosts, Friezes And Fairs – Chronicles Of The Frozen Thames And Harsh Winters In Britain by Ian Currie partially inspired this novel and stayed on my desk throughout the writing of it. Jonathan Myerson, Gill Coleridge and Dan Franklin are – and I hope always will be – my ideal first readers. Alex Bowler gave it the kind of thorough and sensitive page-editing that most authors dream of, but rarely get. And then there were all the kind people – family and friends but also many strangers – who buoyed me up so generously through a dark year. Without you I really am not sure this book would exist.

Plan Your Trip
Spain's Top 12

Madrid
Fine art and irresistible street life

Madrid (p35) is one of the fine-arts capitals of the world. Housing works by Goya, Velázquez and El Greco, the showpiece is the Museo del Prado, but within a short stroll are the Centro de Arte Reina Sofía, with works by Picasso, Dalí and Miró, and the Museo Thyssen-Bornemisza. Few European cities can match the intensity and street clamour of Madrid's nightlife with its wall-to-wall bars (including at Mercado de San Miguel p48; pictured right), small clubs and live venues.

1

Welcome to Spain

Passionate, sophisticated and devote to living the good life, Spain is both a stereotype come to life and a country more diverse than you ever imagined.

Poignantly windswept Roman ruins, cathedrals of rare power and incomparable jewels of Islamic architecture speak of a country where the great civilisations of history have risen, fallen and left behind their indelible mark. More recently, what other country could produce such rebellious and relentlessly creative spirits as Salvador Dalí, Pablo Picasso and Antoni Gaudí? Here, grand monuments to the past coexist alongside architectural creations of such daring that it becomes clear Spain's future will be every bit as original as its past.

But for all the talk of Spain's history, this is a country that lives very much in the present and there's a reason 'fiesta' is one of the best-known words in the Spanish language – life itself is a fiesta here and everyone seems to be invited. Perhaps you'll sense it along a crowded, post-midnight street when all the world has come out to play. Or maybe that moment will come when a flamenco performer touches something deep in your soul.

Food and wine are national obsessions in Spain, and with good reason. The touchstones of Spanish cooking are deceptively simple: incalculable variety, traditional recipes handed down through the generations, and an innate willingness to experiment and see what comes out of the kitchen laboratory.

there's a reason 'fiesta' is one of the best-known words in the Spanish language

Park Güell (p96), Barcelona

Contents

Welcome to Spain

Passionate, sophisticated and devoted to living the good life, Spain is both a stereotype come to life and a country more diverse than you ever imagined.

Poignantly windswept Roman ruins, cathedrals of rare power and incomparable jewels of Islamic architecture speak of a country where the great civilisations of history have risen, fallen and left behind their indelible mark. More recently, what other country could produce such rebellious and relentlessly creative spirits as Salvador Dalí, Pablo Picasso and Antoni Gaudí? Here, grand monuments to the past coexist alongside architectural creations of such daring that it becomes clear Spain's future will be every bit as original as its past.

But for all the talk of Spain's history, this is a country that lives very much in the present and there's a reason 'fiesta' is one of the best-known words in the Spanish language – life itself is a fiesta here and everyone seems to be invited. Perhaps you'll sense it along a crowded, post-midnight street when all the world has come out to play. Or maybe that moment will come when a flamenco performer touches something deep in your soul.

Food and wine are national obsessions in Spain, and with good reason. The touchstones of Spanish cooking are deceptively simple: incalculable variety, traditional recipes handed down through the generations, and an innate willingness to experiment and see what comes out of the kitchen laboratory.

> *there's a reason 'fiesta' is one of the best-known words in the Spanish language*

Park Güell (p96), Barcelona
MANFRED GOTTSCHALK / GETTY IMAGES ©

Bay of Biscay

FRANCE

BASQUE COUNTRY p220

bao

Irún

San Sebastián

Vitoria

Pamplona

Logroño

Val d'Aran

ANDORRA LA VELLA ANDORRA

THE PYRENEES p286

Parc Nacional d'Aigüestortes i Estany de Sant Maurici

COSTA BRAVA p110

LA RIOJA WINE REGION p273

Huesca

Girona

Soria

Zaragoza

Lleida

Río Segre

BARCELONA p68

ro

Río Ebro

Tarragona

Golfo de Valencia

Guadalajara

SPAIN

Teruel

Cuenca

Castellón de la Plana

Palma de Mallorca

Valencia

Río Júcar

Albacete

Río Segura

MEDITERRANEAN SEA

que Natural as de Cazorla, ra y las Villas

Murcia

DA p128

cional vada

Almería

ALGERIA

N

0   200 km
0   100 miles

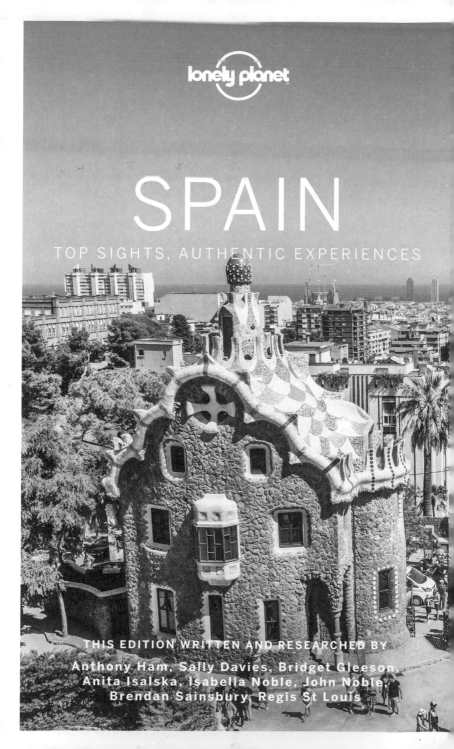

lonely planet

SPAIN

TOP SIGHTS, AUTHENTIC EXPERIENCES

THIS EDITION WRITTEN AND RESEARCHED BY

Anthony Ham, Sally Davies, Bridget Gleeson,
Anita Isalska, Isabella Noble, John Noble,
Brendan Sainsbury, Regis St Louis

Contents

Plan Your Trip

Plan Your Trip
Spain's Top 12

GLENN VAN DER KNIJFF / GETTY IMAGES ©

Madrid

Fine art and irresistible street life

Madrid (p35) is one of the fine-arts capitals of the world. Housing works by Goya, Velázquez and El Greco, the showpiece is the Museo del Prado, but within a short stroll are the Centro de Arte Reina Sofía, with works by Picasso, Dalí and Miró, and the Museo Thyssen-Bornemisza. Few European cities can match the intensity and street clamour of Madrid's nightlife with its wall-to-wall bars (including at Mercado de San Miguel p48; pictured right), small clubs and live venues.

1

VISIONE OF OUR LAND / GETTY IMAGES ©

EMRE TURAN / GETTY IMAGES ©

Barcelona

One of Europe's coolest cities

Home to cutting-edge architecture, world-class dining and pulsating
nightlife, Barcelona (p69) has long been one of Europe's most alluring
destinations. Days are spent wandering the cobblestone lanes of the
Gothic quarter, visiting La Catedral (p80; pictured bottom) basking on
Mediterranean beaches such as La Barceloneta (p88; pictured top)
or marvelling at Gaudí masterpieces. By night, it's all vintage cocktail
bars, gilded music halls, innovative eateries and dance-loving clubs.

Costa Brava

Beautiful beaches with echoes of Salvador Dalí

Filled with villages, such as Tossa de Mar (p116; pictured) and beaches of the kind that spawned northern Europe's summer obsession with the Spanish coast, the Costa Brava (p111) in Catalonia is one of our favourite corners of the Mediterranean. Beyond this, the spirit of Salvador Dalí lends so much personality and studied eccentricity to the Costa Brava experience, from his one-time home in Port Lligat near Cadaqués to Dalí-centric sites in Figueres and Castell de Púbol.

Granada

The exotic jewel in Andalucía's crown

Granada (p129) is an extraordinary place. The city's Alhambra (p132; pictured right) is close to architectural perfection and perhaps the most refined example of Islamic art anywhere in the world. Magnificent from afar, exquisite in its detail up close, the Alhambra is a singular jewel that's worth crossing the country to see. But Granada is also about so much more, from the Middle Eastern touches of the whitewashed Albayzín to its gilded monuments to Christian rule, not to mention one of the most dynamic and accessible tapas scenes anywhere in Spain.

Andalucía's Hill Towns

The whitewashed essence of Spain's rural south

The splendid cities of Andalucía (p147) find their luminous counterpoint in the *pueblos blancos* (white towns) that lie scattered across Spain's south. In Andalucía's east, in the Sierra Nevada, the fascinating villages of Las Alpujarras rank among the region's finest, resembling as they do charming outposts of North Africa, oasis-like and set amid woodlands and the deep ravines for which the region is renowned. Others such as Comares (p157; pictured right), Arcos de la Frontera and Vejer de la Frontera also vie for the title of Andalucía's most engaging hamlets.

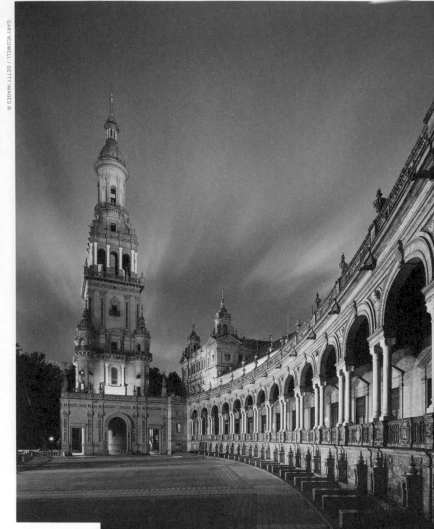

Seville

Spain's Andalucian city par excellence

Nowhere is as quintessentially Spanish as Seville (p175), a city of capricious moods and soulful secrets, which has played a pivotal role in flamenco, bullfighting, baroque art and Mudéjar architecture, including the Alcázar (p180; pictured). Blessed with year-round sunshine and fuelled by an unending schedule of festivals, everything seems more amorous here, a feeling not lost on legions of 19th-century aesthetes, who used the city as a setting in their romantic works of fiction.

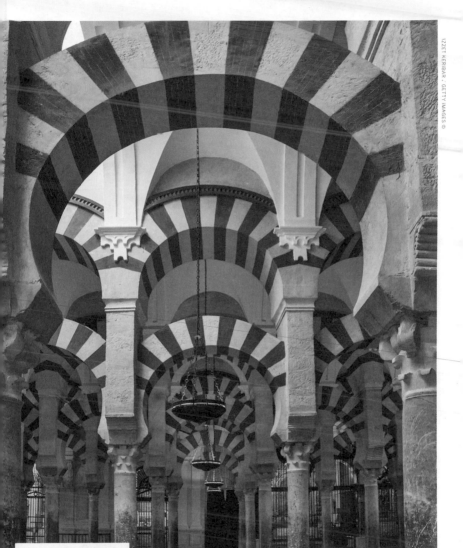

Córdoba

Architectural jewels and vibrant, life-filled streets

The sublime Mezquita (p198; pictured) at the heart of Córdoba (p195) is both a high point of Moorish architecture in Europe and symbol of Andalucía's fascinating history. Its features include perfectly proportioned horseshoe arches, an intricate mihrab, and a veritable 'forest' of 856 columns, many recycled from Roman ruins. Elsewhere in the city, there's a storied old Jewish quarter, fabulous food and many landmarks to the days back in the 10th century.

Salamanca

Stunning architecture, storied history and constant clamour

Luminous when floodlit, the elegant central square of Salamanca (p207), the Plaza Mayor (p212; pictured right), is possibly the most attractive in all of Spain. It is just one of many highlights in a city whose architectural splendour has few peers in the country. Salamanca is home to one of Europe's oldest and most prestigious universities, so student revelry also lights up the nights. It's this combination of grandeur and energy that makes so many people call Salamanca their favourite city in Spain.

STEFANO POLITI MARKOVINA / GETTY IMAGES ©

9

Basque Country
Fine food and cultural excellence

The Basque Country (p221) has its own unique flavour. Chefs here have turned bar snacks into an art form. Sometimes called 'high cuisine in miniature', *pintxos* (Basque tapas; pictured left) are piles of flavour and the choice lined up along the counter in any San Sebastián bar will leave first-time visitors gasping: this is Spain's most memorable eating experience. But this is also a relentlessly dynamic cultural region with visitors drawn to Bilbao's shimmering titanium fish, the Museo Guggenheim Bilbao, as well as riverside promenades, clanky funicular railways, an iconic football team and quality museums.

RAMÓN M. COVELO / GETTY IMAGES ©

JIL PHOTO / SHUTTERSTOCK ©

PEETERV / GETTY IMAGES ©

Northwest Coast

Dramatic coastal scenery and the Camino

From Cantabria in the east to Asturias and Galicia in the west, Spain's northern shore (p253) is a succession of stunning beaches, postcard-pretty villages and wild Atlantic cliffs. These are also some of Spain's most celebrated foodie destinations, while the hinterland is a rugged spine of mountains and one of the world's most popular sacred walks, the Camino de Santiago all the way into Santiago de Compostela. Top and bottom right: Cudillero (p266)

NICK LEDGER / GETTY IMAGES ©

La Rioja Wine Region

Spain's premier wine region bar none

La Rioja (p273) is the sort of place where you could spend weeks meandering along quiet roads in search of the finest drop. Bodegas (pictured above) offering wine tastings and picturesque villages that shelter excellent wine museums are the mainstay in this region. The Frank Gehry–designed Hotel Marqués de Riscal, close to Elciego, has been likened to Bilbao's museum in architectural scale and ambition, and has become the elite centre for wine tourism in the region.

JEKATERINA NIKITINA / GETTY IMAGES ©

The Pyrenees

Spectacular mountains and Spain's best hiking

Spain is a walker's destination of exceptional variety, but we reckon the Pyrenees (p287) in Navarra, Aragón and Catalonia offer the most special hiking country. Aragón's Parque Nacional de Ordesa y Monte Perdido is one of the high points (pun intended), while its glories are mirrored across the provincial frontier of Parc Nacional d'Aigüestortes i Estany de Sant Maurici in Catalonia.

Plan Your Trip
Need to Know

When to Go

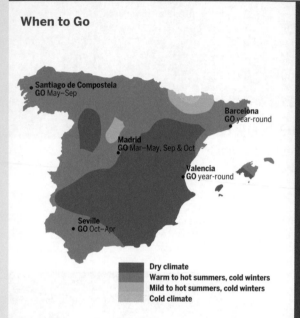

Santiago de Compostela
GO May–Sep

Barcelona
GO year-round

Madrid
GO Mar–May, Sep & Oct

Valencia
GO year-round

Seville
GO Oct–Apr

Dry climate
Warm to hot summers, cold winters
Mild to hot summers, cold winters
Cold climate

High Season (Jun–Aug, public holidays)

○ Accommodation books out and prices increase up to 50%.

○ Low season in parts of inland Spain.

○ Warm, dry and sunny; more humid in coastal areas.

Shoulder (Mar–May, Sep & Oct)

○ A good time with mild, clear weather and fewer crowds.

○ Local festivals can send prices soaring.

Low Season (Nov–Feb)

○ Cold in central Spain; rain in the north and northwest. This is high season in ski resorts.

○ Mild temperatures in Andalucía and the Mediterranean coast.

○ Many hotels are closed in beach areas, elsewhere prices plummet.

Currency
Euro (€)

Language
Spanish (Castilian). Also Catalan, Basque and Galician.

Visas
Generally not required for stays up to 90 days; some nationalities need a Schengen visa.

Money
ATMs widely available. Visa and Mastercard are generally accepted; American Express is less common.

Mobile Phones
Local SIM cards widely available and can be used in European and Australian mobile phones.

Time
GMT/UTC plus one hour during winter and GMT/UTC plus two hours during daylight saving.

Daily Costs

Budget: Less than €80
o Dorm bed: €20 to €30

o Double room in *hostal*: €55 to €65 (more in Madrid and Barcelona)

o Self-catering and lunch *menú del día*: €10 to €15

o Use museum and gallery 'free admission' afternoons

Midrange: €80–175
o Double room in midrange hotel: €65–140

o Lunch and/or dinner in local restaurant: €20–40

o Car rental: per day from €25

Top End: More than €175
o Double room in top-end hotel: from €140 (€200 in Madrid, Barcelona and the Balearics)

o Fine dining for lunch and dinner: €150–250

o Regularly stay in *paradores* (luxurious state-owned hotels): €120–200

Useful Websites

Fiestas.net (www.fiestas.net) Festivals around the country.

Lonely Planet (www.lonelyplanet.com/spain) Destination information, hotel bookings, traveller forums and more.

Renfe (www.renfe.com) Spain's rail network.

Tour Spain (www.tourspain.org) Culture, food and links to hotels and transport.

Turespaña (www.spain.info) Spanish tourist office's site.

Arriving in Spain

Adolfo Suárez Madrid-Barajas Airport, Madrid (p65)
Metro (€4.50, 30 minutes to the centre) Runs from 6.05am to 1.30am
Exprés Aeropuerto bus (€5; 40 minutes) Runs 24 hours between the airport and Puerta de Atocha train station or Plaza de Cibeles
Private minibuses (€30)
Taxis (€30)

El Prat Airport, Barcelona (p107)
Buses (€5.90, 30 to 40 minutes to the centre) Run every five to 10 minutes from 6.10am to 1.05am
Trains (€4.10, 25 to 30 minutes to the centre) Run half-hourly from 5.42am to 11.38pm
Taxis (€30, 30 minutes to the centre)

Getting Around

Spain's public transport system is one of the best in Europe.

Train Extremely efficient, from slow inter-city regional trains to some of the fastest trains on the planet. More routes are added yearly.

Car Vast network of motorways radiating from Madrid, shadowed by smaller but often more picturesque minor roads.

Bus The workhorses of the Spanish roads, from slick express coaches to stop-everywhere village-to-village buses.

For more on **getting around**, see p342 ➡

Plan Your Trip
Hot Spots For...

Spanish Food

Spain's food is one of the most varied and innovative on the planet, and sampling it will likely be one of the most memorable experiences of your trip.

Moorish Architecture

Almost seven centuries of Islamic rule on Iberian soil left behind an extraordinary legacy of architectural magnificence. The cities of Andalucía in particular house so many glittering jewels.

Hiking

Fabulous hiking trails criss-cross Spain's mountain regions, and the summer possibilities are endless, from the Pyrenees and Picos de Europa in the north to the Sierra Nevada in the south.

Medieval Villages

Spain's pretty pueblos (villages) are something special, from the stone-and-wood villages of the north to the luminous white hamlets that cling to rocky crags in the Andalucian south.

San Sebastián (p243) Without doubt one of Europe's gastronomic stars, from Michelin-starred restaurants to Spain's best tapas scene.

Casco Viejo Go on a *pintxo* crawl in the *casco viejo* (old quarter; p226).

Barcelona (p93) Catalan cooking is both bastion of tradition and laboratory for many weird and wonderful creations.

Tickets A tapas bar (p100) by one of Spain's most creative chefs, Ferran Adrià.

Madrid (p48) Spain's capital takes the best of Spain's myriad regional cuisines and brings them together.

Mercado de San Miguel Sample fine food (p48) and the buzz of eating, Spanish-style.

Granada (p129) No city in Spain feels more like the Middle East, from the Albayzín to Europe's most beautiful palace.

Alhambra No building (p132) captures Al-Andalus' sophistication quite like it.

Córdoba (p195) This sultry city was once the Moorish heartland and remains awash in monuments from the age.

Mezquita The forest of columns and horseshoe arches (p195) is simply sublime.

Seville (p175) Seville's Islamic monuments are worthy complements to the stars of Granada and Córdoba.

Alcázar The exquisite detail of Moorish decoration dominates the Alcázar (p180).

Parc Nacional d'Aigüestortes i Estany de Sant Maurici (p290) Classic Pyrenean national park combining peaks, lakes and churches just outside the park boundaries.

Estany Llong A natural amphitheatre (p291) surrounded by high mountains.

Las Alpujarras (p150) Hike from one charming white-washed village to the next along trails clinging to the Sierra Nevada slopes.

Barranco de Poqueira Explore Las Alpujarras most appealing corner (p150) on foot.

Parque Nacional de Ordesa y Monte Perdido (p292) The most spectacular corner of the Pyrenees? This stunning park has some of Spain's most celebrated hikes.

Circo de Soaso A seven-hour trek (p292) into the heart of the range.

Western Andalucía (p147) The villages of Andalucía's west have few peers when it comes to the hill towns.

Arcos de la Frontera Postcard-perfect hill town (p152) atop a dizzying perch.

The Aragonese Pyrenees (p300) The Pyrenean foothills shelter numerous candidates for the title of Spain's most beautiful village.

Sos del Rey Católico Twisting cobblestone lanes (p303) climb along a ridge.

Sierra de Grazalema (p160) Set amid rolling hill country, the villages here are little-known, and all the better for it.

Zahara de la Sierra Topped by a castle and looking like part of the mountain (p161).

Plan Your Trip
Local Life

ETHAN WELTY / GETTY IMAGES ©

✻ Activities

Spain's landscapes provide the backdrop to some of Europe's best hiking, most famously the Camino de Santiago. The Pyrenees are also stellar, while hiking from one Las Alpujarras village to the next is a memorable way to explore the white villages of the south. Skiing, again in the Pyrenees, is a much-loved Spanish pastime, but the Sierra Nevada, accessible from Granada, is also brilliant. Other highlights include surfing Spain's northwestern coast, wildlife-watching in the north and south, and snorkelling off the Costa Brava. Cyclists of all levels will likely find countless suitable trails.

ᗉ Shopping

Shopping takes you from one extreme to the other – at the most visible end, frilly flamenco dresses, bullfighting posters with your name on them or bulls in a variety of poses seem to overflow from souvenir shops across the country. But look a little harder and you'll find high-quality crafts and cer-

amics, genuine flamenco memorabilia, the finest Spanish foods and all manner of fabulous things. Spain is one of Europe's most style-conscious places and its designers are some of the most accessible yet innovative you'll find anywhere. Madrid and Barcelona offer the most choice, but shopping here is almost a national sport and you're never far from a small shop selling the perfect gift.

☆ Entertainment

Live flamenco is an undoubted highlight, but the breadth of Spain's live-music scene is almost as appealing. Watching Real Madrid or FC Barcelona live alongside nearly 100,000 passionate fans is another experience that features on many bucket lists.

✕ Eating

Spain is one of Europe's culinary powerhouses, a foodie destination of the highest order. So much of Spanish cuisine has colonised the world, from tapas, paella, *jamón* and churros to Spanish wines and olive oils. But by visiting Spain you can go to

MAREMAGNUM / GETTY IMAGES ©

the source and enjoy Spanish cooking at its best, and in all its infinite variety. Better still, you'll get to experience one ingredient that is missing from eating Spanish food beyond Spain's shores – in Spain, the culture of eating and passion for good food and all things gastronomical can be as enjoyable as the food itself. Barcelona and the Basque Country are the undoubted stars of the show, while Galicia and Andalucía are known at once for their love of tradition and fine seafood. Anywhere along Spain's Mediterranean coast is good for paella, while tapas is a highlight in Barcelona, Madrid, San Sebastián, Seville, Granada and Bilbao. Madrid also deserves special mention – its own cuisine may be unremarkable but you can still find all that's wonderful about the Spanish kitchen.

♟ Drinking & Nightlife

Spanish nightlife is the stuff of legend – Madrid, for example, has more bars per capita than any other city on earth, and even the smallest village will likely have at least

★ Best Flamenco

Casa de la Memoria (p192)

Casa Patas (p62)

Centro Flamenco Fosforito (p200)

Jardines de Zoraya (p144)

Peña Cultural Flamenca 'Aguilar de Vejer' (p173)

one local watering hole. Yes, these bars are places to drink, but they're much more – they're meeting places, places to order tapas, hubs of community life, and the starting point of seemingly endless Spanish nights. Nightclubs will keep you going until dawn (and sometimes even beyond), from mega-clubs to indie hangouts for people-in-the-know. Most Spanish cities have nonstop nightlife, none more so than Madrid and Barcelona.

From left: Mountain biking, Las Alpujarras (p150); Madrid bar (p57)

Plan Your Trip
Month by Month

LUGVI / SHUTTERSTOCK ©

January

Ski resorts in the Pyrenees in the northeast and the Sierra Nevada, close to Granada in the south, are in full swing. Snow in Catalonia is usually better in the second half of the month. School holidays run until around 8 January, so book ahead.

February

This is often the coldest month in Spain, with temperatures close to freezing, especially in the north and inland regions.

🎊 Contemporary Art Fair

One of Europe's biggest celebrations of contemporary art, Madrid's Feria Internacional de Arte Contemporánea (Arco; www.ifema.es) draws gallery reps and exhibitors from all over the world.

🎊 Barcelona's Winter Bash

Around 12 February, the Festes de Santa Eulàlia (www.bcn.cat/santaeulalia) celebrates Barcelona's first patron saint with a week of cultural events, from parades of giants to *castells* (human castles).

April

Spain has a real spring in its step with wildflowers in full bloom, Easter celebrations and school holidays. It requires some advance planning (book ahead), but it's a great time to be here.

🎊 Semana Santa (Holy Week)

Easter (the dates change each year) entails parades of *pasos* (holy figures), hooded penitents and huge crowds. It's extravagantly celebrated in Seville (p191).

🎊 Feria de Abril (April Fair)

This week-long party (p191), held in Seville in the second half of April, is the biggest of Andalucía's fairs. *Sevillanos* dress up in their traditional finery, ride around on horseback and in elaborate horse-drawn carriages and dance late into the night.

May

A glorious time to be in Spain, May sees the countryside carpeted with spring wildflowers and the weather can feel like summer is just around the corner.

☘ Córdoba's Courtyards Open Up

Scores of beautiful private courtyards in Córdoba are opened to the public for the Fiesta de los Patios de Córdoba (p201). It's a rare chance to see an otherwise hidden side of Córdoba, strewn with flowers and freshly painted.

⚘ Fiesta de San Isidro

Madrid's major fiesta (www.esmadrid.com) celebrates the city's patron saint with bullfights, parades, concerts and more.

★ Best Festivals

Semana Santa (Holy Week), usually March or April

Feria de Abril, April

Festival de la Guitarra de Córdoba, July

Fiestas del Apóstol Santiago, July

Bienal de Flamenco, September

Locals dress up in traditional costumes, and some of the events, such as the bullfighting season, last for a month.

June

By June the north is shaking off its winter chill and the Camino de Santiago's trails are becoming crowded. In the south, it's warming up as the coastal resorts ready themselves for the summer onslaught.

From left: Feria de Abril (p191), Seville; Semana Santa, Córdoba

✵ Bonfires & Fireworks

Midsummer bonfires, fireworks and roaming giants feature on the eve of the Fiesta de San Juan (24 June; Dia de Sant Joan), notably along the Mediterranean coast, particularly in Barcelona (www.santjoan.bcn.cat).

☆ Electronica Festival

Performers and spectators come from all over the world for Sónar (www.sonar.es), Barcelona's two-day celebration of electronic music, which is said to be Europe's biggest festival of its kind. Dates vary each year.

♟ Wine Battle

Haro, one of the premier wine towns of La Rioja, enjoys the Batalla del Vino (p282) on 29 June, squirting wine all over the place in one of Spain's messiest play fights, pausing only to drink the good stuff.

July

Temperatures in Andalucía and much of the interior can be fiercely hot, but July is a great time to be at the beach and is one of the best months for hiking in the Pyrenees.

✵ Festival de la Guitarra de Córdoba

Córdoba's contribution to Spain's impressive calendar of musical events, this fine international two-week guitar festival (www.guitarracordoba.org) ranges from flamenco and classical to rock, blues and beyond. Headline performances take place in the city's theatres and Plaza de Toros.

✵ Fiestas del Apóstol Santiago

The Día de Santiago (http://www.santiagoturismo.com/festas-e-tradicions/festas-do-apostolo-santiago) on 25 July marks the day of Spain's national saint (St James) and is spectacularly celebrated in Santiago de Compostela. With so many pilgrims around, it's the city's most festive two weeks of the year.

August

Spaniards from all over the country join Europeans in converging on the coastal resorts of the Mediterranean.

✵ Barcelona Street Festival

Locals compete for the most elaborately decorated street in the popular week-long Festa Major de Gràcia (www.festamajordegracia.org), held around 15 August. People pour in to listen to bands in the streets and squares, fuel up on snacks, and drink at countless street stands.

September

This is the month when Spain returns to work after a seemingly endless summer. Weather generally remains warm until late September at least.

☆ Bienal de Flamenco

There are flamenco festivals all over Spain throughout the year, but this is the most prestigious of them all. Held in Seville (p191) in even-numbered years (and Málaga every other year), it draws the biggest names in the genre.

♟ La Rioja's Grape Harvest

Logroño celebrates the feast day of St Matthew (Fiesta de San Mateo) and the year's grape harvest. There are grape-crushing ceremonies and endless opportunities to sample the fruit of the vine in liquid form.

✵ Barcelona's Big Party

Barcelona's co-patron saint is celebrated with fervour in the massive four-day Festes de la Mercè (www.bcn.cat/merce) in September. The city stages special exhibitions, free concerts and street performers galore.

December

The weather turns cold, but Navidad (Christmas) is on its way. There are Christmas markets, turrón (nougat) in abundance, an extra long weekend at the beginning of the month and a festive period that lasts until early January.

Plan Your Trip
Get Inspired

Read

The New Spaniards (2006) Updated version of John Hooper's classic portrait of contemporary Spain.

The Ornament of the World (2003) Fascinating look at Andalucía's Islamic centuries.

Ghosts of Spain (2007) Giles Tremlett's take on contemporary Spain and its tumultuous past.

Getting to Mañana (2004) Miranda Innes' take on starting a new life in an Andalucian farmhouse.

A Late Dinner (2007) Paul Richardson's beautifully written journey through Spanish food.

Sacred Sierra: A Year on a Spanish Mountain (2009) Jason Webster's excellent alternative to the expat-renovates-a-Spanish-farmhouse genre.

Watch

Todo sobre mi madre (All About My Mother; 1999) Considered by many to be Pedro Almodóvar's masterpiece.

Broken Embraces (2009) Pedro Almodóvar's film noir–inspired movie.

Mar adentro (The Sea Inside; 2004) Alejandro Amenábar's touching movie filmed in Galicia.

Jamón jamón (1992) Launched the careers of Javier Bardem and Penélope Cruz.

Listen

Paco de Lucía antología (1995) Collected works by Spain's most celebrated flamenco guitarist.

Lagrimas negras (2003) Bebo Valdés and Diego El Cigala in stunning flamenco-Cuban fusion.

Sueña la Alhambra (2005) Enrique Morente, one of flamenco's most enduring and creative voices.

La luna en el río (2003) Carmen Linares, flamenco's foremost female voice in the second half of the 20th century.

Pokito a poko (2005) Flamenco meets electronica in this fabulous fusion band from Málaga.

Above: Puente Romano (p201), Córdoba

Plan Your Trip
Five-Day Itineraries

Madrid, Barcelona & Costa Brava

On offer here are fantastic art galleries, architecture and endlessly fascinating streetlife, with a day trip to the Costa Brava for good measure.

3 Costa Brava (p110) Visit Cadaqués and Figueres to understand how Salvador Dalí made the region his own, then return to Barcelona by night.

2 Barcelona (p68) Modernista architecture, fabulous food and a sense that anything is possible: welcome to Barcelona.
🚗 2 hrs to Figueres

1 Madrid (p34) Madrid has mastered the art of living the good life with galleries and feel-good streets. ✈ 1 hr or 🚗 2½ hrs to Barcelona

Andalucía's Moorish Heartland

Andalucía's trio of vibrant, soulful cities – Seville, Córdoba and Granada – goes to the heart of the region's modern, and historical, appeal.

2 Córdoba (p194) Córdoba's medieval heart is filled with reminders of the city's sophisticated past, with the Mezquita as a centrepiece.
🚆 2¾ hrs to Granada

1 Seville (p174) When most people think of Andalucía at its passionate, beautiful, traditional best, they're probably thinking of Seville.
🚆 1 hr to Córdoba

3 Granada (p128) Filled with echoes of Al-Andalus and framed by the snowcapped mountains of the Sierra Nevada, Granada is unlike anywhere else in Spain.

Plan Your Trip
10-Day Itinerary

Best of Spain

Spain's two most dynamic cities, a duo of Andalusian beauties, and the pick of the hill towns of the south. Put them all together and this itinerary is Spain at its most memorable.

1 Barcelona (p68) Spend two days here and you'll soon be making plans to return. Focus on food and Gaudí.
🚆 2 hrs to Madrid

2 Madrid (p34) Take your pick of the art galleries, spend time soaking up the atmosphere in its plazas, and go on a tapas crawl.
🚆 2½ hrs to Seville

3 Seville (p174) Two days is a minimum for getting the most out of this gutsy, beautiful cliché of the Andalusian south.
🚆 3 hrs to Granada

4 Granada (p128) A day in the Alhambra and Albayzín should leave a day for exploring the town's tapas culture and fine Christian buildings.
🚗 2 hrs to Las Alpujarras

5 Las Alpujarras (p150) Spend a day exploring the whitewashed villages and pretty valleys that inhabit the Sierra Nevada's southern flank.
🚗 2-3 hrs to Ronda

6 Ronda (p154) Ronda has gravitas, great food and marvellous views from atop its impossibly high perch.

Plan Your Trip
Two-Week Itinerary

Spain's North

From Barcelona to Santiago de Compostela, this journey across the country's north takes in the Pyrenees, the Basque Country and Spain's most rugged stretch of coast. You'll enjoy some of the best food of your trip, too.

8 Cudillero (p266) Perhaps Spain's loveliest fishing village, Cudillero lies close to some of the country's finest beaches too.
🚗 5-7 hrs to Cabo Ortegal

9 Cabo Ortegal (p270) Wild, windswept and downright dramatic, the coast around Cabo Ortegal will simply take your breath away.
🚗 5-6 hrs to Santiago de Compostela

10 Santiago de Compostela (p260) The endpoint of many a pilgrim's journey, Santiago has loads of charm, glorious architecture and fine food to enjoy at the end of this epic trip.

7 Santillana del Mar (p262) An impossibly picturesque place, Santillana del Mar is many visitors' choice for Spain's prettiest *pueblo* (village).
🚗 1-2 hrs to Cudillero

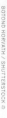
BOTOND HORVATH / SHUTTERSTOCK ©

6 Bilbao (p228) A couple of days in Bilbao should allow enough time for the Guggenheim Museum Bilbao and some serious tapas indulgence.
🚗 2-3 hrs to Santillana del Mar

5 San Sebastián (p239) Beautiful beyond compare and Spain's undisputed culinary capital, San Sebastián is worth at least two days...at *least*.
🚗 2 hrs to Bilbao

3 Aínsa (p301) There are no more beautiful mountain villages than stone-built Aínsa, with its splendid panoramic views.
🚗 2-3 hrs to Sos del Rey Católico

2 Taüll (p295) The pick of Catalonia's Pyrenean hamlets, Taüll has Romanesque churches and serves as gateway to a stunning national park.
🚗 4 hrs to Aínsa

4 Sos del Rey Católico (p303) Just when you run out of superlatives, you arrive in Sos del Rey Católico, the essence of a medieval mountain village. 🚗 6 hrs to San Sebastián

1 Barcelona (p68) The starting point of so many wonderful journeys and destination in itself, Barcelona is Spain's most celebrated city.
🚗 6 hrs to the Pyrenees

Plan Your Trip
Family Travel

STEFANO POLITI MARKOVINA / GETTY IMAGES ©

Spain is a family-friendly destination with excellent transport and accommodation infrastructure, food to satisfy even the fussiest of eaters, and an extraordinary range of attractions that appeal to both adults and children. Visiting as a family does require some careful planning, but no more than for visiting any other European country.

Children's Highlights

Spain has a surfeit of castles, horse shows, fiestas and ferias, interactive museums, flamenco shows and even the Semana Santa processions.

Spain's beaches, especially those along the Mediterranean coast, are custom-made for children – many along the Costa Brava are sheltered from the open ocean by protective coves. Try San Sebastián's Playa de la Concha, Spain's most easily accessible city beach, or any of the sheltered, beautiful Costa Brava coves.

Many museums have started to incorporate an interactive element into what were once staid and static exhibits. Numerous major sights (such as the Alhambra and most art galleries) also have guidebooks aimed specifically at children. Children will be impressed by Gaudí's weird-and-wonderful Park Güell and Casa Batlló. Football fans will love Camp Nou.

When to Go

If you're heading for the beach, summer (especially July and August) is the obvious choice – but it's also when Spaniards undertake a mass pilgrimage to the coast, so book well ahead. It's also a good time to travel to the Pyrenees. The interior can be unbearably hot during the summer months, however – Seville and Córdoba regularly experience daytime temperatures of almost 50°C.

Our favourite time for visiting Spain is in spring and autumn, particularly May, June, September and October. In all but the latter month, you might be lucky and get weather warm enough for the beach, but temperatures in these months are generally mild and the weather often fine.

CHRISTIAN BERTRAND / SHUTTERSTOCK ©

Eating Out

Food and children are two of the great loves for Spaniards, and Spanish fare is rarely spicy so kids tend to like it.

○ Children are usually welcome, whether in a sit-down restaurant or in a chaotically busy bar.

○ You cannot rely on restaurants having *tronas* (high chairs), although many do these days. There is rarely more than one, though, so make the request as early as possible.

○ Very few restaurants (or other public amenities) have nappy-changing facilities.

○ A small but growing number of restaurants offer a *menú infantil* (children's menu).

○ Adapting to Spanish eating hours can be a challenge. Carry emergency supplies for those times when there's simply nothing open.

★ Best Destinations for Kids

Barcelona (p69)
Basque Country (p221)
Costa Brava (p111)
Madrid (p34)
Northwest Coast (p253)

Tips

○ Always ask for extra tapas in bars, such as olives or cut, raw carrots.

○ Adjust your children to Spanish time (ie late nights) as quickly as you can; otherwise they'll miss half the fun.

○ Crayons and paper are rarely given out in restaurants – bring your own.

○ If you're willing to share your bed with your child, you won't incur a supplement. Extra beds usually incur a €20 to €30 charge.

Above left: Playa de la Concha (p241), San Sebastián;
Above: Camp Nou (p90), Barcelona

Teatro Real

Palacio Real

Ca

MADRID

edral de la Almundena

Río Manzanares

Palacio Real (p40)

Arriving in Madrid

Adolfo Suárez Madrid-Barajas Airport (p65) The airport is connected to central Madrid by **metro** (www.metro madrid.es; ☺6.05am-1.30am) and 24-hour **bus** (www.emtmadrid.es) or minibus; taxis cost €30.

Puerta de Atocha Metro and buses run from Atocha train station to central Madrid; taxis cost from €8.

Estación de Chamartín Metro and buses run from Chamartín train station to central Madrid; taxis cost around €13.

Sleeping

Madrid has high-quality accommodation at prices that haven't been seen in the centre of other European capitals in decades. Five-star temples to good taste and a handful of buzzing hostels bookend a fabulous collection of midrange hotels and cheaper family-run *hostales* (cheap hotels); most of the midrangers are creative originals.

For more on where to stay, see p67.

Cloisters

Museo del Prado

Welcome to one of the world's elite art galleries. Visiting is the ultimate artistic indulgence, with Spanish masters (Goya, Velázquez and El Greco) and big names from across Europe.

Great For...

☑ **Don't Miss**

Goya's *Las pinturas negras* (The Black Paintings) or his *El dos de mayo,* or...

The more than 7000 paintings held in the Museo del Prado's collection (only around 1500 are currently on display) are like a window onto the historical vagaries of the Spanish soul, at once grand and imperious in the royal paintings of Velázquez, darkly tumultuous in *Las pinturas negras* (The Black Paintings) of Goya, and outward looking with sophisticated works of art from all across Europe.

Goya

Francisco José de Goya y Lucientes (Goya) is found on all three floors of the Prado, but start at the southern end of the ground or lower level. In Room 65, Goya's *El dos de mayo* and *El tres de mayo* rank among Madrid's most emblematic paintings. Alongside, in Rooms 67 and 68, are some of

Veláquez monument

FELIPE RODRIGUEZ 2 / 500PX ©

❶ Need to Know

Map p47; www.museodelprado.es; Paseo del Prado; adult/child €14/free, 6-8pm Mon-Sat & 5-7pm Sun free, audioguides €3.50, admission plus official guidebook €23; ⊙10am-8pm Mon-Sat, 10am-7pm Sun; Ⓜ Banco de España

✕ Take a Break

The Prado's inhouse cafeteria is next to the bookshop. Otherwise cross the road to **Estado Puro** (p54).

★ Top Tip

Purchase your ticket online and avoid the queues.

whom features in *Las meninas*), *El Príncipe Baltasar Carlos* and *Isabel de Francia* – on horseback.

Spanish & Other European Masters

If Spanish painters have piqued your curiosity, look for the stark figures of Francisco de Zurbarán or the vivid, almost surreal works by the 16th-century master and adopted Spaniard El Greco.

Another alternative is the Prado's outstanding collection of Flemish art, with highlights including the fulsome figures and bulbous cherubs of Peter Paul Rubens, *The Triumph of Death* by Pieter Bruegel, Rembrandt's *Artemisa*, and those by Anton Van Dyck. And on no account miss the weird and wonderful *The Garden of Earthly Delights* (Room 56A) by Hieronymus Bosch.

And then there are the paintings by Dürer, Rafael, Tiziano (Titian), Tintoretto, Sorolla, Gainsborough, Fra Angelico, Tiepolo...

his darkest and most disturbing works, *Las pinturas negras*.

There are more Goyas on the 1st floor in Rooms 34 to 37 (among them are the enigmatic *La maja vestida* and *La maja desnuda*) and on the top floor.

Velázquez

Diego Rodríguez de Silva y Velázquez (Velázquez) is another of the grand masters of Spanish art who brings so much distinction to the Prado. Of all his works, *Las meninas* (Room 12) is what most people come to see. The rooms surrounding *Las meninas* contain more fine works by Velázquez: watch in particular for his paintings of various members of royalty who seem to spring off the canvas – *Felipe II*, *Felipe IV*, *Margarita de Austria* (a younger version of

⊙ SIGHTS

Madrid has three of the finest art galleries in the world. Beyond museum walls, there is nowhere easier to access the combination of stately architecture and feel-good living than in the beautiful plazas, where *terrazas* (cafes or bars with outdoor tables) provide a front-row seat for Madrid's fine cityscape and endlessly energetic street life. Throw in areas like Chueca, Malasaña and Salamanca, each with their own personality, and you'll wonder why you decided to spend so little time here.

⊙ Plaza Mayor & Royal Madrid

These *barrios* (districts) are where the story of Madrid began. As the seat of royal power, this is where the splendour of imperial Spain was at its most ostentatious and where Spain's overarching Catholicism was at its most devout – think expansive palaces, elaborate private mansions, ancient churches and imposing convents amid the clamour of modern Madrid.

Plaza Mayor   Square

(Map p42; Ⓜ Sol) Madrid's grand central square, a rare but expansive opening in the tightly packed streets of central Madrid, is one of the prettiest open spaces in Spain; a combination of imposing architecture, historic tales and vibrant street life coursing across its cobblestones. At once beautiful, and a reference point for so many Madrid days, it hosts the city's main tourist office, a Christmas market in December and arches leading to laneways leading out into the labyrinth.

Palacio Real   Palace

(Map p42; 🖉 91 454 88 00; www.patrimonio nacional.es; Calle de Bailén; adult/concession €11/6, guide/audioguide €4/4, EU citizens free last 2hr Mon-Thu; ◷ 10am-8pm Apr-Sep, 10am-6pm Oct-Mar; Ⓜ Ópera) Spain's lavish Palacio Real is a jewel box of a palace, although it's used only occasionally for royal ceremonies; the royal family moved to the modest Palacio de la Zarzuela years ago. When the *alcázar* (Muslim-era fort) burned down on Christmas Day 1734, Felipe V, the first Bourbon king, decided to build a palace that would dwarf all its European counterparts. Felipe died before

Plaza Mayor

S-F / SHUTTERSTOCK ©

the palace was finished, which is perhaps why the Italianate baroque colossus has a mere 2800 rooms, just one-quarter of the original plan.

Plaza de Oriente Square

(Map p42; MÓpera) A royal palace that once had aspirations to be the Spanish Versailles. Sophisticated cafes watched over by apartments that cost the equivalent of a royal salary. The Teatro Real, Madrid's opera house and one of Spain's temples to high culture. Some of the finest sunset views in Madrid... Welcome to Plaza de Oriente, a living, breathing monument to imperial Madrid.

Plaza de la Villa & Around Square

(MÓpera) There are grander plazas in Madrid, but this intimate little square is one of the prettiest. Enclosed on three sides by wonderfully preserved examples of 17th-century Madrid-style baroque architecture (barroco madrileño), it was the permanent seat of Madrid's city government from the Middle Ages until recent years when Madrid's city council relocated to the grand Palacio de Comunicaciones on Plaza de la Cibeles.

Convento de las Descalzas Reales Convent

(Convent of the Barefoot Royals; Map p42; www.patrimonionacional.es; Plaza de las Descalzas 3; €6, incl Convento de la Encarnación €8, EU citizens free Wed & Thu afternoon; 10am-2pm & 4-6.30pm Tue-Sat, 10am-3pm Sun; MÓpera, Sol) The grim plateresque walls of the Convento de las Descalzas Reales offer no hint that behind the facade lies a sumptuous stronghold of the faith. The compulsory guided tour (in Spanish) leads you up a gaudily frescoed Renaissance stairway to the upper level of the cloister. The vault was painted by Claudio Coello, one of the most important artists of the Madrid School of the 17th century and whose works adorn San Lorenzo de El Escorial.

◎ La Latina & Lavapiés

El Rastro Market

(Calle de la Ribera de los Curtidores; 8am-3pm Sun; MLa Latina) A Sunday morning at El Ra-

stro is a Madrid institution. You could easily spend an entire morning inching your way down the hill and through the maze of streets that hosts the flea market every Sunday morning. Cheap clothes, luggage, old flamenco records, even older photos of Madrid, faux designer purses, grungy T-shirts, household goods and electronics are the main fare. For every 10 pieces of junk, there's a real gem (a lost masterpiece, an Underwood typewriter) waiting to be found.

Basílica de San Francisco El Grande Church

(Map p42; Plaza de San Francisco 1; adult/concession €3/2; mass 8-10.30am Mon-Sat, museum 10.30am-12.30pm & 4-6pm Tue-Sun Sep-Jun, 10.30am-12.30pm & 5-7pm Tue-Sun Jul & Aug; MLa Latina, Puerta de Toledo) Lording it over the southwestern corner of La Latina, this imposing and recently restored baroque basílica is one of Madrid's grandest old churches. Its extravagantly frescoed dome is, by some estimates, the largest in Spain and the fourth-largest in the world, with a height of 56m and diameter of 33m.

◎ Sol, Santa Ana & Huertas

Plaza de Santa Ana Square

(Map p42; MSevilla, Sol, Antón Martín) Plaza de Santa Ana is a delightful confluence of elegant architecture and irresistible energy. It presides over the upper reaches of the Barrio de las Letras and this literary personality makes its presence felt with the statues of the 17th-century writer Calderón de la Barca and Federíco García Lorca, and in the **Teatro Español** (91 360 14 84; www.teatroespanol.es; Calle del Príncipe 25), formerly the Teatro del Príncipe, at the plaza's eastern end. Apart from anything else, the plaza is the starting point for many a long Huertas night.

Real Academia de Bellas Artes de San Fernando Museum

(Map p42; 91 524 08 64; www.realacademia bellasartessanfernando.com; Calle de Alcalá 13; adult/child €6/free, Wed free; 10am-3pm Tue-Sun Sep-Jul; MSol, Sevilla) Madrid's 'other' art gallery, the Real Academia de Bellas Artes has for centuries played a pivotal role in the

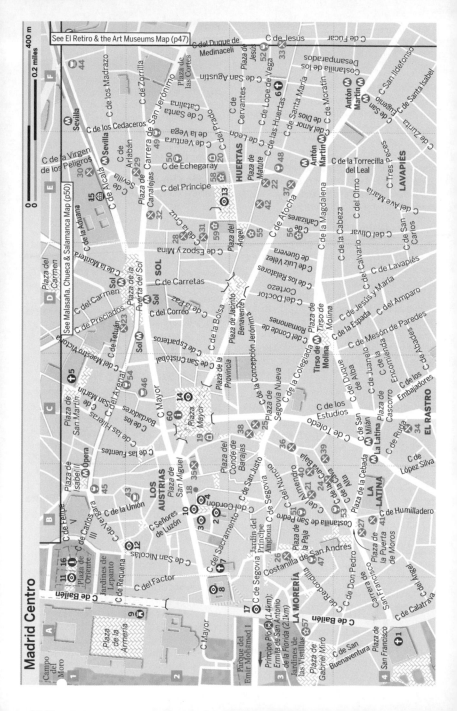

Madrid Centro

Madrid Centro

artistic life of the city. As the royal fine arts academy, it has nurtured local talent, thereby complementing the royal penchant for drawing the great international artists of the day into their realm. The pantheon of former alumni reads like a Who's Who of Spanish art, and the collection that now hangs on the academy's walls is a suitably rich one.

◎ El Retiro & the Art Museums

Centro de Arte Reina Sofía   Museum

(Map p47; ☑91 774 10 00; www.museoreina sofia.es; Calle de Santa Isabel 52; adult/concession €8/free, 1.30-7pm Sun, 7-9pm Mon & Wed-Sat free; ⊙10am-9pm Mon & Wed-Sat, 10am-7pm Sun; ⓜAtocha) Home to Picasso's *Guernica,* arguably Spain's single-most famous artwork, the Centro de Arte Reina Sofía is Madrid's premier collection of contemporary art. In addition to plenty of paintings by Picasso, other major drawcards are works by Salvador Dalí (1904–89) and Joan Miró (1893–1983). The collection principally spans the 20th century up to the 1980s. The occasional non-Spaniard artist makes an appearance (including Francis Bacon's *Lying Figure;* 1966), but most of the collection is strictly peninsular.

Museo Thyssen-Bornemisza
Museum

(Map p47; ✆902 760511; www.museothyssen.org; Paseo del Prado 8; adult/child €10/free, Mon free; ◷10am-7pm Tue-Sun, noon-4pm Mon; Ⓜ Banco de España) The Thyssen is one of the most extraordinary private collections of predominantly European art in the world. Where the Prado or Reina Sofía enable you to study the body of work of a particular artist in depth, the Thyssen is the place to immerse yourself in a breathtaking breadth of artistic styles. Most of the big names are here, sometimes with just a single painting, but the Thyssen's gift to Madrid and the art-loving public is to have them all under one roof.

Parque del Buen Retiro
Gardens

(Map p47; ◷6am-midnight May-Sep, to 11pm Oct-Apr; Ⓜ Retiro, Príncipe de Vergara, Ibiza, Atocha) The glorious gardens of El Retiro are as beautiful as any you'll find in a European city. Littered with marble monuments, landscaped lawns, the occasional elegant building (the Palacio de Cristal is especially worth seeking out) and abundant greenery, it's quiet and contemplative during the week but comes to life on weekends. Put simply, this is one of our favourite places in Madrid.

Mirador de Madrid
Viewpoint

(Map p47; www.centrocentro.org; 8th fl, Palacio de Comunicaciones, Plaza de la Cibeles; adult/child €2/0.50; ◷10.30am-1.30pm & 4-7pm Tue-Sun; Ⓜ Banco de España) The views from the summit of the Palacio de Comunicaciones are arguably Madrid's best, sweeping west down over Plaza de la Cibeles, up the hill towards the sublime Edificio Metrópolis and out to the mountains. But the views are splendid whichever way you look. Take the lift up to the 6th floor, from where the gates are opened every half hour. From there you can either take another lift or climb the stairs up to the 8th floor.

◉ Salamanca

Plaza de Toros & Museo Taurino
Stadium

(✆91 356 22 00; www.las-ventas.com; Calle de Alcalá 237; ◷10am-5.30pm; Ⓜ Ventas) **FREE** East of central Madrid, the Plaza de Toros Monumental de Las Ventas (Las Ventas) is

Parque del Buen Retiro

ALEX SEGRE / 500PX ©

the most important and prestigious bullring in the world. A visit here – especially as part of a guided tour, which must be booked through **Las Ventas Tour** ([☎]687 739032; www.lasventastour.com; adult/child €14/8; ⊙10am-5.30pm, days of bullfight 10am-1.30pm) in advance – is a good way to gain an insight into this very Spanish tradition. There's also the fine **Museo Taurino** ([☎]91 725 18 57) [FREE], and the architecture will be of interest even to those with no interest in *la corridas* (bullfights).

Museo Lázaro Galdiano   Museum

([☎]91 561 60 84; www.flg.es; Calle de Serrano 122; adult/concession/child €6/3/free, last hour free; ⊙10am-4.30pm Mon & Wed-Sat, 10am-3pm Sun; [M]Gregorio Marañón) This imposing early 20th-century Italianate stone mansion, set discreetly back from the street, belonged to Don José Lázaro Galdiano (1862–1947), a successful businessman and passionate patron of the arts. His astonishing private collection, which he bequeathed to the city upon his death, includes 13,000 works of art and objets d'art, a quarter of which are on show at any time.

◎ Parque del Oeste & Northern Madrid

Ermita de San Antonio de la Florida   Gallery

([☎]91 542 07 22; www.sanantoniodelaflorida.es; Glorieta de San Antonio de la Florida 5; ⊙10am-8pm Tue-Sun, hours vary Jul & Aug; [M]Príncipe Pío) [FREE] The frescoed ceilings of the Ermita de San Antonio de la Florida are one of Madrid's most surprising secrets. It's been recently restored and is also known as the Panteón de Goya. The southern of the two small chapels is one of the few places to see Goya's work in its original setting, as painted by the master in 1798 on the request of Carlos IV. Simply breathtaking.

Plaza de Olavide   Plaza

([M]Bilbao, Iglesia, Quevedo) Plaza de Olavide hasn't always had its current form. From 1934, the entire plaza was occupied by a covered, octagonal market. In November 1974, the market was demolished in a spectacular

📖 Where Are They Buried?

While other countries have turned the graves of famous locals into tourist attractions, Spain has been slow to do the same. But that may be because mystery surrounds the final resting places of some of Spain's most towering historical figures.

According to records, Spain's master painter Diego Velázquez (1599–1660) was buried in the Iglesia de San Juanito, but the church was destroyed in the early 19th century by Joseph Bonaparte to make way for what would later become **Plaza de Ramales** (Map p42; [M]Ópera). Excavations in 2000 revealed the crypt of the former church, but Velázquez was nowhere to be found. Meanwhile, in 1919 the remains Francisco Goya (1746–1828) were entombed in the Ermita de San Antonio de la Florida, the small chapel still adorned by some of Goya's most celebrated frescoes. But his head was never found.

Miguel de Cervantes Saavedra (1547–1616), author of *Don Quijote*, lived much of his life in Madrid and on his death was buried at the **Convento de las Trinitarias** (Map p42; Calle de Lope de Vega 16; [M]Antón Martín). In the centuries that followed, his body was misplaced until, in early 2015, archaeologists announced that they had discovered his bones in a crypt in the convent. Currently the convent is closed to the public, but authorities are considering opening part of it.

Relief of Miguel de Cervantes Saavedra

controlled explosion, opening up the plaza as one of Madrid's most agreeable public spaces. To see the plaza's history told in pictures, step into Bar Méntrida at No 3 for a drink and admire the photos on the wall.

⚙ TOURS

Visitas Guiadas Oficiales   Tour
(Official Guided Tours; Map p42; ☑902 221424; www.esmadrid.com/programa-visitas-guiadas-oficiales; Plaza Mayor 27; per person €17-21; ⓂSol) More than 40 highly recommended walking, cycling and rollerblading tours conducted in Spanish and English. Organised by the Centro de Turismo de Madrid (p64). Stop by the office and pick up its *M – Visitas Guiadas/Guided Tours* catalogue.

Insider's Madrid   Walking Tour
(☑91 447 38 66; www.insidersmadrid.com; tours from €70) An impressive range of tailor-made tours, including walking, shopping, fashion, fine arts, tapas and flamenco tours.

Spanish Tapas Madrid   Tour
(☑672 301231; www.spanishtapasmadrid.com; per person from €40) Local boy Luis Ortega takes you through some iconic Madrid tapas bars; also has tours that take in Old Madrid, flamenco and the Prado.

Wellington Society   Walking Tour
(☑609 143203; www.wellsoc.org; tours €65-90) A handful of quirky historical tours laced with anecdotes and led by the inimitable Stephen Drake-Jones. Membership costs €65 and includes a day or evening walking tour.

Bike Spain   Bicycle Tour
(Map p42; ☑91 559 06 53; www.bikespain.info; Calle del Codo; bike rental half-/full day from €12/18, tours from €35; ☺10am-2pm & 4-7pm Mon-Fri daily Apr-Oct, 10am-2pm & 3-6pm Mon-Fri Nov-Mar; ⓂÓpera) Bicycle hire plus English-language guided city tours by bicycle, by day or (Friday) night, as well as longer expeditions.

🔒 SHOPPING

Our favourite aspect of shopping in Madrid is the city's small boutiques and quirky shops.

Often run by the same families for generations, they counter the over-commercialisation of mass-produced Spanish culture with everything from fashions and rope-soled espadrilles to old-style ceramics and gourmet Spanish food and wine. On Sunday morning, don't forget El Rastro (p41), Madrid's epic flea market.

Antigua Casa Talavera   Ceramics
(Map p50; ☑91 547 34 17; www.antiguacasatalavera.com; Calle de Isabel la Católica 2; ☺10am-1.30pm & 5-8pm Mon-Fri, 10am-1.30pm Sat; ⓂSanto Domingo) The extraordinary tiled facade of this wonderful old shop conceals an Aladdin's cave of ceramics from all over Spain. This is not the mass-produced stuff aimed at a tourist market, but comes from the small family potters of Andalucía and Toledo, ranging from the decorative (tiles) to the useful (plates, jugs and other kitchen items). The couple who run the place are delightful.

El Arco Artesanía   Handicrafts
(Map p42; ☑913 65 26 80; www.artesaniaelarco.com; Plaza Mayor 9; ☺10am-9pm Mon-Sat, 10am-5pm Sun; ⓂSol, La Latina) This original shop in the southwestern corner of Plaza Mayor sells an outstanding array of homemade designer souvenirs, from stone, ceramic and glass work to jewellery and home fittings. The papier-mâché figures are gorgeous, but there's so much else here to turn your head.

Agatha Ruiz de la Prada   Fashion
(Map p50; ☑91 319 05 01; www.agatharuizdelaprada.com; Calle de Serrano 27; ☺10am-8.30pm Mon-Sat; ⓂSerrano) This boutique has to be seen to be believed, with pinks, yellows and oranges everywhere you turn. It's fun and exuberant, but not just for kids. It also has serious and highly original fashion. Agatha Ruiz de la Prada is one of the enduring icons of *la movida,* Madrid's 1980s outpouring of creativity (see p318 for more).

Loewe   Fashion
(Map p50; ☑91 522 68 15; www.loewe.com; Gran Vía 8; ☺10am-8.30pm Mon-Sat, 11am-8pm Sun; ⓂGran Vía) Born in 1846 in Madrid, Loewe is arguably Spain's signature line in high-end

El Retiro & the Art Museums

fashion and its landmark store on Gran Vía is one of the most famous and elegant stores in the capital. Classy handbags and accessories are the mainstays and prices can be jaw-droppingly high, but it's worth stopping by here, even if you don't plan to buy. There's another branch in **Salamanca** (Map p50; ☏91 426 35 88; Calle de Serrano 26 & 34; ☺10am-8.30pm Mon-Sat; Ⓜ Serrano).

María Cabello   Wine
(Map p42; ☏91 429 60 88; Calle de Echegaray 19; ☺9.30am-2.30pm & 5.30-9pm Mon-Fri, 10am-2.30pm & 6.30-9.30pm Sat; Ⓜ Sevilla, Antón Martín) All wine shops should be like this. This family-run corner shop really knows its wines and the interior has scarcely changed since 1913, with wooden shelves and even a faded ceiling fresco. There are fine wines in

abundance (mostly Spanish, and a few foreign bottles), with some 500 labels on show or tucked away out the back.

Tienda Real Madrid — Sports
(☎91 458 72 59; www.realmadrid.com; Gate 55, Estadio Santiago Bernabéu, Avenida de Concha Espina 1; ⊗10am-9pm Mon-Sat, 11am-7.30pm Sun; Ⓜ Santiago Bernabéu) The club shop of Real Madrid sells replica shirts, posters, caps and just about everything else under the sun to which it could attach a club logo. From the shop window, you can see down onto the stadium itself.

⊗ EATING

Madrid has transformed itself into one of Europe's culinary capitals, not least because the city has long been a magnet for people (and cuisines) from all over Spain. Travel from one Spanish village to the next and you'll quickly learn that each has its own speciality; travel to Madrid and you'll find them all.

⊗ Plaza Mayor & Royal Madrid

Casa Revuelta — Tapas €
(Map p42; ☎91 366 33 32; Calle de Latoneros 3; tapas from €2.80; ⊗10.30am-4pm & 7-11pm Tue-Sat, 10.30am-4pm Sun, closed Aug; Ⓜ Sol, La Latina) Casa Revuelta puts out some of Madrid's finest tapas of *bacalao* (cod) bar none – unlike elsewhere, *tajadas de bacalao* don't have bones in them and slide down the throat with the greatest of ease. Early on a Sunday afternoon, as the Rastro crowd gathers here, it's filled to the rafters.

Mercado de San Miguel — Tapas €€
(Map p42; www.mercadodesanmiguel.es; Plaza de San Miguel; tapas from €1; ⊗10am-midnight Sun-Wed, 10am-2am Thu-Sat; Ⓜ Sol) One of Madrid's oldest and most beautiful markets, the Mercado de San Miguel has undergone a stunning major renovation. Within the early 20th-century glass walls, the market has become an inviting space strewn with tables. You can order tapas and sometimes more substantial plates at most of the counter bars, and everything here (from caviar to

Casa Patas (p62)

BRUCE YUANYUE BI / GETTY IMAGES ©

chocolate) is as tempting as the market is alive.

Taberna La Bola   Madrileño €€

(Map p50; ☎91 547 69 30; www.labola.es; Calle de la Bola 5; mains €16-24; ⓘ1.30-4.30pm & 8.30-11pm Mon-Sat, 1.30-4.30pm Sun, closed Aug; MSanto Domingo) Taberna La Bola (going since 1870 and run by the sixth generation of the Verdasco family) has a much-loved trad- itional Madrid cuisine. If you're going to try *cocido a la madrileña* (chickpea-and-meat stew; €21), this is a good place to do so. It's busy and noisy and very Madrid.

Restaurante Sobrino
de Botín   Castilian €€€

(Map p42; ☎91 366 42 17; www.botin.es; Calle de los Cuchilleros 17; mains €19-27; ⓘ1-4pm & 8pm-midnight; MLa Latina, Sol) It's not every day that you can eat in the oldest restaurant in the world (the *Guinness Book of Records* has recognised it as the oldest – established in 1725). The secret of its staying power is fine *cochinillo asado* (roast suckling pig; €25) and *cordero asado* (roast lamb; €25) cooked in wood-fired ovens. Eating in the vaulted cellar is a treat.

😮 La Latina & Lavapiés
Almendro 13   Tapas €

(Map p42; ☎91 365 42 52; Calle del Almendro 13; mains €7-15; ⓘ1-4pm & 7.30pm-midnight Sun-Thu, 1-5pm & 8pm-1am Fri & Sat; MLa Latina) Almendro 13 is a charming *taberna* (tavern) where you come for traditional Spanish tapas with an emphasis on quality rather than frilly elaborations. Cured meats, cheeses, omelettes and variations on these themes dominate the menu.

Taberna Txakolina   Tapas €

(Map p42; ☎91 366 48 77; www.tabernatxakolina madrid.com; Calle de la Cava Baja 26; tapas from €4; ⓘ8pm-midnight Tue, 1-4pm & 8pm-midnight Wed-Sat, 1-4pm Sun; MLa Latina) Taberna Txako- lina calls its *pintxos* 'high cuisine in miniature'. If ordering tapas makes you nervous be- cause you don't speak Spanish or you're not quite sure how it works, it couldn't be easier here – they're lined up on the bar, Basque

style, in all their glory, and you can simply point. Whatever you order, wash it down with *txacoli*, a sharp Basque white.

Juana La Loca   Tapas €€

(Map p42; ☎91 364 05 25; Plaza de la Puerta de Moros 4; tapas from €5, mains €8-19; ⓘnoon-1am Tue-Sun, 8pm-1am Mon; MLa Latina) Juana La Loca does a range of creative tapas with tempting options lined up along the bar, and more on the menu that they prepare to order. But we love it above all for its *tortilla de patatas,* which is distinguished from others of its kind by the caramelised onions – yum!

Txirimiri   Tapas €€

(Map p42; ☎91 364 11 96; www.txirimiri.es; Calle del Humilladero 6; tapas from €4; ⓘnoon 4.30pm & 8.30pm-midnight Mon-Sat, closed Aug; MLa Latina) This *pintxos* (Basque tapas) bar is a great little discovery just down from the main La Latina tapas circuit. Wonderful wines, gorgeous *pintxos* (tapas; the *tortilla de patatas* – potato and onion omelette – is superb) and fine risottos add up to a pretty special combination.

Taberna
Matritum   Modern Spanish €€

(Map p42; ☎91 365 82 37; Calle de la Cava Alta 17; mains €12-22; ⓘ1.30-4pm & 8.30pm-midnight Wed-Sun, 8.30pm-midnight Mon & Tue; MLa Lati- na) This little gem is reason enough to detour from the more popular Calle de la Cava Baja next door. The seasonal menu here encom- passes terrific tapas, salads and generally creative cooking – try the *cocido* croquettes or the winter *calçots* (large spring onions) from Catalonia. The wine list runs into the hundreds and it's sophisticated without being pretentious. Highly recommended.

Malacatín   Madrileño €€

(Map p42; ☎91 365 52 41; www.malacatin.com; Calle de Ruda 5; mains €11-15; ⓘ11am-5.30pm Mon-Sat & 8.15-11pm Thu & Fri, closed Aug; MLa Latina) If you want to see *madrileños* (people from Madrid) enjoying their favourite local food, this is one of the best places to do so. The clamour of conversation bounces off the tiled walls of the cramped dining area adorned with bullfighting memorabilia. The

Malasaña, Chueca & Salamanca

0 500 m
0.25 miles

See El Retiro & the Art Museums Map (p47)

See Madrid Centro Map (p42)

Malasaña, Chueca & Salamanca

speciality is as much *cocido* as you can eat
(€20). The *degustación de cocido* (taste of
cocido; €5) at the bar is a great way to try
Madrid's favourite dish.

El Estragón
Vegetarian €€

(Map p42; ✆91 365 89 82; www.elestragon
vegetariano.com; Plaza de la Paja 10; mains
€8-15; ⊙11.30am-midnight; ✓; ⓂLa Latina) A
delightful spot for crêpes, vegie burgers and
other vegetarian specialities, El Estragón
is undoubtedly one of Madrid's best
vegetarian restaurants, although attentive
vegans won't appreciate the use of butter.
Apart from that, we're yet to hear a bad
word about it, and the *menú del día* (daily
set menu; from €9) is one of Madrid's best
bargains.

Casa Lucio
Spanish €€€

(Map p42; ✆91 365 82 17, 91 365 32 52; www.
casalucio.es; Calle de la Cava Baja 35; mains €18-
28; ⊙1-4pm & 8.30pm-midnight, closed Aug; ⓂLa
Latina) Lucio has been wowing *madrileños*
with his light touch, quality ingredients and
home-style local cooking since 1974 – think
eggs (a Lucio speciality) and roasted meats

in abundance. There's also *rabo de toro*
(bull's tail) during the Fiestas de San Isidro
Labrador and plenty of *rioja* (red wine) to
wash away the mere thought of it.

Posada de la Villa
Madrileño €€€

(Map p42; ✆91 366 18 80; www.posadadelavilla.
com; Calle de la Cava Baja 9; mains €19-28; ⊙1-
4pm & 8pm-midnight Mon-Sat, 1-4pm Sun, closed
Aug; ⓂLa Latina) This wonderfully restored
17th-century *posada* (inn) is something of a
local landmark. The atmosphere is formal,
the decoration sombre and traditional
(heavy timber and brickwork), and the cuisine decidedly local – roast meats, *cocido*,
callos (tripe) and *sopa de ajo* (garlic soup).

🍴 Sol, Santa Ana & Huertas

Casa Labra
Tapas €

(Map p42; ✆91 532 14 05; www.casalabra.es;
Calle de Tetuán 11; tapas from €1.25; ⊙11.30am-
3.30pm & 6-11pm; ⓂSol) Casa Labra has been
going strong since 1860, an era that the
decor strongly evokes. Locals love their
bacalao (cod) and ordering it here – either
as deep-fried tapas (*una tajada de bacalao*

🍽️ Madrid Culinary Specialities

When the weather turns chilly in Madrid that traditionally means *sopa de ajo* (garlic soup) and *legumbres* (legumes) such as *garbanzos* (chickpeas), *judías* (beans) and *lentejas* (lentils). Hearty stews are the order of the day and there are none more hearty than *cocido a la madrileña;* it's a kind of hotpot that starts with a noodle broth and is followed by or combined with carrots, chickpeas, chicken, *morcilla* (blood sausage), beef, lard and possibly other sausage meats – there are as many ways of eating *cocido* as there are *madrileños*. *Repollo* (cabbage) sometimes makes an appearance. Madrid shares with much of the Spanish interior a love of roasted meats. More specifically, *asado de cordero lechal* (spring lamb roasted in a wood-fired oven) is a winter obsession in Madrid. Less celebrated (it's all relative), is *cochinillo asado* (roast suckling pig) from the Segovia region northwest of Madrid.

Cocido a la madrileña
ARCHEOPHOTO / GETTY IMAGES ©

goes for €1.30) or as *una croqueta de bacalao* – is a Madrid rite of initiation. As the lunchtime queues attest, Casa Labra goes through more than 700kg of cod every week.

Las Bravas   Tapas €

(Map p42; ☑91 522 85 81; www.lasbravas. com; Callejón de Álvarez Gato 3; raciones €3.75-12; ⊗12.30-4.30pm & 7.30pm-12.30am; Ⓜ Sol, Sevilla) Las Bravas has long been the place

for a *caña* (small glass of beer) and some of the best *patatas bravas* (fried potatoes with a spicy tomato sauce; €3.75) in town. In fact, their version of the *bravas* sauce is so famous that they patented it. Other good orders include *calamares* (calamari) and *oreja a la plancha* (grilled pig's ear).

La Finca de Susana   Spanish €

(Map p42; ☑91 369 35 57; www.grupandilana. com/es/restaurantes/la-finca-de-susana; Calle de Arlabán 4; mains €7-12; ⊗1-3.45pm & 8.30-11.30pm Sun-Wed, 1-3.45pm & 8.15pm-midnight Thu-Sat; Ⓜ Sevilla) It's difficult to find a better combination of price, quality cooking and classy atmosphere anywhere in Huertas. The softly lit dining area is bathed in greenery and the sometimes innovative, sometimes traditional food draws a hip young crowd. The duck confit with plums, turnips and couscous is a fine choice. No reservations.

Casa Alberto   Tapas €€

(Map p42; ☑91 429 93 56; www.casaalberto.es; Calle de las Huertas 18; tapas €4-10, raciones €6.50-16, mains €14-21; ⊗restaurant 1.30-4pm & 8pm-midnight Tue-Sat, 1.30-4pm Sun, bar 12.30pm-1.30am Tue-Sat, 12.30-4pm Sun, closed Sun Jul & Aug; Ⓜ Antón Martín) One of the most atmospheric old *tabernas* (taverns) in Madrid, Casa Alberto has been around since 1827 and occupies a building where Cervantes is said to have written one of his books. The secret to its staying power is vermouth on tap, excellent tapas at the bar and fine sit-down meals.

Ramiro's Tapas Wine Bar   Tapas €€

(Map p42; ☑91 843 73 47; Calle de Atocha 51; tapas from €4.50, raciones from €10; ⊗1-4.30pm & 8-11.30pm Mon-Sat, 1-4.30pm Sun; Ⓜ Antón Martín) One of the best tapas bars to open in Madrid in recent years, this fine gastrobar offers up traditional tapas with subtle but original touches. Most of the cooking comes from Castilla y León but they do exceptional things with cured meats, foie gras and prawns. Highly recommended.

Vi Cool
Modern Spanish €€

(Map p42; ☑91 429 49 13; www.vi-cool.com; Calle de las Huertas 12; mains €8-19; ⊕1.30-4.15pm & 8.30pm-12.15am Tue-Sun; MAntón Martín) Catalan master chef Sergi Arola is one of the most restless and relentlessly creative culinary talents in the country. Aside from his showpiece **Sergi Arola Gastro** (☑91 310 21 69; www.sergiarola.es; Calle de Zurbano 31; mains €49-58, set menus €49-195; ⊕2-3.30pm & 9-11.30pm Tue-Sat Sep-May; MAlonso Martínez), he has dabbled in numerous new restaurants around the capital and in Barcelona, and this is one of his most interesting yet.

Los Gatos
Tapas €€

(Map p42; ☑91 429 30 67; Calle de Jesús 2; tapas from €3.50; ⊕11am-2am; MAntón Martín) Tapas you can point to without deciphering the menu and eclectic old-world decor (from bullfighting memorabilia to a fresco of skeletons at the bar) make this a popular choice down the bottom end of Huertas. The most popular orders are the canapés (tapas on toast), which, we have to say, are rather delicious.

La Casa del Abuelo
Tapas €€

(Map p42; ☑902 027334; www.lacasadel abuelo.es; Calle de la Victoria 12; raciones from €9.50; ⊕noon-midnight Sun-Thu, noon-1am Fri & Sat; MSol) The 'House of the Grandfather' is an ageless, popular place, which recently passed its centenary. The traditional order here is a *chato* (small glass) of the heavy, sweet El Abuelo red wine (made in Toledo province) and the heavenly *gambas a la plancha* (grilled prawns) or *gambas al ajillo* (prawns sizzling in garlic on little ceramic plates).

Lhardy
Spanish €€€

(Map p42; ☑91 521 33 85; www.lhardy. com; Carrera de San Jerónimo 8; mains €19-38; ⊕1-3.30pm & 8.30-11pm Mon-Sat, 1-3.30pm Sun, closed Aug; MSol, Sevilla) This Madrid landmark (since 1839) is an elegant treasure trove of takeaway gourmet tapas downstairs, while the six upstairs dining areas are the upmarket preserve of traditional Madrid dishes with an occasional hint of French influence. House specialities include *cocido a la madrileña* (meat-and-chickpea stew;

Convento de las Descalzas Reales (p41)

€36), pheasant and wild duck in an orange perfume.

⊗ El Retiro & the Art Museums

Estado Puro Tapas €€

(Map p47; ☎91 330 24 00; www.tapasenestado puro.com; Plaza Neptuno/Plaza de Cánovas del Castillo 4; tapas €5-16, mains €13-22; ⊙noon-midnight Mon-Sat, noon-4pm Sun; Ⓜ Banco de España, Atocha) A slick but casual tapas bar, Estado Puro serves up fantastic tapas, such as the *tortilla española siglo XXI* (21st-century Spanish omelette, served in a glass...), lobster gazpacho and Parmesan ice cream. The kitchen here is overseen by Paco Roncero, the head chef at **La Terraza del Casino** (Map p42; ☎91 532 12 75; www. casinodemadrid.es; Calle de Alcalá 15; mains €35-45, lunch set menu €69; ⊙1-4pm & 9pm-midnight Mon-Sat; Ⓜ Sevilla), who learned his trade with master chef Ferran Adrià.

⊗ Salamanca

Platea Spanish €€

(Map p50; ☎91 577 00 25; www.plateamadrid. com; Calle de Goya 5-7; ⊙12.30pm-12.30am Sun-Wed, 12.30pm-2.30am Thu-Sat; Ⓜ Serrano, Colón)

Platea is one of the most exciting things to happen in Madrid's eating scene in years. The ornate Carlos III cinema opposite the Plaza de Colón has been artfully transformed into a dynamic culinary scene with more than a hint of burlesque. There are 12 restaurants (among them the outstanding Arriba), three gourmet food stores and cocktail bars. The chefs here boast six Michelin stars among them.

Working with the original theatre-style layout, the developers have used the multi-level seating to array a series of restaurants that seem at once self-contained yet connected to the whole through the soaring open central space, with all of them in some way facing the stage area where cabaret-style or 1930s-era performances or live cooking shows provide a rather glamorous backdrop. It's where food court meets haute cuisine, a daring combination of lunch or dinner with floorshow without the formality that usually infuses such places.

Biotza Tapas, Basque €€

(Map p50; ☎91 781 03 13; Calle de Claudio Coello 27; cold/hot pintxos €2.80/3.40, raciones from

From left: Scallops; Vermouth, Casa Alberto (p52); Mercado de San Miguel (p48)

€6, set menus from €18; ⊘1-5pm & 8pm-midnight Mon-Sat; ⓂSerrano) This breezy Basque tapas bar is one of the best places in Madrid to sample the creativity of bite-sized *pintxos* (Basque tapas) as only the Basques can make them. It's the perfect combination of San Sebastián–style tapas, Madrid-style pale-green/red-black decoration and unusual angular benches. The prices quickly add up, but it's highly recommended nonetheless. There's also a more formal Basque restaurant out the back.

José Luis · Spanish €€

(☎91 563 09 58; www.joseluis.es; Calle de Serrano 89; tapas from €5; ⊘8.30am-1am Mon-Fri, 9am-1am Sat, 12.30pm-1am Sun; ⓂGregorio Marañón) With numerous branches around Madrid, José Luis is famous for its fidelity to traditional Spanish recipes. It wins many people's vote for Madrid's best *tortilla de patatas* (Spanish potato omelette), but it's also good for *croquetas* (croquettes) and *ensaladilla rusa* (Russian salad). This outpost along Calle de Serrano has a slightly stuffy, young-men-in-suits feel to it, which is, after all, *very* Salamanca.

⊗ Malasaña & Chueca

Bazaar · Modern Spanish €

(Map p50; ☎91 523 39 05; www.restaurant bazaar.com; Calle de la Libertad 21; mains €6.50-10; ⊘1.15-4pm & 8.30-11.30pm Sun-Wed, 1.15-4pm & 8.15pm-midnight Thu-Sat; ⓂChueca) Bazaar's popularity among the well-heeled Chueca set shows no sign of abating. Its pristine white interior design, with theatre-style lighting and wall-length windows, may draw a crowd that looks like it's stepped out of the pages of *¡Hola!* magazine, but the food is extremely well priced and innovative, and the atmosphere is casual.

Casa Julio · Spanish €

(Map p50; ☎91 522 72 74; Calle de la Madera 37; 6/12 croquetas €5/10; ⊘1-3.30pm & 6.30-11pm Mon-Sat Sep-Jul; ⓂTribunal) A city-wide poll for the best *croquetas* (croquettes) in Madrid would see half of those polled voting for Casa Julio and the remainder not doing so only because they haven't been yet. They're that good that celebrities and mere mortals from all over Madrid come here, along with the crusty old locals.

Basílicia de San Francisco El Grande (p41)

Baco y Beto — Tapas €

(Map p50; 📞91 522 84 41; Calle de Pelayo 24; tapas from €4; ⏰8pm-1am Mon-Fri, 2-4.30pm & 8.30pm-1am Sat; Ⓜ Chueca) Friends of ours in Madrid begged us not to include this place in our reviews and we must admit that we were tempted to keep this secret all to ourselves. Some of the tastiest tapas in the city are what you'll find here. The clientele is predominantly gay, and they, like our friends, can't have it all to themselves.

Bodega de la Ardosa — Tapas €

(Map p50; 📞91 521 49 79; www.laardosa.es; Calle de Colón 13; tapas & raciones €4-11; ⏰8.30am-2am Mon-Fri, 12.45pm-2.30am Sat & Sun; Ⓜ Tribunal) Going strong since 1892, the charming, wood-panelled bar of Bodega de la Ardosa is brimful of charm. To come here and not try the *salmorejo* (cold tomato soup made with bread, oil, garlic and vinegar), *croquetas* or *tortilla de patatas* (potato and onion omelette) would be a crime. On weekend nights there's scarcely room to move.

Albur — Tapas €€

(Map p50; 📞91 594 27 33; www.restaurante albur.com; Calle de Manuela Malasaña 15; mains €11-16; ⏰1-5pm & 8pm-12.30am Mon-Fri, 1pm-1am Sat & Sun; Ⓜ Bilbao) One of Malasaña's best deals, this place has a wildly popular tapas bar and a classy but casual restaurant out the back. The restaurant waiters never seem to lose their cool, and their extremely well-priced rice dishes are the stars of the show, although in truth you could order anything here and leave well satisfied.

Bon Vivant & Co — Seafood €€

(Map p50; 📞91 704 82 86; www.bonvivantco.es; Calle de San Gregorio 8; mains €9-15; ⏰9am-1am Mon-Fri, 10am-2am Sat & Sun; Ⓜ Chueca) What a lovely little spot this is. Set on a tiny square, its wooden tables flooded with natural light through the big windows, Bon Vivant & Co is ideal for a casual meal, a quietly intimate encounter or simply an afternoon spent reading the papers. Food is simple but tasty – tapas, focaccias, salads, brunch...

La Musa
Spanish, Fusion €€

(Map p50; ✆91 448 75 58; www.grupolamusa. com; Calle de Manuela Malasaña 18; cold/hot tapas from €4/6, mains €11-16; ⊗9am-midnight Mon-Thu, 9am-1am Fri, 1pm-2am Sat, 1pm-midnight Sun; ⓂSan Bernardo) Snug, loud and unpretentious, La Musa is all about designer decor, lounge music and memorably fun food. The menu is divided into three types of tapas – hot, cold and barbecue. Among the hot varieties is the fantastic *jabalí con ali-oli de miel y sobrasada* (wild boar with honey mayonnaise and *sobrasada* – a soft and spreadable mildly spicy sausage from Mallorca).

Maricastaña
Spanish €€

(Map p50; ✆91 082 71 42; www.maricastana madrid.com; Corredera Baja de San Pablo 12; mains €9-19; ⊗9am-2am Mon-Thu, 9am-2.30am Fri & Sat, 10am-2am Sun; ⓂCallao) This fabulous find sits in the increasingly cool corner of Malasaña that is flourishing just off the back of Gran Vía. The decor is quite lovely, all potted plants, creative lighting, iron pillars and rustic brickwork. The food is simple but excellent – try the pumpkin croquettes or the tuna pieces with bean shoots and strawberries.

La Tasquita de Enfrente
Modern Spanish €€€

(Map p50; ✆91 532 54 49; www.latasquitade enfrente.com; Calle de la Ballesta 6; mains €17-32, set menus €45-69; ⊗1.30-4.30pm & 8.30pm-midnight Mon-Sat; ⓂGran Vía) It's difficult to overstate how popular this place is among people in the know in Madrid's food scene. The seasonal menu prepared by chef Juanjo López never ceases to surprise while also combining simple Spanish staples to stunning effect. His *menú de degustación* (tasting menu; €50) or *menú de Juanjo* (€65) would be our choice if this is your first time. Reservations are essential.

🍷 DRINKING & NIGHTLIFE

Nights in the Spanish capital are the stuff of legend. They're invariably long and loud most nights of the week, rising to a deafening crescendo as the weekend nears. And what Ernest Hemingway wrote of the city in the 1930s remains true to this day: 'Nobody goes to bed in Madrid until they have killed the night.'

🍷 Plaza Mayor & Royal Madrid

Teatro Joy Eslava
Club

(Joy Madrid; Map p42; ✆91 366 37 33; www. joy-eslava.com; Calle del Arenal 11; ⊗11.30pm-6am; ⓂSol) The only things guaranteed at this grand old Madrid dance club (housed in a 19th-century theatre) are a crowd and the fact that it'll be open (it claims to have operated every single day for the past 29 years). The music and the crowd are a mixed bag, but queues are long and invariably include locals and tourists, and even the occasional *famoso* (celebrity).

Chocolatería de San Ginés
Cafe

(Map p42; ✆91 365 65 46; www.chocolateria sangines.com; Pasadizo de San Ginés 5; ⊗24hr; ⓂSol) One of the grand icons of the Madrid night, this *chocolate con churros* cafe sees a sprinkling of tourists throughout the day, but locals pack it out in their search for sustenance on their way home from a nightclub somewhere close to dawn. Only in Madrid...

The Sherry Corner
Wine Bar

(Map p42; ✆681 007700; www.sherry-corner. com; Stall 24, Mercado de San Miguel, Plaza de San Miguel; ⊗10am-9pm; ⓂSol) The Sherry Corner, inside the Mercado de San Miguel, has found an excellent way to give a crash course in sherry. For €25, you get six small glasses of top-quality sherry to taste, each of which is matched to a different tapa. Guiding you through the process is an audioguide in eight languages (Spanish, English, German, French, Italian, Portuguese, Russian and Japanese).

Charada
Club

(Map p50; ✆663 230504; www.charada.es; Calle de la Bola 13; ⊗midnight-6am Wed-Sun; ⓂSanto Domingo) Charada is a reliable regular on the Madrid clubbing scene. Its two rooms (one red, the other black) are New York chic with no hint of the building's former

What's On in Madrid?

EsMadrid Magazine (www.esmadrid.com) Monthly tourist office listings.

Guía del Ocio (www.guiadelocio.com) Weekly magazine available for €1 at news kiosks.

In Madrid (www.in-madrid.com) Free monthly English-language expat publication.

Metropoli (www.elmundo.es/metropoli) *El Mundo* newspaper's Friday supplement magazine.

existence as a brothel. The cocktails are original and we especially like it when they turn their attention to electronica, but they also do disco and house. Admission is €12.

Anticafé   Cafe
(Map p42; Calle de la Unión 2; ⊗5pm-2am Tue-Sun; MÓpera) Bohemian kitsch in the best sense is the prevailing theme here and it runs right through the decor, regular cultural events (poetry readings and concerts) and, of course, the clientele. As such, it won't be to everyone's taste, but we think that it adds some much-needed variety to the downtown drinking scene.

Café del Real   Bar
(Map p42; ⌨91 547 21 24; Plaza de Isabel II 2; ⊗8am-1am Mon-Thu, 8am-2.30am Fri, 9am-2.30am Sat, 10am-11.30pm Sun; MÓpera) A cafe and cocktail bar in equal parts, this intimate little place serves up creative coffees and a few cocktails to the soundtrack of chill-out music. The best seats are upstairs, where the low ceilings, wooden beams and leather chairs make for a great place to pass an afternoon with friends.

🍸 La Latina & Lavapiés
Taberna Tempranillo   Wine Bar
(Map p42; Calle de la Cava Baja 38; ⊗1-3.30pm & 8pm-midnight Tue-Sun, 8pm-midnight Mon; MLa Latina) You could come here for the tapas, but we recommend Taberna Tempranillo

primarily for its wines, of which it has a selection that puts numerous Spanish bars to shame; many wines are sold by the glass. It's not a late-night place, but it's always packed in the early evening and on Sundays after El Rastro.

Delic   Bar
(Map p42; ⌨91 364 54 50; www.delic.es; Costanilla de San Andrés 14; ⊗11am-2am Sun & Tue-Thu, 11am-2.30am Fri & Sat; MLa Latina) We could go on for hours about this long-standing cafe-bar, but we'll reduce it to its most basic elements: nursing an exceptionally good mojito (€8) or three on a warm summer's evening at Delic's outdoor tables on one of Madrid's prettiest plazas is one of life's great pleasures. Bliss.

Taberna Chica   Bar
(Map p42; ⌨683 269114; Costanilla de San Pedro 7; ⊗8pm-2am Mon-Thu, 5pm-2am Fri, 1pm-2am Sat & Sun; MLa Latina) Most of those who come to this narrow little bar are after one of two things: the famous Santa Teresa rum that comes served in an extra-large mug, or some of the finest mojitos in Madrid. The music is chill-out with a nod to lounge, which makes it an ideal pit stop if you're hoping for conversation.

🍸 Sol, Santa Ana & Huertas
La Venencia   Bar
(Map p42; ⌨91 429 73 13; Calle de Echegaray 7; ⊗12.30-3.30pm & 7.30pm-1.30am; MSol, Sevilla) La Venencia is a *barrio* classic, with fine sherry from Sanlúcar and *manzanilla* from Jeréz poured straight from the dusty wooden barrels, accompanied by a small selection of tapas with an Andalucian bent. Otherwise, there's no music, no flashy decorations; it's all about you, your *fino* (sherry) and your friends. As one reviewer put it, it's 'a classic among classics'.

Taberna La Dolores   Bar
(Map p42; ⌨91 429 22 43; Plaza de Jesús 4; ⊗11am-1am; MAntón Martín) Old bottles and beer mugs line the shelves behind the bar at this Madrid institution (1908), known for its blue-and-white-tiled exterior and for a thirty-

Plaza de Santa Ana (p41)

something crowd that often includes the odd *famoso* (celebrity) or two. It claims to be 'the most famous bar in Madrid' – that's pushing it, but it's invariably full most nights of the week, so who are we to argue?

It serves good house wine, great anchovies and what Spaniards like to call 'well-poured beer'.

El Imperfecto   Cocktail Bar

(Map p42; Plaza de Matute 2; ☺5pm-2.30am Mon-Thu, 3pm-2.30am Fri & Sat; Ⓜ Antón Martín) Its name notwithstanding, the 'Imperfect One' is our ideal Huertas bar, with occasional live jazz and a drinks menu as long as a saxophone, ranging from cocktails (€7, or two *mojitos* for €10) and spirits to milkshakes, teas and creative coffees. Its pina colada is one of the best we've tasted and the atmosphere is agreeably buzzy yet chilled.

La Terraza del Urban   Cocktail Bar

(Map p42; ☑91 787 77 70; Carrera de San Jerónimo 34; ☺noon-8pm Sun & Mon, noon-3am Tue-Sat mid-May–Sep; Ⓜ Sevilla) A strong contender with The Roof and **Splash Óscar** (La Terraza de Arriba; Map p50; Plaza de Vázquez de

Mella 12; ☺6.30pm-2.30am Wed & Thu, 4.30pm-2.30am Fri-Sun mid-May–mid-Sep; Ⓜ Gran Vía) for the prize for best rooftop bar in Madrid, this indulgent terrace sits atop the five-star Urban Hotel and has five-star views with five-star prices. Worth every euro, but it's only open while the weather's warm, usually from sometime in May to latish September.

🍷 Malasaña & Chueca

Café Belén   Bar

(Map p50; ☑91 308 27 47; www.elcafebelen. com; Calle de Belén 5; ☺3.30pm-3am Tue-Thu, 3.30pm-3.30am Fri, 1pm-3.30am Sat, 1-10pm Sun; Ⓜ Chueca) Café Belén is cool in all the right places – lounge and chill-out music, dim lighting, a great range of drinks (the mojitos are especially good) and a low-key crowd that's the height of casual sophistication. It's one of our preferred Chueca watering holes.

Museo Chicote   Cocktail Bar

(Map p50; ☑91 532 67 37; www.grupomercado delareina.com/en/museo-chicote-en/; Gran Vía 12; ☺5pm-3am Mon-Thu, to 3.30am Fri & Sat; Ⓜ Gran Vía) This place is a Madrid landmark, complete with its 1930s-era interior, and its founder is said to have invented more than 100 cocktails, which the likes of Hemingway, Ava Gardner, Grace Kelly, Sophia Loren and Frank Sinatra have all enjoyed at one time or another. It's at its best after midnight, when a lounge atmosphere takes over, couples cuddle on the curved benches and some of the city's best DJs do their stuff.

1862 Dry Bar   Cocktail Bar

(Map p50; ☎609 531151; Calle del Pez 27; ⏱3.30pm-2am Mon-Thu, 3.30pm-2.30am Fri & Sat, 3.30-10.30pm Sun; Ⓜ Noviciado) Fab cocktails, muted early 20th-century decor and a refined air make this one of our favourite bars down Malasaña's southern end. Prices are reasonable, the cocktail list extensive and new cocktails appear every month.

Café-Restaurante El Espejo   Cafe

(Map p50; ☎91 308 23 47; www.restaurante elespejo.com; Paseo de los Recoletos 31; ⏱8am-midnight; Ⓜ Colón) Once a haunt of writers and intellectuals, this architectural gem blends Modernista and art-deco styles and its interior could well overwhelm you

with all the mirrors, chandeliers and bow-tied service of another era. The atmosphere is suitably quiet and refined, although our favourite corner is the elegant glass pavilion out on the Paseo de los Recoletos.

Le Cabrera   Cocktail Bar

(Map p50; ☎91 319 94 57; www.lecabrera.com; Calle de Bárbara de Braganza 2; ⏱7pm-2am Sun, Wed & Thu, 7pm-2.30am Fri & Sat; Ⓜ Colón, Alonso Martínez) In the basement below the exciting **tapas bar** (tapas €3.50-22; ⏱8pm-midnight Wed, Thu & Sun, 8pm-2.30am Fri & Sat) of the same name, this cocktail bar is every bit as appealing. The 60-plus different cocktail varieties are the work of Diego Cabrera, the long-standing barman of renowned master chef Sergi Arola.

Café de Mahón   Cafe

(Map p50; ☎91 532 47 56; Plaza del Dos de Mayo 4; ⏱noon-1.30am Mon-Thu, to 3am Fri-Sun; Ⓜ Bilbao) If we had to choose our favourite slice of Malasaña life, this engaging little cafe, whose outdoor tables watch out over Plaza del Dos de Mayo, would be a prime candidate. It's beloved by *famosos*

Calle de las Huertas

(celebrities) as much as by the locals catching up for a quiet drink with friends.

El Jardín Secreto — Bar

(Map p50; 91 541 80 23; www.eljardinsecreto madrid; Calle del Conde Duque 2; ⊗5.30pm-12.30am Sun-Wed, 6.30pm-1.30am Thu, 6.30pm-2.30am Fri & Sat; M Plaza de España) 'The Secret Garden' is intimate and romantic in a *barrio* that's one of Madrid's best-kept secrets. Lit by Spanish designer candles, draped in organza from India and serving up chocolates from the Caribbean, El Jardín Secreto ranks among our most favoured drinking corners in Conde Duque. It serves milkshakes, cocktails and everything in between.

Fábrica Maravillas — Bar, Brewery

(Map p50; 915 21 87 53; www.fmaravillas. com; Calle de Valverde 29; ⊗6pm-midnight Mon-Fri, 12.30pm-midnight Sat & Sun; M Tribunal, Gran Vía) Spain has taken its time in getting behind the worldwide trend of boutique or artisan beers, but it's finally starting to happen. The finest example of this in Madrid is Fábrica Maravillas, a microbrewery known for its 'Malasaña Ale'.

Café Manuela — Cafe

(Map p50; 91 531 70 37; Calle de San Vicente Ferrer 29; ⊗4pm-2am Sun-Thu, 4pm-2.30am Fri & Sat; M Tribunal) Stumbling into this graciously restored throwback to the 1950s along one of Malasaña's grittier streets is akin to discovering hidden treasure. There's a luminous quality to it when you come in out of the night and, like so many Madrid cafes, it's a surprisingly multifaceted space, serving cocktails, delicious milkshakes and offering board games atop the marble tables.

Bar El 2D — Bar

(Map p50; 91 445 88 39; Calle de Velarde 24; ⊗noon-2am; M Tribunal) One of the enduring symbols of *la movida madrileña*, El 2D's fluted columns, 1970s-brown walls and 1980s music suggest that it hasn't quite arrived in the 21st century yet. No one seems to care.

El Rincón de Jerez

Out in the eastern reaches of Salamanca, the Andalucian bar **El Rincón de Jerez** (91 112 30 80; www.elnuevorincon dejerez.es; Calle de Rufino Blanco 5; raciones €7-13; ⊗1-4.30pm & 7pm-midnight Tue-Sat, 1-4.30pm Sun Sep-Jul; M Manuel Bacerra) is utterly unlike anywhere else in Madrid. At 11pm from Tuesday to Saturday, they turn off the lights, light the candles and sing as one 'La Salve Rociera', a near mythical song with deep roots in the flamenco and Catholic traditions of the south. It'll send chills down your spine.

Cerveza (beer)
CARLOS GOGGIO / GETTY IMAGES ©

Café Acuarela — Cafe

(Map p50; 91 522 21 43; www.cafeacuarela. es; Calle de Gravina 10; ⊗11am-2am Sun-Thu, 11am-3am Fri & Sat; M Chueca) A few steps up the hill from Plaza de Chueca and long a centrepiece of gay Madrid – a huge statue of a nude male angel guards the doorway – this is an agreeable, dimly lit salon decorated with, among other things, religious icons.

Antigua Casa Ángel Sierra — Taverna

(Map p50; 91 531 01 26; Calle de Gravina 11; ⊗noon-1am; M Chueca) This historic old *taberna* is the antithesis of modern Chueca chic – it has hardly changed since it opened in 1917. As Spaniards like to say, the beer on tap is very 'well poured' here and there's also vermouth on tap. Fronting onto the vibrant Plaza de Chueca, it can get pretty lively of a weekend evening when it spills over onto the plaza.

Football Celebrations

The battle for football supremacy in Madrid is rarely confined to the stadiums. Whenever Real Madrid wins a major trophy, crowds head for the **Plaza de la Cibeles** (Map p50; MBanco de España) to celebrate in their hundreds and thousands. To protect the fountain, the city council boards up the statue and surrounds it with police on the eve of important matches. A little further down the Paseo del Prado, **Plaza de Neptuno** (Plaza de Cánovas del Castillo; Map p47; MBanco de España) is where fans of Atlético de Madrid hold equally popular (and every bit as destructive) celebrations.

Spanish football fans, Plaza de la Cibeles
PEDRO RUFO / SHUTTERSTOCK ©

Bar Cock   Cocktail Bar

(Map p50; ☎91 532 28 26; www.barcock. com; Calle de la Reina 16; ⏱4pm-3am Mon-Fri, 7pm-3am Sat & Sun; MGran Vía) With a name like this, Bar Cock could go either way, but it's definitely cock as in 'rooster', so the atmosphere is elegant and classic rather than risqué. The decor evokes an old gentlemen's club, but it is beloved by A-list celebrities and A-list wannabes, and a refined thirty-something crowd who come here for the lively atmosphere and great cocktails. On weekends all the tables seem to be reserved, so be prepared to hover on the fringes of fame.

Del Diego   Cocktail Bar

(Map p50; ☎91 523 31 06; www.deldiego.com; Calle de la Reina 12; ⏱7pm-3am Mon-Thu, 7pm-3.30am Fri & Sat; MGran Vía) Del Diego is one of the city's most celebrated cocktail bars. The decor blends old-world cafe with New York style, and it's the sort of place where the music rarely drowns out the conversation. Even with around 75 cocktails to choose from, we'd still order the signature 'El Diego' (vodka, advocaat, apricot brandy and lime).

Why Not?   Club

(Map p50; ☎91 521 80 34; www.whynotmadrid. com; Calle de San Bartolomé 7; ⏱10.30pm-6am; MChueca) Underground, narrow and packed with bodies, gay-friendly Why Not? is the sort of place where nothing's left to the imagination (the gay and straight crowd who come here are pretty amorous) and it's full nearly every night of the week. Pop and Top 40 music are the standard here, and the dancing crowd is mixed and serious about having a good time. We're not huge fans of the bouncers here, but once you get past them it's all good fun. Admission is €10.

⭐ ENTERTAINMENT

Madrid has a happening live-music scene that owes a lot to the city's role as the cultural capital of the Spanish-speaking world. There's flamenco, world-class jazz and a host of performers you may never have heard of who may just be Spain's next big thing. For a dose of high culture, there's opera and *zarzuela* (satirical musical comedy).

Casa Patas   Flamenco

(Map p42; ☎91 369 04 96; www.casapatas.com; Calle de Cañizares 10; ⏱shows 10.30pm Mon-Thu, 9pm & midnight Fri & Sat; MAntón Martín, Tirso de Molina) One of the top flamenco stages in Madrid, this *tablao* (flamenco venue) always offers flawless quality that serves as a good introduction to the art. It's not the friendliest place in town, especially if you're only here for the show, and you're likely to be crammed in a little, but no one complains about the standard of the performances (admission including drink €36).

Corral de la Morería   Flamenco

(Map p42; ☎91 365 84 46; www.corraldela moreria.com; Calle de la Morería 17;

🕐7pm-12.15am, shows 9pm & 10.55pm;
Ⓜ️Ópera) This is one of the most prestigious
flamenco stages in Madrid, with 50 years'
experience as a leading venue and top
performers most nights. The stage area has
a rustic feel, and tables are pushed up close.
Admission including drink costs from €39;
set menus from €40.

Villa Rosa   Flamenco
(Map p42; 📞91 521 36 89; www.tablaoflamenco
villarosa.com; Plaza de Santa Ana 15; 🕐11pm-6am
Mon-Sat, shows 8.30pm & 10.45pm Sun-Thu,
8.30pm, 10.45pm & 12.15am Fri & Sat; Ⓜ️Sol) Villa
Rosa has been going strong since 1914 and
has seen many manifestations – it made its
name as a flamenco venue and has recently
returned to its roots with well-priced shows
and meals that won't break the bank.
Admission (show and drink) costs from
€32/17 per adult/child.

Café Central   Jazz
(Map p42; 📞91 369 41 43; www.cafecentral
madrid.com; Plaza del Ángel 10; 🕐12.30pm-
2.30am Sun-Thu, 12.30pm-3.30am Fri & Sat,
performances 9pm; Ⓜ️Antón Martín, Sol) In 2011

the respected jazz magazine *Down Beat*
included this art-deco bar on its list of the
world's best jazz clubs, the only place in
Spain to earn the prestigious accolade (said
by some to be the jazz equivalent of earning
a Michelin star). With well over 9000 gigs
under its belt, it rarely misses a beat. Admission costs from €12 to €18.

Sala El Sol   Live Music
(Map p50; 📞91 532 64 90; www.elsolmad.com;
Calle de los Jardines 3; 🕐midnight-5.30am Tue-
Sat Jul-Sep; Ⓜ️Gran Vía) Madrid institutions
don't come any more beloved than Sala
El Sol. It opened in 1979, just in time for *la
movida madrileña* (the Madrid scene), and
quickly established itself as a leading stage
for all the icons of the era, such as Nacha
Pop and Alaska y los Pegamoides.

Las Tablas   Flamenco
(📞91 542 05 20; www.lastablasmadrid.com; Plaza
de España 9; 🕐shows 8pm & 10pm; Ⓜ️Plaza de
España) Las Tablas has a reputation for
quality flamenco and reasonable prices
(admission including drink is €27); it could
just be the best choice in town. Most nights

Centro de Arte Reina Sofía (p43)

Rooftop view of Madrid

you'll see a classic flamenco show, with plenty of throaty singing and soul-baring dancing. Antonia Moya and Marisol Navarro, leading lights in the flamenco world, are regular performers here.

Estadio Santiago Bernabéu
Stadium, Football
(tickets 902 324324, tours 91 398 43 00/70; www.realmadrid.com; Avenida de Concha Espina 1; tour adult/child €19/13; tours 10am-7pm Mon-Sat, 10.30am-6.30pm Sun, except match days; Santiago Bernabéu) Football fans and budding Madridistas (Real Madrid supporters) will want to make a pilgrimage to the Estadio Santiago Bernabéu, a temple to all that's extravagant and successful in football. The self-guided tours take you up into the stands for a panoramic view of the stadium, then pass through the presidential box, press room, dressing rooms, players' tunnel and even onto the pitch itself. The tour ends in the extraordinary Exposición de Trofeos (trophy exhibit). Better still, attend a game alongside 80,000 delirious fans.

For bigger games, tickets are difficult to find unless you're willing to take the risk with scalpers. For less important matches, you shouldn't have too many problems. Tickets can be purchased online, by phone or in person from the ticket office at Gate 42 on Avenida de Concha Espina; for the last option, turn up early in the week before a scheduled game (eg a Monday morning for a Sunday game).

The football season runs from September (or the last weekend in August) until May, with a two-week break just before Christmas until early in the New Year.

For tours of the stadium, buy your ticket at window 10 (next to gate 7).

ℹ INFORMATION

TOURIST INFORMATION
Centro de Turismo de Madrid (91 454 44 10; www.esmadrid.com; Plaza Mayor 27; 9.30am-8.30pm) Housed in the Real Casa de la Panadería on the northern side of Plaza Mayor, it allows free access to its outstanding website and city

database, and offers free downloads of the metro map to your mobile.

Centro de Turismo Colón (www.esmadrid.com; Plaza de Colón 1; ⊙9.30am-8.30pm) Accessed via the underground stairs on the corner of Calle de Goya and the Paseo de la Castellana.

Punto do Información Turística Centro Centro (www.esmadrid.com, Plaza de la Cibeles 1; ⊙10am-8pm Tue-Sun)

Punto de Información Turística del Paseo del Arte (www.esmadrid.com; cnr Calle de Santa Isabel & Plaza del Emperador Carlos V; ⊙9.30am-8.30pm)

ℹ GETTING THERE & AWAY

AIR

Madrid's **Adolfo Suárez Madrid-Barajas Airport** (📞902 404704; www.aena.es, www. aeropuertomadrid-barajas.com) lies 15km northeast of the city. It's Europe's sixth-busiest hub, with almost 50 million passengers passing through here every year.

Barajas has four terminals. Terminal 4 (T4) deals mainly with flights of Iberia and its partners, while the remainder leave from the conjoined T1, T2 and (rarely) T3. To match your airline with a terminal, visit website and click on 'Airlines'. There are car rental services, ATMs, money-exchange bureaus, pharmacies, tourist offices, left luggage offices and parking services at T1, T2 and T4.

BUS

The city's principal bus station **Estación Sur de Autobuses** (📞91 468 42 00; www.estacionde autobuses.com; Calle de Méndez Álvaro 83; Ⓜ Méndez Álvaro) is just south of the M30 ring road. It serves most destinations to the south and many in other parts of the country. Most bus companies have a ticket office here, even if their buses depart from elsewhere.

CAR & MOTORCYCLE

Madrid is surrounded by two main ring roads, the outermost M40 and the inner M30; there are also two partial ring roads, the M45 and the more

distant M50. The R5 and R3 are part of a series of toll roads built to ease traffic jams.

TRAIN

Madrid is served by two main train stations. The bigger of the two is **Puerta de Atocha** (www. renfe.es; Ⓜ Atocha Renfe), at the southern end of the city centre, while **Chamartín** (📞902 432343; Ⓜ Chamartín) lies in the north of the city. The bulk of trains for Spanish destinations depart from Atocha, especially those going south. International services arrive at and leave from Chamartín.

High-speed Tren de Alta Velocidad Española (AVE) services connect Madrid with Barcelona, Burgos, Cádiz, Córdoba, Cuenca, Huesca, León, Lerida, Málaga, Palencia, Salamanca, Santiago de Compostela, Seville, Valencia, Valladolid, Zamora and Zaragoza. For bookings, contact **Renfe** (📞902 320320; www.renfe.es/cercanias/ madrid).

ℹ GETTING AROUND

TO/FROM THE AIRPORT

BUS

The **Exprés Aeropuerto** (Airport Express; www. emtmadrid.es; per person €5; ⊙24hr; 🚍) runs between Puerta de Atocha train station and the airport; the trip takes 40 minutes. From 11.30pm to 6am, departures are from the Plaza de Cibeles, not the train station. Departures take place every 13 to 20 minutes from the station or at night-time every 35 minutes from Plaza de Cibeles. There's also a free bus service connecting all four airport terminals.

METRO

The easiest way into town from the airport is line 8 of the metro to the Nuevos Ministerios transport interchange, which connects with lines 10 and 6 and the local overground *cercanías* (local trains serving suburbs and nearby towns). It operates from 6.05am to 1.30am. A single ticket costs €4.50 including the €3 airport supplement. If you're buying a 10-ride Metrobús ticket (€12.20), you'll need to top it up with the €3 supplement if you're travelling to/from the

Madrid Card

If you intend to do some intensive sightseeing and travelling on public transport, consider the **Madrid Card** (www.madridcard.com; 1/2/3/5 days adult €47/60/67/77, child 6-12yr €34/42/44/47). It includes entry to over 50 museums in and around Madrid (including the Museo del Prado, Museo Thyssen-Bornemisza, Centro de Arte Reina Sofía, Estadio Santiago Bernabéu and Palacio Real), walking tours and discounts in a number of restaurants, shops and bars, as well as for car rental. The Madrid Card can be bought online (slightly cheaper), at the Centro de Turismo de Madrid (p64) or at any of the sales outlets listed on the website.

airport. The journey to Nuevos Ministerios takes around 15 minutes, around 25 minutes from T4.

MINIBUS

AeroCITY (91 747 75 70, 902 151654; www.aerocity.com; per person from €17.85, express service from €34 per minibus) is a private minibus service that takes you door-to-door between central Madrid and the airport (T1 in front of Arrivals Gate 2; T2 between gates 5 and 6; and T4 arrivals hall). It operates 24 hours and you can book by phone or online. You can reserve a seat or the entire minibus; the latter option operates like a taxi.

TAXI

A taxi to the centre (around 30 minutes, depending on traffic; 35 to 40 minutes from T4) costs a fixed €30 for anywhere inside the M30 motorway (which includes all of downtown Madrid). There's a minimum €20, even if you're only going to an airport hotel.

BUS

Buses operated by Empresa Municipal de Transportes de Madrid travel along most city routes regularly between about 6.30am and 11.30pm. Twenty-six night-bus *búhos* (owls) routes operate from 11.45pm to 5.30am, with all routes originating in Plaza de la Cibeles. Fares for day and night trips are the same as for the metro: €1.50 for a single trip, €12.20 for a 10-trip Metrobús ticket. Single-trip tickets can be purchased on board.

METRO

Madrid's modern **metro** (www.metromadrid.es), Europe's second-largest, is a fast, efficient and safe way to navigate Madrid, and generally easier than getting to grips with bus routes. There are 11 colour-coded lines in central Madrid, in addition to the modern southern suburban MetroSur system as well as lines heading east to the population centres of Pozuelo and Boadilla del Monte. Colour maps showing the metro system are available from any metro station or online. The metro operates from 6.05am to 1.30am.

The short-range *cercanías* operated by Renfe (www.renfe.es/cercanias/madrid) are handy for making a quick, north–south hop between Chamartín and Atocha train stations (with stops at Nuevos Ministerios and Sol).

TAXI

You can pick up a taxi at ranks throughout town or simply flag one down. Flag fall is €2.40 from 7am to 9pm daily, €2.90 from 9pm to 7am and all day Saturday and Sunday. You pay between €1.05 and €1.20 per kilometre depending on the time of day. Several supplementary charges, usually posted inside the taxi, apply; these include €5.50 to/from the airport (if you're not paying the fixed rate); €3 from taxi ranks at train and bus stations, €3 to/from the Parque Ferial Juan Carlos I; and €6.70 on New Year's Eve and Christmas Eve from 10pm to 6am. There's no charge for luggage. Among the 24-hour taxi services are **Tele-Taxi** (91 371 21 31; www.tele-taxi.es) and **Radio-Teléfono Taxi** (91 547 82 00; www.radiotelefono-taxi.com).

A green light on the roof means the taxi is *libre* (available). Usually a sign to this effect is also placed in the lower passenger side of the windscreen.

Where to Stay

Madrid has quality accommodation at prices not seen in other European capitals in decades. Five-star temples to good taste and a handful of buzzing hostels bookend a fabulous collection of creative, original midrange hotels, blending comfort with a quirky sense of style.

Neighbourhood	Atmosphere
Plaza Mayor & Royal Madrid	Walking distance to most sights, shops and restaurants; good metro connections elsewhere. Can be noisy from night-time revellers.
La Latina & Lavapiés	Excellent central location, combining medieval architecture with terrific restaurants and tapas bars. Can be noisy in the evening (less so later at night), and it's a walk uphill from the art galleries.
Sol, Santa Ana & Huertas	Close to most attractions and eating, drinking and entertainment options. Possibly Madrid's noisiest neighbourhood, with all-night revellers, especially on weekends. Steep hills test weary legs.
El Retiro & the Art Museums	Right next door (or just around the corner) from Madrid's big three art galleries, although traffic noise can be a problem. Most restaurants are at least a 10-minute walk away.
Salamanca	In the heart of fantastic shopping and close to good eating options. A decent walk from the rest of the city, it's quieter by night than most Madrid neighbourhoods.
Malasaña & Chueca	Lively streets and wonderful places to eat and drink – a sense of Madrid beyond the tourist crowds. A noisy nighttime neighbourhood. Chueca is gay-friendly.
Parque del Oeste & Northern Madrid	Removed from the clamour of downtown, just a short metro ride away, this neighbourhood provides an immersion in local Madrid life.

BARCELONA

Barcelona at a Glance...

Barcelona is a mix of sunny Mediterranean charm and European urban style. The city bursts with art and architecture (from Gothic to Gaudí), Catalan cooking is among the country's best, summer sun seekers fill the beaches in and beyond the city, and the bars and clubs heave year-round. The city began as a middle-ranking Roman town, of which vestiges can be seen today, and its old centre constitutes one of the greatest concentrations of Gothic architecture in Europe. Beyond this core are some of the world's more bizarre buildings: surreal spectacles capped by Gaudí's church, La Sagrada Família. Barcelona has been breaking ground in art, architecture and style since the late 19th century. Equally busy are the city's avant-garde chefs, who compete with old-time classics for the gourmet's attention.

Barcelona in Two Days

Start with the **Barri Gòtic** (p80), then stroll **La Rambla** (p74) to the **Museu d'Història de Barcelona** (p80) on historic **Plaça del Rei** (p81). Visit the **Museu Picasso** (p85) and round off with a meal and cocktails in **El Born** (p103). On day two, experience **Park Güell** (p96) and **La Sagrada Família** (p72). Afterwards, go for dinner at **Disfrutar** (p99) followed by drinks at **Bar Marsella** (p103).

Barcelona in Four Days

Start the third day with more Gaudí, visiting **Casa Batlló** (p79) and **La Pedrera** (p78), followed by beachside relaxation and seafood in **Barceloneta** (p88). Day four should be dedicated to **Montjuïc** (p76), with its museums, galleries, fortress, gardens and Olympic stadium.

See Central Barcelona Map (p82)
La Sagrada & L'Eixample Map (p89)
See Montjuïc Map (p98)

Arriving in Barcelona

El Prat Airport (p107) Frequent *aerobúses* make the 35-minute run into town (€5.90) from 6am to 1am; taxis cost around €25.

Estació Sants Metro connections between the long-distance train station and other neighbourhoods.

Estació del Nord In L'Eixample, 1.5km northeast of Plaça de Catalunya, the long-haul bus station is a short walk from several metro stations.

Sleeping

Barcelona has some fabulous accommodation, but never arrive in town without a reservation. Designer digs are something of a Barcelona speciality, with midrange and top-end travellers particularly well served. Apartments are also widespread and a fine alternative to hotels. Prices in Barcelona are generally higher than elsewhere in the country. Wherever you stay it's wise to book well ahead, particularly if you travel around holidays.

For more on where to stay, see p109.

Ambulatory

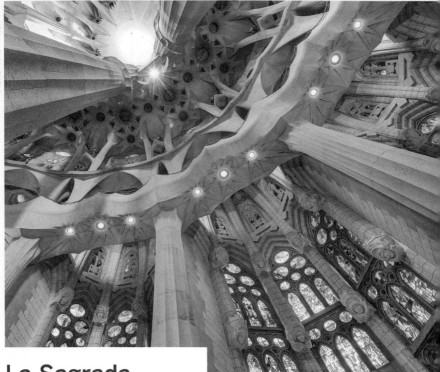

JASON WALTMAN / 500PX ©

La Sagrada Família

If you can only visit one place in Barcelona, this should be it. Still under construction, La Sagrada Família inspires awe by its sheer verticality in the manner of the medieval cathedrals.

Great For...

☑ Don't Miss

The extraordinary pillars and stained glass, the Nativity Facade, the Passion Facade...

Gaudí's Vision

The Temple Expiatori de la Sagrada Família (Expiatory Temple of the Holy Family) was Antoni Gaudí's all-consuming obsession. Given the commission by a conservative society that wished to build a temple as atonement for the city's sins of modernity, Gaudí saw its completion as his holy mission.

Gaudí devised a temple 95m long and 60m wide, able to seat 13,000 people, with a central tower 170m high above the transept (representing Christ) and another 17 of 100m or more. The 12 along the three facades represent the Apostles, while the remaining five represent the Virgin Mary and the four evangelists. With his characteristic dislike for straight lines (there were none in nature, he said), Gaudí gave his towers swelling outlines inspired by the weird peaks of the holy mountain Montserrat outside

VISIONS OF OUR LAND / GETTY IMAGES ©

❶ Need to Know

Map p89; ☑ 93 208 04 14; www.sagrada familia.cat; Carrer de Mallorca 401; adult/ concession/under 11yr €15/13/free; ◷ 9am-8pm Apr-Sep, to 6pm Oct-Mar; Ⓜ Sagrada Família

✕ Take a Break

Cerveseria Catalana (p99) is a great choice at any time of the day.

> ★ **Top Tip**
> Book tickets online to avoid what can be very lengthy queues.

Barcelona. At Gaudí's death, only the crypt, the apse walls, one portal and one tower had been finished.

The Nativity Facade

The Nativity Facade is the artistic pinnacle of the building, mostly created under Gaudí's personal supervision. You can climb high up inside some of the four towers by a combination of lifts and narrow spiral staircases – a vertiginous experience. The towers are destined to hold tubular bells capable of playing complex music at great volume. Their upper parts are decorated with mosaics spelling out 'Sanctus, Sanctus, Sanctus, Hosanna in Excelsis, Amen, Alleluia'.

Passion Facade

The southwest Passion Facade, on the theme of Christ's last days and death, was

built between 1954 and 1978 based on surviving drawings by Gaudí, with four towers and a large, sculpture-bedecked portal. The main series of sculptures, on three levels, are in an S-shaped sequence, starting with the Last Supper at the bottom left and ending with Christ's burial at the top right.

Glory Facade

The Glory Facade is under construction and will, like the others, be crowned by four towers – the total of 12 representing the Twelve Apostles. Gaudí wanted it to be the most magnificent facade of the church. Inside will be the narthex, a kind of foyer made up of 16 'lanterns', a series of hyperboloid forms topped by cones.

Museu Gaudí

The Museu Gaudí, below ground level, includes interesting material on Gaudí's life and other works, as well as models and photos of La Sagrada Família.

KARSOL / SHUTTERSTOCK ©

La Rambla

One of the world's most famous thoroughfares, La Rambla is a stirring vision of Barcelona's polyglot soul. With the Barri Gòtic on one side, and gritty El Raval on the other, there's interest at every turn.

Great For...

☑ Don't Miss

The Mercat de la Boqueria, one of the world's most celebrated markets on La Rambla's western shore.

Barcelona's most famous street is both a tourist magnet and a window into Catalan culture. Set between narrow traffic lanes and flanked by plane trees, the middle of La Rambla is a pedestrian boulevard, crowded daily until the wee hours with a wide cross section of society. A stroll here is pure sensory overload, with souvenir hawkers, buskers, pavement artists, mimes and living statues all part of the ever-changing street scene.

What's in a Name?

La Rambla takes its name from a seasonal stream (*raml* in Arabic) that once ran here. From the early Middle Ages on, it was better known as the Cagalell (Stream of Shit) and lay outside the city walls until the 14th century. Monastic buildings were then built and, subsequently, mansions of the well-to-do from the 16th to the early 19th centuries.

❶ Need to Know

Metro stations include Catalunya (north), Liceu (middle) and Drassanes (south).

✕ Take a Break

Bar Pinotxo (p96) is a brilliant tapas bar at the Mercat de la Boqueria.

★ Top Tip

Pickpockets and con artists love La Rambla – keep your wits about you.

to I a Rambla dels Estudis (officially) or La Rambla dels Ocells (Birds, unofficially) in Barcelona's twittering bird market (under threat from ice-cream and pastry stands) where you'll be serenaded by birdsong.

Plaça de la Boqueria

At around La Rambla's midpoint lies one of Europe's greatest markets, the Mercat de la Boqueria (p80), while almost opposite is your chance to walk on a Miró: the colourful Mosaïc de Miró in the pavement, with one tile signed by the artist. Look also for the grandiose Gran Teatre del Liceu (p81), then rest in the lovely Plaça Reial. The lamp posts by the central fountain are Antoni Gaudí's first known works in the city.

Unofficially, La Rambla is divided into five sections, which explains why many know it as Las Ramblas.

La Font de Canaletes

From Plaça de Catalunya, La Rambla unfurls down the hill to the southeast. Its first manifestation, La Rambla de Canaletes, is named after a pretty 19th-century, wrought-iron fountain, La Font de Canaletes. Local legend has it anyone who drinks from its waters will return to Barcelona. More prosaically, delirious football fans gather here to celebrate whenever FC Barcelona wins something.

Bird Market

In keeping with its numerous contradictory impulses, La Rambla changes personality as it gains momentum down the hill. Stalls crowd in from the side as the name changes

La Rambla de Santa Mònica

The final stretch, La Rambla de Santa Mònica, widens out to approach the **Mirador de Colom** (☎93 302 52 24; www.barcelonaturisme. com; Plaça del Portal de la Pau; adult/concession €6/4; ☉8.30am-8.30pm summer, 8.30am-7.30pm winter; MDrassanes) overlooking Port Vell. And just off La Rambla's southwestern tip, don't miss the sublime Museu Marítim (p88).

Museu Nacional d'Art de Catalunya

RICH THOMPSON / GETTY IMAGES ©

Montjuïc

The Montjuïc hillside, crowned by a castle and gardens, overlooks the port with some of the city's finest art collections: the Museu Nacional d'Art de Catalunya, the Fundació Joan Miró and CaixaForum.

Great For...

☑ Don't Miss

The Romanesque frescoes in the Museu Nacional d'Art de Catalunya.

Museu Nacional d'Art de Catalunya

From across the city, the bombastic neo-baroque silhouette of the **Museu Nacional d'Art de Catalunya** (Map p98; ☑93 622 03 76; www.museunacional.cat; Mirador del Palau Nacional; adult/student/child €12/8.40/free, after 3pm Sat & 1st Sun of month free; ⊙10am-8pm Tue-Sat, to 3pm Sun May-Sep, to 6pm Tue-Sat Oct-Apr; MEspanya) can be seen on the slopes of Montjuïc. Built for the 1929 World Exhibition and restored in 2005, it houses a vast collection of mostly Catalan art spanning the early Middle Ages to the early 20th century. The high point is the collection of extraordinary Romanesque frescoes, rescued from neglected country churches across northern Catalonia in the early 20th century.

Castell de Montjuïc

VITOMARIGO / SHUTTERSTOCK ©

Montjuïc

ⓘ Need to Know

The metro stops at the foot of Montjuïc; buses and funiculars go all the way

✕ Take a Break

Montjuïc eateries tend to be over-priced. The gardens surrounding the Fundació Joan Miró are perfect for a picnic.

★ Top Tip

Ride the Transbordador Aeri from Barceloneta for a bird's-eye approach to Montjuïc.

Fundació Joan Miró

Joan Miró, the city's best-known 20th-century artistic progeny, bequeathed the **Fundació Joan Miró** (Map p98; ☎93 443 94 70; www.fmirobcn.org; Parc de Montjuïc; adult/child €12/free; ☉10am-8pm Tue-Sat, to 9pm Thu, to 2.30pm Sun & holidays; ☐55, 150, funicular Paral·lel) to his hometown in 1971. Its light-filled buildings, designed by close friend and architect Josep Lluís Sert, are crammed with seminal works, from Miró's earliest timid sketches to paintings from his last years. Highlights include Sala Joan Prats, with works spanning the early years until 1919; Sala Pilar Juncosa, which covers his surrealist years 1932–55; and Rooms 18 and 19 which contain masterworks of the years 1956–83.

CaixaForum

The Caixa building society prides itself on its involvement in (and ownership of) art, in particular all that is contemporary. at **Caixa Forum** (Map p98; ☎93 476 86 00; www.fundacio.lacaixa.es; Avinguda de Francesc Ferrer i Guàrdia 6-8; adult/student & child €4/free, 1st Sun of month free; ☉10am-8pm; Ⓟ; ⓂEspanya), its pre-mier art expo space in Barcelona. The setting is a renovated former factory, an outstanding Modernista brick structure designed by Puig i Cadafalch. On occasion portions of La Caixa's own collection of 800 works of modern and contemporary art go on display, but more often than not major international exhibitions are the key draw.

Castell de Montjuïc

This forbidding *castell* (castle or fort) domi-nates the southeastern heights of Montjuïc and enjoys commanding views over the Mediterranean. It dates, in its present form, from the late 17th and 18th centuries. For most of its dark history, it has been used to watch over the city and as a political prison and killing ground.

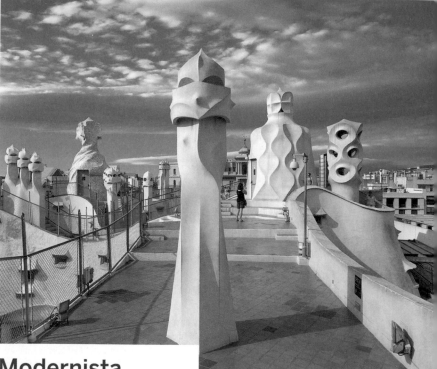

La Pedrera

Modernista Masterpieces

The elegant, if traffic-filled, district of L'Eixample (pronounced 'lay-sham-pluh') is a showcase for Modernista architecture, including some of Gaudí's most treasured masterpieces.

Great For...

☑ Don't Miss

Casa Batllo is quite simply one of the weirdest and most wonderful buildings in Spain.

La Pedrera

An undulating beast, **La Pedrera** (Casa Milà; Map p89; ☎90 220 21 38; www.lapedrera.com; Passeig de Gràcia 92; adult/concession/under 13yr/under 7yr €20.50/16.50/10.25/free; ⊙9am-8.30pm Mar-Oct, to 6.30pm Nov-Feb; Ⓜ Diagonal) is another madcap Gaudí masterpiece, built from 1905 to 1910 as a combined apartment and office block. Formally called Casa Milà after the businessman who commissioned it, it is better known as La Pedrera (the Quarry) because of its uneven grey stone facade.

The Fundació Caixa Catalunya has opened the top-floor apartment, attic and roof, called the Espai Gaudí (Gaudí Space), to visitors. The roof is the most extraordinary element, with its giant chimney pots looking like multi-coloured medieval knights. Gaudí wanted to put a tall statue of the Virgin up here too: when the Milà family said no, Gaudí resigned from the project in disgust.

Casa Batlló

MAREK STEPAN / GETTY IMAGES ©

Modernista
Masterpieces

ℹ️ Need to Know

Four metro lines criss-cross L'Eixample, with Passeig de Gràcia and Diagonal the most useful.

✖️ Take a Break

Tapas 24 (p99), one of Barcelona's best tapas bars, is close to Casa Batlló.

★ Top Tip

Get started early in the day to stay one step ahead of the crowds.

The next floor down is the apartment (El Pis de la Pedrera). It's fascinating to wander around this elegantly furnished home, done up in the style a well-to-do family might have enjoyed in the early 20th century. There are sensuous curves and unexpected touches in everything from light fittings and door handles, bedsteads and balconies.

Casa Batlló

One of the strangest residential buildings in Europe, **Casa Batlló** (Map p89; 📞93 216 03 06; www.casabatllo.es; Passeig de Gràcia 43; adult/concession/under 7yr €22.50/19.50/free; ⊙9am-9pm, last admission 8pm; Ⓜ Passeig de Gràcia) is Gaudí at his hallucinatory best. The facade, sprinkled with blue, mauve and green tiles and studded with wave-shaped window frames and balconies, rises to an uneven blue-tiled roof. Locals know Casa Batlló

variously as the *casa dels ossos* (house of bones) or *casa del drac* (house of the dragon). The balconies look like the bony jaws of some strange beast and the roof represents Sant Jordi (St George) and the dragon. The internal light wells shimmer with tiles of deep sea blue. Everything swirls: the ceiling is twisted into a vortex around its sunlike lamp; the doors, window and skylights are dreamy waves of wood and coloured glass.

Beyond Gaudí

Casa Batlló is one of the three houses on the block between Carrer del Consell de Cent and Carrer d'Aragó that gave it the playful name Manzana de la Discordia. The other houses are the Casa Amatller (p88), one of Puig i Cadafalch's most striking bits of Modernista fantasy, and the Casa Lleó Morera (p89), Domènech i Montaner's 1905 creation and perhaps the least odd-looking of the three main buildings on the block.

Other Modernista icons to watch out for include Puig i Cadafalch's Palau del Baró Quadras (p90) and Palau Montaner (p90).

◉ SIGHTS
◉ La Rambla & Barri Gòtic

La Rambla, Barcelona's most famous pedestrian strip, is always a hive of activity, with buskers, peddlers, tourists and con artists (watch out!) mingling amid the sunlit cafes and shops on the boulevard. The adjoining Barri Gòtic is packed with historical treasures – relics of ancient Rome, 14th-century Gothic churches and atmospheric cobblestone lanes lined with shops, bars and restaurants.

Mercat de la Boqueria   Market

(Map p82; ☎93 412 13 15; www.boqueria.info; La Rambla 91; ☺8am-8.30pm Mon-Sat; Ⓜ Liceu) The Mercat de la Boqueria is possibly La Rambla's most interesting building, not so much for its Modernista-influenced design (it was actually built over a long period, from 1840 to 1914, on the site of the former St Joseph Monastery), but for the action of the food market within.

La Catedral   Cathedral

(Map p82; ☎93 342 82 62; www.catedralbcn.org; Plaça de la Seu; admission free, 'donation entrance' €7, choir €3, roof €3; ☺8am-12.45pm & 5.15-7.30pm Mon-Fri, 8am-8pm Sat & Sun, 'donation entrance' 1-5pm Mon-Sat, 2-5pm Sun; Ⓜ Jaume I) Barcelona's central place of worship presents a magnificent image. The richly decorated main facade, laced with gargoyles and the stone intricacies you would expect of northern European Gothic, sets it quite apart from other churches in Barcelona. The facade was actually added in 1870, although the rest of the building was built between 1298 and 1460. The other facades are sparse in decoration, and the octagonal, flat-roofed towers are a clear reminder that, even here, Catalan Gothic architectural principles prevailed.

Museu d'Història de Barcelona   Museum

(MUHBA; Map p82; ☎93 256 21 00; www.museuhistoria.bcn.cat; Plaça del Rei; adult/concession/child €7/5/free, 3-8pm Sun & 1st Sun of month free; ☺10am-7pm Tue-Sat, 10am-8pm Sun; Ⓜ Jaume I) One of Barcelona's most fascinating museums takes you back through the centuries to the very foundations of Roman Barcino. You'll stroll over ruins of the old streets, sewers, laundries and wine- and

Mercat de la Boqueria

TUPUNGATO / SHUTTERSTOCK ©

fish-making factories that flourished here following the town's founding by Emperor Augustus around 10 BC. Equally impressive is the building itself, which was once part of the Palau Reial Major (Grand Royal Palace) on Plaça del Rei, among the key locations of medieval princely power in Barcelona.

Museu Frederic Marès   Museum

(Map p82; ☑93 256 35 00; www.museumares. bcn.cat; Plaça de Sant Iu 5; adult/concession/child €4.20/2.40/free, after 3pm Sun & 1st Sun of month free; ☺10am-7pm Tue-Sat, 11am-8pm Sun; ⓜJaume I) One of the wildest collections of historical curios lies inside this vast medieval complex, once part of the royal palace of the counts of Barcelona. A rather worn coat of arms on the wall indicates that it was also, for a while, the seat of the Spanish Inquisition in Barcelona. Frederic Marès i Deulovol (1893–1991) was a rich sculptor, traveller and obsessive collector, and displays of religious art and vast varieties of bric-a-brac litter the museum.

Gran Teatre del Liceu   Architecture

(Map p82; ☑93 485 99 00; www.liceubarcelona. cat; La Rambla 51-59; tours 50/25min €16/6; ☺50min tours 9.30am & 10.30am, 25min tours schedule varies; ⓜLiceu) If you can't catch a night at the opera, you can still have a look around one of Europe's greatest opera houses, known to locals as the Liceu. Smaller than Milan's La Scala but bigger than Venice's La Fenice, it can seat up to 2300 people in its grand horseshoe auditorium.

Plaça del Rei   Square

(Map p82; ⓜJaume I) Plaça del Rei (King's Sq) is a picturesque plaza where Fernando and Isabel received Columbus following his first New World voyage. It is the courtyard of the former Palau Reial Major. The palace today houses a superb history museum (p80), with significant Roman ruins underground.

◉ El Raval

The once down-and-out district of El Raval is still seedy in parts, though it has seen remarkable rejuvenation in recent years, with the addition of cutting-edge museums

📖🍴 Gaudí: A Catholic & a Catalan

Antoni Gaudí (1852–1926) was a devout Catholic and Catalan nationalist. In addition to nature, Catalonia's great medieval churches were a source of inspiration to him, and he took pride in using local building materials. In contrast to his architecture, Gaudí's life was simple; he was not averse to knocking on doors, literally begging for money to help fund construction of the cathedral. As he became more adventurous he appeared as a lone wolf. With age he became almost exclusively motivated by stark religious conviction, and he devoted much of the latter part of his life to what remains Barcelona's call sign – the unfinished La Sagrada Família. He died in 1926, hit by a streetcar while taking his daily walk to the Sant Felip Neri church. Wearing ragged clothes, and with empty pockets, Gaudí was initially taken for a beggar and sent to a hospital where he was left in a pauper's ward, dying two days later. Thousands attended his funeral forming a half-mile procession to La Sagrada Família, where he was buried in the crypt. Like his work in progress, La Sagrada Família, Gaudí's story is far from over. In March 2000 the Vatican decided to proceed with the case for canonising him, and pilgrims stop by the crypt to pay him homage. One of the key sculptors at work on the church, the Japanese Etsuro Sotoo, converted to Catholicism because of his passion for Gaudí.

Casa Batlló (p79)

Central Barcelona

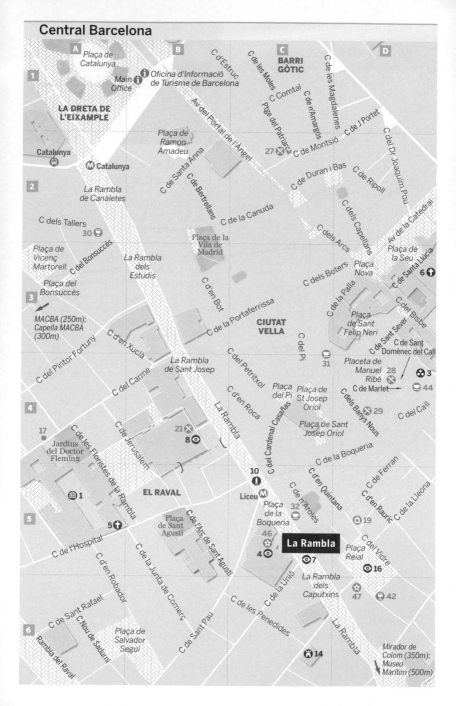

Plaça de Catalunya

A B C D

BARRI GÒTIC

C d'Estruc
C de les Moles
C Comtal
C de les Magdalenes
C de J Portet
C de n'Amargós
Ptge del Patriarca

1

Main Office
Oficina d'Informació de Turisme de Barcelona

LA DRETA DE L'EIXAMPLE

Av del Portal de l'Àngel

C de Montsió
27

C del Dr Joaquim Pou

Plaça de Ramon Amadeu

Catalunya

Ⓜ Catalunya

C de Santa Anna
C de Bertrellans

C de Duran i Bas
C de Ripoll

2

La Rambla de Canaletes

C de la Canuda

C dels Capellans

C dels Tallers
30

C dels Arcs

Av de la Catedral

Plaça de Vicenç Martorell

C del Bonsuccés

Plaça de la Vila de Madrid

C dels Boters

Plaça Nova

Plaça de la Seu

La Rambla dels Estudis

C de Santa Llúcia
6

Plaça del Bonsuccés

3

C en Bot

C de la Palla

C del Bisbe

MACBA (250m);
Capella MACBA (300m)

C de la Portaferrissa

CIUTAT VELLA

Plaça de Sant Felip Neri

C de Sant Sever

C d'en Xuclà

C del Pintor Fortuny

C del Pi

31

Placeta de Manuel Ribé
28

C de Sant Domènec del Call
3

La Rambla de Sant Josep

C del Petritxol

Plaça del Pi

Plaça de St Josep Oriol

C de Marlet
44

C del Carme

C d'en Roca

C dels Banys Nous
29

C del Call

4

17

C de Jerusalem

C en Quintana

Plaça de Sant Josep Oriol

Jardins del Doctor Fleming

C de les Floristes de la Rambla

21
8

La Rambla

C del Cardenal Casañas

C de la Boqueria

C de Ferran

EL RAVAL

10

C d'en Raurig

C d'en Rauric
C de la Lleona

1

5

Liceu Ⓜ

Plaça de la Boqueria

C de n'Aroles
32

19

5

Plaça de Sant Agustí

C de l'Arc de Sant Agustí

46

La Rambla

Plaça Reial

C del Vidre

C de l'Hospital

4

7

16

C d'en Robador

C de la Junta de Comerç

La Rambla dels Caputxins

47
42

C de Sant Rafael

C Nou de Sadurní

Plaça de Salvador Seguí

C de Sant Pau

C de la Unió

C de les Penedides

La Rambla

Rambla del Raval

14

Mirador de Colom (350m);
Museu Marítim (500m)

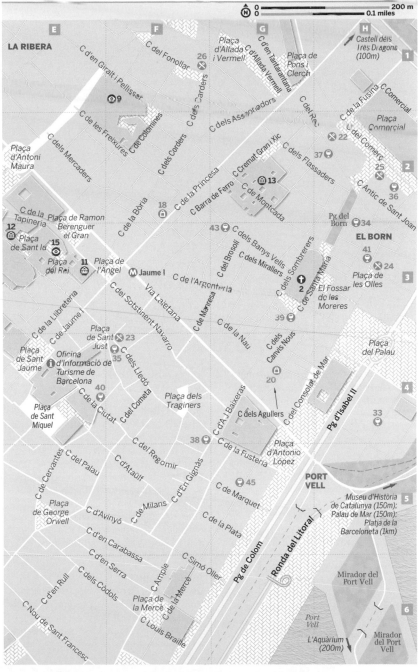

Central Barcelona

and cultural centres, including the Richard Meier–designed MACBA (Museu d'Art Contemporani de Barcelona). Other highlights not to be missed include the bohemian nightlife and the sprawling culinary delights of the Mercat de la Boqueria.

MACBA   Arts Centre

(Museu d'Art Contemporani de Barcelona; ☑93 481 33 68; www.macba.cat; Plaça dels Àngels 1; adult/concession/under 12yr €10/8/free; ◎11am-7.30pm Mon & Wed-Fri, 10am-9pm Sat, 10am-3pm Sun & holidays; ⓂUniversitat) Designed by Richard Meier and opened in 1995, MACBA has become the city's foremost contemporary art centre, with captivating exhibitions for the serious art lover. The permanent collection is on the ground floor and dedicates itself to Spanish and Catalan art from the second half of the 20th century, with works by Antoni Tàpies, Joan Brossa and Miquel Barceló, among others, though international

artists, such as Paul Klee, Bruce Nauman and John Cage, are also represented.

Palau Güell   Palace

(Map p82; ☑93 472 57 75; www.palauguell.cat; Carrer Nou de la Rambla 3-5; adult/concession/under 10yr €12/9/free; ◎10am-8pm Tue-Sun; ⓂDrassanes) Finally reopened in its entirety in 2012 after several years of refurbishment, this is a magnificent example of the early days of Gaudí's fevered architectural imagination. The extraordinary neo-Gothic mansion, one of the few major buildings of that era raised in the Ciutat Vella, gives an insight into its maker's prodigious genius.

Antic Hospital
de la Santa Creu   Historic Building

(Former Hospital of the Holy Cross; Map p82; ☑93 270 16 21; www.bcn.cat; Carrer de l'Hospital 56; ◎9am-8pm Mon-Fri, to 2pm Sat; ⓂLiceu) Behind La Boqueria stands the Antic Hospital de la

Santa Creu, which was once the city's main hospital. Begun in 1401, it functioned until the 1930s, and was considered one of the best in Europe in its medieval heyday – it is famously the place where Antoni Gaudí died in 1926. Today it houses the Biblioteca de Catalunya and the Institut d'Estudis Catalans (Institute for Catalan Studies). The hospital's Gothic chapel, **La Capella** (☑93 256 20 44; www.bcn.cat/lacapella; ⊘noon-8pm Tue-Sat, 11am-2pm Sun & holidays) **FREE**, shows temporary exhibitions.

◎ La Ribera

This medieval quarter has a little of everything, from high-end shopping to some of Barcelona's liveliest tapas bars. Key sights include the superb Museu Picasso, the awe-inspiring Gothic Basílica de Santa Maria del Mar and the artfully sculpted Modernista concert hall of Palau de la Música Catalana. For a bit of fresh air, locals head to the manicured gardens of Parc de la Ciutadella.

Museu Picasso   Museum

(Map p82; ☑93 256 30 00; www.museupicasso. bcn.cat; Carrer de Montcada 15-23; adult/concession/child all collections €14/7.50/free, permanent collection €11/7/free, temporary exhibitions €4.50/3/free, 3-7pm Sun & 1st Sun of month free; ⊘9am-7pm Tue, Wed & Fri-Sun, to 9.30pm Thu; ⓂJaume I) The setting alone, in five contiguous medieval stone mansions, makes the Museu Picasso unique (and worth the probable queues). The pretty courtyards, galleries and staircases preserved in the first three of these buildings are as delightful as the collection inside. While the collection concentrates on the artist's formative years – sometimes disappointing for those hoping for a feast of his better-known later works – there is enough material from subsequent periods to give you a thorough impression of the man's versatility and genius. Above all, you come away feeling that Picasso was the true original, always one step ahead of himself (let alone anyone else), in his search for new forms of expression.

Basílica de Santa
Maria del Mar   Church

(Map p82; ☑93 310 23 90; www.santamariadel marbarcelona.org; Plaça de Santa Maria del Mar; incl guided tour 1-5pm €8; ⊘9am-8pm; ⓂJaume I) At the southwest end of Passeig del Born stands the apse of Barcelona's finest Catalan Gothic church, Santa Maria del Mar (Our Lady of the Sea). Built in the 14th century with record-breaking alacrity for the time (it took just 54 years), the church is remarkable for its architectural harmony and simplicity.

Palau de la
Música Catalana   Architecture

(☑93 295 72 00; www.palaumusica.cat; Carrer de Palau de la Música 4-6; adult/concession/child €18/11/free; ⊘guided tours 10am-3.30pm, to 6pm Easter, Jul & Aug; ⓂUrquinaona) This concert hall is a high point of Barcelona's Modernista architecture, a symphony in tile, brick, sculpted stone and stained glass. Built by Domènech I Montaner between 1905 and 1908 for the Orfeó Català musical society, it was conceived as a temple for the Catalan Renaixença (Renaissance).

Mercat de Santa Caterina   Market

(Map p82; ☑93 319 57 40; www.mercatsanta caterina.com; Avinguda de Francesc Cambó 16; ⊘7.30am-3.30pm Mon, Wed, Sat, to 8.30pm Tue, Thu, Fri, closed afternoons Jul & Aug; ⓂJaume I) Come shopping for your tomatoes at this extraordinary-looking produce market, designed by Enric Miralles and Benedetta Tagliabue to replace its 19th-century predecessor. Finished in 2005, it is distinguished by its kaleidoscopic and undulating roof, held up above the bustling produce stands, restaurants, cafes and bars by twisting slender branches of what look like grey steel trees.

Castell dels
Tres Dragons   Architecture

(ⓂArc de Triomf) The Passeig de Picasso side of Parc de la Ciutadella is lined by several buildings constructed for, or just before, the Universal Exposition of 1888. The medieval-looking caprice at the top end is the most engaging. Known as the Castell dels Tres Dragons (Castle of the Three Dragons), it

Walking Tour: Barri Gòtic

This walk through the Barri Gòtic will take you back in time, from the early days of Roman-era Barcino through to the medieval era.

Start La Catedral
Distance 1.5km
Duration 1½ hours

Classic Photo: La Catedral

1 Before entering the cathedral, look for the three Picasso friezes on the building facing the square. Next, wander through the magnificent **La Catedral** (p80). Keep an eye out for the flock of 13 geese in the cloister.

2 Pass through the former city gates and turn right into **Plaça de Sant Felip Neri**. The shrapnel-scarred church was damaged by pro-Francist bombers in 1939.

3 Head west to the looming 14th-century **Església de Santa Maria del Pi** (☎93 318 47 43; www.basilicadelpi.com; ◷10am-6pm; adult/concession/under 6yr €4/3/free) famed for its magnificent rose window.

4 Follow the curving road to **Plaça Reial**, one of Barcelona's prettiest squares. Flanking the fountain are Gaudí-designed lamp posts.

La Rambla de Sant Josep

C d'en Roca

C. del Petritxol

Plaça del Pi

Plaça de St Josep Oriol

3 Plaça de Sant Josep Oriol

C del Cardenal Cassañas

La Rambla

C de la Boqueria

C d'en Quintana

Plaça de la Boqueria

Ⓜ Liceu

C de n'Arolas

C de Sant Pau

La Rambla dels Caputxins

C de la Unió

N
0.1 miles
200 m

Plaça d'Antoni Maura

C del Dr Joaquim Pou

Av de la Catedral

Via Laietana

C de la Tapineria

Plaça de la Seu

Plaça Nova

Plaça de Sant Iu

C dels Comtes

1 START

7 FINISH

C de Santa Llúcia

C de Sant Sever

C del Paradís

C del Bisbe

C de la Llibreteria

2

Baixada de Santa Eulàlia

C de Sant Honorat

6

Placeta de Manuel Ribé

C de Marlet

5

Plaça de Sant Jaume

C dels Banys Nous

C del Call

C d'en Raurıc

C de Ferran

C de les Heures

C de la Lleona

C dels Escudellers Blancs

4

C del Vidre

7 The final stop is picturesque **Plaça del Rei** (p81). The former palace today houses a superb history museum, with significant Roman ruins.

6 Cross Plaça de Sant Jaume and turn left after Carrer del Bisbe. You'll pass the entrance to a ruined **Roman Temple**, with four columns hidden in a small courtyard.

Take a Break...
In the heart of El Call, the medieval Jewish quarter, **Alcoba Azul** (☑93 302 81 41; Carrer de Sant Domènec del Call 14; ⊙6pm-2.30am winter, noon-2am summer) is atmospheric.

5 Nearby you'll find **Sinagoga Major** (☑93 317 07 90; www.callde barcelona.org; Carrer de Marlet 5; ⊙11am-5.30pm Mon-Fri, to 3pm Sat & Sun winter, 10.30am-6.30pm Mon-Fri, to 2.30pm Sat & Sun summer; ⓂLiceu) **FREE**, one of Europe's oldest synagogues.

long housed the Museu de Zoologia, which has since been transferred to the Fòrum area.

◉ La Barceloneta & Waterfront

The formerly industrial waterfront has experienced a dramatic transformation in the last three decades, with sparkling beaches and seaside bars and restaurants, elegant sculptures, a 4.5km-long boardwalk, ultra-modern high-rises and yacht-filled marinas. Your gateway to the Mediterranean is the gridlike neighbourhood of Barceloneta, an old-fashioned fishing quarter full of traditional seafood eateries.

Museu Marítim   Museum
(☎93 342 99 20; www.mmb.cat; Avinguda de les Drassanes; adult/child €7/3.50, 3-8pm Sun free; ⊗10am-8pm; ⓂDrassanes) These mighty Gothic shipyards shelter the Museu Marítim, a remarkable relic from Barcelona's days as the seat of a seafaring empire. Highlights include a full-sized replica (made in the 1970s) of Don Juan of Austria's 16th-century flagship, fishing vessels, antique navigation charts and dioramas of the Barcelona waterfront.

Platjes   Beach
(🚌36, 41, ⓂCiutadella Vila Olímpic, Bogatell, Llacuna, Selva de Mar) A series of pleasant beaches stretches northeast from the Port Olímpic marina. They are largely artificial, but this doesn't stop an estimated seven million bathers from piling in every year!

Museu d'Història
de Catalunya   Museum
(Museum of Catalonian History; ☎93 225 47 00; www.mhcat.net; Plaça de Pau Vila 3; adult/child €4.50/3.50, last Tue of the month Oct-Jun free; ⊗10am-7pm Tue & Thu-Sat, to 8pm Wed, to 2.30pm Sun; ⓂBarceloneta) Inside the Palau de Mar, this worthwhile museum takes you from the Stone Age through to the early 1980s. It is a hotchpotch of dioramas, artefacts, videos, models, documents and interactive bits: all up, an entertaining exploration of 2000 years of Catalan history. Signage is in Catalan/Spanish.

L'Aquàrium   Aquarium
(☎93 221 74 74; www.aquariumbcn.com; Moll d'Espanya; adult/child €20/15, dive €300; ⊗9.30am-11pm Jul & Aug, to 9pm Sep-Jun; ⓂDrassanes) It is hard not to shudder at the sight of a shark gliding above you, displaying its toothy, wide-mouthed grin. But the 80m shark tunnel here is the highlight. One of Europe's largest marine exhibits, L'Aquàrium has the world's best Mediterranean collection and plenty of colourful fish from as far off as the Red Sea, the Caribbean and the Great Barrier Reef. All up, some 11,000 fish (including a dozen sharks) of 450 species reside here.

Platja de la Barceloneta   Beach
(ⓂBarceloneta) This beach, just east of its namesake neighbourhood, has obvious appeal, with Mediterranean delights, plus ample eating and drinking options inland from the beach when you need a bit of refreshment.

Edge Brewing   Brewery
(www.edgebrewing.com; Carrer de Llull 62; tours including beer tastings €20; ⊗tours by appointment; ⓂBogatell) Founded by two Americans in 2013, Edge Brewing has already racked up some impressive awards for its craft beers (among other things it was named top new brewer in the world in 2014 by RateBeer.com). On a brewery tour, you'll get a behind-the-scenes look at Edge's operations, and get to taste some of its classic (like the Hoptimista, an award-winning 6.6% IPA) and seasonal brews (the summertime Apassion-ada is a passionfruit sour ale).

◉ L'Eixample

As well as being a showcase for Modernista architecture, including Gaudí's La Sagrada Família, L'Eixample has a celebrated dining scene, along with high-end boutiques and wildly diverse nightlife: university party spots, gilded cocktail lounges and the buzzing gay club scene of 'Gaixample' are all part of the mix.

Casa Amatller   Architecture
(Map p89; ☎93 461 74 60; www.amatller.org; Passeig de Gràcia 41; adult/child 6-12yr/under 6yr

La Sagrada & L'Eixample

La Sagrada & L'Eixample

⊙ Sights	
1 Casa Amatller	C3
2 Casa Batlló	C3
3 Casa de les Punxes	C2
4 Casa Lleó Morera	C3
5 La Pedrera	B3
6 La Sagrada Família	D1
7 Palau del Baró Quadras	B2
8 Palau Montaner	C2

⊗ Eating	
9 Cerveseria Catalana	B3
10 Speakeasy	A3
11 Tapas 24	C3

⊖ Drinking & Nightlife	
Dry Martini	(see 10)
12 Les Gens Que J'Aime	C3

1hr tours €15/7.50/free, 30min tours €12/7/free; ⊙11am-6pm; Ⓜ Passeig de Gràcia) One of Puig i Cadafalch's most striking bits of Modernista fantasy, Casa Amatller combines Gothic window frames with a stepped gable borrowed from Dutch urban architecture. But the busts and reliefs of dragons, knights and other characters dripping off the main facade are pure caprice. The pillared foyer and staircase lit by stained glass are like the inside of some romantic castle. The building was renovated in 1900 for the chocolate baron and philanthropist Antoni Amatller (1851–1910).

Casa Lleó Morera   Architecture

(Map p89; ☎ 93 676 27 33; www.casalleo morera.com; Passeig de Gràcia 35; guided tours adult/concession/under 12yr €15/13.50/free, express tours adult/under 12yr €12/free; ⊙10am-1.30pm & 3-7pm Tue-Sun; Ⓜ Passeig de Gràcia) Domènech i Montaner's 1905 contribution to the Manzana de la Discordia, with Modernista carving outside and a bright, tiled lobby in which floral motifs predominate, is perhaps the least odd-looking of the three main buildings on the block. Since 2014 part of the building has been open to the public (by guided tour only – a one-hour tour in

Tickets to FC Barcelona Matches

Tickets to FC Barcelona matches are available at Camp Nou (p107), online (through FC Barcelona's official website: www.fcbarcelona.com), and through various city locations. Tourist offices sell them – the branch at Plaça de Catalunya is a centrally located option – as do FC Botiga stores. Tickets can cost anything from €39 to upwards of €250, depending on the seat and match. On match day the ticket windows (at gates 9 and 15) open from 9.15am until kick-off. Tickets are not usually available for matches with Real Madrid.

FC Barcelona logo
CHARNSITR / SHUTTERSTOCK ©

English at 11am, and 'express tours' every 30 minutes), so you can appreciate the 1st floor, giddy with swirling sculptures, rich mosaics and whimsical decor.

Casa de les Punxes Architecture
(Casa Terrades; Map p89; Avinguda Diagonal 420; MDiagonal) Puig i Cadafalch's Casa Terrades is better known as the Casa de les Punxes (House of Spikes) because of its pointed turrets. This apartment block, completed in 1905, looks like a fairy-tale castle and has the singular attribute of being the only fully detached building in L'Eixample.

Palau Montaner Architecture
(Map p89; ☑93 317 76 52; www.fundaciotapies. org; Carrer de Mallorca 278; adult/child €7/free; ⊙guided tours 11am Sat; MPasseig de Gràcia) Interesting on the outside and made all the more enticing by its gardens, this creation by Domènech i Montaner is spectacular on the

inside. Completed in 1896, its central feature is a grand staircase beneath a broad, ornamental skylight. The interior is laden with sculptures (some by Eusebi Arnau), mosaics and fine woodwork. It is currently only open by guided tour, organised by the Fundació Tàpies and in Catalan only.

Palau del Baró Quadras Architecture
(Map p89; ☑93 467 80 00; www.llull.cat; Avinguda Diagonal 373; ⊙8am-8pm Mon-Fri; MDiagonal) FREE Puig i Cadafalch designed Palau del Baró Quadras (built 1902–06) in an exuberant Gothic-inspired style. The main facade is its most intriguing, with a soaring, glassed-in gallery. Take a closer look at the gargoyles and reliefs – the pair of toothy fish and the sword-wielding knight clearly have the same artistic signature as the architect behind Casa Amatller. Decor inside is eclectic, but dominated by Middle Eastern and East Asian themes.

Recinte Modernista de Sant Pau Architecture
(☑93 553 78 01; www.santpaubarcelona.org; Carrer de Sant Antoni Maria Claret 167; adult/concession/under 16yr €10/7/free; ⊙10am-6.30pm Mon-Sat, to 2.30pm Sun; MSant Pau/Dos de Maig) Domènech i Montaner outdid himself as architect and philanthropist with the Modernista Hospital de la Santa Creu i de Sant Pau, redubbed in 2014 the 'Recinte Modernista'. It was considered one of the city's most important hospitals, and only recently repurposed, its various spaces becoming cultural centres, offices and something of a monument. The complex, including 16 pavilions – together with the Palau de la Música Catalana, a joint World Heritage site – is lavishly decorated and each pavilion is unique.

◎ Camp Nou, Pedralbes & La Zona Alta

Several of Barcelona's most sacred sights nestle inside the huge expanse beyond L'Eixample. One is the peaceful monastery of Pedralbes, another is the great shrine to Catalan football, Camp Nou. Other attractions include the amusement park and great views atop Tibidabo, the wooded trails of Parc de Collserola and a kid-friendly science museum.

Camp Nou Experience Museum

(☏902 189900; www.fcbarcelona.com; Gate 9, Avinguda de Joan XXIII; adult/child €23/18; ⊗9.30am-7.30pm daily Apr-Sep, 10am-6.30pm Mon-Sat, to 2.30pm Sun Oct-Mar; ⓂPalau Reial) A pilgrimage site for football fans from around the world, Camp Nou (p107) is one of Barcelona's most hallowed grounds. While nothing compares to the excitement of attending a live match, the Camp Nou Experience is a must for FC Barcelona fans. On this self-guided tour, you'll get an in-depth look at the club, starting with a museum filled with multimedia exhibits, trophies and historical displays, followed by a tour of the stadium.

⊙ TOURS

Oficina d'Informació de Turisme de Barcelona Walking Tour

(Map p82; ☏93 285 38 34; www.barcelona turisme.com; Plaça de Catalunya 17; ⊗9.30am-9.30pm; ⓂCatalunya) Organises a series of guided walking tours of the Barri Gòtic (adult/child €16/free); Picasso's footsteps, winding up at the Museu Picasso to which entry is included in the price (€22//); and jewels of Modernisme (€16/free). There's also a 'gourmet' tour of traditional purveyors of fine foodstuffs across the Ciutat Vella (€22/7). Tours typically last two hours and start at the tourist office.

Barcelona Metro Walks Walking Tour

(€16 including a walk guide, two-day transport pass and map) Consists of seven self-guided routes combining public transport as well as stretches on foot. Sold at tourist information points at Plaça de Catalunya and Plaça de Sant Jaume.

My Favourite Things Tour

(☏637 265405; www.myft.net; tours from €26) Offers tours for no more than 10 participants based on numerous themes: anything from design to food. Other activities include flamenco and salsa classes, and bicycle rides in and out of Barcelona.

Camp Nou

Runner Bean Tours   Walking Tour

(Map p82; ☑636 108776; www.runnerbeantours.
com; Carrer del Carme 44; ⊙tours 11am year-round
& 4.30pm Apr-Sep; MLiceu) Daily thematic
tours. It's a pay-what-you-wish tour, with
a collection taken at the end for the guide.
The Old City tour explores the Roman and
medieval history of Barcelona, visiting
highlights in the Ciutat Vella. The Gaudí
tour takes in the great works of Modernista
Barcelona; it involves two trips on the metro.
Also has ghostly evening tours and a Kids &
Family walking tour. Check the website for
departure times.

🅐 SHOPPING

If your doctor has prescribed an intense
round of retail therapy to deal with the blues,
then Barcelona is the place. Across the
Ciutat Vella (the Barri Gòtic, El Raval and La
Ribera), L'Eixample and Gràcia is spread a
thick mantle of boutiques, historic shops,
original one-off stores, gourmet corners,
wine dens and more designer labels than
you can shake your gold card at. You name it,
you'll find it here.

El Rei de la Màgia   Magic

(Map p82; ☑93 319 39 20; www.elreydelamagia.
com; Carrer de la Princesa 11; ⊙10.30am-2pm
& 4-7.30pm Mon-Sat; MJaume I) For more
than 100 years, the people behind this box
of tricks have been keeping locals both
astounded and amused. Should you decide
to stay in Barcelona and make a living as a
magician, this is the place to buy levitation
brooms, glasses of disappearing milk and
decks of magic cards.

Vila Viniteca   Wine

(Map p82; ☑902 327777; www.vilaviniteca.es;
Carrer dels Agullers 7; ⊙8.30am-8.30pm Mon-Sat;
MJaume I) One of the best wine stores in
Barcelona (and there are a few...), this place
has been searching out the best local and
imported wines since 1932. On a couple of
November evenings it organises what has
become an almost riotous wine-tasting
event in Carrer dels Agullers and surrounding lanes, at which cellars from around Spain
present their young new wines.

Herboristeria del Rei   Beauty

(Map p82; ☑93 318 05 12; www.herboristeria
delrei.com; Carrer del Vidre 1; ⊙2-8.30pm Mon,

Els Encants Vells

10am-8.30pm Tue-Sat; MLiceu) Once patronised by Queen Isabel II, this timeless corner store flogs all sorts of weird and wonderful herbs, spices and medicinal plants. It's been doing so since 1823 and the decor has barely changed since the 1860s. However, some of the products have, and you'll find anything from fragrant soaps to massage oil nowadays.

Cereria Subirà   Homewares
(Map p82; ☑93 315 26 06; Baixada de la Llibreteria 7; ⊙9.30am-1.30pm & 4-8pm Mon-Thu, 9.30am-8pm Fri, 10am-8pm Sat; MJaume I) Even if you're not interested in myriad mounds of colourful wax, pop in just so you've been to the oldest shop in Barcelona. Cereria Subirà has been churning out candles since 1761 and at this address since the 19th century; the interior has a beautifully baroque quality, with a picturesque *Gone With the Wind* staircase.

Els Encants Vells   Market
(Fira de Bellcaire; ☑93 246 30 30; www.encants bcn.com; Plaça de les Glòries Catalanes; ⊙9am-8pm Mon, Wed, Fri & Sat; MGlòries) In a gleaming open-sided complex near Plaça de les Glòries Catalanes, the 'Old Charms' flea market is the biggest of its kind in Barcelona. More than 500 vendors ply their wares beneath massive mirror-like panels. It's all here, from antique furniture through to secondhand clothes. A lot of it is junk, but occasionally you'll stumble across a *ganga* (bargain).

🍽 EATING

Barcelona has a celebrated food scene fuelled by a combination of world-class chefs, imaginative recipes and magnificent ingredients fresh from farms and the sea. Catalan culinary masterminds like Ferran Adrià and Carles Abellan have become international icons, reinventing the world of haute cuisine, while classic old-world Catalan recipes continue to earn accolades in dining rooms and tapas bars across the city.

🛍 Shopping Strips

Avinguda del Portal de l'Àngel This broad pedestrian avenue is lined with high-street chains, shoe shops, bookshops and more. It feeds into Carrer dels Boters and Carrer de la Portaferrissa, characterised by stores offering light-hearted costume jewellery and youth-oriented streetwear.

Avinguda Diagonal This boulevard is loaded with international fashion names and design boutiques, suitably interspersed with cafes to allow weary shoppers to take a load off.

Carrer d'Avinyó Once a fairly squalid old city street, Carrer d'Avinyó has morphed into a dynamic young fashion street.

Carrer de la Riera Baixa The place to look for a gaggle of shops flogging preloved threads.

Carrer del Petritxol Best for chocolate shops and art.

Carrer dels Banys Nous Along with nearby Carrer de la Palla, this is the place to look for antiques.

Passeig de Gràcia This is the premier shopping boulevard, chic with a capital 'C', and mostly given over to big-name international brands.

✪ La Rambla & Barri Gòtic

Xurreria   Churros €
(Map p82; ☑93 318 76 91; Carrer dels Banys Nous 8; cone €1.20; ⊙7.30am-1.30pm & 3.30-8.15pm; MJaume I) It doesn't look much from the outside, but this brightly lit street joint is Barcelona's best spot for paper cones of piping-hot churros − long batter sticks fried and sprinkled with sugar and best enjoyed dunked in hot chocolate.

Cafè de l'Acadèmia   Catalan €€
(Map p82; ☑93 319 82 53; Carrer dels Lledó 1; mains €14-18; ⊙1-3.30pm & 8-11pm Mon-Fri; 🛜; MJaume I) Expect a mix of traditional Catalan dishes with the occasional creative twist.

Walking Tour: Gràcia's Squares

One of Barcelona's most vibrant districts, Gràcia was an independent town until the 1890s. Explore the }barrio's picturesque squares and experience its beauty, history and culture.

Start Plaça de Joan Carles I
Distance 1.9km
Duration 50 minutes

Take a Break...
La Nena (☏ 93 285 14 76; www.chocolaterialanena.com; Carrer de Ramon y Cajal 36; ☻9am-10pm) is a chaotic, exuberant, gem of a cafe.

7 Busy, elongated **Plaça de la Revolució de Setembre de 1868** commemorates the toppling of Queen Isabel II.

4 Plaça de la Llibertat is home to a Modernista produce market (pictured), designed by Francesc Berenguer i Mestres, Gaudí's long-time assistant.

Gràcia Ⓜ

3 Plaça de Galla Placidia recalls the brief sojourn of the Roman empress-to-be Galla Placidia in the 5th century AD.

2 Where **Carrer Gran de Gràcia** leads you into Gràcia proper, the grand Modernista Casa Fuster (p94) rises in all its glory.

GRÀCIA

FINISH

8

SANT
GERVASI

START

Av Diagonal

Diagonal Ⓜ

8 Pleasant terraces adorn pedestrianised **Plaça de la Virreina**, presided over by the 17th-century Església de Sant Joan.

6 Possibly the rowdiest of Gràcia's squares, **Plaça del Sol** is lined with bars and eateries, which buzz on summer nights.

5 Popular **Plaça de la Vila de Gràcia** is home to the Torre del Rellotge (Clock Tower), long a symbol of Republican agitation.

1 The obelisk at **Plaça de Joan Carles I** honours Spain's present king for stifling an attempted coup d'état in 1981.

Park Güell

North of Gràcia and about 4km from Plaça de Catalunya, **Park Güell** (⌨93 409 18 31; www.parkguell.cat; Carrer d'Olot 7; admission to central area adult/child €8/6; ☺8am-9.30pm May-Aug, to 8pm Sep-Apr; ☐24, 32, MLesseps, Vallcarca) is where Gaudí turned his hand to landscape gardening. It's a strange, enchanting place where his passion for natural forms really took flight – to the point where the artificial almost seems more natural than the natural.

Gaudí-designed fountain
ELI_ASENOVA / GETTY IMAGES ©

At lunchtime, local Ajuntament (town hall) office workers pounce on the *menú del día* (€14.30). In the evening it is rather more romantic, as low lighting emphasises the intimacy of the beamed ceiling and stone walls. On warm days you can also dine on the pretty square at the front.

La Vinateria del Call   Spanish €€
(Map p82; ⌨93 302 60 92; www.lavinateriadel call.com; Carrer de Sant Domènec del Call 9; small plates €7-12; ☺7.30pm-1am; MJaume I) In a magical setting in the former Jewish quarter, this tiny jewel box of a restaurant (recently extended to add another dining room) serves up tasty Iberian dishes including Galician octopus, cider-cooked chorizo and the Catalan *escalivada* (roasted peppers, aubergine and onions) with anchovies. Portions are small and made for sharing, and there's a good and affordable selection of wines.

Els Quatre Gats   Catalan €€€
(Map p82; ⌨93 302 41 40; www.4gats.com; Carrer de Montsió 3; mains €21-29; ☺12.30-4.30pm & 6.30pm-1am; ☎; MUrquinaona) Once the lair of Barcelona's Modernista artists, Els Quatre Gats is a stunning example of the movement, inside and out, with its colourful tiles, geometric brickwork and wooden fittings. The restaurant is not quite as thrilling as its setting, though you can just have a coffee and a croissant in the cafe (open from 9am to 1am) at the front.

✖ El Raval
Mam i Teca   Catalan €€
(⌨93 441 33 35; Carrer de la Lluna 4; mains €9-12; ☺1-4pm & 8pm-midnight Mon, Wed-Fri & Sun, 8pm-midnight Sat; MSant Antoni) A tiny place with half a dozen tables, Mam i Teca is as much a lifestyle choice as a restaurant. Locals drop in and hang at the bar, and diners are treated to Catalan dishes made with locally sourced products that adhere to Slow Food principles (such as cod fried in olive oil with garlic and red pepper, or pork ribs with chickpeas).

Bar Pinotxo   Tapas €€
(Map p82; www.pinotxobar.com; Mercat de la Boqueria; mains €8-17; ☺6am-4pm Mon-Sat; MLiceu) Bar Pinotxo is arguably La Boqueria's, and even Barcelona's, best tapas bar. It sits among the half-dozen or so informal eateries within the market, and the popular owner, Juanito, might serve up chickpeas with pine nuts and raisins, a soft mix of potato and spinach sprinkled with salt, soft baby squid with cannellini beans, or a quivering cube of caramel-sweet pork belly.

✖ La Ribera
Bormuth   Tapas €
(Map p82; ⌨93 310 21 86; Carrer del Rec 31; tapas from €4; ☺1pm-midnight; ☎; MJaume I) Opened on the pedestrian Carrer del Rec in 2013, Bormuth has tapped into the vogue for old-school tapas with modern service and decor, and serves all the old favourites – *patatas bravas* (fried potato with a spicy tomato sauce), *ensaladilla* (Russian salad), tortilla

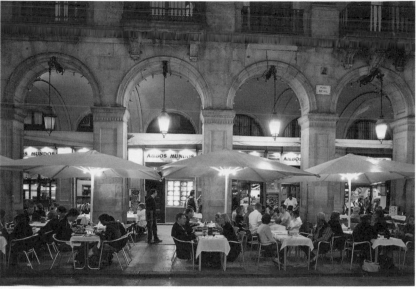

Plaça Reial

– along with some less predictable and superbly prepared numbers (try the chargrilled red pepper with black pudding).

El Atril International €€

(Map p82; ☑93 310 12 20; www.atrilbarcelona. com; Carrer dels Carders 23; mains €11-15; ⊗noon-midnight Mon-Thu, to 1am Fri & Sat, 11.30am-11.30pm Sun; ☎; MJaume I) Aussie owner Brenden is influenced by culinary flavours from all over the globe, so while you'll see plenty of tapas (the *patatas bravas* are recommended for their homemade sauce), you'll also find kangaroo fillet, salmon and date rolls with mascarpone, chargrilled turkey with fried yucca, and plenty more.

Casa Delfín Catalan €€

(Map p82; ☑93 319 50 88; www.tallerdetapas. com; Passeig del Born 36; mains €10-15; ⊗8am-midnight Sun-Thu, to 1am Fri & Sat; ☎; MBarceloneta) One of Barcelona's culinary delights, Casa Delfín is everything you dream of when you think of Catalan (and Mediterranean) cooking. Start with the tangy and sweet *calçots* (a cross between a leek and an onion; February and March only) or salt-strewn *padron* peppers, moving on to grilled sardines speckled with parsley, then tackle the meaty monkfish roasted in white wine and garlic.

Cal Pep Tapas €€

(Map p82; ☑93 310 79 61; www.calpep.com; Plaça de les Olles 8; mains €13-20; ⊗7.30-11.30pm Mon, 1-3.45pm & 7.30-11.30pm Tue-Sat, closed last 3 weeks Aug; MBarceloneta) It's getting a foot in the door of this legendary fish restaurant that's the problem – there can be queues out into the square. And if you want one of the five tables out the back, you'll need to call ahead. Most people are happy elbowing their way to the bar for some of the tastiest seafood tapas in town.

❌ La Barceloneta & Waterfront

La Cova Fumada Tapas €

(☑93 221 40 61; Carrer del Baluard 56; tapas €4-8; ⊗9am-3.20pm Mon-Wed, 9am-3.20pm & 6-8.15pm Thu & Fri, 9am-1pm Sat; MBarceloneta) There's no sign and the setting is decidedly downmarket, but this tiny, buzzing family-run tapas spot always packs in a crowd.

Montjuïc

Montjuïc

The secret? Mouthwatering *pulpo* (octopus), *calamar, sardinias* and 15 or so other small plates cooked to perfection in the small open kitchen. The *bombas* (potato croquettes served with *alioli*) and grilled *carxofes* (artichokes) are good, but everything is amazingly fresh.

Can Recasens   Catalan €€
(☏93 300 81 23; Rambla del Poblenou 102; mains €7-15; ☺9pm-1am Mon-Fri, 1-4pm & 9pm-1am Sat; ⓂPoblenou) One of Poblenou's most romantic settings, Can Recasens hides a warren of warmly lit rooms full of oil paintings, flickering candles, fairy lights and

baskets of fruit. The food is outstanding, with a mix of salads, fondues, smoked meats, cheeses, and open-faced sandwiches piled high with delicacies like wild mushrooms and brie, *escalivada* (grilled vegetables) and Gruyère, and spicy chorizo.

El 58   Tapas €€
(Le Cinquante Huit; Rambla del Poblenou 58; sharing plates €4-11; ☺1.30pm-midnight Tue-Sat; ⓂLlacuna) This French-Catalan eatery serves imaginative, beautifully prepared tapas dishes that earn rave reviews from both locals and expats. Solo diners can grab a seat at the marble-topped front bar and get

dining tips from the friendly multilingual baristas. The back dining room with its exposed brick walls, industrial light fixtures and curious artworks is a lively place to linger over a long meal.

Kaiku   Seafood €€

(☏93 221 90 82; www.restaurantkaiku.cat; Plaça del Mar 1; mains for 2 €28-36; �
1-3.30pm Tue-Sun; MBarceloneta) Overlooking the waterfront at the south end of Barceloneta, Kaiku has a solid reputation for its creative seafood plates. Mouth-watering ingredients are sourced from the nearby fish market, and artfully prepared in dishes like crayfish with mint, swordfish carpaccio with avocado and sundried tomatoes, chilli-smeared tuna with green apples and mushrooms, and the outstanding rice dishes for two.

✖ L'Eixample
Tapas 24   Tapas €€

(Map p89; ☏93 488 09 77; www.carlesabellan.com; Carrer de la Diputació 269, tapas €4-9; �
9am-midnight; ☎; MPasseig de Gràcia) Carles Abellan, master of the now-defunct Comerç 24 in La Ribera, runs this basement tapas haven known for its gourmet versions of old faves. Specials include the *bikini* (toasted ham and cheese sandwich – here the ham is cured and the truffle makes all the difference) and a thick black *arròs negre de sípia* (squid-ink black rice).

Cerveseria Catalana   Tapas €€

(Map p89; ☏93 216 03 68; Carrer de Mallorca 236; tapas €4-11; ☎8am-1.30am Mon-Fri, 9am-1.30am Sat & Sun; MPasseig de Gràcia) The 'Catalan Brewery' is good for breakfast, lunch and dinner. Come for your morning coffee and croissant, or enjoy the abundance of tapas and *montaditos* (tapas on a slice of bread) at lunch. You can sit at the bar, on the pavement terrace or in the restaurant at the back. The variety of hot tapas, salads and other snacks draws a well-dressed crowd of locals and outsiders.

Cata 1.81   Tapas €€

(☏93 323 68 18; www.cata181.com; Carrer de València 181; tapas €5.50-8; ☎6pm-midnight

Mon-Sat; MPasseig de Gràcia) A beautifully designed venue (with lots of small lights, some trapped in birdcages), this is the place to come for fine wines and dainty gourmet dishes like *raviolis amb bacallà* (salt-cod dumplings) or *truita de patates i tòfona negre* (thick potato tortilla with a delicate trace of black truffle). The best idea is to choose from one of several tasting-menu options.

Disfrutar   Modern European €€€

(☏93 348 68 96; www.en.disfrutarbarcelona.com; Carrer de Vilarroel 163; tasting menus €75/105/135; ☎1-4pm & 8-11pm Tue-Sat; MHospital Clínic) In its first few months of life, Disfrutar rose stratospherically to become the city's finest restaurant – book now while it's still possible to get a table. Run by alumni of Ferran Adrià's game-changing El Bulli restaurant, it operates along similar lines.

Cinc Sentits   International €€€

(☏93 323 94 90; www.cincsentits.com; Carrer d'Aribau 58; tasting menus €100/120; ☎1.30-3pm & 8.30-10pm Tue-Sat; MPasseig de Gràcia) Enter the realm of the 'Five Senses' to indulge in a jaw-dropping tasting menu consisting of a series of small, experimental dishes (there is no à la carte, although dishes can be tweaked to suit diners' requests). There is a lunch *menú* for €55.

✖ Montjuïc & Poble Sec
Quimet i Quimet   Tapas €€

(Map p98; ☏93 442 31 42; Carrer del Poeta Cabanyes 25; tapas €4-10, montaditos around €3; ☎noon-4pm & 7-10.30pm Mon-Fri, noon-4pm Sat; MParal·lel) Quimet i Quimet is a family-run business that has been passed down from generation to generation. There's barely space to swing a *calamar* in this bottle-lined, standing-room-only place, but it is a treat for the palate, with *montaditos* (tapas on a slice of bread) made to order.

Palo Cortao   Tapas €€

(Map p98; ☏93 188 90 67; www.palocortao.es; Carrer de Nou de la Rambla 14; mains €10-15; ☎8pm-1am Tue-Sun, & 1-5pm Sat & Sun; MParal·lel) Palo Cortao has a solid reputation for its beautifully executed seafood and meat dishes,

🍽 Catalan Main Courses

Arròs a la cassola/arroz a la catalana Catalan paella, cooked without saffron.

Arròs negre Rice cooked in black cuttlefish ink.

Bacallà a la llauna Salted cod baked in tomato, garlic, parsley, paprika and wine.

Botifarra amb mongetes Pork sausage with fried white beans.

Cargols/Caracoles Snails, often stewed with *conill/conejo* (rabbit) and chilli.

Fideuà Similar to paella but with vermicelli noodles as the base. Often accompanied by *allioli* (pounded garlic with olive oil), which you can mix in as you wish.

Fricandó Pork and vegetable stew.

Sarsuela/zarzuela Mixed seafood cooked in *sofregit* (fried onion, tomato and garlic sauce) with seasonings.

Suquet de peix Fish and potato hotpot.

Fideuà
VOLANTHEVIST / GETTY IMAGES ©

served at fair prices. Highlights include octopus with white bean hummus, skirt steak with foie armagnac, and tuna tataki tempura. You can order half sizes of all plates – which will allow you to try more dishes.

Casa Xica   Fusion €€
(Map p98; ☎93 600 58 58; Carrer de la França Xica 20; sharing plates €9-15; ☉1.30-3pm & 8.30-11.30pm Mon-Sat; ⓂPoble Sec) On the parlour floor of an old house, Casa Xica is a casual, but artfully designed space that fuses elements of the Far East with fresh Catalan

ingredients (owners Marc and Raquel lived and travelled in Asia).

Tickets   Modern Spanish €€€
(Map p98; ☎606 225545; www.ticketsbar.es; Avinguda del Paral·lel 164; tapas €5-27; ☉6.30-10.30pm Tue-Fri, 1-3pm & 7-10.30pm Sat, closed Aug; ⓂParal·lel) This is, literally, one of the sizzling tickets in the restaurant world, a tapas bar opened by Ferran Adrià, of the legendary El Bulli, and his brother Albert. And unlike El Bulli, it's an affordable venture – if you can book a table, that is: you can only book online, and two months in advance (or call for last-minute cancellations).

🍷 DRINKING & NIGHTLIFE

Barcelona is a nightlife lovers' town, with an enticing spread of candlelit wine bars, old-school taverns, stylish lounges and bright nightclubs where the party continues until daybreak. For something a little more sedate, the city's atmospheric cafes and teahouses make a fine retreat when the skies turn grey.

🍸 La Rambla & Barri Gòtic

La Rambla holds little interest, so leave it to those content to settle for expensive pints, and plunge into the narrow streets and back alleys of the lower end of the Barri Gòtic. Check out Carrer dels Escudellers, Carrer Ample (and the parallel Carrer d'en Gignàs and Carrer del Correu Vell) and the area around Plaça Reial.

Ginger   Cocktail Bar
(Map p82; ☎93 310 53 09; www.ginger.cat; Carrer de Palma de Sant Just 1; ☉7.30pm-2.30am Tue-Thu, 7.30pm-3am Fri & Sat; ⓂJaume I) Tucked away just off peaceful Plaça de Sant Just, Ginger is an art deco–style multilevel drinking den with low lighting, finely crafted cocktails and good ambient sounds (provided by vinyl-spinning DJs some nights). It's a mellow spot that's great for sipping wine and sampling from the gourmet tapas menu.

Caelum   Cafe
(Map p82; ☎93 302 69 93; www.caelum barcelona.com; Carrer de la Palla 8; ☉10.30am-

8.30pm Mon-Thu, to 11pm Fri & Sat, to 9pm Sun; Ⓜ Liceu) Centuries of heavenly gastronomic tradition from across Spain are concentrated in this exquisite medieval space in the heart of the city. The upstairs cafe is a dainty setting for decadent cakes and pastries, while descending into the underground chamber with its stone walls and flickering candles is like stepping into the Middle Ages.

Cafè de l'Òpera
Cafe

(Map p82; ☎ 93 317 75 85; www.cafeoperabcn.com; La Rambla 74; ⊗ 8.30am-2.30am; ☎; Ⓜ Liceu) Opposite the Gran Teatre del Liceu is La Rambla's most intriguing cafe. Operating since 1929, it is pleasant enough for an early evening libation or coffee and croissants. Head upstairs for an elevated seat above the busy boulevard. Can you be tempted by the *cafè de l'Òpera* (coffee with chocolate mousse)?

L'Ascensor
Bar

(Map p82; ☎ 93 318 53 47; Carrer de la Bellafila 3; ⊗ 6pm-2.30am Sun-Thu, to 3am Fri & Sat; ☎; Ⓜ Jaume I) Named after the lift (elevator) doors that serve as the front door, this elegant drinking den with its vaulted brick ceilings, vintage mirrors and marble-topped bar gathers a faithful crowd that comes for old-fashioned cocktails and lively conversation against a soundtrack of up-tempo jazz and funk.

Salterio
Cafe

(Map p82; Carrer de Sant Domènec del Call 4; ⊗ 11am-midnight, to 1am Fri & Sat; ☎; Ⓜ Jaume I) A wonderfully photogenic candlelit spot tucked down a tiny lane in El Call, Salterio serves refreshing teas, Turkish coffee, authentic mint teas and snacks amid stone walls, incense and ambient Middle Eastern music. If hunger strikes, try the *sardo* (grilled flatbread covered with pesto, cheese or other toppings).

Sor Rita
Bar

(Map p82; ☎ 93 176 62 66; www.sorritabar.es; Carrer de la Mercè 27; ⊗ 7pm-3am Sun-Thu, to 3.30am Fri & Sat; ☎; Ⓜ Jaume I) A lover of all things kitsch, Sor Rita is pure eye candy, from its leopard-print wallpaper to its high-heel-festooned ceiling and deliciously irreverent decorations inspired by the films

Platja de la Barceloneta (p88)

ALAN COPSON / GETTY IMAGES ©

of Pedro Almodóvar. It's a fun and festive scene, with special-event nights including tarot readings on Mondays, €5 all-you-can-eat snack buffets on Tuesdays, karaoke or cabaret on Wednesdays, and gin specials on Thursdays.

Ocaña   Bar

(Map p82; 📞93 676 48 14; www.ocana.cat; Plaça Reial 13; ⏰noon-2.30am Mon-Fri, 11am-2.30am Sat & Sun; 🛜; Ⓜ Liceu) Named after a flamboyant artist who once lived on Plaça Reial, Ocaña is a beautifully designed space with chandeliers and plush furnishings. Have a seat on the terrace and watch the passing people parade, or head downstairs to the Moorish-inspired Apotheke bar or the chic lounge a few steps away, where DJs spin for a mix of beauties and bohemians on weekend nights.

La Cerveteca   Bar

(Map p82; www.lacerveteca.com; Carrer d'en Gignàs 25; ⏰6pm-midnight Tue-Fri, noon-3.30pm & 6pm-midnight Sat, noon-3.30pm Sun; Ⓜ Jaume I) An unmissable stop for beer lovers, La Cerveteca serves an impressive variety of global craft brews. In addition to scores of bottled beers, there's a frequent rotation

of what's on draught. Cheeses, *jamón ibérico* and other charcuterie selections are on hand, including *cecina* (cured horse meat).

🍷 El Raval

Bars and clubs have been opening up along the shadowy side streets of El Raval for the past two decades, and despite its vestigial edginess, it's now a great place to go out. You'll find super-trendy places alongside some great old taverns that still thrive – there are joints that have been the hang-outs of the city's bohemia since Picasso's time. The lower end of El Raval has a history of insalubriousness and the area around Carrer de Sant Pau retains its seedy feel: drug dealers, pickpockets and prostitutes mingle with nocturnal hedonists. Keep your wits about you if walking around here late at night.

La Confitería   Bar

(Map p98; Carrer de Sant Pau 128; ⏰7.30pm-2.30am Mon-Thu, 6pm-3.30am Fri, 5pm-3.30am Sat, 12.45pm-2.45am Sun; Ⓜ Paral·lel) This is a trip into the 19th century. Until the 1980s it was a confectioner's shop, and although the original cabinets are now lined with booze,

From left: Sangría; Paella (p329); *Botifarra amb mongetes* (p100)

the look of the place barely changed with its conversion into a laid back bar. A quiet enough spot for a house *vermut* (vermouth, €3; add your own soda) in the early evening.

Boadas
Cocktail Bar

(Map p82; www.boadascocktails.com; Carrer dels Tallers 1; ⏱noon-2am Mon-Thu, noon-3am Fri & Sat; ⓜCatalunya) One of the city's oldest cocktail bars, Boadas is famed for its daiquiris. Bow-tied waiters have been serving up unique, drinkable creations since Miguel Boadas opened it in 1933 – in fact Miró and Hemingway both drank here. Miguel was born in Havana, where he was the first barman at the immortal La Floridita.

Casa Almirall
Bar

(www.casaalmirall.com; Carrer de Joaquín Costa 33; ⏱6pm-2.30am Mon-Thu, 6.30pm-3am Fri, noon-3am Sat, noon-12.30am Sun; ⓜUniversitat) In business since the 1860s, this unchanged corner bar is dark and intriguing, with Modernista decor and a mixed clientele. There are some great original pieces in here, such as the marble counter, and the cast-iron statue of the muse of the Universal Exposition, held in Barcelona in 1888.

Bar Marsella
Bar

(☎93 442 72 63; Carrer de Sant Pau 65; ⏱10pm-2.30am Mon-Thu, 10pm-3am Fri & Sat; ⓜLiceu) This bar has been in business since 1820, and has served the likes of Hemingway, who was known to slump here over an *absenta* (absinthe). The bar still specialises in absinthe, a drink to be treated with respect.

🅞 La Ribera

There are several bars along Passeig del Born and the web of streets winding off it and around the Basílica de Santa Maria del Mar – the area has an ebullient, party feel.

El Born Bar
Bar

(Map p82; ☎93 319 53 33; Passeig del Born 26; ⏱10am-2am Mon-Sat, noon-1.30am Sun; 🛜; ⓜJaume I) El Born Bar effortlessly attracts everyone from cool thirty-somethings from all over town to locals who pass judgment on Passeig del Born's passing parade. Its staying power depends on a good selection of beers, spirits, and *empanadas* and other snacks.

🏛 Domènech i Montaner

Although overshadowed by Gaudí, Lluís Domènech i Montaner (1850–1923) was one of the great masters of Modernisme. He was a widely travelled man of prodigious intellect, with knowledge of everything from mineralogy to medieval heraldry, and he was an architectural professor, a prolific writer and a nationalist politician. The question of Catalan identity and how to create a national architecture consumed Domènech i Montaner, who designed more than a dozen large-scale works in his lifetime.

The exuberant, steel-framed Palau de la Música Catalana is one of his masterpieces. Adorning the facade are elaborate Gothic-style windows, floral designs (Domènech i Montaner also studied botany) and sculptures depicting characters from Catalan folklore and the music world as well as everyday citizens of Barcelona. Inside, the hall leaves visitors dazzled with delicate floral-covered colonnades, radiant stained-glass walls and ceiling, and a rolling, sculpture-packed proscenium referencing the epics of musical lore.

His other great masterpiece is the Hospital de la Santa Creu i de Sant Pau (p90; Recinte Modernista de Sant Pau), with sparkling mosaics on the facade and a stained-glass skylight which fills the vestibule with golden light (like Matisse, Domènech i Montaner believed in the therapeutic powers of colour).

Palau de la Música Catalana (p85)
RODRIGO GARRIDO / SHUTTERSTOCK ©

Guzzo   Cocktail Bar
(Map p82; ☑93 667 00 36; www.guzzo.es; Plaça Comercial 10; ⊙6pm-3am Tue-Thu, to 3.30am Fri & Sat, noon-3am Sun; 🛜; MBarceloneta) A swish but relaxed cocktail bar, run by much-loved Barcelona DJ Fred Guzzo, who is often to be found at the decks, spinning his delicious selection of funk, soul and rare groove. You'll also find frequent live-music acts of consistently decent quality, and a funky atmosphere at almost any time of day.

Juanra Falces   Cocktail Bar
(Map p82; ☑93 310 10 27; Carrer del Rec 24; ⊙8pm-3am Tue-Sat, 10pm-3am Sun & Mon; MJaume I) Transport yourself to a Humphrey Bogart movie in this narrow little bar, formerly (and still, at least among the locals) known as Gimlet. White-jacketed bar staff with all the appropriate aplomb will whip you up a gimlet or any other classic cocktail (around €10) that your heart desires.

La Vinya del Senyor   Wine Bar
(Map p82; ☑93 310 33 79; www.lavinyadel senyor.com; Plaça de Santa Maria del Mar 5; ⊙noon-1am Mon-Thu, noon-2am Fri & Sat, noon-midnight Sun; 🛜; MJaume I) Relax on the *terrassa*, which lies in the shadow of the Basílica de Santa Maria del Mar, or crowd inside at the tiny bar. The wine list is as long as *War and Peace* and there's a table upstairs for those who opt to sample by the bottle rather than the glass.

Mudanzas   Bar
(Map p82; ☑93 319 11 37; Carrer de la Vidrieria 15; ⊙10am-2am Sun-Thu, to 3am Fri & Sat; 🛜; MJaume I) This was one of the first bars to get things into gear in El Born and it still attracts a crowd. With its chequered floor and marble-topped tables, it's an attractive, lively place for a beer and a tapa. It also has a nice line in rums and malt whisky.

Rubí   Bar
(Map p82; ☑647 773707; Carrer dels Banys Vells 6; ⊙7.30pm-2.30am Sun-Thu, to 3am Fri & Sat; MJaume I) With its boudoir lighting and cheap mojitos, Rubí is where the Born's cognoscenti head for a nightcap – or several. It's a narrow, cosy space – push through to the

Recinte Modernista de Sant Pau (p90)

back where you might just get one of the coveted tables, with superior bar food, from Vietnamese rolls to more traditional selections of cheese and ham.

🍷 La Barceloneta & Waterfront

The northeastern end of the beach on the Barceloneta waterfront near Port Olímpic is a pleasant corner of evening chic that takes on a balmy, almost Caribbean air in the warmer months. A selection of restaurant-lounges and trendy bar-clubs vies for your attention. Further north, the seaside beach bars draw a laid-back crowd when summertime arrives. Head inland to explore the emerging night spots of Poblenou, which has a mix of cocktail lounges, brewpubs and outdoor places along Rambla del Poblenou.

Absenta   Bar

(www.absentabar.es; Carrer de Sant Carles 36; ⊙7pm-1am Tue & Wed, from 11am Thu-Mon; MᴍBarceloneta) Decorated with old paintings, vintage lamps and curious sculpture (including a dangling butterfly woman and face-painted TVs), this whimsical and creative drinking den takes its liquor seriously. Stop in for the

house-made vermouth or for more bite try one of the many absinthes on hand. Just go easy: with an alcohol content of 50% to 90%, these spirits have kick!

Can Paixano   Wine Bar

(Map p82; ☑93 310 08 39; Carrer de la Reina Cristina 7; ⊙9am-10.30pm Mon-Sat; MᴍBarceloneta) This lofty old champagne bar (also called La Xampanyeria) has long been run on a winning formula. The standard poison is bubbly rosé in elegant little glasses, combined with bite-sized *bocadillos* (filled rolls) and tapas (€3 to €7). Note that this place is usually jammed to the rafters, and elbowing your way to the bar can be a titanic struggle.

🍷 L'Eixample

Much of middle-class L'Eixample is dead at night, but several streets are exceptions. Noisy Carrer de Balmes is thronged with an adolescent set. More interesting is the cluster of locales lining Carrer d'Aribau between Avinguda Diagonal and Carrer de Mallorca. They range from quiet cocktail bars to '60s retro joints. Few get going much before midnight and are generally closed or dead

Barcelona on Film

All about my Mother (director Pedro Almodóvar, 1999) One of Almodóvar's best-loved films is full of plot twists and dark humour, complete with transsexual prostitutes and doe-eyed nuns.

Vicky Cristina Barcelona (director Woody Allen, 2008) Allen gives Barcelona the *Manhattan* treatment, showing a city of startling beauty and neuroticism.

L'Auberge Espagnole (director Cédric Klapisch, 2002) Warmly told coming-of-age story about a mishmash of foreign-exchange students thrown together in Barcelona.

Barcelona (director Whit Stillman, 1994) A sharp and witty romantic comedy about two Americans living in Barcelona during the end of the Cold War.

from Sunday to Wednesday. Lower down, on and around Carrer del Consell de Cent and Carrer de la Diputació, is the heart of the 'Gaixample', with several gay bars and clubs.

Dry Martini   Bar
(Map p89; ☑93 217 50 80; www.drymartiniorg. com; Carrer d'Aribau 162-166; ⊗1pm-2.30am Mon-Thu, 6pm-3am Fri & Sat, 7pm-2.30am Sun; MDiagonal) Waiters with a knowing smile will attend to your cocktail needs and make uncannily good suggestions, but the house drink, taken at the bar or in one of the plush green leather banquettes, is a safe bet. The gin and tonic comes in an enormous mug-sized glass – one will take you most of the night.

Monvínic   Wine Bar
(☑93 272 61 87; www.monvinic.com; Carrer de la Diputació 249; ⊗1-11pm Tue-Fri, 7-11pm Mon & Sat; MPasseig de Gràcia) Apparently considered unmissable by El Bulli's sommelier, Monvínic is an ode, a rhapsody even, to wine loving. The interactive wine list (on a digital tablet) sits on the bar for you to browse, and boasts more than 3000 varieties.

Les Gens Que J'Aime   Bar
(Map p89; ☑93 215 68 79; www.lesgensquejaime. com; Carrer de València 286; ⊗6pm-2.30am Sun-Thu, 7pm-3am Fri & Sat; MPasseig de Gràcia) This intimate basement relic of the 1960s follows a deceptively simple formula: chilled jazz music in the background, minimal lighting from an assortment of flea-market lamps and a cosy, cramped scattering of red-velvet-backed lounges around tiny dark tables.

Milano   Cocktail Bar
(☑93 112 71 50; www.camparimilano.com; Ronda de la Universitat 35; ⊗noon-2.30am Mon-Sat, 6pm-2.30am Sun; MCatalunya) A gem of hidden Barcelona nightlife, Milano is a subterranean old-school cocktail bar with velvet banquettes and glass-fronted cabinets, presided over by white-jacketed waiters, and completely invisible from street level. Check the website for details on occasional live music.

Napar BCN   Brewery
(☑606 546467; www.naparbcn.com; Carrer de la Diputació 223; ⊗noon-midnight Tue-Thu, to 2am Fri & Sat, noon-5pm Sun; ☏; MUniversitat) The latest bar to open as part of Barcelona's burgeoning craft-beer scene, Napar has 12 beers on tap, six of which are beers brewed on-site, including a mix of IPAs, pale ale and stout. There's also an accomplished list of bottled beers. It's a stunning space, with a gleaming steampunk aesthetic, and serves some excellent food should hunger strike.

☻ ENTERTAINMENT

Palau de la Música Catalana   Classical Music
(☑93 295 72 00; www.palaumusica.cat; Carrer de Palau de la Música 4-6; from €15; ⊗box office 9.30am-9pm Mon-Sat, 10am-3pm Sun; MUrquinaona) A feast for the eyes, this Modernista confection is also the city's most traditional venue for classical and choral music, although it has a wide-ranging program, including flamenco, pop and – particularly – jazz. Just being here for a performance is an experience. In the foyer, its tiled pillars all a-glitter, sip a pre-concert tipple.

Gran Teatre
del Liceu
Theatre, Live Music

(Map p82; ☎93 485 99 00; www.liceubarcelona.com; La Rambla 51-59; ☺box office 9.30am-8pm Mon-Fri, 9.30am-6pm Sat & Sun; Ⓜ Liceu) Barcelona's grand old opera house, restored after fire in 1994, is one of the most technologically advanced theatres in the world. To take a seat in the grand auditorium, returned to all its 19th-century glory but with the very latest in acoustics, is to be transported to another age.

Camp Nou
Football

(☎902 189900; www.fcbarcelona.com; Carrer d'Arístides Maillol; Ⓜ Palau Reial) Among Barcelona's most-visited sites is the massive stadium of Camp Nou (which means New Field in Catalan), home to the legendary Futbol Club Barcelona. Attending a game amid the roar of the crowds is an unforgettable experience. Football fans who aren't able to see a game can get a taste of all the excitement at the Camp Nou Experience (p91), which includes a visit to interactive galleries and a tour of the stadium. The season runs from September to May. See p90 for information about tickets.

Sala Tarantos
Flamenco

(Map p82; ☎93 304 12 10; www.masimas.com/tarantos; Plaça Reial 17; €15; ☺shows 8.30pm, 9.30pm & 10.30pm; Ⓜ Liceu) Since 1963, this basement locale has been the stage for up-and-coming flamenco groups performing in Barcelona. These days Tarantos has become a mostly tourist-centric affair, with half-hour shows held three times a night. Still, it's a good introduction to flamenco, and not a bad setting for a drink.

ⓘ INFORMATION

SAFE TRAVEL

○ Violent crime is rare in Barcelona, but petty crime (bag-snatching, pickpocketing) is a major problem.

○ You're at your most vulnerable when dragging around luggage to or from your hotel; make sure you know your route before arriving.

○ Be mindful of your belongings, particularly in crowded areas.

○ Avoid walking around El Raval and the southern end of La Rambla late at night.

○ Don't wander down empty city streets at night. When in doubt, take a taxi.

○ Take nothing of value to the beach, and don't leave anything unattended.

TOURIST INFORMATION

Several tourist offices operate in Barcelona. Two general information telephone numbers worth bearing in mind are ☎010 and ☎012. The first is for Barcelona and the other is for all Catalonia (run by the Generalitat). You sometimes strike English speakers, although for the most part operators are Catalan/Spanish bilingual. Information booths operate at Estació del Nord bus station and at Portal de la Pau, at the foot of the Mirador de Colom at the port end of La Rambla. Others set up at various points in the city centre in summer.

Plaça de Catalunya (Map p82; ☎93 285 38 34; www.barcelonaturisme.com; Plaça de Catalunya 17; ☺9.30am-9.30pm; Ⓜ Catalunya)

Plaça Sant Jaume (☎93 285 38 32; Carrer de la Ciutat 2; ☺8.30am-8.30pm Mon-Fri, 9am-7pm Sat, 9am-2pm Sun & holidays; Ⓜ Jaume I)

Estació Sants (☺8am-8pm)

El Prat Airport (☺8.30am-8.30pm)

Palau Robert Regional Tourist Office (☎93 238 80 91; www.palaurobert.gencat.cat; Passeig de Gràcia 107; ☺10am-8pm Mon-Sat, to 2.30pm Sun) Offers a host of material on Catalonia, audiovisual resources, a bookshop and a branch of Turisme Juvenil de Catalunya (for youth travel).

ⓘ GETTING THERE & AWAY

AIR

After Madrid, Barcelona is Spain's busiest international transport hub. Many airlines fly directly to **El Prat airport** (☎902 404704; www.aena.es) including budget carriers from around Europe. Ryanair uses Girona and Reus airports (buses link Barcelona to both). Most intercontinental flights require passengers to change flights in Madrid or another major European hub. Iberia, Air Europa,

Spanair and Vueling all have dense networks across the country, and while flights can be costly, you can save considerable time by flying from Barcelona to distant cities like Seville or Málaga.

BUS

Long-distance buses leave from **Estació del Nord** (902 26 06 06; www.barcelonanord.cat; Carrer d'Ali Bei 80; Arc de Triomf). A plethora of companies service different parts of Spain; many come under the umbrella of **Alsa** (902 422242; www.alsa.es). For other companies, ask at the bus station.

Eurolines (93 367 44 07; www.eurolines. com), in conjunction with local carriers all over Europe, is the main international carrier; its website provides links to national operators. It runs services across Europe and to Morocco from Estació del Nord, and from **Estació d'Autobusos de Sants** (93 339 73 29; Carrer de Viriat; Estació Sants), next to Estació Sants Barcelona.

Much of the Pyrenees and the entire Costa Brava are served only by buses, as train services are limited to important railheads such as Girona, Figueres, Lleida, Ripoll and Puigcerdà.

TRAIN

Train is the most convenient overland option for reaching Barcelona from major Spanish centres. It can be a long haul from other parts of Europe – budget flights frequently offer a saving in time and money. A network of *rodalies/cercanías* serves towns around Barcelona (and the airport). Contact **Renfe** (902 320320; www.renfe.es).

Eighteen high-speed Tren de Alta Velocidad Española (AVE) trains between Madrid and Barcelona run daily in each direction, nine of them in under three hours. Most long-distance (*largo recorrido* or *Grandes Línias*) trains have 1st and 2nd classes (known as *preferente* and *turista*). After the AVE, Euromed and several other similarly modern trains, the most common long-distance trains are the slower, all-stops Talgos.

The main train station in Barcelona is **Estació Sants** (Plaça dels Països Catalans; Estació Sants), 2.5km west of La Rambla. Direct overnight trains from Paris, Geneva, Milan and Zurich arrive here.

(i) GETTING AROUND

Barcelona has abundant options for getting around town. The excellent metro can get you most places, with buses and trams filling in the gaps. Taxis are the best option late at night.

Metro The most convenient option. Runs 5am to midnight Sunday to Thursday, till 2am on Friday and 24 hours on Saturday. Targeta T-10 (10-ride passes; €10.30) are the best value; otherwise, it's €2.15 per ride.

Bus A hop-on, hop-off **Bus Turístic** (93 298 70 00; www.barcelonabusturistic.cat; day tickets adult/child €28/16; 9am-8pm), departing from Plaça de Catalunya, is handy for those wanting to see the city's highlights in one or two days.

Taxi You can hail taxis on the street (try La Rambla, Via Laietana, Plaça de Catalunya and Passeig de Gràcia) or at taxi stands.

On foot To explore the old city, all you need is a good pair of walking shoes.

Where to Stay

Barcelona has a wide range of sleeping options, from inexpensive hostels hidden in the old quarter to luxury hotels overlooking the waterfront. The small-scale B&B-style apartment rentals scattered around the city are a good value choice.

Neighbourhood	Atmosphere
La Rambla & Barri Gòtic	Great location, close to major sights, with good nightlife and dining options, this is the perfect area for exploring on foot. It can be very touristy and noisy, while some hotel rooms are small and lack windows.
El Raval	Central option, with good local nightlife and access to sights; it has a bohemian vibe with few tourists. However, it can be noisy, seedy and run-down in parts, with many fleapits best avoided.
La Ribera	Great restaurant scene and neighbourhood exploring, La Ribera is central and close to top sights including the Museu Picasso and the Palau de la Música Catalana. It can be noisy, overcrowded and touristy.
La Barceloneta & Waterfront	Excellent seafood restaurants, with an easy-going local vibe and handy to the promenade and beaches, but it has few sleeping options, and can be far from the action. Better suited to business travellers.
L'Eixample	Offering a wide range of options for all budgets, it is close to Modernista sights, good restaurants and nightlife, and is a prime neighbourhood for the LGBT scene (in the 'Gaixample'). Can be very noisy with lots of traffic though, and is not a great area for walking as it is a little far from the old city.

COSTA BRAVA

Costa Brava at a Glance...

Stretching north to the French border, the Costa Brava, or 'rugged coast', is by far the prettiest of Spain's three principal holiday coasts. Although you'll find plenty of tourism development and English breakfasts, there are also unspoiled coves, charming seaside towns with quality restaurants, spectacular scenery, and some of Spain's best diving around the protected Illes Medes. Nestling in the hilly backcountry – green and covered in umbrella pine in the south, barer and browner in the north – are charming stone villages and the towering monastery of Sant Pere de Rodes. Further inland are the bigger towns of Girona, with its strikingly well-preserved medieval centre, and Figueres, famous for its bizarre Teatre-Museu Dalí, foremost of sites associated with the eccentric surrealist artist Salvador Dalí.

Costa Brava in Two Days

Base yourself in **Cadaqués** (p117) and fall in love with this town that Dalí made his own, most memorably in the **Casa Museu Dalí** (p118) in nearby Port Lligat. Use the town as a base for exploring **Cap de Creus** (p119) and visit the **Teatre-Museu Dalí** (p114) in Figueres.

Costa Brava in Four Days

With a couple of extra days, spend at least a night in **Girona** (p122), basing yourself within its medieval core to immerse yourself in its storied history. To complete a triumverate of Dalí masterpieces, visit the **Castell de Puból** (p126), then sleep in the charming coastal town of **Tossa de Mar** (p116).

Arriving on the Costa Brava

Girona-Costa Brava airport is 11km south of central Girona. Sagalés (www.sagales.com) connects it with Girona's main bus/train station, while direct buses from Barcelona go to most towns on or near the Costa Brava. If driving, the AP7 tollway and the NII highway both run from Barcelona via Girona and Figueres to the French border.

Sleeping

The Costa Brava has outstanding accommodation, from beachfront hotels to boutique-style places in the old centre of Girona. Girona draws visitors year-round, but many of the coastal towns are very quiet – and we mean *very* quiet – outside of the peak summer months. Carnaval in February/March is the exception. During weekends and public holidays, particularly in peak season, accommodation should be booked well ahead of time.

KIWISOLL / SHUTTERSTOCK ©

Teatre-Museu Dalí

Welcome to one of the weirdest and most wonderful art museums anywhere on earth. 'Theatre-museum' is an apt label for this trip through the incredibly fertile imagination of one of the great showmen of the 20th century.

Great For...

☑ Don't Miss

Dalí's heavenly re-imagining of the Sistine Chapel in the Palace of the Wind Room.

From the moment you lay eyes on this place, the building aims to surprise – from its entrance watched over by medieval suits of armour balancing baguettes on their heads, to bizarre sculptures outside the entrance on Plaça de Gala i Salvador Dalí, to the pink wall along Pujada del Castell. The Torre Galatea, added in 1983, is where Dalí spent his final years. Exhibits within these walls range from enormous installations to the more discreet, such as a tiny mysterious room with a mirrored flamingo.

The interior contains a substantial portion of Dalí's life's work, though you won't find his most famous pieces here: they are scattered around the world. Even so, it's an entirely appropriate final resting place for the master of surrealism, and has assured his immortality.

Avinguda Salvador Dalí
Pujada del Castell
⊙ **Teatre-Museu Dalí**
C de Castelló
Av de Vilallonga
Train Station ⊙

❶ Need to Know

www.salvador-dali.org; Plaça de Gala i Salvador Dalí 5, Figueres; incl Museu de l'Empordà adult/under 9yr €12/free; ⊙9am-8pm Tue-Sun Jul-Sep, 10.30am-6pm Tue-Sun Oct-Jun

✕ Take a Break

A few streets away, **Sidrería Txot's** (p121) serves cider from the barrel and *pintxos* (Basque tapas).

★ Top Tip

This is one museum where you'll need to book ahead online.

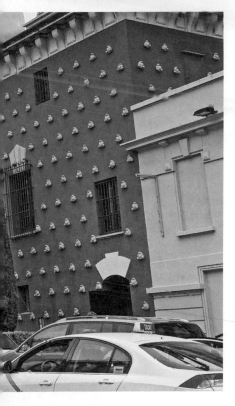

The Essentials

Where to start? Choice exhibits include *Taxi Plujós* (Rainy Taxi), composed of an early Cadillac, surmounted by statues. Put a coin in the slot and water washes all over the occupant of the car. The Sala de Peixateries (Fishmongers' Hall) holds a collection of Dalí oils, including the famous *Autoretrat tou amb tall de bacon fregit* (Soft Self-Portrait with Fried Bacon) and *Retrat de Picasso* (Portrait of Picasso). Beneath the former stage of the theatre is the crypt with Dalí's plain tomb, located at 'the spiritual centre of Europe' as Dalí modestly described it.

Gala, Dalí's wife and lifelong muse, is seen throughout – from the *Gala mirando el mar mediterráneo* (Gala Looking at the Mediterranean Sea) on the 2nd level, which also appears to be a portrait of Abraham Lincoln from afar, to the classic *Leda atómica* (Atomic Leda).

Other Highlights

After you've seen the more notorious pieces, such as climbing the stairs in the famous Mae West Room, see if you can find a turtle with a gold coin balanced on its back, peepholes into a tiny mysterious room with a mirrored flamingo amid fake plants, and Dalí's re-imagining of the Sistine Chapel in the Palace of the Wind Room.

A separate entrance (same ticket and opening times) leads into Dalí Joies, a collection of 37 jewels, designed by Dalí. He designed these on paper (his first commission was in 1941) and the jewellery was made by specialists in New York. Each piece, ranging from the disconcerting *Ull del temps* (Eye of Time) through to the *Cor reial* (Royal Heart), is unique.

Tossa de Mar

Tossa de Mar curves around a boat-speckled bay, guarded by a headland crowned with impressive defensive medieval walls and towers. Tourism has bolted a larger, modern extension onto this picturesque village of crooked, narrow streets, though its old town and clifftop views retain their magic.

Tossa was one of the first places on the Costa Brava to attract foreign visitors: a small colony of artists and writers gravitated towards what painter Marc Chagall dubbed 'Blue Paradise' in the 1930s. It was made famous by Ava Gardner in the 1951 film *Pandora and the Flying Dutchman;* you'll find a statue of the silver-screen queen along the path towards the lighthouse. In July and August it's hard to reach the water's edge without tripping over oily limbs. Out of high season it is still an enchanting place to visit.

⊙ SIGHTS

The deep-ochre fairy-tale walls and towers on pine-dotted Mont Guardí, the headland at the end of the main beach, were built between the 12th and 14th centuries. The area they girdle is known as the Vila Vella (old town), full of steep little cobbled streets and whitewashed houses, garlanded with flowers. The main town beach, fine shingle Platja Gran, tends to be busy. Beyond the headland, at the end of Avinguda de Sant Ramon Penyafort, is the quieter and smaller Platja Mar Menuda, popular with divers.

⊗ EATING

Look out for *cim i tomba,* a hearty one-pot fish-and-vegetable stew harking back to Tossa's fishing days. There are plenty of paella-and-sangría restaurant clichés, but a lot of good seafood as well.

Restaurant Bahia   Seafood €€
(📋972 34 03 22; www.restaurantbahiatossa. com; Passeig del Mar 19; mains €13; ⊙1-3.30pm & 7-10.30pm) Grilled sardines and pans of paella crowd the tables of this charming seafood place. The interior is decorated with local ceramics and tables spilling onto the road allow a glimpse of the beach.

Tossa de Mar

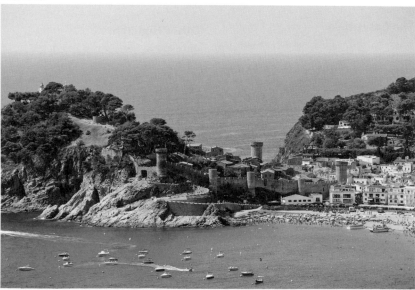

VVOEVALE / GETTY IMAGES ©

La Cuina de Can Simon
Catalan €€€

(☎972 34 12 69; www.restaurantcansimon. com; Carrer del Portal 24; mains €22-35, taster menus €68-98; ☺1-3.30pm Wed-Sun, 8-10.30pm Wed-Sat) This is the standout star of a slew of restaurants hugging the stretch of old wall along Carrer del Portal. Within a former fisherman's stone house, La Cuina de Can Simon credits its innovative dishes to a dual heritage: the owner's grandfathers were a fisherman and an artist. Flavoursome fusions such as tuna with wasabi gnocchi, or crunchy pineapple with cinnamon ice cream, are money well spent. Opens daily in summer.

🍷 DRINKING & NIGHTLIFE

Bar el Far de Tossa
Cocktail Bar

(☺11am-late) Perched on Mont Guardí next to the lighthouse is this bar with a terrace overhanging a steep drop. Views of cliffs speckled with cacti plummeting towards the inky sea can inspire vertigo, so take the edge off with a cocktail (€8.50). The 'Ava Gardner' is a blend of strawberry, vodka and Cointreau; but you're here for the best views in town, rather than the mixology.

ℹ️ INFORMATION

Tourist Office (www.infotossa.com; ☎972 34 01 08; Avinguda del Pelegrí 25; ☺10am-2pm & 4-7pm Mon-Sat, 9am-9pm in high season) Located next to the bus station.

ℹ️ GETTING THERE & AWAY

Sarfa (www.sarfa.com) runs buses to/from Barcelona's Estació del Nord (€12.15, 1¼ hours, five to seven daily) and also has direct airport services. The bus station is next to the tourist office. The C32 *autopista* connects Tossa to Barcelona, while the picturesque GI682 snakes spectacularly 23km northeast to Sant Feliu de Guíxols.

🥾 The Costa Brava Way

The 255km-long stretch of cliffs, coves, rocky promontories and pine groves that make up the signposted Costa Brava Way, stretching from Blanes to Culliure in France, unsurprisingly offers some of the best walks in Catalonia, ranging from gentle rambles to high-octane scrambles (or one long, demanding hike if you want to do the whole thing). For the most part, the trail follows the established GR92, but it also includes a number of coastal deviations.

A choice route is Cadaqués to the Cap de Creus lighthouse (2½ hours), a relatively easy walk that begins in the centre of Cadaqués, then passes Port Lligat, continuing along windswept, scrub-covered, rocky ground past several isolated beaches before it reaches the lighthouse.

Cadaqués

Cadaqués gleams above the cobalt-blue waters of a rocky bay on Catalonia's most easterly outcrop. This whitewashed village owes its allure in part to its windswept pebble beaches and meandering lanes, and the easy-going atmosphere that draws throngs of summer visitors. But it's the artist Salvador Dalí who truly gave Cadaqués its sparkle.

The artist spent family holidays here during his youth, and lived much of his later life at nearby Port Lligat. Thanks to Dalí and other luminaries, such as his friend Federico García Lorca, Cadaqués pulled in a celebrity crowd and still does.

⊙ SIGHTS

Cadaqués' main beach, and several others along the nearby coast, are small, with more pebbles than sand, but their pictur-esqueness and beautiful blue waters make up for that. Overlooking Platja Llané, to the

Palafrugell & Around

Halfway up the coast from Barcelona to the French border begins one of the most beautiful stretches of the Costa Brava. The town of Palafrugell, 4km inland, is the main access point for a cluster of enticing beach spots. Calella de Palafrugell, Llafranc and Tamariu, one-time fishing villages squeezed into small bays, are three of the Costa Brava's most charming, low-key resorts.

Begur, 7km northeast of Palafrugell, is a handsomely conserved, castle-topped village with a cluster of less-developed beaches nearby. Inland, seek out charming Pals and the fabulous village of Peratallada.

Llafranc
MICHAL KRAKOWIAK / GETTY IMAGES ©

south of the town centre, is Dalí's parents' holiday home. All the beaches around here experience strong winds, so caution is recommended. Even in high summer, swimming can be far from relaxing.

Casa Museu Dalí　　　　　Museum
(☑972 25 10 15; www.salvador-dali.org; adult/under 8yr €11/free; ☺10.30am-6pm Tue-Sun, closed Jan–mid-Feb) Located by a peaceful cove in Port Lligat, a tiny fishing settlement a 20-minute walk from Cadaqués, the Casa Museu Dalí was the residence and sanctuary of Salvador Dalí. This splendid whitewashed structure is a mishmash of cottages and sunny terraces, linked together by narrow labyrinthine corridors and containing an assortment of offbeat furnishings. Access is by semi-guided tour only. It's essential to book ahead, by phone or via the website.

Dalí lived in this magnificent seaside complex with his wife Gala from 1930 to 1982. The cottage was originally a mere fisherman's hut, but it was steadily altered and enlarged by its owners. Every corner reveals a new and wondrous folly or objet d'art: a taxidermied polar bear with jewellery to rival Mr T's, stuffed swans (an obsession for the artist) perched on bookshelves, and the womb-like Oval Room. The artist's workshop and the boudoir-like resting room for models are especially interesting. Meanwhile Dalí's bedroom still has a suspended mirror, positioned to ensure he was the first person to see the glint of sunrise each morning. If the Teatre-Museu Dalí in Figueres is the mask that the showman presented to the world, then this is an intimate glimpse of Dalí's actual face. It's open longer hours in the high season.

🍽 EATING

The seafront is lined with fairly pricey seafood eateries. Cadaqués' signature dish is *suquet de peix* – a hearty, traditional potato-based fish-and-shellfish stew.

Casa Nun　　　　　Seafood €€
(☑972 25 88 56; Plaça des Portitxó 6; mains €15-25; ☺12.30-3.30pm & 7.30-11pm daily Apr-Oct, Sat & Sun Nov-Mar) Head for the cute upstairs dining area or take one of the few tables outside overlooking the port. Everything is prepared with care, from the seafood dominating the menu to generous steaks and a little dessert selection with *tarta de limón* and homemade flans.

Es Baluard　　　　　Seafood €€
(☑972 25 81 83; www.esbaluard-cadaques.net; Carrer de la Riba Nemesi Llorens; mains €16-22; ☺1-3.30pm & 8.30-11pm) There may be roe, deer, carpaccio and salt-sprinkled grilled asparagus on the menu, but the family behind Es Baluard clearly worships at the throne of Poseidon. Fish dishes such as *anchoas de Cadaqués* (anchovies from Cadaqués) and *suquet de peix* (local fish

SIMON GREENWOOD / GETTY IMAGES ©

Casa Museu Dalí

stew) dominate the menu. Plus there is a formidable selection of desserts including syrup-soaked figs and cream cheese ice cream with orange marmalade.

ℹ️ INFORMATION

Tourist Office (📞972 25 83 15; www.visit cadaques.org; Carrer del Cotxe 2; ⊙9am-1pm & 3-6pm Mon-Thu, to 7pm Fri & Sat, 10am-1pm Sun) Longer opening hours in high season.

ℹ️ GETTING THERE & AWAY

Sarfa (www.sarfa.com) buses connect Cadaqués to Barcelona (€24.50, 2¾ hours, one to two weekdays, plus weekends in summer), Figueres (€5.50, one hour, four weekdays) via Castelló d'Empúries, and Girona (€10.80, 1¾ hours, one weekdays).

Cap de Creus

Cap de Creus is the most easterly point of the Spanish mainland and is a place of sublime, rugged beauty, battered by the merciless *tramuntana* wind and reachable by a lonely, 8km-long road that winds its way through the moonscapes. With a steep, rocky coastline indented by coves of turquoise water, it's a wonderful place to be at dawn or sunset.

The odd-shaped rocks, barren plateaux and deserted shorelines that litter Dalí's famous paintings were not just a product of his fertile imagination. This is the landscape that inspired the artist, which he described as a 'grandiose geological delirium'. See if you can find the huge rock that morphed into the subject of his painting *The Great Masturbator*, half-way between the main road and the lighthouse at the top.

⚡ ACTIVITIES

Declared a nature reserve in 1998, the Cap de Creus peninsula is now much loved for the walking trails along its craggy cliffs; find route maps at the **Espai Cap de Creus** (⊙10am-7pm summer) information centre. The lighthouse glinting from the top of the cape dates to 1853.

🍴 EATING

If the clifftop **Bar Restaurant Cap de Creus** (📞972 19 90 05; restcapdecreus@yahoo. es; mains €15-19; 🕙9.30am-8pm Sun-Thu, to midnight Fri & Sat Nov-Apr, 9.30am-midnight daily May-Oct) doesn't appeal, bring a picnic or dine down in Cadaqués.

ℹ️ GETTING THERE & AWAY

Cap de Creus is most easily accessed by car, along an 8km winding gravel road from Cadaqués via Port Lligat.

Figueres

Twelve kilometres inland from Catalonia's glistening Golf de Roses lies Figueres, birthplace of Salvador Dalí and now home to the artist's flamboyant theatre-museum (p114). Although Dalí's career took him to Madrid, Barcelona, Paris and the US, Figueres remained close to his heart; so in the 1960s and '70s he created the extraordinary Teatre-Museu Dalí – a monument to surrealism and a legacy that outshines any

other Spanish artist, both in terms of popularity and sheer flamboyance. Whatever your feelings about this complex, egocentric man, this museum is worth every cent and minute you can spare.

Beyond this star attraction, busy Figueres has a couple of interesting museums, pleasant shopping streets around Carrer de Peralada, and a whopping 18th-century fortress. It's well worth staying to see the city breathe after Dalí day trippers board their buses at sundown.

◎ SIGHTS

Castell de Sant Ferran   Fort

(www.lesfortalesescatalanes.info; adult/child €3/ free; 🕙10am-8p, Jul–mid-Sep, 10.30am-6pm mid-Sep–Oct & Apr-Jun, 10.30am-3pm Nov-Mar) This sturdy 18th-century fortress commands the surrounding plains from a low hill 1km northwest of the centre. The complex is a wonder of military engineering: it sprawls over 32 hectares, with the capacity for 6000 men to march within its walls and snooze in military barracks that are on display today. The admission fee includes

From left: Stables at Castell de Sant Ferran; Cap de Creus (p119); Figueres a clanking audioguide (nearly as old as the castle) to help navigate the site. Book ahead for group guided tours (€10 to €15 per person). Opening hours vary seasonally.

Museu del Joguet   Museum

(www.mjc.cat; Carrer de Sant Pere 1; adult/child €6/free; ◷10am-6pm Tue-Sat, 11am-2pm Sun, closed Jan) This museum has more than 3500 toys from throughout the ages – from the earliest board games involving coloured stones to ball-in-a-cup to intricate dolls' houses to 1920s dolls with baleful stares that may haunt your dreams to Catalonia- and Valencia-made religious processions of tiny figures. It's a mesmerising display, with plenty to amuse the kids... that is, unless you're the kind to associate blank-eyed Victorian dolls with horror movies. Admission is half-price if you flash a Teatre-Museu Dalí ticket.

Museu de l'Empordà   Museum

(www.museuemporda.org; La Rambla 2; adult/child €4/free; ◷11am-8pm Tue-Sat, to 2pm Sun) Across four floors, this local museum time travels from ancient amphorae to 7th-century sculptures to rotating installations of contemporary art. The region's culture and history are presented in a rather fragmented way, but it's an enjoyable romp. The 17th-century religious art is especially worthy of attention. There are signs in Spanish and Catalan, plus explanation on laminated cards in English and French. Admission is free with a Teatre-Museu Dalí ticket.

🍴 EATING

Beware the mediocre tourist traps near the Teatre-Museu Dalí. There are a few good restaurants along Carrer Nou de Dalt and outside the centre. There is a rich seam of *mar i muntanya* (sea and mountain) cuisine in Figueres. In this Catalonian spin on surf and turf, meat and fish are combined into a single dish, from mixed paellas to casseroles of shrimp and chicken.

Sidrería Txot's   Catalan, Basque €

(www.sidreriatxots.com; Avinguda Salvador Dalí 114; mains €10; ◷noon-midnight; 🛜) Perch on a wooden seat and watch your Basque cider poured from on high from the barrel before tucking into cold and hot *pintxos*, tasty

🐢 Centre de Reproducció de Tortugues de l'Albera

For 21 years, wildlife sanctuary **Centre de Reproducció de Tortugues de l'Albera** (📞972 55 22 45; www.tortugues.cat; Garriguella; €6; ⏱10am-1pm & 3-5pm Tue-Sat, 10am-1pm Sun late Mar-Oct; 🅿) has been a haven for Hermann's tortoises, and a force for educating people about these little armoured tanks of the Pyrenees. There's an introductory film (Catalan, Spanish, English, French or German) explaining threats to the region's tortoises, but the biggest thrill is a stroll around the boardwalk to peep at the scores of critters ambling among rocks and flower beds. The sanctuary is just north of Garriguella, a teeny town 15km northeast of Figueres.

The Hermann's tortoise is a tragic victim of its own cuteness. Not only is this armoured Pyrenees native felled by forest fires, its population is dwindling as people nab them as pets. Tortoises have been native to this part of the Pyrenees for thousands of years, and the Albera Massif, jutting along the France–Spain border in northern Catalonia, is the last stronghold for these threatened animals.

To see tortoises at peak activity (that is, a pacy stumble), time your visit for a sunny morning. The sanctuary is well signposted from the centre of Garriguella. It makes an easy half-day excursion from Figueres, Llançà or El Port de la Selva. It opens continuously between 10am and 6pm during July and August, and shuts in winter.

Hermann's tortoise
CYNOCLUB / GETTY IMAGES ©

burgers, cured meats, cheeses and salads, as well as dishes such as chorizo in cider and L'Escala anchovies on toast. The kitchen's open all afternoon – handy for a post-Dalí meal.

El Motel   Catalan €€€
(Hotel Empordà; 📞972 50 05 62; www.elmotel. cat; Avinguda Salvador Dalí i Domènech 170; tasting menu €39.70; ⏱7.30-11am, 12.45-3.45pm & 9-11pm; 🅿🛜) Jaume Subirós, the chef and owner of this hotel-restaurant on a busy road 1km north of the centre, is a seminal figure of the transition from traditional Catalan home cooking to the polished, innovative affair it is today. Highlights are such dishes as sea urchins from Cadaqués, cod with truffle and calf's cheek in red wine. There are also appealing rooms in which to sleep off the gastronomic indulgence (single €94, double €109, suite €140).

ℹ INFORMATION

Tourist Office (www.visitfigueres.cat; 📞972 50 31 55; Plaça del Sol; ⏱9.30am-2pm & 4-6pm Tue-Sat, 10am-2pm Sun & Mon, longer in high season) On the busy main road.

ℹ GETTING THERE & AWAY

Sarfa (www.sarfa.com) buses serve Cadaqués (€5.50, one to 1½ hours, four on weekdays) via Castelló d'Empúries. There are half-hourly train connections to Girona (€4.10 to €5.45, 30 minutes) and Barcelona (€12 to €16, 1¾ to 2½ hours). Hourly trains chug towards Portbou (€3.40, 30 minutes) for connections across the French border.

Girona

Northern Catalonia's largest city is a jewellery box of museums, galleries and Gothic churches, strung around a tangle of cobbled lanes and medieval walls. Reflections of Modernista mansions shimmer in the Riu Onyar, which demarcates the historical centre on its right bank from the gleaming commercial centre on the left.

VENTURA CARMONA / GETTY IMAGES ©

Girona Catedral

The Roman town of Gerunda lay on Vía Augusta, the highway from Cádiz all the way to the Pyrenees. Taken from the Muslims by the Franks in the late 8th century, Girona became the capital of one of Catalonia's most important counties, falling under the sway of Barcelona in the late 9th century.

Girona's wealth in medieval times produced many fine Romanesque and Gothic buildings that have survived repeated attacks and sieges. There are also traces of a Jewish community that flourished in Girona until their expulsion in 1492. These cultural riches are packed into Girona's walkable centre. With Catalonia's most diverse nightlife and dining scene outside Barcelona, Girona makes a delicious distraction for a few days, before you're helplessly drawn to the coast.

◉ SIGHTS

Catedral Cathedral
(www.catedraldegirona.org; Plaça de la Catedral; adult/student incl Basílica de Sant Feliu €7/5, Sun

free; ⊙10am-7.30pm Apr-Oct, 10am-6.30pm Nov-Mar) Towering over a flight of 86 steps rising from Plaça de la Catedral, this edifice is far more ancient than its billowing baroque facade suggests. Built over an old Roman forum, parts of the cathedral's foundations date from the 5th century. Today, Gothic styling – built over the Romanesque church during the 14th century – dominates, though a fine, double-columned Romanesque cloister dates from the 12th century. It's a surprisingly formidable sight to explore, but an audioguide is included in the price.

Highlights include the 14th-century silver altarpiece, studded with gemstones, portraying 16 scenes from the life of Christ. Also find the bishop's throne and the museum, which holds the masterly Romanesque *Tapís de la creació* (Tapestry of the Creation).

The tapestry shows God at the epicentre and in the circle around him are the creation of Adam, Eve, the animals, the sky, light and darkness. There is also a Mozarabic illuminated Beatus manuscript, dating from 975.

Museu d'Història dels Jueus de Girona · Museum

(www.girona.cat/call; Carrer de la Força 8; adult/child €4/free; ⊘10am-6pm Mon-Sat, to 2pm Sun) Until 1492 Girona was home to Catalonia's second most important medieval Jewish community (after Barcelona), and one of the finest Jewish quarters in the country. The Call (as the quarter was known) was centred on the narrow Carrer de la Força for 600 years, until relentless persecution forced the Jews out of Spain. This excellent museum shows genuine pride in Girona's Jewish heritage without shying away from the less salubrious aspects, such as persecution by the Inquisition and forced conversions.

Museu d'Art · Gallery

(www.museuart.com; Plaça de la Catedral 12; €4.50; ⊘10am-7pm Tue-Sat May-Sep, to 6pm Oct-Apr, 10am-2pm Sun) Next door to the cathedral, in the 12th- to 16th-century Palau Episcopal, this art museum impresses with the scale and variety of its collection. Around 8500 pieces of art, mostly from this region, make up the collection, which ranges from Romanesque woodcarvings and stained-glass tables to modernist paintings of the city by Mela Mutter and early 20th-century sculptures by the influential Rafael Masó i Valentí.

Banys Àrabs · Ruin

(www.banysarabs.cat; Carrer de Ferràn el Catòlic; adult/child €2/1; ⊘10am-7pm Mon-Sat, to 2pm Sun Apr-Sep, 10am-2pm daily Oct-Mar) Although modelled on earlier Muslim and Roman bathhouses, the Banys Àrabs are a finely preserved, 12th-century Christian affair in Romanesque style. The baths contain an *apodyterium* (changing room), followed by a *frigidarium* and *tepidarium* (with respectively cold and warm water) and a *caldarium* (a kind of sauna) heated by an underfloor furnace.

Passeig Arqueològic · Walls

(Passeig de la Muralla; ⊘10am-8pm) **FREE** A walk along Girona's medieval walls is a wonderful way to appreciate the city landscape from above. There are several points of access, the most popular being across the street

Banys Àrabs

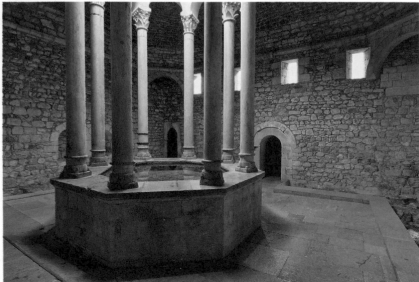

KAROL KOZLOWSKI / GETTY IMAGES ©

from the Banys Àrabs, where steps lead up into some heavenly gardens where town and plants merge into one organic masterpiece. The southernmost part of the wall ends right near Plaça de Catalunya.

❷ EATING

There's extraordinary variety in Girona's dining scene, from casual tapas bars to hip late-night purveyors of ham, and even the world's best restaurant. Unlike other parts of Catalonia, vegetarians, vegans and diners with food allergies will enjoy plenty of choice.

+Cub   Cafe €

(www.mescub.cat; Carrer de l'Albereda 15; mains €10-14; ⊙8am-9pm Mon-Thu, 8am-midnight Fri, 9am-midnight Sat; 🅿🏀) This trendy cafe-bar is as good for a takeaway coffee as it is for a full-blown nosh on speciality burgers and vegie crêpes. Thirst-quenchers include fresh fruit-juice combos and shakes, and there's a range of Scottish, German and other beers, plus local Moska homebrew.

L'Alqueria   Spanish, Catalan €€

(☑972 22 18 82; www.restaurantalqueria.com; Carrer de la Ginesta 8; mains €14-20; ⊙1-4pm Tue-Sun, 9-11pm Wed-Sat) This smart minimalist *arrocería* serves the finest *arròs negre* (rice cooked in cuttlefish ink) and *arròs a la catalan* in the city, as well as around 20 other superbly executed rice dishes, including paellas. Eat your heart out, Valencia! It's wise to book ahead for dinner, though it also offers takeaway.

Nu   Catalan €€

(☑972 22 52 30; www.nurestaurant.cat; Carrer d'Abeuradors 4; mains €16-18; ⊙1.15-3.45pm & 8.15-10.45pm Mon-Sat; 🏀) Sleek and confident, this handsome contemporary old-town spot has innovative, top-notch plates prepared in view by the friendly team. Flavour combinations keep things interesting: sample tuna *tataki* with red fruit glaze, tandoori pork cheeks with mango, and orange flower crème brûlée. Great value for this quality.

🍽◖ The World's Best Restaurant?

Ever-changing avant-garde takes on Catalan dishes have catapulted **El Celler de Can Roca** (☑972 22 21 57; www.cellercanroca.com; Calle Can Sunyer 48; degustation menus €150-180; ⊙1-4pm & 8.30-11pm Wed-Sat, 8.30-11pm Sun) to global fame: it was named the best restaurant in the world in 2015 by The World's 50 Best Restaurants. Each year brings new innovations from molecular gastronomy to multisensory food-art interplay to sci-fi dessert trolleys, all with mama's home cooking as the core inspiration.

Run by three brothers, El Celler de Can Roca is set in a refurbished country house, 2km northwest of central Girona. Book online 11 months in advance or join a standby list.

Foie gras stuffed figs
WESTEND61 / GETTY IMAGES ©

Occi   Fusion €€

(☑972 22 71 54; www.restaurantocci.com; Carrer dels Mercaders 3; mains €15-23; ⊙1-3.30pm & 8.30-11pm, closed Wed) With elegant contemporary styling and quality glassware and service, Occi has many elements of a pricier place but remains accessible and welcoming. The menu incorporates Catalan, French and Asian influences, such as squid lavished with *romesco* (pepper and nut) sauce and bite-sized tuna heaped with wasabi. Reserve ahead as the day it closes can vary.

❶ INFORMATION

GironsMuseus (www.gironamuseus.cat) This card covers six Girona museums including the

Girona's Jews

In its 13th-century heyday, Girona was home to one of Catalonia's largest Jewish communities, which lived by and large peacefully alongside its Christian neighbours, gaining in prosperity and contributing to fields as diverse as astronomy and medicine.

Nevertheless the Jewish community came under attack, especially during the later crusades of the 12th and 13th centuries. The Call – a maze of tiny alleys, surrounded by a stone wall – went from refuge to ghetto as Jews were gradually confined to their tiny corner of the town. Especially stomach-churning were the 'Disputes', rigged debates intended to ridicule pillars of the Jewish community against the supposedly superior logic of Christians. The spin of the day reported that these debates led to mass conversions, but the likelier story is that Jews converted out of heavy pressure and fear. Slander against Jews became increasingly grotesque.

Things came to a head during a riot in 1391, when a mob broke into the ghetto, massacring 40 residents. Since the Jews were still under the king's protection, troops were sent in and the survivors were confined to the Galligants Tower 'for their own safety' for 17 weeks, only to find their houses and possessions destroyed when they came out. Many converted to Christianity during the 15th century. In 1492 those who remained were expelled from Spain, ending a story that had been over 1500 years in the making.

Museu d'Història dels Jueus de Girona, Museu d'Art, Museu d'Història de Girona, Monestir de Sant Pere de Galligants, Museu del Cinema and Casa Masó. It provides good savings – you pay the full entrance fee at the first museum you visit and then get a 50% discount at the remainder. It's valid for six months.

Tourist Office (www.girona.cat/turisme; ☑972 22 65 75; Rambla de la Llibertat 1; ◷9am-8pm Mon-Fri, 9am-2pm & 4-8pm Sat, 9am-2pm Sun) Helpful, multilingual staff; located by the river.

ⓘ GETTING THERE & AROUND

AIR

Girona-Costa Brava airport (www.girona-airport.net), a Ryanair hub, is located 11km south of the centre, with **Sagalés** (www.sagales.com) connecting it to Girona's main bus/train station (€2.75, 30 minutes, hourly), as well as Barcelona's Estació del Nord (one way/return €16/25, 1¼ hours). Other direct bus services run to various Costa Brava destinations, including Lloret de Mar (€10, 35 minutes). A **taxi** (☑672 081830, 636 431300) to central Girona costs around €27 during the day and €35 at night.

BUS

Teisa (www.teisa-bus.com) runs from Girona to Besalú (€4.10 to €4.70, one hour, four to 12 daily) and Olot (€7.45 to €8.50, 1½ hours, four to 15 daily). **Sarfa** (www.sarfa.com) serves Cadaqués (€10.80, 1¾ hours, one on weekdays) and other coastal destinations. The **bus station** (☑972 21 23 19; Plaça d'Espanya) is next to the train station.

TRAIN

Girona is on the train line between Barcelona (€11.25 to €16.20, 40 minutes to 1¼ hours, up to 24 daily), Figueres (€4.10 to €5.45, 30 minutes, two to three daily) and Portbou, on the French border (€6.15 to €8.25, one hour, one daily). There are several through trains to France and beyond.

Castell de Púbol

If you're intrigued by artist Salvador Dalí, the **Castell de Púbol** (www.salvador-dali.org; Plaça de Gala Dalí; adult/concession €8/6; ◷10am-5pm Tue-Sun mid-Mar–Dec) is an essential piece of the puzzle. Between Girona and Palafrugell (22km northwest of the latter, south of the

Castell de Púbol

C66), this castle was Dalí's gift to his wife and muse Gala. The Gothic and Renaissance building, with creepers tracing its walls, spiral stone staircases and a shady garden, was decorated according to Gala's tastes. Nonetheless there are surrealist touches such as the grimacing anglerfish fountain and a sofa shaped like pouting lips.

The life of Gala Dalí is fascinating in its own right, due to her entanglement with several pivotal figures of the first half of the 20th century. Gala married poet Paul Éluard, had a two-year affair with pioneer of Dadaism Max Ernst, and then met Dalí in 1929. With Dalí's approval she continued to take lovers, though their loyalty to each other remained fierce. Russian-born Gala was as admired for her elegance as much as she was feared for her imposing manners.

Having promised to make Gala 'queen of the castle', in 1969 Dalí finally found the ideal residence to turn into Gala's refuge. At the age of 76, Gala preferred to flit in and out of Dalí's decadent lifestyle. Dalí was only permitted to visit the castle with advance written permission, a restriction that held considerable erotic charge for the artist.

Today the Castell de Púbol forms the southernmost point of the 'Salvador Dalí triangle', the other stops being the Teatre-Museu Dalí in Figueres (p114) and his home in Port Lligat (p118) near Cadaqués. The sombre castle is almost an antithesis to the flamboyance of the Teatre-Museu Dalí and Dalí's seaside home.

To get here, catch a bus to Cruïlla de la Pera from Girona (€3, 40 minutes, eight daily) or Palafrugell (€3.05, 25 minutes, seven to 14 daily), and alight at the stop on the C66 then walk the 2km to the castle. Alternatively, take a train from Girona to Flaçà (€3.30, 12 minutes, two to three daily), then catch a taxi the last 5km. Opening hours vary: there are early closures in November and December, longer hours from June to September, and the attraction goes into hibernation from January to March. Check the website before visiting.

IAKOV FILIMONOV / SHUTTERSTOCK ©

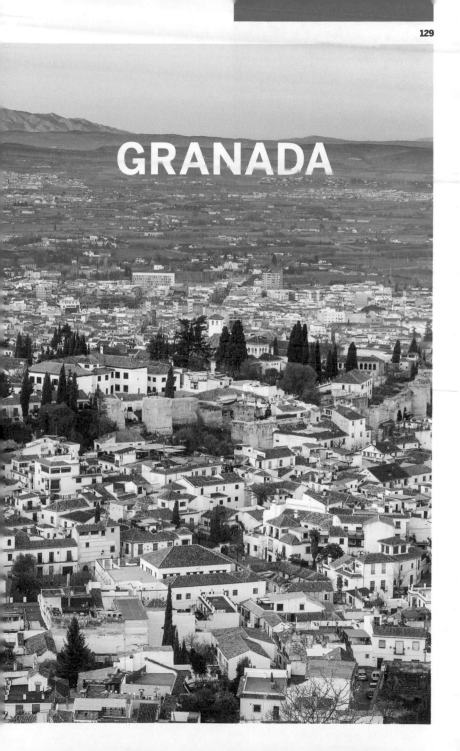

GRANADA

Granada at a Glance...

Revered for its lavish Alhambra palace, and enshrined in medieval history as the last stronghold of the Moors in Western Europe, Granada is the darker, more complicated cousin of sunny, exuberant Seville. Humming with a feisty cosmopolitanism and awash with riddles, question marks, contradictions and myths, this is a place to put down your guidebook and let your intuition lead the way. But 21st-century Granada is anything but straightforward. Instead, this stunning city set spectacularly in the crook of the Sierra Nevada is an enigmatic place where – if the mood is right – you sense you might find something that you've long been looking for. A free tapa, perhaps? A flamenco performance that finally unmasks the spirit of duende? Granada has all of this and more.

Granada in Two Days

Spend the best part of a day in the **Alhambra** (p132) – no matter how long you spend here, it won't be enough. Near sunset, head up to the **Mirador San Nicolás** (p136) for wonderful views back across the valley to the Alhambra. Devote the second day to the **Albayzín** (p135), exploring its palaces, teahouses and restaurants.

Granada in Four Days

Dive into the city's **tapas culture** (p144), especially along Calle de Elvira and Calle Navas, and explore the magnificent Christian monuments of the **Catedral de Granada** (p137), **Capilla Real** (p137) and the gilded **Basílica San Juan de Díos** (p138). And make sure you leave time for exploring the signposts to **Lorca's Legacy** (p142). For sustenance, don't miss **Carmela Restaurante** (p140), **Bodegas Castañeda** (p141) and **Arrayanes** (p142).

See Granada Map (p134)

Arriving in Granada

Granada is well connected to the rest of Spain by air, bus, train and a network of motorways. Aeropuerto Federico García Lorca is 17km west of the city, to which it is connected by Autocares J González (www.autocaresjosegonzalez.com) buses. The train station, 1.5km north-west of the centre, is connected to downtown by regular buses.

Sleeping

Granada has accommodation that ranges from brilliant boutique conversions of medieval mansions to business hotels, from flower-strewn, family-run *hostales* (cheap hotels) to palatial digs fit for a king. High season can be any time of the year, but weekends and festivals are particularly busy. And unlike Seville and Córdoba, which bake in summer, Granada is lovely at any time.

For more on where to stay, see p145.

Generalife gardens

YURIY BIRYUKOV / GETTY IMAGES ©

Alhambra

The Alhambra is part palace, part fort, part World Heritage Site, and part lesson in medieval architecture. It is unlikely that, as a historical monument, it will ever be surpassed.

Great For...

☑ Don't Miss

The Patio de los Leones, the Alhambra's centrepiece and gateway to the inner sanctum.

Palacio Nazaríes

The central palace complex, the Palacio Nazaríes, is the pinnacle of the Alhambra's design. Highlights include the Patio de Arrayanes where rooms look onto the rectangular pool edged in myrtles, and the Salón de los Embajadores, where the marvellous domed marquetry ceiling uses more than 8000 cedar pieces to create its intricate star pattern representing the seven heavens.

The adjacent Patio de los Leones (Courtyard of the Lions), built in the second half of the 14th century, has as its centrepiece, a fountain that channelled water through the mouths of 12 marble lions. The stucco work hits its apex here, with almost lacelike detail. On the patio's northern side is the Sala de Dos Hermanas (Hall of Two Sisters) whose dizzying ceiling is a fantastic *muqarnas* dome with some 5000 tiny cells. A reflecting

Detail of a column, Generalife gardens

RUTH TOMLINSON / ROBERTHARDING / GETTY IMAGES ©

ℹ Need to Know

Map p134; ☎902 44 12 21; www.alhambra-tickets.es; adult/under 12yr €14/free, Generalife only €7; ⊙8.30am-8pm mid-Mar–mid-Oct, to 6pm mid-Oct–mid-Mar, night visits 10-11.30pm Tue-Sat mid-Mar–mid-Oct, 8-9.30pm Fri & Sat mid-Oct–mid-Mar

✕ Take a Break

Bring a picnic and behave like royalty by relaxing in the Generalife gardens.

★ Top Tip

Reserve tickets online at www.alhambratickets.es. See p137 for more information.

pool and terraced garden front the small Palacio del Partal (Palace of the Portico), the oldest surviving palace in the Alhambra, from the time of Mohammed III (r 1302–09).

Generalife

From the Arabic *jinan al-'arif* (the overseer's gardens), the Generalife is a soothing arrangement of pathways, patios, pools, fountains, tall trees and, in season, flowers. At the north end is the emirs' summer palace, a whitewashed structure on the hillside facing the Alhambra. The courtyards here are particularly graceful; in the second courtyard, the trunk of a 700-year-old cypress tree suggests what delicate shade once graced the patio. Climb the steps outside the courtyard to the Escalera del Agua, a delightful bit of garden engineering, where water flows along a shaded staircase.

Alcazaba & Christian Buildings

The western end of the Alhambra grounds are the remnants of the Alcazaba, chiefly its ramparts and several towers. The Torre de la Vela (Watchtower), with a narrow staircase leading to the top terrace, is where the cross and banners of the Reconquista were raised in January 1492.

By the Palacios Nazaríes, the hulking Renaissance-era Palacio de Carlos V, built in 1527 after the Reconquista, clashes spectacularly with its surroundings. Inside, the **Museo de la Alhambra** (⊙8.30am-8pm Wed-Sat, to 2.30pm Tue & Sun) **FREE** has a collection of Alhambra artefacts and the **Museo de Bellas Artes** (Fine Arts Museum; non-EU/EU citizen €1.50/free; ⊙2.30-8pm Tue, 9am-8pm Wed-Sat, to 2.30pm Sun) displays paintings and sculptures from Granada's Christian history.

Granada

Granada

⊙ SIGHTS

Most major sights are an easy walk within the city centre, and there are buses for when the hills wear you out. Rectangular Plaza Nueva is Granada's main nexus. The Albayzín sits on a hill immediately to the north and is roughly demarcated by Gran Via de Colón and the Río Darro. The Alhambra lies on a separate hill on the opposite side of the Darro. Granada's former Jewish quarter, the Realejo, occupies the southwestern slope of the Alhambra hill and some of the flat land beyond. Central Granada is laid out in a grid on the flat land west of the Albayzín and northwest of the Realejo. Its main square is Plaza Bib-Rambla.

⊙ Realejo

Museo Sefardí   Museum

(☏958 22 05 78; www.museosefardidegranada.es; Placeta Berrocal 5; €5; ◷10am-2pm & 5-9pm) Since being expelled en masse in 1492, there are very few Sephardi Jews left living in Granada today. But this didn't stop one

enterprising couple from opening up a museum to their memory in 2013, the year that the Spanish government began offering Spanish citizenship to any Sephardi Jew who could prove their Iberian ancestry. The museum is tiny, but the selected artefacts make excellent props to the passionate and fascinating historical portrayal related by the owners.

⊙ Near Plaza Nueva

Baños Árabes
El Bañuelo   Hammam

(Carrera del Darro 31; ◷10am-5pm Tue-Sat) **FREE**
Located along narrow Carrera del Darro is this simple, yet well-preserved, 11th-century Islamic bathhouse.

⊙ Albayzín

On the hill facing the Alhambra across the Darro valley, Granada's old Muslim quarter (the Albayzín) is a place for aimless wandering; you'll get lost regularly whatever map you're using. The cobblestone streets are lined with signature only-in-Granada *cármenes* (large mansions with walled gardens, from the Arabic *karm* for garden). The Albayzín survived as the Muslim quarter for several decades after the Christian conquest in 1492.

Bus C1 runs circular routes from Plaza Nueva around the Albayzín about every seven to nine minutes, from 7.30am to 11pm.

Palacio de Dar-al-Horra — Palace
(Callejón de las Monjas) Close to the Placeta de San Miguel Bajo, off Callejón del Gallo and down a short lane, is the 15th-century Palacio de Dar-al-Horra, a romantically dishevelled mini-Alhambra that was home to the mother of Boabdil, Granada's last Muslim ruler. It's not open to the public, but viewable from the outside.

Calle Calderería Nueva — Street
Linking the upper and lower parts of the Albayzín, Calle Calderería Nueva is a narrow street famous for its *teterías* (teahouses), but also a good place to shop for slippers, hookahs, jewellery and North African

pottery from an eclectic cache of shops redolent of a Moroccan souk.

Colegiata del Salvador — Church
(Plaza del Salvador; €0.75; ⊙10am-1pm & 4.30-6.30pm) Plaza del Salvador, near the top of the Albayzín, is dominated by the Colegiata del Salvador, a 16th-century church on the site of the Albayzín's former main mosque, the patio of which still survives at the church's western end.

Mirador San Nicolás — Viewpoint
Callejón de San Cecilio leads to the Mirador San Nicolás, a lookout with unbeatable views of the Alhambra and Sierra Nevada. Come back here for sunset (you can't miss the trail then!). At any time of day take care: skilful, well-organised wallet-lifters and bag-snatchers operate here. Don't be put off though – it is still a terrific atmosphere, with buskers and local students intermingling with camera-toting tourists.

Palacio de los Olvidados — Museum
(☑655 553340; www.palaciodelosolvidados.com; Cuesta de Santa Inés 6; €5; ⊙10am-7pm)

Calle Calderería Nueva

Lest we forget, Jews played a vital role in the glorious Nasrid Emirate of Granada that reigned from the 1200s to 1492, built on peaceful Christian, Muslim and Jewish coexistence. The aptly named 'palace of the forgotten', which opened in 2014 in the Albayzín, revisits this oft-ignored Jewish legacy. It's the second and best of Granada's new Jewish-related museums, with seven rooms filled with attractively displayed relics (scrolls, costumes and ceremonial artefacts) amassed from around Spain.

Carmen Museo Max Moreau
Museum

(☑958 29 33 10; Camino Nuevo de San Nicolás 12; ◷10.30am-1.30pm & 4-6pm Tue-Sat) FREE Most of the Albayzín's *cármenes* are true to their original concept – quiet, private houses with high walls that hide beautiful terraced gardens. But you can get a rare (and free) glimpse of one of these secret domains at the former home of Belgium-born portrait painter and composer Max Moreau. His attractive house has been made into a museum displaying his former living quarters and work space, along with a gallery that showcases his best portraits.

◉ Plaza Bib-Rambla & Around

Capilla Real
Historic Building

(www.capillarealgranada.com; Calle Oficios; €4; ◷10.15am-1.30pm & 3.30-6.30pm Mon-Sat, 11am-1.30pm & 2.30-5.30pm Sun) Here they lie, Spain's notorious Catholic Monarchs, entombed in a chapel adjoining Granada's cathedral; far more peaceful in death than their tumultuous lives would have suggested. Isabel and Fernando commissioned the elaborate Isabelline-Gothic-style mausoleum that was to house them, but it was not completed until 1521, hence their temporary interment in the Alhambra's Convento de San Francisco.

Catedral de Granada
Cathedral

(☑958 22 29 59; www.catedraldegranada.com; Gran Vía de Colón 5; €4; ◷10.45am-7.45pm Mon-Sat, 4-7pm Sun) Too boxed in by other buildings to manifest its full glory to observers at ground level, Granada's cavernous

ⓘ Alhambra Practicalities

Some areas of the Alhambra (p132) can be visited at any time free of charge, but the highlight areas (the Palacios Nazaríes) can be entered only with a ticket at a pre-allocated time slot. Up to 6600 tickets are available each day. About one third of these are sold at the ticket office on the day, but they sell out early, especially in high season (March to October), when you need to start queuing by 7am to be reasonably sure of getting one.

Fortunately, it's also possible to buy tickets up to three months ahead online or by phone from **Alhambra Advance Booking** (☑902 88 80 01, for international calls +34 958 92 60 31; www.alhambra-tickets. es). Advance tickets can also be purchased (or prepaid tickets picked up) at the bookshop, Tienda Librería de la Alhambra (p139), just off Plaza Nueva, which has less manic queues than the complex itself. All advance tickets incur a 13% surcharge. When full-access tickets are sold out, you can still buy a ticket to the Generalife and gardens (€7). The Palacios Nazaríes is also open for **night visits** (€8; ◷10-11.30pm Tue-Sat mid-Mar–mid-Oct, 8-9.30pm Fri & Sat mid-Oct–mid-Mar), good for atmosphere rather than detail. There is no explanatory signage in the complex, but a reasonable audio-guide is available for €6.50.

The best access on foot is to walk up the Cuesta de Gomérez from Plaza Nueva through the *bosque* (woods) to the Puerta de la Justicia. Enter here if you already have your ticket, otherwise proceed further along to the ticket office. Buses C3 and C4 run up to the ticket office from Plaza Isabel la Católica.

From 2016 a €45-million entrance gate and visitors centre is due to be built and is expected to take five years. A temporary exhibition of the winning design by Portuguese architect Álvaro Siza Vieira is on the site of the ticket office.

Granada's Moorish History

Granada came into its own late in Spain's Islamic era. As Córdoba and Seville fell to the Catholics in the mid-13th century, a minor potentate called Mohammed ibn Yusuf ibn Nasr established an independent state based in Granada, which became the last bastion of Al-Andalus.

The Alhambra was developed as royal court, palace, fortress and miniature city, and the Nasrids ruled from this increasingly lavish complex for 250 years, developing it to became one of the richest cities in Europe, with a population of more than 350,000.

But decadent palace life bred a violent rivalry over succession. One faction supported the emir Abu al-Hasan and his Christian concubine, Zoraya, while the other backed Boabdil (Abu Abdullah). In 1482 Boabdil started a civil war and, following Abu al-Hasan's death in 1485, won control of the city. With the emirate weakened by infighting, the Catholics pounced. Queen Isabel particularly had been smitten by Granada and she wanted it for herself. After an eight-month siege, Boabdil agreed to surrender the city in return for the Alpujarras valleys, 30,000 gold coins and political and religious freedom for his subjects. Boabdil hiked out of town – letting out the proverbial 'Moor's last sigh' as he looked over his shoulder in regret – and on 2 January 1492, Isabel and Fernando entered the city ceremonially in Muslim dress, to set up court in the Alhambra.

Detail of a mosaic, Alhambra (p132)
BETHUNE CARMICHAEL / GETTY IMAGES ©

cathedral is, nonetheless, a hulking classic that sprang from the fertile imagination of the 17th-century painter cum sculptor cum architect Alonso Cano. Although commissioned by the Catholic Monarchs in the early 1500s, construction began only after Isabel's death, and didn't finish until 1704.

◉ Outside the Centre

Basílica San Juan de Díos   Church

(Calle San Juan de Díos; €4; ⊘10am-1pm & 4-7pm)
Bored of baroque churches? Seen every gilded altarpiece you want to see? Come to the Basilica of St John of God. If Seville cathedral is the world's most voluminous church, this basilica is surely one of the most opulently decorated. Barely a square inch of the interior lacks embellishment, most of it rich and glittering.

Monasterio de San Jerónimo   Monastery

(Calle Rector López Argüeta 9; €4; ⊘10am-1.30pm & 4-8pm Mon-Fri, 10am-2.30pm & 4-7.30pm Sat & Sun) Another of Granada's stunning Catholic buildings is a little out of the centre. At the 16th-century Monasterio de San Jerónimo, where nuns still sing vespers, every surface of the church has been painted – the stained glass literally pales in comparison.

✪ ACTIVITIES

Hammam de Al Andalus   Hammam

(☑902 33 33 34; www.granada.hammamalandalus.com; Calle Santa Ana 16; bath/bath & massage €24/36; ⊘10am-midnight) With three pools of different temperatures, plus a steam room and option of a proper skin-scrubbing massage, this is the best of Granada's three Arab-style baths. Sessions are booked for two-hour sessions (reserve) and the dim, tiled rooms are sybaritic and relaxing.

✪ TOURS

Pancho Tours   Cultural Tour

(☑664 642904; www.panchotours.com) FREE Excellent free tours of Granada by the guys in the orange T-shirts. Choose from the

daily Albayzín tour (11am), or the more eso-
teric 'street art tour' (Monday, Wednesday,
Friday at 5pm). Guides are knowledgeable
and humorous, and tours are loaded with
interesting anecdotes. Book online.

Cicerone Cultura
y Ocio   Walking Tour
(📞958 56 18 10; www.ciceronegranada.com; tours
€15) Informative walking tours of central Granada and the Albayzín leave daily from Plaza
Bib-Rambla at 10.30am and 5pm (10am and
4pm in winter) Wednesday to Sunday.

Play Granada   Cultural Tour
(www.playgranada.com; Calle Santa Ana 2; Segway
tours €30) 🕐 The make or break of a good
tour is the tour guide, and Play Granada's
are truly fantastic. Even if you don't do a
tour, you'll see the congenial guides buzzing
around Plaza Nueva on their Segways, stopping to chat with anyone and everyone.

🅐 SHOPPING

Granada's craft specialities include *taracea*
(marquetry). The best work has shell, silver

or mother-of-pearl inlay, applied to boxes,
tables, chess sets and more.

Alcaicería   Souvenirs
(Calle Alcaicería) Formerly a grand Moorish
bazaar where silk was made and sold, the
stalls are now taken up with souvenir shops.
The setting is still very reminiscent of the
past, however, especially in the early morning before the coach tours descend. You can
still see where the gates once stood at the
entrances, there to guard against looting
and closed at night. Opening hours vary,
depending on the individual shops.

Artesanías González   Arts & Crafts
(Cuesta de Gomérez 12; ⊙11am-8pm) Specialises in exceptionally fine examples of
marquetry, ranging from small and easy-to-
pack boxes to larger pay-the-overweight-
allowance chess sets.

Tienda Librería
de la Alhambra   Souvenirs
(📞958 22 78 46; Calle Reyes Católicos 40;
⊙9.30am-8.30pm) This is a fabulous shop
for Alhambra aficionados, with a tasteful

Catedral de Granada (p137)

From left: Detail of a wall painting, Monasterio de San Jerónimo (p138); Hammam de Al Andalus (p138); Monasterio de San Jerónimo

selection of quality gifts, including excellent coffee table–style tomes, children's art books, hand-painted fans, arty stationery and stunning photographic prints, which you select from a vast digital library (from €14 for A4 size).

🍴 EATING

Granada's a place where gastronomy remains reassuringly down to earth – and cheap. What it lacks in flashy *alta cocina* (haute cuisine) it makes up for in generous portions of Andalucian standards. The city has a wealth of places serving decent tapas and *raciones* (large tapas servings). It also excels in Moroccan cuisine.

🍴 Alhambra & Realejo

Hicuri Art Restaurant   Vegan €

(Plaza de los Girones 3; mains €7-12; ⏱10am-10pm Mon-Sat; 🖉) Granada's leading graffiti artist, El Niño de las Pinturas, has been let loose on the inner and outer walls of Hicuri, and the results are positively psychedelic. The food used to be vegetarian with a few

dishes for diehard carnivores, but it recently went full-on vegan.

Carmela Restaurante   Tapas €€

(☎958 22 57 94; www.restaurantecarmela.com; Calle Colcha 13; tapas €5-10; ⏱12.30pm-midnight) Long a bastion of traditional tapas, Granada has taken a leaf out of Seville's book and come up with something a little more out-of-the-box at this new streamlined restaurant, guarded by the statue of Jewish philosopher Yehuba ibn Tibon at the jaws of the Realejo quarter. The best of Carmela's creative offerings is the made-to-order tortilla and cured-ham croquettes the size of tennis balls.

La Botillería   Tapas €€

(☎958 22 49 28; Calle Varela 10; mains €13-20; ⏱1pm-1am Wed-Sun, 1-8pm Mon) Establishing a good reputation for nouveau tapas, La Botillería is just around the corner from the legandary La Tana bar, to which it has family connections. It's a more streamlined modern place than its cousin, where you can *tapear* (eat tapas) at the bar or sit down for the full monty Andalucian-style.

DAVID CABRERA / GETTY IMAGES ©

The *solomillo* (pork tenderloin) comes in a rich, wine-laden sauce.

Los Diamantes
Seafood €€

(www.barlosdiamantes.com; Calle Navas 26; raciones €8-10; ⊗noon-6pm & 8pm-2am Mon-Fri, 11am-1am Sat & Sun) Granada's great tapas institution has two central outlets. This old-school scruffy joint in tapa bar–lined Calle Navas, and a newer, hipper Ikea-esque version in Plaza Nueva. What doesn't change is the tapa specialty – fish, which you'll smell sizzling in the fryer as soon as you open the door.

Parador de Granada
International €€€

(☑958 22 14 40; Calle Real de la Alhambra; mains €19-22; ⊗1-4pm & 8.30-11pm) On one side, the Parador de Granada is a hushed, swanky dinner experience, with a Moroccan-Spanish-French menu that also features local goat and venison. On the other, it's a stylish little canteen for sightseers, where even your *bocadillo de jamón* tastes special – and it ought to, considering its €12 price

tag. Overall, a bit inflated, but a lovely treat for the location.

✖ Near Plaza Nueva

La Bella y la Bestia
Andalucian, Tapas €

(☑958 22 51 87; www.bodegaslabellaylabestia. com; Calle Carcel Baja 14; tapas €2-3; ⊗noon-midnight) Lots of beauty, but no real beast – this place wins the prize for Granada's most generous free tapas: a huge plate of bagels, chips and pasta arrives with your first drink. There are four branches, though this one is particularly well placed, just off Calle de Elvira.

Bodegas Castañeda
Tapas €

(Calle Almireceros; tapas €2-3, raciones €6-8; ⊗11.30am-4.30pm & 7.30pm-1.30am) A much-loved relic among locals and tourists alike, the buzzing Castañeda is the Granada tapas bar to trump all others. Don't expect any fancy new stuff here, but do expect lightning-fast service, booze from big casks mounted on the walls, and eating as a physical contact sport.

Lorca's Legacy

Spain's greatest poet and playwright, Federico García Lorca (1898–1936), epitomised many of Andalucía's potent hallmarks – passion, ambiguity, exuberance and innovation – and brought them to life in a multitude of precocious works. Early popularity was found with *El romancero gitano* (Gypsy Ballads), a 1928 collection of verses on Roma themes, full of startling metaphors yet crafted with the simplicity of flamenco song. Between 1933 and 1936 he wrote the three tragic plays for which he is best known: *Bodas de sangre* (Blood Wedding), *Yerma* (Barren) and *La casa de Bernarda Alba* (The House of Bernarda Alba) – dramatic works dealing with themes of entrapment and liberation. Lorca was murdered at the start of the civil war in August 1936. Although his remains have proved elusive, recent research reaffirms the longstanding notion that he was executed by military authorities loyal to Franco.

Lorca's summer house, **Huerta de San Vicente** (☏958 25 84 66; Calle Virgen Blanca; admission only by guided tour in Spanish €3, Wed free; ☉9.15am-1.30pm & 5-7.30pm Tue-Sun), is now a museum, 15 minutes' walk from Puerta Real (head 700m down Calle de las Recogidas). In 2015 it was joined by **Centro Lorca** (Plaza de la Romanilla), the new home of the Lorca foundation that hosts a library, 424-seat theatre and expo space in a super-modern building.

Huerta de San Vicente
AGE FOTOSTOCK / ALAMY STOCK PHOTO ©

⊗ Albayzín

Arrayanes Moroccan €€

(☏958 22 84 01; www.rest-arrayanes.com; Cuesta Marañas 4; mains €15; ☉1.30-4.30pm & 7.30-11.30pm Sun-Fri, to 4.30pm Sat; ☑) The best Moroccan food in a city that is well known for its Moorish throwbacks? Recline on lavish patterned seating, try the rich, fruity tagines and make your decision. Note that Arrayanes does not serve alcohol.

⊗ Plaza Bib-Rambla & Around

Gran Café Bib-Rambla Cafe €

(Plaza Bib-Rambla 3; chocolate & churros €4; ☉8am-11pm; ⊞) It's 5pm, you've just traipsed around five vaguely interesting churches and hypoglycemia is rapidly setting in. Time to hit Plaza Bib-Rambla, where Granada's best churros (fried dough strips) are served in a no-nonsense 1907-vintage cafe. Check their freshness by watching Mr Churro-maker lower them into the fryer behind the bar, and then enjoy them dipped in cups of ultra-thick hot chocolate.

La Bicicleta Bistro €€

(☏958 25 86 36; Plaza Pescadería 4; raciones €8-15; ☉11am-11.30pm Thu-Tue) For something new and a bit different, head to this lovely bistro, which adds a touch of Parisian panache to Granada – truly the best of both worlds. It's small and intimate, and good for many things, including an excellent *huevos a la flamenca* (tomato sauce and eggs). Placed strategically by the door, the cake tray is perfect for an afternoon *merienda* (afternoon snack).

La Fábula Restaurante Modern European €€€

(☏958 25 01 50; www.restaurantelafabula.com; Calle San Antón 28; mains €22-28; ☉1.30-4.30pm & 8.30-11pm Tue-Sat) In Fábula it's hard to avoid the pun – the place is pretty fabulous. Hidden in the highly refined confines of the Hotel Villa Oniria, the setting matches the food, which is presented like art and tastes equally good. Standouts are the venison with chestnuts and quince, or the baby eels with basil in venere (black) rice. The 11-course tasting menu is €65 (€80 with wine pairing) and there's a lovely garden out back. Be sure to book ahead.

🍸 DRINKING & NIGHTLIFE

The best street for drinking is the rather scruffy Calle de Elvira, but other chilled bars line Río Darro at the base of the Albayzín and Calle Navas. Just north of Plaza de Trinidad are a bunch of cool hipster-ish bars.

Old stalwarts on the drinking and tapas scene are the two branches of Los Diamantes (p141), four branches of La Bella y la Bestia (p141), including one in Calle de Elvira, and the eternal classic Bodegas Castañeda (p141).

Taberna La Tana   Bar
(Calle Rosario; ⊙12.30-4pm & 8.30pm-midnight) Possibly the friendliest family-run bar in Granada, La Tana specialises in Spanish wines and backs it up with some beautifully

paired tapas. You can't go wrong with the 'surtido' plate of Spanish hams. Ask the bartender about the 'wines of the month' and state your preference – a *suave* (smooth) red, or a *fuerte* (strong).

The small interior is old-fashioned, packed to the rafters (usually) and filled with the aroma of fine wine.

El Bar de Eric   Bar
(Calle Escuelas 8; ⊙8.30am-2am Sun-Thu, to 3am Fri & Sat) Imagine Keith Moon reincarnated as a punk rocker and put in charge of a modern tapas restaurant. Eric's is the brainchild of Spanish rock'n'roll drummer Eric Jiménez, of Los Planetas – but in this new bastion of rock chic, things aren't as chaotic as you might think.

Albayzín Abaco Té   Teahouse
(☑958 22 19 35; Calle Álamo de Marqués 5; 🔊) Hidden high up in the Albayzín maze, Abaco's Arabian minimalist interior allows you to enjoy Alhambra views from a comfy-ish floor mat. Health freaks hog the carrot juice; sweet tooths bag the excellent cakes.

Capilla Real (p137)

🍴 Tapas for Free

Granada – bless its generous heart – is one of the last bastions of that fantastic practice of free tapas with every drink. Place your drink order at the bar and, hey presto, a plate will magically appear with a generous portion of something delicious-looking on it. Order another drink and another plate will materialise. The process is repeated with every round you buy – and each time the tapa gets better. As Spanish bars serve only small glasses of beer (cañas measure just 250mL), it is perfectly easy to fill up on free tapas over an enjoyable evening without getting totally inebriated. Indeed, some people 'crawl' from bar to bar getting a drink and free tapa in each place. Packed shoulder to shoulder with tapas institutions, Calle de Elvira and Calle Navas are good places for bar crawls. If you're hungry you can always order an extra plate or two to soak up the cervezas.

WESTEND61 / GETTY IMAGES ©

⭐ ENTERTAINMENT

Do not miss the nightly shows (8pm; €30) in the Palacio de los Olvidados (p136), which combine Lorca's plays with some magnificent self-penned flamenco. Best night out in Granada. No contest!

Casa del Arte Flamenco   Flamenco
(📞958 56 57 67; www.casadelarteflamenco. com; Cuesta de Gomérez 11; tickets €18; ⏰shows 7.30pm & 9pm) A small newish flamenco venue that is neither tablao (tourist show)

nor peña (private club), but something in between. The performers are invariably top-notch, while the atmosphere depends largely on the tourist-local make-up of the audience.

Peña La Platería   Flamenco
(www.laplateria.org.es; Placeta de Toqueros 7) Buried in the Albayzín warren, Peña La Platería claims to be the oldest flamenco aficionados' club in Spain, founded in 1949. Unlike other more private clubs, it regularly opens it doors to nonmembers for performances on Thursday nights (and sometimes Saturdays) at 10.30pm.

Jardines de Zoraya   Flamenco
(📞958 20 60 66; www.jardinesdezoraya.com; Calle Panaderos 32; tickets with drink/dinner €20/45; ⏰shows 8pm & 10.30pm) A little larger than some of Andalucía's new flamenco cultural centres, and hosted in a restaurant that serves food and drink, the Jardines de Zoraya appears, on first impression, to be a touristy flamenco tablao. But reasonable entry prices, top-notch performers and a highly atmospheric patio make the Albayzín venue a worthwhile stop for any aficionado.

ℹ️ INFORMATION

Bono Turístico Granada Valid for five days this €32 card gives admission to the city's major sights, plus 10 rides on city buses, use of the sightseeing bus for a day and discounts on the Cicerone Cultura y Ocio walking tour (p139) and a city audioguide. You can buy the Bono at this.is:granada (the orange kiosk opposite Plaza Nueva, where the bus to the Albazyín stops). For a €2.50 surcharge, you can pre-order by phone from the Bono information line or online at www. caja-granada.es, then pick it up at the **Caja Granada** (Plaza Isabel La Católica 6; ⏰8.30am-2.15pm Mon-Fri) bank. Buying in advance gives you the advantage of choosing your Alhambra entrance time, rather than being assigned one.

Provincial Tourist Office (📞958 24 71 28; www. turismodegranada.org; Plaza de Mariana Pineda 10; ⏰9am-8pm Mon-Fri, 10am-7pm Sat, 10am-3pm Sun) Information on all of Granada province.

Where to Stay

Central Granada – the level ground from the Realejo across to Plaza de la Trinidad – is very compact, so hotel location doesn't matter much. The prettiest lodgings are the Albayzín courtyard houses, though these call for some hill walking, and many aren't accessible by taxi. The handful of hotels up by the Alhambra are scenic but a hassle for sightseeing further afield. Rates are highest in spring and fall, spiking over Easter. Parking, where offered, costs €15 to €20 per day, and is usually at a municipal parking lot, not on the hotel grounds.

Tourist Office (958 22 10 22; Calle Santa Ana 1; 9am-7.30pm Mon-Sat, 9.30am-3pm Sun) Close to Plaza Nueva.

GETTING THERE & AWAY

AIR

Aeropuerto Federico García Lorca (www.aena. es) is 17km west of the city, near the A92. Links to destinations outside Spain are limited to **British Airways** (www.ba.com), who run thrice-weekly flights to London City Airport.

BUS

Granada's **bus station** (Carretera de Jaén) is 3km northwest of the city centre. Take city bus SN2 to Cruz del Sur and change to the LAC bus for the Gran Via de Colón in the city centre. Taxis cost around €7 to €9. **Alsa** (www.alsa.es)

handles buses in the province and across the region, plus a night bus direct to Madrid's Barajas airport (€25, six hours).

TRAIN

The **train station** (958 24 02 02; Avenida de Andaluces) is 1.5km northwest of the centre, off Avenida de la Constitución. For the centre, walk straight ahead to Avenida de la Constitución and turn right to pick up the LAC bus to Gran Via de Colón; taxis cost about €5. There are regular services to Madrid (€69, 2½ hours), Barcelona (€60, seven to 11 hours), Córdoba (€36, 2½ hours) and Seville (€30, three hours).

GETTING AROUND

BUS

Individual tickets are €1.20; you can pay the bus driver with notes or coins. The most useful lines are C1, which departs from Plaza Nueva and does a full circuit of the Albayzín; C2, which runs from Plaza Nueva up to Sacramonte; and C3, which goes from Plaza Isabel II up through the Realejo quarter to the Alhambra.

METRO

Stalled by the economic crisis, Granada's long-awaited new metro (scheduled initially to be completed by 2012) was still not operational at the time of writing this guide, although the lines have been built. The 16km route, which will run between Albolote in the north and Amarilla in the southwest, includes 26 stations and will take 45 minutes to ride in its entirety. As only 2.5km of the route in central Granada will travel beneath the ground, the metro is better described as a light-rail link.

ANDALUCÍA'S HILL TOWNS

In this Chapter

Andalucía's Hill Towns at a Glance...

The hill towns of Andalucía rank among Spain's most memorable attractions. From afar, these pueblos blancos (white villages) seem to cling to impossibly steep hillsides and rocky crags, ancient village fortresses rising up from the plains. Up close, in the twisting laneways and pretty squares, there is an intimacy to the experience, a sense of having discovered some hidden world unchanged in centuries. Explore with your own wheels to cover as many as you can – take your pick from boutique Vejer de la Frontera, magnificent Ronda, unique Setenil de las Bodegas or the towns of the Sierra de Grazalema.

Andalucía's Hill Towns in Three Days

Las Alpujarras (p150) has the densest concentration of whitewashed hill towns anywhere in Andalucía – spend at least two days exploring the area, mixing in some short day hikes with driving between the villages to sample the local cuisine. On your third day, make a bee-line for **Ronda** (p154), one of the most beautiful villages anywhere in Spain.

Andalucía's Hill Towns in One Week

After visiting Las Alpujarras and Ronda, spend at least a night in **Arcos de la Frontera** (p152), preferably sleeping in the *parador*. Add a couple of extra nights exploring the **Sierra de Grazalema** (p160) – Zahara de la Sierra, Olvera and Grazalema are stunning hill towns with some great hiking in the vicinity. Don't miss **Carmona** (p168) and **Vejer de la Frontera** (p172) to round out your week.

Arriving in Andalucía's Hill Towns

There are numerous gateways to Andalucía's Hill Towns. Málaga is ideal if Ronda is your starting point; it receives flights from all over Europe. Granada works for Las Alpujarras, while Seville or Jerez de la Frontera are convenient to Arcos de la Frontera. All of these airports and train stations have car rental offices, although we recommend reserving your vehicle in advance.

Sleeping

Every village and town across the region has accommodation, from peerless *paradors* (luxury, state-owned hotels) to welcoming, family-run *hostales* (cheap hotels) and *casas rurales* (rural homes), with plenty of midrange places in between. Ronda, Arcos de la Frontera, Vejer de la Frontera and the villages of Las Alpujarras have the widest selection.

Capileira

FRAN MARIN / GETTY IMAGES ©

Las Alpujarras

The icy sentinels of the Sierra Nevada lord it over Las Alpujarras, a jumble of deep green valleys and stunning white, pocket-sized villages. Together they represent some of the most breathtaking scenery in Spain.

Las Alpujarras' 70km-long jumble of valleys consists of arid hillsides split by deep ravines and alternating with oasis-like white villages set beside rapid streams and surrounded by gardens, orchards and woodlands. Las Alpujarras has a historical personality all its own: it was the last part of Spain to retain a strong Muslim population and it shows in everything from the architecture to the cuisine.

Barranco de Poqueira

When seen from the bottom of the Poqueira gorge, the three villages of Pampaneira, Bubión and Capileira, 14km to 20km northeast of Órgiva, look like splatters of white paint flicked Jackson Pollock–style against the grey stone behind. They're the most beautiful villages of Las Alpujarras, and the

---

Great For...

☑ Don't Miss

Trevélez, home to some of Andalucía's finest *jamón serrano*.

Jamón serrano

CARLOS SANCHEZ PEREYRA / GETTY IMAGES ©

most visited. The Poqueira is famous for its multitude of artisan crafts; leather, weaving and tilework are all practiced using age-old methods. Then there is the unique cuisine made using locally produced ham, jam, cheese, honey, mushrooms and grapes. Equally alluring are the hiking trails that link the villages, many of them perfectly doable in a day.

Trevélez

To gastronomes, Trevélez equals ham (*jamón serrano* to be more precise), one of Spain's finest cured hams that matures perfectly in the village's rarefied mountain air. It is the second-highest village in Spain, sitting at 1486m on the almost treeless slopes of the Barranco de Trevélez.

La Tahá

In the next valley east from Poqueira, life gets substantially more tourist-free. Still known by the Arabic term for the administrative districts into which the Islamic caliphate divided the Alpujarras, this region consists of the town of Pitres and its six outlying villages – Mecina, Capilerilla, Mecinilla, Fondales, Ferreirola and Atalbéitar – in the valley just below, all of Roman origin. Day trippers are few.

Las Alpujarras Walking Trails

The alternating ridges and valleys of Las Alpujarras are criss-crossed with a network of mule paths, irrigation ditches and hiking routes, for a near-infinite number of good walks between villages or into the wild. The villages in the Barranco de Poqueira are the most popular starting point, but even there, you'll rarely pass another hiker on the trail. Colour-coded routes ranging from 4km to 23km (two to eight hours) run up and down the gorge, and you can also hike to Mulhacén (mainland Spain's highest peak) from here.

View from the Parador de Arcos de la Frontera

CAROLINE VON TUEMPLING / GETTY IMAGES ©

Arcos de la Frontera

Everything you've ever dreamed a pueblo blanco (white town) to be materialises in Arcos de la Frontera, with its thrilling clifftop location and old town full of winding streets and mystery.

Great For...

☑ Don't Miss

The lookout on Plaza del Cabildo at the heart of the old town.

The appeal of Arcos de la Frontera lies in walking its stunning streets and catching glimpses of the glorious views out across the plains that surround the town. There are, however, a few attractions worth seeking out as you explore the town.

Basílica Menor de Santa María de la Asunción

A Gothic-cum-baroque creation, the **Basilica of Santa María** (Plaza del Cabildo; €2; ⊙10am-1pm & 4-6.30pm Mon-Fri, 10am-2pm Sat Mar-Dec) is one of Andalucía's more beautiful and intriguing small churches, built over several centuries on the site of a mosque. Check out the ornate gold-leaf altarpiece (a miniature of the one in Seville cathedral) carved between 1580 and 1608, a striking painting of San Cristóbal

Basílica Menor de Santa María de la Asunción

© AD PERSHOUSE / GETTY IMAGES ©

(St Christopher), a 14th-century mural uncovered in the 1970s, an ornate wood-carved choir and the lovely Isabelline ceiling tracery.

Plaza del Cabildo

Lined with fine ancient buildings, Plaza del Cabildo is the centre of the old town, its vertiginous *mirador* (lookout) affording exquisite vistas over the Río Guadalete. The 11th-century, Moorish-built Castillo de los Duques is closed to the public, but its outer walls frame classic Arcos views. On the square's eastern side, the **Parador de Arcos de la Frontera** (📞956 70 05 00; www. parador.es; r €100-170; ❄ @ 🛜) is a recon-struction of a 16th-century magistrate's house.

Mirador de Abadés

Less famous than the mirador on Plaza del Cabildo, the Mirador de Abadés offers a sweeping panorama of Arcos and the surrounding country from the southeastern end of the old town.

Convento de las Mercedarias

It's not often that buying biscuits feels like going to confession, but step into the vestibule of this ancient **convent** (Plaza Boticas; ☺hours vary), push a bell, and a concealed nun on the other side of a wooden partition will invite you to buy a bag of sweet treats. Place your money in a revolving compartment, and within a couple of minutes it will flip back round with your order on it.

A Frontier Town

Arcos' strategic position made it an important prize and, for a brief period during the 11th century, Arcos was an independent Berber-ruled *taifa* (small kingdom). In 1255 it was claimed by Christian king Alfonso X El Sabio for Seville and it remained 'de la Frontera' (on the frontier) between Moorish and Christian Spain until the fall of Granada in 1492.

Ronda

Perched on an inland plateau riven by the 100m fissure of El Tajo gorge, Ronda is one of Andalucía's most spectacular towns. It has a superbly dramatic location, and owes its name ('surrounded' by mountains) to the encircling Serranía de Ronda.

◎ SIGHTS

La Ciudad, the historic old town on the southern side of El Tajo gorge, is an atmospheric area for a stroll with its evocative, still-tangible history, Renaissance mansions and wealth of museums. But don't forget the newer town, which has its distinctive charms and is home to the emblematic bullring, plenty of good tapas bars and restaurants, and the leafy Alameda del Tajo gardens. Three bridges crossing the gorge connect the old town with the new.

Puerta de Almocábar   Gate
The old town is surrounded by massive fortress walls pierced by two ancient gates: the Islamic Puerta de Almocábar, which in the 13th century was the main gateway to the castle, and the 16th-century Puerta de Carlos V. Inside, the Islamic layout remains intact, and its maze of narrow streets now takes its character from the Renaissance mansions of powerful families whose predecessors accompanied Fernando el Católico in the taking of the city in 1485.

Iglesia de Santa
María La Mayor   Church
(Calle José M Holgado; adult/child €4/1.50; ◎10am-8pm) The city's original mosque metamorphed into this elegant church. Inside the entrance is an arch covered with Arabic inscriptions, which was part of the mosque's mihrab (prayer niche indicating the direction of Mecca). The church has been declared a national monument, and its interior is an orgy of decorative styles and ornamentation. A huge central, cedar choir stall divides the church into two sections: aristocrats to the front, everyone else at the back.

La Mina   Historic Site
This Islamic stairway comprises more than 300 steps which are cut into the rock all the way down to the river at the bottom of the gorge. These steps enabled Ronda to maintain water supplies when it was under attack.

Plaza de Toros   Bullring
(Calle Virgen de la Paz; €7, incl audioguide €8.50; ◎10am-8pm) Ronda's Plaza de Toros is a mecca for bullfighting aficionados. In existence for more than 200 years, it is one of the oldest and most revered bullrings in Spain and has been the site of some of the most important events in bullfighting history.

The on-site **Museo Taurino** is crammed with memorabilia such as blood-spattered costumes worn by 1990s star Jesulín de Ubrique. It also includes artwork by Picasso and photos of famous fans such as Orson Welles and Ernest Hemingway.

Baños Arabes   Historic Site
(Arab Baths; Hoyo San Miguel; €3, Mon free; ◎10am-7pm Mon-Fri, to 3pm Sat & Sun) Enjoy the pleasant walk here from the centre of town. Backing on to Ronda's river, these 13th- and 14th-century Arab baths are in good condition, with horseshoe arches, columns and clearly designated divisions between the hot and cold thermal baths. They're some of the best-preserved Arab baths in Andalucía.

Museo del Bandolero   Museum
(www.museobandolero.com; Calle de Armiñán 65; adult/child €3.75/free; ◎10.30am-8pm) This small museum is dedicated to the banditry for which central Andalucía was once renowned. Old prints reflect that when the youthful *bandoleros* (bandits) were not being shot, hanged or garrotted by the authorities, they were stabbing each other in the back, literally as much as figuratively. You can pick up your fake pistol or catapult at the gift shop.

✕ EATING

Typical Ronda food is hearty mountain fare, with an emphasis on stews (called *cocido*,

Ronda

Ronda

estofado or cazuela), trucha (trout), rabo de toro (bull's-tail stew) and game such as conejo (rabbit), perdiz (partridge) and codorniz (quail).

Casa María   Andalucian €

(☑951 083 663; Plaza Ruedo Alameda 27; menú €20; ☺noon-3.30pm & 7.30-10.30pm Thu-Tue; ⛪) This no-frills restaurant has a kitchen run by a passionate cook who prepares dishes strictly according to what is fresh in the market. There is no menu. The selection is not huge but most diners opt for the five-course poco de todo tasting menú reflecting María's delicious homestyle cooking.

Faustino   Andalucian €

(Calle Santa Cecilía; tapas €1.50, raciones €6-8; ☺11.30am-midnight Tue-Sun) This is the real deal: a lively atmospheric tapas bar with plenty of seating in the open traditional atrium decorated with plants, feria posters, and bullfighting and religious pictures. Tapas and raciones are generous. Go with the recommendations like champingnones a la plancha (grilled mushrooms with lashings of garlic). The only downside is the uncomfortable, if pretty, rustic-style painted chairs. Ouch!

Ronda Wine Route

The Ronda region was a major wine-producing area in Roman times; **Ronda la Vieja** (⊙9am-3pm Tue-Sat, 8am-2pm Sun) **FREE** is the archaeological site of the great Roman city of Acinipo, which means 'among the vineyards'. Coins have been found here embellished with bunches of grapes. Other viticultural relics include remains of ceramic kilns and even a bronze head of Bacchus at a Roman villa in nearby Los Villares. Since 1990 there has been a renaissance of the wine industry in these parts and today you can visit up to 21 wineries in the region (by prior appointment). Check www.ruta-vinos-ronda.com for more details.

Local wine to purchase
KARL BLACKWELL / GETTY IMAGES ©

Restaurante Albacara International €€€

(☑952 16 11 84; www.hotelmontelirio.com; Calle Tenorio 8; mains €15-22) One of Ronda's best restaurants, the Albacara is in the old stables of the Montelirio palace and teeters on the edge of the gorge. It serves up delicious meals – try the beef stroganoff or classic magret of duck. Be sure to check out the extensive wine list. Reserve your table in advance.

Restaurante Tragabuches Modern Spanish €€€

(☑952 19 02 91; Calle José Aparício 1; menús €59-87; ⊙1.30-3.30pm & 8-10.30pm Tue-Sat) Ronda's most famous restaurant is a 180-degree-turn away from the ubiquitous 'rustic' look and cuisine. Tragabuches is

modern and sleek with an innovative menu to match. Choose from three set menus. People flock here from miles away to taste the food prepared by its creative chef.

❶ INFORMATION

Tourist Office (www.turismoderonda.es; Paseo de Blas Infante; ⊙10am-7pm Mon-Fri, to 5pm Sat, to 2pm Sun) Helpful staff with a wealth of information on the town and region.

❶ GETTING THERE & AROUND

BUS

The bus station is at Plaza Concepción García Redondo 2. **Comes** (www.tgcomes.es) has buses to Arcos de la Frontera (€9.60, two hours, one to two daily), Jerez de la Frontera (€13, three hours, one to three daily) and Cádiz (€18, two hours, one to three daily). **Los Amarillos** (www.losamarillos.es) goes to Seville via Algodonales and Grazalema, and to Málaga via Ardales.

CAR & MOTORCYCLE

There are a number of underground car parks and some hotels have parking deals for guests. Parking charges are about €1.50 per hour, or €18 to €25 for 14 to 24 hours.

TRAIN

Ronda's **train station** (☑952 87 16 73; www.renfe.es; Avenida de Andalucía) is on the line between Bobadilla and Algeciras. Trains run to Algeciras via Gaucín and Jimena de la Frontera. This train ride is incredibly scenic and worth taking just for the views. Other trains depart for Málaga, Córdoba, Madrid, and Granada via Antequera. For Seville change at Bobadilla or Antequera. It's less than 1km from the train station to most accommodation. A taxi will cost around €7.

Gaucín

Gaucín is a picturesque whitewashed village located on the edge of the Serranía de Ronda mountain range with views to Gibraltar and Morocco. The village was impoverished until the late 1970s when it gradually became discovered by a group of footloose bohemians and artists mainly

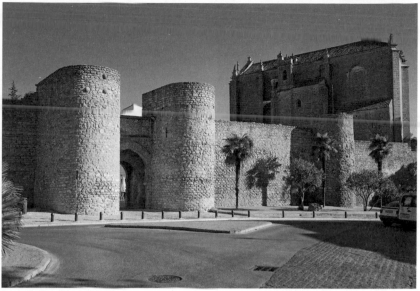

Puerta de Almocábar (p154). Ronda

from chilly northern European climes. Since then Gaucín has continued to grow as an artist's colony. Every year **Art Gaucín** (www.artgaucin.com; ⊗May) takes place, with around 25 local painters, sculptors and photographers opening their studios to the public.

The village is also home to boutique hotel **La Fructuosa** (☑617 692784; www.lafructuosa. com; Calle Luís de Armiñán 67; s/d incl breakfast €80/90; ❄️🔊) and several restaurants, ranging from the super-chic **La Granada Divino** (☑951 70 90 75; www.lagranadadivino.com; Calle de las Piedras; mains €13-23; ⊗noon-3pm & 7-11pm Wed-Sun, 7-11pm Mon & Tue), famously overhauled by Gordon Ramsay (try his signature King prawn dish), to the earthy local **Casa Antonia** (Plaza del Santo Niño 10; mains €7-9; ⊗9am-11pm Tue-Sun), with its terrace seating on the main square watched over by a quaint 17th-century six-spout fountain. Gaucín is also an excellent spot for bird-watchers and there are handy identification plaques throughout the meandering narrow lanes; look skywards and you may spy vultures and booted eagles circling above.

To get here take the signposted A377 from the A7 (or AP7 toll road) at Manilva, signposted Casares and Gaucín; the village is approximately 25km from the turn-off.

Comares

Comares sits like a snowdrift atop its lofty hill. The adventure really is in getting there. You see it for kilometre after kilometre before a final twist in an endlessly winding road lands you below the hanging garden of its cliff. From a little car park you can climb steep, winding steps to the village. Look for ceramic footprints underfoot and simply follow them through a web of narrow, twisting lanes past the Iglesia de la Encarnación and eventually to the ruins of Comares' castle and a remarkable summit cemetery.

The village has a history of rebellion, having been a stronghold of Omar ibn Hafsun, but today there is a tangible sense of contented isolation, enjoyed by locals and many newcomers. The views across the Axarquía are stunning.

Have lunch at **El Molino de los Abuelos** (☑952 50 93 09; Plaza de la Axarquía; mains

From left: Gaucín (p156); Cómpeta; Comares (p157)

€8-16, menú €9), a converted olive mill on the main plaza, which serves Spanish cuisine, including several rice dishes (the owner is from Valencia), and doubles as a charming small **hotel** (www.hotelmolinodelosabuelos.com; d with/without bathroom from €75/55, ste €120; P 🛜). There are a couple of friendly bars at the heart of the village.

On weekdays only, a bus leaves Málaga for Comares at 6pm and starts back at 7am the next morning (€3.20, 1½ hours).

Cómpeta

This picturesque village with its panoramic views, steep winding streets and central bar-lined plaza, overlooking the 16th-century church, has long attracted a large, mixed foreign population. Not only has this contributed to an active cultural scene, but Cómpeta is also home to one or two above-*pueblo*-average restaurants serving contemporary cuisine. It also has a couple of charity shops (rare in Spain) and a foreign-language bookshop. The village is a good base for hiking and other similar adrenalin-fuelled activities.

🏃 ACTIVITIES

El Lucero   Walking
An exhilarating long walk from Cómpeta is up the dramatically peaked El Lucero (1779m), from whose summit, on a clear day, you can see both Granada and Morocco. This is a demanding full-day return walk from Cómpeta, but it's possible to drive as far up as Puerto Blanquillo pass (1200m) via a slightly hairy mountain track from Canillas de Albaida. From Puerto Blanquillo a path climbs 200m to another pass, the Puerto de Cómpeta. One kilometre down from there, past a quarry, the summit path (1½ hours), marked by a signboard, diverges to the right across a stream bed.

Los Caballos
del Mosquin   Horse Riding
(📞608 658108; www.horseriding-andalucia.com; Canillas del Albaida; half-day trek incl picnic €65) Offers guided horse-riding treks ranging from one hour to three days (including full board and accommodation) in the surrounding countryside.

ANDREAS POERTNER / SHUTTERSTOCK ©

❌ EATING

Taberna de
Oscar   Modern Andalucian €

(☑952 51 66 31; www.tabernadeoscar.es; Plaza
Pantaleón Romero 1; medias raciones €3.50-5.50;
☺restaurant 11am-11pm Wed-Mon, bar 6pm-late
Wed-Mon; ☒) The olive oil and produce used
in dishes at this restaurant tucked behind
the church is organic (as far as possible),
and the robust house wine comes from the
family bodega. There's a vegetarian menu
with ingredients such as roast beetroot
and marinated tofu as well as Andalucian
staples, including gazpacho and *zarzuela*
(fish and seafood stew).

Dishes are served in *medias raciones*
(half rations, about double a *tapa* size). Upstairs on the terrace there is a cocktail bar
with great rooftop views and even better
strawberry daiquiris.

Museo del Vino   Andalucian €€

(Avenida Constitución; mains €9.50-17; ☺1-4pm
& 7.30-10.30pm) Exuding rustic warmth with
exposed bricks and beams, this long-time
tourist favourite serves excellent ham,

cheese and sausage *raciones* and wine
from the barrel. It's also something of an
Aladdin's cave of regional crafts and produce, plus Moroccan bits and pieces.

El Pilón   International €€

(☑952 55 35 12; www.restauranteelpilon.
com; Calle Laberinto; mains €13-18; ☺7-11pm
Mon, Wed-Sat, 1-3.30pm Sun; ☒) This former
carpenter's workshop is one of the village's
most popular restaurants. Dishes are created using locally sourced ingredients, whenever possible, and reflect an eclectic range
including tandoori chicken, Burgo's black
pudding and plenty of vegetarian options.
There's a cocktail lounge with sweeping
views and regular events, including wine
tastings and live music.

ℹ INFORMATION

Tourist Office (☑952 55 36 85; Avenida de la
Constitución; ☺10am-3pm Mon-Sat, to 2pm Sun)
Located beside the bus stop at the foot of the
village. It has plenty of information about the
town and region.

Hiking the Sierra de Grazalema

The Sierra de Grazalema is criss-crossed by beautiful trails, many of which require a free permit from the **Centro de Visitantes El Bosque** (956 70 97 33; cv_elbosque@agenciamedio ambienteyagua.es; Calle Federico García Lorca 1; 9.30am-2pm Sun-Tue, 9.30am-2pm & 4-6pm Wed-Sat). In peak season (April to June and September to October) you'll need to contact the centre at least a week before your hike.

El Torreón (1654m) is the highest peak in Cádiz province and from the summit on a clear day you can see Gibraltar, the Sierra Nevada and the Rif Mountains of Morocco. The usual route starts 100m east of the Km40 marker on the Grazalema–Benamahoma road, about 8km from Grazalema. It takes about 2½ hours of walking to reach the summit and 1½ hours back down.

The 14km Pinsapar walk runs between Grazalema and Benamahoma and takes around six hours. The trailhead is signposted off the CA531 (the road to Zahara de la Sierra), a 40-minute uphill walk from Grazalema. The path into the Garganta del Verde (literally 'Green Throat'), a lushly vegetated ravine more than 100m deep, starts 3.5km from Zahara de la Sierra on the Grazalema road. Allow three to four hours' walking if you drive to the start.

The information centres in El Bosque and Grazalema have general maps outlining the main walking possibilities. Far better, equip yourself with a good walking guide such as *Walking in Andalucía* by Guy Hunter-Watts or *Eight Walks from Grazalema* by RE Bradshaw. The best map is Editorial Alpina's *Sierra de Grazalema* (1:25,000), with a walking-guide booklet in English and Spanish. Some of these are sold locally, but don't count on it.

ⓘ GETTING THERE & AWAY

Three buses travel daily from Malaga to Cómpeta (€4.60, 1½ hours), stopping via Torre del Mar. There's a free car park up the hill from the tourist office.

Sierra de Grazalema

The rugged pillar-like peaks of the Parque Natural Sierra de Grazalema rise abruptly from the plains northeast of Cádiz, revealing sheer gorges, rare firs, wild orchids and the province's highest summits against a beautifully green backdrop. This is the wettest part of Spain – stand aside Galicia and Cantabria, Grazalema village logs an average 2000mm annually. It's gorgeous walking country (best in May, June, September and October). For the more intrepid, adventure activities abound. The 534-sq-km park, named Spain's first Unesco Biosphere Reserve in 1977, extends into northwestern Málaga province, where it includes the **Cueva de la Pileta** (952 16 73 43; www. cuevadelapileta.org; Benaoján; adult/child €8/5; hourly tours 10am-1pm & 4-6pm; ⓟ).

Grazalema

Few white towns are as generically perfect as Grazalema, with its spotless white-washed houses sporting rust-tiled roofs and wrought-iron window bars, sprinkled on the steep rocky slopes of its eponymous mountain range. With hikes fanning out in all directions, Grazalema is the most popular base for adventures into the Parque Natural Sierra de Grazalema. It's also an age-old producer of blankets, honey, cheese, meat-filled stews and an adrenaline-filled bull-running festival, and has its own special mountain charm.

⊙ SIGHTS

Plaza de España   Square
The centre of the village is this plaza overlooked by the 18th-century **Iglesia de la Aurora** (11am-1pm) and refreshed by a four-spouted Visigothic fountain.

⊗ EATING

Cafetería Rumores
Cafe €

(Plaza de España; ⊙7am-8pm) 'Rumores' is where most of the local ones start judging by the loquaciousness of the clientele. Drop by for breakfast churros. There's also an on-site pastry shop.

Restaurante El Torreón
Andalucian €€

(☑956 13 23 13; www.restauranteeltorreon-grazalema.com; Calle Agua 44; mains €7-15; ⊙1-3.30pm & 7.30-11.30pm Thu-Tue) This cosy, friendly restaurant with a log fire specialises in traditional mountain cuisine, from local chorizo and cheese platters to *tagarnina* (thistle) scrambles (a Cádiz delicacy), sirloin in green-pepper sauce, and a tasty spinach blended with pine nuts. Tables spill out on to the street when it's sunny.

❶ INFORMATION

Tourist Office (www.grazalema.es; Plaza de Asomaderos; ⊙10am-2pm & 4-7pm Mon-Sat) Has Parque Natural Sierra de Grazalema walking information.

❶ GETTING THERE & AWAY

Los Amarillos (www.losamarillos.es) runs two daily buses to/from Ronda (€2.90, one hour); three daily to/from Ubrique (€2.35, 30 minutes) via Benaocaz (€1.60, 20 minutes); and one daily Monday to Friday to El Bosque (€1.45, 30 minutes), where you can change for Arcos de la Frontera.

Zahara de la Sierra

Rugged Zahara, strung around a vertiginous crag at the foot of the Grazalema mountains, overlooking the turquoise Embalse de Zahara, hums with Moorish mystery. For over 150 years in the 14th and 15th centuries, it stood on the old medieval frontier facing off against Christian Olvera, clearly visible in the distance. These days Zahara ticks all the classic white-town boxes and is a great base for hiking the Garganta Verde, so it's popular. Come during the afternoon siesta, however, and you can still hear a pin drop.

The precipitous CA9104 road over the ultra-steep 1331m Puerto de las Palomas (Doves' Pass) links Zahara with Grazalema

Sculpture, Grazalema

(17km) and is a spectacular drive full of white-knuckle switchbacks.

◎ SIGHTS

With vistas framed by tall palms and bougainvillea, Zahara's streets invite exploration. The village centres on Calle San Juan; towards its eastern end stands the 18th-century baroque **Iglesia de Santa María de Mesa** (⊙hours vary). To climb to the 12th-century castle **keep** (⊙24hr) 𝐅𝐑𝐄𝐄, a hike of about 10 to 15 minutes, take the path almost opposite the Hotel Arco de la Villa. The castle's recapture from the Christians by Abu al-Hasan of Granada, in a 1481 night raid, provoked the Reyes Católicos (Catholic Monarchs) to launch the last phase of the Reconquista, which ended with the fall of Granada.

❶ INFORMATION

Punto de Información Zahara de la Sierra
(☏956 12 31 14; Plaza del Rey 3; ⊙9am-2.30pm & 4-6pm Tue-Fri, 11am-3pm & 4-6pm Sat & Sun) Official Parque Natural Sierra de Grazalema information.

❶ GETTING THERE & AWAY

Comes (www.tgcomes.es) runs two daily buses to/from Ronda (€4.50, one hour).

Olvera

Dramatically topped by an Arabic castle, Olvera (27km northeast of Zahara de la Sierra) beckons from miles away across olive-covered country. A bandit refuge until the mid-19th century, the town now supports more family-run farming cooperatives than anywhere else in Spain. Most come to Olvera for the Vía Verde de la Sierra (p164), but as a white town par excellence, it's renowned for its olive oil, striking neoclassical church and roller-coaster history, which probably started with the Romans.

◎ SIGHTS

Castillo Árabe   Castle
(Plaza de la Iglesia; adult/child €2/1; ⊙10.30am-2pm & 4-7pm Tue-Sun) Perched on a crag high

atop town is Olvera's late 12th-century Arabic castle, which later formed part of Nasrid Granada's defensive systems.

Iglesia Parroquial Nuestra Señora de la Encarnación   Church
(Plaza de la Iglesia; €2; ⊙11am-1pm Tue-Sun) Built over a Gothic-Mudéjar predecessor, Olvera's neoclassical top-of-town church was commissioned by the Dukes of Osuna and completed in 1843.

La Cilla   Museum
(Plaza de la Iglesia; adult/child €2/1; ⊙10.30am-2pm & 4-7pm Tue-Sun) The old grain store of the Dukes of Osuna, beside the castle, houses the tourist office, the Museo La Frontera y los Castillos, and an exposition on Olvera's Vía Verde de la Sierra cycling/hiking path.

✗ EATING

Taberna Juanito Gómez   Tapas €
(Calle Bellavista; tapas €2-3; ⊙1.30-4.30pm & 8.30-11.30pm Mon-Sat) A simple little place that does tasty, decent-value tapas and *montaditos* (bite-sized filled rolls) taking in all your usual faves: garlic prawns, grilled mushrooms, Manchego cheese and Iberian ham.

Hotel Sierra y Cal   Andalucian €
(☏956 13 03 03; Calle Nuestra Señora de los Remedios 2; mains €8-12) A decent hotel cafe-restaurant that pulls in locals, especially on football nights.

❶ INFORMATION

Tourist Office (☏956 12 08 16; www.turism olvera.es; Plaza de la Iglesia; ⊙10.30am-2pm & 4-7pm Tue-Sun)

❶ GETTING THERE & AWAY

Los Amarillos (www.losamarillos.es) runs one or two daily buses to/from Jerez de la Frontera (€9.18, two hours) and Málaga (€12, three hours), and one daily Monday to Friday to/from Ronda (€5.44, 1½ hours). **Comes** (www.tgcomes. es) has one daily bus Monday to Friday to/from Cádiz (€15, three hours).

Antequera

Antequera is a fascinating town, both architecturally and historically, yet it has somehow avoided being on the coach-tour circuit – which only adds to its charms. The three major influences in the region (Roman, Moorish and Spanish) have left the town with a rich tapestry of architectural gems. The highlight is the opulent Spanish-baroque style that gives the town its character and which the civic authorities have worked hard to restore and maintain. There is also an astonishing number of churches here – more than 30, many with wonderfully ornate interiors. Little wonder that the town is often referred to as the 'Florence of Andalucía'.

And there's more! Some of Europe's largest and oldest dolmens (burial chambers built with huge slabs of rock), from around 2500 BC to 1800 BC, can be found just outside the town's centre.

The flip side to all this antiquity is a vibrant city centre with some of the best tapas bars this side of Granada.

◉ SIGHTS

The substantial remains of the Alcazaba, a Muslim-built hilltop castle, dominate Antequera's historic quarter and are within easy (if uphill) distance of the town centre.

Alcazaba   Fortress
(adult/child incl Colegiata de Santa María la Mayor €6/3; ◷10am-7pm Mon-Sat, 10.30am-3pm Sun) Favoured by the Granada emirs of Islamic times, Antequera's hilltop Moorish fortress has a fascinating history and covers a massive 62,000 sq metres. The main approach to the hilltop is from Plaza de San Sebastián, up the stepped Cuesta de San Judas and then through an impressive archway, the Arco de los Gigantes, built in 1585 and formerly bearing huge sculptures of Hercules. All that is left today are the Roman inscriptions on the stones.

Colegiata de Santa
María la Mayor   Church
(Plaza Santa María; adult/child incl Alcazaba €6/3; ◷10am-7pm Mon-Sat, 10.30am-3pm Sun) Just

⌐⊃ꟼ Unspoiled Andalucía:
La Axarquía

The region of La Axarquía has deep valleys lined with terraces and irrigation channels that date to Islamic times – nearly all the villages dotted among the olive-, almond- and vine-planted hills date from this era. Nowadays, its chief attractions include fantastic scenery; pretty white villages; strong, sweet, local wine; and good walking in spring and autumn. The 'capital' of La Axarquía, Vélez Málaga, 4km north of Torre del Mar, is a busy but unspectacular town, although its restored hilltop castle is worth a look. From Vélez the A335 heads north past the turquoise Embalse de la Viñuela reservoir and up through the Boquete de Zafarraya (a dramatic cleft in the mountains). One bus a day makes its way over this road between Torre del Mar and Granada. Some of the most dramatic La Axarquía scenery is up around the highest villages of Alfarnate (925m) and Alfarnatejo (858m), with towering, rugged crags such as Tajo de Gomer and Tajo de Doña Ana rising to their south. You can pick up information on La Axarquía at the tourist offices in Málaga, Nerja, Torre del Mar or Cómpeta. Prospective walkers should ask for the leaflet on walks in the Parque Natural Sierras de Tejeda, Almijara y Alhama. Good maps for walkers are *Mapa Topográfico de Sierra Tejeda* and *Mapa Topográfico de Sierra Almijara* by Miguel Ángel Torres Delgado, both at 1:25,000. You can also follow the links at www.axarquia.es for walks in the region.

Embalse de la Viñuela

Vía Verde de la Sierra

Regularly touted as the finest of Spain's *vías verdes* (greenways which have transformed old railway lines into traffic-free thoroughfares for bikers, hikers and horse-riders), the **Vía Verde de la Sierra** (www.fundacionviaverdedelasierra. com) between Olvera and Puerto Serrano is one of 23 such schemes in Andalucía. Aside from the wild, rugged scenery, the 36km-route is notable for four spectacular viaducts, 30 tunnels (with sensor-activated lighting) and three old stations-turned-hotel-restaurants. Ironically, the train line itself was never actually completed. It was constructed in the 1920s as part of the abortive Jerez to Almargen railway, but the Spanish Civil War put a stop to construction works. The line was restored in the early 2000s.

The **Hotel-Restaurante Estación Verde** (✆661 463207; Calle Pasadera 4; s/d/tr €25/40/60) just outside Olvera is the official starting point. Here you can hire bikes, including tandems, kids' bikes and chariots, from €12 per day, and check out the **Centro de Interpretación Vía Verde de la Sierra** (adult/child €2/1; ⊗9.30am-5.30pm Thu-Mon). Bike hire is also available at Coripe and Puerto Serrano stations. Other services include the **Patrulla Verde** (✆638 280184; ⊗9am-5pm Sat & Sun), a staff of bike experts who help with info and mechanical issues.

A highlight of the Vía Verde is the Peñón de Zaframagón, a distinctive crag that's a prime breeding ground for griffon vultures. The **Centro de Interpretación y Observatorio Ornitológico** (✆956 13 63 72; adult/child €2/1; ⊗11am-4pm Sat & Sun), in the former Zaframagón station building 16km west of Olvera, allows close-up observations activated directly from a high-definition camera placed up on the crag.

below the Alcazaba is the large 16th-century Colegiata de Santa María la Mayor. This church-cum-college played an important part in Andalucía's 16th-century humanist movement, and boasts a beautiful Renaissance facade, lovely fluted stone columns inside and a Mudéjar *artesonado* (a ceiling of interlaced beams with decorative insertions). It also plays host to some excellent musical events and exhibitions.

Iglesia del Carmen   Church
(Plaza del Carmen; €2; ⊗11am-1.30pm & 4.30-5.45pm Tue-Fri, 11am-2pm Sat & Sun) Only the most jaded would fail to be impressed by the Iglesia del Carmen and its marvellous 18th-century churrigueresque retable. Magnificently carved in red pine by Antequera's own Antonio Primo, it's spangled with statues of angels by Diego Márquez y Vega, and saints, popes and bishops by José de Medina. While the main altar is unpainted, the rest of the interior is a dazzle of colour and design, painted to resemble traditional tilework.

Museo de la Ciudad de Antequera   Museum
(www.antequera.es; Plaza del Coso Viejo; compulsory guided tour €3; ⊗9.30am-2pm & 4.30-6.30pm Tue-Fri, 9.30am-2pm Sat, 10am-2pm Sun) Located in the town centre, the pride of the Museo Municipal is the elegant and athletic 1.4m bronze statue of a boy, *Efebo*. Discovered on a local farm in the 1950s, it is possibly the finest example of Roman sculpture found in Spain.

Maqueta de Antequera   Museum
(www.maquetadeantequera.es; €1; ⊗8am-11pm, to midnight Fri & Sat) A huge scale model of the city in the 18th century, unveiled in 2013. It is said to be the largest model of its kind in Spain.

✖ EATING

Local specialities you'll encounter on almost every Antequera menu include *porra antequerana* (a thick and delicious garlicky soup, similar to gazpacho); *bienmesabe* (literally 'tastes good to me'; a sponge dessert);

Alcazaba (p163)

and *angelorum* (a dessert incorporating meringue, sponge and egg yolk). Antequera also does a fine breakfast *mollete* (soft bread roll), served with a choice of fillings.

Rincón de Lola   Tapas €

(www.rincondelola.net; Calle Encarnación 7; tapas €2, raciones €7; ☺noon-11.30pm Tue-Sun) A great place for inexpensive, varied tapas that can give you a taster of local dishes such as *cochinillo* (suckling pig), or *porra antequerana*. There are also piled-high *tostas* (open sandwiches on toasted bread) and *raciones* such as tomatoes filled with cheese, salmon, wild mushrooms and prawns.

Arte de Cozina   Andalucian €€

(www.artedecozina.com; Calle Calzada 27-29; mains €12-15, tapas €2; ☺1-11pm) The *simpática* (friendly) owner of this hotel-restaurant has her own garden that provides fresh ingredients for her dishes. Traditional dishes are reinterpreted, like gazpacho made with green asparagus or *porra* with oranges, plus meat, fish and Antequeran specialities. On Thursday and Friday evenings classical musicians provide entertainment.

The adjacent tapas bar serves unusual light bites such as snails in a spicy almond sauce or river crab with chilli and peppers. There are plenty of dessert choices, which is unusual in these parts.

Reina Restaurante   Contemporary Andalucian €€

(☏952 70 30 31; Calle San Agustín 1; mains €14-18, menú €14; ☺1-4pm & 8-11pm Tue-Sun) Located in a pretty restaurant-flanked cul-de-sac off Calle Infante Don Fernando, this restaurant also runs a cooking school, La Espuela, so they know what they're doing. The menu includes a fine selection of Antequeran specialities, such as chicken in almond sauce and partridge pâté, along with more daring dishes like strawberry gazpacho with goats' cheese.

⊖ DRINKING & NIGHTLIFE

El Angelote   Bar

(Plaza del Carmen 10; ☺12.30pm-late Tue-Sat; ☏) A lively bar with terrace seating on the picturesque square; it offers occasional live music.

Setenil de las Bodegas

While most white towns sought protective status atop lofty crags, the people of Setenil did the opposite and burrowed into the dark caves beneath the steep cliffs of the Río Trejo. The strategy clearly worked. It took the Christian armies a 15-day siege to dislodge the Moors from their well-defended positions in 1484. Many of the original cave-houses remain and some have been converted into bars and restaurants. Further afield, you can hike along the 6km Ruta de los Molinos past ancient mills to the next village of Alcalá del Valle.

The tourist office is near the top of the town in the 16th-century Casa Consistorial, which exhibits a rare wooden Mudéjar ceiling. A little higher up is the 12th-century castle (opening hours are sporadic; check at the tourist office), captured by the Christians just eight years before the fall of Granada.

Setenil has some great tapas bars that make an ideal pit-stop while you study its unique urban framework. Start in Restaurante Palermo in Plaza de Andalucía at the top of town and work your way down.

Old Town, Setenil de las Bodegas
DESIGN PICS / PETER ZOELLER / GETTY IMAGES ©

❶ INFORMATION

Municipal Tourist Office (☑952 70 25 05; www.antequera.es; Plaza de San Sebastián 7; ⊙11am-2pm & 5-8pm Mon-Sat, to 2pm Sun) A helpful tourist office with information about the town and region.

❶ GETTING THERE & AWAY

BUS

The **bus station** (Paseo Garcí de Olmo) is 1km north of the centre. **Alsa** (www.alsa.es) runs buses to Seville (€14, 2½ hours, five daily), Granada (€9, 1½ hours, five daily), Córdoba (€11, 2¾ hours, one daily), Almería (€23, six hours, one daily) and Málaga (€6, 1½ hours, two daily).

Three daily buses run between Antequera and Fuente de Piedra village (€2.45, 25 minutes).

CAR & MOTORCYCLE

A toll road (AP-46) running from Torremolinos to Las Padrizas (€5) is located around 21km southeast of Antequera.

TRAIN

The **train station** (www.renfe.es; Avenida de la Estación) is 1.5km north of the centre. Six trains a day run to/from Granada (€11, 1½ hours), and there are four daily to Seville (€18, 1½ hours). Another three run to Málaga or Córdoba, but you'll need to change at Bobadilla.

Sierras de Cazorla, Segura y Las Villas

One of the biggest drawcards in Jaén province – and, for nature lovers, in all of Andalucía – is the mountainous, lushly wooded Parque Natural Sierras de Cazorla, Segura y Las Villas. This is the largest protected area in Spain – 2099 sq km of craggy mountain ranges, deep, green river valleys, canyons, waterfalls, remote hilltop castles and abundant wildlife, with a snaking, 20km-long reservoir, the Embalse del Tranco, in its midst. The abrupt geography, with altitudes varying between 460m at the lowest point to 2107m at the summit of Cerro Empanadas, makes for dramatic changes in the landscape. The Río Guadalquivir, Andalucía's longest river, begins in the south of the park, and flows northwards into the reservoir, before heading west across Andalucía to the Atlantic Ocean.

The best times to visit the park are spring and autumn, when the vegetation is at its most colourful and temperatures pleasant.

Waterfall, Parque Natural Sierras de Cazorla, Segura y Las Villas

The park is hugely popular with Spanish tourists and attracts several hundred thousand visitors each year. The peak periods are Semana Santa, July, August, and weekends from April to October.

Exploring the park is easier if you have a vehicle; the network of paved and unpaved roads and footpaths reaches some pretty remote areas and offers plenty of scope for panoramic day walks or drives. If you don't have a vehicle, you have the option of guided walks, 4WD excursions and wildlife-spotting trips, which will get you out into the wild areas. There are plenty of places to stay within the park as well as in Cazorla town.

Cazorla

This picturesque, bustling white town sits beneath towering crags, just where the Sierra de Cazorla rises up from a rolling sea of olive trees, 45km east of Úbeda. It makes the perfect launching pad for exploring the beautiful Parque Natural Sierras de Cazorla, Segura y Las Villas, which begins dramatically among the cliffs of Peña de los Halcones (Falcon Crag) directly above the town.

◎ SIGHTS

The heart of town is Plaza de la Corredera, with busy bars and the elegant *ayuntamiento* (town hall) and clock tower looking down from the southeastern corner. Canyonlike streets lead south to the Balcón de Zabaleta. This little mirador is like a sudden window in a blank wall, with stunning views up to the Castillo de la Yedra and beyond. From here another narrow street leads down to Cazorla's most picturesque square, Plaza de Santa María.

Castillo de la Yedra Castle

(Museo del Alto Guadalquivir; EU citizen/other free/€1.50; ⊘9am-7.30pm Tue-Sat, to 3.30pm Sun & daily mid-Jun–mid-Sep) Cazorla's dramatic Castle of the Ivy, a 700m walk above Plaza de Santa María, has great views and is home to the interesting Museum of the Upper Guadalquivir, whose diverse collections include traditional agricultural tools and kitchen utensils, religious art, models of an old olive mill, and a small chapel featuring a life-size Romanesque-Byzantine crucifixion sculpture. The castle is of Muslim origin, comprehensively rebuilt in the 14th century after the Reconquista.

⊗ EATING

There are good bars on Cazorla's main squares, where you can choose tapas and *raciones*.

Bar Las Vegas   Tapas €
(Plaza de la Corredera 17; tapas €1-2, raciones €10-12; ☉10am-midnight) It's tiny but it's the best of Cazorla's central bars, with barrel tables outside (and packed tables inside when the weather's poor). It does great tapas including one called *gloria bendita* (blessed glory), which turns out to be scrambled eggs with prawns and capsicum, as well as *raciones* of local favourites such as cheese, ham, venison and *lomo de orza*.

Mesón
Leandro   Contemporary Spanish €€
(www.mesonleandro.com; Calle Hoz 3; mains €9-20; ☉1.30-4pm & 8.30-11pm Wed-Mon) Just behind the Iglesia de Santa María, Leandro brings a touch of sophistication to Cazorla dining – professional, friendly service in a bright, attractive dining room with lazy music, and just one token set of antlers on the wall. The broad menu of nicely presented dishes encompasses the likes of *fettuccine a la marinera,* as well as partridge-and-pheasant pâté and a terrific *solomillo de ciervo* (venison sirloin).

❶ INFORMATION

Oficina Municipal de Turismo (📞953 71 01 02; www.cazorla.es; Plaza de Santa María; ☉10am-1pm & 4-8pm, to 7pm Oct-Mar) Inside the remains of Santa María church, with useful information on the natural park as well as the town.

❶ GETTING THERE & AROUND

BUS

Alsa (www.alsa.es) runs three to five daily buses to Úbeda (€4, one hour), Baeza (€4.80, 1¼ hours), Jaén (€9.25, two to 2½ hours) and Granada (€18, 3¾ hours). The bus stop is on Calle Hilario Marco,

500m north of Plaza de la Corredera via Plaza de la Constitución.

CAR & MOTORCYCLE

Parking and driving in the old, central part of town is near impossible, but there's a reasonable amount of free parking around the periphery. **Parking Hogar Sur** (Calle Cronista Lorenzo Polaino; ☉7am-11pm; per 1/24hr €1.25/10), just down from Plaza de la Constitución, is convenient.

Hornos

Like better-known Segura de la Sierra, little Hornos is fabulously located – atop a crag backed by a sweep of mountains, with marvellous views over the shimmering Embalse del Tranco and the lush, green countryside, richly patterned with olive, pine and almond trees and the occasional tossed dice of a farmhouse. Hornos dates back to the Bronze Age when there was a settlement here; the castle on the crag was built by Christians in the mid-13th century, probably on the site of an earlier Muslim fortification. Don't expect colour-coordinated geraniums, souvenir shops or a tourist office: Hornos' charms lie in exploring the narrow, winding streets and wondering at the view from several strategically placed miradors. Seek out the early 16th-century Iglesia de la Asunción, which has the oldest, albeit crumbling, plateresque portal in the province, plus a vibrant 1589 *retablo* (altarpiece) with nine painted panels.

There are a couple of restaurants and basic lodgings should you want to stay. If you want to stride out, a plaque at the village entrance shows local trails, including two of about 4km each to tiny outlying villages – the PRA152 south down to Hornos El Viejo and the PRA148 east up to La Capellanía. To get to Hornos, take the A319 12km north of the Tranco dam to a T-junction; from here the A317 winds 4km up to Hornos village.

Carmona

Perched on a low hill 35km east of Seville, overlooking a hazy *vega* (valley) that sizzles in the summer heat, and dotted with ancient palaces and majestic monuments, Carmona comes as a surprise highlight of western Andalucía. This strategic site was important as long ago as Carthaginian times. The Romans laid out a street plan that survives to this day: the Vía Augusta, running from Rome to Cádiz, entered Carmona by the eastern Puerta de Córdoba and left by the western Puerta de Sevilla (both of which are still standing strong). The Muslims built a strong defensive wall around Carmona, but the town fell in 1247 to Fernando III. Later on Mudéjar and Christian artisans constructed grand churches, convents and mansions.

◎ SIGHTS

From the Puerta de Sevilla, it's an easy stroll through the best of old-town Carmona. Inside the **town hall** (📞954 14 00 11; Calle El Salvador; ⊙8am-3pm Mon-Fri) **FREE** is a large, very fine Roman mosaic of the gorgon Medusa.

Necrópolis Romana   Historic Site

(Roman cemetery; 📞600 143632; www.museos deandalucia.es; Avenida de Jorge Bonsor 9; ⊙9am-7pm Tue-Sat & 9am-3.30pm Sun Apr-May, 9am-3.30pm Tue-Sun Jun–mid-Sep, 9am-5.30pm Tue-Sat & 9am-3.30pm Sun mid-Sep–Mar) **FREE**
On the southwestern edge of Carmona lie the remains of a Roman city of the dead. A dozen or more family tombs, some elaborate and many-chambered, were hewn into the rock here in the 1st and 2nd centuries AD. Most of the inhabitants were cremated, and in the tombs are wall niches for the boxlike stone urns. You can enter the huge Tumba de Servilia, the tomb of a family of Hispano-Roman VIPs, and climb down into several others.

Convento de Santa Clara   Convent

(📞954 14 21 02; www.clarisasdecarmona.word press.com; Calle Torno de Santa Clara; adult/child €2/1; ⊙11am-2pm & 4-6pm Thu-Mon) With its Gothic ribbed vaulting, carved Mudéjar-style ceiling and dazzling altarpiece – a shining example of Sevillan baroque – the Santa Clara convent appeals to both art and architecture buffs. Visits start with a spiral ascent of the tower, an 18th-century addition. Don't miss the pretty arch-lined cloister out the back.

🥾 Cazorla Walks

There are some great walks from Cazorla town – all uphill to start with, but your reward is beautiful forest paths and fabulous panoramas of cliffs, crags, circling vultures and lonely monasteries. Good maps and information in anything except Spanish are hard to come by, but the main routes are signposted and waymarked. Cazorla's tourist office has maps with descriptions in Spanish. Editorial Alpina's *Sierra de Cazorla* map is useful and sold in some shops in Cazorla.
Sendero del Gilillo (PRA313) The best walk for the fit and energetic is the full-day 21km loop from Cazorla up to the Puerto del Gilillo pass (nearly 1100m higher than the town and with stupendous views) and back via the Loma de los Castellones ridge, Puerto del Tejo pass, Prado Redondo forest house and Ermita Virgen de la Cabeza chapel. The route ascends from Cazorla's Iglesia de Santa María via the Ermita de San Sebastián chapel (2.2km, about two hours return) and the Riogazas picnic area (3.5km, about three hours return), either of which makes a scenic there-and-back walk if you fancy something shorter.
Sendero de Ermitas y Monasterios (SLA7) An 11km loop (four hours) passing a few isolated chapels and monasteries in the hills, the SLA7 follows the PRA313 (Sendero del Gilillo) for 4km before diverging to the right along the La Iruela–El Chorro road, then descending back to town via the Monasterio de Montesión.

From left: Paella; Iglesia de San Pedro, Carmona; Carmona town (p168)

Iglesia Prioral de Santa María de la Asunción   Church

(☑954 19 14 82; Plaza Marqués de las Torres; €3; ⏰9.30am-2pm & 5.30-6.30pm Tue-Fri, to 2pm Sat) This splendid church was built mainly in the 15th and 16th centuries on the site of the former main mosque. The Patio de los Naranjos by which you enter has a Visigothic calendar carved into one of its pillars. Inside, the plateresque altar is detailed to an almost perverse degree, with 20 panels of biblical scenes framed by gilt-scrolled columns.

Iglesia de San Pedro   Church

West of the Puerta de Sevilla, the 15th-century Iglesia de San Pedro has a rich baroque interior; its tower was modelled on Seville's Giralda.

Iglesia de Santiago   Church

At the northeastern end of the old-town tangle is this fine 14th- to 18th-century church, with a Mudéjar tower.

Alcázar de la Puerta de Sevilla   Gate

(adult/child €2/1, Mon free; ⏰10am-6pm Mon-Sat, to 3pm Sun) The impressive main gate of Carmona's old town is one element of a fortification that had already been standing for five centuries when the Romans reinforced it and built a temple on top. The Muslim Almohads added an *aljibe* (cistern) to the upper patio, which remains a hawklike perch from which to admire the typically Andalucian tableau of white cubes and soaring spires.

⏩ TOURS

Carmona Bike Tours   Bicycle Tour

(☑617 265798; www.carmonabiketours.com; Calle Mimosa 15; tours per person €18, bicycle hire per day €10) This energetic operation is run by two keen local cyclists. Tours (English or Spanish) take historical routes through town or venture out into the beautiful, little-explored surrounding Campiña. Book ahead.

✖ EATING

Tapeando – tapas noshing – is such a pastime here that Carmona has made it official by establishing a tapas route. The Ruta de la Tapa includes 17 eateries, an impressive number for a town this size. Pick up a

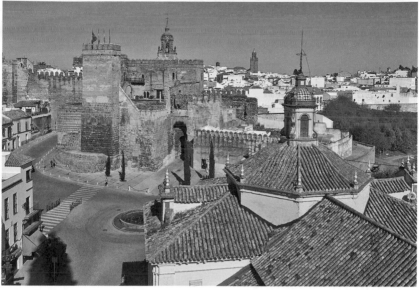

ANDREA PISTOLESI / GETTY IMAGES ©

brochure with maps and descriptions of the bars at the tourist office and hit the trail!

Mingalario
Tapas €

(954 14 38 93; Calle El Salvador; montaditos €2.50, tapas €2-4; 1-4pm & 7.30pm-midnight Wed-Mon) This small, old eatery with hams hanging from the rafters is big on *montaditos* – small toasted sandwiches stuffed with goodies like roast pork or garlic prawns. You'll find all kinds of homemade local favourites like *presa ibérica* (Iberian pork), spinach with chickpeas (a Carmona special) and *bacalao* (cod) gratin.

Molino de la Romera
Tapas €€

(954 14 20 00; www.molinodelaromera.com; Calle Sor Ángela de la Cruz 8; mains €17-20; 1-4pm & 8-11pm Tue-Sat, 1-4pm Sun) Housed in a cosy 15th-century olive-oil mill with wonderful views across the *vega* (valley), this popular restaurant serves hearty, well-prepped meals with a splash of contemporary flair. Traditional Andalucian flavours rule (try the Carmona spinach), but tasty novel variations include fish flambéed in vodka, and *secreto ibérico* (a succulent section of Iberian pork loin) with candied pumpkin.

Bar Goya
Tapas, Raciones €€

(Calle Prim 2; raciones €5-12; 8am-11pm Sat-Mon & Thu, 8am-3pm Tue, noon-11pm Fri;) From the kitchens of this ever-crammed bar on Plaza de San Fernando comes forth a fabulous array of tasty tapas. Apart from such carnivores' faves as *carrillada* (pigs' cheeks) and *menudo* (tripe), chef Isabel offers pure vegetarian treats such as *alboronía* (a delicious veg stew) and an excellent Carmona spinach (blended with chickpeas).

Casa Curro Montoya
Tapas €€

(657 903629; Calle Santa María de Gracia 13; tapas €2-6, mains €12-19; 1.15-5pm & 8pm-midnight) This friendly, family-run joint opposite the Convento de Santa Clara occupies a narrow hall littered with memorabilia. Long-cultivated family traditions find expression in such items as fresh tuna in a luscious onion sauce, foie-gras-stuffed eggplant and fried *pizcota* (small sardine-like fish).

ⓘ INFORMATION

Tourist Office (954 19 09 55; www.turismo.carmona.org; Alcázar de la Puerta de Sevilla; 10am-6pm Mon-Sat, to 3pm Sun)

Courses in Vejer de la Frontera

Annie B's Spanish Kitchen (☑620 560649; www.anniebspain.com; Calle Viñas 11; 1-day course €135) This is your chance to master the fine art of Andalucian cooking with top-notch local expertise. Annie's popular day classes (Andalucian-, Moroccan- or seafood-focused) end with lunch by the pool or on the fabulous roof terrace at her gorgeous old-town house. She also does a great selection of full-board six-day courses, including 'Low-Carb Deliciousness' and 'Spanish Culinary Classics'.

La Janda (☑956 44 70 60; www.lajanda. org; Calle José Castrillón 22; per 20hr week €180) Who wouldn't want to study Spanish in Vejer, with its winding streets, authentic bars and mysterious feel? La Janda's courses emphasise cultural immersion, integrating everything from flamenco, yoga and cooking classes to Almodóvar movie nights in a lovely 18th-century village mansion.

🛈 GETTING THERE & AROUND

BUS

From Monday to Friday, **Casal** (www.autocares casal.com) runs hourly buses to Seville (€2.80, one hour) from the stop on Paseo del Estatuto, less often on weekends. **Alsa** (www.alsa.es) has three daily buses to Córdoba (€9.72, 1½ hours) via Écija (€4.71, 35 minutes) from the car park next to the Puerta de Sevilla.

CAR & MOTORCYCLE

There's 24-hour underground parking on Paseo del Estatuto (€1.20 per hour).

Vejer de la Frontera

Vejer – the jaw drops, the eyes blink, the eloquent adjectives dry up. Looming moodily atop a rocky hill above the busy N340, 50km south of Cádiz, this serene, compact white town is something very special. Yes, there's a labyrinth of twisting old-town streets plus some serendipitous viewpoints, a ruined castle, a surprisingly elaborate culinary scene and a tangible Moorish influence. But Vejer has something else – an air of magic and mystery, an imperceptible touch of *duende* (spirit).

◎ SIGHTS

Castillo   Castle
(Calle del Castillo; tours per person €4-6; ⊙10am-2pm & 4-8pm) Vejer's much-reworked castle, once home of the Duques de Medina Sidonia, dates from the 10th or 11th century. Its small, erratically open museum preserves one of the black cloaks that Vejer women wore until just a couple of decades ago (covering everything but the eyes).

Currently, the only way to visit the castle is by private guided tour; check with the tourist office.

Plaza de España   Square
With its elaborate 20th-century, Seville-tiled fountain and perfectly white town hall, Vejer's palm-studded Plaza de España is a favourite hang-out. There's a small lookout above its western side (accessible from Calle de Sancho IV El Bravo).

Walls   Walls
Enclosing the 40,000-sq-metre old town, Vejer's imposing 15th-century walls are particularly visible between the Arco de la Puerta Cerrada and the Arco de la Segur, two of the four original gateways to survive. The Arco de la Segur area was, in the 15th century, the *judería* (Jewish quarter).

Iglesia del Divino Salvador   Church
(Plaza Padre Ángel; ⊙mass 6.30pm Mon, Wed & Fri, 7pm Sat, 10am Sun) Built atop an earlier mosque, this unusual church is 14th-century Mudéjar at the altar end and 16th-century Gothic at the other. In the late afternoon the sun shines surreally through the stained-glass windows, projecting multicoloured light above the altar.

Casa del Mayorazgo   House

(Callejón de la Villa; admission by donation; ☉hours vary) If the door's open, pop into this private 18th-century house to find two stunning flower-filled patios and one of just three original towers that kept watch over the city, with panoramic views down to Plaza de España and across town.

❌ EATING

Vejer has quietly morphed into a gastro-nomic highlight of Andalucía, where you can just as happily tuck into traditional, age-old recipes as Moroccan fusion dishes.

La Posada   Andalucian, Tapas €

(Avenida Los Remedios; raciones €6.50-12; ☉8am-11pm; 🛜) La Posada is an old local hang-out where you can get simple tapas with zero ceremony in a bar filled with *mucho ruido* (a lot of noise). Dig in!

El Jardín
del Califa   Moroccan, Fusion €€

(📞956 44 77 30; www.jardin.lacasadelcalifa. com; Plaza de España 16; mains €12-18; ☉1-4pm & 8-11.30pm mid-Feb–mid-Dec; 🍴) The sizzling atmosphere matches the food at this exotically beautiful restaurant – also a **hotel** (www.lacasadelcalifa.com; incl breakfast s €88-123, d €99-148, ste €169-220; ☉mid-Feb–mid-Dec; 🅿🌣🛜) and *tetería* (teahouse). It's buried away in a cavernous house where even finding the toilets is a full-on adventure. The menu is Moroccan/Middle Eastern – tagines, couscous, hummus, falafel – and, while the presentation is fantastic, it's the Maghreb flavours (saffron, figs, almonds) that linger the longest. Book ahead.

Valvatida   Andalucian, Fusion €€

(📞622 468594; Calle Juan Relinque 3; dishes €7-12; ☉noon-4pm & 8-11.30pm; 🍴) Creative cookery meets market-fresh Andalucian ingredients at this cute modern-rustic spot with fold-out chairs, dangling fishing nets and posters in the window. The short seasonal menu plays with contemporary twists on local fish and meats (fancy pigs' cheeks fajitas?), but also features delicious vegie-friendly pastas, salads and stir-fries. Your *café* is served on a tiny wooden tray.

Mesón Pepe Julián   Andalucian €€

(📞956 45 10 98; Calle Juan Relinque 7; dishes €7-12; ☉12.30-5pm & 7.30-11.30pm Thu-Tue) Opposite the market, family-run Pepe Julián shines for its wholesome traditional home-cooking. It's a hit with local Spaniards, who pack in for the carefully prepped meats, fish, *platos combinados* (meat-and-three-veg dishes) and tortillas (try the cheese one), as well as for perfectly simple *jamón* and *ensaladilla* (Russian salad) tapas in the tile-walled bar.

⭐ ENTERTAINMENT

Peña Cultural Flamenca
'Aguilar de Vejer'   Flamenco

(Calle Rosario 29) Part of Vejer's magic is its genuine small-town flamenco scene, best observed in this atmospheric old-town bar/performance space. Free shows usually happen on Saturdays at 9.30pm; ask at the tourist office.

ℹ️ INFORMATION

Oficina Municipal de Turismo (📞956 45 17 36; www.turismovejer.es; Avenida Los Remedios 2; ☉8am-3pm Mon-Fri) About 500m below the town centre, beside a big free car park.

ℹ️ GETTING THERE & AROUND

From Avenida Los Remedios, **Comes** (www. tgcomes.es) runs services to Cádiz (€5.70, 1½ hours, five daily), Barbate (€1.35, 15 minutes, six daily), Jerez de la Frontera (€7.80, 1½ hours, one daily Mon-Fri) and Seville (€15-16, 2 hours, four to five daily).

Other destinations include Algeciras (€7.20, 1¼ hours, six daily), La Línea (for Gibraltar, €9.05, 1¾ hours, five daily), Málaga (€22, 3¼ hours, two daily) and Tarifa (€4.50, 45 minutes, eight daily). More buses stop at La Barca de Vejer, on the N340 at the bottom of the hill. From here, it's a steep 20-minute walk or €6 taxi ride up to town.

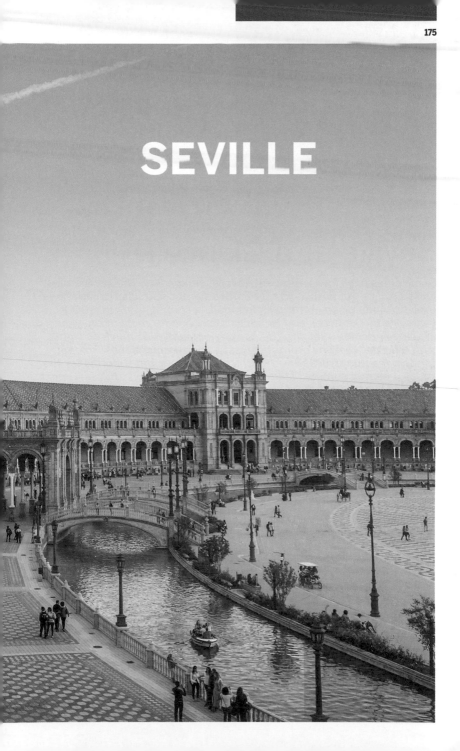

SEVILLE

Seville at a Glance...

Some cities have looks, other cities have personality. The sevillanos – lucky devils – get both, courtesy of their flamboyant, charismatic, ever-evolving Andalucian metropolis founded, according to myth, 3000 years ago by the Greek god Hercules. Drenched for most of the year in spirit-enriching sunlight, this is a city of feelings as much as sights, with different seasons prompting vastly contrasting moods: solemn for Semana Santa, flirtatious for the spring fiesta and soporific for the gasping heat of summer. Like all great cities, Seville also has historical layers. Yet, one of the most remarkable things about modern Seville is its ability to adapt and etch fresh new brushstrokes onto an ancient canvas.

Seville in One Day

Get moving in the **Barrio de Santa Cruz** (p182), then visit the **Alcázar** (p180). Come up for air in El Centro and brave a crowded **tapas bar** (p188) near Plaza de la Alfalfa. Admire (or not) the whimsical **Metropol Parasol** (p183) and the shopping chaos of **Calle Sierpes** (p183). Then roll up for night-time **drinks** (p191) in the Alameda de Hércules.

Seville in Two Days

Buy your ticket for the **cathedral** (p178), which deserves at least two hours. Afterwards have lunch in **El Arenal** (p187) and stroll the river banks down to **Parque de María Luisa** (p186). Return to Santa Cruz and book a ticket for a musical performance at the **Museo del Baile Flamenco** (p183). Browse the exhibits until showtime at 7pm.

Arriving in Seville

Seville's airport has loads of domestic (and some international) flights. The city is also connected by super-fast AVE trains to Madrid and Córdoba. Buses and taxis connect the airport and Estación Santa Justa with the city centre.

Sleeping

Seville has fine accommodation choices, from boutique marvels to flower-filled *hostales* (cheap hotels). High season typically runs from March to June and again in September and October. During Semana Santa and the Feria de Abril rates are doubled – at least! – and sell out completely. Book well ahead at this time.

For more on where to stay, see p193.

Interior of the Catedral

MATTEO COLOMBO / GETTY IMAGES ©

Catedral & Giralda

Seville's immense cathedral, officially the biggest in the world by volume, is awe-inspiring in its scale and sheer majesty. Its former minaret, the Giralda, is an architectural jewel.

Great For...

☑ Don't Miss

The Capilla Mayor contains the cathedral's greatest treasure: a sublime gold-plated altarpiece.

After Seville fell to the Christians in 1248, the mosque was used as a church until 1401. Then, in view of its decaying state, the church authorities decided to knock it down and start again. 'Let's construct a church so large future generations will think we were mad,' they quipped (or so legend has it). When it was completed in 1502 after 100 years of hard labour, the Catedral de Santa María de la Sede, as it is officially known, pretty much defined the word 'Gothic'. It's also a veritable art gallery replete with notable works by Zurbarán, Murillo, Goya and others.

Tomb of Columbus

Inside the Puerta de los Príncipes (Door of the Princes) stands the monumental tomb of Christopher Columbus (Cristóbal Colón in Spanish) – the subject of a continuous

Giralda

JEAN-PIERRE LESCOURRET / GETTY IMAGES ©

ⓘ Need to Know

Map p184; www.catedraldesevilla.es; adult/child €9/free; ⊘11am-3.30pm Mon, 11am-5pm Tue-Sat, 2.30-6pm Sun

✕ Take a Break

The gilded and much-loved pastry cafe of **Horno de San Buenaventura** (p189) sits just opposite the cathedral.

★ Top Tip

Take time to admire the cathedral from the outside. It's particularly stunning at night from the Plaza Virgen de los Reyes, and from across the river in Triana.

riddle – containing what were long believed to be the great explorer's bones, brought here from Cuba in 1898. Even though there were suggestions that the bones kept in Seville's cathedral were possibly those of his son Diego (who was buried with his father in Santo Domingo, Hispaniola), recent DNA tests seemed to finally prove that it really is Christopher Columbus lying in that box.

Capilla Mayor

East of the choir is the Capilla Mayor (Main Chapel). Its Gothic retable is the jewel of the cathedral and reckoned to be the biggest altarpiece in the world. Begun by Flemish sculptor Pieter Dancart in 1482 and finished by others in 1564, this sea of gilt and polychromed wood holds over 1000 carved biblical figures.

Sacrista Mayor

This large room with a finely carved stone dome was created between 1528 and 1547; the arch over its portal has carvings of 16th-century foods. Pedro de Campaña's 1547 *Descendimiento* (Descent from the Cross), above the central altar at the southern end, and Francisco de Zurbarán's *Santa Teresa,* to its right, are two of the cathedral's most precious paintings.

Giralda

In the northeastern corner of the cathedral you'll find the passage for the climb up to the belfry of the Giralda. The decorative brick tower which stands 104m tall was the minaret of the mosque, constructed between 1184 and 1198 at the height of Almohad power. At the very top is El Giraldillo, a 16th-century bronze weather vane representing 'faith' that has become a symbol of Seville.

Patio de las Doncellas

Alcázar

If heaven really does exist, let's hope it looks a little like the inside of Seville's Alcázar. Built primarily in the 1300s, the castle marks one of history's architectural high points.

Great For...

☑ Don't Miss

The Patio de las Doncellas is the highlight of the peerless Palacio de Don Pedro.

Originally founded as a fort for the Cordoban governors of Seville in 913, the Alcázar has been expanded or reconstructed many times in its 11 centuries of existence. In the 11th century Seville's prosperous Muslim *taifa* (small kingdom) rulers developed the original fort by building a palace called Al-Muwarak (the Blessed) in what's now the western part of the Alcázar. The 12th-century Almohad rulers added another palace east of this, around what's now the Patio del Crucero. Christian Fernando III moved into the Alcázar when he captured Seville in 1248, and several later Christian monarchs used it as their main residence. Fernando's son Alfonso X replaced much of the Almohad palace with a Gothic one. Between 1364 and 1366, Pedro I created the Alcázar's crown jewel, the sumptuous Mudéjar Palacio de Don Pedro.

Garden of the Alcoba Real

JOSEPH SOHM / SHUTTERSTOCK ©

❶ Need to Know

Map p184; ✎tours 954 50 23 24; www.alcazar
sevilla.org; adult/child €9.50/free; ⏱9.30am-
7pm Apr-Sep, to 5pm Oct-Mar

✖ Take a Break

Just north of the Alcázar, **Bodega
Santa Cruz** (p187) is forever crowded
and good for tapas.

★ Top Tip

Don't visit the Alcázar and cathedral
on the same day. There is far too
much to take in.

First Steps

From the ticket office inside the Puerta
del León (Lion Gate) you'll emerge into
the Patio del León (Lion Patio), which
was the garrison yard of the original Al-
Muwarak palace. Just off here is the Sala de
la Justicia (Hall of Justice), with beautiful
Mudéjar plasterwork and an *artesonado*
(ceiling of interlaced beams with decorative
insertions).

Palacio de Don Pedro

Posterity owes Pedro I a big thank you for
creating the Palacio de Don Pedro (also
called the Palacio Mudéjar), the single most
stunning architectural feature in Seville. At
the heart of the palace is the wonderful Patio de las Doncellas (Patio of the Maidens),
surrounded by beautiful arches, plasterwork and tiling. The sunken garden in the

centre was uncovered by archaeologists in
2004 from beneath a 16th-century marble
covering.

The Cámara Regia (King's Quarters),
on the northern side of the patio, has
stunningly beautiful ceilings and wonderful
plaster- and tilework. Its rear room was
probably the monarch's summer bedroom.
From here you can move west into the little
Patio de las Muñecas (Patio of the Dolls),
the heart of the palace's private quarters,
featuring delicate Granada-style decoration. Indeed, plasterwork was actually
brought here from the Alhambra in the
19th century when the mezzanine and top
gallery were added for Queen Isabel II.

Gardens

Formal gardens with pools and fountains
sit closest to the palace. The gardens' most
arresting feature is the Galeria de Grutesco,
a raised gallery with porticoes fashioned in
the 16th century out of an old Muslim-era
wall.

⊙ SIGHTS

◉ Barrio de Santa Cruz

Seville's medieval *judería* (Jewish quarter), east of the cathedral (p178) and Alcázar (p180), is today a tangle of atmospheric, winding streets and lovely plant-decked plazas perfumed with orange blossom. Among its most characteristic plazas is Plaza de Santa Cruz, which gives the *barrio* (district) its name. Nearby, Plaza de Doña Elvira is perhaps the most romantic small square in Andalucía, especially in the evening.

Hospital de los Venerables Sacerdotes   Gallery

(Map p184; ☑954 56 26 96; www.focus. abengoa.es; Plaza de los Venerables 8; adult/child €5.50/2.75, Sun afternoon free; ☺10am-2pm & 4-8pm) Inside this 17th-century baroque mansion once used as a hospice for ageing priests, you'll find one of Seville's greatest and most admirable art collections. The onsite Centro Velázquez was founded in 2007 by the local Focus-Abengoa Foundation with the intention of reviving Seville's erstwhile artistic glory. Its collection of masterpieces anchored by Diego Velázquez' *Santa Rufina* is one of the best and most concise art lessons the city has to offer. The excellent audio commentary explains how medieval darkness morphed into Velázquezian realism.

Centro de Interpretación Judería de Sevilla   Museum

(Map p184; ☑954 04 70 89; www.juderiade sevilla.es; Calle Ximenez de Enciso; €6.50; ☺10.30am-3.30pm & 5-8pm Mon-Sat, 10.30am-7pm Sun) A reinterpretation of Seville's weighty Jewish history has been long overdue and what better place to start than in the city's former Jewish quarter. This museum is in an old Sephardic Jewish house in the higgledy-piggledy Santa Cruz quarter, the one-time Jewish neighbourhood that never recovered from a brutal pogrom and massacre in 1391. The events of the pogrom and other historical happenings are catalogued inside, along with a few surviving mementos including documents, costumes and books. It's small but poignant.

Plaza de San Francisco

⊙ El Centro

Museo del Baile Flamenco   Museum

(Map p184; www.museoflamenco.com; Calle
Manuel Rojas Marcos 3; adult/seniors & students
€10/8; ⊙10am-7pm) The brainchild of
sevillano flamenco dancer Cristina Hoyos,
this museum spread over three floors of an
18th-century palace makes a noble effort to
showcase the mysterious art with sketches,
paintings and photos of erstwhile (and
contemporary) flamenco greats, plus a
collection of dresses and shawls. Even better
than that are the fantastic nightly concerts
(7pm; €20) in the on-site courtyard.

Plaza de San Francisco   Square

(Map p184) Plaza de San Francisco has been
Seville's main public square since the 16th
century. The southern end of the Ayuntamiento (Town Hall) here is encrusted with lovely
Renaissance carving from the 1520–30s.

Calle Sierpes   Street

(Map p184) Pedestrianised Calle Sierpes,
heading north from Plaza de San Francisco,
and the parallel Calle Tetuán/Velázquez are
the hub of Seville's fanciest shopping zone.
This being Andalucía, it's busiest in the evenings between about 6pm and 9pm.

Palacio de la
Condesa de Lebrija   Museum, Palace

(Map p184; Calle Cuna 8; ground fl €5, whole
bldg €8, ground fl 9am-noon Wed free; ⊙10.30am-
7.30pm Mon-Fri, 10am-2pm & 4-6pm Sat, 10am-
2pm Sun) A block east of Calle Sierpes, this
16th-century mansion has a rich collection
of art and a beautiful Renaissance-Mudéjar
courtyard. The late Countess of Lebrija was
an archaeologist, and she remodelled the
house in 1914, filling many of the rooms with
treasures from her travels.

Metropol Parasol   Museum

(Map p184; www.metropolsevilla.com; Plaza de la
Encarnación; €3; ⊙10.30am-midnight Sun-Thu, to
1am Fri & Sat) Smarting with the audacity of a
modern-day Eiffel Tower, the opinion-dividing
Metropol Parasol, which opened in March
2011 in Plaza de la Encarnación, claims
to be the largest wooden building in the

📖 Seville's History

Founded by the Romans, the city of Seville didn't really flower until the Moorish
Almoravid period, which began in 1085.
They were replaced by the Almohads
in the 12th century; Caliph Yacub Yusuf
made Seville capital of the Almohad
realm and built a great mosque where
Seville's cathedral now stands. But
Almohad power dwindled after the dis-
astrous defeat of Las Navas de Tolosa
in 1212, and Castilla's Fernando III (El
Santo; the Saint) went on to capture
Seville in 1248. Fernando brought
24,000 settlers to Seville and by the
14th century it was the most important
Castilian city. Seville's biggest break was
Columbus' discovery of the Americas
in 1492. In 1503 the city was awarded
an official monopoly on Spanish trade
with the new-found continent. It rapidly
became one of the biggest, richest and
most cosmopolitan cities on earth.

Plaza de España
SYLVAIN SONNET / GETTY IMAGES ©

world. Its undulating honeycombed roof is
held up by five giant mushroom-like pillars,
earning it the local nickname *Las setas de la
Encarnación* (the mushrooms of Plaza de la
Encarnación).

⊙ El Arenal & Triana

Colonising caballeros made rich on New
World gold once stalked the streets of El
Arenal on the banks of the Río Guadalquivir,
watched over by Spanish galleons offloading
their American booty. There's no port here
today, but the compact quarter retains

Seville

⊙ N 0 ___ 500 m
      0 ___ 0.25 miles

Camino de los Descubrimientos
Puente de la Cartuja
C del Torneo
C Juan Rabadán
C Pascual de Gayangos
C de Barños
C Alfonso XII
C de San Vicente
C de Abad Gordillo
C de Marqués de Paradas
C Marqués de Paradas
Río Guadalquivir
Estación de Autobuses Plaza de Armas
Puente del Cachorro
C de Arjona
C Santa Ana
Plaza de San Lorenzo
24
C San Juan
C Jesús del Gran Poder
C Trajano
C Amor de Dios
Alameda de Hércules
C de la Feria
36
C Arrayán
C Castellar
C San Luis
C Viriato
C Gerona
C Bustos Tavera
C del Sol
Plaza de la Encarnación
8
C Laraña
C Imagen
Plaza Cristo de Burgos
27
C Alhóndiga
C Santiago
C Imperial
Plaza Padre Jerónimo Córdoba
Plaza Concordia
31
C Tarifa
26
Plaza del Duque de la Victoria
C San Eloy
C Monsalves
41
C Sierpes
10
Plaza de la Magdalena
C Tetuán
EL CENTRO
3
19 Plaza de la Alfalfa
39
C Águilas
Plaza de Pilatos
Plaza del Museo
Plaza del Salvador
34
23
El Palacio Andaluz (1km);
Train Station (1.5km)
C Canalejas
C Reyes Católicos
C Zaragoza
C Bilbao
C Albareda
Plaza Nueva
2
Plaza de San Francisco
9
C Federico Rubio
16
C Santa María La Blanca
C Aire
25
29
28
Plaza de Malviedro
18
13
Av de la Constitución
30
33
Patio de los Naranjos
BARRIO DE SANTA CRUZ
C Reyes Católicos
Puente de Triana (Puente de Isabel II)
C de Adriano
14
C Antonia Díaz
22
4
Turismo Sevilla
21
20
7
6
35
Paseo de Nuestra Señora de la O
C de Castilla
C Alfarería
5
38
37
40
Plaza del Altozano
C de la Pureza
32
17
Paseo de Cristóbal Colón
Catedral & Giralda
Plaza del Triunfo
1
Alcázar
Alcázar Gardens
C Gloria
Av de Menéndez Pelayo
C San Jacinto
C Pagés del Corro
TRIANA
C Evangelista
15
Archivo de Indias
Regional Tourist Office
Puerta de Jerez
Jardines de Murillo
Estación de Autobuses Prado de San Sebastián
Plaza de Cuba
Puente de San Telmo
Plaza de Cuba
Puerta de Jerez
C San Fernando
Av de Roma
Av de Portugal
C del Trabajo
Av de la República Argentina
C del Niebla
C de la Asunción
C del Turia
C Juan Sebastián Elcano
C Palos de la Frontera
Av del Cid
Prado de San Sebastián
Prado de San Sebastián
Parque de los Príncipes
LOS REMEDIOS
C Santa Fe
C Virgen de Luján
Paseo de las Delicias
La Rábida
Av María Luisa
12
Plaza de España
11
Parque de María Luisa
Av de Isabel la Católica
Av de Borbolla
Parque de los Remedios

Seville

plenty of rambunctious bars and a seafaring spirit. The legendary *barrio* of Triana sits on the west bank of the Río Guadalquivir. This atmospheric quarter was once home to many of Seville's most quintessential characters and still hosts some of its most poignant sights.

Torre del Oro   Museum

(Map p184; Paseo de Cristóbal Colón; €3, Mon free; ◎9.30am-6.45pm Mon-Fri, 10.30am-6.45pm Sat & Sun) This 13th-century Almohad watchtower by the river supposedly had a dome covered in golden tiles, hence its name, 'Tower of Gold'. Today, it hosts a small maritime museum spread over two floors and a rooftop viewing platform. The tower was also once used to store the booty siphoned off the colonial coffers by the returning conquistadors from Mexico and Peru. Since then it has become one of the most recognisable architectural symbols of Seville.

Plaza de Toros de la Real Maestranza   Bullring, Museum

(Map p184; ☑954 22 45 77; www.realmaestranza.com; Paseo de Cristóbal Colón 12; tours adult/child €7/4; ◎half-hourly 9.30am-8pm, to 3pm bullfight days) In the world of bullfighting Seville's bullring is the Old Trafford and Camp Nou. In other words, if you're selected to fight here then you've made it. In addition to being regarded as a building of almost religious significance to fans, it's also the oldest ring in Spain (building began in 1758) and it was here, along with the bullring in Ronda, that bullfighting on foot began in the 18th century. Slightly rushed guided visits, in English and Spanish, take you into the ring and its museum.

Centro Cerámica Triana   Museum

(Map p184; Antillano Campos 14; €2.10; ◎10am-2pm & 5-8pm Mon-Sat, 10am-3pm Sun) Triana's – and Seville's – newest museum is an attempt

DAVID C TOMLINSON / GETTY IMAGES ©

Wall tiles depicting Triana (p188)

to rekindle the flames that once lit the kilns of the neighbourhood's erstwhile ceramic industry. It cleverly mixes the methodology and history of ceramic production with the wider history of Triana and its people.

◎ South of the Centre

Parque de María Luisa   Park

(Map p184; ◷8am-10pm Sep-Jun, to midnight Jul & Aug; ⛄🐾) The lungs of central Seville are the dreamy Parque de María Luisa, which is a delightful place to escape from the noise of the city, with duck ponds, snoozing *sevillanos* and paths snaking under the trees.

If you'd rather continue your cultural education than commune with the flowers, the park contains a couple of sites that'll keep you smiling. Curving round Plaza de España, with its fountains and mini-canals, is the most grandiose of the buildings built for the 1929 Exposición Iberoamericana, a brick-and-tile confection featuring Seville tilework at its gaudiest, with a map and historical scene for each Spanish province.

You can hire row boats to ply the canals from only €5.

🟢 ACTIVITIES

Aire Baños Árabes   Hammam

(Map p184; ☏955 01 00 25; www.airedesevilla. com; Calle Aire 15; bath/bath with massage €26/41; ◷every 2hr 10am-midnight) Jumping on the *hammam* bandwagon, Seville's Arabic-style baths win prizes for atmosphere, historic setting (in the Barrio de Santa Cruz) and Moroccan riad-style decor – living proof that those Moors knew a thing or two about how to relax. It's best to book baths and massages one day in advance.

🟢 TOURS

**Cruceros Turísticos
Torre del Oro**   Boat Tour

(Map p184; ☏954 56 16 92; www.crucerostorre deloro.com; adult/child under 14yr €16/free) One-hour sightseeing river cruises every half-hour from 11am departing from the river bank by the Torre del Oro. Last departure can range from 6pm in winter to 10pm in summer.

Sevilla Tour   Bus Tour

(☏902 10 10 81; www.sevillatour.com; adult €17, child €7; ☺7am-8pm) One-hour city tours in open-topped double-decker buses and converted trams with earphone commentary in a choice of languages. The ticket is valid for 48 hours and you can hop on or off at a number of stops. Buses typically leave every 30 minutes from 7am to 8pm.

Sevilla Walking Tours   Walking Tour

(☏902 15 82 26; www.sevillawalkingtours.com; per person €15) English-language tours of the main monumental area, lasting about two hours, at 10.30am daily. It also offers tours of the cathedral and the Alcázar.

🄰 SHOPPING

Shopping in Seville is a major pastime, and shopping for clothes is at the top of the list for any sevillano. Shoe fetishists beware: Seville possibly has the densest quota of shoe shops on the planet. Calles Sierpes, Velázquez/Tetuán and Cuna have retained their charm with a host of small shops selling everything from polka-dot trajes de flamenca (flamenco dresses) to antique fans. Most shops open between 9am and 9pm, but expect it to be ghostly quiet between 2pm and 5pm when they close for siesta.

For a more alternative choice of shops, head for Calles Amor de Dios and Doctor Letamendi, close to Alameda de Hércules.

Triana is famous for its pottery and tile-making. A dozen shops and workshops still sell charming and artistic ceramics on the corner of Calles Alfarería and Antillano Campos.

Cerámica Santa Ana   Ceramics

(Map p184; ☏954 33 39 90; Calle San Jorge 31; ☺10am-8.30pm Mon-Fri, to 3pm Sat) Seville specialises in distinctive azulejos (ceramic tiles) and they are best seen in Triana. Cerámica Santa Ana has been around for more than 50 years and the shop itself almost qualifies as a tourist attraction.

🖒 Tours with a Difference

The ingenious augmented-reality video tour by **Past View** (Map p184; ☏954 32 66 46; www.pastview.es; Plaza de la Encarnación; tours €15; ☺10.30am & 1pm; ♿) takes you on a guided walk using 3D video glasses that re-create scenes from the past in the actual locations they happened. The ticket office and starting point is in the Metropol Parasol (p183) and the two-hour walk (with a guide) proceeds through Seville's main sights to the Torre del Oro.

Padilla Crespo   Accessories, Clothing

(Map p184; ☏954 21 29 88; Calle Adriano 18B; ☺10am-8.30pm Mon-Sat) If you're really immersing yourself in the culture, you can pick up your wide-brimmed hat and riding outfit for the Feria de Abril right here.

🍴 EATING

Seville produces Andalucía's most inventive tapas – end of story. If you're not enamoured with the new culinary alchemists, there are plenty of decent salt-of-the-earth tapas bars too. The **Mercado del Arenal** (Map p184; Calle Pastor y Landero) and **Mercado de la Encarnación** (Map p184; Plaza de la Encarnación) are central Seville's two food markets. The Encarnación, which mainly sells fruit, vegies and fish, is located under the giant mushroom pillars of the Metropol Parasol (p183).

🚫 Barrio de Santa Cruz

Bodega Santa Cruz   Tapas €

(Map p184; Calle Mateos Gago; tapas €2; ☺11.30am-midnight) This forever crowded bodega is where eating tapas becomes a physical contact sport. Watch out for flying elbows and admire those dexterous waiters who bob and weave like prizefighters amid the chaos. The fiercely traditional tapas are best enjoyed alfresco with a cold beer as

Triana: The Outsider in Seville

To understand the modern montage that makes up Seville there are several essential pilgrimages. Arguably, the most important is to Triana, the neighbourhood situated on the west bank of the Río Guadalquivir, a place whose past is littered with stories of sailors, ceramicists, bullfighters, flamenco artists, religious zealotry and a strong working-class identity. Triana's 'outsider' reputation was first cemented in the Middle Ages when it was labelled *extramuros* (outside the walls) by Seville's authorities, a place where 'undesirables' were sent to live. In 1481 infamy was established when the seat of the Inquisition Court was set up in the Castillo de San Jorge on the banks of the Guadalquivir from where it began trying suspected religious deviants for heresy. The outsider myth burgeoned in the 15th century as itinerant Roma people drifted in from the east and started to put down roots, an influx that gave Triana much of its musical personality.

By the 19th century, Triana's interlinked Roma families were producing the finest bullfighters and flamenco singers of the age. Most of Seville's Roma were resettled in Seville's new suburbs in the 1960s, a move that altered the demographics of Triana, but not its essence. Unlike the more sanitised Santa Cruz quarter, Triana has kept much of its authenticity. Its outdoor living room in summer is the bar-filled Calle del Betis overlooking the river.

Triana
ZU SANCHEZ PHOTOGRAPHY / GETTY IMAGES ©

you watch marching armies of Santa Cruz tourists go squeezing past.

Casa Tomate Tapas €€
(Map p184; ☑954 22 04 21; Calle Mateos Gago 24; tapas €3-4, raciones €12; ☺9am-midnight) Hams swing from ceiling hooks, old feria posters are etched with art-nouveau and art-deco designs, and outdoor blackboards relay what's cooking in the kitchen of Casa Tomate on Santa Cruz' most intense tourist strip. The staff recommend dishes like garlic prawns and pork sirloin in a white-wine-and-pine-nut sauce, and who are you to argue?

Vinería San Telmo Tapas €€
(Map p184; ☑954 41 06 00; www.vineriasan telmo.com; Paseo Catalina de Ribera 4; tapas €3.50, medias raciones €10; ☺1-4.30pm & 8pm-midnight) San Telmo invented the *rascacielo* (skyscraper) *tapa*, an 'Empire State' of tomatoes, aubergine, goat's cheese and smoked salmon. If this and other creative nuggets such as foie gras with quail's eggs and lychees, or exquisitely cooked bricks of tuna, don't make you drool with expectation then you're probably dead.

⊗ El Centro

Plaza de la Alfalfa is the hub of the tapas scene and has some excellent bars.

Redhouse Art & Food International €
(Map p184; ☑661 615 646; www.redhousespace. com; Calle Amor de Dios 7; snacks from €4; ☺11.30am-12.30am Tue-Sun; ☏) It's hard to classify Redhouse. With its mismatched chairs and abstract wall art, it's flirting with hipster territory, yet inside you'll find families, seniors, college geeks and the obviously not-so-hip enjoying a whole variety of food from casual coffee to romantic meals. Whatever you opt for, save room for the best homemade cakes in Andalucía.

Bar Europa Tapas €
(Map p184; ☑954 22 13 54; www.bareuropa.info; Calle Siete Revueltas 35; tapas €3, media raciones €6-8; ☺8am-1am) An old-school bar with no pretensions that's been knocking out tapas

lapas bar, Barrio Santa Cruz (p187)

since 1925. Notwithstanding, Europa isn't afraid to experiment. Its signature *tapa* is the *quesadilla los balanchares gratinada sobre manzana* which turns a boring old Granny Smith apple into a taste sensation by covering it in goat's cheese and laying it on a bed of strawberries.

Horno de San Buenaventura Cafe €

(Map p184; www.hornosanbuenaventura.com; Avenida de la Constitución; pastries from €1; ⏰7.30am-10pm Mon-Fri, 8am-10pm Sat & Sun) There are actually two of these gilded pastry/coffee/snack bars in Seville, one here on Avenida de la Constitución opposite the cathedral and the other (inferior one) at the **Plaza de la Alfalfa** (Map p184; ⏰9am-9pm). All kinds of fare are on show though it's probably best for its lazy continental breakfasts (yes, the service can be slow) or a spontaneous late-night cake fix.

La Pepona Tapas, Modern €€

(Map p184; ☏954 21 50 26; Javier Lasso de la Vega 1; tapas €3.50-6.50; ⏰1.30-4.30pm & 8pm-midnight Mon-Sat) One of the best newcomer restaurants of 2014, La Pepona gets all the basics right, from the bread (doorstop-sized rustic slices), to the service (fast but discreet), to the decor (clean Ikea lines and lots of wood). Oscar status is achieved with the food, which falls firmly into the nouveau tapas camp.

The Room International €€

(Map p184; ☏619 200946; www.theroomart cuisine.com; Calle Cuesta del Rosario 15; tapas €2.75-5; ⏰noon-4.30pm & 8pm-1am; 🛜) Another new 'art-cuisine' place, The Room sticks its succinct menu on a blackboard and circumnavigates the globe with everything from British-style fish and chips to pad thai noodles, Peruvian ceviche and Italian risotto. The interior is mega-casual with Chaplin movies often projected onto a wall.

Los Coloniales Contemporary Andalucian €€

(Map p184; www.tabernacoloniales.es; cnr Calle Dormitorio & Plaza Cristo de Burgos; mains €10-12; ⏰12.30pm-midnight) The quiet ones are always the best. It might not look like much from the outside, but Los Coloniales

Hermandades (penitents) celebrate during Semana Santa

is something very special. The quality plates line up like models on a catwalk: *chorizo a la Asturiana,* a divine spicy sausage in an onion sauce served on a bed of lightly fried potato; aubergine in honey; and pork tenderloin *al whisky* (in a whisky-flavoured sauce).

La Azotea   Fusion, Andalucian €€

(Map p184; ☑955 11 67 48; Jesús del Gran Poder 31; raciones €10; ☺1.30-4.30pm & 8.30pm-midnight Thu-Mon) The latest word in *nueva cocina* comes from Azotea, whose proliferating empire – there are now four branches – testifies to a growing legend. The decor is Ikea-friendly, staff wear black, and the *raciones* (full servings of tapas items), which are sweetened and spiced with panache, arrive like pieces of art in a variety of plates, dishes and boxes.

✖ El Arenal & Triana

Mercado Lonja del Barranco   International €

(Map p184; www.mercadodelbarranco.com; Calle Arjona; snacks €5-12; ☺10am-midnight Sun-Thu, to 2am Fri & Sat) ❢ Fabulous new food court in an Eiffel-esque structure near the Isabel

II bridge, with posh stalls stashed with the full cornucopia of *sevillano* food products. Float through the stalls and load up on cakes, fried fish, beer, miniburgers and tapas. There are plenty of nooks and crannies filled with shared tables. It's a mouthwatering and highly sociable experience.

La Brunilda   Tapas €€

(Map p184; ☑954 22 04 81; Calle Galera 5; tapas €3.50-6.50; ☺1-4pm & 8.30-11.30pm Tue-Sat, 1-4pm Sun) Seville's crown as Andalucía's tapas capital is regularly attacked by well-armed rivals from the provinces, meaning it constantly has to reinvent itself and offer up fresh competition. Enter La Brunilda, a newish font of fusion tapas sandwiched into an inconspicuous backstreet in the Arenal quarter where everything – including the food, staff and clientele – is pretty.

Mesón Cinco Jotas   Tapas €€

(Map p184; www.mesoncincojotas.com; Calle Castelar 1; medias raciones €10; ☺8am-midnight Mon-Fri, from noon Sat & Sun) In the world of *jamón* (ham) making, if you are awarded Cinco Jotas (Five Js) for your *jamón,* it's like getting an Oscar. The owner of this place, Sánchez Romero Carvajal, is the biggest producer of Jabugo ham, and has a great selection on offer.

T de Triana   Andalucian €€

(Map p184; ☑954 33 12 03; Calle Betis 20; ☺8pm-2am) The T is Triana being itself: simple fish-biased tapas, walls full of history, *fútbol* on the big screen whenever local boys Sevilla or Real Betis are playing, and live, gutsy flamenco shows every Friday night at 10pm.

🍷 DRINKING & NIGHTLIFE

Drinking neighbourhoods are legion. Classic spots include drinks on the banks of the Río Guadalquivir in Triana (the wall along Calle del Betis forms a fantastic makeshift bar), Plaza de la Alfalfa (cocktail and dive bars), the Barrio de Santa Cruz and the Alameda de Hércules. The latter is the hub for young *sevillanos* and the city's gay nightlife.

El Garlochi   Bar

(Map p184; Calle Boteros 4; ☺10pm-6am) Dedicated entirely to the iconography, smells and sounds of Semana Santa, the ultra-camp El Garlochi is a marvel. Taste the rather revolting sounding cocktail, Sangre de Cristo (Blood of Christ), and the Agua de Sevilla, both laced with vodka, whisky and grenadine, and pray they open more bars like this.

Cervezas Taifa   Microbrewery

(Map p184; ☑954 04 27 31; www.cervezastaifa. es; Mercado de Triana 36; ☺7.30am-3pm Mon-Fri, 12.30pm-5pm Sat & Sun) A tiny nano-brewery in Triana market, Taifa is at the forefront of Andalucía's newborn craft-beer movement that is slowly challenging the monopoly of Cruzcampo et al (Cruzcampo is Spain's bestselling beer). Its diminutive market stall (equivalent to that of a small fruit stall) also serves as a factory, shop and bar.

Drop by for a bottle of pilsen, pale ale or IPA, and you'll probably end up chatting about how to start brewing your own with the friendly bilingual owners.

Seville's Festivals

Bienal de Flamenco (www.labienal.com) Most of the big names of the flamenco world participate in this major flamenco festival. Held in September in even-numbered years.

Feria de Abril The April fair, held in the second half of the month (sometimes into May), is the jolly counterpart to the sombre Semana Santa. The biggest and most colourful of all Andalucía's ferias (fairs) is less invasive (and less inclusive) than the Easter celebration. It takes place on El Real de la Feria, in the Los Remedios area west of the Río Guadalquivir.

Semana Santa (www.semana-santa.org) Every day from Palm Sunday to Easter Sunday, large, life-sized *pasos* (sculptural representations of events from Christ's Passion) are carried from Seville's churches through the streets to the cathedral, accompanied by processions that may take more than an hour to pass. The processions are organised by more than 50 different *hermandades* or *cofradías* (brotherhoods, some of which include women).

Bulebar Café   Bar

(Map p184; ☑954 90 19 54; Alameda de Hércules 83; ☺9am-2am) This place gets pretty *caliente* (hot) at night but is pleasantly chilled in the early evening, with friendly staff. Don't write off its spirit-reviving alfresco breakfasts that pitch early birds with up-all-nighters. It's in the uber-cool Alameda de Hércules.

Café de la Prensa   Bar

(Map p184; ☑954 00 29 69; Calle del Betis 8; ☺3pm-2.30am Mon-Thu, 2pm-3.30am Fri-Sun) Calle del Betis is second only to the Alameda de Hércules as a communal Seville watering hole and Café de la Prensa is a fine place to kick off a riverside bar crawl. You can sit inside and stare at walls covered in old newspapers or squeeze outside for better

Calle Sierpes (p183)

views of the river with the Giralda beckoning in the background.

⚘ ENTERTAINMENT

The Museo del Baile Flamenco (p183) stages excellent nightly concerts.

Casa de la Memoria   Flamenco

(Map p184; ☑954 56 06 70; www.casadela memoria.es; Calle Cuna 6; €18; ⓧshows 7.30pm & 9pm) Neither a *tablao* (choreographed flamenco show) nor a private *peña* (club, usually of flamenco aficionados), this cultural centre offers what are, without doubt, the most intimate and authentic nightly flamenco shows in Seville. It's accommodated in the old stables of the Palacio de la Condesa de Lebrija. It's perennially popular and space is limited to 100, so reserve tickets a day or so in advance by calling or visiting the venue.

El Palacio Andaluz   Flamenco

(☑954 53 47 20; www.elpalacioandaluz.com; Calle de María Auxiliadora; admission with drink/dinner €38/76; ⓧshows 7pm & 9.30pm) The purists will, no doubt, tell you that these highly choreographed performances in a 400-seat theatre are for tourists, but go along anyway and decide for yourself. You may be surprised. The Palacio's performers are absolute masters of their art with talent to write home about. What a show!

Casa de la Guitarra   Flamenco

(Map p184; ☑954 22 40 93; Calle Mesón del Moro 12; adult/child €17/10; ⓧshows 7.30pm & 9pm) Tiny newish flamenco-only venue in Santa Cruz (no food or drinks served) where a missed step from the dancers would land them in the front row of the audience. Glass display cases filled with guitars of erstwhile flamenco greats adorn the walls.

Casa Anselma   Flamenco

(Map p184; Calle Pagés del Corro 49; ⓧmidnight-late Mon-Sat) True, the music is often more folkloric than flamenco, but Casa Anselma is the antithesis of a touristy flamenco *tablao,* with cheek-to-jowl crowds, zero amplification and spontaneous outbreaks of dexterous dancing. Beware: there's no sign, just a doorway embellished with *azulejos* (tiles).

ℹ INFORMATION

Infhor (☏954 54 19 52; Estación Santa Justa; ⊙8am-10pm, closes for lunch Sat & Sun) Independent tourist office at the train station.

Regional Tourist Office (Map p184; Avenida de la Constitución 21; ⊙9am-7pm Mon-Fri, 10am-2pm & 3-7pm Sat, 10am-2pm Sun, closed holidays) The Constitución office is well informed but often very busy. There is also a branch at the airport.

Sevilla Card (24/48/72hr €30/48/64; www.sevillacard.es) Allows discounted access to city sights, tours, and some shops and restaurants. Purchase online.

Turismo Sevilla (Map p184; www.turismosevilla.org; Plaza del Triunfo 1; ⊙10.30am-7pm Mon-Fri) Information on all of Sevilla province.

ℹ GETTING THERE & AWAY

AIR

Seville's **airport** (☏954 44 90 00; www.aena.es) has a fair range of international and domestic flights. Numerous international carriers fly in and out of Seville; carrier and schedule information changes frequently, so it's best to check with specific airlines or major online booking agents.

BUS

Seville has two main bus stations serving different destinations and bus companies. Plaza de Armas is the larger of the two.

Estación de Autobuses Plaza de Armas (www.autobusesplazadearmas.es; Avenida del Cristo de la Expiración) The main HQ for Spain's intercity bus company, Alsa, linking to other major cities in Andalucía including Málaga (€19, three hours, eight daily), Granada (€23, three hours, nine daily), Córdoba (€12, two hours, seven daily) and Almería (€37, 5½ hours, three daily). Damas runs buses to Huelva province and Eurolines has international services to Germany, Belgium, France and beyond.

Estación de Autobuses Prado de San Sebastián (Plaza San Sebastián) Primarily home to smaller companies running buses to lesser towns in west-

🛏 Where to Stay

There's a good range of places to stay in all three of the most attractive areas – Barrio de Santa Cruz (within walking distance of Prado de San Sebastián bus station), El Arenal and El Centro (both convenient for Plaza de Armas bus station). Anywhere in the centre can be noisy, especially on weekends, so if you're a light sleeper and unless you've a view you can't bear to give up, ask for an interior-facing room.

ern Andalucía. Of note are Amarillos serving the provinces of Sevilla, Cádiz and parts of Málaga, and Comes who run to some of the harder-to-reach 'white towns'.

TRAIN

Seville's **Estación Santa Justa** (☏902 43 23 43; Avenida Kansas City) is 1.5km northeast of the centre. High-speed AVE trains go to/from Madrid (from €79, 2½ hours, 20 daily) and Córdoba (from €30, 40 minutes, 30 daily). Slower trains head to Cádiz (€16, 1¾ hours, 15 daily), Huelva (€12, 1½ hours, three daily), Granada (€30, three hours, four daily) and Málaga (€44, two hours, 11 daily).

ℹ GETTING AROUND

Seville offers a multitude of ways to get around, though walking still has to be the best option, especially in the centre. The **Sevici** (☏902 011032; www.sevici.es) bike-sharing scheme has made cycling easy and bike lanes are now almost as ubiquitous as pavements. The tram has recently been extended to the station of San Bernardo but its routes are still limited. Buses are more useful than the metro to link the main tourist sights. The recent 'greening' of the city has made driving increasingly difficult as whole roads in the city centre are now permanently closed to traffic; park on the periphery.

CÓRDOBA

Córdoba at a Glance...

One building alone is enough to put Córdoba high on any traveller's itinerary: the mesmerising multiarched Mezquita. One of the world's greatest Islamic buildings, it's a symbol of the sophisticated Islamic culture that flourished here more than a millennium ago when Córdoba was the capital of Islamic Spain, and Western Europe's biggest and most cultured city. But there's much more to this city. Córdoba is a great place for exploring on foot or by bicycle, staying and eating well in old buildings centred on verdant patios, diving into old wine bars, and feeling millennia of history at every turn. The narrow streets of the old judería (Jewish quarter) and Muslim quarter stretch out from the great mosque like capillaries (to the northwest and northeast respectively).

Córdoba in Two Days

You could easily spend a day in the **Mezquita** (p198). When you can finally tear yourself away, head for the **Centro Flamenco Fosforito** (p200), **Museo Arqueológico** (p200) and **Alcázar de los Reyes Cristianos** (p200). Otherwise, wander the charming streets of the **Judería** (p205) and dine at **Taberna Salinas** (p204) and **La Boca** (p205).

Córdoba in Four Days

With extra time, make an excursion to evocative **Madinat al-Zahra** (p203). Back in town, take in a flamenco performance at **Centro Flamenco Fosforito** (p200), wander along the riverbank from the **Puente Romano** (p201), visit the **Palacio de Viana** (p201), and eat and drink well at **Bodegas Campos** (p204) and **Bodega Guzmán** (p205).

See Córdoba Map (p202)

Arriving in Córdoba

Super-fast AVE train services connect Córdoba with Madrid (€38 to €71, 1¾ hours) and Seville (€14 to €30, 45 minutes). The train station is close to the city centre, 1.2km northwest of Plaza de las Tendillas; either walking distance or a short taxi ride away depending on your level of luggage. Taxis from the train station to the Mezquita cost around €7.

Sleeping

Córdoba's many accommodation options span the spectrum of economy to deluxe. Even some of the lower-end places offer elegantly styled and spacious rooms, while others are laden with antiques and history. Booking ahead is essential. Expect prices to rise during Semana Santa, the May festivals and some weekends. Stay as close as you can to the Mezquita or the atmospheric *judería*.

NAUGHTY NUT / SHUTTERSTOCK ©

Mezquita

It's impossible to overemphasise the beauty of Córdoba's great mosque. With all its lustrous decoration, it evokes the city's golden age of sophistication and peaceful coexistence between faiths.

Great For...

☑ **Don't Miss**

The mosque's greatest treasure, the 10th-century *mihrab,* a scallop-shell-shaped prayer niche facing Mecca.

Patio de los Naranjos

This lovely courtyard, with its orange, palm and cypress trees and fountains, forms the entrance to the Mezquita. It was formerly the site of ritual ablutions before prayer in the mosque. Its most impressive entrance is the Puerta del Perdón, a 14th-century Mudéjar archway in the base of the bell tower. The courtyard can be enjoyed free of charge at any time.

Bell Tower (Minaret)

The 54m-high bell tower reopened to visitors in 2014 after 24 years of intermittent restoration work, and you can climb up to its bells for fine panoramas. Originally built in 951–52, it was encased in a strengthened outer shell, and heightened, by the Christians in the 16th and 17th centuries. The original minaret would have looked something like the Giralda in Seville. Córdoba's minaret

ⓘ Need to Know

Map p202; ⌖957 47 05 12; www.catedralde cordoba.es; Calle Cardenal Herrero; adult/ child €8/4, 8.30-9.30am Mon-Sat free; ☉8.30-9.30am & 10am-7pm Mon-Sat, 8.30-11.30am & 3-7pm Sun Mar-Oct, to 6pm daily Nov-Feb

✕ Take a Break

Legendary little **Bar Santos** (p204) serves Córdoba's best *tortilla de patata* (potato omelette) under the Mezquita's walls.

★ Top Tip

Get here early: free entry 8.30am and 9.30am (except Sunday) and no groups before 10am.

influenced all minarets built thereafter throughout the western Islamic world.

Columns & Arches

The main prayer hall consists of 'naves' lined by two-tier arches striped in red brick and white stone. The columns used for the Mezquita were a mishmash of material collected from earlier Visigothic and Roman buildings. Later enlargements of the mosque extended these lines of arches to cover an area of nearly 120 sq metres and create one of the biggest mosques in the world. The arcades are one of the much-loved Islamic architectural motifs. Their simplicity and number give a sense of endlessness to the Mezquita.

Mihrab & Maksura

Just past the cathedral's western end, the approach to the glorious *mihrab* begins,

marked by heavier more elaborate arches. Immediately in front of the *mihrab* is the *maksura* (royal prayer enclosure), with its intricately interwoven arches and lavishly decorated domes created by Caliph Al-Hakam II in the 960s. The decoration of the *mihrab* portal incorporates 1600kg of gold mosaic cubes, a gift from the Christian emperor of Byzantium, Nicephoras II Phocas.

Cathedral

Following the Christian conquest of Córdoba in 1236, the Mezquita was used as a cathedral but remained largely unaltered for nearly three centuries. But in the 16th century King Carlos I gave the cathedral authorities permission to rip out the centre of the Mezquita in order to construct the Capilla Mayor (the main altar area) and *coro* (choir). Legend has it that when the king saw the result he was horrified, exclaiming: 'You have destroyed something that was unique in the world.'

Córdoba's History

Although founded by the Romans in 152 BC, the city took centre stage in AD 756 when Abd ar-Rahman I set himself up as the emir of Al-Andalus (the Muslim-controlled parts of the Iberian Peninsula), founding the Omayyad dynasty, which more or less unified Al-Andalus for two and a half centuries. Abd ar-Rahman I founded the Mezquita in 785. The city's – and Al-Andalus' – heyday came under Abd ar-Rahman III (912–61). He named himself caliph (the title of the Muslim successors of Mohammed) in 929, ushering in the era of the Córdoba caliphate.

Córdoba was by now the biggest city in Western Europe, with a flourishing economy based on agriculture and skilled artisan products, and a population somewhere around 250,000. The city shone with hundreds of dazzling mosques, public baths, patios, gardens and fountains. This was the famed 'city of the three cultures', where Muslims, Jews and Christians coexisted peaceably, and Abd ar-Rahman III's court was frequented by scholars from all three communities. Córdoba's university, library and observatories made it a centre of learning whose influence was still being felt in Christian Europe many centuries later.

⊙ SIGHTS

Picture a city 500,000 strong, embellished with fine architecture and fuelled by a prosperous and diverse economy – with universities and libraries filled with erudite artists and wise philosophers, an Islamic caliphate more advanced and civilised than anything else the world had ever known. OK, so this slightly grainy image may be more than 1000 years old now, but enough of ancient Córdoba remains to place it in the contemporary elite drawcards of Andalucía. The centrepiece is the gigantic Mezquita, an architectural anomaly and one of the only places in the world where you can worship Mass in a mosque.

Surrounding it is an intricate web of winding streets, flower boxes and cool intimate patios that are at their most beguiling in late spring.

Alcázar de los Reyes Cristianos   Fortress, Gardens

(Fortress of the Christian Monarchs; Map p202; www.alcazardelosreyescristianos.cordoba.es; Campo Santo de Los Mártires; admission 8.30am-2.30pm €4.50, other times incl water, light & sound show adult/child €7/free; ⊙8.30am-8.45pm Tue-Fri, to 4.30pm Sat, to 2.30pm Sun Sep-Jun, to 3pm Tue-Sun Jul-Aug; 🚼) Built under Castilian rule in the 13th and 14th centuries on the remains of a Moorish predecessor, this fort-cum-palace hosted both Fernando and Isabel, who first met Columbus here in 1486. One hall displays some remarkable Roman mosaics, dug up from Plaza de la Corredera in the 1950s. The Alcázar's terraced gardens, full of fish ponds, fountains, orange trees and flowers, are a delight to stroll around. Also interesting to visit is the nearby **Baños del Alcázar Califal** (€2.50; ⊙8.30am-8.45pm Tue-Fri, to 4.30pm Sat, to 2.30pm Sun mid-Sep–mid-Jun, to 3pm Tue-Sat, to 2.30pm Sun mid-Jun–mid-Sep), the impressive 10th-century bathhouse of the Moorish Alcázar.

Centro Flamenco Fosforito   Museum

(Map p202; ☎957 47 68 29; www.centroflamenco fosforito.cordoba.es; Plaza del Potro; €2; ⊙8.30am-7.30pm Tue-Fri, 8.30am-2.30pm Sat, 9.30am-2.30pm Sun) Possibly the best flamenco museum in Andalucía, the Fosforito centre has exhibits, film and information panels in English and Spanish telling you the history of the guitar and all the flamenco greats. Touch-screen videos demonstrate the important techniques of flamenco song, guitar, dance and percussion – you can test your skill at beating out the *compás* (rhythm) of different *palos* (song forms). Regular live flamenco performances are held here too.

Museo Arqueológico   Museum

(Map p202; Plaza de Jerónimo Páez 7; EU citizen/other free/€1.50; ⊙9am-7.30pm Tue-Sat, to 3.30pm Sun mid-Sep–mid-Jun, 9am-3.30pm Tue-Sun mid-Jun–mid-Sep) The excellent Archaeo-

Visitors to the Fiesta de los Patios de Córdoba

logical Museum traces Córdoba's change in size, appearance and lifestyle from pre-Roman to early Reconquista times, with some fine sculpture, an impressive coin collection, and interesting exhibits on domestic life and religion. In the basement you can see the excavated remains of a Roman theatre.

Palacio de Viana   Museum

(Map p202; www.palaciodeviana.com; Plaza de Don Gome 2; whole house/patios €8/5; ⏱10am-7pm Tue-Sat, to 3pm Sun Sep-Jun, 9am-3pm Tue-Sun Jul & Aug) A stunning Renaissance palace set around 12 beautiful patios, the Viana Palace is a particular delight to visit in spring. Occupied by the aristocratic Marqueses de Viana until 1980, the large building is packed with art and antiques. The whole-house charge covers a one-hour guided tour of the rooms and access to the patios and garden. It's an 800m walk northeast from Plaza de las Tendillas.

Puente Romano   Bridge

(Map p202) Spanning the Río Guadalquivir just below the Mezquita, this handsome 16-arched Roman bridge formed part of the ancient Vía Augusta, which ran from Girona in Catalonia to Cádiz. Rebuilt several times down the centuries, it's now traffic-free and makes for a lovely stroll.

Patios   Historic Buildings

Studded with pots of geraniums, bougainvillea cascading down the walls and a trickling fountain in the middle, the famed patios of Córdoba have provided shade and cool during the searing heat of summer for centuries. The origin of these courtyards probably lies in the Roman atrium (open spaces inside buildings). The tradition was continued by the Arabs, for whom the internal courtyard was an area where women went about their family life and household jobs. The addition of a central fountain and multitudes of plants heightened the sensation of coolness.

Beautiful patios can be glimpsed – often tantalisingly through closed wrought-iron gates – in Córdoba's *judería* and many other parts of town. They are at their prettiest in spring, and happily dozens of them open up for free public viewing during the popular **Fiesta de los Patios de Córdoba** (www.patios.cordoba.es; ⏱early May). The **Asociación**

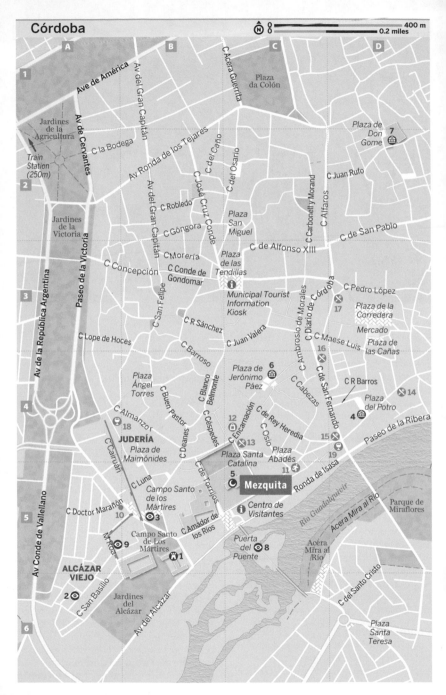

Córdoba

N 0 400 m
0.2 miles

Ave de América

Av del Gran Capitán

C Acera Guerrita

Plaza da Colón

Jardines de la Agricultura

Av de Cervantes

C la Bodega

Plaza de Don Gome 7

Train Station (250m)

Av Ronda de los Tejares

C del Caño

C del Osario

C Juan Rufo

Jardines de la Victoria

Av del Gran Capitán

C Robledo

C José Cruz Conde

Plaza San Miguel

C Carbonell y Morand

C Alfaros

C de San Pablo

C Góngora

Paseo de la Victoria

C Concepción

C Morería

C Conde de Gondomar

Plaza de las Tendillas

C de Alfonso XIII

C Pedro López

Plaza de la Corredera 17

Av de la República Argentina

C San Felipe

Municipal Tourist Information Kiosk

C Ambrosio de Morales

C Diario de Córdoba

C Lope de Hoces

C R Sánchez

C Juan Valera

Mercado

Plaza de las Cañas

C Barroso

C Maese Luis

16

C R Barros

Plaza Ángel Torres

C Buen Pastor

C Blanco Belmonte

Plaza de Jerónimo Páez 6

C Cabezas

C de San Fernando

Plaza del Potro 14

C Almanzor

C Céspedes

4

18

C Deanes

12

C Encarnación

C de Rey Heredia

15

JUDERÍA

Plaza de Maimónides

C Carruán

C de Torrijos

13

C Osio

Plaza Abadés

19

11

C Luna

Campo Santo de los Mártires

Plaza Santa Catalina

5 **Mezquita**

Ronda de Isasa

C Doctor Marañón

10

3

Centro de Visitantes

Río Guadalquivir

Parque de Miraflores

M Roca

Campo Santo de Los Mártires

C Amador de los Ríos

Puerta del Puente 8

Acera Mira al Río

9

1

Acera Mira al Río

ALCÁZAR VIEJO

2

C San Basilio

Jardines del Alcázar

C del Santo Cristo

Av Conde de Vallellano

Av del Alcázar

Plaza Santa Teresa

Córdoba

de Amigos de los Patios Cordobeses (Map p202; Calle San Basilio 44; ⊙11am-2pm & 5.30-8pm, closed Tue Nov-Feb & Sun evening year-round) **FREE** is a particularly lovely patio and can be visited free year-round. **Ruta de Patios del Alcázar Viejo** (Map p202; www.patiosdelalcazarviejo.com; Calle San Basilio 14; €6, ⊙11am-2pm & 5-8pm Wed-Mon Mar-Apr & Oct, 11am-2pm & 6-9pm Wed-Mon May, Jun & 2nd half Sep, 11am-2pm & 5-8pm Fri-Mon Nov–mid-Dec, closed Jul–mid-Sep, mid-Dec–Feb & Sun evenings year-round) offers the chance to enter six patios in the Alcázar Viejo district outside of the patio festival season.

Madinat al-Zahra
Archaeological Site

(Medina Azahara; ☑957 10 49 33; www.museosdeandalucia.es; Carretera Palma del Río Km 5.5; EU citizen/other free/€1.50; ⊙9am-7.30pm Tue-Sat Apr–mid-Jun, to 3.30pm mid-Jun–mid-Sep, to 5.30pm mid-Sep–Mar, 9am-3.30pm Sun year-round; ℗) Eight kilometres west of Córdoba stands what's left of the sumptuous palace-city built by Caliph Abd ar-Rahman III in the 10th century. The complex spills down a hillside with the caliph's palace (the area you visit today) on the highest levels overlooking what were gardens and open fields. The residential areas (still unexcavated) were on each side. A fascinating modern museum has been installed below the site.

🅐 ACTIVITIES

Hammam Baños Árabes
Hammam

(Map p202; ☑957 48 47 46; http://cordoba.hammamalandalus.com; Calle del Corregidor Luis de la Cerda 51; bath/bath & massage €24/36; ⊙2hr sessions 10am, noon, 2pm, 4pm, 6pm, 8pm & 10pm) Follow the lead of the medieval Cordobans and dip your toe in these beautifully renovated Arab baths, where you can enjoy an aromatherapy massage, with tea, hookah and Arabic sweets in the cafe afterwards.

🅖 TOURS

Córdoba Vision
Tour

(Map p202; ☑957 23 17 34; Calle Doctor Marañón 1; tours €10; ⊙tours 4pm Tue-Sat Oct-May, 6pm Tue-Sat Jun-Sep, 10.30am Sat & Sun year-round) Offers a three-hour guided tour to Medina Azahara, conducted in Spanish, French and English. The bus departs from Avenida del Alcázar from in front of the Alcázar de los Reyes Cristianos. It also does a combined tour of the city and Medina for around €30.

🅐 SHOPPING

Córdoba's craft specialities are colourful embossed leather (cuero repujado), silver jewellery and some attractive pottery. The embossed leather is also known as guadamecí (sheepskin) or cordobán (goatskin). Calles Cardenal González and Manríquez have some of the classier craft shops.

Meryan   Handicrafts
(Map p202; ☎957 47 59 02; Calleja de las Flores
2; ⊙9am-8pm Mon-Fri, to 2pm Sat) Has
a particularly good range of embossed leather goods: wallets, bags, boxes, notebooks,
even copies of Picasso paintings.

🍴 EATING

Córdoba's signature dish is *salmorejo*, a
delicious, thick, chilled soup of blended
tomatoes, garlic, bread, lemon, vinegar and
olive oil, sprinkled with hard-boiled egg and
strips of ham. Along with *rabo de toro* (bull's
tail stew), it appears on every menu. There's
traditional meaty and fishy Andalucian fare
aplenty here – but also a good sprinkling
of creative contemporary eateries putting
successful fresh twists on Spanish and Mediterranean ingredients. Don't miss the wine
from nearby Montilla and Moriles.

Bar Santos   Tapas €
(Map p202; Calle Magistral González Francés 3;
tortilla €2; ⊙10am-midnight) Most restaurants
close to the Mezquita are geared to an
undiscriminating tourist market. But this
legendary little bar serves the best *tortilla
de patata* (potato omelette) in town – and
don't the *cordobeses* know it. Thick wedges
are deftly cut from giant wheels of the stuff
and customarily served with plastic forks
on paper plates to eat outside under the
Mezquita's walls. Don't miss it.

Taberna Salinas   Andalucian €
(Map p202; www.tabernasalinas.com; Calle Tun-
didores 3; raciones €7-8; ⊙12.30-4pm & 8-11.30pm
Mon-Sat, closed Aug) A historic bar-restaurant
(since 1879), with a patio and several rooms,
Salinas is adorned in classic Córdoba fashion
with tiles, wine barrels, art and photos of
bullfighter Manolete. It's popular with tourists (and offers a five-language menu), but
it retains a traditional atmosphere and the
waiters are very helpful. Not least, the food is
very good, from the orange-and-cod salad to
the pork loin in hazelnut sauce.

Bodegas Campos   Andalucian €€
(Map p202; ☎957 49 75 00; www.bodegas
campos.com; Calle de Lineros 32; mains & raciones
€11-23; ⊙1.30-4.30pm daily, 8-11.30pm Mon-Sat)
This atmospheric warren of rooms and patios
is popular with smartly dressed *cordobeses*.

Salmorejo, a Córdoban speciality

The restaurant and more informal *taberna* (tavern) serve up delicious dishes, putting a slight creative twist on traditional Andalucian fare – the likes of cod-and-cuttlefish ravioli or pork sirloin in grape sauce. Campos also produces its own house Montilla.

La Boca   Fusion €€

(Map p202; ☑957 47 61 40; www.restaurante laboca.com; Calle San Fernando 39; mains €10-15; ☺noon-midnight Wed-Sun, to 5pm Mon) Trendy for a reason, this cutting-edge eatery whips up exciting global variations from traditional ingredients, then presents them in eye-catching ways: Iberian pork cheeks with red curry and basmati? Battered cod chunks with almonds and garlic? It's very well done, though portions are not for giant appetites. Reservations advisable at weekends.

Garum   Contemporary
2.1   Andalucian €€

(Map p202; Calle San Fernando 122; tapas €3-7, raciones €7-17; ☺noon-4pm & 8pm-midnight, to 2am Fri & Sat) Garum serves up traditional meaty, fishy and vegie ingredients in creative, tasty new concoctions. We recommend the *presa ibérica con herencia del maestro* (Iberian pork with potatoes, fried eggs and ham). Service is helpful and friendly.

🍷 DRINKING & NIGHTLIFE

Bodega Guzmán   Wine Bar

(Map p202; Calle de los Judíos 7; ☺noon-4pm & 8.15-11.45pm Fri-Wed) This atmospheric *judería* drinking spot bedecked with bullfighting memorabilia is frequented by both locals and tourists. Montilla wine is dispensed from three giant barrels behind the bar: don't leave without trying some *amargoso* (bitter).

La Bicicleta   Bar

(Map p202; ☑666 544690; Calle Cardenal González 1; ☺10am-late Mon-Fri, noon-late Sat & Sun) 🚲 This friendly, informal bar welcomes cyclists (and anyone else who's thirsty) with an array of drinks, tasty snacks (light dishes €4 to €9) and – best of all – long, cool, multi-fruit juices. There's 20% off some drinks if you come by bike.

📖 Córdoba's Judería

The old Jewish quarter west and north of the Mezquita is a labyrinth of narrow streets and small squares, whitewashed buildings and wrought-iron gates allowing glimpses of plant-filled patios. The importance of the medieval Jewish community is illustrated by the *judería's* proximity to the Mezquita and the city's centres of power. Spain had one of Europe's biggest Jewish communities, recorded from as early as the 2nd century AD. Persecuted by the Visigoths, the Jews allied themselves with the Muslims following the Arab conquests. By the 10th century they were established among the most dynamic members of society, holding posts as administrators, doctors, jurists, philosophers and poets.

ℹ INFORMATION

Centro de Visitantes (Map p202; ☑957 35 51 79; www.andalucia.org; Plaza del Triunfo; ☺9am-7.30pm Mon-Fri, 9.30am-3pm Sat & Sun) The main tourist information centre.

Córdoba Tourist Information (www.cordoba turismo.es) Tourist information for the province.

Municipal Tourist Information Kiosk
(Map p202; ☑902 20 17 74; www.turismode cordoba.org; Plaza de las Tendillas; ☺9am-2pm & 5-7.30pm)

Municipal Tourist Information Office (☑902 20 17 74; www.turismodecordoba.org; ☺9am-2pm & 4.30-7pm) In the train station's main entry hall.

ℹ GETTING THERE & AWAY

Most travellers arrive in Córdoba by train. Its modern **train station** (www.renfe.com; Glorieta de las Tres Culturas), 1.2km northwest of Plaza de las Tendillas, is served both by fast AVE services and by some slower regional trains. There are services to Granada (€38, 2¾ hours, six daily), Madrid (€38 to €71, 1¾ to two hours, 30 daily) and Seville (€14 to €30, 45 to 80 minutes, 35 daily).

SALAMANCA

Salamanca at a Glance...

Whether floodlit by night or bathed in late afternoon light, there's something magical about Salamanca, one of Spain's most alluring provincial cities. This is where the history of one of Europe's oldest universities meets rare beauty in a city awash with golden sandstone overlaid with Latin inscriptions. The result is an extraordinary virtuosity of plateresque and Renaissance styles without peer anywhere in Spain. The highlights are many, with the exceptional Plaza Mayor (illuminated to stunning effect at night) an unforgettable highlight, not to mention the cathedral and university facades. But this is also Castilla's liveliest city, home to a massive Spanish and international student population that provides the city with so much vitality.

Salamanca in One Day

Begin in the **Plaza Mayor** (p212), the glorious beating heart of the city. Join the crowds and head for the **Catedral Nueva** (p210), then the staggering altarpiece of the **Catedral Vieja** (p211). Round out your day with visits to the **Universidad Civil** (p212) and **Convento de San Esteban** (p213), sandwiched between meals at **La Cocina de Toño** (p215) and the up-market **Victor Gutierrez** (p217).

Salamanca in Three Days

Admire the **Casa de las Conchas** (p214) and **Real Clericía de San Marcos** (p213), then climb the **Puerta de la Torre** (p211) for exceptional views out over the city's rooftops. Don't miss also the outstanding **Museo de Art Nouveau y Art Decó** (p213) or the cloister at the **Convento de las Dueñas** (p214). On day three, head to the **Sierra de Francia** (p219).

Arriving in Salamanca

Salamanca has no airport. The bus and train stations are a 10- and 15-minute walk, respectively, from Plaza Mayor. Bus 4 runs past the bus station and around the old-city perimeter to Calle Gran Vía, an easy walk from Plaza Mayor. From the train station, the best bet is bus 1, which heads into the centre along Calle de Azafranal.

Sleeping

Salamanca has excellent accommodation across a range of budgets. In the city centre close to Plaza Mayor, boutique hotels rub shoulders with simpler, often family-run *hostales* (cheap hotels) and apartments. The more upmarket hotels aren't far away, but generally inhabit quieter streets south of the more clamorous streets of the centre. Even so, you're still within walking distance.

For more on where to stay, see p219.

Catedral Nueva

JULIAN ELLIOTT PHOTOGRAPHY / GETTY IMAGES ©

Salamanca's Cathedrals

Most Spanish cities can boast one cathedral. Salamanca has two. The city's conjoined old and new cathedrals have virtuosic facades and glorious interiors in keeping with Salamanca's reputation for architectural magic.

Great For...

☑ Don't Miss

The extraordinary altarpiece in the Catedral Vieja. It's one of Spain's most beautiful.

A better name for these twin towers of worship would be the 'old cathedral' and 'even older cathedral' – the Catedral Nueva is a mere babe having been completed in 1733. Then again, Salamanca nearly had no cathedrals at all. The 1755 Lisbon earthquake wrought devastation across the region and you can still see cracks and broken windows from that time. On 31 October every year, locals climb to the cupola, there to play flutes and drums in riotous commemoration of the day the cathedrals nearly fell.

Catedral Nueva

The tower of this late-Gothic cathedral lords over the city centre, its compelling churrigueresque (an ornate style of baroque) dome visible from almost every angle. The interior is similarly impressive, with elaborate choir stalls, main chapel and

Altarpiece, Catedral Vieja

❶ Need to Know

Map p215; ☎923 21 74 76; Plaza de Anaya; adult/child €4/3 incl audioguide & admission to both cathedral; ⏰10am-5.15pm Oct-Mar, 10am-8pm Apr-Sep

✖ Take a Break

You're never far from anywhere in Salamanca. **Mandala Cafe** (Map p215; ☎923 12 33 42; www.mandalasalamanca.com; Calle de Serranos 9-11; set menu €12.50; ⏰8am-11pm; 🐾) is just a few blocks away.

★ Top Tip

Come to Plaza de Anaya after sunset for stunning facade views.

retrochoir, much of it courtesy of the prolific José Churriguera. The ceilings are also exceptional, along with the Renaissance doorways – particularly the Puerta del Nacimiento on the western face, which stands out as one of several miracles worked in the city's native sandstone.

The Puerta de Ramos, facing Plaza de Anaya, contains an encore to the 'frog spotting' challenge on the university facade. Look for the little astronaut and ice-cream cone chiselled into the portal by stonemasons during restoration work in 1992.

Catedral Vieja

The Catedral Nueva's largely Romanesque predecessor, the Catedral Vieja is adorned with an exquisite 15th-century altarpiece, one of the finest outside Italy. Its 53 panels depict scenes from the lives of Christ

and Mary and are topped by a haunting representation of the Final Judgment. The cloister was largely ruined in an earthquake in 1755, but the Capilla de Anaya houses an extravagant alabaster sepulchre and one of Europe's oldest organs, a Mudéjar work of art from the 16th century.

The cathedral was begun in 1120 and remains something of a hybrid. There are Gothic elements, while the unusual ribbed cupola, the Torre del Gallo, reflects a Byzantine influence.

Puerta de la Torre

For fine views over Salamanca, head to the tower at the southwestern corner of the Catedral Nueva's facade. From here, stairs lead up through the tower, past labyrinthine but well-presented exhibitions of cathedral memorabilia, then – a real bonus – along the interior balconies of the sanctuaries of the Catedral Nueva and Catedral Vieja and out onto the exterior balconies.

From left: Convento de San Estaban; wall bas-relief, University of Salamanca; Plaza Mayor

⊙ SIGHTS

Plaza Mayor
Square

(Map p215) Built between 1729 and 1755, Salamanca's exceptional grand square is widely considered to be Spain's most beautiful central plaza. The square is particularly memorable at night when illuminated (until midnight) to magical effect. Designed by Alberto Churriguera, it's a remarkably harmonious and controlled baroque display. The medallions placed around the square bear the busts of famous figures. Look for the controversial inclusion of Franco in the northeast corner – it's often either covered or vandalised. Bullfights were held here well into the 19th century; the last ceremonial *corrida* (bullfight) took place in 1992.

Universidad Civil
Historic Building

(Map p215; ☏923 29 44 00, ext 1150; Calle de los Libreros; adult/concession €10/5, audioguide €2; ⊙10am-6.30pm Mon-Sat, to 1.30pm Sun) Founded initially as the Estudio General in 1218, the university reached the peak of its renown in the 15th and 16th centuries. The visual feast of the entrance facade is a tap-estry in sandstone, bursting with images of mythical heroes, religious scenes and coats of arms. But one of the compulsory tasks facing visitors to Salamanca is to search out the frog sculpted into the facade. Once pointed out, it's easily seen, but the uninitiated can spend considerable time searching. They say that those who detect it without help can be assured of good luck and even marriage within a year; some hopeful students believe they'll be guaranteed to ace their examinations. If you believe all this, stop reading now – spoilers ahead.

If you need help, look at the busts of Fernando and Isabel. From there, turn your gaze to the largest column on the extreme right. Slightly above the level of the busts is a series of skulls, atop the leftmost of which sits our little amphibious friend (or what's left of his eroded self).

Behind the facade, the highlight of an otherwise modest collection of rooms lies upstairs: the extraordinary university library, the oldest one in Europe and containing some 2800 manuscripts. Note also

FULCANELLI / SHUTTERSTOCK ©

the fine late-Gothic features and beautiful *techumbre* (carved wooden ceiling).

The Escalera de la Universidad (University Staircase) that connects the two floors has symbols carved into the balustrade, seemingly of giant insects having a frolic with several bishops – to decode them was seen as symbolic of the quest for knowledge.Expect big celebrations in 2018, when the university celebrates its 800th anniversary.

Convento de San Esteban
Convent

(Map p215; ☑923 21 50 00; Plaza del Concilio de Trento; adult/concession/child €3/2/free; ⏲10am-1.15pm & 4-7.15pm) Just down the hill from the cathedral, the lordly Dominican Convento de San Esteban's church has an extraordinary altar-like facade, with the stoning of San Esteban (St Stephen) as its central motif. Inside is a well-presented museum dedicated to the Dominicans, a splendid Gothic-Renaissance cloister and an elaborate church built in the form of a Latin cross and adorned by an overwhelming 17th-century altar by José Churriguera.

Museo de Art Nouveau y Art Decó
Museum

(Casa Lis; Map p215; ☑923 12 14 25; www.museocasalis.org; Calle de Gibraltar; adult/under 12yr €4/free, Thu morning free; ⏲11am-2pm & 4-8pm Tue-Fri, 11am-8pm Sat & Sun Apr–mid-Oct plus Mon 11am-2pm & 4-8pm Aug, 11am-2pm & 4-7pm Tue-Fri, 11am-8pm Sat & Sun mid-Oct–Mar; ▦) Utterly unlike any other Salamanca museum, this stunning collection of sculpture, paintings and art deco and art nouveau pieces inhabits a beautiful, light-filled Modernista (Catalan art nouveau) house. There's abundant stained glass and exhibits that include Lalique glass, toys by Steiff (inventor of the teddy bear), Limoges porcelain, Fabergé watches, fabulous bronze and marble figurines and a vast collection of 19th-century children's dolls (some strangely macabre), which kids will love. There's also a cafe and an excellent gift shop.

Real Clericía de San Marcos
Church, Tower

(San Marcos; Map p215; ☑923 27 71 14/00; Calle de la Compañia; San Marcos €3, Scala Coeli

€3.75, 10am-2pm Tue free, combined ticket €6; ☺San Marcos 10.30am-12.45pm & 5-6.30pm Tue-Fri, 10am-1pm & 5-7.15pm Sat, 10.30am-1.30pm Sun, Scala Coeli 10am-5.15pm) Visits to this colossal baroque church and the attached Catholic university are via obligatory guided tours (in Spanish), which run every 45 minutes. You can also climb the Scala Coeli – some 166 steps, including the bell tower – to enjoy superb panoramic views.

Casa de las Conchas
Historic Building

(House of Shells; Map p215; ☎923 26 93 17; Calle de la Compañía 2; ☺9am-9pm Mon-Fri, 9am-2pm & 4-7pm Sat & Sun) FREE One of the city's most endearing buildings, Casa de las Conchas is named after the 300 scallop shells clinging to its facade. The house's original owner, Dr Rodrigo Maldonado de Talavera, was a doctor at the court of Isabel and a member of the Order of Santiago, whose symbol is the shell. It now houses the public library, entered via a charming colonnaded courtyard with a central fountain and intricate stone tracery.

Convento de las Dueñas
Convent

(Map p215; ☎923 21 54 42; Calle Gran Vía; €2; ☺10.30am-12.45pm & 4.30-5.30pm Mon-Sat) This Dominican convent is home to the city's most beautiful cloister, with some decidedly ghoulish carvings on the capitals.

☻ TOURS

Guided Tours
Walking Tour

(☎622 52 46 90; visitasplaza@hotmail.es; tours per person €8-10; ☺11am Mon-Thu, 11am & 8pm Fri, 10.30am, 11.30am, 4.30pm, 5pm & 8pm Sat, 10.30am Sun) Two-hour guided tours run from the tourist office on Plaza Mayor. Although there are variations, daytime tours take in the main monumental highlights of Salamanca, while the 8pm Friday and Saturday tour is all about local legends and curiosities. Buy your ticket in advance from the tourist office (p218).

⊙ SHOPPING

Mercatus
Souvenirs

(Map p215; ☎923 29 46 48; www.mercatus. usal.es; Calle de Cardenal Pla y Deniel; ☺10am-8.15pm Mon-Sat, 10.15am-2pm Sun) The official shop of the University of Salamanca has a stunning range of stationery items, leather-bound books and other carefully selected reminders of your Salamanca visit.

La Galatea
Books

(Map p215; ☎689 41 87 89; www.lagalatea.es; Calle de los Libreros 28; ☺10.30am-2pm & 5-8.30pm Tue-Sat) The first bookshop in decades to open along Salamanca's 'Street of the Booksellers' (there were once more than 50), this fine space combines a bargain table (with some books in English), some gorgeous Spanish-language rare antique books and a carefully chosen collection of LP records.

Convento de las Dueñas
Food

(Map p215; Calle Gran Vía; ☺10.30am-12.45pm & 4.30-5.30pm Mon-Sat) The time-honoured tradition of monks and nuns making sweets and selling them to a paying public is alive at this convent.

La Nave
Books, Jewellery

(Map p215; ☎923 62 29 59; Calle de la Compañía 14; ☺10am-2.15 & 5.30-9pm Mon-Sat, 11am-3pm Sun) Secondhand books (mostly in Spanish) and designer jewellery may seem like a strange combination but this narrow little shop is always full and deservedly so.

⊗ EATING

Salamanca has an excellent range of restaurants to suit all budgets. Restaurants in and around Plaza Mayor concentrate on traditional grilled meats and tend to be more expensive, although the quality is generally high. Prices drop the further away you are from the square. Pedestrian Calle Meléndez and Rúa Mayor are home to more restaurants with outside seating, while the streets around the university, including

Salamanca

◉ Sights

1 Casa de las Conchas	B2
2 Catedral Nueva	B3
3 Catedral Vieja	B3
4 Convento de las Dueñas	C3
5 Convento de San Esteban	C3
6 Museo de Art Nouveau y Art Decó	B3
7 Plaza Mayor	C1
8 Puerta de la Torre	B3
9 Real Clerecía de San Marcos	B2
10 Universidad Civil	B3

⊕ Shopping

Convento de las Dueñas	(see 4)
11 La Galatea	B2
12 La Nave	B2
13 Mercatus	B3

✗ Eating

14 Igüazú Gastrobar	C1
15 La Cocina de Toño	D1
16 Mandala Café	B2
17 Mesón Cervantes	C2
18 Mesón Las Conchas	C2
19 Victor Gutierrez	A2
20 Zazu Bistro	C1

⊜ Drinking & Nightlife

21 Café El Corrillo	B2
22 Doctor Cocktail	C1
23 Garamond	C1
24 Tío Vivo	C1
25 Vinodiario	D3

Calle de Serranos, are a good, inexpensive bet as restaurants here cater more to a student crowd.

La Cocina de Toño Tapas €€

(Map p215; ✆923 26 39 77; www.lacocina-detoño.es; Calle Gran Via 20; tapas from €1.60,

mains €7-22; ⊗noon-4.30pm & 8-11.30pm Tue-Sat, noon-4.30pm Sun) This place owes its loyal following to its creative *pinchos* (tapas-like snacks) and half-servings of dishes such as escalope of foie gras with roast apple and passionfruit gelatin. The restaurant serves more traditional fare

Casa de las Conchas (p214)

as befits the decor, but the bar is one of Salamanca's gastronomic stars. Slightly removed from the old city, it draws a predominantly Spanish crowd.

Zazu Bistro   Italian €€

(Map p215; www.restaurantezazu.com; Plaza de la Libertad 8; mains €11-17; ⏰2-4pm & 8.30pm-midnight) Enjoy a romantic intimate ambience and Italian-inspired dishes like asparagus, mint and cheese risotto or farfalle with tomato, bacon, vodka and Parmesan. The culinary surprises extend to desserts, like that delectable British standard, sticky toffee pudding. Every dish is executed to perfection. Snag a table by the window overlooking this tranquil square.

Igüazú Gastrobar   Tapas €€

(Map p215; ☑923 21 27 21; www.igüazú-gastrobar.com; Calle de Toro 7; tapas from €1.50, raciones €6-15; ⏰8am-midnight) This slick bar effortlessly segues from breakfast to all-day tapas with some terrific choices on the menu – try the Russian salad with red-pepper foam, for example. It's a good place

to try *farinato,* a local pork sausage made with spices and, in this case, quail egg, almonds and honey. The wine list is excellent and the atmosphere cool and classy.

Mesón Las Conchas   Castilian €€

(Map p215; ☑923 21 21 67; Rúa Mayor 16; mains €10-21; ⏰bar 8am-midnight, restaurant 1-4pm & 8pm-midnight; ⏸) Enjoy a choice of outdoor tables, an atmospheric bar or the upstairs, wood-beamed dining area. The bar caters mainly to locals who know their *embutidos* (cured meats). For sit-down meals, there's a good mix of roasts, *platos combinados* and *raciones* (full-size tapas). The restaurant serves a highly rated oven-baked turbot.

Mesón Cervantes   Castilian €€

(Map p215; ☑923 21 72 13; www.meson cervantes.com; Plaza Mayor 15; mains €12-23, set menu €14.50; ⏰10am-1.30am) Although there are outdoor tables on the square, the dark wooden beams and atmospheric buzz of the Spanish crowd on the 1st floor should be experienced at least once; if you snaffle a window table in the evening, you've hit the jackpot. The food's a mix of *platos combinados*, salads and *raciones*.

Victor Gutierrez
Contemporary Spanish €€€

(Map p215; ✆923 26 29 73; www.restaurante-victorgutierrez.com; Calle de Empedrada 4; set menus €65-80; ⏱1.30-4pm & 8.30-11.30pm Tue-Thu, 1.30-4pm & 9-11.30pm Fri & Sat, 2-4pm Sun; 🖥) They may have moved premises but this is still the best table in town. Chef Victor Gutierrez has a Michelin star and his place has a justifiably exclusive vibe, with an emphasis on innovative dishes with plenty of colourful drizzle. The choice of what to order is largely made for you with some excellent set menus that change regularly. Reservations essential.

🍸 DRINKING & NIGHTLIFE

Salamanca's large student population equals lively nights. Nightlife here starts very late, with many bars not filling until after midnight, when many cafe-bars morph into dance clubs. The so-called 'litre bars' on Plaza de San Juan Bautista are fun nighttime hang-outs mainly for students (who clearly have better things to do than hit the books).

Doctor Cocktail
Cocktail Bar

(Map p215; ✆923 26 31 51; Calle del Doctor Piñuela 5; ⏱4pm-late) Excellent cocktails, friendly bar staff and a cool crowd make for a fine mix just north of Plaza Mayor. Apart from the creative list of cocktails, there are 32 different kinds of gin to choose from and above-average tonic to go with it.

Tío Vivo
Music Bar

(Map p215; ✆923 215 768; www.tiovivosalamanca.com; Calle del Clavel 3-5; ⏱3.30pm-late) Sip drinks by flickering candlelight to a background of '80s music, enjoying the whimsical decor of carousel horses and oddball antiquities. There's live music Tuesday to Thursday from midnight, sometimes with a €5 cover charge.

Vinodiario
Wine Bar

(Map p215; ✆923 01 40 25; Plaza de los Basilios 1; ⏱10am-1am Sun-Thu, to 1.30am Fri & Sat) Away from the crowds of the old-city centre, this quiet but classy neighbourhood wine bar is staffed by knowledgeable bartenders and loved by locals who, in summer, fill the outdoor tables for early-evening drinks. The tapas are good and wine by the glass starts from €2.50.

Café El Corrillo
Bar

(Map p215; ✆923 27 19 17; www.cafecorrillo.com; Calle de Meléndez; ⏱8.30am-3am) Great for a beer and tapas at any time, with live music (especially jazz or singer-songwriters) on Sunday and Thursday nights from 10pm; concerts sometimes take place on other

---

📖 Salamanca's History

In 220 BC, Celtiberian Salamanca was besieged by Hannibal. Later, under Roman rule, it was an important staging post on the Ruta de la Plata (Silver Route) from the mines in Asturias to Andalucía. After the Muslim invasion of Spain, the city repeatedly changed hands. The greatest turning point was the founding of the university in 1218, which grew to became the equal of Oxford and Bologna. The city followed the rest of Castilla into decline in the 17th century, although by the time Spanish literary hero Miguel de Unamuno became rector at the university in 1900, Salamanca had essentially recovered.

Throughout the 20th century, especially during the civil war, Salamanca's university became both the centre for liberal resistance to fascism and the object of Franco's efforts to impose a compliant academic philosophy at Spain's most prestigious university. To a small degree, that liberal/conservative tension still defines the character of the town.

nights. The *terraza* out back is perfect on a warm summer's evening.

Garamond   Club
(Map p215; ☑923 26 88 98; www.garamond-salamanca.es; Calle del Prior 24; ☺9pm-late)
A stalwart of Salamanca nightlife with medieval-style decor. Garamond has music that's good to dance to without straying too far from the mainstream. No cover.

ⓘ INFORMATION

The **municipal tourist office** (☑923 21 83 42; www.salamanca.es; Plaza Mayor 14; ☺9am-2pm & 4.30-8pm Mon-Fri, 10am-8pm Sat, 10am-2pm Sun Easter–mid-Oct, 9am-2pm & 4-6.30pm Mon-Fri, 10am-6.30pm Sat, 10am-2pm Sun mid-Oct–Easter) shares an office with the regional office. An audioguide to city sights can be accessed on your smartphone from www.audioguiasalamanca.es.

ⓘ GETTING THERE & AWAY

BUS

Bus services include Madrid (regular/express €15.80/23, 2½ to three hours, hourly), Ávila (€7.10, 1½ hours, five daily), Segovia (€14.75, 2½ hours, four daily) and Valladolid (€8.60, 1½ hours, eight daily). There is a limited service to smaller towns with just one daily bus – except on Sunday – to La Alberca (€5.50, around 1½ hours), with stops in the villages of the Sierra de Francia, such as Mogarraz and San Martín del Castañar.

TRAIN

Regular departures to Madrid's Chamartín station (€24.10, 2½ hours), Ávila (€12.25, 1¼ hour) and Valladolid (from €10.45, 1½ hours).

ⓘ GETTING AROUND

Bus 4 runs past the bus station and around the old-city perimeter to Calle Gran Vía. From the train station, the best bet is bus 1, which heads into the centre along Calle de Azafranal.

Salamancan architecture, La Alberca

JOSE ANTONIO CARAVACA / GETTY IMAGES ©

Sierra de Francia

Hidden away in the hills around an hour's drive south of Salamanca, the Sierra de Francia is one of Spain's most rewarding collections of medieval villages. Until recently secluded for centuries, this mountainous region with wooded hillsides and pretty stone-and-timber villages was once one of Spain's most godforsaken regions, but it is today among the country's best-kept secrets.

La Alberca is one of the largest and most beautifully preserved of the Sierra de Francia's villages; a historical and harmonious huddle of narrow alleys flanked by gloriously ramshackle houses built of stone, wood beams and plaster.

Mogarraz, east of La Alberca, has some of the most evocative old houses in the region. It's also famous for its embutidos (cured meats). Further east, Miranda del Castañar is similarly intriguing, strung out along a narrow ridge, but San Martín del Castañar is the most enchanting, with half-timbered stone houses, flowers cascading from balconies, a bubbling stream and a small village bullring at the top of the town, next to the renovated castle. Villanueva del Conde is another lovely hamlet.

Where to Stay

A recent improvement in train services between Salamanca and Madrid means that you could conceivably visit here on a day trip from the capital, but this is one city that definitely deserves more time. Staying close to Plaza Mayor is high on atmosphere, but rooms can be noisy and the centre's system of one-way streets can make arrival difficult if you're driving. If you will be arriving with your own wheels, get detailed directions from your hotel before entering the city. Options south of the city centre are quieter but require a steepish uphill walk to the main sights.

The main natural attraction of the region is the highest peak in the area, Peña de Francia (1732m). Topped by a monastery and reached by a sinuous 12km climb from close to La Alberca, it's a stunning place with views that extend east to the Sierra de Gredos, south into Extremadura and west towards Portugal.

BASQUE COUNTRY

In this Chapter

Basque Country at a Glance...

No matter where you've just come from – be it the hot, southern plains of Spain or gentle and pristine France – the Basque Country is different. Known to Basques as Euskadi or Euskal Herria ('the land of Basque Speakers') and called El Pais Vasco in Spanish, this is where mountain peaks reach for the sky and sublime rocky coves are battered by mighty Atlantic swells. Food is an obsession in this part of the country, whether it's three-Michelin-starred restaurants of San Sebastián or the fabulous pintxo (Basque tapas) bars in the same city or in Bilbao. And the Basque Country has reinvented itself as one of Spain's style and culture capitals, with Bilbao's Museo Guggenheim Bilbao leading the way.

Basque Country in Two Days

With so little time, you've little choice but to spend a day in **Bilbao** (p228) with the **Museo Guggenheim Bilbao** (p224) as your visit's centrepiece, as well as time spent in the town's old centre and food market. Spend your second day in **San Sebastián** (p239), sampling some of the best food Europe has to offer and wandering along the sublime **Playa de la Concha** (p241).

Basque Country in Four Days

Four days would be a minimum to get the best out of the Basque Country. Add an extra day in San Sebastián, and factor in a day trip to **Guernica** (Gernika; p237) or a night in **Vitoria** (p248). If you've time, squeeze a side trip to **Hondarribia** (p246) or **Lekeitio** (p238) from San Sebastián. Better still, stay a few days longer and do it all.

Arriving in Basque Spain

Bilbao is connected by air to numerous European and other Spanish cities; an airport bus connects the airport with the city centre. Otherwise, train and bus services connect Bilbao and San Sebastián with other Basque towns and villages, as well as to Madrid, Barcelona and other northern Spanish cities.

Sleeping

Such is the region's popularity that hotel rooms are at a premium in the Basque Country, particularly in San Sebastián, where advance bookings are essential. Both here and Bilbao are popular weekend getaways so you may have better luck on weekdays, although year-round could almost be considered one long high season. Many coastal towns have good-value guesthouses run by families.

For more on where to stay, see p251.

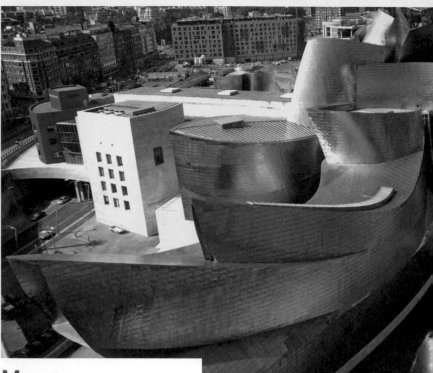

© FMGB. GUGGENHEIM BILBAO MUSEUM. PHOTO: ERIKA BARAHONA EDE

Museo Guggenheim Bilbao

Bilbao's titanium Museo Guggenheim Bilbao is one of modern architecture's most iconic buildings. It almost single-handedly lifted Bilbao into the international art and tourism spotlight.

Great For...

☑ **Don't Miss**

The atrium – the interior counterpoint to the facade's flights of fancy.

The Exterior

Some might say, probably quite rightly, that the Museo Guggenheim Bilbao is more famous for its architecture than its content. But Canadian architect Frank Gehry's inspired use of flowing canopies, cliffs, promontories, ship shapes, towers and flying fins is irresistible. Gehry designed the museum with historical and geographical contexts in mind. The site was an industrial wasteland, part of Bilbao's wretched and decaying warehouse district on the banks of the Ría del Nervión. The city's historical industries of shipbuilding and fishing reflected Gehry's own interests, not least his engagement with industrial materials in previous works. The gleaming titanium tiles that sheathe most of the building like giant herring scales are said to have been inspired by the architect's childhood fascination with fish.

Museo Guggenheim Bilbao

ⓘ Need to Know

Map p230; www.guggenheim-bilbao.es; Avenida Abandoibarra 2; adult/student/child from €13/7.50/free; ⊙10am-8pm, closed Mon Sep-Jun)

✕ Take a Break

The museum has a high-class restaurant (p233), but also try **Bistró**, with *menús* from €20.

★ Top Tip

The Artean Pass joint ticket for the Museo Guggenheim Bilbao and Museo de Bellas Artes de Bilbao offers a reduction of €2 off the admission price.

Beyond Gehry

Other artists have added their touch as well. Lying between the glass buttresses of the central atrium and the Ría del Nervión is a simple pool of water that emits a mist installation by Fuyiko Nakaya. Near the riverbank is Louise Bourgeois' *Maman*, a skeletal spider-like canopy said to symbolise a protective embrace. In the open area west of the museum, the fountain sculpture randomly fires off jets of water. Jeff Koons' kitsch whimsy *Puppy*, a 12m-tall Highland terrier made up of thousands of begonias, is on the city side of the museum.

The Interior

The museum's interior is purposefully vast. The cathedral-like atrium is more than 45m high, with light pouring in through the glass cliffs. Permanent exhibits fill the ground floor and include such wonders as mazes of metal and phrases of light reaching for the skies.

For most people, though, it is the temporary exhibitions that are the main attraction. Recent exhibitions featured the life work of Yoko Ono and the extraordinary sculptures of Brazilian Ernesto Neto.

Museum Essentials

Admission prices vary depending on special exhibitions and the time of year. The last ticket sales are half an hour before closing. Free guided tours in Spanish take place at 12.30pm and 5pm. Tours can be conducted in other languages, but you must ask at the information desk beforehand. Excellent self-guided audio tours in various languages are free with admission and there is also a special children's audioguide. Entry queues can be horrendous, with wet summer days and Easter almost guaranteeing you a wait of more than an hour. The museum is wheelchair accessible.

Bodega Donostiarra

Pintxos in San Sebastián

San Sebastián stands atop a pedestal as one of the planet's culinary capitals. The city overflows with bars, almost all of which have bar tops weighed down under a mountain of Spain's best pintxos.

Great For...

☑ Don't Miss

Bar Nagusía – for the essence of *pintxos* San Sebastián style. For more of San Sebastián's best *pintxo* bars, see (p244).

The Basque version of a tapa, the *pintxo* transcends the commonplace by the sheer panache of its culinary campiness. Usually savoured in two elegant bites *pintxos* are often bedded on small pieces of bread or tiny half-baguettes, upon which towering creations are constructed. Some bars specialise in seafood, others deal in pepper or mushroom delicacies, or simply offer a mix of everything. And the choice isn't normally limited to what's on the bar top in front of you: many of the best *pintxos* are the hot ones you need to order.

The following *pintxo* bars all charge between €2.50 to €3.50 for one *pintxo*. Not so bad if you just take one, but is one ever enough?

La Cuchara de San Telmo

This unfussy, hard-to-find **bar** (Map p240; www.lacucharadesantelmo.com; Calle de 31 de

Pintxos ready for eating

---

❶ Need to Know

Tell the barman what you want first; never just help yourself!

✕ Take a Break

Go for a stroll along Playa de la Concha to compensate for over-eating.

★ Top Tip

Pace yourself: try the speciality in each bar then move on to the next.

---

most highly regarded *pintxo* bars in Gros and has a mouthwatering array of delights piled onto the bar counter, as well as others chalked up onto the board.

Astelena

The *pintxos* draped across the counter in this **bar** (Map p240; Calle de Iñigo 1; ⊙1-4.30pm & 8-11pm Tue & Thu-Sat, 1-4.30pm Wed), tucked into the corner of Plaza de la Constitución, stand out. Many of them are a fusion of Basque and Asian inspirations, but the best of all are the foie-gras-based treats. The great positioning means that prices are slightly elevated.

Bar Nagusía

This **bar** (Map p240; Nagusía Kalea 4), reminiscent of old San Sebastián, has a counter that moans under the weight of its *pintxos*. You'll be moaning after a few as well – in sheer pleasure.

Bodega Donostiarra

The stone walls, potted plants and window ornaments give this **bodega** (Map p240; www.bodegadonostiarra.com; Calle de Peña y Goñi 13; mains €9; ⊙9.30am-midnight Mon-Sat) a real old-fashioned French bistro look, but at the same time it feels very up to date and modern. Although initial impressions make you think the food would be very snooty, it's actually best known for humble *jamón*, chorizo and, most of all, tortilla.

Agosto 28; ⊙7.30-11pm Tue, noon-3.30pm & 7.30-11pm Wed-Sun) offers miniature *nueva cocina vasca* (Basque nouvelle cuisine) from a supremely creative kitchen. Unlike many San Sebastián bars, this one doesn't have any *pintxos* laid out on the bar top; instead you must order from the blackboard menu behind the counter.

Bar Borda Berri

This mustard-yellow place is a *pintxo* **bar** (Map p240; Calle Fermín Calbetón 12; ⊙noon-midnight) that really stands out. The house specials are pig's ears served in garlic soup (much better than it sounds!), braised veal cheeks in wine, and a mushroom and *idiazabal* (a local cheese) risotto.

Bergara Bar

This **bar** (Map p240; www.pinchosbergara.es; General Artetxe 8; ⊙9am-11pm) is one of the

Bilbao

Bilbao isn't the kind of city that knocks you out with its physical beauty – head on over to San Sebastián for that particular pleasure – it's a city that slowly wins you over. Bilbao, after all, has had a tough upbringing. Surrounded for years by an environment of heavy industry and industrial wastelands, its riverfront landscapes and quirky architecture were hardly recognised or appreciated by travellers on their way to more pleasant destinations. But Bilbao's graft paid off when a few wise investments left it with a shimmering titanium landmark, the Museo Guggenheim Bilbao – and a horde of art-world types from around the globe started coming to see what all the fuss was about.

The Botxo (Hole), as it's fondly known to its inhabitants, has now matured into its role of major European art centre. But at heart it remains a hard-working town, and one that has real character. It's this down-to-earth soul, rather than its plethora of art galleries, that is the real attraction of the vital, exciting and cultured city of Bilbao.

◎ SIGHTS

Many first-time visitors associate Bilbao with its world-famous art museum, the Museo Guggenheim Bilbao. But there's a wide variety of interesting sights around town, from architectural highlights to landmark bridges, from bustling plazas to the winding streets of the Casco Viejo (historic centre).

Museo de Bellas Artes   Gallery
(Map p230; www.museobilbao.com; Plaza del Museo 2; adult/student/child €7/5/free, Wed free; ◎10am-8pm Wed-Mon) The Museo de Bellas Artes houses a compelling collection that includes everything from Gothic sculptures to 20th-century pop art. There are three main subcollections: classical art, with works by Murillo, Zurbarán, El Greco, Goya and van Dyck; contemporary art, featuring works by Paul Gauguin, Francis Bacon and Anthony Caro; and Basque art, with works of the great sculptors Jorge de Oteiza and Eduardo Chillida, and strong paintings by the likes of Ignacio Zuloaga and Juan de Echevarria.

Zubizuri

NITO / SHUTTERSTOCK ©

Casco Viejo   Old Town

The compact Casco Viejo, Bilbao's atmospheric old quarter, is full of charming streets, boisterous bars and plenty of quirky and independent shops. At the heart of the Casco are Bilbao's original seven streets, Las Siete Calles, which date from the 1400s.

The 14th-century Gothic **Catedral de Santiago** (Map p230; Plaza de Santiago; ⊙10am-1pm & 5-7.30pm Tue-Sat, 10am-1pm Sun & holidays) has a splendid Renaissance portico and pretty little cloister. Further north, the 19th-century arcaded **Plaza Nueva** (Map p230) is a rewarding *pintxo* haunt. There's a lively Sunday-morning flea market here, which is full of secondhand book and record stalls, and pet 'shops' selling chirpy birds (some kept in old-fashioned wooden cages), fluffy mice and tiny baby terrapins. Elsewhere in the market, children and adults alike swap and barter football cards and old stamps from countries you've never heard of; in between weave street performers and waiters with trays piled high. The market is much more subdued in winter. A sweeter-smelling flower market takes place on Sunday mornings in the nearby Plaza del Arenal.

Basilica de Begoña   Basilica

(Map p230; Calle Virgen de Begoña; ⊙8.30am-1.30pm & 5-8.30pm Mon-Sat, 9am-2pm & 5-9pm Sun) This 16th-century basilica towers over the Casco Viejo from atop a nearby hill. It's mainly Gothic in look, although Renaissance touches, such as the arched main entrance, crept in during its century-long construction. The austere vaulted interior is brightened by a gold altarpiece which contains a statue of the Virgin Begoña, the patron saint of Biscay who's venerated locally as Amatxu (Mother).

Euskal Museoa   Museum

(Museo Vasco; Map p230; www.euskal-museoa.org/es/hasiera; Plaza Miguel Unamuno 4; adult/child €3/free, Thu free; ⊙10am-7pm Mon & Wed-Fri, 10am-1.30pm & 4-7pm Sat, 10am-2pm Sun) This is probably the most complete museum of Basque culture and history in

👍 Las Siete Calles

Forming the heart of Bilbao's Casco Viejo are seven streets known as the Siete Calles (Basque: Zazpi Kaleak). These dark, atmospheric lanes – Barrenkale Barrena, Barrenkale, Carnicería Vieja, Belostikale, Tendería, Artekale and Somera – date to the 1400s when the east bank of the Ría del Nervión was first developed. They originally constituted the city's commercial centre and river port; these days they teem with lively cafes, *pintxo* bars and boutiques.

all of Spain. The story begins in prehistory; from this murky period the displays bound rapidly up to the modern age, in the process explaining just how long the Basques have called this corner of the world home.

Alas, unless you read Spanish (or perhaps you studied Euskara at school?), it's all a little meaningless as there are no English translations.

The museum is housed in a fine old building, at the centre of which is a peaceful cloister that was part of an original 17th-century Jesuit college. In the cloister is the Mikeldi Idol, a powerful pre-Christian symbolic figure, possibly from the Iron Age.

Zubizuri   Bridge

(Map p230) The most striking of the modern bridges that span the Ría del Nervión, the Zubizuri (Basque for 'White Bridge') has become an iconic feature of Bilbao's cityscape since its completion in 1997. Designed by Spanish architect Santiago

Bilbao

Calatrava, it has a curved walkway suspended under a flowing white arch to which it's attached by a series of steel spokes.

⊕ TOURS

There are a number of different city tours available. Some are general-interest tours, others focus on specific aspects of the city such as architecture or food. The following are recommended.

Bilbao Tourist Office   Walking Tour
(☏944 79 57 60; www.bilbaoturismo.net; Plaza Circular 1; ⊙9am-9pm) Organises 1½-hour walking tours covering either the old town or the architecture in the newer parts of town. At busy times tours can run with more frequency.

Bilboats   Boat Tour
(Map p230; ☏946 42 41 57; www.bilboats.com; Plaza Pío Baroja; adult/child from €12/7) Runs boat cruises along the Nervión several times a day.

Bilbao Greeters   Tour
(www.bilbaogreeters.com; adult €12) An original and interesting way to see the city and get to know a local person, who gives you a tour of the city showing you their favourite

sights, places to hang out and, of course, *pintxo* bars. You need to reserve through the website at least a fortnight in advance.

⊜ SHOPPING

For major department stores and big-name fashion labels trawl the streets of El Ensanche. For more one of a kind, independent boutiques, Casco Viejo is the place to look (although even here the chain shops are increasingly making their presence felt). Bilbao is also a great place for food shopping (of course!).

Mercado de la Ribera   Market
(Map p230; Calle de la Ribera) Overlooking the river, the Mercado de la Ribera is supposedly one of the largest covered food markets in Spain. It's had a recent makeover which has sanitised it somewhat, but many of the city's top chefs still come here to select fresh produce each morning.

Arrese   Food
(Map p230; www.arrese.biz; Calle Lopez de Haro 24; ⊙9am-9pm Mon-Sat, 9am-3pm & 5-9pm Sun) With 160 years of baking experience you'd hope the cakes at this little patissiere would taste divine, but frankly, they're even better than expected.

Pintxo Bars in Bilbao

Bilbao may lack San Sebastián's reputation for *pintxos* (Basque tapas), but prices are generally lower here (from around €2.50 per *pintxo*) and the quality is equal. Some of the city's standouts include: in no particular order:

Sorginzulo (Plaza Nueva 12; ⊙9.30am-12.30am) Matchbox-sized bar with an exemplary spread of *pintxos*. The house special is calamari (served on weekends).

Berton Sasibil (Calle Jardines 8; ⊙8.30am-midnight Mon-Sat, 10am-4pm Sun) Watch informative films on the crafting of the same *pintxos* you're munching on.

Claudio: La Feria del Jamón (Calle Iparragirre 9-18; ⊙10am-2pm & 5-9pm Mon-Fri, 10am-2pm & 6-9.30pm Sat) As you'll guess from the name and the dozens of legs of ham hanging from the ceiling, it's all about pigs.

La Viña del Ensanche (Calle de la Diputación 10; ⊙8.30am-11pm Mon-Fri, noon-1am Sat) Hundreds of bottles of wine line the walls of this outstanding *pintxo* bar – it could well be the best place to eat *pintxos* in the city.

Museo del Vino (Calle de Ledesma 10; ⊙1-5pm & 8-11pm Mon-Fri) Delicious octopus *pintxos* and an excellent wine selection (as you'd hope with a name like this). This place makes us smile.

Bitoque de Albia (Alameda Mazarredo 6; ⊙1.30-4pm Mon-Wed, 1.30-4pm & 8.30-11.15pm Thu-Sat) Award-winning modern *pintxo* bar that also offers a *pintxos* tasting menu (€12).

Chocolates de Mendaro Food
(Map p230; www.chocolatesdemendaro.com; Calle de Licenciado Poza 16; ⊙10am-2pm & 4-8pm Mon-Sat) This old-time chocolate shop created its first chocolate treats way back in 1850 and is hands down the best place to ruin a diet in Bilbao.

🍴 EATING

In the world of trade and commerce, the Basques are an outward-looking lot, but when it comes to food they refuse to believe that any other people could possibly match their culinary skills (and they may well have a point). This means that eating out in Bilbao is generally a choice of Basque, Basque or Basque food. Still, life could be worse and there are some terrific places to eat.

The porticoed Plaza Nueva is a good spot for coffee and people-watching, especially in summer.

Agape Restaurante Basque €€
(Map p230; ✆944 16 05 06; www.restauranteagape.com; Calle de Hernani 13; menú del día €12.20, menús €14.80-36; ⊙1-4pm Sun-Wed, 1-4pm & 8.30-11.30pm Thu-Sat) With a solid reputation among locals for good-value meals that don't sacrifice quality, this is a great place for a slice of real Bilbao culinary life. It's well away from the standard tourist circuit, but is worth the short walk. The lunch menu, at €12.20, is exceptional value, comprising starters such as mushroom risotto and mains like fried anchovies with sweet ratatouille. Book ahead.

Casa Rufo Basque €€
(Map p230; ✆944 43 21 72; www.casarufo.com; Hurtado de Amézaga 5; mains €10-15; ⊙1.30-4pm & 8.30-11pm Mon-Sat) Despite the emergence of numerous glitzy restaurants that are temples to haute cuisine, this resolutely old-fashioned place, with its shelves full of dusty bottles of top-quality olive oil and wine, still stands out as one of the best places to eat traditional Basque food in Bil-

Mercado de la Ribera (p231)

bao. The house special is steak – lovingly cooked over hot coals.

Mina Restaurante
Contemporary Basque €€€

(Map p230; ☑944 79 59 38; www.restaurante mina.es; Muelle Marzana; tasting menu €60-110; ⊗2-3.30pm & 9-10.30pm Wed-Sat, 2-3.30pm Sun & Tue) Offering unexpected sophistication and fine dining in an otherwise fairly grimy neighbourhood, this riverside restaurant has some critics citing it as the current *número uno* in Bilbao. Expect serious culinary creativity: think along the lines of spider crab with passion fruit or frozen 'seawater' with seaweed and lemon sorbet. Reservations are essential.

Nerua Guggenheim Bilbao
Contemporary Basque €€€

(Map p230; ☑944 00 04 30; www.nerua guggenheimbilbao.com; tasting menu from €65, mains €30-35; ⊗1-3pm & 8.30-9.30pm Thu-Sat, 1-3pm Tue, Wed & Sun) The museum's modernist, chic, and very white restaurant is under the direction of Michelin-starred chef Josean Alija (a disciple of

Ferran Adrià). Needless to say, the *nueva cocina vasca* (Basque nouvelle cuisine) is breathtaking – even the olives are vintage classics: all come from 1000-year-old olive trees! Reservations are essential. If the gourmet restaurant is too extravagant for you, try El Goog's Bistró, which has *menús* from €20.

🍷 DRINKING & NIGHTLIFE

In the Casco Viejo, around Calles Barrenkale, Ronda and de Somera, there are plenty of terrific hole-in-the-wall, no-nonsense bars with a generally youthful crowd.

Across the river, in the web of streets around Muelle Marzana and Bilbao la Vieja, are scores more little bars and clubs. This is gritty Bilbao as it used to be in the days before the arty makeover. It's both a Basque heartland and the centre of the city's ethnic community. The many bars around here are normally welcoming, but one or two can be a bit seedy. It's not a great idea for women to walk here alone at night.

Lamiak — Cafe

(Map p230; Calle Pelota 8; ⊙4pm-midnight Sun-Thu, 3.30pm-2.30am Fri & Sat) Lamiak, a long-standing Casco Viejo favourite, is a buzzing cafe with a cavernous red and black hall, cast-iron columns and upstairs seating on a mezzanine floor. Good for coffees and cocktails, it exudes an arty, laid-back vibe and pulls in a cool weekend crowd.

Geo Cocktail Lounge — Cocktail Bar

(Map p230; ☑944 66 84 42; Calle Maximo Aguirre 12; ⊙3pm-1.30am Tue-Sun) For a re-fined post-dinner cocktail, search out this lounge bar in the area south of the Museo Guggenheim Bilbao. Expect subdued lighting, low-key tunes and expertly crafted cocktails.

Cotton Club — Club

(Map p230; ☑944 10 49 51; www.cottonclub bilbao.es; Calle de Gregorio de la Revilla 25; ⊙8.30pm-3am Tue & Wed, to 5am Thu, to 6.30am Fri & Sat, 7pm-1.30am Sun) A historic Bilbao nightspot, the Cotton Club draws a mixed crowd to its DJ-stoked nights and regular gigs – mainly blues, jazz and rock.

It's a tiny place so prepare to get up close with your fellow revellers.

☻ ENTERTAINMENT

There are plenty of clubs and live venues in Bilbao, and the vibe is friendly and general-ly easy-going. Venue websites usually have details of upcoming gigs.

Bilbao offers regular performances of dance, opera and drama at the city's principal theatre and the Kafe Antzokia. Check the theatre websites for current information.

Kafe Antzokia — Live Music

(Map p230; ☑944 24 46 25; www.kafeantzokia. com; Calle San Vicente 2) This is the vibrant heart of contemporary Basque Bilbao, fea-turing international rock, blues and reggae, as well as the cream of Basque rock-pop. Weekend concerts run from 10pm to 1am, followed by DJs until 5am. During the day it's a cafe, restaurant and cultural centre all rolled into one and has frequent exciting events on.

From left: Teatro Arriaga; Bodega window showing *pintxos*; Eating out is a way of life in Basque Country

ALAN COPSON / GETTY IMAGES ©

CULTURA EXCLUSIVE / RUSS ROHDE / GETTY IMAGES ©

Euskalduna Palace   Live Music

(Map p230; ☑944 03 50 00; www.euskalduna.
net; Avenida Abandoibarra) About 600m
downriver from the Museo Guggenheim
Bilbao is this modernist gem, built on the
riverbank in a style that echoes the great
shipbuilding works of the 19th century.
The Euskalduna is home to the Bilbao
Symphony Orchestra and the Basque
Symphony Orchestra, and hosts a wide
array of events.

Teatro Arriaga   Theatre

(Map p230; ☑944 79 20 36; www.teatroarria-
ga.com; Plaza Arriaga) The baroque facade of
this venue commands the open spaces of
El Arenal between the Casco Viejo and the
river. It stages theatrical performances and
classical-music concerts.

❶ INFORMATION

Friendly staff at Bilbao's tourist office are
extremely helpful, well informed and, above all,
enthusiastic about their city. Ask for the free
bimonthly *Bilbao Guía*, which has entertainment listings plus tips on restaurants, bars and
nightlife.

At the newly opened, state-of-the-art **main
tourist office** (☑944 79 57 60; www.bilbao
turismo.net; Plaza Circular 1; ⊗9am-9pm),
there's free wi-fi access, a bank of touch-screen
information computers and, best of all, some
humans to help answer questions. There are
also branches at the **airport** (☑944 71 03 01;
⊗9am-9pm Mon-Sat, 9am-3pm Sun) and the
Museo Guggenheim Bilbao (Alameda Mazarredo 66; ⊗10am-7pm daily, to 3pm Sun Sep-Jun).
The Bilbao tourism authority has a very useful
reservations service (☑902 87 72 98; www.
bilbaoreservas.com).

❶ GETTING THERE & AWAY

AIR

Bilbao's **airport** (☑902 404 704; www.aena.es)
is near Sondika, to the northeast of the city. A
number of European flag carriers serve the city.
Of the budget airlines, **EasyJet** (www.easyjet
com) and **Vueling** (www.vueling.com) cover the
widest range of destinations.

BUS

Bilbao's main bus station, **Termibus** (944 39 50 77; Gurtubay 1, San Mamés), is west of the centre. There are regular services to the following destinations: Barcelona (€50, seven to eight hours), Biarritz (France; €19.50, three hours), Logroño €14, 2¾ hours), Madrid (€34, 4¾ hours), Oñati (€6.50, 1¼ hours), Pamplona (€18, 2¾ hours, San Sebastián (€9, one hour), Santander (€9, 1¼ hours) and Vitoria (€9, 1½ hours).

Bizkaibus travels to destinations throughout the rural Basque Country, including coastal communities such as Mundaka and Guernica (€2.50). Euskotren buses serve Lekeitio (€6.65).

TRAIN

The Abando train station is just across the river from Plaza Arriaga and the Casco Viejo. There are frequent trains to Barcelona (from €19.60, 6¾ hours), Burgos (from €7, three hours), Madrid (from €20, five hours) and Valladolid (from €12.55, four hours).

Nearby is the Concordia train station, with its handsome art-nouveau facade of wrought iron and tiles. It is used by the **FEVE** (www.feve.es), a formerly private rail company that was recently purchased by renfe. It has trains running west into Cantabria. There are three daily trains to Santander (from €12.55, three hours) where you can change for stations in Asturias.

The Atxuri train station is just upriver from Casco Viejo. From here, **Eusko Tren/Ferrocarril Vasco** (www.euskotren.es) operates services every half-hour to Bermeo (€3.70, 1½ hours), Guernica (€3.70, one hour) and Mundaka (€3.70, 1½ hours).

ⓘ GETTING AROUND

TO/FROM THE AIRPORT

The airport bus departs from a stand on the extreme right as you leave arrivals. It runs through the northwestern section of the city, passing the Museo Guggenheim Bilbao, stopping at Plaza de Federico Moyúa and terminating at the Termibus (bus station). It runs from the airport every 20 minutes in summer and every 30 minutes in winter from 6.20am to midnight. There is also a direct hourly bus from the airport to

Guernica (Gernika)

TICHR / SHUTTERSTOCK ©

San Sebastián (€16.85, 1¼ hours). It runs from 7.45am to 11.45pm. Taxis from the airport to the Casco Viejo cost about €23 to €30 depending on traffic.

METRO

There are metro stations at all the main focal points of El Ensanche and at Casco Viejo. Tickets start at €1.65. The metro runs to the north coast from a number of stations on both sides of the river and makes it easy to get to the beaches closest to Bilbao.

TRAM

Bilbao's Eusko Tren tramline is a boon to locals and visitors alike. It runs to and fro between Basurtu, in the southwest of the city, and the Atxuri train station. Stops include the Termibus station, the Museo Guggenheim Bilbao and Teatro Arriaga by the Casco Viejo. Tickets cost €1.50 and need to be validated in the machine next to the ticket dispenser before boarding.

Guernica (Gernika)

Guernica (Basque: Gernika) is a state of mind. At a glance it seems no more than a modern and not-too-attractive country town. Apparently, prior to the morning of 26 April 1937, Guernica wasn't quite so ugly, but the horrifying events of that day meant that the town was later reconstructed as fast as possible with little regard for aesthetics.

⊙ SIGHTS

Museo de la Paz de Gernika   Museum

(Guernica Peace Museum; ☎946 27 02 13; www.museodelapaz.org; Plaza Foru 1; adult/child €5/3; ⊗10am-7pm Tue-Sat, 10am-2pm Sun Mar-Sep, shorter hours rest of year) Guernica's seminal experience is a visit to the peace museum, where audiovisual displays calmly reveal the horror of war and hatred, both in the Basque Country and around the world. Displays are in Basque, but guided tours in other languages are available: log

📖 Guernica's Story

The reasons Franco wished to destroy Guernica are pretty clear. The Spanish Civil War was raging and WWII was looming on the horizon. Franco's Nationalist troops were advancing across Spain, but the Basques, who had their own autonomous regional government consisting of supporters of the Left and Basque nationalists, stood opposed to Franco and Guernica was the final town between the Nationalists and the capture of Bilbao.

On that fateful April morning planes from Hitler's Condor Legion flew backwards and forwards over the town demonstrating their newfound concept of saturation bombing. In the space of a few hours, the town was destroyed and many people were left dead or injured. Exactly how many people were killed remains hard to quantify, with figures ranging from a couple of hundred to well over a thousand. The Museo de la Paz de Gernika claims that around 250 civilians were killed and several hundred injured.

The tragedy of Guernica gained international resonance with Picasso's iconic painting *Guernica*, which has come to symbolise the violence of the 20th century. A copy of the painting now hangs in the entrance hall of the UN headquarters in New York, while the original hangs in the Centro de Arte Reina Sofía (p43) in Madrid.

Reproduction of Pablo Picasso's *Guernica*

Mundaka's Wave

Universally regarded as the home of the best wave in Europe, Mundaka is a name of legend for surfers across the world. The wave breaks on a perfectly tapering sandbar formed by the outflow of the Río Urdaibai and, on a good day, offers heavy, barrelling lefts that can reel off for hundreds of metres. Fantastic for experienced surfers, Mundaka is not a place for novices to take to the waves.

Despite all the focus being on the waves, Mundaka remains a resolutely Basque port with a pretty main square and harbour area.

Mundaka
MARK DAFFEY / GETTY IMAGES ©

onto the website and fill out the visitor's booking form ahead of your visit.

Parque de los Pueblos de Europa
Park

(Allende Salazar) The Parque de los Pueblos de Europa contains a couple of typically curvaceous sculptures by Henry Moore and other works by renowned Basque sculptor Eduardo Chillida. The park leads to the attractive Casa de Juntas, where the provincial government has met since 1979. Nearby is the Tree of Guernica, under which the Basque parliament met from medieval times to 1876.

There are plenty of bars in Guernica serving good *pintxos,* and several restaurants offering set menus that cater to day trippers from Bilbao visiting Guernica's caves or museums.

Locals will tell you that **Zallo Barri** (☑946 25 18 00; www.zallobarri.com; Juan Calzada 79; mains €15-22; ☺noon-3.30pm Sun-Thu, noon-3.30pm & 8-11pm Fri & Sat), something of a dining institution, is the best place in town for authentic Basque cuisine.

ℹ INFORMATION
Tourist Office (☑946 25 58 92; www.gernika-lumo.org; Artekalea 8; ☺10am-2pm & 4-7pm Mon-Sat, 10am-2pm Sun) This helpful office has friendly multilingual staff.

ℹ GETTING THERE & AWAY
Guernica is an easy day trip from Bilbao by ET/FV train from Atxuri train station (€3.10, one hour). Trains run every half-hour; buses also make the journey.

Lekeitio

Bustling Lekeitio is gorgeous. The attractive old core is centred on the unnaturally large and slightly out of place late-Gothic Iglesia de Santa María de la Asunción and a busy harbour lined by multicoloured, half-timbered old buildings – some of which house fine seafood restaurants and *pintxo* bars. But for most visitors, it's the two beaches that are the main draw. The one just east of the river, with a small rocky mound of an island offshore, is one of the finest beaches in the Basque Country. In many ways the town is like a miniature version of San Sebastián, but for the moment at least, Lekeitio remains a fairly low-key and predominantly Spanish and French holiday town.

✖ EATING
Lekeitio has some good places to eat, including a handful of bars with outdoor seating across from the harbour. Self-caterers can pick up fish, straight from the boats, from nearby stalls.

Lekeitio beach

A big hit with the locals, **Taberna Bar Lumentza** (www.lumentza.com; Buenaventura Zapirain 3; pintxos €2-5; ⊘noon-late Tue-Sun), is a no-fuss *pintxo* bar tucked away in the side streets. Try the octopus cooked on the *plancha* (grill) washed down with a glass of wine or two.

ℹ INFORMATION

Tourist Office (⍾946 84 40 17; Plaza Independencia; ⊘10am 2pm & 4-8pm)

ℹ GETTING THERE & AWAY

Bizkaibus buses (€3.50) leave from Calle Hurtado de Amézaga, by Bilbao's Abando train station, about eight times a day (except Sunday) and go via Guernica and Elantxobe. Buses also run four times daily from Lekeitio to San Sebastián (€6.65). Drivers take note: finding a parking space can be borderline impossible in the summer.

San Sebastián

It's impossible to lay eyes on stunning San Sebastián (Basque: Donostia) and not fall madly in love. This city is cool and happening by night, charming and well mannered by day. It's a city filled with people that love to indulge – and with Michelin stars apparently falling from the heavens onto its restaurants, not to mention a *pintxo* (tapas) culture almost unmatched anywhere else in Spain, San Sebastián frequently tops lists of the world's best places to eat.

Just as good as the food is the summertime fun in the sun. For its setting, form and attitude, Playa de la Concha is the equal of any city beach in Europe. Then there's Playa de Gros (also known as Playa de la Zurriola), with its surfers and sultry beach-goers. As the sun falls on another sweltering summer's day, you'll sit back with a drink and an artistic *pintxo* and realise that, yes, you too are in love with San Sebastián.

San Sebastián has four main centres of action. The lively Parte Vieja (old town) lies

San Sebastián

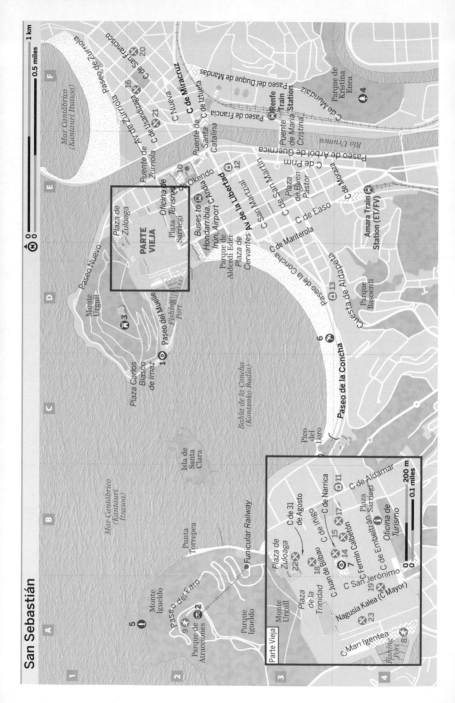

0.5 miles
1 km

Mar Cantábrico
(Kantauri Itsasoa)

Paseo Nuevo

Monte
Urgull

Plaza Carlos
Blasco
de Imaz

Paseo del Muelle

Fishing
Port

Bahía de la Concha
(Kontxako Badia)

Isla de
Santa
Clara

Mar Cantábrico
(Kantauri
Itsasoa)

Punta
Torrepea

Monte
Igueldo

Paseo del Faro

Parque de
Atracciones

Funicular Railway

Parque de
Igueldo

Pico
del
Loro

Paseo de la Concha

C de San Francisco

Paseo de Zurriola

Av de Zurriola

C de Usandizaga

C de Zurriola

Puente de
Zurriola

Plaza de
Zuloaga

Oficina de
Turismo

Plaza de
Sarriegi

PARTE
VIEJA

Paseo de Okendo

Buses to
Hondarribia,
Irún, Airport

C de Andía

Parque de
Alderdi Eder

Plaza de
Cervantes

C Nueva

C de Miracruz

C de Iztueta

Puente de
Santa
Catalina

Paseo del Duque de Mandas

Parque de
Kristina
Enea

Renfe
Train
Station

Paseo de Francia

Río Urumea

Puente
de María
Cristina

Paseo de Árbol de Guernica

C de Prim

C de Moraza

C de Mundaiz

Río Urumea

Av de la Libertad

C de San Martín

C de San Martín

Plaza
de Buen
Pastor

C de Easo

C de Manterola

Cuesta de Aldapeta

Parque
Baserdi

Amara Train
Station (ET/FV)

PASEO DE LA CONCHA

Parte Vieja

200 m
0.1 miles

C de Aldamar

C de Narrica

C de 31
de Agosto

C de Iñigo

C Juan de Bilbao

Plaza de
Zuloaga

Plaza
de la
Trinidad

Monte
Urgull

Nagusia Kalea (C Mayor)

C San Jerónimo

C San Fermín Calbetón

C de Embeltrán Sarriegi

Plaza
Sarriegi

Oficina de
Turismo

C Mari Igentea

Fishing
Port

San Sebastián

across the neck of Monte Urgull, the bay's eastern headland, and is where the most popular *pintxo* bars and many of the cheap lodgings are to be found. South of the Parte Vieja is the commercial and shopping district, the Área Romántica, its handsome grid of late 19th-century buildings extending from behind Playa de la Concha to the banks of the Río Urumea. On the eastern side of the river is the district of Gros, a pleasant enclave that, with its relaxed ambience and the surfing beach of Playa de Gros, makes a cheerful alternative to the honeypots on the western side of the river. Right at the opposite, western end of the city is Playa de Ondarreta (essentially a continuation of Playa de la Concha), a very upmarket district known as a millionaires' belt on account of its lavish holiday homes.

⊙ SIGHTS

San Sebastián is more about the beautiful beach – and the world-famous *pintxo* bars, and the quaint streets of the historic quarter – than it is about specific sights and attractions. Still, there's plenty to keep visitors busy here when you tire of sun and sand.

Aquarium   Aquarium
(Map p240; www.aquariumss.com; Plaza Carlos Blasco de Imaz 1; adult/child €13/6.50; ⊙10am-

9pm daily Jul & Aug, 10am-8pm Mon-Fri, 10am-9pm Sat & Sun Easter-Jun & Sep, shorter hours rest of year) Fear for your life as huge sharks bear down behind glass panes, or gaze in disbelief at tripped-out fluoro jellyfish. The highlights of a visit to the city's excellent aquarium are the cinema-screen-sized deep-ocean and coral-reef exhibits and the long tunnel, around which swim monsters of the deep. The aquarium also contains a maritime museum section. Allow at least 1½ hours for a visit.

Parque de Cristina Enea   Park
(Map p240; Paseo del Duque de Mandas) Created by the Duke of Mandas in honour of his wife, the Parque de Cristina Enea is a favourite escape for locals. This formal park, the most attractive in the city, contains ornamental plants, ducks and peacocks, and open lawns.

Playa de la Concha   Beach
(Map p240) Fulfilling almost every idea of how a perfect city beach should be formed, Playa de la Concha (and its westerly extension, Playa de Ondarreta), is easily among the best city beaches in Europe. Throughout the long summer months a fiesta atmosphere prevails, with thousands of tanned and toned bodies spread across the sands. The swimming is almost always safe.

Aquarium (p241), San Sebastián

Plaza de la Constitución · Plaza

(Map p240) One of the most attractive city squares in the Basque Country, the Plaza de la Constitución sits at the heart of the old town. The square dates from 1813 but sits on the site of an older square. It was once used as a bullring; the balconies of the fringing houses were rented to spectators.

Peine del Viento · Sculpture

(Map p240) A symbol of the city, the *Peine del Viento* (Wind Comb) sculpture, which sits at the far western end of the Bahía de la Concha, below Monte Igueldo, is the work of the famous Basque sculptor Eduardo Chillida and architect Luis Peña Ganchegui.

Monte Igueldo · Viewpoint

(Map p240; www.monteigueldo.es; ☺10am-10pm Jun-Sep, shorter hours rest of year) The views from the summit of Monte Igueldo, just west of town, will make you feel like a circling hawk staring down over the vast panorama of the Bahía de la Concha and

the surrounding coastline and mountains. The best way to get there is via the old-world **funicular railway** (Map p240; Plaza del Funicular; return adult/child €3.15/2.35; ☺10am-9pm Jun-Aug, shorter hours rest of year) to the **Parque de Atracciones** (Map p240; €2.20; ☺11.15am-2pm & 4-8pm Mon-Fri, to 8.30pm Sat & Sun Jul-Sep, shorter hours rest of year), a slightly tacky theme park at the top of the hill.

Monte Urgull · Castle, Park

(Map p240) You can walk to the summit of Monte Urgull, topped by the low walls of the Castillo de la Mota and a grand statue of Christ, by taking a path from Plaza de Zuloaga or from behind the aquarium. The views are breathtaking and the shady parkland on the way up is a peaceful retreat from the city.

🜚 ACTIVITIES

Boats · Boating

(Map p240; www.motorasdelaisla.com; Lasta Plaza; normal boat €4, glass-bottom boat €6;

⊙10am-8pm Jun-Sep) Isla Santa Clara is accessible by boats from the fishing port. Normal boats, which go directly to the island, run every half-hour; glass-bottom boats, which take a far more roundabout route, run roughly every hour.

🔵 TOURS & COURSES

The tourist office (p245) runs several different city tours (including a cinema tour) starting at €10.

Sabores de San Sebastián   Tour

(Flavours of San Sebastián; ☑902 44 34 42; www.sansebastianreservas.com; tours €18; ⊙11.30am Tue & Thu Jul & Aug) The tourist office runs the Sabores de San Sebastián, a two-hour tour (in Spanish and English; French tours are available on request) of some of the city's *pintxo* haunts. Tours are also held with less frequency outside high season – contact the tourist office for dates.

San Sebastián Food   Tour, Cooking Course

(Map p240; ☑943 42 11 43; www.sansebastian food.com; Hotel María Cristina, Paseo de la República Argentina 4) The highly recommended San Sebastián Food runs an array of *pintxo* tasting tours (from €95) and cookery courses (from €145) in and around the city, as well as wine tastings (from €45). The shop/booking office also sells an array of high-quality local food and drink products.

🔒 SHOPPING

The Parte Vieja is awash with small independent boutiques, while the Área Romántica has all your brand-name and chain-store favourites.

Aitor Lasa   Food

(Map p240; www.aitorlasa.com; Calle de Aldamar 12) This high-quality deli is the place to stock up on ingredients for a gourmet picnic you'll never forget. It specialises in cheeses, mushrooms and seasonal products.

> 💬 **Basque Language**
>
> Victor Hugo described the Basque language as a 'country', and it would be a rare Basque who'd disagree with him. The language, known as *euskara,* is the oldest in Europe and has no known connection to any Indo-European languages. Suppressed by Franco, Basque was subsequently recognised as one of Spain's official languages, and it has become the language of choice among a growing number of young Basques.

Playa de la Concha (p241)

Follow Me San Sebastián   Food & Drink

(Map p240; www.justfollowme.com; Calle de Zubieta 7; ⊙10am-2pm & 4-8pm Mon-Sat) A small selection of top-quality regional wine and foodstuffs. You can also learn all about the products on one of the gastronomic tours.

Chocolates de Mendaro   Food

(Map p240; www.chocolatesdemendaro.com; Calle de Echaide 6; ⊙10am-2pm & 4-8pm) We dare you to walk past this fabulous old chocolate shop and resist the temptation to walk inside.

❌ EATING

With 16 Michelin stars (including three restaurants with the coveted three stars), San Sebastián stands atop a pedestal as one of the culinary capitals of the planet. As if that alone weren't enough, the city

🍴🍽️ More of San Sebastián's Best Pintxo Bars

Bar Goiz-Argi (Map p240; Calle de Fermín Calbetón 4; pintxos from €2.50; ⊙9.30am-3.30pm & 6.30-11.30pm Wed-Sun, 9.30-3.30pm Mon) *Gambas a la plancha* (prawns cooked on a hotplate) are the house speciality. Sounds simple, we know, but never have we tasted prawns cooked quite as perfectly as this.

La Mejíllonera (Map p240; Calle del Puerto 15; pintxos from €2.50; ⊙11.30am-3pm & 6-11pm) If you thought mussels only came with garlic sauce, come here to discover mussels (from €3.50) by the thousand in all their glorious forms. Mussels not for you? Opt for the calamari and *patatas bravas* (fried potatoes with a spicy tomato and mayo sauce). We promise you won't regret it.

Bar Martinez (Map p240; Calle 31 de Agosto 13; pintxos from €2.50; ⊙9.30am-11pm Tue-Sun, open late Fri & Sat) This small bar, with dusty bottles of wine stacked up, has won awards for its *morros de bacalao* (delicate slices of cod balanced atop a piece of bread) and is one of the more character-laden places to dip into some *pintxos*.

Bar Diz (Map p240; Calle Zabaleta 17; pintxos from €2.50; ⊙8am-late) In beach-blessed Gros, tiny Bar Diz has massively good *pintxos* (and the breakfast isn't bad either), and other foreign tourists are rare, so it's a totally local affair. If you're hungry opt for a *ración* (plate).

is overflowing with bars – almost all of which have bar tops weighed down under a mountain of *pintxos* that almost every Spaniard will (sometimes grudgingly) tell you are the best in country. These statistics alone make San Sebastián's CV look pretty impressive. But it's not just us who thinks this: a raft of the world's best chefs, including such luminaries as Catalan super-chef Ferran Adrià, have said that San Sebastián is quite possibly the best place on the entire planet to eat.

La Fábrica Modern Basque €€ (Map p240; ☎943 98 05 81; www.restaurante lafabrica.es; Calle del Puerto 17; mains €15-20, menús from €25; ⊙12.30-4pm & 7.30-11.30pm Mon-Fri, 1-4pm & 8-11pm Sat-Sun) The red-brick interior walls and white tablecloths lend an air of class to this restaurant, whose modern takes on Basque classics have been making waves with San Sebastián locals over the last couple of years. At just €25, the multi-dish tasting *menú* is about the best-value deal in the city. Advance reservations are essential.

Arzak Contemporary Basque €€€ (☎943 27 84 65; www.arzak.info; Avenida Alcalde Jose Elosegui 273; meals around €195; ⊙Tue-Sat, closed Nov & late Jun) With three shining Michelin stars, acclaimed chef Juan Mari Arzak is king when it comes to *nueva cocina vasca* and his restaurant is considered one of the best in the world. Arzak is now assisted by his daughter Elena, and they never cease to innovate. Reservations, well in advance, are obligatory. The restaurant is located just east of San Sebastián.

Martín Berasategui
Restaurant Basque €€€ (☎943 36 64 71; www.martinberasategui. com; Calle Loidi 4, Lasarte-Oria; tasting menu €195; ⊙Wed-Sun lunch) This superlative restaurant, about 9km southwest of San Sebastián, is considered by foodies to be one of the best restaurants in the world. The chef, Martín Berasategui, approaches cuisine as a science and the results are tastes you never knew existed. Reserve well ahead.

Akelañe Basque €€€ (☎943 31 12 09; www.akelarre.net; Paseo Padre Orcolaga 56; tasting menu €170; ⊙1-3.30pm & 8.30-11pm Tue-Sat Jul-Dec, Wed-Sat Jan-Jun) This is where chef Pedro Subijana creates cuisine that is a feast for all five senses. As with most of the region's top *nueva cocina* vasca restaurants, the emphasis here is on using fresh, local produce and turning it into something totally unexpected. It's in the suburb of Igeldo, just west of the city.

🍷 DRINKING & NIGHTLIFE

It would be hard to imagine a town with more bars than San Sebastián. Most of the city's bars mutate through the day from calm morning-coffee hang-outs to *pintxo*-laden delights, before finally finishing up as noisy bars full of writhing, sweaty bodies. Nights in San Sebastián start late and go on until well into the wee hours.

ℹ️ INFORMATION

Oficina de Turismo (Map p240; ☏943 48 11 66; www.sansebastianturismo.com; Alameda del Boulevard 8; ⊙9am-8pm Mon-Sat, 10am-7pm Sun Jul-Sep, shorter hours rest of year) This friendly office offers comprehensive information on the city and the Basque Country in general.

ℹ️ GETTING THERE & AROUND

AIR

The city's **airport** (☏902 404704; www.aena. es) is 22km out of town, near Hondarribia. There are regular flights to Madrid and Barcelona and occasional charters to other major European cities. Biarritz, just over the border in France, is served by Ryanair and EasyJet, among various other budget airlines, and is generally much cheaper to fly into.

Buses to Hondarribia (€2.35, 45 minutes) and the airport (€2.35, 45 minutes) depart from Plaza de Gupúzkoa.

BUS

The main bus stop is a 20-minute walk south of the Parte Vieja, between Plaza de Pío XII and the river. Local buses 28 and 26 connect the bus station with Alameda del Boulevard (€1.65, 10 minutes), but it's also a pleasant stroll into the historic centre from here, especially if you walk along the river. There's no real station here, but all the bus companies have offices and ticket booths near the bus stop.

Bars line Parte Vieja (old town)

There are daily bus services to the following: Biarritz (France; from €6.75, 1¼ hours), Bilbao (from €3.30, one hour), Bilbao Airport (€16.85, 1¼ hours), Madrid (from €36, five to six hours), Pamplona (from €7.80, one hour) and Vitoria (from €6.20, 1½ hours).

TRAIN

The main **Renfe train station** (Paseo de Francia) is just across the Río Urumea, on a line linking Paris to Madrid. There are several services daily to Madrid (from €27, 5½ hours) and two to Barcelona (from €19.25, six hours).

Hondarribia

Lethargic Hondarribia (Castilian: Fuen-terrabía), staring across the estuary to France, has a heavy Gallic fragrance, a charming *casco antiguo* (old city) and, in contrast to the quiet old city, a buzzing beach scene.

You enter the *casco* through an archway at the top of Calle San Compostela to reach the pretty Plaza de Gipuzkoa. Head straight on to Calle San Nicolás and go left to reach the bigger Plaza de Armas and the Gothic **Iglesia de Santa María de la Asunción** (Calle Mayor).

For La Marina, head the other way from the archway. This is Hondarribia's most picturesque quarter. Its main street, Calle San Pedro, is flanked by typical fishermen's houses, with facades painted bright green or blue and wooden balconies gaily decorated with flower boxes.

The beach is about 1km from the town. Lined by bars and restaurants, it's not the prettiest stretch of coastline, but it does offer some of the calmest waters in the entire region.

🍴 EATING

The main *casco* plaza is home to a number of excellent *pintxo* bars and restaurants.

Ardoka Pintxos €

(☏943 64 31 69; www.ardokavinoteka.com; Calle San Pedro 30, Hondarribia; pintxos €1.80-4; ⊗noon-3.30pm & 6-11pm Wed-Mon) A modern set-up on Hondarribia's main bar strip with black-grey decor and a great selection of

Iglesia de Santa María de la Asunción, Hondarribia

local wines and ciders. The *pintxos* menu lists hot and cold offerings, including grilled scallops and flavoursome mushrooms.

Arroka Berri   Basque €€

(☑943 64 27 12; www.arrokaberri.com; Calle Higer Bidea 6; mains €15-25; ☺1-3.30pm & 8-11pm) Arroka Berri isn't yet well known outside of town, but we're certain that news of its fabulous cuisine will one day spread far and wide. As with many trend-setting Basque restaurants, this one takes high-quality local produce and turns old-fashioned recipes on their head with a fun, theatrical twist. Unusually, it's open every day.

La Hermandad de Pescadores   Seafood €€

(☑943 64 27 38; www.facebook.com/la hermandadDePescadores; Calle Zuloaga 12; mains €18-21; ☺1-3.30pm & 8-11pm, closed evenings Mon & Sun) Locals in the know travel from San Sebastián to eat at this historic Hondarribia restaurant. Housed in a traditional white-and-blue cottage, it serves an array of seafood classics but is best known for its *sopa de pecsado* (fish soup), said by some to be the best in the area.

Restaurante Sebastián   Basque €€

(☑943 64 01 67; www.sebastianhondarribia. com; Calle Mayor 11; mains €15-25; ☺1-3.30pm & 8-11pm Wed-Sun, 8-11pm Tue) In a beautiful historic building in the middle of the old quarter, the regarded (and rather self-regarding) Restaurante Sebastián serves perfectly executed traditional Basque fare and seafood without any of the fancy, arty touches of some other Basque restaurants.

Alameda   Basque €€€

(☑943 64 27 89; www.restaurantealameda. net; Calle Minasoroeta 1; tasting menus €38-80; ☺1-3.30pm & 8-11pm, closed evenings Sun, Mon & Tue) Hondarribia is rapidly gaining fame as a gourmet hot spot and this Michelin-starred restaurant is leading the way.

⌐r Santuario de Arantzazu

About 10km south of Oñati, the **Santuario de Arantzazu** (☑943 78 09 51; www.arantzazu.org; Barrio de Arantzazu 8) is a busy Christian pilgrimage site that's a fabulous conflation of piety and avant-garde art. The sanctuary was built in the 1960s on the site where, in 1468, a shepherd found a statue of the Virgin under a hawthorn bush. The sanctuary's design is based on this. The overwhelming impression of the building is of spiky towers and halls guarded by fourteen chiselled apostles and, in the crypt, a devil-red Christ.

What started life as a simple tavern is now a sophisticated fine-dining restaurant, complete with garden and terrace, serving creative takes on traditional Basque cuisine, all prepared with fresh, locally sourced ingredients.

❶ INFORMATION

Tourist Office (☑943 64 36 77; www. hondarribia.org; Plaza de Armas 9; ☺9.30am-7.30pm daily Jul–mid-Sep, shorter hours rest of year)

❶ GETTING THERE & AWAY

Buses run frequently to nearby Irún and on to San Sebastián (€2.50, one hour); catch them from Sabin Arana.

Oñati

With a flurry of magnificent architecture and a number of interesting sites scattered throughout the surrounding green hills, the small and resolutely Basque town of Oñati is a great place to get to know the rural Basque heartland. Many visitors pass through on their way to or from the nearby Santuario de Arantzazu.

From left: *Bacalao al pil-pil*; Artium museum, Vitoria;
Plaza de la Virgén Blanca, Vitoria

◎ SIGHTS

Iglesia de San Miguel   Church

(☑943 78 34 53; Avenida de Unibertsitate 2;
⊙hours vary) This late-Gothic confection
has a cloister built over the river. The
church faces the main square, Foruen En-
parantza, dominated by the eye-catching
baroque *ayuntamiento* (town hall). Contact
the tourist office for guided tours.

Monastery of Bidaurreta   Monastery

(☑943 78 34 53; Kalea Lazarraga; ⊙hours vary)
Founded in 1510, this monastery contains
a beautiful baroque altarpiece. It's at the
opposite end of town from the tourist
office and Iglesia de San Miguel. Hours
aren't regular; contact the tourist office for
the latest details.

❶ INFORMATION

Tourist Office (☑943 78 34 53; Calle San Juan
14; ⊙10am-2pm & 3.30-7.30pm Mon-Fri, 10am-
2pm & 4-6.30pm Sat, 10am-2pm Sun)

❶ GETTING THERE & AWAY

PESA buses serve Oñati from many destinations
in the Basque Country, including Bilbao (€6.65,
45 minutes to one hour).

Vitoria

Vitoria (Basque: Gasteiz) has a habit of
falling off the radar, yet it's actually the
capital of not just the southern Basque
province of Álava (Basque: Araba) but also
the entire Basque Country. Maybe it was
given this honour precisely because it is
so forgotten, but if that's the case, prepare
for a pleasant surprise. With an art gallery
whose contents frequently surpass those
of the more famous Bilbao galleries, a delightful old quarter, dozens of great *pintxo*
bars and restaurants, a large student
contingent and a friendly local population,
you have the makings of a lovely city.

◎ SIGHTS

At the base of Vitoria's medieval Casco
Viejo is the delightful Plaza de la Virgén

Blanca. It's lorded over by the 14th-century **Iglesia de San Miguel** (☉10.30am-1pm & 5.30-7pm Mon-Fri), whose statue of the Virgen Blanca, the city's patron saint, lends its name to the plaza below.

The 14th-century **Iglesia de San Pedro Apóstol** (☏945 25 41 93; Fundadora de las Siervas de Jesús) is the city's oldest church and has a fabulous Gothic frontispiece on its eastern facade.

Artium
Museum
(☏945 20 90 00; www.artium.org; Calle de Francia 24; adult/child €6/free, Wed by donation; ☉11am-2pm & 5-8pm Tue-Fri, 11am-8pm Sat & Sun; ♿) Unlike some more famous Basque art galleries, Vitoria's palace of modern art doesn't need to dress to impress. It knows that what's on the inside is all that really counts. It's daring, eccentric and challenging in a way other museums could never get away with.

😵 EATING
Internationally Vitoria might not have the same culinary cachet as San Sebastián,

but among in-the-know Spaniards this is a city with serious culinary pedigree. How serious? Well, in 2014 it was awarded the title of Capital Nacional de la Gastronomia (National Gastronomic Capital) on account of its stellar array of *pintxo* bars and highly creative chefs. What makes Vitoria even

---

🍽️ Basque Food Specialities

Food and drink is almost the cornerstone of life in this part of Spain. Basque food is generally considered about the best in the country. Seafood is big on the coast: *bacalao al pil-pil* (salted cod and garlic in an olive-oil emulsion) and *chipirones en su tinta* (baby squid served in its own ink) are both popular. Further into the hills and mountains people tuck into *chuleton de buey* (steaks – never less than massive). Look out also for fine mountain cheese in the Pyrenees and tiny baby elvers on the coast (although nowadays a substitute is often used due to the rarity of elvers).

more enticing as a foodie destination is that unlike San Sebastián, where the price of *pintxos* is starting to get a bit silly, eating out here is very affordable. Even more so on Thursday evenings when many bars offer a *pintxo* and drink for €1 to €2.

La Malquerida — Pintxos €

(Calle de la Correría 10; pintxos from €2; ☺10am-10.30pm Mon-Thu, 10am-midnight Fri & Sat) A fantastic *pintxo* bar hidden away under the shadows of the church spires. Many locals consider it the best in town.

Bar El Tabanco — Pintxos €

(www.eltabanco.es; Calle de la Korrería 46; pintxos from €2; ☺7-11.30pm Tue-Fri, 12.30-4pm & 7-11.30pm Sat-Sun) Taking its cue, in terms of both decoration and food, from the steamy southern region of Andalucía, this is another ever busy, ever reliable *pintxo* bar.

Asador Sagartoki — Pintxos €

(www.sagartoki.com; Calle del Prado 18; mains €8-12, set menu €42; ☺10am-11pm Mon-Fri, 9am-midnight Sat-Sun) A marvellous *pintxo*

bar and *sidrería* (cider house) that has one of the most creative menus around and an atmosphere to go with it. The house specials, which have won awards, are the tortilla and the fried-egg *pintxos*. Sit back and marvel as the bar staff orchestrate jets of cider from big barrels to the glasses in their outstretched hands.

Arkupe — Basque €€€

(☎945 23 00 80; www.restaurantearkupe.com; Calle Mateo Benigno de Moraza 13; mains €15-21, menús €40-47; ☺1.30-3.30pm & 8.30-11pm) For modern, creative Basque cooking, check out stylish Arkupe, just around the corner from the main plaza. There's an extensive wine list, with all the offerings racked up against the back wall. Reserve in advance for meals. It's also a great place to stop for people-watching and a quick drink or bite, standing at one of the high outdoor tables.

🍷 DRINKING & NIGHTLIFE

There's a strong politico-arty vibe in the Casco Viejo, where a lively student cadre keeps things swerving with creative street

Calamares (calamari)

MARIONTXA / SHUTTERSTOCK ©

posters and action. The main action is at Calle de la Cuchillería/Aiztogile and neighbouring Cantón de San Francísco Javier, both of which are packed with busy bars that attract a wide range of age groups. There's a heavy Basque nationalist atmosphere in some bars.

ℹ INFORMATION

Tourist Office (📞945 16 15 98; www.vitoria-gasteiz.org/turismo; Plaza de España 1; ⏲10am-8pm Jul-Sep, shorter hours Oct-Jun) In the central square of the old town. It can organise guided tours of the city, including fascinating tours taking in the numerous giant wall murals of the city and tours out to the extensive green spaces and birdwatching sites that fringe the city.

ℹ GETTING THERE & AWAY

There are car parks by the train station, by the Artium, and just east of the cathedral.

BUS

Vitoria's **bus station** (Calle de los Herrán) has regular services to the following:

Barcelona (from €21.50, seven hours)

Bilbao (€6.30, 1¼ hours)

Madrid (€27, 4½ hours)

🛏 Where to Stay

Bilbao and San Sebastián have the largest selection of places to stay, but you'll need to book ahead at any time of the year. Apart from being fantastic destinations in their own right, these two cities make good bases for exploring the region – most other towns within the Basque Country are an easy day trip from one of these two cities. The Bilbao tourism authority has a very useful **reservations department** (p235); if you do turn up in San Sebastián without a booking, head to the **tourist office** (p245), which keeps a list of available rooms.

Pamplona (€ 7.50 to €8.50, 1¾ hours)

San Sebastián (€12, 1¼ hours)

TRAIN

Trains go to the following destinations:

Barcelona (from €31, five hours, one daily)

Madrid (from €41, four to six hours, five daily)

Pamplona (from €6, one hour, five daily)

San Sebastián (from €12, 1¾ hours, up to 10 daily)

NORTHWEST
COAST

Northwest Coast at a Glance...

The regions of Cantabria, Asturias and Galicia are unlike anywhere else in Spain. The coastline from Santander in the east to the Portuguese border is a succession of sheer cliffs, beautiful beaches and quiet fishing ports. Behind it at the eastern end, gorgeous river valleys dotted with stone-built villages rise to the 2000m-plus mountain wall of the Picos de Europa. To the west, Galicia is home to Santiago de Compostela, the goal of several hundred thousand people who set out yearly on the storied Camino de Santiago pilgrim trail. Throw in some of Spain's best seafood and a host of engaging villages and cities and you'll want to stay.

Northwest Coast in Three Days

With three days at your disposal, spend them meandering along the coast of **Asturias** (p265) and **Cantabria** (p265), perhaps basing yourself in **Santillana del Mar** (p262) or **Cudillero** (p266). Plan for some beach sightseeing (don't expect warm weather – you're more likely to be admiring the view than swimming), and a day excursion into the **Picos de Europa** (p256).

Northwest Coast in One Week

Use your extra time for a half day at the **Museo de Altamira** (p264), then drive slowly along Galicia's coast, taking in the breathtaking scenery around the **Cabo Ortegal** (p270) and pausing at the smaller fishing villages with their fine, fresh-off-the-boat seafood en route. Don't miss the **Costa da Morte** (p271), a dramatic Atlantic coastline, on your way into **Santiago de Compostela** (p260).

Arriving on Spain's Northwest Coast

There are international airports at Santander, Castrillon (between Oviedo and Gijón) and Santiago de Compostela, with additional domestic airports at A Coruña and Vigo. Santander has overnight ferries to/from the UK, while all cities of the area are connected to the rest of the country by regular bus and train services.

Sleeping

There's good accommodation across the region, from Santander to Santiago, with the widest selection in the cities. Summer is the high season, and bookings are always recommended in Santiago or anywhere along the coast. The Picos de Europa are also popular in summer and on weekends, but virtually deserted in winter. Oviedo and Gijón can be good value on weekends.

For more on where to stay, see p271.

ARSENIY ROSSIKHIN / SHUTTERSTOCK ©

Picos de Europa

The jagged, deeply fissured Picos de Europa mountains straddle southeast Asturias, southwest Cantabria and northern Castilla y León, and amount to some of the most spectacular country in Spain.

Great For...

☑ Don't Miss

The **Teleférico Fuente Dé** (☎942 73 66 10; www.cantur.com; adult/child return €16/6; ⏱9am-8pm Easter & Jul–mid-Sep, 10am-6pm mid-Sep–Jun, closed 2nd half Jan; ℗) for superlative views.

Western Picos

Approaching the Picos from the Asturian (western) side, the Macizo Occidental (El Cornión) unfolds in a series of gorgeous high-altitude lakes, green-on-green pastures and bald rock panoramas. Plain Cangas de Onís is the area's main base, with a host of outdoor activities, while unassuming Arriondas, 8km northwest of Cangas, is the starting point for kayak and canoe rides down the Río Sella. About 10km southeast of Cangas lies holy Covadonga, famous as the first spot in Spain where the Muslims were defeated. From Covadonga, a twisting mountain road zips up to the beautiful (and incredibly popular) Lagos de Covadonga, where several fine hiking trails begin.

humdrum town of Panes. South of Panes, the N621 follows the Río Deva upstream through the impressive Desfiladero de la Hermida gorge. You cross into Cantabria at Urdón, 2km north of the hamlet of La Hermida, then continue 18km south to Potes, the major base and activity hub for the eastern Picos. About 23km west of Potes lies Fuente Dé, with its cable car providing the main Picos access point in this area.

Central Picos

The star attraction of the Picos' central massif is the gorge that divides it from the western Macizo El Cornión. The popular Garganta del Cares (Cares Gorge) trail through it gets busy in summer, but the walk is always an exhilarating experience. This part of the Picos, however, also has plenty of less heavily tramped paths and climbing challenges. Arenas de Cabrales, on the AS114 between Cangas de Onís and Panes, is a popular base, but Poncebos, Sotres, Bulnes and Caín also offer facilities.

Bears in the Picos de Europa

The wild mountain area of southwest Asturias and northwestern Castilla y León, including the Parque Natural de Somiedo, is the main stronghold of Spain's biggest animal, the *oso pardo* (brown bear). Bear numbers in the Cordillera Cantábrica have climbed to over 200 from as low as 70 in the mid-1990s, including a smaller population of 30 to 40 in a separate easterly area straddling southeast Asturias, southwest Cantabria and northern Castilla y León. You can see bears in semi-liberty at the **Cercado Osero** (☑985 96 30 60; www.osodeasturias.es) 🐾 on the Senda del Oso.

Eastern Picos

The AS114 east from Cangas de Onís and Arenas de Cabrales in Asturias meets the N621, running south from the coast, at the

Walkers, Camino Francés

Camino de Santiago

For more than 1000 years, people have taken up the Camino de Santiago's age-old symbols (the scallop shell and staff) and walked to the tomb of St James the Apostle, in Santiago de Compostela.

Great For...

☑ **Don't Miss**

The final march into Santiago de Compostela.

Camino Francés

Although there are many *caminos* (paths) to Santiago in Spain, by far the most popular is, and was, the Camino Francés, which originated in France, crossed the Pyrenees at Roncesvalles and then headed west for 783km across the regions of Navarra, La Rioja, Castilla y León and Galicia. Way-marked with cheerful yellow arrows and scallop shells, the 'trail' is a mishmash of rural lanes, paved secondary roads and footpaths all strung together. Starting at Roncesvalles, the Camino takes roughly two weeks cycling or five weeks walking.

Camino History

In the 9th century a remarkable event occurred in the poor Iberian hinterlands: following a shining star, Pelayo, a religious hermit, unearthed the tomb of the

Santillana del Mar (p262)

J. ERGEN RICHTER / LOOK-FOTO → GETTY IMAGES ©

❶ Need to Know

People walk and cycle the Camino year-round, but June to August is most popular.

✕ Take a Break

There are around 300 *refugios* (pilgrim hostels) along the Camino.

★ Top Tip

Get your *Credencial* (like a pilgrims' passport) stamped at various points along the route.

apostle James the Greater (or, in Spanish, Santiago). The news was confirmed by the local bishop, the Asturian king and later the Pope. Its impact is hard to truly imagine today, but it was instant and indelible: first a trickle, then a flood of Christian Europeans began to journey towards the setting sun in search of salvation.

Compostela later became the most important destination for Christians after Rome and Jerusalem. Its popularity increased with an 11th-century papal decree granting it Holy Year status: pilgrims could receive a plenary indulgence – a full remission of your lifetime's sins – during a Holy Year; the next one is in 2021.

Other Routes

The Camino Francés is by no means the only route, and the summer crowds along the Camino Francés have prompted some to look at alternative routes. Increasingly popular routes include the following:

○ **Camino Portugués** North to Santiago through Portugal.

○ **Camino del Norte** Via the Basque Country, Cantabria and Asturias.

○ **Via de la Plata** From Andalucía north through Extremadura, Castilla y León and on to Galicia.

A very popular alternative is to walk only the last 100km (the minimum distance allowed) from Sarria in Galicia in order to earn a *Compostela* certificate of completion given out by the Catedral de Santiago de Compostela (p260).

Another possibility is to continue on beyond Santiago to the dramatic, 'Land's End' outpost of Fisterra (Finisterre), an extra 88km.

Catedral de Santiago de Compostela

ECG / SHUTTERSTOCK ©

Santiago de Compostela

Locals say the arcaded, stone streets of Santiago de Compostela are most beautiful in the rain, when the Old Town glistens. However, it's hard to catch Santiago in a bad pose.

Great For...

  ⵏⵓⵍ

☑ **Don't Miss**

The **Cathedral Rooftop Tour** (☑902 557812; www.catedraldesantiago.es; adult/ senior, pilgrim, unemployed & student/child €12/10/free; ⊘tours hourly 10am-1pm & 4-6pm or 7pm; 👪), for unforgettable views.

Catedral de Santiago de Compostela

The heart of Santiago, the **cathedral** (www. catedraldesantiago.es; ⊘7am-8.30pm) soars above the city centre in a splendid jumble of spires and sculpture. Built piecemeal over several centuries, its beauty is a mix of the original Romanesque structure (constructed between 1075 and 1211) and later Gothic and baroque flourishes. The tomb of Santiago beneath the main altar is the magnet. The artistic high point is the Pórtico de la Gloria inside the west entrance, featuring 200 masterly Romanesque sculptures.

Praza do Obradoiro

The grand square in front of the cathedral's western facade earned its name (Workshop Sq) from the stonemasons' workshops set up here while the cathedral was being built.

Statue of St James, Catedral de Santiago de Compostela

❶ Need to Know

May, June and September are good months to come.

✕ Take a Break

Mercado de Abastos (www.mercadode abastosdesantiago.com; Rúa das Ameas 5-8; ⊙7am-2pm Mon-Sat) ⌖, Santiago's main market and foodie central.

★ Top Tip

Visit the cathedral early in the morning to avoid the crowds.

Stretching across the northern end of the plaza, the Renaissance-style **Hostal dos Reis Católicos** (adult/child €3/free; ⊙noon-2pm & 4-6pm Sun-Fri) was built in the early 16th century by order of the Catholic Monarchs, Isabel and Fernando, as a recuperation centre for exhausted pilgrims. Today it's a *parador* (luxurious state-owned hotel). Along the western side of the plaza stretches the elegant 18th-century Pazo de Raxoi, now Santiago's city hall. At the southern end stands the Colexio de San Xerome, a 17th-century building with a 15th-century Romanesque/Gothic portal.

Museo das Peregrinacións e de Santiago

Recently installed in a newly converted premises on Praza das Praterías, the brightly displayed **Museum of Pilgrim-** **ages & Santiago** (http://museoperegrinacions. xunta.gal; adult/pilgrim & student/senior & child €2.40/1.20/free; Sat afternoon & Sun free; ⊙9.30am-8.30pm Tue-Sat, 10.15am-2.45pm Sun) gives fascinating insights into the phenomenon of Santiago (man and city). Much of the material is in English as well as Spanish and Galician. There are also great close-up views of some of the cathedral's towers from the 3rd-floor windows.

Santiago's Food Scene

Central Santiago is packed with eateries and the city can be a wonderful place to sample Galicia's celebrated cuisine. For typical, no-frills local cooking, try **O Filandón** (Rúa Acibechería 6; raciones €15-20, medias raciones €10-12; ⊙1-4pm & 8pm-1am, to 2am Fri & Sat) or **O Piorno** (www.opiorno.com; Rúa da Caldeirería 24; dishes €7-14; ⊙8.30am-midnight Mon-Sat, kitchen 12.30-4pm & 7.30pm-midnight), while the local obsession with octopus is nowhere better sampled than at **Pulpería Sanjurjo** (Mercado de Abastos; small plate €8; ⊙11.30am-3.30pm Tue-Sat approx Apr-Oct, Thu-Sat Nov-Mar).

Camino Resources

Caminolinks (www.caminolinks.co.uk) Complete, annotated guide to many Camino websites.

Mundicamino (www.mundicamino.com) Excellent, thorough descriptions and maps.

Camino de Santiago (www.caminodesantiago.me) Contains a huge selection of news groups, where you can get all of your questions answered.

Cantabria

Santillana del Mar

This medieval jewel is in such a perfect state of preservation, with its bright cobbled streets, flower-filled balconies and tanned stone and brick buildings huddling in a muddle of centuries of history, that it seems too good to be true. It's a film set, surely? Well, no. People still live here, passing their grand precious houses down from generation to generation. In summer, the streets get busy with curious visitors.

Strict town planning rules were first introduced back in 1575, and today they include the stipulation that only residents or guests in hotels with garages may bring vehicles into the old heart of town. Other hotel guests may drive to unload luggage and must then return to the car park at the town entrance.

Santillana is a bijou in its own right, but also makes the obvious base for visiting nearby Altamira (p264).

◉ SIGHTS

Colegiata de Santa Juliana   Church
(Plaza del Abad Francisco Navarro; adult/child €3/free; ☺10am-1.30pm & 4-7.30pm, closed Mon Oct-Jun) A stroll along Santillana's cobbled main street, past solemn 15th- to 18th-century nobles' houses, leads you to this beautiful 12th-century Romanesque ex-monastery.

The big drawcard is the cloister, a formidable storehouse of Romanesque handiwork, with the capitals of its columns finely carved into a huge variety of figures. The monastery originally grew up around the relics of Santa Juliana, a 3rd-century Christian martyr from Turkey (and the real source of the name Santillana), whose sepulchre stands in the centre of the church.

✖ EATING

Los Blasones   Cantabrian €€
(☎942 81 80 70; Plaza La Gándara 8; tapas €2.50, mains €16-24; ☺1-4pm & 8-10.30pm daily Mar-Sep, 1-4pm Sat-Thu Oct-Feb) A warm yellow dining room lined with chestnut wood, Los Blasones has been proudly dishing up the usual Cantabrian selection since 1970. Hearty offerings from the open-plan kitchen include *cocido montañés* (a hearty stew), giant beef chops and fresh fish of the day, plus a choice of three-course set menus (€16 to €25).

Restaurante Gran Duque   Cantabrian €€
(☎942 84 03 86; www.granduque.com; Calle del Escultor Jesús Otero 7; mains €15-19; ☺1-3.30pm & 8-10.30pm, closed Sun & Mon lunch Sep-May) The food is high-quality local fare and what sets it apart is the setting, a grand stone house with noble trappings and lovely decorative touches such as the exposed brick and beams. There's a reasonable balance of surf or turf options including *mariscadas* for two (seafood feasts; from €50) and a decent €19 *menú del día*, available for lunch and dinner.

ℹ INFORMATION

Oficina Regional de Turismo (☎942 81 82 51/12; Calle del Escultor Jesús Otero; ☺9am-9pm Jul–mid-Sep, 9.30am-2pm & 4-7pm mid-Sep–Jun)

ℹ GETTING THERE & AWAY

Autobuses La Cantábrica (☎942 72 08 22; www.lacantabrica.net) runs three or more buses from Santander to Santillana (€2.65, 40 minutes), continuing to Comillas (20 minutes) and San Vicente

Cloisters, Colegiata de Santa Juliana

de la Barquera (40 minutes). Buses stop by Campo del Revolgo, just south of the main road.

Comillas

Sixteen kilometres west of Santillana through verdant countryside, Comillas is set across hilltops crowned by some of the most original and beautiful buildings in Cantabria. For these, the town is indebted to the first Marqués de Comillas (1817–83), who was born here as plain Antonio López, made a fortune in Cuba as a tobacco planter, shipowner, banker and slave trader, and then returned to commission leading Catalan Modernista architects to jazz up his home-town in the late 19th century. This, in turn, prompted the construction of other quirky mansions in Comillas. And there's more too: a lovely golden beach, a tiny fishing port and a pleasant, cobbled old centre.

◉ SIGHTS

Comillas' compact medieval centre is built around several cobbled plazas, with a vernacular architecture of solid sandstone houses with wooden, geranium-loaded balconies or glassed-in galleries.

Palacio de Sobrellano   Historic Building

(☑942 72 03 39; http://centros.culturade cantabria.com; Barrio de Sobrellano; adult/child €3/1.50, grounds free; ⊗9.30am-2.30pm & 3.30-7.30pm Tue-Sun mid-Jun–mid-Sep, reduced hours mid-Sep–mid-Jun) In hillside parkland stands the Marqués de Comillas' fabulous neo-Gothic palace. With this 1888 building, Modernista architect Joan Martorell truly managed to out-Gothic real Gothic. On the 25-minute guided tour (in Spanish), you'll see the grand lounge featuring ornate wood-carved fireplaces with Gaudí-designed dragons, the elaborate dining room with its gold-wood *artesonado* (ceiling of interlaced beams with decorative insertions), beautiful stained-glass windows and vibrant original murals detailing the marquis' story. Martorell also designed the marquis' majestic family tomb, next door.

Museo de Altamira

The highlight of the **Museo de Altamira** (☑942 81 88 15; http://museodealtamira. mcu.es; Avenida Marcelino Sanz de Sautuola, Santillana del Mar; adult/child, EU senior or EU student €3/free, Sun & from 2.30pm Sat free; ⊗9.30am-8pm Tue-Sat May-Oct, to 6pm Tue-Sat Nov-Apr, to 3pm Sun & holidays; P⛟) is the Neocueva, a full-sized re-creation of the real Cueva de Altamira's most interesting chamber, the Sala de Polícromos (Polychrome Hall), covered in exquisite 15,000-year-old ochre-and-black bison paintings created using the natural rock relief. Other excellent displays cover prehistoric humanity and cave art around the world, from Altamira to Australia. The museum is incredibly popular, so it's best to reserve tickets in advance, especially for Easter, July, August and September.

Book tickets at any Banco Santander branch in Spain or online via the Altamira website – the final stages for online payment are available in Spanish only. Advance tickets cost €3 for everybody (children, students and seniors included) and are not available for Saturday afternoon or Sunday. Same-day tickets are sold only at the museum ticket office. With all tickets you are assigned an exact time for entering the Neocueva, where visits can be guided or independent. If you're visiting before 10.30am on Friday, you'll be offered an application form to enter into the ballot for visiting the real cave later that day.

Cave painting detail
ROBERT FRERCK/GETTY IMAGES ©

Capricho de Gaudí Architecture
(☑942 72 03 65; www.elcaprichodegaudi. com; Barrio de Sobrellano; adult/child €5/2.50; ⊗10.30am-9pm Jul-Sep, to 8pm Mar-Jun & Oct, to 5.30pm Nov-Feb, closed 1 week Jan) Antoni Gaudí left few reminders of his genius beyond Catalonia, but, of those that he did, the 1885 Gaudí Caprice is easily the most flamboyant. This brick building, one of Gaudí's earliest works and originally a summer playpad for the Marqués de Comillas' sister-in-law's brother, is striped all over the outside with ceramic bands of alternating sunflowers and green leaves. The elegant interior is comparatively restrained, with quirky touches like *artesonado* ceilings (interlaced beams with decorative insertions), stained-glass windows and slim spiral staircases.

✖ EATING

Restaurante Gurea Cantabrian, Basque €
(☑942 72 24 46; Calle Ignacio Fernández de Castro 11; mains €8-14, menú €14.50; ⊗1-3.45pm & 8.15-11pm, closed Tue dinner & Wed) This friendly, elegant restaurant and social bar, hidden in a small street a few blocks east of the town centre, dishes up Basque-Cantabrian fare and can throw together excellent salads and *raciones*. There's a varied *menú especial* (€24) and a set menu for two (€50), available for lunch or dinner.

ⓘ INFORMATION

Oficina de Turismo (☑942 72 25 91; www. comillas.es; Plaza de Joaquín del Piélago 1; ⊗9am-9pm Jul-Sep, 9am-2pm & 4-6pm Mon-Sat, 9am-3pm Sun Oct-Jun) Just off the main plaza.

ⓘ GETTING THERE & AWAY

Autobuses La Cantábrica (☑942 72 08 22; www.lacantabrica.net) runs three to four daily buses between Comillas and Santander (€4, one hour), via Santillana del Mar. The main stop is on Calle del Marqués de Comillas, just west of the town centre.

Asturias

Llanes

Inhabited since ancient times, Llanes was for a long time an independent-minded town and whaling port with its own charter, awarded by Alfonso IX of León in 1206. Today, with a small medieval centre, a bustling harbour and some sensational beaches within easy reach, it's one of northern Spain's more popular holiday destinations – a handy base for the Asturias coast (Ribadesella is just 28km west), with the Picos de Europa close at hand, if not particularly exciting in itself.

◎ SIGHTS

More than 20 sandy stretches and concealed coves lie scattered along the dramatic coastline between Llanes and Ribadesella.

Cueva del Pindal — Cave

(☏608 175284; http://artepaleoliticoenasturias. com; Pimiango; adult/senior & child €3.13/1.62, Wed free; ◒10am-4pm Wed-Sun) The World Heritage–listed Cueva del Pindal, 2km north-east of Pimiango (past a spectacular coastal lookout), contains 31 Palaeolithic paintings and engravings of animals, mostly ochre, including bison, horses and rare depictions of a mammoth and a fish. It's not in the same league as Cantabria's Altamira or Ribadesella's Tito Bustillo caves, but it was Asturias' first-discovered prehistoric cave art. With its setting among wooded sea-cliffs, close to a 16th-century chapel, ruined Romanesque monastery and interpretation centre, it's an appealing visit.

❌ EATING

Plenty of lively *marisquerías* (seafood eateries) and *sidrerías* (cider houses) line Calles Mayor and Manuel Cué, so finding a place to tuck into sea critters and wash them down with cascades of cider is no problem.

Restaurante Siete Puertas — Seafood €€

(☏686 859412, 985 40 27 51; Calle de Manuel Cué 7; mains €15-30, menús €12-30; ◒1-4pm & 8-11pm, closed Mon-Thu & Sun dinner Nov-Mar) The Siete Puertas is a cut above your average Llanes

Capricho de Gaudí

KARSOL / GETTY IMAGES ©

Cudillero

restaurant, with neat white tablecloths, efficient service, a canopied summer terrace and elegantly prepared local dishes. Fish and homemade desserts are its fortes, and there's a variety of *menús* to suit different budgets.

ℹ️ INFORMATION

Oficina de Turismo (☎985 40 01 64; www.llanes.es; Calle Marqués de Canillejas, Antigua Lonja; ⏰10am-2pm & 5-9pm mid-Jun–mid-Sep, 10am-2pm & 4-6.30pm Mon-Sat, 10am-2pm Sun mid-Sep–mid-Jun) Advice on walking routes in the area, including the 5000km E9 coastal path that passes through here on its journey from Russia to Portugal.

ℹ️ GETTING THERE & AWAY

Three or four FEVE trains arrive daily from Oviedo (€8.55, three hours), Arriondas (€4, one hour) and Ribadesella (€2.55, 40 minutes), two of them continuing to Santander (€7.80, 2¼ hours).

Cudillero

Cudillero, 60km northwest of Oviedo, is the most picturesque fishing village on the Asturian coast – and it knows it. The houses, painted in a rainbow of pastels, cascade down to a tiny port on a narrow inlet. Despite its touristy feel, Cudillero is reasonably relaxed and makes an appealing stop, even in mid-August when every room in town is taken. The surrounding coastline is a dramatic sequence of sheer cliffs and fine beaches.

The main activity in town is watching the fishing boats come in to unload their catch (between 5pm and 8pm), and then sampling fish, molluscs and urchins at local *sidrerías* (cider bars) and restaurants. You can also head out along well-made paths to several nearby lookout points.

Ribadesella

Split in two by the Río Sella's estuary, Ribadesella is a low-key fishing town and lively beach resort. Its two halves are joined by the long, low Sella bridge. The western part (where most hotels are) has an expansive golden beach, Playa de Santa Marina, while the older part of town and fishing harbour are on the eastern side. Between Ribadesella and Llanes, 28km east along the coast, more than 20 sandy beaches and pretty coves await discovery.

Unless you've booked far ahead, it's best to stay away from Ribadesella on the first weekend of August, when the whole place goes mad for the Descenso Internacional del Sella canoeing festival.

◎ SIGHTS

Cueva de Tito Bustillo   Cave

(☑985 18 58 60, reservations 902 306600; www.centrotitobustillo.com; Avenida de Tito Bustillo; incl Centro de Arte Rupestre adult/senior, student & child €7.34/5.30, Wed free; ◷10.15am-5pm mid-Mar–Oct; P) To admire some of Spain's finest cave art, including superb horse paintings probably done around 15,000 to 10,000 BC, visit this World Heritage–listed cave, 300m south of the western end of the Sella bridge. Daily visitor numbers are limited, so online or phone reservations are essential. Even if you miss the cave itself, the modern **Centro de Arte Rupestre Tito Bustillo** (☑985 18 58 60, reservations 902 306600; www.centrotitobustillo.com; Avenida de Tito Bustillo; adult/senior, student & child €5.30/3.16, Wed free; ◷10am-7pm Wed-Sun Jul & Aug, reduced hours Sep-Jun; P), 200m south, is well worth a visit for its displays, video and replicas.

✖ EATING

The lively waterfront *sidrerías* (cider bars) on the eastern side of the Río Sella are a good bet for seafood. Ribadesella also has some excellent top-end restaurants.

Carroceu   Sidrería, Asturian €

(☑985 86 14 19; Calle Marqués de Argüelles 25; dishes €7-14; ◷1-4pm & 8pm-midnight Fri-Wed) A popular choice in central Ribadesella, this laid-back, stone-walled *sidrería* is perfect for snacking on simple seafood-focused tapas like deep-fried calamari, steamed cockles and tuna-stuffed onions, plus Asturian cheese and meat *raciones*.

〜 Pick of
the Playas

Playa del Silencio (Castañeras) This is one of Spain's most beautiful beaches: a long, silver, sandy cove backed by a natural rock amphitheatre. It isn't particularly good for swimming due to underwater rocks, but it's a stunning spot for a stroll and, weather permitting, some sun-soaking. It's 15km west of Cudillero: take the A8 west, then exit 441 for Santa Marina, and head west on the N632 to Castañeras, from where the beach is signposted. The last 500m down is on foot.

Playa de Torimbia (Niembro) This beautiful gold-blonde crescent bounded by rocky headlands and a bowl of green hills, 9km west of Llanes, is truly spectacular. It's also a particularly popular nudist beach. Turn off the AS263 at Posada to reach Niembro (2km), from where it's a further 2km to the beach; it's well signposted through Niembro's narrow streets. You have to walk the last kilometre or so, which keeps the crowds down.

Playa de Toranda (Niembro) About 8km west of Llanes, Playa de Toranda is dramatically backed by fields and a forested headland. To get here, turn off the AS263 at Posada and head 2km northwest to Niembro; the beach is 500m beyond Niembro and well signed.

Playa del Silencio
BORJAREYES / GETTY IMAGES ©

🍴 The Food of Asturias & Cantabria

Fabada asturiana No dish better represents Asturias' taste for simplicity than the humble *fabada,* a hearty bean dish jazzed up with meat and sausage.

Ultra-tangy blue cheeses from the Picos de Europa King of Asturian cheeses is the powerful – but surprisingly moreish – bluey-green *queso de Cabrales,* made from untreated cow's milk, or a blend of cow, goat and sheep milk, and matured in mountain caves. It often pops up in meat sauces or poured on top of potatoes *(patatas al Cabrales).*

Seafood There is a wealth of fresh seafood in Asturias, while inland rivers provide trout, salmon and eels. Spain's best anchovies come from Santoña in Cantabria.

Cocido montañés Inland Cantabria's dish is a filling stew of white beans, cabbage, potato, chorizo, black pudding and, sometimes, port.

Double-layered stuffed tortilla Cantabria's *tortillas de patatas* (potato omelettes) come topped with an extra plain omelette and a layer of stuffing – anything from tuna or ham to crunchy salad.

Casa Gaspar   Sidrería, Asturian €€
(📞985 86 06 76; www.restaurantecasagaspar. com; Calle de López Muñiz 6; dishes €9-18; ⏰1-4.30pm & 8pm-midnight, closed Jan-Mar) At busy little Casa Gaspar, in the heart of old-town Ribadesella, take a break from seafood and go for grilled meats, *sartenes* (frying pans) of eggs, chorizo and bacon, or other *raciones,* and cider in copious quantities.

Arbidel   Contemporary Asturian €€€
(📞985 86 14 40; www.arbidel.com; Calle Oscura 1; mains €23-35, set menus €40-70; ⏰1.30-4pm & 8.30-11pm Wed-Sat, 1.30-4pm Tue & Sun, closed Jan) Tucked into an old-town corner, much-loved Michelin-starred Arbidel is famous for chef Jaime Uz' reinvention of classic Astu-

rian flavours and ingredients with distinctly modern flair – at non-exorbitant prices (relatively speaking). Exquisitely prepped local-inspired delights might feature green-apple gazpacho, baked *pixín* (anglerfish) with squid noodles or a giant beef chop for two, but the good-value degustation menus are the way to go.

ℹ️ INFORMATION

Oficina de Turismo de Ribadesella (📞985 86 00 38; www.ribadesella.es; Paseo Princesa Letizia; ⏰10am-2pm & 4-8pm daily Jul & Aug, 10am-2pm & 4-6.30pm Tue-Sat, 11am-2pm Sun Sep-Jun) At the eastern end of the Sella bridge.

ℹ️ GETTING THERE & AWAY

Three or four FEVE trains run daily to/from Oviedo (€6.65, two hours), Arriondas (€1.85, 30 minutes) and Llanes (€2.55, 40 minutes), and two to/from Santander (€9.65, three hours). There are also buses to Gijón (€6.90, 1½ hours) from the bus station, 300m south of the Sella bridge, east of the river.

Gijón

Gijón has emerged like a phoenix from its industrial roots, having given itself a thorough face-lift with pedestrianised streets, parks, seafront walks, cultural attractions and lively eating, drinking and shopping scenes. It's a surprisingly engaging city, and a party and beach hot spot too, with endless summer entertainment. Though it's no quaint Asturian fishing port, Gijón sure knows how to live.

◎ SIGHTS

Gijón's ancient core is concentrated on the headland known as Cimadevilla, the old fishermen's quarter. The harmonious, porticoed Plaza Mayor marks the southern end of this promontory. To the west stretch the Puerto Deportivo (marina) and the broad golden Playa de Poniente, while to the south is the busy, more modern, 19th- to 20th-century city centre, bounded on its eastern side by Playa de San Lorenzo.

Cimadevilla, Gijón

😵 EATING

The most atmospheric area to eat is Cimadevilla, though the newer city centre also offers plenty of choice. Newly pedestrianised Calle Begoña, on *la ruta de los vinos,* is popular for tapas and wine.

La Galana   Sidrería, Asturian €€

(☑985 17 24 29; www.restauranteasturianolagalana.es; Plaza Mayor 10; mains & raciones €15-24; ⏱1.30-4pm & 8pm-midnight; 🌱) The front bar is a boisterous *sidrería* for snacking on tapas (€6.50 to €16) accompanied by free-flowing cider. For a smarter dining experience, head to the spacious back dining room with ceilings covered in murals. Fish, such as wild sea bass or *pixín* (anglerfish) with clams, is the strong suit. It also does excellent vegetarian dishes, including giant veg-tempura platters and beautifully prepared salads.

Tierra Astur   Sidrería, Asturian €€

(☑985 32 74 48; www.tierra-astur.com; Playa de Poniente; mains €9-25; ⏱11am-2am; 🍷) Brave the ugly apartment-block exterior and jump in line at this buzzing *sidrería*-restaurant, a favourite among locals and tourists alike.

The focus is on sizzling meats and grilled seafood, but platters of Asturian cheese, sausage or ham are a good bet too. There's a great-value €9.80 weekday lunch *menú,* along with a seafood-focused *menú* (€20). Book ahead for seats inside a cider barrel.

Casa Gerardo   Asturian €€€

(☑985 88 77 97; www.restaurantecasagerardo.es; Carretera AS19, Km 9, Prendes; mains €19-35, set menus €60-120; ⏱1-3.45pm Tue-Thu & Sun, 1-3.45pm & 9-10.45pm Fri & Sat; 🅿) About 12km west of Gijón, this stone-fronted modern-rustic house has been serving top-quality local cooking since 1882. Five generations of the Morán family have refined their art to the point of snagging a Michelin star. The *fabada,* fish and shellfish are famously delectable. To best sample the Morán blend of tradition and innovation go for one of the set menus.

🍷 DRINKING & NIGHTLIFE

Hit the *sidrerías* in Cimadevilla, along Cuesta del Cholo (Tránsito de las Ballenas) and around town. Further up in Cimadevilla, a student scene flourishes around Plaza

Praia do Picón & the 'Best Bank of the World'

A few kilometres southwest of the Bares Peninsula, some of Spain's most dramatic and least-known beaches are strung along the foot of the spectacular Acantilados de Loiba cliffs. Easiest to reach is Praia do Picón, 2km from Loiba FEVE station. By road, turn off the AC862 at Km 63.4 and follow the DP6104 for 3km to Picón village, where a sharp left turn leads to a small picnic area and a path down to the beach.

West along the clifftop from Praia do Picón, two benches after 200m and 400m afford inspiringly expansive panoramas along the rocky coast from the Punta da Estaca de Bares to Cabo Ortegal.

The second bench has acquired considerable renown under the curious English name 'best bank of the world', thanks to a confusion between different meanings of the Spanish word *banco*, which means both bench and bank. More prosaically it's also known as the Banco de Loiba.

Its fame increased exponentially when it featured in an honourable-mention photo in the 2015 International Earth & Sky Photo Contest of The World At Night (www.twanight.org).

Cliffs near Praia do Picón
IRANTZU ARBAIZAGOITIA / SHUTTERSTOCK ©

Corrada. South of Cimadevilla, lively bars abound along *la ruta de los vinos* (Calles del Buen Suceso, Santa Rosa and Begoña). Naútico, near Playa de San Lorenzo, and Fomento, parallel to Playa de Poniente, host plenty more drinking spots.

ℹ INFORMATION

Gijón Turismo (☎985 34 17 71; www.gijon.info; Espigón Central de Fomento; ⏱10am-9pm daily Aug, 10am-2.30pm & 4.30-7.30pm Sep-Jul) The main tourist office, on a Puerto Deportivo pier, is very helpful. A summer information booth also opens at Playa de San Lorenzo from May to September.

ℹ GETTING THERE & AWAY

All **Renfe** (☎902 320320; www.renfe.com) and **FEVE** (☎902 320320; www.renfe.com/viajeros/feve) trains depart from the **Estación Sanz Crespo** (Calle de Sanz Crespo), 1km west of the city centre. Destinations include Cudillero (€3.30, 1¾ hours, five to 10 direct FEVE trains daily) and Oviedo (€3.40, 30 minutes, two to three Renfe *cercanías* hourly 6am to 11.30pm). Renfe also has several daily trains to León (€13, 2½ hours) and Madrid (€33, five hours).

Galicia

Cabo Ortegal

The wild, rugged coastline for which the Rías Altas are famous begins above Cedeira. No public transport serves the main places of interest, but if you have wheels (and, even better, time for some walks), Galicia's northwestern corner is a spectacular place to explore, with lush forests, vertigo-inducing cliffs, stunning oceanscapes and horses roaming free over the hills.

◎ SIGHTS

Cabo Ortegal   Cape
Four kilometres north of the workaday fishing town of Cariño looms the mother of Spanish capes, Cabo Ortegal, where the Atlantic Ocean meets the Bay of Biscay. Great stone shafts drop sheer into the ocean from such a height that the waves crashing

on the rocks below seem pitifully benign. Os Tres Aguillóns, three jagged rocky islets, provide a home to hundreds of marine birds, and with binoculars you might spot dolphins or whales.

Garita de Herbeira   Viewpoint

From San Andrés de Teixido the DP2205 winds up and across the Serra da Capelada towards Cariño for incredible views. Six kilometres from San Andrés is the must-see Garita de Herbeira, a naval lookout post built in 1805, 615m above sea level and the best place to be wowed over southern Europe's highest ocean cliffs.

✸ EATING

San Andrés de Teixido has several cafes, where you can sample the area's famed *percebes* (goose barnacles): the minimum serve is usually 250g, costing anything from €8 upwards. Cariño has several restaurants and bars with food.

Mesón O Barómetro   Galician €

(Rúa Fraga Iribarne 23, Cariño; raciones €6-12; ⊗1-4pm & 8.30pm-midnight Wed-Mon) A good choice for well-priced fish, seafood and Galician meat dishes, with half a dozen tables in the bar and a small dining room inside. A good range of Galician wines too.

❶ GETTING THERE & AWAY

Arriva (www.arriva.es) runs three buses each way, Monday to Friday only, between Cariño and Mera (20 minutes, €1.40), 10km south. Some of these services connect with Arriva buses at Mera along the AC862 between Ferrol and Viveiro. From Cedeira the 1pm (Monday to Friday) Arriva bus to Mera connects with the 1.30pm Mera–Cariño bus.

🛏 Where to Stay

There are plenty of accommodation options along the coast, but it's more about small hotels and family-run guesthouses than large hotels. Gijón is a notable exception with a full range of accommodation of all kinds – since it's a business-oriented city, you're more likely to find good deals on the weekend here. Elsewhere, you'll need to book weeks, perhaps even months, in advance for most places along the coast in July and August, when Spaniards flock here for their summer holidays.

Costa da Morte

Rocky headlands, winding inlets, small fishing towns, plunging cliffs, wide sweeping bays and many a remote, sandy beach – this is the eerily beautiful 'Coast of Death'. One of the most enchanting parts of Galicia, this relatively isolated and unspoilt shore runs from Muros, at the mouth of the Ría de Muros y Noia, round to Caión, just before A Coruña. It's a coast of legends, like the one about villagers who used to put out lamps to lure passing ships on to deadly rocks. This treacherous coast has certainly seen a lot of shipwrecks, and the idyllic landscape can undergo a rapid transformation when ocean mists blow in.

❶ GETTING THERE & AWAY

There is reasonable bus service from Santiago de Compostela to Fisterra (via Muros, Carnota and O Pindo) and Muxía, but limited services into the area from A Coruña.

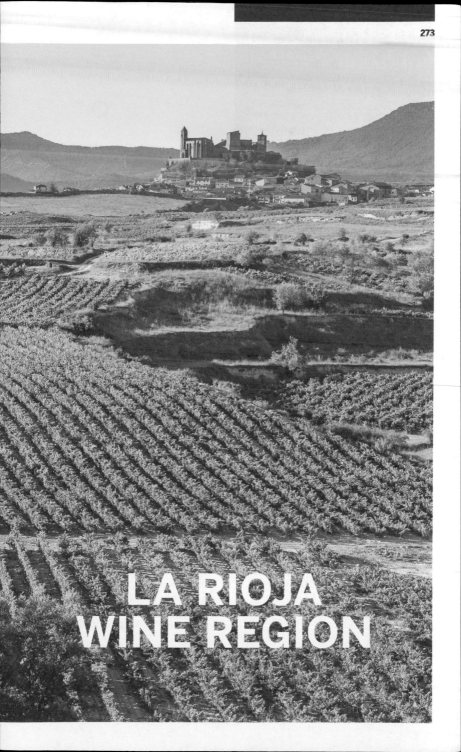

LA RIOJA
WINE REGION

La Rioja Wine Region at a Glance...

Get out the copas (glasses) for La Rioja and some of the best red wines produced in the country. Wine goes well with the region's ochre earth and vast blue skies, which seem far more Mediterranean than the Basque greens further north. In fact, it's hard not to feel as if you're in a different country altogether. The bulk of the vineyards line the Río Ebro around the town of Haro, but some also extend into neighbouring Navarra and the Basque province of Álava. This diverse region offers more than just the pleasures of the grape, though, and a few days here can see you mixing it up in lively towns and quiet pilgrim churches, and even hunting for the remains of giant reptiles.

La Rioja in Two Days

With just two days, take a tour of the **Bodegas Marqués de Riscal** (p276) and stay for dinner. Also visit **Vivanco** (p277) and **Bodegas Ysios** (p277), and take the tour run by **Rioja Trek** (p277). Base yourself in **Laguardia** (p280), the prettiest of La Rioja's small wine towns.

La Rioja in Four Days

A couple of extra days allows you to spend a day in **Logroño** (p278), enjoying its excellent eating scene and shopping for your very own animal skin wine carrier and the best Rioja wines. An extra day could be spent visiting the **Catedral de Santo Domingo de la Calzada** (p282), as well as the fine monasteries in **Nájera** (p283) and **San Millán de Cogolla** (p284).

Arriving in La Rioja

Most travellers choose to explore this region by car. There are no air links to the regional capital of Logroño, but regular trains connect the city with Madrid, Bilbao and other cities. There are also buses to/from nearby towns. Logroño's old town lies just north of the bus and train stations.

Sleeping

There are many charming guesthouses and B&Bs scattered throughout La Rioja's wine country, plus a handful of good hotels in Logroño. Besides Logroño, the best range of accommodation is in the wine towns of Haro and charming Laguardia, with some good choices also in Santo Domingo de la Calzada.

Hotel Marqués de Riscal

Wine Tasting in La Rioja

La Rioja is Spain's most celebrated (and most accessible) wine region, best known for its high-quality reds, charming villages and good mix of wine-centred activities.

Great For...

☑ **Don't Miss**

The Hotel Marqués de Riscal, a Guggenheim for the Basque Country.

Hotel Marqués de Riscal

When the owner of Elciego's Bodegas Marqués de Riscal wanted to create something special, he didn't hold back. The result is the spectacular Frank Gehry–designed **Hotel Marqués de Riscal** (☎945 18 08 80; www.hotel-marquesderiscal.com; Calle Torrea 1, Elciego; r from €330; 🅿❄🛜). Costing around €85 million, the building is a flamboyant wave of multicoloured titanium sheets that stand in utter contrast to the village behind. Unless you're staying at the hotel, join one of the bodega's wine tours or reserve a table at one of the two superb in-house restaurants (mains €24 to €30).

Bodegas Muga

Close to Haro, this **bodega** (☎941 30 60 60; www.bodegasmuga.com; Barrio de la Estación; winery tours €10; ⊘tours by reservation Mon-Sat)

Bodegas Ysios

WALTER BIBIKOW / GETTY IMAGES ©

is particularly receptive and gives daily guided tours (except Sunday) and tastings in Spanish. Although technically you should book in advance in high season, you can often just turn up and join a tour.

Bodegas Ysios

A couple of kilometres north of Laguardia, **Bodegas Ysios** (☏941 27 99 00; www.ysios. com; Camino de la Hoya; per person €12; ⊘tours 11am, 1pm & 4pm Mon-Fri, 11am & 1pm Sat & Sun) was designed by Santiago Calatrava as a 'temple dedicated to wine'. It features an aluminium wave for a roof and a cedar exterior that blends into the mountainous backdrop, and looks its best at night when pools of light flow out of it. Daily tours of the bodega are an excellent introduction to wine production; book ahead.

Vivanco

Vivanco (Museo de la Cultura del Vino; www. vivancoculturadevino.es; Carretera Nacional, Km 232; guided winery & museum visit with wine tasting €20; ⊘11am-6pm Tue-Fri & Sun, 10am-8pm Sat Jul-Aug, shorter hours rest of year) is a must for wine lovers. Tour the winery before a visit to the excellent, interactive Museum of the Culture of Wine, where you'll learn all there is to know about the history and production of wine. The treasures on display include Picasso-designed wine jugs and wine-inspired religious artefacts.

Rioja Trek

Based in the small village of Fuenmayor, 10 minutes west of Logroño, **Rioja Trek** (☏941 58 73 54; www.riojatrek.com; wine experience per person €28) offers three-hour wine 'experiences' where you visit a vineyard and bodega and participate in the process of actually making some wine yourself (and keeping the bottle afterwards).

🍷 La Rioja Wines

Wine categories in La Rioja are termed Young, Crianza, Reserva and Gran Reserva. Young wines are in their first or second year and are inevitably a touch 'fresh'. Crianzas must have matured into their third year and have spent at least one year in the cask, followed by a few months resting in the bottle. Reservas pay homage to the best vintages and must mature for at least three full years in cask and bottle, with at least one year in the cask. Gran Reservas depend on the very best vintages and are matured for at least two years in the cask followed by three years in the bottle. These are the 'velvet' wines.

Experts have developed a classification system for the years in which the wine was particularly good. Five stars (the maximum) were awarded in 1982, 1994, 1995, 2001, 2004, 2005 and 2010. Four-star years include 1981, 1987, 1991, 1996, 1998, 2006, 2007, 2008 and 2009.

Wine tasting
NICK LEDGER / GETTY IMAGES ©

Logroño

Logroño is a stately wine country town with a heart of tree-studded squares, narrow streets and hidden corners. There are few monuments here, but perhaps more importantly to some, a great selection of *pintxo* (tapas) bars. In fact, Logroño is quickly gaining a culinary reputation to rival anywhere in Spain.

◉ SIGHTS

A stroll around the old town and down to the river is a thoroughly pleasant way to spend an afternoon.

Museo de la Rioja   Museum
(📞941 29 12 59; www.larioja.org; Plaza San Agustín 23; ☉10am-2pm & 4-9pm Tue-Sat, 10am-2pm Sun) **FREE** In both Spanish and English, this superb museum in the centre of Logroño takes you on a wild romp through Riojan history and culture – from the days when dinner was killed with arrows to recreations of the kitchens that many a Spanish *abuela* (grandmother) grew up using.

Iglesia de San Bartolomé   Church
(Calle de Rodríguez Paterna) The impressive main entrance to this 13th-century church has a splendid portico of deeply receding borders and an expressive collection of statuary.

Catedral de Santa María de la Redonda   Cathedral
(Calle de Portales; ☉8am-1pm & 6-8.45pm Mon-Sat, 9am-2pm & 6.30-8.45pm Sun) The Catedral de Santa María de la Redonda started life as a Gothic church before maturing into a full-blown cathedral in the 16th century.

🛍 SHOPPING

Félix Barbero Botas Rioja   Handicrafts
(http://botasrioja.artesaniadelarioja.org; Calle de Sagasta 8; ☉10am-2pm & 4-8pm Mon-Sat) Maintaining a dying craft, Félix Barbero handmakes the classic Spanish animal skin wine carriers in which farmers carried their daily rations of wine while working in the fields. The standard one-litre model starts around €22.

Vinos El Peso   Wine
(Calle del Peso 1; ☉9.30am-2pm Mon-Sat) There are countless wine outlets in town, but this one is excellent. In addition to local varietals, it's a good place to pick up some *vermút* (vermouth) de la Rioja.

🍴 EATING

Make no mistake about it: Logroño is a foodie's delight. There are a number of very good restaurants and then there are the *pintxos* – few cities have such a dense concentration of excellent *pintxo* bars. Most of the action takes place on Calle del Laurel and Calle de San Juan. *Pintxos* cost around €2 to €4, and most of the *pintxo* bars are open from about 8pm through to midnight, except on Monday.

Bar Torrecilla Pintxos €

(Calle del Laurel 15; pintxos from €2; ⊙1-4pm & 8-11pm) The best *pintxos* in town? You be the judge. Go for the pyramid of *jamón* or the mini-burgers, or anything else that strikes your fancy, at this modern bar on buzzing Calle del Laurel.

La Taberna del Laurel Pintxos €

(Calle del Laurel 7; pintxos from €2; ⊙noon-4pm & 8pm-late) The speciality at La Taberna del Laurel is *patatas bravas* (potatoes in a spicy tomato sauce). They're not just good: they're divine. The restaurant takes its name from its location on Calle del Laurel, informally known as the 'street of *pintxos*.'

La Taberna de Baco Pintxos €

(Calle de San Agustín 10; pintxos from €2) This popular bar has a list of around 40 different *pintxos*, including *bombitas* (potatoes stuffed with mushrooms) and toast topped with pâté, apple, goat cheese and caramel.

La Cocina de Ramon Spanish €€€

(☎941 28 98 08; www.lacocinaderamon.es; Calle de Portales 30; menús €28-37; ⊙1.30-4pm & 8.30-11pm Tue-Sat, 1.30-4pm Sun) It looks unassuming from the outside, but Ramon's mixture of high-quality, locally grown market-fresh produce and tried-and-tested family recipes gives this place a lot of fans. But it's not just the food that makes it so popular: the service is outstanding, and Ramon likes to come and explain the dishes to each and every guest.

ℹ️ INFORMATION

Tourist Office of La Rioja (☎941 29 12 60; www.lariojaturismo.com; Calle de Portales 50;

Vivanco (p277)

⊘9am-2pm & 5-8pm Mon-Fri, 10am-2pm & 5-8pm Sat, 10am-2pm & 5-7pm Sun Jul-Sep, shorter hours Oct Jun) This office can provide lots of information on both the city and La Rioja in general.

ℹ️ GETTING THERE & AROUND

There are no air links to the regional capital of Logroño, but trains and buses run regularly. If you arrive at the **train** or **bus station** (🖉941 23 59 83; Av de España 1), first head up Avenida de España and then Calle del General Vara de Rey until you reach the Espolón, a large, park-like square lavished with plane trees (and with an underground car park). The Casco Viejo starts just to the north.

Buses go to the following destinations: Bilbao (€14, 2¾ hour), Vitoria (€9, 2¼ hours), Haro (€6, 40 minutes), Pamplona (€9, 1¾ hours) and Santo Domingo de la Calzada (€3.50, 45 minutes).

By train, Logroño is regularly connected to the following: Bilbao (from €13.50, 2½ hours), Burgos (from €13, 2½ hours), Madrid (from €31, 3¼ hours) and Zaragoza (from €14, 2½ hours).

Laguardia

It's easy to spin back the wheels of time in the medieval fortress town of Laguardia, or the 'Guard of Navarra' as it was once appropriately known, sitting proudly on its rocky hilltop. The walled old quarter, which makes up most of the town, is virtually traffic-free and a sheer joy to wander around. As well as memories of long-lost yesterdays, the town further entices visitors with its wine-producing present and striking scenery.

◎ SIGHTS & ACTIVITIES

Maybe the most impressive feature of the town is the castle-like Puerta de San Juan, one of the most stunning city gates in Spain.

Iglesia de Santa
María de los Reyes   Church

(🖉945 60 08 45; Travesía Mayor 1; tours €2; ⊘guided tours 1.15am, 12.15pm, 1.15pm, 5pm & 6.30pm Mon-Fri in summer) The impressive Iglesia de Santa María de los Reyes has a breathtaking late 14th-century Gothic doorway, adorned with beautiful sculptures of

Laguardia

the disciples and other motifs. If the church doors are locked, pop down to the tourist office where you can get a key. Otherwise, guided tours (in Spanish) run throughout the day in summer.

Centro Temático
del Vino Villa Lucia   Museum

(☑945 60 00 32; www.villa-lucia.com; Carretera de Logroño; tours incl tasting €11; ☺11am-6.30pm Tue-Fri, 10.15am-6.30pm Sat, 11am-12.30pm Sun) Just outside Laguardia is this impressive wine museum and shop selling high-quality vino from small local producers. Museum visits are by guided tour only and include a tasting.

Bodegas Palacio   Winery

(☑945 60 01 51; www.bodegaspalacio.com; Carretera de Elciego; tours €5; ☺tours 1pm Mon-Sat, other times by appointment) Bodegas Palacio, only 1km from Laguardia on the Elciego road, runs tours in Spanish, English and German. Reservations are not essential, but they are a good idea, especially out of season. The same bodega also runs excellent wine courses. Check the website for more information.

✖ EATING

Restaurante
Amelibia   Spanish €€

(☑945 62 12 07; www.restauranteamelibia.com; Barbacana 14; menú del día €17; ☺1-3.30pm Sun-Mon & Wed-Thu, 1-3.30pm & 9-10.30pm Fri-Sat) This classy restaurant is one of Laguardia's highlights: stare out the windows at a view over the scorched plains and distant mountain ridges while dining on sublime traditional Spanish cuisine – the meat dishes in particular are of exquisitely high quality.

Castillo el
Collado Restaurant   Spanish €€

(www.hotelcollado.com; Paseo El Collado 1; menus from €25) There's an old-world feeling to the place, and classic Riojan dishes like roasted suckling pig. There's also an English-language menu, and, naturally, a great wine selection.

 Spanish Wine Classification

Spanish wine is subject to a complicated system of classification. If an area meets certain strict standards for a given period, covering all aspects of planting, cultivating and ageing, it receives Denominación de Origen (DO; Denomination of Origin) status. There are currently over sixty DO recognised wine-producing areas in Spain.

An outstanding wine region gets the much-coveted Denominación de Origen Calificada (DOC), a controversial classification that some in the industry argue should apply only to specific wines, rather than every wine from within a particular region. At present, the only DOC wines come from La Rioja and the small Priorat area in Catalonia.

Wine barrel
OLIVER STREWE / GETTY IMAGES ©

❶ INFORMATION

Tourist Office (☑945 60 08 45; www.laguardia-alava.com; Calle Mayor 52; ☺10am-2pm & 4-7pm Mon-Fri, 10am-2pm & 5-7pm Sat, 10.45am-2pm Sun) Has a list of local bodegas that can be visited.

❶ GETTING THERE & AWAY

Eight or nine daily buses leave Logroño for Vitoria (€8, 1½ hours), stopping in Laguardia (€3, 25 to 30 minutes) on the way. There's no bus station: buses stop at the covered shelters along the main road that runs through town, near the lookout point.

Battle of the Wine

The otherwise mild-mannered citizens of Haro go temporarily berserk during the **Batalla del Vino** (Wine Battle; www.batalladelvino.com; ☺29 Jun), squirting and chucking wine all over each other in the name of San Juan, San Felices and San Pedro. Plenty of it goes down the right way, too.

Batalla del Vino, Haro
IAKOV FILIMONOV / SHUTTERSTOCK ©

Haro

Despite its fame in the wine world, there's not much of a heady bouquet to Haro, the capital of La Rioja's wine-producing region. But the town has a cheerful pace and the compact old quarter, leading off Plaza de la Paz, has some intriguing alleyways with bars and wine shops aplenty.

There are plenty of wine bodegas in the vicinity of the town, some of which are open to visitors (almost always with advance reservation). The tourist office keeps a full list.

There are plenty of cafes and bars around Plaza de la Paz and the surrounding streets, and several good restaurants attached to hotels. During the weekends, there is often live music playing in venues.

❶ INFORMATION

Tourist Office (☏941 30 35 80; www.haro turismo.org; San Martín 26; ☺10am-2pm & 4-7pm Mon-Sat, 10am-2pm Sun mid-Jun–Sep, 10am-2pm Mon-Fri, 10am-2pm & 4-6pm Sat Oct–mid-Jun) A

couple of hundred metres along the road from Plaza de la Paz.

❶ GETTING THERE & AROUND

Regular trains connect Haro with Logroño (from €5.95, 40 minutes). Buses additionally serve Logroño, Nájera, Vitoria, Bilbao, Santo Domingo de la Calzada and Laguardia. The bus station, which has a small indoor space with a cafe, is located four to five blocks south of the historic centre. Walk along Avenida de la Rioja to get there.

Santo Domingo de la Calzada

Santo Domingo is small-town Spain at its very best. A large number of the inhabitants continue to live in the partially walled old quarter, a labyrinth of medieval streets where the past is alive and the sense of community is strong. It's the kind of place where you can be certain that the baker knows all his customers by name and that everyone will turn up for María's christening. Santiago-bound pilgrims have long been a part of the fabric of this town, and that tradition continues to this day, with most visitors being foot-weary pilgrims. All this helps to make Santo Domingo one of the most enjoyable places in La Rioja.

◎ SIGHTS

Catedral de Santo Domingo de la Calzada   Cathedral

(www.catedralsantodomingo.es; Plaza del Santo 4; adult/student/child €4/3/free; ☺10am-8.30pm Mon-Fri, 9am-7.10pm Sat, 9am-12.20pm & 1.45-7.10pm Sun Apr-Oct, shorter hours Nov-Mar) The morose, monumental cathedral and its attached museum glitter with the gold that attests to the great wealth the Camino has bestowed on otherwise backwater towns. An audioguide to the cathedral and its treasures is €1. Guided tours, including a night-time tour, are also available.

The cathedral's most eccentric feature is the white rooster and hen that forage in a

Catedral de Santo Domingo de la Calzada

glass-fronted cage opposite the entrance to the crypt (look up!). Their presence celebrates a long-standing legend, the Miracle of the Rooster, which tells of a young man who was unfairly executed only to recover miraculously, while the broiled cock and hen on the plate of his judge suddenly leapt up and chickened off, fully fledged.

❌ EATING

The food scene here isn't very exciting. There are a few lacklustre cafes and bars in the modern centre of town by the bus stop, and a few more near the cathedral.

❶ GETTING THERE & AWAY

Frequent buses run to Nájera (€1.60, 30 minutes) and onward to Logroño. The bus stop, where you'll find posted bus schedules, is located on Avenida Juan Carlos I (also known as Calle San Roque), just across the street from the historic centre.

Nájera

The main attraction of this otherwise unexciting town is the Gothic **Monasterio de Santa María la Real** (€3; ⊙10am-1pm & 4-7pm Tue-Sat, 10am-12.30pm & 4-6pm Sun), in particular its fragile-looking, early 16th-century cloisters.

You'll find a few simple bars and restaurants around the main plaza and its side streets, on the other side of the footbridge from the bus station.

❶ GETTING THERE & AROUND

Nájera's bus station is a travel hub: from here, you can catch buses to Haro, Santo Domingo de la Calzada and Logroño. Though the different companies' bus schedules are posted, they can be difficult to understand – and since the station is not staffed, there's no one to ask about departures and arrivals except other travellers. Even though you can go pretty much anywhere in the La Rioja region from here, it's wise to allow yourself plenty of time.

Monasterio de Yuso, San Millán de Cogolla

The bus station is located across the river from the monastery. To get to the town's main attraction, cross one of the pedestrian bridges behind the station, then follow the signs (or just look for the church's imposing outline).

San Millán de Cogolla

About 16km southwest of Nájera, the hamlet of San Millán de Cogolla, home to only a few hundred people, is set in a lush valley. Like Nájera, San Millán de Cogolla has a long and fascinating Jewish history that dates back to the 10th century. But most people come here to see two remarkable monasteries that helped give birth to the Castilian language. On account of their linguistic heritage and artistic beauty, they have been recognised as Unesco World Heritage Sites.

There are a few simple but worthwhile restaurants in the village, including a good one attached to San Millán de Cogolla's only *hostería*.

◉ SIGHTS

Monasterio de Yuso Monastery
(☑941 37 30 49; www.monasteriodesanmillan.
com; adult/child €6/2; ⊙10am-1.30pm &
4-6.30pm Tue-Sun) The Monasterio de Yuso,
sometimes called El Escorial de La Rioja,
contains numerous treasures in its museum. You can only visit as part of a guided
tour (in Spanish only; non-Spanish speakers will be given an information sheet in
English and French). Tours last 50 minutes
and run every half-hour or so. In August it's
also open on Mondays.

Monasterio de Suso Monastery
(☑941 37 30 82; www.monasteriodesanmillan.
com/suso; €4; ⊙9.30am-1.30pm & 3.30-6.30pm
Tue-Sun) Built above the caves where San
Millán once lived, the Monasterio de Suso
was consecrated in the 10th century. It's
believed that in the 13th century a monk
named Gonzalo de Berceo wrote the first
Castilian words here. It can only be visited
on a guided tour. Tickets must be bought in

advance and include a short bus ride up to the monastery.

You can reserve tickets by calling ahead, or you can pick them up at the very helpful tourist office at the Monasterio de Yuso. Maps detailing short walks in the region can also be obtained at the tourist office.

ⓘ GETTING THERE & AWAY

Most travellers drive here. The village is located about an hour's drive west of La Rioja via the A12.

Arnedillo

The delightful spa village of Arnedillo, surrounded by slowly eroding hills, terraced in olive groves and watched over by circling hawks and vultures, is an ideal place to spend a peaceful day or two walking and dinosaur hunting. It's famous for the warm thermal waters known as Las Fuentes de Arnedillo. Just beyond Arnedillo is the hamlet of Peroblasco, confidently perched on the crown of a hill and well worth a wander.

In addition to a few restaurants and bars in town, there are restaurants at many area wineries.

A good bet for steaks, fish, and classic Spanish dishes, **Bar Restaurante La Pista** (www.restaurantelapista.es; Av del Cidacos 32; mains €10-15; ⊙9am-11pm) is a favourite with locals and Spanish tourists passing through wine country.

ⓘ GETTING THERE & AWAY

Most visitors arrive here in their own cars. Arnedillo is a 66km drive southeast of Logroño via N-232a.

Hunting for Dinosaurs

For those with their own transport, heading south of Logroño towards Soria via Arnedo and Arnedillo leads through some stunning semi-desert countryside riven by red-tinged gorges. Today eagles and vultures are commonly seen prowling the skies. But if you had been travelling these parts some 120 million years ago, it wouldn't have been vultures you'd need to keep an eye out for but prowling tyrannosauruses. The dinosaurs are long gone, but if you know where to look, you can still find clues to their passing.

A short way south of Arnedillo is the small and pretty hill village of Enciso, which is the centre of Jurassic activity in these parts. **El Barranco Perdido** (☑941 39 60 80; www.barrancoperdido.com; Carretera Navalsaz; over 12yr/4-12yr from €20/15; ⊙11am-8pm, shorter hours Sep-May) is a dino theme park containing a museum with complete dinosaur skeletons, various climbing frames, zip-wire slides and an outdoor swimming-pool complex. The real highlight of a visit to Enciso, though, is the chance to see some real-life dinosaur footprints scattered across former mudflats (now rock slopes) in the surrounding countryside. The nearest prints can be found just a kilometre or so east of El Barranco Perdido and the village – look for the terrifying T-Rex and dippy diplodocus on the hillside and you're in the right place.

Further dinosaur footprints can be found – get hold of a map indicating sites from any nearby tourist office.

Dinosaur footprint, Enciso

THE
PYRENEES

The Pyrenees at a Glance...

The crenellated ridges of the Pyrenees fill Spain's northern horizon, offering magnificent scenery, medieval stone-built villages, ski resorts and great walking. From Navarra in the west to Catalonia in the east, this dramatic mountain range is awash in greens and often concealed in mists. Each region has its calling card, from the prim Basque pueblos (villages) of Navarra to the stunning Romanesque churches of Catalonia. Beyond, where the paved road ends and narrow hiking trails take over, two national parks are the jewel in the Pyrenean crown – Catalonia's Parc Nacional d'Aigüestortes i Estany de Sant Maurici and Aragón's Parque Nacional de Ordesa y Monte Perdido.

The Pyrenees in Three Days

With just three days, focus your attention on the **Catalan Pyrenees** (p294), spending a day on foot exploring the **Parc Nacional d'Aigüestortes i Estany de Sant Maurici** (p290), and another day meandering among the Romanesque churches around **Boí-Taüll** (p295). On your third day, head over to Aragón to spend a night in **Aínsa** (p301), a lovely stone village with fine Pyrenean views.

The Pyrenees in One Week

Add to your three-day itinerary an extra day in Catalonia around the **Parc Natural de la Zona Volcànica de la Garrotxa** (p305), and a day's hiking in Aragón's **Parque Nacional de Ordesa y Monte Perdido** (p292). Also factor in a night each in **Sos del Rey Católico** (p303) and **Torla** (p300), plus many pleasurable hours driving quiet Pyrenean back roads, spilling over into the valleys of **Navarra** (p305).

Arriving in the Pyrenees

Almost everyone arrives in the Pyrenees with their own car. The nearest international airports, a day's drive away, are in Zaragoza, Girona and Barcelona. From here, you can reach many of the villages by bus, but you'll miss the best the region has to offer if you don't get behind the wheel yourself.

Sleeping

The Aragonese Pyrenees has the largest selection of accommodation, especially in Aínsa and Torla. Down-to-earth *hostales* (budget hotels) or *casas rurales* (rural homes) lie scattered throughout the smaller villages. Ski area towns have more modern ski-lodge accommodation, while *refugios* (mountain huts) service hikers in the mountains. Accommodation is open pretty much year-round, expect for in ski towns.

ARCAS / GETTY IMAGES ©

Parc Nacional d'Aigüestortes i Estany de Sant Maurici

There are few more beautiful national parks in Europe: the park's rugged terrain sparkles with hundreds of lakes and countless streams and waterfalls, combined with a backdrop of pine and fir forests.

Great For...

☑ Don't Miss

Estany Llong, a natural amphitheatre at the heart of the park.

Sculpted by glaciers over two million years, the park is essentially two U-shaped, east–west valleys that begin at an altitude of 1600m and don't stop until they reach the dizzy heights of close to 3000m. Against its backdrop of jagged granite shards and transparent mountain waters, forests of pine and fir and high mountain pastures carpeted with wildflowers in spring, are found natural features with mythical names like Agujas Perdut (Lost Peaks) and Estany Perdut (Lost Lake). There's even a 600-year-old black pine tree with a birth date that predates Columbus.

You could cross the park in a day – it's a 30km hike between Boí and Espot – but you don't have to go to such lengths to enjoy the park's best scenery and you'll be amply rewarded if you spend your day

Estany Llong

Parc Nacional d'Aigüestortes
i Estany de Sant Maurici

Espot ⊙
(1300m)

⊙ Boí (1240m)

ℹ️ Need to Know

You'll need your own vehicle to reach gateway towns. Taxis run into the park from Boí (p294).

✕ Take a Break

In Taüll, **Sedona** (p295) serves Catalan dishes and tapas.

★ Top Tip

Stay at least one night in Taüll, a gorgeous mountain village.

exploring Llong and Llobreta, the two main valleys in the park's west.

Estany Llong

Estany Llong, in the heart of the park, captures the essence of the park's appeal with lammergeiers invariably soaring high above on the thermals and the valley's bowl – at once vast and intimate – a natural amphitheatre. Climb the moraine off the lake's northeastern tip and watch for the fortress-like outcrops of Agujas Perdut away to the southeast. It's here that you'll find the iconic, 600-year-old black pine tree.

Estany Llobreta

On your way between Estany Llong and the valley of Llobreta, watch along the side of

the main trail for a celebrated dwarf pine growing out of a rock. There's a dramatic lookout where the road up from Taüll ends. Llobreta is fed by the Cascada de Sant Esperit (a waterfall) and its shoreline turns autumnal yellow in September.

Day Hikes

Numerous good walks of three to five hours return will take you up into spectacular side valleys from Estany de Sant Maurici or Aigüestortes.

From the eastern end of Estany de Sant Maurici, one path heads south 2.5km up the Monastero valley to Estany de Monastero (2171m), passing the two peaks of Els Encantats on the left. Another goes 3km northwest up by Estany de Ratero to Estany Gran d'Amitges (2350m).

From Planell Gran (1850m), 1km up the Sant Nicolau valley from Aigüestortes, a path climbs 2.5km southeast to Estany de Dellui (2370m). You can descend to Estany Llong (3km); it takes about four hours from Aigüestortes to Estany Llong.

Valle de Ordesa

GLENN VAN DER KNIJFF / GETTY IMAGES ©

Parque Nacional de Ordesa y Monte Perdido

This is where the Spanish Pyrenees really take your breath away. Shapely peaks rise to impossible heights. It's best explored on foot, but there are numerous fine vantage points for those on wheels.

Great For...

☑ Don't Miss

The view from the 13th-century Iglesia de San Salvador in Torla.

Your first sighting of Parque Nacional de Ordesa y Monte Perdido is one that never quite leaves you, evoking as it does the jagged ramparts of some hidden mountain kingdom. Perhaps it's the name – Monte Perdido translates as 'Lost Mountain' – that lends these mountains their cachet. Or perhaps it's because the park's impossibly steep summits and often-impassable mountain passes have always served as a barrier to France and to the rest of Europe, which lies just beyond, preserving until well into the 20th century that sense of Spain as a place apart. Then again, perhaps it's altogether simpler than that – this is one of Europe's most beautiful corners.

Challenging Hikes

The classic hike in this part of the Pyrenees is the Circo de Soaso, a difficult but infinite-

Iglesia de San Salvador (p300), Torla

❶ Need to Know

Torla, 3km southwest of the park, is the main gateway town.

✕ Take a Break

Restaurante el Duende (p301) in Torla serves fabulous meals.

★ Top Tip

At Easter and in summer, you can't drive beyond Torla; take the shuttle bus.

ly rewarding day walk (seven hours return, 15km) that follows the Valle de Ordesa to the Circo de Soaso, a rocky balcony whose centrepiece is the Cola del Caballo (Horsetail) waterfall. Another famous hike on the other side of the park is the Balcón de Pineta. This eight-hour-return hike begins close to the village of Bielsa and climbs via a series of steep switchbacks up to the 'Pineta Balcony' for stunning glacier and mountain views.

Pretty Drives

Numerous roads circle and dip into the park, so get a set of wheels and get ready to explore. Begin at ridge-top Aínsa, one of northern Spain's most beautiful stone villages, and drive north to Escalona where the road branches. First take the northern branch (turn right at the fork) for the drive up to Bielsa, from where a 12km paved road runs up the Valle de Pineta in the park's northeastern corner with stunning views all the way.

Return to Escalona, then follow the HU631 that runs, bucks and weaves west over the mountains to Sarvisé, crossing the park's southern tip in the process and passing through the dramatic, sinuous road through the Bellos Valley. If you're here from July to mid-September, or during Easter week, a one-way system operates on part of the Escalona–Sarvisé road. Continue on to Torla, then north to the Pradera de Ordesa, the starting point of so many trails and a pretty spot in the shadow of high mountains in its own right; in summer and at Easter, private vehicles cannot drive this road so take the shuttle bus.

JOHN ELK III / GETTY IMAGES ©

Wall mural, Sant Joan de Boí

The Catalan Pyrenees

Catalonia's Pyrenees are more than an all-season adventure playground. Certainly, the Val d'Aran draws skiers and snowboarders in winter, with resorts ranging from red-carpet to family-friendly. Summer and autumn lure hikers to the jewel-like lakes and valleys of the Parc Nacional d'Aigüestortes i Estany de Sant Maurici and the climbing terrain of the Serra del Cadí.

But there is also Catalan heritage to be discovered amid the breathtaking scenery. Centuries-old monasteries slumber in these mountains, meaning treks in the Pyrenees are as likely to bypass ruined Romanesque churches as offer a valley panorama. Taste buds yearning for more than hiking fodder will find satisfaction in the rich gastronomy of Garrotxa's volcanic zone. Beyond the big-ticket sights and major resorts, Catalonia's Pyrenees conceal a raw beauty that awaits discovery.

Boí

The valley location of petite Boí draws trekkers and winter-sports lovers, while its bell tower is one of the jewels of the region's Romanesque architecture. With its angular stone belltower, which was restored after a major fire in the 13th century, the 11th-century **Sant Joan de Boí** (€2; ⏰10am-2pm & 4-7pm Dec-Oct, to 8pm Jul & Aug) church gives an air of romance to the village. The wall paintings that brighten the interior are copies of the Romanesque originals, which are today preserved in Barcelona.

A handful of Catalan restaurants and grills keep outdoorsy visitors well fed, though many close their doors outside skiing and hiking seasons.

ⓘ INFORMATION

National Park Information Office (☎973 69 61 89; Carrer de les Graieres 2; ⏰9am-2pm & 3.30-5.45pm Mon-Sat, 9am-2pm Sun) Tourism hub with trekking and winter-sports information.

ⓘ GETTING THERE & AWAY

Buses between Barcelona/Lleida and Vielha stop at El Pont de Suert year-round. From here a daily hus runs to Boí (€1 to €1.75, 25 minutes), leaving in the afternoon on weekdays and in the morning on weekends. In summer, there's a daily park bus connecting Espot with Boí via Vielha. There are also nine-person **taxis** (Boí Jeep-Taxis; ☑973 69 63 14; www.taxisvalldeboi.com; Plaça del Treio, Boí; ☺8am-7pm summer, 9am-6pm rest of year) between Boí and the Parc Nacional d'Aigüestortes.

Taüll

Three kilometres uphill from Boí, Taüll is by far the most picturesque place to stay on the western side of the Parc Nacional d'Aigüestortes i Estany de Sant Maurici.

◎ SIGHTS

Sant Climent de Taüll   Church
(€5; ☺10am-2pm & 4-7pm, to 8pm Jul & Aug, closed Mon Nov) At the entrance to Taüll, this church is a gem not only for its elegant, simple lines and its slender six-storey bell-tower, but also for the art that once graced its interior. The central apse contains a copy of a famous 1123 mural that now resides in Barcelona's Museu Nacional d'Art de Catalunya. At the church's centre is a Pantocrator (Christ figure), whose rich Mozarabic-influenced colours, and expressive but superhuman features, have become a virtual emblem of Catalan Romanesque art. An audiovisual presentation gives background.

Santa Maria de Taüll   Church
(☺10am-7pm) `FREE` Up in the old village centre of Taüll and crowned with a five-storey tower, the original artwork from this 11th-century church has been whisked away to Barcelona (like many of the churches in the region).

✖ EATING

There is a handful of restaurants in the village, though some close their doors outside tourist season.

Sedona   International €
(☑973 69 62 54; Les Feixes 2; mains €10; ☺noon-4pm & 7-11.30pm Tue-Sun; 🛜🍴) Catalan fish dishes, Tex-Mex and mixed tapas

🏛 The Romanesque Churches of Boí-Taüll

The Vall de Boí, southwest of Parc Nacional d'Aigüestortes i Estany de Sant Maurici, is dotted with some of Catalonia's loveliest Romanesque churches – unadorned stone structures sitting in the crisp alpine air. Together these 11th- to 14th-century constructions were declared a Unesco World Heritage Site in 2000. Start your architectural odyssey with a visit to the interpretation centre, **Centre del Romànic de la Vall de Boí** (☑973 69 67 15; www.centreromanic.com; Carrer del Batalló 5, Erill la Vall; €2; ☺9am-2pm & 5-7pm Easter–mid-Oct). There is a small art collection and you can organise guided church tours and buy combined tickets (three churches for €7). Two of the finest churches are in Taüll, 3km east of Boí. Other worthwhile Romanesque churches are at Barruera (Sant Feliu) and Durro (Nativitat).

The Romanesque churches in Vall de Boí and around are now largely free of adornment, but they used to sport beautiful 12th- and 13th-century frescoes, such as the rather severe Christ from the Sant Climent church in Taüll. But when art nouveau came into being, those frescoes suddenly became ultra-fashionable and there was a danger that foreigners would make off with them (in fact, some had). To prevent this happening, they were instead painstakingly removed and taken to the Museu Nacional d'Art de Catalunya in Montjuïc, Barcelona, where they reside still.

Altar mural, Santa Maria de Taüll
JOHN ELK III / GETTY IMAGES ©

pile the plates at this food and après-ski hang-out.

❶ GETTING THERE & AWAY

Buses from Barcelona (€34.90, five to six hours, seven daily) and Lleide (€13.90, 2½ to three hours, four or five daily) go to Vielha via El Pont de Suert, year-round. From here, irregular local buses reach Taüll. Driving is a much better option.

Espot

Scenic Espot is an excellent gateway to exploring the Parc Nacional d'Aigüestortes i Estany de Sant Maurici, which begins 4km west of this little town. Stone buildings add charm to Espot, which is well-equipped with places to eat and stay, while mountain views from the town centre will make you eager to lace up your hiking boots.

The road into Espot from the C13, joining Carrer Barranco Solau, is the town's main drag with a small choice of restaurants and fast-food places. A popular spot on the main square **Restaurant Juquim** (📞973 62 40 09; Plaća San Martí 1; mains €11-20; ⊗12.45-

4pm & 7.30-10.30pm, closed Tue mid-Oct–May) has a varied menu concentrating largely on filling country food, with generous winter warmers like pig's trotters slathered in garlic and olive oil, or *civet de senglar* (wild boar stew). The adjacent **bar** (⊗8am-11pm Thu-Tue) does simpler fare and sandwiches.

Otherwise, some of the best food locally is found in hotel restaurants.

❶ INFORMATION

National Park Information Office (📞973 62 40 36; www.gencat.cat/parcs/aiguestortes; Carrer de Sant Maurici 5; ⊗9am-2pm & 3.30-5.45pm Mon-Sat, 9am-2pm Sun) Find hiking tips, maps, transport advice and more in this helpful tourist office.

❶ GETTING THERE & AWAY

ALSA (www.alsa.es) buses headed to Esterri d'Áneu from Barcelona (€38.50, five hours, one daily) and Lleida (€13.10, three hours, three daily) stop at the Espot turn-off on the C13. From there it's a 7km uphill walk to Espot.

Monestir de Santa Maria

You can visit the Parc Nacional d'Aigüestortes with a little help from a fleet of 25 **4WDs** (Fspot Jeep-Taxis; ☑973 62 41 05; www.taxisespot.com; ⊙8am-7pm summer, 9am-6pm rest of year) with fixed-rate tours to the park, lake and beyond.

Val d'Aran

Catalonia's northernmost region, famous for its plunging valleys and snowy peaks, is an adventure playground for skiers and snowboarders. Baqueira-Beret's pistes lure the winter-sports jet-set. Meanwhile, charming villages like Salardú enchant hikers with views of cloud-scraping mountains. From Aran's pretty side valleys, walkers can go over the mountains in any direction, notably southward to the Parc Nacional d'Aigüestortes i Estany de Sant Maurici.

Thanks in part to its geography, Aran's native language is not Catalan but Aranese (Aranés), which is a dialect of Occitan or the *langue d'oc*, the old Romance language of southern France.

Ripoll

With an impressive monastery at Ripoll's heart, and another close by in tiny Sant Joan de les Abadesses, this otherwise unremarkable town is a worthy stopover for admirers of Romanesque art.

Ripoll can claim, with some justice, to be the birthplace of Catalonia. In the 9th century it was the power base from which local strongman Guifré el Pilós (Wilfred the Hairy) succeeded in uniting several counties of the Frankish March along the southern side of the Pyrenees. Guifré went on to become the first in a line of hereditary counts of Barcelona. To encourage re-population of the Pyrenean valleys, he founded the Monestir de Santa Maria, the most powerful monastery of medieval Catalonia – and was buried there after death.

Ripoll is well situated for rambling the dormant volcanoes of Garrotxa, 30km east, or the vertiginous hiking and skiing terrain around the Vall de Ribes, 13km north.

Consecrated in AD 888, the **Monestir de Santa Maria** (www.monestirderipoll.cat; Plaça

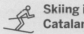

Skiing in the Catalan Pyrenees

Baqueira-Beret-Bonaigua Ski Resort
(www.baqueira.es; day lift pass adult/child €49/27.50; ⊙late Nov-early Apr) Pound the pistes at Catalonia's top winter-sports resort, beloved of Spanish royals, European celebrities and loyal skiers. Its quality lift system gives access to pistes totalling around 150km (larger than any other Spanish resort), amid fine scenery at between 1500m and 2510m.

Boí-Taüll Ski Resort (www.boitaullresort.com; day pass adult/child €39/29; ⊙Dec-early Apr) High up at altitudes from 2020m to 2751m, this medium-sized ski resort has 45km of pistes, including a few slopes suitable for beginners and plenty more to please intermediate and advanced skiers and snowboarders. There is also a freestyle area and snowpark for practising those jumps.

Núria Ski Resort (☑972 73 20 20; www.valldenuria.cat/hivern; day lift pass with train adult/child €27/20.20; ⊙Dec-Mar; 🚠) In winter, Núria transforms into a small-scale ski resort with 11 short runs. Much of the terrain is geared towards beginners, though there are two red (intermediate) and black (advanced) slopes to keep more experienced skiers and boarders busy for an afternoon. There's also a separate kids' activity area with tobogganing in winter and pony rides in summer.

Baqueira-Beret-Bonaigua ski resort

Dragons, Giants & Big-Heads

Fire and fireworks play a big part in many Spanish festivals, but Catalonia adds a special twist with the *correfoc* (fire-running), in which devil and dragon figures run through the streets spitting fireworks at the crowds.

Correfocs are often part of the *festa major* (a town or village's main annual festival), which usually takes place in July or August. Part of the *festa major* fun are the *sardana* (Catalonia's national folk dance) and *gegants* (splendidly attired 5m-high giants that parade through the streets or dance in the squares). Giants tend to come in male-and-female pairs, such as a medieval king and queen. Almost every town and village has its own pair, or up to six pairs, of giants. They're accompanied by grotesque 'dwarfs' (known as *capsgrossos*, or 'big-heads').

On La Nit de Sant Joan (23 June), big bonfires burn at crossroads and town squares in a combined midsummer and St John's Eve celebration, and fireworks explode all night. The supreme fire festival is the Patum in Berga, 30km west of Ripoll. An evening of dancing and firework-spitting angels, devils, mulelike monsters, dwarfs, giants and men covered in grass culminates in a mass frenzy of fire and smoke. Patum happens on Corpus Christi (the Thursday 60 days after Easter Sunday).

Correfoc participant
OSCAR SÁNCHEZ PHOTOGRAPHY / GETTY IMAGES ©

de l'Abat Oliba; adult/child €5.50/2.75; ⊙10am-2pm & 4-7pm Mon-Sat, 10am-2pm Sun Apr-Sep, 10am-1.30pm & 3.30-6pm Mon-Sat, 10am-2pm Sun Oct-Mar) was Catalonia's spiritual and cultural heart from the mid-10th to mid-11th centuries. The five-naved basilica was adorned in about 1100 with a stone portal that ranks among the most splendid Romanesque art in Spain. The well-restored basilica interior has admirable floor mosaics, a display about the Bibles of Ripoll (rare illustrated manuscripts created between AD 1008 and 1020), and the tomb of Guifré el Pilós, who founded the monastery.

ℹ INFORMATION

Tourist Office (☑972 70 23 51; www.ripoll.cat/turisme; Plaça del Abat Oliba; ⊙10am-1.30pm & 3.30-6pm Mon-Sat, to 7pm summer, 10am-2pm Sun) Next door to the Monestir de Santa Maria. Opening hours vary seasonally.

ℹ GETTING THERE & AWAY

Daily rodalies trains (line R3) run from Ripoll to Barcelona (€8.40, two hours, 12 to 16 daily) via Vic (€4.10, 40 minutes). Heading north from Ripoll, trains reach Ribes de Freser (€2.50, 20 minutes, up to seven daily) and Puigcerdà (€4.90, one hour, seven daily).

Sant Joan de les Abadesses

Sleepy Sant Joan de les Abadesses, 10km northeast of Ripoll, entices travellers with its splendid Romanesque **Monestir de Sant Joan de les Abadesses** (www.monestirsantjoanabadesses.cat; Plaça de l'Abadia; €3; ⊙10am-2pm & 4-6pm Mon-Sat Mar-Oct, 10am-2pm Mon-Sat Nov-Feb) and dark tales that swirl through the surrounding hills.

Who gallops through the hills around Sant Joan de les Abadesses on stormy nights, engulfed in flames and accompanied by ravenous black dogs? If you believe the stories, it's the legendary cursed Count Arnau, whose association with the monastery has bequeathed it a heritage of brooding fairy tales alongside its centuries of spiritual activity. The monastery is worth a visit for both its architectural treasures and the count's legend, richly illustrated in a permanent display.

Aside from the monastery and some pleasant biking and hiking terrain – walkers should seek out the pretty Gorg de Malatosca – there is little to detain you long in this tiny town.

ℹ️ INFORMATION

Tourist Office (☑972 72 05 99; Plaça de l'Abadia; ⏰10am-2pm & 4-7pm Mon-Sat, 10am-2pm Sun) This tourist office is tucked within the monastery complex.

ℹ️ GETTING THERE & AWAY

Sant Joan de les Abadesses is 10km east of Ripoll on the N260 to Olot; there is a small free car park for tourists just north of the main road, signposted as you enter the town centre. **Teisa** (www.teisa-bus.com) operates buses more than hourly weekdays and twice-hourly at weekends from Ripoll (€1.95, 15 minutes).

Vall de Núria & Ribes de Freser

A trio of little towns populate the Vall de Ribes and Vall de Núria, southeast of Cerdanya and north of Ripoll. Here spectacular ragged hills, pine forests and plummeting dales are squeezed between the Serra Cavallera and Serra de Montgrony ranges, rippling north to the Capçaleres del Ter i del Freser mountains. Sheltered within the Vall de Ribes is the small but well-equipped town of Ribes de Freser, 13km north of Ripoll. A further 6km north lies Queralbs, a charming stone village perched at an altitude of 1180m. Beyond here, and accessible only by *cremallera* (rack railway), is Núria (1960m to 2252m). This lofty valley holds the sanctuary of the Mare de Déu de Núria icon, though in winter it draws as many winter-sports devotees as pilgrims. Reaching Núria by *cremallera* is a worthy day trip for its views alone as it rattles past lichen-streaked rubble, waterfalls, patches of forest and gaping valleys.

🎯 SIGHTS

Santuari de la Mare de Déu   Church
(www.valldenuria.cat; Núria; ⏰8am-6.30pm) **FREE**

Monestir de Sant Joan de les Abadesses

TEOCARAMEL / GETTY IMAGES ©

From left: Aínsa; Vall de Núria (p299); Torla

The sanctuary (1911) sits incongruously in the centre of a building (now a hotel) that emits an unfortunate boarding-school vibe. A pastel-painted passageway trimmed with gold leads visitors from the main church to the upper level, housing the Mare de Déu de Núria behind a glass screen above the altar. Mary, with a regal expression, sits in star-spangled robes, clasping a grown-up Jesus. The icon is in 12th-century Romanesque style, despite believers insisting that Sant Gil sculpted it back in AD 700.

🛈 INFORMATION

Núria Tourist Office (☎972 73 20 20; www.valldenuria.com; Núria; ⏱8.30am-4.45pm) This tourist info place within Núria's sanctuary is open extended hours during high season.

🛈 GETTING THERE & AWAY

There are two train stations in Ribes de Freser. Ribes-Enllaç, just south of town, has connecting trains to Barcelona (€9.10, two to 2½ hours, seven daily) and Ripoll (€2.50, 20 minutes, seven daily).

The Aragonese Pyrenees

The Aragonese Pyrenees are well over the 3000m mark and among the most dramatic peaks of the range. And the villages here are some of the prettiest in this corner of the country.

Torla

Torla is a lovely Alpine-style village of stone houses with slate roofs, although it does get overrun in July and August. Walkers use Torla as a gateway to the national park, but the setting is also delightful, with the houses clustered above the Río Ara under a backdrop of the national park's mountains. In your ramblings around town, make for the 13th-century Iglesia de San Salvador; there are fine views from the small park on the church's northern side.

For simple home-style dishes such as *jarretes* (hock of ham), the speciality of this bustling local bar and restaurant, try **La Brecha** (☎974 48 62 21; www.lucienbriet.com; Calle Francia; mains €8-10; ⏱1.30-4pm & 8-10.30pm). Don't forget to sample the

JOSE LLEDO / SHUTTERSTOCK ©

homemade *pacharan* (traditional local liq-
uoeur said to help with digestion). It's open
all year – another bonus.

For food you'll want to photograph, served
out of a building you'll probably want to
photograph also, **Restaurante el Duende**
(📞974 48 60 32; www.elduenderestaurante.com;
Calle de la Iglesia; mains €15-22; ⏱1.30-3.30pm
& 8-10.30pm) just might inspire that mythical
spirit flamenco aficionados know as *duende*.
Encased in a 19th-century building made
from local stone and serving a variety fantastic meats right off the grill, it's undoubtedly the best restaurant in town.

ℹ️ INFORMATION

Centro de Visitantes de Torla (📞974 48 64
72; ⏱9am-2pm & 4.15-7pm Apr-Oct, 8am-3pm
Nov-Mar)

ℹ️ GETTING THERE & AWAY

One daily bus operated by **Alosa** (📞902 21 07
00; www.alosa.es) connects Torla to Aínsa (€4.30,
one hour).

Aínsa

The beautiful hilltop village of medieval
Aínsa, which stands above the small modern
town of the same name, is one of Aragón's
gems, a medieval masterpiece hewn from
uneven stone. From its perch, you'll have
commanding panoramic views of the mountains, particularly the great rock bastion of
La Peña Montañesa.

◎ SIGHTS

Simply wander down through the village
along either Calle de Santa Cruz or Calle
Mayor, pausing in the handful of artsy shops
en route; note the drain pipes carved into
the shape of gargoyles.

Castle   Castle
(⏱7am-11pm) **FREE** The castle and fortifica-
tions off the western end of the Plaza de
San Salvador mostly date from the 1600s,
though the main tower is 11th century;
there are some reasonable views from the
wall. It contains an **Ecomuseo** (€4; ⏱11am-
2pm & 4-8pm) on Pyrenean fauna with an
aviary that is 'home' to various

A Drive North of Sos del Rey Católico

From just north of Sos, the engaging A1601 begins its 34km-long snaking journey west and then northwest en route to the N240. It passes the pretty villages of Navardún and Urriés, before climbing over the Sierra de Peña Musera and down to the gorgeous abandoned village of Ruesta – medieval murals from the ruined church here can be viewed at Jaca's fine **Museo Diocesano** (Museum of Sacred Art; www.diocesisdejaca. org; Plaza de la Catedral; adult/concession €6/4.50; ⊙10am-1.30pm & 4-7pm Tue-Sat, 10am-1.30pm Sun). The final stretch passes some unusual rock formations and wheat fields, with fine views of the hilltop village of Milanos away to the east.

Ruesta
AGUSTIN PEÑA - RASPAKAN32 / GETTY IMAGES ©

rescued birds of prey, including the majestic *quebrantahuesos* (bearded vulture), and the **Espacio del Geoparque de Sobrarbe** (www.geoparquepirineos.com; ⊙9.30am-2pm & 4.30-7.30pm) **FREE** with displays on the region's intriguing geology, as well as good views from the tower.

Iglesia de Santa María   Church
(belfry €1; ⊙belfry 11am-1.30pm & 4-7pm Sat & Sun) Aínsa's main church – austere and sober by Spanish standards – bears all the hallmarks of unadulterated Romanesque. Few embellishments mark its thick, bare walls which date from the 11th century. Don't leave without exploring the crypt and the belfry.

⊗ EATING

In summer, there are plenty of outdoor tables around Plaza Mayor, a delightful place to eat in the cool of the evening, although prices can be steep.

L'Alfil   Tapas €
(Calle Traversa; raciones €5.80-18.50; ⊙11am-4pm & 7pm-midnight Thu-Tue May-Oct, shorter hours Nov-Apr) This pretty little cafe-bar, with floral accompaniment to its outside tables, is in a side street along from the church. It has a whole heap of *raciones* that are more creative than you'll find elsewhere, from ostrich chorizo, snails and deer sausage to wild-boar pâté and cured duck. Also specialises in local herbal liquors.

Bodegas del Sobrarbe   Aragonese €€
(☏974 50 02 37; www.bodegasdelsobrarbe.com; Plaza Mayor 2; mains €18-22; ⊙noon-4pm & 8-11pm) Unless you're a vegetarian, you won't want to wave *adiós* to Aragon before you've tasted the local lamb, known as *ternasco*, which is slow-roasted and best served with some Pyrenean mushrooms and/or *patatas a lo pobre* (potatoes sautéed with onions and garlic). Bodegas del Sobrarbe overlooking Aínsa's archaic main square is a fine place to try it.

Restaurante Callizo   Contemporary Spanish €€€
(☏974 50 03 85; Plaza Mayor; set menus €25-42; ⊙1-3pm & 7-11pm Tue-Sat, 1-4pm Sun) Tap a local and they'll probably tell you this is the best place in town, if not the region. It pulls off that difficult trick off marrying Aragonese tradition with modern gastronomic theatre. The result: a true eating experience, especially if you opt for the five-course tasting menu. Typical dishes include wild boar and roast suckling lamb, as well as a few fish dishes.

❶ INFORMATION

Municipal Tourist Office (☏974 50 07 67; www. ainsasobrarbe.net; Avenida Pirenáica 1; ⊙10am-

2pm & 4-7.30pm) Located in the new town down the hill.

Regional Tourist Office (📞974 50 05 12; www. turismosobrarbe.com; Plaza del Castillo 1, Torre Nordeste; ⊘9.30am-2pm & 4-7pm Sun-Thu, 9.30am-2pm & 4.30-7.30pm Sun) The extremely helpful regional tourist office is within the castle walls.

🛈 GETTING THERE & AWAY

Alosa (📞902 21 07 00; www.alosa.es) runs daily buses to/from Barbastro (€5.90, one hour) and Torla (€4.30, one hour).

Sos del Rey Católico

If King Fernando II of Aragon were reincarnated in the 21st century, he'd probably still recognise his modest birthplace in Sos del Rey Católico. Take away the petrol station and the smattering of parked Peugeots and Fiats, and little has changed in this small, tightly packed hilltop village since 1452, when the future king of a united Spain was born in the Sada palace. Legend has it that Fernando's mother risked going into labor by travelling on horseback from nearby Navarra (5km away as the crow flies), purely to ensure her son was born Aragonese.

Royalty aside, Sos is a fine place to soak up the tranquil essence of Aragonese village life. When you've finished having historical hallucinations in its labyrinthine streets, you can investigate the intricate network of mossy walking paths that dissolve into the surrounding countryside.

⊙ SIGHTS

Casa Palacio de Seda
Historic Building

(Plaza de la Hispanidad; adult/child €2.90/1.90, incl tour of village €4.90/2.90; ⊘10am-1pm & 4-7pm Tue-Fri, 10am-2pm & 4-7pm Sat & Sun) Fernando is said to have been born in this building in 1452. It's an impressive noble mansion, which now contains an interpretative centre, with fine exhibits on the history of Sos and the life of the king. The tourist office, also housed here, runs guided tours of the building.

Sos del Rey Católico

ASIFE / GETTY IMAGES ©

Valle del Baztán

Iglesia de San Esteban   Church
(€1; ⊙10am-1pm & 3.30-5.30pm) This Gothic church with a weathered Romanesque portal, has a deliciously gloomy crypt decorated with medieval frescoes.

Castillo de la Peña Feliciano   Ruin
The 12th-century watchtower is all that remains of the castle that once guarded the frontier between the two Christian kingdoms of Aragón and Navarra. Climb up for views of the countryside in all directions.

⊗ EATING

La Cocina
del Principal   Aragonese €€
(☑948 88 83 48; www.lacocinadelprincipal.com; Calle Fernando el Católico 13; mains €14-17.50; ⊙1.30-3.30pm & 8.30-10.30pm Tue-Sat) Generally hailed as having the best food in town, this place wins plaudits for its rib-eye steak, apple-doused veal, and pig's trotters. The setting, inside a typically medieval Sos house, is enhanced by some interesting art, including a graffiti-etched rendering of Goya's *Third of May* masterpiece hung up on the stairway.

Vinacua   Aragonese €€
(www.vinacua.com; Calle Goya 24; mains €8-16, set menus €12-20; ⊙1-3.30pm & 9-11pm Mon-Fri, 1.30-3.30pm Sat & Sun; ⊛) Hearty local cuisine is served in a contemporary space with raspberry-pink walls and glossy-black furnishings. The menu includes rabbit with snails, *garbanzo* (chickpea) stew, grilled meats and, for lightweights, some excellent salads with toppings like warm goat's cheese or partridge and pâté.

❶ INFORMATION

Tourist Office (☑948 88 85 24; Plaza Hispanidad; ⊙10am-2pm & 4-8pm) Housed in the Casa Palacio de Seda, the tourist office runs twice-daily guided tours (one/two hours €2.90/4.90) of the village on weekends.

❶ GETTING THERE & AWAY

Autobuses CincoVillas (📞976 70 05 90; www.
autobusescincovillas.com) departs from Zaragoza (€10.50, 2½ hours) for Sos at 5pm Monday to
Friday. It returns from Sos at 7am.

The Navarran Pyrenees

Awash in greens and often concealed in
mists, the rolling hills, ribboned cliffs, clammy forests and snow-plastered mountains
that make up the Navarran Pyrenees are
a playground for outdoor enthusiasts.
They are, without doubt, some of the most
delightful and least exploited mountains in
Western Europe.

Navarra's most spectacular mountain
area is around the Valle del Roncal, an eastern valley made up of seven villages.

Valle del Baztán

This is the rural Pyrenees at its most
Basque, a landscape of splotchy reds and
greens. Minor roads take you in and out
of charming little villages, such as Arraioz,
known for the fortified Casa Jaureguizar, and
Ziga, with its 16th-century church.

Just beyond Irurita on the N121B is the
valley's biggest town, Elizondo, given a
distinctly urban air by its tall half-timbered
buildings. It's a good base for exploring the
area.

Beyond Elizondo, the NA2600 road
meanders dreamily amid picturesque farms,
villages and hills before climbing sharply to
the French border pass of Puerto de Izpegui,
where the world becomes a spectacular
collision of crags, peaks and valleys. At the
pass, you can stop for a short, sharp hike up
to the top of Mt Izpegui.

The N121B continues northwards to the
Puerto de Otxondo and the border crossing

🐦 Parc Natural de la Zona Volcànica de la Garrotxa

The hills around Olot are volcanic in
origin, making up the 120-sq-km Parc
Natural de la Zona Volcànica de la
Garrotxa. Volcanic eruptions began here
about 350,000 years ago; the last one
was 11,500 years ago. As the African
and Eurasian tectonic plates nudge ever
closer (at a rate of 2cm per year), the
occasional mild earthquake still sends
a shiver across Garrotxa. But the volcanoes have long snoozed under a blanket
of meadows and oak forests.

The park completely surrounds Olot,
but the most interesting area is between
Olot and the village of Santa Pau, 10km
southeast. In the park there are about
40 volcanic cones, up to 160m high and
1.5km wide. Together with the lush vegetation, a result of fertile soils and a damp
climate, these create a landscape of
verdant beauty. Between the woods are
crop fields, a few hamlets and scattered
old stone farmhouses and Romanesque
churches.

Hamlet located within the park

PILAR ANDREU ROVIRA / SHUTTERSTOCK ©

into France at Dantxarinea. Just before
the border, a minor road veers west to the
almost overly pretty village of Zugarramurdi.

In Focus

Port Vell, Barcelona (p70)

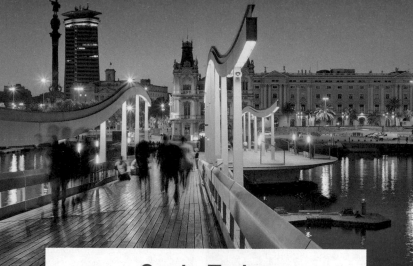

Spain Today

Spain has turned a corner. Unemployment may remain stubbornly high and the scars of a long, deep and profoundly damaging economic crisis may still be evident, but there is light at the end of the tunnel. The economy is making baby steps towards recovery, a new kind of politics is emerging and there is a widespread feeling that the worst may finally be over.

Economic Crisis

Spain's economy went into free fall in late 2008. Unemployment, which had dropped as low as 6% as Spain enjoyed 16 consecutive years of growth, rose above 26%, which equated to six million people, with catastrophic youth unemployment rates nudging 60%. Suicide rates were on the rise, Spain's young professionals fled the country in unprecedented numbers and Oxfam predicted that a staggering 18 million Spaniards – 40% of the population – were at risk of social marginalisation. Finally, in 2014, the tide began to turn.

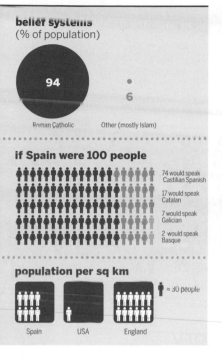

belief systems
(% of population)

94 — Roman Catholic

6 — Other (mostly Islam)

if Spain were 100 people

74 would speak Castilian Spanish

17 would speak Catalan

7 would speak Galician

2 would speak Basque

population per sq km

≈ 30 people

Spain   USA   England

That was the first year in seven in which the country enjoyed a full year of positive economic growth, and unemployment dipped below 25%. That this growth was largely fuelled by the increased spending of Spaniards led many to hope that life was improving for ordinary citizens. Spain remains a country in dire economic straits, and many Spaniards are still doing it tough. But most Spaniards think that the next decade will be better than the last.

A New Politics

Spain's political spoils have for decades been divided between the left (the Socialist Workers' Party, or PSOE) and the right (the conservative People's Party, or PP). Not any more. A radical shift in the way that Spain does politics began in Madrid on 15 May 2011, when IOS *indignados* ('the indignant ones' – a social movement) took over the iconic Plaza de la Puerta del Sol in the city centre with a peaceful sit-in protest. Maintaining popularity through social-media networks, they stayed for months, in what was the forerunner to numerous similar movements around the world, including Occupy Wall Street and its offshoots. In 2015, that groundswell of community activism took on the form of a revolution when left-leaning Podemos and the centrist Ciudadanos won scores of seats across the country, first in municipal and regional elections, and then nationally.

Uncertain Times

If there is a downside to Spain's bold new political future, it is the uncertainty that many Spaniards feel at a time when they need certainty the most. Bubbling away in the background is the issue of Catalan independence. In November 2014, a referendum organised by the Catalan regional government (but not recognised by Spain's national government or Spain's Constitutional Court) saw 80% vote in favour of independence; opinion polls suggest that any official referendum would be much closer. Catalonia's regional parliament promises to secede by mid-2017, though major political parties the PP and PSOE are threatening to block any such moves. At the same time, elections on 20 December 2015 produced no clear winners and negotiations for forming a new government dragged on well into 2016 before new elections were called. Exciting as it may be to see new voices emerging in the national debate, this political instability – which may well be the way of the future – has economists worried at a time when a steady hand is needed to help guide the Spanish economy towards prosperity.

History

Spain's story is one of Europe's grand epics. It is a tale shaped by ancient and not-so-ancient civilisations sweeping down through the Iberian Peninsula, and by the great ideological battles between Muslims and Christians of the Middle Ages. The 20th century was a match for anything that went before with civil war, dictatorship and a stunning return to democracy.

c 1.2 million BC	c 15,000–10,000 BC	218 BC
Europe's earliest-known humans leave their fossilised remains in the Sima del Elefante at Atapuerca, near the northern city of Burgos.	Palaeolithic hunters paint sophisticated animal images in caves at Altamira and other sites along Spain's northern coastal strip.	Roman legions arrive in Spain during the Second Punic War against Carthage, initiating the 600-year Roman occupation of the Iberian Peninsula.

Plaza Mayor (p40), Madrid

Ancient Civilisations

To the ancient Greeks and Romans, the dramatic limestone ridge at Gibraltar, together with Jebel Musa in Morocco, were the Pillars of Hercules and represented the limits of the known world. But the Phoenicians, who came before them, knew differently. From their base on what is now the southern coast of Lebanon, the seafaring Phoenicians were the first to rule the Mediterranean: in the 8th century BC, they established the port of Gadir, the site of modern Cádiz in southwestern Andalucía.

In the 7th century BC, Greek traders arrived along the Mediterranean coast and brought with them several things now considered quintessentially Spanish – the olive tree, the grapevine and the donkey – along with writing, coins, the potter's wheel and poultry. But the Romans, who ruled Hispania (as Roman Iberia was known) for 600 years until the 5th century AD, would go on to leave a far more lasting impression. By AD 50, most of Hispania had adopted the Roman way of life. The Romans gave the country a road system, aqueducts, temples,

AD 711	718	1218
Muslims invade Iberia from North Africa and become the dominant force for nearly four centuries, then a potent one for four centuries more.	Pelayo establishes the Kingdom of Asturias. With victory over a Muslim force at the Battle of Covadonga, Reconquista begins.	The University of Salamanca is founded by Alfonso IX, King of León, making it Spain's oldest and most prestigious university.

Seville (p175)

★ **Moorish Monuments**

Alhambra (p132), Granada

Mezquita (p198), Córdoba

Albayzín (p135), Granada

Alcázar (p180), Seville

Giralda (p179), Seville

MATTEO COLOMBO / GETTY IMAGES ©

theatres, amphitheatres and bathhouses, but they began the process of deforestation as they culled the extensive forests that in their time covered half the *meseta* (plateau; the high tableland of central Spain). Even more than these, their cultural impact was profound. They brought Christianity to Spain, planted olive trees on a massive scale, introduced olive oil production and may even have invented *jamón* (cured ham). The basis of most of the languages still spoken here – Castilian, Catalan, Galician and Portuguese – are versions of the vernacular Latin spoken by Roman legionaries and colonists, filtered through 2000 years of linguistic mutation. The Roman era also saw the arrival of Jewish people in Spain, who were to play a big part in Spanish life for more than 1000 years.

Islamic Spain

In AD 711, Tariq ibn Ziyad, the Muslim governor of Tangier, landed at Gibraltar with around 10,000 men, mostly Berbers (indigenous North Africans). Within a few years the Muslims (often referred to as Moors) had conquered the whole Iberian Peninsula, except small areas in the Asturian mountains in the north. Their advance into Europe was only checked by the Franks at the Battle of Poitiers in 732.

The name given to Muslim territory on the peninsula was Al-Andalus. Political power and cultural developments centred initially on Córdoba (756–1031), then Seville (c 1040–1248) and lastly Granada (1248–1492).

Muslim rule left an indelible imprint upon the country. Great architectural monuments such as the Alhambra in Granada and the Mezquita in Córdoba are the stars of the Moorish legacy, but thousands of other buildings large and small are Moorish in origin. The tangled, narrow street plans of many a Spanish town and village, especially in the south, date back to Moorish times, and the Muslims also developed the Hispano-Roman agricultural base by improving irrigation and introducing new fruits and crops, many of which are still widely grown today. The Spanish language contains many common words of Arabic origin, including the names

1229–38	1469	October 1492
Catalonia enjoys its golden age under King Jaume I of Aragón, who makes Catalonia the major power in the western Mediterranean.	Isabel, the 18-year-old heir to Castilla, marries 17-year-old Fernando, heir to Aragón, uniting Spain's two most powerful Christian states.	Christopher Columbus, funded by Isabel and Fernando, lands in the Bahamas, opening up the Americas to Spanish colonisation.

of some of those new crops – *naranja* (orange), *azúcar* (sugar) and *arroz* (rice). Flamenco, though brought to its modern form by Roma people in post-Moorish times, has clear Moorish roots. It was also through Al-Andalus that much of the learning of ancient Greece and Rome – picked up by the Arabs in the eastern Mediterranean – was transmitted to Christian Europe, where it would exert a profound influence on the Renaissance.

The Reconquista

The Christian Reconquest of Iberia began in about 718 at Covadonga, Asturias, and ended with the fall of Granada in 1492. It was a stuttering affair, conducted by Christian kingdoms that were as often at war with each other as with the Muslims.

An essential ingredient in the Reconquista was the cult of Santiago (St James), one of the 12 apostles. In 813 the saint's supposed tomb was discovered in Galicia. The city of Santiago de Compostela grew here, to become the third most popular medieval Christian pilgrimage goal after Rome and Jerusalem. Santiago became the inspiration and special protector of soldiers in the Reconquista, earning the sobriquet Matamoros (Moor-slayer). By 757, Christians occupied nearly a quarter of the Iberian Peninsula, although progress thereafter was slow.

The year 1212, when the combined Christian armies routed a large Muslim force at Las Navas de Tolosa in Andalucía, marked the beginning of the end for Islamic Al-Andalus. The royal wedding of Isabel (of Castilla) and Fernando (of Aragón) in 1469 united two of the most powerful Christian kingdoms, enabling the armies of the Reconquista to make a final push. On 2 January 1492, Isabel and Fernando entered Granada. The surrender terms were fairly generous to Boabdil, the last emir, who was given the Alpujarras valleys south of Granada and 30,000 gold coins. The remaining Muslims were promised respect for their religion, culture and property, but this promise was quickly discarded.

The Golden Age of Empire

Isabel and Fernando were never going to be content with Spain alone. In April 1492, Los

(i) The Spanish Inquisition

An ecclesiastical tribunal set up by Fernando and Isabel in 1478, the Spanish Inquisition in Al-Andalus focused first on *conversos* (Jews converted to Christianity), accusing many of continuing to practise Judaism in secret. In April 1492, Isabel and Fernando expelled all Jews who refused Christian baptism. Up to 100,000 converted, but some 200,000 (the first Sephardic Jews) fled into exile. The Inquisitors also carried out forced mass baptisms of Muslims, burnt Islamic books and banned the Arabic language. In 1500, Muslims were ordered to convert to Christianity or leave. Those who converted *(moriscos)* were later expelled between 1609 and 1614.

1512	**1521**	**1556–98**
Fernando, ruling as regent after Isabel's death, annexes Navarra, bringing all of Spain under one rule for the first time since the Romans.	Hernán Cortés, from Medellín, Extremadura, conquers the Aztec empire in present-day Mexico and Guatemala.	Reign of Felipe II; the zenith of Spanish power. Enormous wealth arriving from the colonies is used for grandiose architectural projects.

Gardens, Alhambra (p132), Granada

HAGENS WORLD PHOTOGRAPHY / GETTY IMAGES ©

★ **Civil War Reads**

For Whom the Bell Tolls, Ernest Hemingway

Homage to Catalonia, George Orwell

Blood of Spain, Ronald Fraser

The Spanish Civil War, Hugh Thomas

The Battle for Spain, Antony Beevor

Reyes Católicos (the Catholic Monarchs) granted the Genoese sailor Christopher Columbus (Cristóbal Colón to Spaniards) funds for his long-desired voyage across the Atlantic in search of a new trade route to the Orient. Columbus set off from the Andalucian port of Palos de la Frontera on 3 August 1492, with three small ships and 120 men.

After a near mutiny as the crew despaired of sighting land, they finally arrived on the island of Guanahaní, in the Bahamas, and went on to find Cuba and Hispaniola. Columbus returned to a hero's reception from the Catholic Monarchs in Barcelona, eight months after his departure.

Brilliant but ruthless conquistadors followed Columbus' trail, seizing vast tracts of the American mainland for Spain. By 1600 Spain controlled Florida, all the biggest Caribbean islands, nearly all of present-day Mexico and Central America, and a large strip of South America. The new colonies sent huge cargoes of silver, gold and other riches back to Spain. Seville enjoyed a monopoly on this trade and grew into one of Europe's richest cities.

Two Spains

Spain was united for the first time in almost eight centuries after Fernando annexed Navarra in 1512, and in 1519 Carlos I (Fernando's grandson) succeeded to the Habsburg lands in Austria and was elected Holy Roman Emperor (as Charles V). He ruled all of Spain, the Low Countries, Austria, several Italian states, parts of France and Germany, and the expanding Spanish colonies in the Americas.

But the storm clouds were brewing. Colonial riches lined the pockets of a series of backward-looking monarchs, a wealthy, highly conservative Church, and idle nobility. Although some of this wealth was used to foster the Golden Age of art, little was done to improve the lot of ordinary Spaniards and food shortages were rife. Spain's overseas possessions were ebbing away, but problems at home were even more pressing. In 1812 a national Cortes (parliament) meeting at Cádiz drew up a new liberal constitution for Spain, prompting a backlash from conservatives (the Church, the nobility and others who

1676	**1809–24**	**1881**
The devastation caused by the third great plague to hit Spain in a century is compounded by poor harvests.	Most of Spain's American colonies win independence as Spain is beset by problems at home.	The Partido Socialista Obrero Español (PSOE; Spanish Socialist Workers' Party) is founded in one of Madrid's most prestigious tapas bars.

preferred the earlier status quo) and liberals (who wanted vaguely democratic reforms). During the next century, Spain alternated between federal republic and monarchy, a liberal-conservative schism that saw the country lurch from one crisis to the next. By the 1930s, Spain was teetering on the brink of war.

The Spanish Civil War

On 17 July 1936, the Spanish army garrison in Melilla, North Africa, rose up against the left-wing government, followed the next day by garrisons on the mainland. The leaders of the plot were five generals, among them Francisco Franco, who on 19 July flew from the Canary Islands to Morocco to take charge of his legionnaires. The civil war had begun.

Wherever the blame lies, the civil war split communities, families and friends, killed an estimated 350,000 Spaniards (some historians put the number as high as 500,000), and caused untold damage and misery. Both sides (Franco's Nationalists and the left-wing Republicans) committed atrocious massacres and reprisals, and employed death squads to eliminate opponents. On 26 April 1937, German planes bombed the Basque town of Guernica (called Gernika in Basque), causing terrible casualties. The USSR withdrew their support from the war in September 1938, and in January 1939 the Nationalists took Barcelona unopposed. The Republican government and hundreds of thousands of supporters fled to France and, on 28 March 1939, Franco's forces entered Madrid.

Franco's Spain

Francisco Franco would go on to rule Spain with an iron fist for almost four decades until his death in 1975. An estimated 100,000 people were killed or died in prison after the war. The hundreds of thousands imprisoned included many intellectuals and teachers; others fled abroad, depriving Spain of a generation of scientists, artists, writers, educators and more. The army provided many government ministers and enjoyed a most generous budget. Catholic supremacy was fully restored, with secondary schools entrusted to the Jesuits, divorce made illegal and church weddings compulsory.

During WWII Franco flirted with Hitler (although Spain watched the war from the sidelines), but Spain was desperately poor to

👍 Why Madrid?

When Felipe II chose Madrid as Spain's capital in 1561, it was hardly the most obvious choice. Madrid (then with a population of 30,000) was much smaller and less powerful than Toledo and Seville (each with more than 80,000 people) or Valladolid, the capital of choice for Isabel and Fernando. Unlike other cities, however, Madrid was described by one king as 'very noble and very loyal': Felipe II chose the path of least resistance. Another reason was the location: 'a city fulfilling the function of a heart located in the middle of the body', as Felipe II was heard to say.

1936	1936–39	1939–50
Left-wing National Front wins a national election. Right-wing 'Nationalist' rebels led by General Francisco Franco rise against it, starting a civil war.	Spanish Civil War: Franco's Nationalist rebels, supported by Nazi Germany and Fascist Italy, defeat the USSR-supported Republicans.	Franco establishes a right-wing dictatorship, imprisoning hundreds of thousands of people.

The International Brigades

The International Brigades never numbered more than 20,000 and couldn't turn the tide against the better armed and organised Nationalist forces. Nazi Germany and Fascist Italy supported the Nationalists with planes, weapons and men (75,000 from Italy and 17,000 from Germany), turning the war into a testing ground for WWII. The Republicans had some Soviet planes, tanks, artillery and advisers, but the rest of the international community refused to become involved (apart from 25,000 French, who fought on the Republican side).

the extent that the 1940s are known as *los años de hambre* (years of hunger). Despite small-scale rebel activity, ongoing repression and international isolation (Spain was not admitted to the UN until 1955), an economic boom began in 1959 and would last through much of the 1960s. The recovery was funded in part by US aid, and remittances from more than a million Spaniards working abroad, but above all by tourism, which was developed initially along Andalucía's Costa del Sol and Catalonia's Costa Brava. By 1965 the number of tourists arriving in Spain was 14 million a year.

But with the jails still full of political prisoners and Spain's restive regions straining under Franco's brutal policies, labour unrest grew and discontent began to rumble in the universities and even in the army and Church. The Basque nationalist terrorist group Euskadi Ta Askatasuna (ETA; Basque Homeland and Freedom) also appeared in 1959. In the midst of it all, Franco chose as his successor Prince Juan Carlos. In 1969 Juan Carlos swore loyalty to Franco and the Movimiento Nacional, Spain's fascist and only legal political party. Franco died on 20 November 1975.

Spain's Democratic Transition

Juan Carlos I, aged 37, took the throne two days after Franco died. The new king's links with the dictator inspired little confidence in a Spain now clamouring for democracy, but Juan Carlos had kept his cards close to his chest and can take most of the credit for the successful transition to democracy that followed.

He appointed Adolfo Suárez, a 43-year-old former Franco apparatchik with film-star looks, as prime minister. To general surprise, Suárez got the Francoist-filled Cortes to approve a new, two-chamber parliamentary system, and in early 1977 political parties, trade unions and strikes were all legalised and the Movimiento Nacional was abolished. After elections in 1977, a centrist government led by Suárez granted a general amnesty

1955–65	1978	1986
Spain is admitted to the UN after agreeing to host US bases. The economy is boosted by US aid and mass tourism to the Costas.	A new constitution establishes Spain as a parliamentary democracy with no official religion and the monarch as official head of state.	Spain joins the European Community (now the EU), a turning point in the country's post-Franco international acceptance.

for acts committed in the civil war and under the Franco dictatorship. In 1978 the Cortes passed a new constitution making Spain a parliamentary monarchy with no official religion and granting a large measure of devolution to Spain's regions. Despite challenges such as the brutal campaign by ETA, which killed hundreds in the 1980s, and an unsuccessful coup attempt by renegade Civil Guards in 1981, Spain's democratic, semi-federal constitution and multiparty system have proved at once robust and durable.

Spain Grows Up

The 1980s saw Spain pass a succession of milestones along the road to becoming a mature European democracy. That they took these steps so quickly and so successfully after four decades of fascism is one of modern Europe's most remarkable stories.

In 1982 the left-of-centre Partido Socialista Obrero Español (PSOE; Spanish Socialist Workers' Party) was elected to power, led by a charismatic young lawyer from Seville, Felipe González. During its 14 years in power, the PSOE brought Spain into mainstream Europe, joining the European Community (now the EU) in 1986. It also oversaw the rise of the Spanish middle class, established a national health system and improved public education, and Spain's women streamed into higher education and jobs, although unemployment was the highest in Europe.

But the PSOE finally became mired in scandal, and in the 1996 elections, the centre-right Partido Popular (PP; People's Party), led by José María Aznar, swept the PSOE from power. Upon coming to power, Aznar promised to make politics dull, and he did, but he also presided over eight years of solid economic progress. Spain's economy grew annually by an average of 3.4%, and unemployment fell from 23% (1996) to 8% (2006). Not surprisingly, the PP won the 2000 election as well, with an absolute parliamentary majority. Aznar's popularity began to wane thanks to his strong support for the US-led invasion of Iraq in 2003 (which was deeply unpopular in Spain) and his decision to send Spanish troops to the conflict.

Troubled Times

On 11 March 2004, Madrid was rocked by 10 bombs on four rush-hour commuter trains heading into the capital's Atocha station. When the dust cleared, 191 people had died and 1755 were wounded, many of them seriously. It was the biggest such terror attack in the nation's history. In a stunning reversal of pre-poll predictions, the PP, who insisted that ETA was responsible despite overwhelming evidence to the contrary, was defeated by the PSOE in elections three days after the attack.

The new Socialist government of José Luis Rodríguez Zapatero gave Spain a makeover by introducing a raft of liberalising social reforms. Gay marriage was legalised, Spain's arcane divorce laws were overhauled, almost a million illegal immigrants were granted

1992	11 March 2004	July 2010
Barcelona holds the Olympic Games, putting Spain in the international spotlight and highlighting the country's progress since 1975.	Terrorist bombings kill 191 people on 10 Madrid commuter trains. The next day 11 million people take to the streets across Spain.	Spain's national football team wins the World Cup for the first time, two years after its maiden European Championship trophy.

La Movida

After the long, dark years of dictatorship and conservative Catholicism, Spaniards, especially those in Madrid, emerged onto the streets with all the zeal of ex-convent schoolgirls. Nothing was taboo in a phenomenon known as *'la movida'* (the scene) or *'la movida madrileña'* (the Madrid scene) as young *madrileños* discovered the 1960s, '70s and early '80s all at once. Drinking, drugs and sex suddenly were OK. All-night partying was the norm, drug taking in public was not a criminal offence (that changed in Madrid in 1992) and Madrid in particular howled. All across Madrid and other major cities, summer terraces roared to the chattering, drinking, carousing crowds and young people from all over Europe (not to mention cultural icons such as Andy Warhol) flocked here to take part in the revelry.

What was remarkable about *la movida* in Madrid is that it was presided over by Enrique Tierno Galván, an ageing former university professor who had been a leading opposition figure under Franco and was affectionately known throughout Spain as 'the old teacher'. A Socialist, he became mayor in 1979 and, for many, launched *la movida* by telling a public gathering *'a colocarse y ponerse al loro'*, which loosely translates as 'get stoned and do what's cool'. Unsurprisingly he was Madrid's most popular mayor ever and when he died in 1986 a million *madrileños* turned out for his funeral.

But *la movida* was also accompanied by an explosion of creativity among the country's musicians, designers and film-makers keen to shake off the shackles of the repressive Franco years. The most famous of these was film director Pedro Almodóvar, whose riotously colourful films captured the spirit of *la movida,* featuring larger-than-life characters who pushed the limits of sex and drugs.

residence, and a law seeking to apportion blame for the crimes of the civil war and Franco dictatorship entered the statute books. Although Spain's powerful Catholic Church cried foul over many of the reforms, the changes played well with most Spaniards. Spain's economy was booming, the envy of Europe. And then it all fell apart.

Spain's economy went into free fall in late 2008 and still remains in precarious straits. Zapatero's government waited painfully long to recognise that a crisis was looming and was replaced, in November 2011, with a right-of-centre one promoting a deep austerity drive and turning back the liberalising reforms of the Socialists.

That the country remains firmly democratic, however, suggests that modern Spaniards have, for the first time in Spain's tumultuous history, found means other than war for resolving the many differences that divide them.

2012
Spain's economic crisis continues with unemployment rising above 25%, with more than 50% of young Spaniards out of work.

June 2014
After a series of Royal family scandals King Juan Carlos, who had reigned since 1975, abdicates in favour of his son, Felipe VI.

December 2015
Ruling People's Party government loses its majority, but no party can form a coalition and new elections are called for June 2016.

Flamenco dancer

Flamenco

*Flamenco's passion is clear to anyone who has heard
its melancholic strains in the background of a crowded
Spanish bar or during an uplifting live performance.
If you're lucky, you'll experience that single sublime
moment when flamenco's raw passion suddenly
transports you to another place (known as* duende*),
where joy and sorrow threaten to overwhelm you.*

The Birth of Flamenco

Flamenco's origins have been lost to time. Some have suggested that it derives from Byzantine chants used in Visigothic churches, but most musical historians agree that it probably dates back to a fusion of songs brought to Spain by the Roma people, with music and verses from North Africa crossing into medieval Muslim Andalucía.

Flamenco as we now know it first took recognisable form in the 18th and early 19th centuries among Roma people in the lower Guadalquivir valley in western Andalucía. The Seville, Jerez de la Frontera and Cádiz axis is still considered flamenco's heartland, and it's here, purists believe, that you'll encounter the most authentic flamenco experience.

Guitarist

★ **Flamenco Festivals**

Festival de Jerez (☉late Feb–early Mar; www.facebook.com/FestivalDeJerez)

Suma Flamenca (☉Jun; www.madrid. org/sumaflamenca)

Bienal de Flamenco (p191)

Festival de la Guitarra de Cordoba (p24)

Flamenco Essentials

A flamenco singer is known as a *cantaor* (male) or *cantaora* (female); a dancer is a *bailaor* or *bailaora*. Most of the songs and dances are performed to a blood-rush of guitar from the *tocaor* or *tocaora* (male or female flamenco guitarist). Percussion is provided by tapping feet, clapping hands and sometimes castanets.

Flamenco *coplas* (songs) come in many different types, from the solemn *soleá* or the intensely despairing *siguiriya* to the livelier *alegría* or the upbeat *bulería*. The first flamenco was *cante jondo* (deep song), an anguished instrument of expression for a group on the margins of society. *Jondura* (depth) is still the essence of pure flamenco.

The traditional flamenco costume – shawl, fan and long, frilly *bata de cola* (tail gown) for women, and flat Cordoban hats and tight black trousers for men – dates from Andalucian fashions in the late 19th century.

Flamenco Legends

The great singers of the 19th and early 20th centuries were Silverio Franconetti and La Niña de los Peines, from Seville, and Antonio Chacón and Manuel Torre, from Jerez de la Frontera. Torre's singing, legend has it, could drive people to rip their shirts open and upturn tables. The dynamic dancing and wild lifestyle of Carmen Amaya (1913–63), from Barcelona, made her the Roma dance legend of all time. Her long-time partner Sabicas was the father of the modern solo flamenco guitar, inventing a host of now-indispensable techniques.

After a trough in the mid-20th century, when it seemed that the *tablaos* (touristy flamenco shows emphasising the sexy and the jolly) were in danger of taking over, *flamenco puro* got a new lease of life in the 1970s through singers such as Terremoto, La Paquera, Enrique Morente, Chano Lobato and, above all, El Camarón de la Isla (whose real name was José Monge Cruz) from San Fernando near Cádiz.

Some say that Madrid-born Diego El Cigala (b 1968) is El Camarón's successor. This powerful singer launched onto the big stage with the extraordinary *Lágrimas negras* (2003), a wonderful collaboration with Cuban virtuoso Bebo Valdés that mixes flamenco with Cuban influences, and its follow-up, *Dos lagrimas* (2008). Other fine Diego El Cigala albums include *Picasso en mis ojos* (2005), *Cigala&Tango* (2010) and *Romance de la luna Tucumana* (2013).

Another singer whose fame endures is Enrique Morente (1942–2010), referred to by one Madrid paper as 'the last bohemian'. While careful not to alienate flamenco purists, Morente, through his numerous collaborations across genres, helped lay the foundations for nuevo flamenco and fusion. His untimely death in 2010 was mourned by a generation of flamenco aficionados.

Paco de Lucía (1947–2014), from Algeciras, was the doyen of flamenco guitarists. By the time he was 14 his teachers admitted that they had nothing left to teach him and for many in the flamenco world, he is the personification of *duende*, that indefinable capacity to transmit the power and passion of flamenco. In 1968 he began flamenco's most exciting partnership with his friend El Camarón de la Isla (1950–92); together they recorded nine classic albums. De Lucía would go on to transform the flamenco guitar into an instrument of solo expression with new techniques, scales, melodies and harmonies that have gone far beyond traditional limits.

Other guitar maestros include Tomatito (b 1958), who also accompanied El Camarón de la Isla, and members of the Montoya family (some of whom are better known by the sobriquet of Los Habichuela), especially Juan (b 1933) and Pepe (b 1944).

> 🎧 **Flamenco Playlist**
>
> ○ Pata Negra, *Blues de la frontera* (1987)
>
> ○ El Camarón de la Isla, *Una leyenda flamenca* (1992)
>
> ○ Paco de Lucía, *Antología* (1995)
>
> ○ Chambao, *Flamenco chill* (2002)
>
> ○ Diego El Cigala & Bebo Valdés, *Lágrimas negras* (2003)
>
> ○ Paco de Lucía, *Cositas buenas* (2004)
>
> ○ Enrique Morente, *Sueña la Alhambra* (2005)
>
> ○ Diego El Cigala, *Romance de la luna tucumana* (2013)

Carmen Linares is said to have flamenco's most enduring voice, while Joaquín Cortés is a dance star fusing flamenco with jazz and ballet.

Seeing Flamenco

The intensity and spontaneity of flamenco have never translated well onto recordings. Instead, to ignite the goosebumps and inspire the powerful emotional spirit known to aficionados as '*duende*,' you have to be there, stamping your feet and passionately yelling '*¡óle!*' It's easiest to catch in Seville, Jerez de la Frontera, Granada and Madrid.

Seeing flamenco can be expensive – at the *tablaos* (restaurants where flamenco is performed) expect to pay €25 to €35 just to see the show. The admission price usually includes your first drink, but you pay extra for meals (up to €50 per person) that aren't always worth the money. For that reason, we often suggest you eat elsewhere and simply pay for the show (after having bought tickets in advance), albeit on the understanding that you won't have a front-row seat. The other important thing to remember is that most of these shows are geared towards tourists. That's not to say that the quality isn't top-notch – on the contrary, often it's magnificent, spine-tingling stuff – it's just that they sometimes lack the genuine, raw emotion of real flamenco.

The best places for live performances are *peñas* (clubs where flamenco fans band together). The atmosphere in such places is authentic and at times very intimate, proof that flamenco feeds off an audience that knows its flamenco. Most Andalucian towns have dozens of *peñas*, and many tourist offices – especially those in Seville, Jerez de la Frontera and Cádiz – have lists of those that are open to visitors.

Festivals are another place to see fabulous live flamenco.

Museo del Prado (p38), Madrid

Master Painters

Spain has an artistic legacy that rivals anything found elsewhere in Europe. In centuries past, this impressive portfolio owed much to the patronage of Spanish kings who lavished money upon the great painters of the day. In the 20th century, it was the relentless creativity of artists such as Pablo Picasso, Salvador Dalí and Joan Miró who became the true masters.

The Golden Century

The star of the 17th-century art scene, which became known as Spain's artistic Golden Age, was the genius court painter, Diego Rodríguez de Silva Velázquez (1599–1660). Born in Seville, Velázquez later moved to Madrid as court painter and composed scenes (landscapes, royal portraits, religious subjects, snapshots of everyday life) that owe their vitality not only to his photographic eye for light, contrast and the details of royal finery, but also to a compulsive interest in the humanity of his subjects so that they seem to breathe on the canvas. His masterpieces include *Las meninas* (Maids of Honour) and *La rendición de Breda* (Surrender of Breda), both in Madrid's Museo del Prado.

Centro de Arte Reina Sofía (p43), Madrid

Francisco de Zurbarán (1598–1664), a friend and contemporary of Velázquez, ended his life in poverty in Madrid and it was only after his death that he received the acclaim that his masterpieces deserved. He is best remembered for the startling clarity and light in his portraits of monks, a series of which hangs in Madrid's Real Academia de Bellas Artes de San Fernando, with other works in the Museo del Prado.

Other masters of the era whose works hang in the Museo del Prado include José (Jusepe) de Ribera (1591–1652), who was influenced by Caravaggio and produced fine chiaroscuro works, and Bartolomé Esteban Murillo (1618–82).

Goya & the 19th Century

Francisco José de Goya y Lucientes (1746–1828) began his career as a cartoonist in the Real Fábrica de Tapices (Royal Tapestry Workshop) in Madrid. Illness in 1792 left him deaf; many critics speculate that his condition was largely responsible for his wild, often merciless style that would become increasingly unshackled from convention. By 1799 Goya was appointed Carlos IV's court painter.

In the last years of the 18th century Goya painted enigmatic masterpieces, such as *La maja vestida* (The Young Lady Dressed) and *La maja desnuda* (The Young Lady Undressed), identical portraits but for the lack of clothes in the latter. The Inquisition was not amused by the artworks, which it covered up. Nowadays all is bared in Madrid's Museo del Prado.

The arrival of the French and the war in 1808 had a profound impact on Goya. Unforgiving portrayals of the brutality of war are *El dos de mayo* (The Second of May) and, more

Museo Guggenheim Bilbao (p224), Bilbao

dramatically, *El tres de mayo* (The Third of May). The latter depicts the execution of Madrid rebels by French troops.

Goya saved his most confronting paintings for the end. After he retired to the Quinta del Sordo (Deaf Man's House) in Madrid, he created his nightmarish *Pinturas negras* (Black Paintings), which now hang in the Museo del Prado. *The Saturno devorando a su hijo* (Saturn Devouring His Son) captures the essence of Goya's genius, and *La romería de San Isidro* (The Pilgrimage to San Isidro) and *El akelarre* (*El gran cabrón*; The Great He-Goat) are profoundly unsettling.

Other places, both in Madrid, to see Goya's works include the Real Academia de Bellas Artes de San Fernando and the Ermita de San Antonio de la Florida; the latter has fabulous ceiling frescoes painted by Goya.

Picasso, Dalí & Miró

Pablo Ruíz Picasso (1881–1973) underwent repeated creative revolutions as he passed from one creative phase to another. From his gloomy Blue Period, through the brighter Pink Period and on to cubism – in which he was accompanied by Madrid's Juan Gris (1887–1927) – Picasso was nothing if not surprising. Cubism, his best-known form, was inspired by the artist's fascination with primitivism, primarily African masks and early Iberian sculpture. This highly complex form reached its high point in *Guernica,* which hangs in Madrid's Centro de Arte Reina Sofía. A good selection of his early work can be viewed in Barcelona's Museu Picasso.

Separated from Picasso by barely a generation, two other artists reinforced the Catalan contingent in the vanguard of 20th-century art: Dalí and Miró. Although he started off dabbling in cubism, Salvador Dalí (1904–89) became more readily identified with the surrealists. This complex character's 'hand-painted dream photographs', as he called them, are virtuoso executions brimming with fine detail and nightmare images dragged up from a feverish and Freud-fed imagination. The single best display of his work can be seen at the Teatre-Museu Dalí in Figueres, but you'll also find important works in the Museu de Cadaqués in Cadaqués, the Casa Museu Dalí in Port Lligat, and Madrid's Centro de Arte Reina Sofía.

Barcelona-born Joan Miró (1893–1983) developed a joyous and almost child-like style. His later period is his best known, characterised by the simple use of bright colours and forms in combinations of symbols that represented women, birds and stars. The Fundació Joan Miró in Barcelona and the Fundació Pilar i Joan Miró in Palma de Mallorca are the pick of the places to see his work, with some further examples in Madrid's Centro de Arte Reina Sofía.

Le Pedrera (p78), Barcelona

VOLANTHEVIST / GETTY IMAGES ©

Architecture

Spain's architectural landscapes are some of the richest of their kind in Europe. The country's architecture tells a beguiling story that takes in the cinematic sweep of its history, from glorious Moorish creations in Andalucía and the singular imagination of Gaudí to soaring cathedrals and temples to contemporary creativity.

The Islamic Era

In 784, with Córdoba well established as the new capital of the western end of the Umayyad dynasty, Syrian architects set to work on the grand Mezquita, conjuring up their homeland with details that echo the Umayyad Mosque in Damascus, such as delicate horseshoe arches and exquisite decorative tiles with floral motifs. But the building's most distinctive feature – more than 500 columns that crowd the interior of the mosque – was repurposed from Roman and Visigothic ruins.

In the centuries that followed, Moorish architecture incorporated trends from all over the Islamic empire. The technique of intricately carved stucco detailing was developed in 9th-century Iraq, while *muqarnas* (honeycomb) vaulting arrived via Egypt in the 10th

Mercat de Santa Caterina (p85), Barcelona

NICOLAS KIPOURAX PAQUET / GETTY IMAGES ©

★ **Gaudí Masterpieces**

La Sagrada Família (p72) A symphony of religious devotion.

La Pedrera (p78) Dubbed 'the Quarry' because of its flowing facade.

Casa Batlló (p79) A fairy-tale dragon.

Park Güell (p98) A park full of Modernista twists.

century. Square minarets, such as the Giralda in Seville (now a church tower), came with the Almohad invasion from Morocco in the 12th century.

Perhaps the most magnificent creation is the core of Granada's Alhambra, the Palacios Nazaríes (Nasrid Palaces). From the 13th to the 15th century, architects reached new heights of elegance, creating a study in balance between inside and outside, light and shade, spareness and intricate decoration. Eschewing innovation, the Alhambra refined well-tried forms, as if in an attempt to freeze time and halt the collapse of Moorish power, which, at the time, was steadily eroding across the peninsula.

Andalucía's Formal Gardens

Paradise, according to Islamic tradition, is a garden. It's an idea that architects took to heart in Al-Andalus, surrounding some of Andalucía's loveliest buildings with abundant greenery, colour, fragrances and the tinkle of water. See some stunning examples at the Alhambra's Generalife gardens in Granada, where the landscaping shows off a near-perfect sophistication. In Seville the Parque de María Luisa is the sprawling green heart of the city, while the gardens of the Alcázar is the classic Islamic palace pleasure garden. Highlights in Córdoba feature the gardens of the Alcázar de los Reyes Cristianos, a lush terrace with abundant water, and the Palacio de Viana with its formal gardens and an emphasis on symmetry.

Modernisme & Art Deco

At the end of the 19th century, Barcelona's prosperity unleashed one of the most imaginative periods in Spanish architecture. The architects at work here, who drew on prevailing art-nouveau trends as well as earlier Spanish styles, came to be called the Modernistas. Chief among them, Antoni Gaudí sprinkled Barcelona with jewels of his singular imagination.

While Barcelona went all wavy, Madrid embraced the rigid glamour of art deco. This global style arrived in Spain just as Madrid's Gran Vía was laid out in the 1920s. One of the more overwhelming caprices from that era is the Palacio de Comunicaciones on Plaza de la Cibeles.

Antoni Gaudí

Born in Reus and initially trained in metalwork, Antoni Gaudí i Cornet (1852–1926) person-ifies, and largely transcends, the Modernisme movement that brought a thunderclap of innovative greatness to turn-of-the-century Barcelona.

He devoted much of the latter part of his life to what remains Barcelona's call sign: the unfinished Sagrada Família. His inspiration in the first instance was Gothic, but he also sought to emulate the harmony he observed in nature, eschewing the straight line and favouring curvaceous forms. Gaudí used complex string models weighted with plumb lines to make his calculations. You can see examples in the upstairs mini-museum in La Pedrera.

The architect's work is an earthy appeal to sinewy movement, but often with a dreamlike or surreal quality. The private apartment house Casa Batlló is a fine example. Not only are straight lines eliminated, but the lines between real and unreal, sober and dream-drunk, good sense and play are all blurred. He seems to have particularly enjoyed himself with rooftops, at La Pedrera and Palau Güell, in particular.

Contemporary Innovation

Post-Franco, Spain has made up for lost time and, particularly since the 1990s, the unifying theme appears to be that anything goes.

Catalan Enric Miralles had a short career, dying of a brain tumour in 2000 at the age of 45, but his Mercat de Santa Caterina in Barcelona shows brilliant colour and inventive use of arches. In 1996 Rafael Moneo won the Pritzker Prize, the greatest international honour for living architects, largely for his long-term contributions to Madrid's cityscape, such as the revamping of the Atocha railway station. His Kursaal Palace in San Sebastían is staunchly functional, but shining, like two giant stones swept up from the sea.

In the years since, Spain has become something of a Pritzker playground. Sir Norman Foster designed the eye-catching metro system in Bilbao and Spain's tallest building the 250m Torre Caja Madrid. But it was Frank Gehry's 1998 Museo Guggenheim Bilbao in the same city that really sparked the quirky-building fever. Now the list of contemporary landmarks includes Jean Nouvel's spangly, gherkin-shaped Torre Agbar, in Barcelona; Richard Rogers' dreamy, wavy Terminal 4 at Madrid's Barajas airport, for which he won the prestigious Stirling Prize in October 2006; Oscar Niemeyer's flying-saucerish Centro Cultural Internacional Avilés in Asturias; and Jürgen Mayer's Metropol Parasol in Seville.

 Spanish Architecture: The Basics

Roman (210 BC–AD 409) Bridges, waterworks, walls and whole cities that inspired later traditions.

Visigothic (409–711) Sturdy stone churches with simple decoration and horseshoe arches.

Moorish (711–1492) Horseshoe arches, square minarets and intricate geometric design.

Mudéjar (1100–1700) Post-Reconquista work by Muslims adapting the Moorish tradition of decoration to more common materials.

Romanesque (1100–1300) Spare decoration and proportions based on Byzantine churches.

Gothic (1200–1600) Flying buttresses enable ceilings to soar, and arches become pointy to match.

Plateresque (1400–1600) A dazzling ornate style of relief carving on facades.

Churrigueresque (1650–1750) Spain's special twist on baroque with spiral columns and gold-leaf everything.

Modernisme (1888–1911) The Spanish version of art nouveau took a brilliant turn in Barcelona.

Contemporary (1975–present) Previously unimaginable directions since the death of Franco.

Paella

DANITA DELIMONT / GETTY IMAGES ©

The Spanish Kitchen

For Spaniards, eating is one of life's more pleasurable obsessions. In this chapter, we'll help you make the most of this fabulous culinary culture, whether it's demystifying the art of ordering tapas or taking you on a journey through the regional specialities of Spanish food.

Regional Specialities

Basque Country & Catalonia

Seafood and steaks are the pillars upon which Basque cuisine were traditionally built. San Sebastián, in particular, showcases the region's diversity of culinary experiences and it was from the kitchens of San Sebastián that *nueva cocina vasca* (Basque nouvelle cuisine) emerged, announcing Spain's arrival as a culinary superpower.

Catalonia blends traditional Catalan flavours and expansive geographical diversity with an openness to influences from the rest of Europe. All manner of seafood, paella, rice and pasta dishes, as well as Pyrenean game dishes, are regulars on Catalan menus. Sauces are more prevalent here than elsewhere in Spain.

Inland Spain

The best *jamón ibérico* comes from Extremadura, Salamanca and Teruel, while *cordero asado lechal* (roast spring lamb) and *cochinillo asado* (roast suckling pig) are winter mainstays. King of the hearty stews, especially in Madrid, is *cocido,* a hotpot or stew with a noodle broth, carrots, cabbage, chickpeas, chicken, *morcilla* (blood sausage), beef and lard.

Galicia & the Northwest

Galicia is known for its bewildering array of seafood, and the star is *pulpo á feira* or *pulpo gallego* (spicy boiled octopus with oil, paprika and garlic).

In the high mountains of Asturias and Cantabria, the cuisine is as driven by mountain pasture as it is by the daily comings and goings of fishing fleets. Cheeses are particularly sought after, with special fame reserved for the *queso de Cabrales* (untreated cow's-milk cheese). *Asturianos* (Asturians) are also passionate about their *fabada asturiana* (a stew made with pork, blood sausage and white beans) and *sidra* (cider) straight from the barrel.

Andalucía

Seafood is a consistent presence the length of the Andalucian coast. Andalucians are famous above all for their *pescaito frito* (fried fish). A particular speciality of Cádiz, fried fish Andalucian-style means that just about anything that emerges from the sea is rolled in chickpea-and-wheat flour, shaken to remove the surplus, then deep-fried ever so briefly in olive oil, just long enough to form a light, golden crust that seals the essential goodness of the fish or seafood within.

In a region where summers can be fierce, there's no better way to keep cool than with a *gazpacho andaluz* (Andalucian gazpacho), a cold soup with many manifestations. The base is almost always tomato, cucumber, vinegar and olive oil.

Paella & Other Rice Dishes

Rice dishes are traditional in Catalonia, Valencia and Andalucía, so that's where they're best eaten. Check out the clientele first. No locals? Walk on by.

Restaurants should take around 20 minutes or more to prepare a rice dish – beware if they don't – so expect to wait. Rice dishes are usually for a minimum of two.

Paella has all the liquid evaporated, *meloso* rices are wet, and *caldoso* rices come with liquid. Traditional Valencian rices can have almost any ingredients, varying by region and season. The base always includes short-grain rice, garlic, olive oil and saffron. The best rice is *bomba,* which opens accordion-like when cooked, allowing for maximum absorption while remaining firm. Paella should be cooked in a large shallow pan to enable maximum contact with flavour. And for the final touch of authenticity, the grains on the bottom (and only those) should have a crunchy, savoury crust known as the *socarrat.*

Jamón

There's no more iconic presence on the Spanish table than cured ham from the high plateau, and the sight of *jamones* hanging from the ceiling is one of Spain's most enduring images. Spanish *jamón* is, unlike Italian prosciutto, a bold, deep red and well marbled with buttery fat. At its best, it smells like meat, the forest and the field.

Like wines and olive oil, Spanish *jamón* is subject to a strict series of classifications. *Jamón serrano* refers to *jamón* made from white-coated pigs introduced to Spain in the 1950s. Once salted and semi-dried by the cold, dry winds of the Spanish sierra, most now go through a similar process of curing and drying in a climate-controlled shed for around a year.

Tapas

★ Cooking Classes

La Espuela, Reina Restaurante (p165), Antequera

Annie B's Spanish Kitchen (p172), Vejer de la Frontera

San Sebastián Food (p243), San Sebastián

Jamón ibérico – more expensive and generally regarded as the elite of Spanish hams – comes from a black-coated pig indigenous to the Iberian Peninsula and a descendant of the wild boar. Gastronomically, its star appeal is its ability to infiltrate fat into the muscle tissue, thus producing an especially well-marbled meat. If the pig gains at least 50% of its body weight during the acorn-eating season, it can be classified as *jamón ibérico de bellota,* the most sought-after designation for *jamón.*

The best-quality *jamón* is most commonly eaten as a starter or a *ración* (large tapa) – on menus it's usually called a *tabla de jamón ibérico* (or *ibérico de bellota*). Cutting it is an art form; it should be sliced so wafer-thin as to be almost transparent. Spaniards almost always eat it with bread.

Tapas

In the Basque Country, and many bars in Madrid, Barcelona and elsewhere, ordering tapas couldn't be easier. With tapas varieties lined up along the bar, you either take a small plate and help yourself or point to the morsel you want. If you do this, it's customary to keep track of what you eat (by holding on to the toothpicks, for example) and then tell the bar staff how many you've had when it's time to pay. Otherwise, many places have a list of tapas, either on a menu or posted up behind the bar. If you can't choose, ask for *'la especialidad de la casa'* (the house speciality) and it's hard to go wrong.

Another way of eating tapas is to order *raciones* (literally 'rations'; large tapas servings) or *media raciones* (half-rations; smaller tapas servings). Remember, however, that after a couple of *raciones* you're likely to be full. In some bars, especially in Granada, you'll also get a small (free) tapa when you buy a drink.

Spanish Wines

La Rioja, in the north, is Spain's best-known wine-producing region. The principal grape of Rioja is the tempranillo, widely believed to be a mutant form of the pinot noir. Its wine is smooth and fruity, seldom as dry as its supposed French counterpart. Look for the 'DOC Rioja' classification on the label and you'll find a good wine.

Not far behind are the wine-producing regions of Ribera del Duero in Castilla y León, Navarra and the Somontano wines of Aragón. For white wines, the Ribeiro wines of Galicia are well regarded. Also from the area is one of Spain's most charming whites – *albariño.*

The Penedès region in Catalonia produces whites and sparkling wine such as *cava,* the traditional champagne-like toasting drink of choice for Spaniards at Christmas.

The best wines are often marked with the designation *'crianza'* (aged for one year in oak barrels), *'reserva'* (aged for two years, at least one of which is in oak barrels) and *'gran reserva'* (two years in oak and three in the bottle).

Barri Gòtic (p80), Barcelona

Survival Guide

Directory A–Z

Accommodation

Spain's accommodation is generally of a high standard, from small, family-run *hostales* (budget hotels) to the old-world opulence of *paradores* (state-owned hotels). Places to stay are classified into *hoteles* (hotels; one to five stars), *hostales* (one to three stars) and *pensiones* (basically small private *hostales*, often family-run; one or two stars). These are the categories used by the annual *Guía Oficial de Hoteles,* which lists almost every establishment in Spain (except for one-star *pensiones*), with approximate prices. Tourist offices also have lists of local accommodation options. Checkout time in most establishments is noon.

Seasons

What constitutes low or high season depends on where and when you're looking. Most of the year is high season in Barcelona or Madrid, especially during trade fairs. August can be dead in the cities, but high season along the coast. Winter is high season in the ski resorts of the Pyrenees and low season along the

coast (indeed, many coastal towns seem to shut down between November and Easter). Weekends are high season for boutique hotels and *casas rurales* (rural homes), but low season for business hotels (which often offer generous specials) in Madrid and Barcelona.

Reservations

Finding a place to stay without booking ahead in July and August along the coast can be difficult and many places require a minimum stay of at least two nights during high season. Always check hotel websites for discounts. Although there's usually no need to book ahead for a room in the low or shoulder seasons (Barcelona is a notable exception), booking ahead is usually a good idea.

Most places will ask for a credit-card number or will hold the room for you until 6pm unless you have provided credit-card details as security or have let them know that you'll be arriving later.

Price Ranges

The following price ranges refer to a double room with private bathroom:

€	less than €65
€€	€65–140
€€€	more than €140

The price ranges for Madrid and Barcelona are inevitably higher:

€	less than €75
€€	€75–200
€€€	more than €200

Book Your Stay Online

For more accommodation reviews by Lonely Planet authors, check out www.lonelyplanet.com/spain/hotels. You'll find independent reviews, as well as recommendations on the best places to stay. Best of all, you can book.

Customs Regulations

Duty-free allowances for travellers entering Spain from outside the EU include 2L of wine (or 1L of wine and 1L of spirits), and 200 cigarettes or 50 cigars or 250g of tobacco.

There are no restrictions on the import of duty-paid items into Spain from other EU countries for personal use. You *can* buy VAT-free articles at airport shops when travelling between EU countries.

Food

The following price ranges refer to a standard main dish:

€	less than €10
€€	€10–20
€€€	more than €20

Climate

Barcelona

Madrid

Seville

Electricity

230V/50Hz   220V/50Hz

GLBT Travellers

Spain has become perhaps the most gay-friendly country in southern Europe. In 2005 same-sex marriages were legalised in Spain

Lesbians and gay men generally keep a fairly low profile, but are quite open in the cities. Madrid and Barcelona have particularly lively scenes. There are also gay parades, marches and events in several cities on and around the last Saturday in June, when **Madrid Pride** (www.madridorgullo.org) takes place. Madrid also hosts the annual **Les Gai Cine Mad** (☏015 930 540; www.lesgai cinemad.com; ☺late Oct or early Nov) festival, a celebration of lesbian, gay and transsexual films.

Useful Resources

Barcelona's tourist board publishes *Barcelona: The Official Gay and Lesbian Tourist Guide* biannually, while Madrid's tourist office has useful information on its website (www.esmadrid. com/lgtb-madrid). See also:

Chueca (www.chueca.com) Useful gay portal with extensive links.

GayBarcelona (www.gay barcelona.com) News, views and a listings section covering bars, saunas, shops and more in Barcelona and Sitges.

Gay Iberia (www.gayiberia.com) Gay guides to Barcelona, Madrid, Sitges and 26 other Spanish cities.

Gay Madrid 4 U (www.gaymadrid4u.com) A good overview of Madrid's gay bars and clubs.

Night Tours.com (www.nighttours.com) A good guide to nightlife and attractions in Madrid, Barcelona and 18 other Spanish locations.

Orgullo Madrid (www.madridorgullo.com) Website for Madrid's gay and lesbian piode march and links to gay organisations across the country.

Shangay (www.shangay.com) For news, events, reviews and contacts. It also publishes *Shanguide*, a Madrid-centric biweekly listings magazine (including saunas and hardcore clubs) and contact ads. Its companion publication *Shangay Express* is better for articles with a handful of listings and ads. They're available in gay bookshops and gay-friendly bars.

Universo Gay (http://guia.universogay.com) A little bit of everything.

Health

Spain has an excellent health-care system.

Availability & Cost of Health Care

If you need an ambulance, call ☎061. For emergency treatment, go straight to the *urgencias* (casualty) section of the nearest hospital.

Farmacias offer valuable advice and sell over-the-counter medication. A system of *farmacias de guardia* (duty pharmacies) operates so that each district has one open all the time. When a pharmacy is closed, it posts the name of the nearest open one on the door.

Medical costs are lower in Spain than many other European countries, but they still mount quickly if you are uninsured. Costs if you attend casualty range from nothing (in some regions) to around €80.

Altitude Sickness

○ If you're hiking at altitude, altitude sickness may be a risk. Lack of oxygen at high altitudes (over 2500m) affects most people to some extent.

○ Symptoms of Acute Mountain Sickness (AMS) usually develop during the first 24 hours at altitude but may be delayed by up to three weeks.

○ Mild symptoms include headache, lethargy, dizziness, difficulty sleeping and loss of appetite.

○ AMS may become more severe without warning and can be fatal. Severe symptoms include breathlessness, a dry cough (which may progress to the production of pink, frothy sputum), severe headache, lack of coordination and balance, confusion, irrational behaviour, vomiting, drowsiness and unconsciousness.

○ Treat mild symptoms by resting at the same altitude until recovery, usually for a day or two.

○ Paracetamol or aspirin can be taken for headaches.

○ If symptoms persist or become worse, immediate descent is necessary; even 500m can help.

○ Drug treatments should never be used to avoid descent or to enable further ascent.

Bites & Stings

○ Beware of the hairy reddish-brown caterpillars of the pine processionary moth – touching their hairs sets off a severely irritating allergic skin reaction.

○ Some Spanish centipedes have a very nasty but non-fatal sting.

○ Jellyfish, which have stinging tentacles, are an increasing problem along the Mediterranean coastline.

○ Lataste's viper is the only venomous snake that is relatively common in Spain. It has a triangular-shaped head, grows up to 75cm long, and is grey with a zigzag pattern. It lives in dry, rocky areas. Its bite can be fatal and needs to be treated with a serum, which state clinics in major towns keep in stock.

Hypothermia

○ The weather in Spain's mountains can be extremely changeable any time of year.

○ Proper preparation will reduce the risks of getting hypothermia: always carry waterproof garments and warm layers, and inform others of your route.

○ Hypothermia starts with shivering, loss of judgment

and clumsiness; unless re-warming occurs, the sufferer deteriorates into apathy, confusion and coma.

• Prevent further heat loss by seeking shelter, wearing warm dry clothing, drinking hot sweet drinks and sharing body warmth.

Water

Tap water is generally safe to drink. If you are in any doubt, ask, '*¿Es potable el agua (de grifo)?*' – Is the (tap) water drinkable? Do not drink water from rivers or lakes as it may contain bacteria or viruses that can cause diarrhoea or vomiting.

Insurance

A travel-insurance policy to cover theft, loss, medical problems and cancellation or delays to your travel arrangements is a good idea. Paying for your ticket with a credit card can often provide limited travel-accident insurance and you may be able to reclaim the payment if the operator doesn't deliver.

Worldwide travel insurance is available at www.lonelyplanet.com/travel-insurance.

Internet Access

Wi-fi is almost universally available at hotels, and in some cafes, restaurants and airports. Generally but not always, it's free. Connection speed often varies from room to room (and coverage is sometimes restricted to the hotel lobby), so always ask when you check-in or make your reservation. Some tourist offices may have a list of wi-fi hot spots in their area.

Legal Matters

If you're arrested, you will be allotted the free services of an *abogado de oficio* (duty solicitor), who may speak only Spanish. You're also entitled to make a phone call. If you use this to contact your embassy or consulate, the staff will probably be able to do no more than refer you to a lawyer who speaks your language. If you end up in court, the authorities are obliged to provide a translator.

You are meant to have your national ID card or passport with you at all times. If asked for it by the police, you should be able to produce it on the spot. In practice it is rarely an issue and many people choose to leave passports in hotel safes.

The Policía Local or Policía Municipal deal with issues such as traffic infringements and minor crime. The Policía Nacional (☎091) is the state police force, dealing with major crime and operating primarily in the cities. The military-linked Guardia Civil (created in the 19th century to deal with banditry) is largely responsible for highway patrols, borders, security, major crime and terrorism. Several regions have their own police forces, such as the Mossos d'Esquadra in Catalonia and the Ertaintxa in the Basque Country.

Cannabis is legal but only for personal use and in very small quantities. Public consumption of any illicit drug is illegal. Travellers entering Spain from Morocco should be prepared for drug searches.

Money

The most convenient way to bring your money is in the form of a debit or credit card, with some extra cash in case of an emergency.

ATMs

Many credit and debit cards can be used for withdrawing money from *cajeros automáticos* (ATMs) that display the relevant symbols. There is usually a charge (around 1.5% to 2%) on ATM cash withdrawals abroad.

Cash

Most banks and building societies will exchange major foreign currencies and offer the best rates. Ask about commissions and take your passport.

Credit & Debit Cards

These can be used to pay for most purchases. Among the most widely accepted are Visa, MasterCard, American

Express (Amex), Cirrus, Maestro, Plus and JCB. Diners Club is less widely accepted. You'll often be asked to show your passport or other identification.

Moneychangers

You can exchange both cash and travellers cheques at *cambio* (exchange) offices. Generally they offer longer opening hours and quicker service than banks, but worse exchange rates and higher commissions.

Taxes & Refunds

○ Value-added tax (VAT) is known as IVA (ee-ba; *impuesto sobre el valor añadido*).

○ Hotel rooms and restaurant meals attract a 10% IVA (usually included in the quoted price but always ask); most other items have 21% added.

○ Visitors are entitled to a refund of the 21% IVA on purchases costing more than €90.16 from any shop, if they are taking them out of the EU within three months. Ask the shop for a cash-back (or similar) refund form showing the price and IVA paid for each item, and identifying the vendor and purchaser.

○ Present your IVA refund form to the customs booth at the airport, port or border when you leave the EU.

Tipping

Tipping is almost always optional.

Bars It's rare to leave a tip in bars (even if the bartender gives you your change on a small dish).

Restaurants Many leave small change, others up to 5%, which is considered generous.

Taxis Optional, most locals round up to the nearest euro.

Travellers Cheques

Travellers cheques can be changed at most banks and building societies, often with a commission. Visa, Amex and Travelex are widely accepted brands with (usually) efficient replacement policies. It's vital to keep your initial receipt, and a record of your cheque numbers and the ones you have used, separate from the cheques themselves.

Opening Hours

Standard opening hours are for high season only and tend to shorten outside that time.

Banks 8.30am to 2pm Monday to Friday; some also open 4 to 7pm Thursday and 9am to 1pm Saturday

Central post offices 8.30am to 9.30pm Monday to Friday, 8.30am to 2pm Saturday; other branches 8.30am to 8.30pm Monday to Friday, 9.30am to 1pm Saturday

Nightclubs Midnight or 1am to 5am or 6am

Restaurants Lunch 1 to 4pm, dinner 8.30 to 11pm or midnight

Shops 10am to 2pm and 4.30 to 7.30pm or 5 to 8pm; big supermarkets and department stores generally open 10am to 10pm Monday to Saturday

Public Holidays

The two main periods when Spaniards go on holiday are Semana Santa (the week leading up to Easter Sunday) and July and August. At these times accommodation can be scarce and transport heavily booked, but other places are often half-empty.

There are at least 14 official holidays a year – some observed nationwide, some locally. When a holiday falls close to a weekend, Spaniards like to make a *puente* (bridge); taking the intervening day off too. Occasionally when some holidays fall close, they make an *acueducto* (aqueduct)! There are the national holidays:

Año Nuevo (New Year's Day) 1 January

Viernes Santo (Good Friday) March/April

Fiesta del Trabajo (Labour Day) 1 May

La Asunción (Feast of the Assumption) 15 August

Fiesta Nacional de España (National Day) 12 October

La Inmaculada Concepción (Feast of the Immaculate Conception) 8 December

Navidad (Christmas) 25 December

Regional governments set five holidays and local councils two more. Common dates include:

Epifanía (Epiphany) or **Día de los Reyes Magos** (Three Kings' Day) 6 January

Juéves Santo (Good Thursday) March/April; not observed in Catalonia and Valencia

Corpus Christi June; the Thursday after the eighth Sunday following Easter Sunday

Día de Santiago Apóstol (Feast of St James the Apostle) 25 July

Día de Todos los Santos (All Saints Day) 1 November

Día de la Constitución (Constitution Day) 6 December

Safe Travel

Most visitors to Spain never feel threatened, but a sufficient number have unpleasant experiences to warrant some care. The main thing to be wary of is petty theft.

Scams

As a rule, talented petty thieves work in groups and capitalise on distraction. Tricks usually involve a team of two or more (sometimes one of them an attractive woman to distract male victims). While one attracts your attention, the other empties your pockets. More imaginative strikes include someone dropping a milk mixture onto the victim from a balcony. Immediately a concerned citizen comes to help you brush off what you assume to be pigeon poo, and thus occupied, you don't notice the contents of your pockets slipping away.

Beware: not all thieves look like the typical idea of a thief. Watch out for an old classic: the ladies offering

flowers for good luck. We don't know how they do it, but if you get too involved in a friendly chat with these people, your pockets almost always wind up empty.

On some highways, especially the AP7 from the French border to Barcelona, bands of thieves occasionally operate. Beware of men distracting you in rest areas, and don't stop along the highway if people driving alongside indicate you have a problem with the car. While one inspects the rear of the car with you, his pals will empty your vehicle. Another gag has them puncturing car tyres stopped in rest areas, then following and 'helping' the victim when they stop to change the wheel. Hire cars and those with foreign plates are especially targeted.

When you do call in at rest stops, try to park close to the buildings and leave nothing of value in view. If you stop to change a tyre and find yourself getting unsolicited aid, make sure doors are all

locked and don't allow yourself to be distracted.

In some towns self-appointed parking attendants operate in central areas directing you to a parking spot. If possible, ignore them and find your own. If unavoidable, you may well want to pay them some token not to scratch or damage your vehicle after you've walked away. You definitely don't want to leave anything visible in the car (or open the boot – trunk – if you intend to leave luggage or anything else in it).

Theft

Theft is mostly a risk in resorts, cities and when you first arrive and may be off your guard. You are at your most vulnerable when dragging around luggage to or from your hotel. Barcelona, Madrid and Seville have the worst reputations for theft and, on very rare occasions, muggings.

Anything left lying on the beach can disappear when

Government Travel Advice

The following government websites offer travel advisories and information for travellers:

Australian Department of Foreign Affairs & Trade (www.smartraveller.gov.au)

Canadian Department of Foreign Affairs & International Trade (www.travel.gc.ca)

French Ministere des Affaires Etrangeres Europeennes (www.diplomatie.gouv.fr/fr/conseils-aux-voyageurs)

New Zealand Ministry of Foreign Affairs & Trade (www.safetravel.govt.nz)

UK Foreign & Commonwealth Office (www.gov.uk/government/organisations/foreign-commonwealth-office)

US Department of State (www.travel.state.gov)

Practicalities

o **Smoking** Banned in all enclosed public spaces.

o **Weights & Measures** The metric system is used.

o **Newspapers** Three main newspapers: centre-left *El País* (www.elpais.com), centre-right *El Mundo* (www.elmundo.es) and right-wing *ABC* (www.abc.es). The widely available *International New York Times* includes an eight-page supplement of articles from *El País* translated into English, or visit www.elpais.com/elpais/inenglish.html.

o **Radio** Nacional de España (RNE) has Radio 1 (general interest and current affairs); Radio 5 (sport and entertainment); and Radio 3 (Radio d'Espop). Stations covering current affairs include the left-leaning Cadena Ser, or the right-wing COPE. The most popular commercial pop and rock stations are 40 Principales, Kiss FM, Cadena 100 and Onda Cero.

o **TV** Spain's state-run Televisión Española (TVE1 and La 2) or the independent commercial stations (Antena 3, Tele 5, Cuatro and La Sexta). Regional governments run local stations, such as Madrid's Telemadrid, Catalonia's TV-3 and Canal 33 (both in Catalan), Galicia's TVG, Basque Country's ETB-1 and ETB-2, Valencia's Canal 9 and Andalucía's Canal Sur.

your back is turned. At night avoid dingy, empty city alleys and backstreets, or anywhere that just doesn't feel 100% safe.

Report thefts to the national police – visit www.policia.es for a full list of *comisarías* (police stations) around the country. You are unlikely to recover your goods, but you need to make this formal *denuncia* for insurance purposes. To avoid endless queues at the *comisaría* make the report by phone (902 102 112) in various languages or online at www.policia.es (click on 'Denuncias por Internet'), though the instructions are in Spanish only. The following day go to the station of your choice to pick up and sign the report, without queuing.

Telephone

There are no area codes in Spain.

Collect Calls

Placing *una llamada a cobro revertido* (international collect call) is simple. Dial 99 00 followed by the code for the country you're calling (numbers starting with 900 are national toll-free numbers).

Mobile Phones

Spain uses GSM 900/1800, which is compatible with the rest of Europe and Australia but not with the North American system, unless you have a GSM/GPRS-compatible phone (some AT&T and T-Mobile cell phones may work), or the system used in Japan. From those countries, you will need to travel with a tri-band or quadric-band phone.

You can buy SIM cards and prepaid time in Spain for your mobile phone, provided you own a GSM, dual- or tri-band cellular phone. This only works if your national phone hasn't been code-blocked; check before leaving home.

All Spanish mobile-phone companies (Telefónica's MoviStar, Orange and Vodafone) offer *prepagado* (prepaid) accounts for mobiles. The SIM card costs from €10, to which you add some prepaid phone time. Phone outlets are scattered across the country. You can then top up in their shops or by buying cards in outlets, such as *estancos* (tobacconists) and newspaper kiosks. Pepephone (www.pepephone.com) is another option.

If you plan on using your own phone while in Spain, check with your mobile provider for information on roaming charges, especially if you're using a phone from outside the EU.

Useful Numbers

Emergencies 112

English-speaking Spanish international operator 1008 (calls within Europe) or 1005 (rest of the world)

International directory enquiries 11825 (calls to this number cost €2)

National directory enquiries 11818

Operator for calls within Spain 1009 (including for domestic reverse-charge – collect – calls)

Time

Spain is in the same time zone as most of Western Europe (GMT/UTC plus one hour during winter and GMT/UTC plus two hours during the daylight-saving period).

Daylight saving runs from the last Sunday in March to the last Sunday in October.

Toilets

Public toilets are rare to nonexistent in Spain and it's not really the done thing to go into a bar or cafe solely to use the toilet; ordering a quick coffee is a small price to pay for relieving the problem, although you can usually get away with it in a larger, crowded place where they can't really keep track of who's coming and going. Another option in some larger cities is the department stores of El Corte Inglés.

Tourist Information

All cities and many smaller towns have an *oficina de turismo* or *oficina de información turística*. In the provincial capitals you will sometimes find more than one tourist office – one specialising in information on the city alone, the other carrying mostly provincial or regional information. National parks also often have their own visitor centres offering useful information.

Turespaña (www.spain.info) is the country's national tourism body, and it operates branches around the world. Check the website for office locations.

Travellers with Disabilities

Spain is not overly accommodating for travellers with disabilities, but things are slowly changing. For example, disabled access to some museums, official buildings and hotels represents a change in local thinking. In major cities more is being done to facilitate disabled access to public transport and taxis; in some cities, wheelchair-adapted taxis are called 'Eurotaxis'. Newly constructed hotels in most areas of Spain are required to have wheelchair-adapted rooms. With older places, you need to be a little wary of hotels who advertise themselves as being disabled-friendly, as this can mean as little as wide doors to rooms and bathrooms, or other token efforts.

Some tourist offices – notably those in Madrid and Barcelona – offer guided tours of the city for travellers with disabilities.

Inout Hostel (93 280 09 85; www.inouthostel.com; Major del Rectoret 2; dm €22; ❄@🛜♿; 🚉FGC Baixador de Vallvidrera) 🐾 Worthy of a special mention is Barcelona's Inout Hostel, which is completely accessible for those with disabilities, and nearly all the staff that work there have disabilities of one kind or another. Facilities and service are first-class.

Museo Tiflológico (Museum for the Blind; 91 589 42 19; http://museo.once.es; Calle de la Coruña 18; ⏱10am-2pm & 5-8pm Tue-Fri, 10am-2pm Sat 1st half of Aug, closed 2nd half of Aug; Ⓜ Estrecho; 💳FREE) This attraction in Madrid is specifically for people who are visually impaired. Run by the National Organisation for the Blind (ONCE), its exhibits (all of which may be touched) include paintings, sculptures and tapestries, as well as more than 40 scale models of world monuments, including Madrid's Palacio Real and Cibeles fountain, as well

---

Accessible Travel Online Resource

Download Lonely Planet's free *Accessible Travel* guide from http://lptravel.to/Accessible Travel.

as the Alhambra in Granada and the aqueduct in Segovia. It also provides leaflets in Braille and audioguides to the museum.

Organisations

Madrid Accesible (Accessible Madrid; www.esmadrid.com/madrid-accesible) First stop for more information on accessibility for travellers in Madrid should be the tourist office website section known as Madrid Accesible, where you can download a PDF of their excellent *Guia de Turismo Accesible* in English or Spanish. It has an exhaustive list of the city's attractions and transport and a detailed assessment of their accessibility, as well as a list of accessible restaurants.

Accessible Travel & Leisure (☑01452-729739; www.accessibletravel.co.uk) Claims to be the biggest UK travel agent dealing with travel for people with a disability, and encourages independent travel.

Barcelona Turisme (☑93 285 38 34; www.barcelona-access.com) Website devoted to making Barcelona accessible for visitors with a disability.

ONCE (Organización Nacional de Ciegos Españoles; ☑91 577 37 56, 91 532 50 00; www.once.es; Calle de Prim 3; Ⓜ Chueca, Colón) Spanish association for those who are blind. You may be able to get hold of guides in Braille to Madrid, although they're not published every year.

Society for Accessible Travel & Hospitality (www.sath.org) Good resource, which gives advice on how to travel with a wheelchair, kidney disease, sight impairment or deafness.

Visas

Spain is one of 26 member countries of the Schengen Convention, under which 22 EU countries (all but Bulgaria, Cyprus, Ireland, Romania and the UK) plus Iceland, Norway, Liechtenstein and Switzerland have abolished checks at common borders. The visa situation for entering Spain is as follows:

Citizens or residents of EU & Schengen countries No visa required.

Citizens or residents of Australia, Canada, Israel, Japan, New Zealand & the USA No visa required for tourist visits of up to 90 days out of every 180 days.

Other countries Check with a Spanish embassy or consulate.

To work or study in Spain A special visa may be required – contact a Spanish embassy or consulate before travel.

Women Travellers

Travelling in Spain is as easy as travelling anywhere in the West. That said, you should be choosy about your accommodation. Bottom-end fleapits with all-male staff can be insalubrious locations to bed down for the night. Lone women should also take care in city streets at night – stick with the crowds. Hitching for solo women travellers, while feasible, is risky.

Spanish men under about 40, who've grown up in the liberated post-Franco era, conform far less to old-fashioned sexual stereotypes, although you might notice that sexual stereotyping becomes a little more pronounced as you move from north to south in Spain, and from city to country.

Transport

Getting There & Away

Spain is one of Europe's top holiday destinations and well linked to other European countries by air, rail and road. Regular car ferries and hydrofoils run to and from Morocco, and there are ferry links to the UK, Italy, the Canary Islands and Algeria.

Flights, cars and tours can be booked online at www.lonelyplanet.com/bookings.

Entering Spain

Immigration and customs checks (which usually only take place if you're arriving from outside the EU) normally involve a minimum of fuss, although there are exceptions.

Your vehicle could be searched on arrival from Andorra. The tiny principality of Andorra is not in the EU, so border controls remain in place. Spanish customs look out for contraband duty-free products destined for illegal resale in Spain. The same may apply to travellers arriving from Morocco or the Spanish North African enclaves of Ceuta and Melilla. In this case the search is for controlled substances. Expect long delays at these borders, especially in summer.

Passports

Citizens of other EU member states as well those from Norway, Iceland, Liechtenstein and Switzerland can travel to Spain with their national identity card alone. If such countries do not issue ID cards – as in the UK – travellers must carry a valid passport. All other nationalities must have a valid passport.

Air

There are direct flights to Spain from most European countries, as well as North America, South America, Africa, the Middle East and Asia. Those coming from Australasia will usually have to make at least one change

All of Spain's airports share the user-friendly website and flight information telephone number of **Aena** (☎91 321 10 00, 902 404 704; www.aena.es) the national airports authority. To find more information on each airport, choose 'English' and click 'Airports' then 'Airport Network'. Each airport's page has details on practical information (including parking and public transport) and

a full list of (and links to) airlines using that airport. It also has current flight information.

Departure tax is included in the price of a ticket.

Land

Spain shares land borders with France, Portugal and Andorra. Apart from shorter cross-border services, **Eurolines** (www.eurolines.com) is the main operator of international bus services to Spain from most of Western Europe and Morocco.

Andorra

Regular buses connect Andorra with Barcelona (including winter ski buses and direct services to the airport) and other destinations in Spain (including Madrid) and France. Regular buses run between Andorra and Barcelona's Estació d'Autobusos de Sants (€29.50, three hours) or Barcelona's Aeroport del Prat (€33.50, 3½ hours).

France

Bus

Eurolines heads to Spain from Paris and more than 20 other French cities and towns. It connects with Madrid (17¾ hours), Barcelona (14¾ hours) and many other destinations. There's at least one departure per day for main destinations.

Train

The principal rail crossings into Spain pierce the Franco-Spanish frontier along the Mediterranean coast and via the Basque Country. Another

minor rail route runs inland across the Pyrenees from Latour-de-Carol to Barcelona.

In addition to the options listed below, two or three TGV (high-speed) trains leave from Paris-Montparnasse for Irún, where you change to a normal train for the Basque Country and on towards Madrid. Up to three TGVs also put you on track to Barcelona (leaving from Paris Gare de Lyon), with a change of train at Montpellier or Narbonne. For more information on French rail services, check out the **SNCF** (www.voyages-sncf.com) website.

There are plans for a high-speed rail link between Madrid and Paris. In the meantime, high-speed services travel via Barcelona. These are the major cross-border services:

Paris to Madrid (€118 to €187, 9¾ to 12½ hours, eight daily) The slow route runs via Les Aubrais, Blois, Poitiers, Irún, Vitoria, Burgos and Valladolid. The quicker route goes via the high-speed AVE train to Barcelona and change from there.

Paris to Barcelona (from €100, 6½ hours, two daily) A recently inaugurated high-speed service runs via Valence, Nimes, Montpellier, Beziers, Narbonne, Perpignan, Figueres and Girona. Also high-speed services run from Lyon (from €96, five hours) and Toulouse (from €66, three to four hours).

Portugal

Bus

Avanza (☎902 020 999; www.avanzabus.com) runs three daily buses between Lisbon and Madrid (€43.30, 7½ hours, two daily).

Other bus services run north via Porto to Tui, Santiago de Compostela and A Coruña in Galicia, while local buses cross the border from towns such as Huelva in Andalucía, Badajoz in Extremadura and Ourense in Galicia.

Train

From Portugal, the main line runs from Lisbon across Extremadura to Madrid; there is one daily train making this route (chair/sleeper class from €60.50/84, 10½ hours) and another from Lisbon to Irún (chair/sleeper class €69/94, 13½ hours).

Sea

A useful website for comparing routes and finding links to ferry companies is www. ferrylines.com.

Algeria

Trasmediterránea (📞902 454645; www.trasmediterranea. es) Runs year-round ferries between Almería and Ghazaouet (twice weekly) and Oran (weekly).

Algérie Ferries (www.algerie ferries.com) Operates year-round services from Alicante to Oran (11 hours, one to three weekly), as well as summer services from Alicante to Algiers and Mostaganem.

Italy

Most Italian routes are operated by **Grimaldi Lines** (www. grimaldi-lines.com) or **Grand Navi Veloci** (www.gnv.it).

Services to Barcelona depart from the following ports:

Civitavecchia (20 hours, six weekly)

Genoa (19 hours, once or twice weekly)

Livorno (21 hours, weekly)

Porto Torres (12 hours, five weekly)

Savona (18 hours, three weekly)

Morocco

Ferries run to Morocco from mainland Spain. Most services are run by the Spanish national ferry company, Trasmediterránea. You can take vehicles on most routes.

Other companies that connect Spain with Morocco include the following:

Baleària (www.baleria.com)

FRS Iberia (www.frs.es)

Grand Navi Veloci (www.gnv.it)

Grimaldi Lines (www.grimaldi-lines.com)

Naviera Armas (www.naviera armas.com)

Services between Spain and Morocco include the following:

Tangier to Algeciras (one to two hours, up to eight daily) Buses from several Moroccan cities converge on Tangier to make the ferry crossing to Algeciras, then fan out to the main Spanish centres.

Tangier to Tarifa (35 to 40 minutes, up to eight daily)

Tangier to Barcelona (32 to 35 hours, one to two weekly)

Tangier to Motril (eight hours, daily)

Nador to Almería (six hours, daily)

Nador to Motril (3½ hours, three weekly)

Al-Hoceima to Motril (3½ hours, weekly)

UK

Brittany Ferries (📞0871 244 0744; www.brittany-ferries.co.uk) runs the following services:

Plymouth to Santander (20½ hours, weekly) Mid-March to November only.

Portsmouth to Santander (24 hours, two weekly)

Portsmouth to Bilbao (24 hours, two to three weekly)

Getting Around

Spain's train and bus network is one of the best in Europe and there aren't many places that can't be reached using one or the other. The tentacles of Spain's high-speed train network are expanding rapidly, while domestic air services are plentiful over longer distances and on routes that are more complicated by land.

Air

Spain has an extensive network of internal flights. These are operated by both Spanish airlines and a handful of low-cost international airlines, which include the following:

Air Europa (www.aireuropa.com) Madrid to A Coruña, Vigo, Bilbao and Barcelona, as well as other routes between Spanish cities.

Iberia (www.iberia.com) Spain's national airline and its subsidiary, Iberia Regional-Air Nostrum, have an extensive domestic network.

Ryanair (www.ryanair.com) Some domestic Spanish routes include

Madrid to Santiago de Compostela or Seville to Barcelona.

Volotea (www.volotea.com) Budget airline that flies domestically and internationally. Domestic routes take in Málaga, Seville, Valencia, Vigo, Bilbao, Zaragoza, Oviedo and the Balearics (but not Madrid or Barcelona).

Vueling (www.vueling.com) Spanish low-cost company with loads of domestic flights within Spain, especially from Barcelona.

Bus

There are few places in Spain where buses don't go. Numerous companies provide bus links, from local routes between villages to fast intercity connections. It is often cheaper to travel by bus than by train, particularly on long-haul runs, but also less comfortable.

Local services can get you just about anywhere, but most buses connecting villages and provincial towns are not geared to tourist needs. Frequent weekday services drop off to a trickle, if they operate at all, on Saturday and Sunday. Often just one bus runs daily between smaller places during the week, and none operate on Sunday. It's usually unnecessary to make reservations; just arrive early enough to get a seat.

For longer trips (such as Madrid to Seville or to the coast), and certainly in peak holiday season, you can (and should) buy your ticket in advance. On some routes you have the choice between express and stopping-all-stations services.

In most larger towns and cities, buses leave from a single *estación de autobuses* (bus station). In smaller places, buses tend to operate from a set street or plaza, often unmarked. Locals will know where to go and where to buy tickets.

Bus travel within Spain is not overly costly. The trip from Madrid to Barcelona starts from around €32 one way. From Barcelona to Seville, which is one of the longest trips (15 to 16 hours), you can pay at least €100 one way.

People under 26 should enquire about discounts on long-distance trips.

Among the hundreds of bus companies operating in Spain, the following have the largest range of services:

ALSA (902 422 242; www.alsa.es) The biggest player, this company has routes all over the country in association with various other companies.

Avanza (902 020 999; www.avanzabus.com) Operates buses from Madrid to Extremadura, western Castilla y León and Valencia via eastern Castilla-La Mancha (eg Cuenca), often in association with other companies.

Socibus (902 229292; www.socibus.es) Operates services between Madrid, western Andalucía and the Basque Country.

Car & Motorcycle

Every vehicle should display a nationality plate of its country of registration and you must always carry proof of ownership of a private vehicle. Third-party motor insurance is required throughout

Europe. A warning triangle and a reflective jacket (to be used in case of breakdown) are compulsory.

Automobile Associations

The **Real Automóvil Club de España** (RACE; 900 100 992; www.race.es; Calle de Eloy Gonzalo 32, Madrid) is the national automobile club. It may well come to assist you in case of breakdown, but in any event you should obtain an emergency telephone number for Spain from your own insurer or car-rental company.

Driving Licence

All EU member states' driving licences are fully recognised throughout Europe. Those with a non-EU licence are supposed to obtain a 12-month International Driving Permit (IDP) to accompany their national licence, which your national automobile association can issue. In practice, however, car-rental companies and police rarely ask for one. People who have held residency in Spain for one year or more should apply for a Spanish driving licence.

Fuel

Gasolina (petrol) is pricey in Spain, but generally slightly cheaper than in its major EU neighbours (including France, Germany, Italy and the UK); *gasoleo* is diesel fuel. You can pay with major credit cards at most service stations.

Hire

To rent a car in Spain you have to have a licence, be

aged 21 or over and, for the major companies at least, have a credit or debit card. Smaller firms in areas where car hire is particularly common sometimes waiver this last requirement. Although those with a non-EU licence should also have an IDP, you will find that national licences from countries such as Australia, Canada, New Zealand and the US are usually accepted without question.

With some of the low-cost companies, beware of 'extras' that aren't quoted in initial prices.

Avis (☎ 902 180854; www.avis.es)

Enterprise Rent-a-Car (☎ 902 100 101; www.enterprise.es)

Europcar (☎ 902 105 030; www.europcar.es)

Firefly (www.fireflycarrental.com)

Hertz (☎ 91 749 77 78; www.hertz.es)

Pepecar (☎ 807 414243; www.pepecar.com)

SixT (☎ 902 491616; www.sixt.es)

Other possibilities include the following:

Auto Europe (www.autoeurope.com) US-based clearing house for deals with major car-rental agencies.

BlaBlaCar (www.blablacar.com) Car-sharing site which can be really useful for outlying towns, and if your Spanish is up to it, you get to meet people too.

Holiday Autos (☎ 900 838 014; www.holidayautos.com) A clearing house for major international companies.

Ideamerge (www.ideamerge.com) Renault's car-leasing plan, motor-home rental and much more.

Insurance

Third-party motor insurance is a minimum requirement in Spain and throughout Europe. Ask your insurer for a European Accident Statement form, which can simplify matters in the event of an accident. A European breakdown-assistance policy such as the AA Five Star Service or RAC Eurocover Motoring Assistance is a good investment. Car-hire companies also provide this minimum insurance, but be careful to understand what your liabilities and excess are, and what waivers you are entitled to in case of accident or damage to the hire vehicle.

Road Rules

Blood-alcohol limit 0.05%. Breath tests are common, and if found to be over the limit, you can be judged, condemned, fined and deprived of your licence within 24 hours. Fines range up to around €600 for serious offences. Nonresident foreigners may be required to pay up on the spot (at 30% off the full fine). Pleading linguistic ignorance will not help – the police officer will produce a list of infringements and fines in as many languages as you like.

Legal driving age (cars) 18 years.

Legal driving age (motorcycles & scooters) 16 (80cc and over) or 14 (50cc and under) years. A licence is required.

Motorcyclists Must use headlights at all times and wear

a helmet if riding a bike of 125cc or more.

Overtaking Spanish truck drivers often have the courtesy to turn on their right indicator to show that the way ahead of them is clear for overtaking (and the left one if it is not and you are attempting this manoeuvre). Make sure, however, that they're not just turning right!

Roundabouts (traffic circles) Vehicles already in the circle have the right of way.

Side of the road Drive on the right.

Speed limits In built-up areas, 50km/h (and in some cases, such as inner-city Barcelona, 30km/h), which increases to 100km/h on major roads and up to 120km/h on *autovías* and *autopistas* (toll-free and tolled dual-lane highways, respectively). Cars towing caravans are restricted to a maximum speed of 80km/h.

Local Transport

Bus

Cities and provincial capitals all have reasonable bus networks. You can buy single tickets (usually between €1 and €2) on the buses or at *estancos* (tobacconists), but in cities such as Madrid and Barcelona, you are better off buying combined 10-trip tickets that allow the use of a combination of bus and metro, and which work out cheaper per ride. These can be purchased in any metro station and from some tobacconists and newspaper kiosks.

Regular buses run from about 6am to shortly before midnight and even as late as

2am. In the big cities a night bus service generally kicks in on a limited number of lines in the wee hours. In Madrid they are known as *búhos* (owls) and in Barcelona more prosaically as *nitbusos* (night buses).

Metro

Madrid has the country's most extensive metro network. Barcelona has a reasonable system. Bilbao and Seville have limited but nonetheless useful metro (or light rail) systems.

○ Tickets must be bought in metro stations (from counters or vending machines), or sometimes from *estancos* (tobacconists) or newspaper kiosks.

○ Single tickets cost the same as for buses (around €1.50).

○ Visitors wanting to move around the major cities over a few days are best off getting 10-trip tickets, known in Madrid as Metrobús (€12.20) and in Barcelona as T-10 (€10.30).

○ Monthly and seasonal passes are also available.

Taxi

You can find taxi ranks at train and bus stations, or you can telephone for radio taxis. In larger cities taxi ranks are also scattered about the centre, and taxis will stop if you hail them in the street – look for the green light and/or the *libre* sign on the passenger side of the windscreen. The bigger cities are well populated with taxis,

although you might have to wait a bit longer on a Friday or Saturday night. No more than four people are allowed in a taxi.

○ Daytime flagfall (generally to 10pm) is, for example, €2.40 in Madrid, and up to €2.90 after 9pm to 7am, and on weekends and holidays. You then pay €1.05 to €1.20 per kilometre depending on the time of day.

○ There are airport and (sometimes) luggage surcharges.

○ A cross-town ride in a major city will cost about €10 – absurdly cheap by European standards – while a taxi between the city centre and airport in either Madrid or Barcelona will cost €30 with luggage.

Train

Renfe (☏902 243 402; www. renfe.com) is the national train system that runs most of the services in Spain. A handful of small private railway lines also operate.

You'll find *consignas* (left-luggage facilities) at all main train stations. They are usually open from about 6am to midnight and charge from €4 to €6 per day per piece of luggage.

Spain has several types of trains, and *largo recorrido* or *Grandes Líneas* (long-distance trains) in particular have a variety of names.

Alaris, Altaria, Alvia, Arco & Avant Long-distance services, intermediate speed.

Cercanías (rodalies in Catalonia) For short hops and services to outlying suburbs and satellite towns in Madrid, Barcelona and 11 other cities.

Euromed Similar to the Tren de Alta Velocidad Española (AVE) trains, they connect Barcelona with Valencia and Alicante.

FEVE (Ferrocarriles de Vía Estrecha) Narrow-gauge network along Spain's north coast between Bilbao and Ferrol (Galicia), with a branch down to León.

Regionales Trains operating within one region, usually stopping all stations.

Talgo & intercity Slower, long-distance trains.

Tren de Alta Velocidad Española (AVE) High-speed trains that link Madrid with Albacete, Barcelona, Burgos, Cádiz, Córdoba, Cuenca, Huesca, León, Lerida, Málaga, Palencia, Salamanca, Santiago de Compostela, Seville, Valencia, Valladolid, Zamora and Zaragoza. There are also Barcelona–Seville, Barcelona–Málaga and Valencia–Seville services. In coming years, Madrid–Bilbao should also come

Cheaper Train Tickets

Train travel can be expensive, but there's one trick worth knowing. Return tickets cost considerably less than two one-way tickets. If you're certain that you'll be returning on the same route sometime over the coming months (three months is usually the limit), buy a return ticket and you can later change the return date.

Rail Passes

InterRail (www.interrailnet.eu) Available to people who have lived in Europe for six months or more. Can be bought at most major stations, student travel outlets and online. Youth passes are for people aged 12 to 25, and adult passes are for those 26 and over. Children aged 11 and under travel for free if travelling on a family pass.

○ **Global Pass** Encompasses 30 countries and comes in seven versions, ranging from five days' travel in 15 days to a full month's travel. Visit the website for prices.

○ **One-Country Pass** Can be used for three, four, six or eight days within one month in Spain. For the eight-day pass you pay €395/252/186 for adult 1st class/adult 2nd class/youth 2nd class.

Eurail (www.eurail.com) For those who've lived in Europe for less than six months. Supposed to be bought outside Europe, either online or from leading travel agencies. Be sure you will be covering a lot of ground to make your Eurail pass worthwhile – check **Renfe** (www.renfe.com) for prices in euros for the places you intend to travel to.

For most of the following passes children aged between four and 11 pay half-price for the 1st-class passes, while those aged under 26 can get a cheaper 2nd-class pass. The Eurail website has a list of prices, including special family rates and other discounts.

○ **Eurail Global Passes** Good for travel in 28 European countries; forget it if you intend to travel mainly in Spain. There are nine different passes.

○ **Eurail Select Pass** Provides between five and 10 days of unlimited travel within a two-month period in two to four bordering countries (eg Spain, France, Italy and Switzerland).

○ **Spain Pass** With the one-country Spain Pass you can choose from three to eight days' train travel in a one-month period. The eight-day Spain Pass costs €406/325/265 for adult 1st class/adult 2nd class/youth 2nd class.

respectively. The latter is 20% to 40% more expensive.

Fares vary enormously depending on the service (faster trains cost considerably more) and, in the case of some high-speed services such as the AVE, on the time and day of travel. Tickets for AVE trains are by far the most expensive. A one-way trip in 2nd class from Madrid to Barcelona (on which route only AVE trains run) could cost as much as €107 (it could work out significantly cheaper if you book well in advance).

Children aged between four and 12 years are entitled to a 40% discount; those aged under four travel for free (except on high-speed trains, for which they pay the same as those aged four to 12). Buying a return ticket often gives you a 10% to 20% discount on the return trip. Students and people up to 25 years of age with a Euro<26 Card (Carnet Joven in Spain) are entitled to 20% to 25% off most ticket prices.

Reservations

Reservations are recommended for long-distance trips, and you can make them in train stations, Renfe offices and travel agencies, as well as online. In a growing number of stations you can pick up prebooked tickets from machines scattered about the station concourse.

on line, and travel times to Galicia should fall.

Trenhotel Overnight trains with sleeper berths.

Classes & Costs

All long-distance trains have 2nd and 1st classes, known as *turista* and *preferente,*

Language

Spanish pronunciation is not difficult as most of its sounds are also found in English. You can read our pronunciation guides below as if they were English and you'll be understood just fine. And if you pronounce 'th' in our guides with a lisp and 'kh' as a throaty sound, you'll even sound like a real Spanish person.

To enhance your trip with a phrasebook, visit **lonelyplanet.com**.

Basics

Hello.
Hola.   o·la
How are you?
¿Qué tal?   ke tal
I'm fine, thanks.
Bien, gracias.   byen gra·thyas
Excuse me. (to get attention)
Disculpe.   dees·kool·pe
Yes./No.
Sí./No.   see/no
Thank you.
Gracias.   gra·thyas
You're welcome./That's fine.
De nada.   de na·da
Goodbye. /See you later.
Adiós./Hasta luego.   a·dyos/as·ta lwe·go
Do you speak English?
¿Habla inglés?   a·bla een·gles
I don't understand.
No entiendo.   no en·tyen·do
How much is this?
¿Cuánto cuesta?   kwan·to kwes·ta
Can you reduce the price a little?
¿Podría bajar un   po·dree·a ba·khar oon
poco el precio?   po·ko el pre·thyo

Accommodation

I'd like to make a booking.
Quisiera reservar   kee·sye·ra re·ser·var
una habitación.   oo·na a·bee·ta·thyon

How much is it per night?
¿Cuánto cuesta   kwan·to kwes·ta
por noche?   por no·che

Eating & Drinking

I'd like ..., please.
Quisiera ..., por favor.   kee·sye·ra ... por fa·vor
That was delicious!
¡Estaba buenísimo!   es·ta·ba bwe·nee·see·mo
Bring the bill/check, please.
La cuenta, por favor.   la kwen·ta por fa·vor

I'm allergic to ...
Soy alérgico/a al ... (m/f)   soy a·ler·khee·ko/a al ...
I don't eat ...
No como ...   no ko·mo ...
   chicken   pollo   po·lyo
   fish   pescado   pes·ka·do
   meat   carne   kar·ne

Emergencies

I'm ill.
Estoy enfermo/a. (m/f)   es·toy en·fer·mo/a
Help!
¡Socorro!   so·ko·ro
Call a doctor!
¡Llame a un médico!   lya·me a oon me·dee·ko
Call the police!
¡Llame a la policía!   lya·me a la po·lee·thee·a

Directions

I'm looking for (a/an/the) ...
Estoy buscando ...   es·toy boos·kan·do ...
   ATM
   un cajero   oon ka·khe·ro
   automático   ow·to·ma·tee·ko
   bank
   el banco   el ban·ko
   ... embassy
   la embajada de ...   la em·ba·kha·da de ...
   market
   el mercado   el mer·ka·do
   museum
   el museo   el moo·se·o
   restaurant
   un restaurante   oon res·tow·ran·te
   toilet
   los servicios   los ser·vee·thyos
   tourist office
   la oficina de   la o·fee·thee·na de
   turismo   too·rees·mo

Behind The Scenes

Acknowledgements

Climate map data adapted from Peel
MC, Finlayson BL & McMahon TA
(2007) 'Updated World Map of the
Köppen-Geiger Climate Classification',
Hydrology and Earth System Sciences,
11, 163344.

This Book

This guidebook was curated by Anthony
Ham, who also researched and wrote
it, along with Sally Davies, Bridget
Gleeson, Anita Isalska, Isabella Noble,
John Noble, Brendan Sainsbury and
Regis St Louis.

This guidebook was produced by the following:

Destination Editors Lorna Parkes, Clifton Wilkinson

Product Editor Amanda Williamson

Senior Cartographer Anthony Phelan

Cartographer Gabe Lindquist

Cartographic Series Designer Wayne Murphy

Book Designer Wibowo Rusli

Assisting Editors Gabrielle Innes, Gabrielle Stefanos

Cover Researcher Naomi Parker

Thanks to Brendan Dempsey-Spencer, Grace Dobell, Chris
Gribble, Paul Harding, James Hardy, Victoria Harrison, Liz
Heynes, Andi Jones, Indra Kilfoyle, Kate Mathews, Campbell
McKenzie, Jenna Myers, Catherine Naghten, Kirsten Rawlings,
Alison Ridgway, Angela Tinson, Dylan Wilson, Tony Wheeler,
Juan Winata

Send Us Your Feedback

We love to hear from travellers – your comments keep us on our
toes and help make our books better. Our well-travelled team reads
every word on what you loved or loathed about this book. Although
we cannot reply individually to postal submissions, we always guar-
antee that your feedback goes straight to the appropriate authors,
in time for the next edition. Each person who sends us information
is thanked in the next edition, the most useful submissions are
rewarded with a selection of digital PDF chapters.

Visit lonelyplanet.com/contact to submit your updates and suggestions or to ask for help. Our award-winning website also features
inspirational travel stories, news and discussions.

Note: We may edit, reproduce and incorporate your comments in
Lonely Planet products such as guidebooks, websites and digital
products, so let us know if you don't want your comments repro-
duced or your name acknowledged. For a copy of our privacy policy
visit lonelyplanet.com/privacy.

A – Z

Index

A

354

Symbols & Map Key

Look for these symbols to quickly identify listings:

- Sights
- Activities
- Courses
- Tours
- Festivals & Events
- Eating
- Drinking
- Entertainment
- Shopping
- Information & Transport

These symbols and abbreviations give vital information for each listing:

- Sustainable or green recommendation
- **FREE** No payment required

- Telephone number
- Opening hours
- Parking
- Nonsmoking
- Air-conditioning
- Internet access
- Wi-fi access
- Swimming pool
- Bus
- Ferry
- Tram
- Train
- English-language menu
- Vegetarian selection
- Family-friendly

Find your best experiences with these Great For... icons.

- Budget
- Food & Drink
- Drinking
- Cycling
- Shopping
- Sport
- Art & Culture
- Events
- Photo Op
- Scenery
- Family Travel
- Short Trip
- Detour
- Walking
- Local Life
- History
- Entertainment
- Beaches
- Winter Travel
- Cafe/Coffee
- Nature & Wildlife

Sights
- Beach
- Bird Sanctuary
- Buddhist
- Castle/Palace
- Christian
- Confucian
- Hindu
- Islamic
- Jain
- Jewish
- Monument
- Museum/Gallery/ Historic Building
- Ruin
- Shinto
- Sikh
- Taoist
- Winery/Vineyard
- Zoo/Wildlife Sanctuary
- Other Sight

Points of Interest
- Bodysurfing
- Camping
- Cafe
- Canoeing/Kayaking
- Course/Tour
- Diving
- Drinking & Nightlife
- Eating
- Entertainment
- Sento Hot Baths/ Onsen
- Shopping
- Skiing
- Sleeping
- Snorkelling
- Surfing
- Swimming/Pool
- Walking
- Windsurfing
- Other Activity

Information
- Bank
- Embassy/Consulate
- Hospital/Medical
- Internet
- Police
- Post Office
- Telephone
- Toilet
- Tourist Information
- Other Information

Geographic
- Beach
- Gate
- Hut/Shelter
- Lighthouse
- Lookout
- Mountain/Volcano
- Oasis
- Park
- Pass
- Picnic Area
- Waterfall

Transport
- Airport
- BART station
- Border crossing
- Boston T station
- Bus
- Cable car/Funicular
- Cycling
- Ferry
- Metro/MRT station
- Monorail
- Parking
- Petrol station
- Subway/S-Bahn/ Skytrain station
- Taxi
- Train station/Railway
- Tram
- Tube Station
- Underground/ U-Bahn station
- Other Transport

355

Anita Isalska

Formerly Lonely Planet's digital editor, Anita surprised no one when she swapped office life for travelling the world with her trusty laptop. Spain has long been an obsession, from hikes in the rugged north via Madrid all-nighters to the full quota of Costas, but it's Catalonia that keeps luring her back. Anita is a freelance copywriter and journalist for a host of international publications, specialising in budget travel, offbeat adventures and food. Check out some of her work on www.anitaisalska.com.

Isabella Noble

English-Australian-Spanish, Isabella has lived and travelled in Spain since 1994. Her in-depth investigations of distant northern regions far from her Andalucian home began at the age of 12. Now based in London, Isabella writes on Spain, India, Southeast Asia and beyond, for Lonely Planet, Telegraph Travel (where she's the Northern Spain expert) and others. Highlights this trip: tapas-touring in Cáceres, rediscovering Cantabria's prehistoric cave paintings and 'researching' Galician wines. Find Isabella on Twitter and Instagram (@isabellamnoble).

John Noble

John, originally from England's Ribble Valley, has lived in an Andalucian mountain village since 1995. He has travelled lengthily all over Andalucía and most of the rest of the Spain and helped write every edition of Lonely Planet's *Spain* and *Andalucía* guides. John finds the diversity of Spain's many distinct regions endlessly fascinating. He loves returning to the green pastures, spectacular coastlines, old stone architecture, warm hospitality and distinctive culture of the far northwest – in many ways almost a different country from the rest of Spain, where the food and wine seem to be getting better and better with every trip!

Brendan Sainsbury

Originally from Hampshire, England, Brendan first went to Spain on an Inter-rail ticket in the 1980s. He went back as a travel guide several years later and met his wife-to-be in a small village in rural Andalucía in 2003. He has been writing books for Lonely Planet for more than a decade, including three previous editions of the *Spain* guide. For this trip, Brendan loved going underground in Zaragoza, reading *Don Quijote* in La Mancha, and walking (and running) ridiculous distances when he ran out of buses.

Regis St Louis

Regis fell in love with Barcelona a decade ago, after arriving in the city and being awestruck by its wild architecture, culinary creativity and warm-hearted people. Since then he has returned frequently, learning Spanish and a smattering of Catalan, and delving into the endless layers of Barcelona's deep cultural heritage. Favourite memories from his most recent trip include fêting the arrival of three bearded kings during Dia de Reis, catching a surreal circus-arts show in a seaside suburb, and exploring far-flung corners of Montjuïc at sunrise. Regis is the author of the two previous editions of *Barcelona*, and he has contributed to *Spain, Portugal* and dozens of other Lonely Planet titles. When not on the road, he lives in New Orleans.

356

Our Story

A beat-up old car, a few dollars in the pocket and a sense of adventure. In 1972 that's all Tony and Maureen Wheeler needed for the trip of a lifetime – across Europe and Asia overland to Australia. It took several months, and at the end – broke but inspired – they sat at their kitchen table writing and stapling together their first travel guide, Across Asia on the Cheap. Within a week they'd sold 1500 copies. Lonely Planet was born.

Today, Lonely Planet has offices in Franklin, London, Melbourne, Oakland, Dublin, Beijing, and Delhi, with more than 600 staff and writers. We share Tony's belief that 'a great guidebook should do three things: inform, educate and amuse'.

Our Writers

Anthony Ham

In 2001, Anthony fell in love with Madrid on his first visit to the city. Less than a year later, he arrived on a one-way ticket, with not a word of Spanish and not knowing a single person. After 10 years living in the city, he recently returned to Australia with his Spanish-born family, but he still adores his adopted country as much as the first day he arrived and returns often. When he's not writing for Lonely Planet, Anthony writes about Spain, Australia and Africa for newspapers and magazines around the world. Find him online at www.anthonyham.com.

Sally Davies

Sally landed in Seville in 1992 with a handful of pesetas and five words of Spanish, and, despite a complete inability to communicate, promptly snared a lucrative job handing out leaflets at Expo '92. In 2001 she settled in Barcelona, where she is still incredulous that her daily grind involves researching fine restaurants, wandering about museums and finding ways to convey the beauty of this spectacular city.

Bridget Gleeson

Based in Buenos Aires, Bridget is a travel writer and occasional photographer. Before her years in South America, she lived in Italy and travelled extensively in Spain; along the way, thanks to her *madrileño* friends, she's learned how to use *vosotros* and *tio*, how to make a proper tortilla, and how to stay out all night.

More Writers

STAY IN TOUCH lonelyplanet.com/contact

AUSTRALIA Levels 2 & 3, 551 Swanston St, Carlton, Victoria 3053
☎ 03 8379 8000,
fax 03 8379 8111

USA 150 Linden Street, Oakland, CA 94607
☎ 510 250 6400,
toll free 800 275 8555,
fax 510 893 8572

UK 240 Blackfriars Road, London SE1 8NW
☎ 020 3771 5100,
fax 020 3771 5101

twitter.com/ lonelyplanet

facebook.com/ lonelyplanet

instagram.com/ lonelyplanet

youtube.com/ lonelyplanet

lonelyplanet.com/ newsletter